AMERICAN MISCHIEF

AMERICAN MISCHIEF

a novel by Alan Lelchuk

farrar, straus and giroux   new york

Selections from Herman Kahn, *On Thermonuclear War*, Copyright © 1960, by Princeton University Press. Reprinted by permission of Princeton University Press.

Selections from *Oedipus Rex* from the book *Dramas* by Sophocles, translated by Sir George Young. Everyman's Library edition. Reprinted by permission of E. P. Dutton & Co., Inc., and J. M. Dent & Sons Limited.

Selections from Norman Mailer's *Advertisements for Myself* reprinted by permission of G. P. Putnam's Sons and André Deutsch Limited. Copyright © 1959, by Norman Mailer.

"Cambridge Talk" originally appeared in *Modern Occasions*.

CONTENTS

To Colonel Smith*

Paris, November 13, 1787

. . . Can history produce an instance of rebellion so honorably conducted? I say nothing of its motives. They were founded in ignorance, not wickedness. God forbid we should ever be twenty years without such a rebellion. The people cannot be all, and always, well informed. The part which is wrong will be discontented, in proportion to the importance of the facts they misconceive. If they remain quiet under such misconceptions, it is a lethargy, the forerunner of death to the public liberty. We have had thirteen states independent for eleven years. There has been one rebellion. That comes to one rebellion in a century and a half, for each state. What country before, ever existed a century and a half without a rebellion? And what country can preserve its liberties, if its rulers are not warned from time to time, that this people preserve the spirit of resistance? Let them take arms. The remedy is to set them right as to facts, pardon and pacify them. What signify a few lives lost in a century or two? The tree of liberty must be refreshed from time to time, with the blood of patriots and tyrants. It is its natural manure. . . .

—Thomas Jefferson

General ideas and great conceit tend always to create horrible mischief.

—Goethe

* Colonel William Stephens Smith was an American diplomat and son-in-law of John Adams. The rebellion discussed was Shays's insurrection in Massachusetts, 1786–7.

AMERICAN MISCHIEF

LENNY'S PREFACE

A man with a woman on his hands, runs the proverb, is a man with his hands full. If this is so, what shall we say of a man with several women on his hands, say more than two or three? And what if that same busy fellow occupied, in this day and age, a position of authority at one of our esteemed universities? Suppose too that we are talking about a relatively young man, still in his early thirties—that watershed age—who is called upon to take sides between agitated students like ourselves and cooler adults like colleagues, administrators, citizens? And that while he *felt* like us, shared our sense of youthful urgent disturbance, he *thought* like them, believing in the language of reason and procedures of calm maturity? As you can see, I'm describing a man in trouble. Such was the situation, perhaps known by now to some of you, of Bernard Kovell, professor of literature and Dean of Students and the School of Humanities at Cardozo College, that prestigious school twelve miles from Cambridge, Massachusetts. It is his personal story, which forms the first part of this book, that I wish briefly to introduce.

I'm Lenny Pincus—the subject of the second part—a name also familiar perhaps, and there are several reasons for my presenting and introducing these texts. One is that Mr. Kovell was my old teacher and friend, and I knew him fairly well. Another is my belief that the Dean's text is an important document in understanding America today, and the reasons for our own special activities of late. Though, to be accurate here, not all my comrades would agree with this. Indeed, many felt that I was wasting my time and labor (on publicizing such decadent materials). Others attributed to me motives of personal aggrandizement for undertaking the project. A charge cited frequently in the bour-

3

geois press and picked up recently by some comrades. All right, I'm used to that. Being a loner among my own kind, an exile among outlaws, is nothing new. (Part of my sympathy, I suppose, for Dean Kovell, also an outsider on his own turf.) I prefer it, perhaps. And accept, with a certain flattery even, the epithet used alike by enemy (in praise) and ally (in derogation), "the Trotsky of the Movement." Though to keep the record straight, I often feel closer to another Russian, that troublesome engineering student of a century ago who developed such an intense interest in morality and justice that he was willing to use an ax on an old lady's head to test his theory. Closer to that brave young madman than to the reasonable old socialist.

While I'm on the subject, let me say a few words about myself. About the boy who a few years ago, while still a senior at Cardozo, had profiles done of him in *Esquire* and *The New York Times*, went on television for several interviews, gave lectures at Princeton and Cornell, among others. Wearing my hearing aid and Cardozo windbreaker all the while. The boy who, while seeking to be a true troublemaker, found himself with the opportunity to become a millionaire. Celebrityhood in America has many functions, not the least of which is to confuse—both the public and the celebrity. Once the industry gets going on you, you begin unwittingly to acquire a new personality. A strange and new Lenny Pincus is born. Not the son of Harry and Rose Pincus of Brooklyn, but a boy with fathers like Reston and Cronkite, mothers such as Mary McCarthy and Diana Trilling. An interesting family. Even Susan Sontag tried to name me ("Little Robin Hood—the Boy of the Future?" *Partisan Review*). Not a bad idea, as things turned out. As you can see, an immaculate conception of Len Pincus, radical, created by media theology.

Confusion and dispersion: which Pincus is real? Even friends doubt their perception and wonder who you are. Which makes self-recognition doubly hard, problematic. Friend or celebrity, man or image? Who's the deceiver, one wonders, I or they? (It is probably one of the reasons that, despite my authentic credentials, I am a fairly isolated member of the committee, distrusted and disliked by many.)

Some examples of what I've been talking about. Item: *Time*

reports that I spent a year in Cuba, training to be a guerrilla in the Sierra Maestra Mountains under the personal tutelage of Che Guevara. Fact: I was badgered into the trip by a fervent female militant, spent one week there suffering from dysentery in my Havana hotel room. I did see Castro; along with twenty thousand Cubans, watching him give a speech. Item: in a *New Leader* profile, it is suggested that at age fifteen, "as a result of reading Conrad's great tale of colonial exploitation, *Heart of Darkness,* the romantic *wunderkind* set off, probably as a stowaway on an American liner, to see for himself the consequences of Western capitalism. It can be assumed that Mr. Pincus, fresh from his two-week survey, was ready to exchange his Conrad for Marx." Fact: at age seventeen I came upon *Two Years Before the Mast,* by a writer I had never heard of, and signed aboard, at the Scandinavian Seaman's Union in Brooklyn, a Norwegian freighter as a *dekksgutt.* The sea and Africa sailed to my head like strong wine: the wild zebras and giraffes loping along the Congo banks, the fierce splendor of the Ghana fishermen, the strange intimacy of the fifty or so Monrovians who lived aboard the ship during the three-month Gold Coast run, the encounters with gold-toothed, black-skinned prostitutes who took me home to floorless shacks and deposited in me gonorrhea and fleas—the magic days on the Atlantic, chatting with Florida missionaries, hauling in the sea-weed-encased anchor with my Norwegian counterpart, taking the ship's wheel in the deckhouse for the midnight watch. Upon my return, I thought about (Sir) Richard Burton and Rimbaud, not Karl Marx; my destiny was to be a sailor or explorer, I was sure, not a guerrilla. Item: David Susskind asked me, on his television show, how it was to grow up in grave poverty with a Russian emigré father who very early forced upon me the basic texts of International Communism. Fact (which I explained patiently to Mr. Susskind, who demands much patience): my father was a millinery operator whose political sympathies embarrassed both of us. He was more interested in having me learn Hebrew in preparation for my bar mitzvah than Lenin in preparation for revolution. Grave poverty was, in fact, a small but comfortable enough apartment, a modest allowance (out of which I bought a fine outfielder's glove and my own spiked shoes), three meals plus snacks every day of my youth. Item:

beneath a *Ramparts* close-up of my face, with focus on my complicated hearing aid, the caption reads, *Police Brutality*. Fact: my near deafness in my right ear is the result of a mistimed explosion by a comrade, a misguided apprentice in the terrorist trade.

About the oft-repeated story of my being radicalized by the Freedom Rides in Alabama and Mississippi, not quite. One summer, taking my cue from Thomas Wolfe, I took the IRT uptown to the George Washington Bridge and hitched south, hoping to buy a motorcycle and go to Mexico. And, of course, *to discover*. I wound up working in Texas, first in a Houston lumberyard and then selling magazines door-to-door in different cities. At the first job, I worked from 6 A.M. to 6 P.M., at 65¢ an hour, all the overtime I wanted at the same price. I was the only white boy among black and Mexican workers—mostly family men who earned up to $1.25 an hour, after years—while the yard was managed by a pleasant enough cracker and run (and part-owned) by a young smiling venal Jew, who had married into the place. The lessons in love and hate were many. My hands were ripped apart by loading steel pipes into low bins without gloves for the first few days; later that week or the next, I passed out while unloading a boxcar of lumber in about 140 degrees. Also during the tenure there (six weeks?), I was almost knifed by a young Chicano for necking with a Mexican girl in a nearby park; and witnessed my first killing, a black shivved by another in a barroom fight. At my door-to-door selling *Ladies' Home Journal, Good Housekeeping, Sports Afield, True Confessions* were among the big sellers, as I recall), I learned a little more about Southerners. Mainly through Neil Whipple, a middle-aged salesman who drank hair tonic in San Antonio gas station bathrooms when nothing else was around (fired from a big job because of alcohol); who prayed to Jesus and to his Nashville mother (while I trembled in the next bed) at 2 A.M., kneeling by the side of the hotel twin bed, naked except for his straw hat; who talked the most enchanting sweet sales talk I ever heard, all Southern gentleman, including a perfect high voice and white shirt and tie, regardless of heat; and who at least twice saved me from being beaten up by dumb and not-so-dumb Jewhaters. Finally, I got my motorcycle, took off for Mexico, hurt my leg in a fall, and ultimately hitched back to Brooklyn, revving with emotion and memories but unsure what it all meant. It was only later that I put people into political categories; and only much later that I took them out again as well. The few times I met civil-rights workers, I'll say in passing, I couldn't take them, since they seemed to me full of missionary thin-bloodedness and suburban arrogance. Later on, when I did some of it in my own back yards (mostly, although once I went South again), I still found them a boring lot. I suppose I have always preferred the Eugene Gants to the Eugene McCarthys.

Do I make my point? Is the tremendous gap between news and real reality painfully apparent? For self-therapy then, if for nothing else, one needs to set down words about oneself once one becomes a success in our land.

Let me say a few words about my beginnings. To begin with, books. No, Mr. Reston, those were not revolutionary texts I "apparently read" early on, but novels, cheap, bad, good, great, indifferent. When I was a sophomore in Thomas Jefferson High School in Brooklyn, I took a job at Schulte's Book Store, a renowned Fourth Avenue second-hand bookstore. For three years, at the heart of adolescence, I worked in Schulte's basement as the Fiction Boy. Not for any symbolic reasons was I implanted below, but rather because of the forty thousand novels that lived down there, waiting how many decades to be filed away! Waiting in piles of bulging cardboard boxes, on rotting wooden shelves bending beneath the sheer weight of those grand illusions, in sagging, ancient bookcases suffocating from last century's dust. My job was to get to know the books—all forty thousand if possible—so that I could immediately answer Will Fuller's buzzer at the head of the stairs with the answer in my head to a customer request. And to keep order, meaning to make sure there was room in the aisles for customers to browse, and that the new waiting-to-be-filed books occasionally moved out to the front lines, the permanent shelves. In that curious Manhattan book mine of choking dust and bare 75-watt light, what could I do but read? Read my eyes red, sore. One and all, indiscriminately: Hervey Allen and Dostoevsky, Maurice Hewlett and Balzac, Ouida and Dickens, Joseph Hergesheimer and Anthony Trollope.

Another room, consisting of broken sets of fine bindings, was also under my charge. Ladies from Park Avenue, who occasionally wished one or two shelves of gold- or maroon-bound books, for purposes of decoration, would be sent to me there.

7

(Also down there were rows of old law books, which we would rent out to TV melodramas for law-office backgrounds.) One Persian-lambed woman in her mid-fifties smiled with approval when I showed her part of a set of Bulwer-Lytton, saying she had read as a child *A Tale of Two Cities*. From these sets, I developed a special affection for books, like a stamp or seashell devotee. My first handling of the eleventh edition of the Encyclopædia Britannica, with its soft black leather covers and tissue-thin India paper text, made me ashamed to touch it with my soot-covered hands. And, before I had ever heard of Henry James, the half-moroccan New York edition of his work, with the Macmillan maple leaves inscribed in gilt on the binding, and the black-and-white photographs of famous international sites (my favorite being the View of St. Paul's Across the Thames, in volume I of *The Princess Casamassima*) awed me. That cellar of fiction became my real school, those Gutenberg-creations my true talismans. A passion of adolescence that sets me apart from many of my comrades. And a subject of interest in the light of what we have been forced to do to the libraries.

To expose my real innocence and interests of that time, I should add that well-known figures visited Schulte's occasionally who might have aided my political education had I been so inclined. Edmund Wilson, the literary critic, used to appear with some regularity. I had never heard of him. Nor had I heard of a thin sprightly elderly man who brandished a cane. When he was pointed out as the man who led Russia for a brief period in its history, it meant as much to me as the day's averages in soybeans. That's what I knew of Kerensky. I'm sure that had Lenin or Trotsky appeared, it would have been no different. My head was too clogged with classifying cheap fiction to take notice.

And clogged with another passion, slowly nurtured down there. One day, in the prestigious Americana room, I was helping a fellow worker put away some Western folklore, when he suddenly put his finger to his lips, told me to switch off the light, and quietly climbed the wooden ladder. Parting a row of books, he peered through a chink in the wall and then motioned me up. Through a small round hole I watched, fascinated, as a circle of four or five people sat around drinking and watching a flickering home-movie screen. My heart fluttered with excitement, and I came to sneak looks regularly. It turned out that pornographic movies were a sort of weekly feature, administered by the black elevator operator who used that part of the basement for his relaxation area. This meant, under Nurlan Thomas's shrewd entrepreneurship, a modest gambling den, whorehouse, and porno-movie scene combined. Once I was working there awhile, and got to know Nurlan, I was invited and encouraged to take part. With fear, trepidation, and excitement, I did, at times. Snatching five- or ten-minute breaks away from dreary filing—always on the alert for Will's buzzer, which signaled that he wanted a book from me—or sneaking there after work for a short time. Frightened by the seedy atmosphere and tough customers (black truck drivers, delivery boys, elevator operators), I was tempted by the women and by the special prices for me (since I was only fifteen). I remember paying three dollars for a blowjob by Ginny, a skinny nineteen-year-old white runaway whose St. Christopher medal swung while she sucked upon me, on her knees. (Once, high on beer, she gave me a "freeby" fuck when Nurlan had stepped out for a while.) There was also a big, good-looking, red-haired lady named Flo, who, according to Nurlan, would come in from her Long Island suburb home to get laid. He said that she was married, with children, but loved him and would do anything he said. The thing I remember about Flo was the way she carried on when I screwed her, on the narrow dirty cot outside the stinking lavatory. Moaning, writhing, flailing, using fantastic obscenities, she terrified me. Clearly, despite Nurlan's words, she was more nympho in motivation than anything else. From the way she dressed when she was ready to leave, in a modest suit or conservative dress, you'd never believe it was the same woman. I guess she simply couldn't get enough degradation on the Island.

Enough. You get an idea of how I was then. Pretty ordinary. Pretty apolitical and susceptible. As intrigued by vice as the next innocent boy. Crummy novels, not manifestoes, consumed me; pornographia, not radical catechism. What chance could Edmund Wilson or the Russian Revolution have next to the lurid glamour of an unprofessional whorehouse, where black limbs and white holes were waiting, hot and true Americana on the other side of the dusty book version?

Two final words here. The first, about my abilities as an

"orator." No, Mr. Sevareid, it did not come from my high-school debating team. If there was such an animal at my high school, I was oblivious to it. I learned about the art of talking from greed, boredom, and fear. Greed, with egotism mixed in, connected with persuading girls to abandon lessons and pieties for adolescent sex. Ever since I fumbled loose the virginity of Rosalie Engelhardt, fifteen-year-old cheerleader, on Jefferson High's rooftop, I became a very active persuader at that school and elsewhere. So I know a bit about Dean Kovell's dilemmas. And in classes, with teachers and subjects and students so dull generally, the only way I could work up interest was to talk out of turn. At least teachers would become passionate then, in their anger and annoyance and even humor. Subjects were *deadly*. Talk was okay. Finally, not being trained or interested in street fighting, and Jefferson and Brownsville having their share of toughs, I had to learn to talk my way out of touchy situations. When an Italian "hardguy" has you up against the wall and is ready to belt you for suggesting something bad to his girl friend—who would have dreamed that Nina, who sat across from me in civics, would sic her boy friend after me for asking her if she ever went down on a boy?—as I say, in such a situation, you better learn to talk persuasively or you'll lose some teeth or worse. Bullies, jealous boy friends, and local tough guys will make an "orator" out of any sensitive fifteen-year-old.

And this last No to mythology. It was not my interest in "new zeitgeist life-styles" and "deep-rooted alienation with the world of words" (Professor Daniel Bell) that led me to occasional moviemaking. The truth is more pedestrian. Saturday afternoons with friends at the Sutter or Pitkin theaters in Brownsville, and Sunday afternoons with my father at the Stanley in Manhattan, were the real source. Saturdays meant gleeful episodes giggling with friends on cracked leather seats, improvising havoc for the huge white-uniformed matron-usherette (whom we nicknamed Sidney, after Mr. Greenstreet), staring in awe at John Wayne in *Red River*, Ray Milland in *Dial M for Murder*, Van Johnson in *Thirty Seconds Over Tokyo*. Saturday joys in that noisy teen-age pleasure-dome were mingled with Sunday fears sitting somberly in the hushed Stanley, where middle-aged Russian emigrés, along with strays and sons, also enjoyed the old-world films. There, Russian melodramas and soap operas played side by side with *Alexander Nevsky, Mother, Potemkin, Ivan the Terrible, Storm Over Asia*. And shorts by Charlie Chaplin played instead of Looney Tunes and Bugs Bunny. (My father, sitting stiffly next to me in striped double-breasted suit, gray fedora in his lap; a figure of authority—three quarters—and affection—one quarter.) So movie theaters were a regular ritual for me, funhouses for play, hothouses for fantasy, incubators of troublemaking (from watching Garfield and Widmark, say). No wonder they remained in my heart like churches or synagogues did for other boys, and in my mind as texts for adventure. Dangerous and thrilling texts which came in handy after all.

Still, despite that boyhood folklore, I never really got interested in making movies seriously. Occasionally, I've taken up a friend's 8-millimeter Bell and Howell, but couldn't resist shooting seagulls, hand-holding couples running in the grass, ghetto faces, and other profundities; only my pals took this seriously and missed my point. Documentaries, on the other hand, can be interesting. To photograph the real in motion, when the real is exciting and momentous, can be irreplaceable. (Imagine catching the real Lenin in action, rather than the manufactured robot of historians and hagiographers.) So that when the Museum Uprising occurred, I was keen on preserving it on celluloid. Not a good idea, as you'll see. Which forced me in part to record the whole thing this way, in the old language. The trade of words, so frail and increasingly out-of-date next to pictures, posters, and song, my comrades' way of explaining and remembering.

As for more about my Childhood and Origins, forget them, for the most part. Read Tolstoy, Goethe, and other literary sentimentalists for such colorings. Nowadays, boys and girls like myself must appear, out of the blue, without parents, without pasts. Suddenly we're *here*, on the scene, *intruding, pushing*. How else can we do what we do, at our age? "History suffocates, Action liberates" is an old poster-saying of mine. I still like it, even though I've had my nose rubbed in it.

But if success doesn't get you, as they say, there are official organizations in this free country that will. In other words, *Esquire, Time, The New York Times* fatten you up, but if you remain unsatisfied and still call for trouble, then the F.B.I. and the police will move in for the kill. So you get to be Wanted, your picture posted in the best post offices (it is to Cambridge's credit that its main branch has decided to advertise for me), and a small biography in J. Edgar's renowned Blue Book. I have even, in the past, gotten to know one or two of his agents on a coffee basis.

And, of course, there's prison. Anyone who's anyone has been there these days. Decent folk, I mean. Headed for grad school, my 2-S was suddenly revoked at the end of my senior year and changed to 1-A. Coincidentally, I had been involved in several well-known political demonstrations that winter and spring. Called to the army—to kill for my country—I stood my ground and said No. Three months of lifting rocks and pick-axing ground was the sane part of my stay in that Connecticut prison. The rest was forced midnight sex and sudden daylight fights (i.e., beatings). Finally Kovell and a Mass. congressman were able to get me out, with A.C.L.U. aid. Just in time; otherwise I'd be no good to anyone by now.

But released from Danbury prison, I had the best summer of my life. Everyone should be put away, I'm convinced, to appreciate walking around loose, free. I just wanted to be alone, on my own, no politicking with groups, just thinking to myself. I took a room in a Back Bay rooming house. Kove, good to have around when the chips are down, paid the rent for the summer and gave me a few hundred dollars' spending money to pull myself together. My case wasn't coming up before late autumn, so I was unburdened (though tailed, hence the coffee with agents). I used to walk up and down along the river embankment, seeing the M.I.T. prodigies with their B.U. or Wellesley dates, or the Harvard Yacht Club boys rigging their white sailfish upon the gleaming Charles. Commonwealth Avenue, the Boston Champs Élysées, was for early-evening sauntering, amid the towering elms and maples, the lazy promenading of elderly dog walkers, white-ducked students, and bell-bottomed coeds, open-shirted executives and long-legged secretaries, released from air-conditioned offices. On one of the ancient stone benches I met my summertime pal, who sat down next to me and opened *The Rebel* by Camus. Abby Hodges, from Muncie, Indiana. She had gone to Antioch, dropped out in her junior year to remain with her boy friend in Boston, but was deserted after she had become pregnant. (Not pleasant behavior for a Movement boy.) Abortion over (Daddy Hodges, general practitioner, cut off relations with her), she worked part-time for Manpower, listened to folk music in the Commons. Large-boned, Midwestern pretty, with wheat-hair and prairie-fresh face; her eyes changed when something affected her, radii of gray spreading the brown pupils; she had an inner life. I had known "Abigail" only from the Bible and felt cheated calling her "Abby," which she insisted upon. When we made love, I compensated, repeating the ancient name over and over as the gray returned.

It was the year the Boston Red Sox won the pennant, and Boston evoked for me Brooklyn sandlot games played in the Parade Grounds, and memories of the Dodgers. Fenway Park and the Commons, Commonwealth Avenue and the Charles, became my Lake District, Abby my Lucy, while I pondered how to live. Once or twice a week I went to day games, using my scorecard for a notebook, a paperback for my own bullpen relief. So, while little Lee Stange made the long walk in, I read two or three pages of Anne Frank's *Diary*, Malraux's *Man's Fate*, Mao's biography in *Red Star Over China* (impressed with his early addiction to folk tales and fiction and poetry, which infuriated his father and lasted throughout his life). Yes, fiction was much more dangerous to the young mind than reality, I decided during that relief-pitcher walk-in reading. Or I would neglect a great peg home by Yastrzemski by jotting down, on top of the Yankee lineup, "Political revolution is a theatrical idea in present-day America. But if so, what then?" Unintentionally, I would blaspheme another Harrelson blast into the left-field screen, to reflect, near a Narragansett ad border, "How can you be a good citizen when the basic strains of the society—political, social, economic—run against your strongest ideals and feelings?" To these games I proceeded alone, but to night games I took Abby. In her yellow linen jumper and white organdy blouse, wearing her brown loafers (with the penny inside), she began to root for the Bosox. Nights at Fenway were like May Day festivals, the smells of horsehide leather and cut grass wafting upward, the red sun dying beyond right field, night arriving, and a thousand yellow eyes suddenly flooding the green oval. The eighth or ninth inning would descend, and the crowd hushed at every pitch for the Boston hit that would begin yet another Cinderella rally. It was a good time to reflect. Glancing over at me, Abby would say, "What are you writing, how you think Reggie'll do?" By the picture of a bloated Volkswagen bus I had scribbled, "Has it always been the situation that, as a reward for not wanting to kill, you wind up forced to degrade yourself in prison in order to stay in one piece?" I nodded toward my braided American Baptist (lapsed), "I think a double." Whereupon the crack of the bat meeting the ball screamed through the night, and Abby jumped and squealed, "Oh, Reggie, run, run!"

I was a prophet that summer all right, and also a swallow, flying about freely, trying to figure out where to go for the winter, and for future winters. Well, I decided to return to earth, where I was eventually jailed (but more decently), read a lot, and began to write (the start of my reputation, I suppose), and was paroled after ten months. It was then, I think, that I started to receive those heroic but false political nicknames. For if they had looked inward, better names would have come from literature. From those protagonists who took dirty plunges in spite of their ideals and against their wills. A decisive political actor I may have appeared on the outside, but my heart trembled in fear at every new decision I took to break the law.

A few words about how we came upon the Dean's manuscript.

When Kove was first taken away, Comrade Pearlman and I went to his apartment to see if there was anything useful to our or the Dean's needs. (That "comrade" stuff is amusing. Like playing soldiers when you're little. But my friends want it that way. They're full of children's games. Okay. But imagine looking at Lauri Pearlman, from Shaker Heights, Cleveland, that dark Semitic face unsmiling beneath her Mao cap, the full ass I used to admire and handle now lost in baggy trousers, and addressing her as comrade? My sweet Gilbert-and-Sullivan revolutionary, who's modeled herself on Mao Tse-tung's latest wife, Comrade Chiang Ching. Does she know that Chiang Ching was no more than a vulgar popular actress before Mao took her up—as if Marcuse were suddenly to marry Ann-Margret! Furthermore, that for

Comrade Chiang to act as an arbiter on Chinese literature and art is like having Ann-M. dictate the rules and regulations of art to Balanchine, Bellow, de Kooning, Stravinsky. Now *she* might find that groovy, but her audiences might not. When I tried to suggest some of this to Lauri, diplomatically, she called me counter-revolutionary. I didn't pursue it.)

Now we had no idea of any "manuscript," apart from his scholarship (on the Victorian novelist Gissing). I had been to the apartment before, but the new condition transformed everything: how I felt and what I saw. It is one thing to be an invited guest and something else to be a secret prowler. Curiously, it inspired a certain perverse thrill, like a native servant suddenly taking over his colonial master's place. Exciting, revealing. Dragging to my surface an unknown latent envy. I guess a part of me had all along wanted to change positions with Kovell. Another point. In poking through that apartment—his academician's shell—I discovered that within the husk of official power lives a voyeurist seed. Opening private letters, boxes of miscellanea, underwear drawers, I found myself trembling. I had a sense of what an F.B.I. agent might get out of his spying, a repressed psychosexual joy. Interesting. Secret investigative work a source of sexual perversity. I say all this because I understand better, then, my abstract theory of reversal of roles, whereby persons of authority exchanged places with those beneath them (professors with students, bosses with workers, masters with servants). A theory of "humanizing" that has been taken up recently and upon which I shall elaborate later.

Catching a man off guard that way, with his pants down so to speak, can result in exposing certain truths about his whole life that were only dimly in evidence before. One such truth about the Dean was immediately apparent: his was a life of proliferation without focus. (Except for one item, which is the subject of his text: girls. But even there, the same destructive principle is at work.) Everywhere you walked in those six rooms there were small deposits of assorted and unrelated matters, a kind of mosaic of compulsive and fundamental restlessness. It was as if his concentration span was limited and he grew bored easily; or else, he simply had too many things on his mind. Take the bedroom. On the surface, pleasant, mundane order. But scribbled remarks and comments were found on tables, in drawers; and there was an incredible jungle of addresses and phone numbers on odd pieces of paper on the mantelpiece. Copies of *New York Review*, *Commentary*, and literary journals lay about unevenly, annotated privately, nervously. Alongside these were subscription issues of *The Living Wilderness*, *Natural History*, and even some *National Geographic*. By the end table, looking out upon a tall oak and a small seedy garden, rested a pair of Japanese binoculars atop a Peterson's Bird Guide with several index cards indicating sightings and locations. The contrasts were more than I had expected: handwritten angry criticisms of literary structuralism alongside the sighting of a "superb rose-breasted grosbeak with extra large patch of rose red at Lexington bird feeder; June 10, 1968." When I tried to interest Comrade Pearlman in this, she shot me her best look of simulated proletarian scorn. I smiled to myself, thinking how cute she looked in her peaked cap and fatigue jacket, realizing that I was the only one in the apartment that day able to appreciate fully my old friend.

In the small guest room you got a strong hint of what was to come later, in the manuscript. It was all rather ordinary, except for a row of orange and black correspondence boxes on the bottom shelf of a tall wooden bookcase. These were filled with letters from girls and women. A voluminous correspondence, from everywhere—Brooklyn and Utah, Ljubljana and San Jose, Houston and London, Indiana, Paris (and Paris, Maine!), and so on. From divorcées, former students, a married woman, a friend's daughter, the very young and very old alike. Oh, he knew them all right, and kept up with them, preserved each and every letter. Not to mention the Cambridge-area letters and notes. It was astonishing. About six boxes of the stuff.

The study was a study in more clutter, hodgepodge, confusion. Hard-backed composition notebooks, with ideas and plans for future work. Maps on the wall and in manila folders—of St. Lucia, Yugoslavia, New England, Cuba, the South Pole. What did it mean? And books: like ants, everywhere, on tables, shelves, in bookcases, and in small piles on the floor, waiting to be put away. (Downstairs in the basement there were thirty to forty unopened cartons that had been shipped from Kovell in California to a girl in Belmont, Massachusetts, evidently years ago.

There simply was no room for them upstairs.) Again, the sheer variety and juxtapositions were unsettling—a *Consumer Reports* on the Russian shelf, three *Want Advertisers* open and marked in the midst of his article reprints, United Farm and Strout Realty catalogues tucked between eight volumes of George Eliot. There were three different lists of "Books to Read." I've kept this one:

Spinoza's Life (center on *cherem*, his ex-communication)
Dost. *A Raw Youth*
Bakunin's pornographic novel (where is it?)
Life of a Mnemonist, Luria (novelistic techniques)
more Roheim, more Herzen
Intelligent Life in Universe, Shklovskii (esp. chs 32–5)
more natural history picture books
Liang Ch'i-chao (a trapped intellectual)
Neuroanatomy, Sidman and Sidman (for brain pix)

Not exactly a consecutive reader, was he?

And finally, tucked furtively into a lower corner bookshelf, I discovered a half-dozen paperbacks of cheap pornography. One, about lesbians, with the cover ripped away. (His action?) Another, with passages marked. Masturbation books? Erotica for his girls? Teaching manuals? Out of male sympathy, I think, I kept the cache to myself. (One wonders if he started this dirty book club after or before Gwen got hold of him?)

More clues to confusion and restlessness: the number of personal memoranda, written on index cards, used envelopes, bits of paper, concerning states of mind, observations, comments (about girls, books). A great talker to himself, it seemed. (And rehasher of his experiences, judging from the use of the notes in his long memoir.) As I said, you found them everywhere, in books and folders, on spindles and shelves. Word clutter. And then there were the file cabinets, stuffed with folders of newspaper and magazine clippings, mostly stories of the time. A mugging in which an old refugee from Belsen was beaten to death in an IND subway station, a man in his sixties. A feature about two new drugs used to control behavior in unruly children. A murder of two mathematics professors by a thirty-four-year-old graduate student, whose thesis they had rejected. An Ortho-

dox son beating up his rabbi-father because he lied to him. And
lots of stories about disordered and chaotic teenagers, teeny-
boppers turning into whores, articulate on-the-loose dropouts,
adult-exposure stories, youthful pornographic rings. On top of
these *New York Times* or Boston *Globe* reports, the Dean had
written (in red marker often, with exclamation points and under-
linings) various comments: "The Official End of Privacy." "The
New Fad for Degradation—or is it Need?" "Daily Murder, New
York, 1968." "America über Alles." This collection went on
through four thick cardboard portfolios (tied with string). For
the third or fourth time that day, I wondered where it was leading to. What did it mean? Who was this guy, on the inside?

I can't resist mentioning an entirely useless item which stuck
in my mind and which I have preserved. It was a letter pinned up
over Kove's desk on a corkboard, with an emblem on top—a
basketball going through a hoop, surrounded by a capital C. It
was signed by the general manager of the Boston Celtics.

> Thanks for your kind encouragement and advice, Pro-
> fessor. We too are looking for a better season next year. And
> we better get it!
> Regarding your present recommendation, I can only say
> that lots of these fellows look sensational in the high-school
> gym or local schoolyard, but that pro ball is a great leap
> upward. That's why we recommend college for them. But
> we'll have one of our scouts check your boy out.
> If I remember rightly, my old friend R. C. Evans, the
> coach at Cardozo, told me about a very enthusiastic professor
> over there who has recommended several local players to
> him. Is that you? (Too bad those boys couldn't get through
> the Cardozo entrance requirements. Why don't you do some-
> thing about that admissions office? Don't they have any local
> civic spirit?)
> And thanks again for your annual letter. You did write
> last year, as I recall? About some Cambridge High and Latin
> youngster? It always pleases me when college profs and
> other professionals show an active interest in our sport. Keep
> it up!
>
> Red Auerbach

In the midst of his personal confusions, he remembered his sports. Clearly Mr. Kovell was an American of parts.

Mechanical parts too. Not one but two cars, an old Ford and a ten-year-old Mercedes. Three radios, a stereo set, a few tape recorders, a pair of electric scissors. A child with his mechanical toys. And yet he was not mechanical at all, I know for a fact, and he was not a music buff. In other words, these things simply piled up. They attached themselves to him, like barnacles. Had he been sixty with this collection of miscellanea, it would be understandable. But in his early thirties? The Dean had too much on his mind; his agenda was too full.

We found the manuscript in a cardboard box in his metal file cabinet. (Actually, there were several drafts or versions, ranging from sixty-odd pages to the present text.) Attached by rubber band to an early version was a series of letters between the Dean and an editor of a New York literary magazine, Gerald Sklar. It seems that Sklar had heard about the Dean's private life from a colleague friend and urged him to write about it in a sort of memoir. In any case, it turned out different from what the editor wanted, as may be seen from this letter.

June 20, 1968

Dear Professor Kovell:

I am very sorry to have to return "Family Talk," since there are many interesting "stories" in it, and since, of course, I encouraged the writing in the first place. Apart from the extraordinary size of it—90 pages is an impossible length for any magazine—I find serious problems with it. One is that it is not what I had hoped for in the way of political reference points. That is, I had anticipated your tying together personal difficulties with public events. Your situation, after all, as dean at a major university where student revolution is in high gear, cannot be simply passed over for the sake of a private story. Furthermore, when you do discuss the students, it is with a peculiarly critical tone that I must say surprises me, since I had thought you were a good friend of theirs. Now, while you don't really elaborate upon the matter, it is clear that the designation "good friend" is misleading. Finally, there is a certain lack of credibility

19

about the story itself. If this were supposed to be fiction and not a *real* memoir, perhaps you could get away with your tale. But the basic situation seems to me to be unbelievable. I simply find it hard to conceive of a man holding together so many women. Perhaps this is because I sense a certain sense of hasty sketchiness in your story. (And the affair with the black girl seems rather unreal.)

I cannot help but believe that you played a subtle trick on yourself here and confused reality with fantasy. This is probably due in part to the newness of the enterprise for you. The act of setting down personal experiences onto the printed page is harder than most people think. At least it was always so for me.

Enclosed please find a check for $250 for having written the piece at my request. I am sorry it didn't work out.

Sincerely,
Gerald Sklar

Obviously the letter of rejection irritated and challenged the Dean, so that he made his memoir almost three times longer, in an effort to explain in more detail and roundness, to remove that sense of "hasty sketchiness." The content changes too, although the basic pattern remains the same, as the tale expands: each version is more sexually explicit and more morally bold than the previous one. It's as if each version loosened him more and motivated him to tell a deeper truth. (For example, in the first sixty-page version, the feeling finally evoked is close to farce and fun, the characters drawn in brushstrokes, and the situation more "literary" than real. It is very different indeed from the steady confusion and unabating self-anguish of the last version.) Nor, finally, should it be missed that the final copy was set in a box and laid to oblivious rest. It seems that the deepest truth was too hard even for Kovell. Even he could not make the final breakthrough beyond bourgeois pride and humiliation.

Unlike the literary-minded editor, however, we believe that the document, though it barely mentions politics, has deep political implications.

A final word about general events and the makeup of this book.

Since the famous Museum Uprising of last June and the notorious events following from it, there has been a lot of excitement everywhere. Fair enough. But the clamor and noise made by the media suggest such grand events as the seizure of the Winter Palace in Petrograd in 1917, or, in our own time, the landing on the moon in 1969. Typical American overpublicity. It so happens that we are neither Lenins nor Armstrongs, but university students making some trouble. To call what's happened a "revolution"—the closing of certain museums, concert halls, theaters, and cinemas, among other things—is to overstate the matter grossly. So to cool the CBS heat (two successive Sunday specials), and to correct the government's inaccuracies (especially our Vice President's recent speeches), to counter the *New York Times* pap (editorial wisdom), we've decided to break the moratorium on words and compile this text. In a sense it is unique. For it is no great secret that books—artifacts written by single individuals in isolation, primarily for the enjoyment of the world's elites—have become obsolete for recording contemporary history (i.e., June 9–10, 1971). Or that films, tapes, and certain music, products of collective hands and accessible to common men everywhere, have replaced them. A change in recording tools that reflects a philosophical and moral change. Because of it, this book, done for the old guard, as it were, may be a unique project.

The text is composed of two voices, that of Dean Kovell and my own. The Dean's words come in two places. The first, Family Talk, is the full chronicle of his hectic private life and forms Book One. The second and smaller document, which I have entitled Barricade Anxiety, reflects his public position as professor and citizen, a man of official authority, and appears later, in its chronological order. This consists of selected portions of the Dean's famous Castroesque speech delivered to the student rebels occupying the university art museum. Its appearance in print will, I hope, dissolve the exaggerated speculation regarding the speech and his role that fateful night, prior to the notorious events which followed.

My own words—those that have been written thus far, at least—come mostly in Book Two. Much of this has been difficult to write since, apart from the obstacle of writing it on the run, I'm speaking of an old personal friend. And also, to take a step further, of another friend, our civilization. Both of whom I have admired in the past and now find obsolete. My aim there is to give some historical perspective to the Dean's situation. It is also to tell a human story. His *and* mine. For this, many political friends will be unhappy. They are interested in political facts, hard analysis, theoretical programs. Sympathy, affection, and grief will strike them as irrelevant or downright bourgeois. I agree, they are both. But they form part of the truth. More, Book Two contains notes on my life and fragments of an ideological manifesto. Fragments because the most one can do nowadays is to describe and annotate contemporary history, let alone buttress it with a full-fledged philosophy. The day of total systems is past. Events in our time change too swiftly and too qualitatively to come to finite conclusions. It is like asking Marx to look in on a nuclear linear accelerator, with atoms crashing and exploding, and explain things. It won't do.

Concerning the narrative of my life, I wish to make it clear that the life of making trouble today—for it's closer to that so far than to overthrowing regimes—is harder than it's ever been. It's no fun and glory any longer playing the radical halfback. Not in America. The opposing linemen make it difficult. Either there are no holes open, or they are strategic illusions. You lower your head, run, and hope for the best. If you're not tackled hard, you suffer a worse fate in some ways: you're tossed in the air, like a child, and toasted and embarrassed. In other words, playing revolution in America in the 1970's is quite a different game from doing it in other places, other times.

And no matter how far we've gone till now with some success, there's little guarantee that we will continue to do so with impunity. I'd like to think that we can go all the way and change America, beginning at the top, but I realize that that's a dream. But is that any reason to give up the pursuit? Not this boy, anyway. So far I've been lucky, moving about with freewheeling bravado and beginner's luck. But who knows how long that will last? Or my arrogance? (And so this preface, before the whole story has been completed.) I have no permanent lease on either, luck or arrogance. And when one or the other runs out . . . I'm in trouble. So, for the time being, first downs not touchdowns are my objective. But they can put you away a long time for those too; after all, twenty-four hours in jail can be like four hundred normal hours. I know, I've been there.

It's fortunate that the Dean's "case" is argued by himself, in his own words. It is one of those rare moments in history when the disintegration of a culture is suggested through an individual biography. The great Russian literary critic Belinsky once wrote, "Historical development is enacted always and everywhere through human personality; and this explains why the history of every nation resembles a combination of the biographies of individuals." This holds true for the Dean's story, a narrative poignant, powerful, and instructive. Interestingly, one of the main reasons for this is to be found in Dean Kovell's remarkable ingenuousness regarding the logical political consequences of his personal dilemma. His political innocence, in other words, is *politically useful*. To my knowledge, no better chronicle exists in recent history that testifies at once to the hopelessness of a culture's values and institutions, and to the necessity for dismantling both.

Indeed, if I may hesitantly move from the particular to the general for a moment, reading Family Talk is like reading a long meditative poem on the state of mind and spirit of (advanced) American man today. It is a mind and spirit in deep trouble, turning and turning in search of a way out, near exhaustion from a futile project. I publish these documents with the hope that they will shed significant light on the personal and public crises of the day. A twin crisis that, according to a Walter Lippmann essay, "threatens the stability of the nation, and perhaps the stability of Western Civilization." A grand statement by the old man. It is not far wrong.

Bernard Kovell was a kind friend and in his own way an honest man. Even the sort of man whom I one time thought of as a model. Now I've come to see him as a different sort of model, a kind of Americanized version of Romanov-Quixote, a European Liberal-Idealist turned Massachusetts sensualist, tilting simultaneously at foolish theories and female bodies. A condition we're working on. Yet, if a dedication were called for, it would go to him—and possibly to his Cambridge girls—for it was that curious family which convinced me that changes had to be made across

23

the board—and bed—as well as on top, in politics. But such
adornment belongs to writers more hopeful than myself—to the
poets and novelists perhaps, whose struggle is with their imagined
worlds and whose basic faith in man thus remains secure. For
my part, I have struggled too much with the real world of
America in the last few years. It has inhibited my fancy,
hardened feelings, blackened hope. It has taught me that only
action will change the real world, and that the only words that
are healthy are those that encourage action. Otherwise, words are
deceptive filigree, used to bolster and protect the cultured and
the privileged.

This is a book for men and women and boys and girls who
believe that such shaking up is necessary for human survival and
human decency; a book for those who are willing to face up to
the actual consequences of their abstract knowledge and instincts
concerning the nation. Our own recent deeds have been based
upon one clear premise: namely, that it is we the student brigands
opposed to America who envision a future, and they, the government and its circles of defenders, who are heading for an end. As
we all know now, the opportunity for choosing a middle road
between us and them, between the justness of rebellious chaos
and the vengeance of government order, between moral violence
and immoral power, has been closed down by our recent siege.

So read these texts, look around you with an honest eye, and
have the courage to make a truthful choice. To live with danger
in these times, with the ache of disorder in one's bones and the
bars of prison down one's horizon, is to live with health.

Lenny Pincus
Hibernation House
In the American mountains

1: FAMILY TALK

*Virtue accompanied by
full potency is usually
felt as a hard task.*
—SIGMUND FREUD

*Whores, mistresses, cooks, wild
beauties, servant girls, typists . . .*
—BERNARD KOVELL

It's not easy having six mistresses, even if two or three lie dormant for a few months at a time, waiting for the phone to ring or that note to arrive which will bring them in from bullpen work to a starting role again. No, it's not all fun and games. Especially if you're a professor and dean. You're kept wildly busy just managing and keeping up, with some of the girls being mothers and working, and I myself lecturing on Conrad or Dickens while attending endless committee meetings, faculty convenings, and student councils. Dinner dates, schedules, birthdays, the right ethnic holiday, not to mention the burden of everyday logistics, game plans—two nights with this girl, a weekend with that one, a heavy month of Gwen and Grace—it's murder! But what could you do these days, with society so nervous, except to take mistresses? Non sequitur? Let me explain. Phone calls, pneumatic drills, jet planes, ambulance and police sirens, trucks and dogs, transistors loose on the streets, and amplified rhythms funneled into the shops—how much can the nervous system stand (or the eardrum)? And the mind: assaulted by endless theories, facts, names; by magazine articles that are essential or a new biochemical discovery drawn in detail in the *Times* that must be understood; by plans, necessities, urgencies, and tactics, new histories and etiologies; and then, when you think you have a subject under control—the origins of the earth or DNA structures or the rise of the Mets—wham! bang! you're hit with the reappraisals, the books of reassessment and reinterpretation, each cutting a finer slice (like a cheese cutter), making yet another qualification, or else overthrowing the whole data cart. Where on earth can one stand with security?

And in the midst of this nonstop disc-jockey intellectuality, what about that antique object, that cornerstone of society, call it what you will, soul, spirit, heart? With Clinical Truth uppermost, what chance does the heart have in Webster's: "a hollow muscular organ which by rhythmic constrictions and relaxations . . ." All of us are familiar enough with the judgments handed down by modern life upon some of its traditional attributes—fidelity: old-fashioned; goodwill: a Victorian hypocrisy; fraternity: a mythology; love: an illusion. Civilization has grown too complex, too knowing, too *filled*. Our globe is bursting at the seams: vast nations on the verge of teeming overflow; policeman-powers on the edge of triggering universal catastrophe; superior minds of both East and West breaking with despair; art, that reflection of our deepest condition, shaking with images of fear and psychosis; air, in which we live, coming down with man-made diseases. Untherapeutic knowledge, failing potentiality, growing complication, mounting waste and misdirection, producing a moral flora and fauna of anxiety and desperation. Meanwhile, the bridge connecting the past with the present sags badly from the endless flow of traffic—history, philosophy, anthropology, universal emotions and frustrations. How much longer before the whole massive structure, that span of civilized identity, collapses into the sea? In the face of it all, the spirit—made obsolete by the efficiency experts who run our land and define the modern character, those engineers of the psyche as well as the highway—withdraws in bewilderment, fatigue, desperation. There, that last: *desperation*. That's what it comes down to in the present moment. People are desperate. Those who care and those who can think. Desperate about their lives, their countries and governments, the future of the earth. Desperate.

From the populace to the intellectuals and artists, there is breakdown. Those inane talk shows that rumble on through morning, noon, and night, touching every subject conceivable from the Six-Day War to UFO's to diaper services to ESP to the generation gap. The euphemistic and pathetic attempt to assuage loneliness by means of three-minute telephone conversations with some "talkmaster" who can barely speak the language, let alone think. And the expensive tidal wave of encounter groups that has flooded the culture. Vulgar substitutes for religious salvation for the wounded, the confused, the simple-minded. Braille touching in place of understanding, predicated upon the absurdity that everyone is Sensitive. A jetsam and flotsam of confusion mirrored by the more serious. Look at those fifty-year-old men and women who have not been lulled by routine or dulled by certitudes. They're going crazy. Scars, pains, children, friends, and ex-mates scattered about like dead autumn leaves. Personal accomplishments like books and paintings suddenly meager and meaningless in the face of the larger situation. The interesting ones are going crazy. Meshuggah. Novelists breaking down and crying at friends' apartments; academics helpless and shrieking in shrinks' offices; poets taken off to asylums for regular winter rests; painters slashing their wrists. All over, the most serious citizens of America (and the world?) breaking down. Over how to run their lives. Over the direction of their society. Over their children. Over their work. It's awful. It's desperate.

Like the body, the spirit is getting mugged day-in, day-out.

So I turn to women. To Angela and Gwen, to Sophie and Grace, to Melissa and Kate. At thirty-four (three days ago), in full control of my rational faculties, a respectable university professor, I live with several ladies at a time. An old habit of mine— late teens, say—that I've made into a precise and permanent way of life—since age thirty-one, say (before it's too late, and I've spent my life in monogamy-boredom, alimony-thralldom, and gone mad like the rest of the middle-aged). A harem for a family soothes and refreshes me. Like Caribbean water, a harem seems to be the perfect medium for keeping a man afloat, his head above water, sane. One woman is impossible these days, everyone knows that. One woman will never keep you off the streets nowadays, or out of mischief. Where it used to take one, it now takes three or four. Naturally, such an arrangement in our society embarrasses me. I'm not fond of boasting of it. And don't. Of course, my personal history is filled with such curious doings, dating from age six and seven when Mrs. Lindner, my first-grade teacher, would sit and hold my face against her great breasts, stirring me to Fellini-like daydreams; or when Miss Kirkpatrick, my slim spinster second-grade teacher, pressed my head against her flat belly, my nose pushing inward just beneath—

But wait, I'm skipping steps.

Society is nervous. More: it is growing eroticized. It is turning into a brothel. Imagine that complicated organism transformed into a *brothel*. In the old days, England in the eighteenth century or America in the 1950's, it was possible to retreat to society to escape from brothels. In fact, that was one of its main purposes for young men. Escape to dinner parties for sophisticated talk and observation of forms, traditions; to leisurely promenades, to view the architecture of the city; to college campuses for study and reflection; to museums and theaters for culture. Naturally, through it all, there was contact with ladies—with wives and secretaries, female professors and checkout clerks, doctors and usherettes—but ladies, not budding whores or husband-cheaters. Ladies not reminding you every moment of their sexuality. In other words, any kind of dull routine would do in order to make a young man forget for a moment his sexual urges. To dull and redirect them. Forays into society were therefore pleasant, tranquilizing, useful. But now look around you: at dinners and walks, parks and universities, playgrounds and movie houses, *it's all a brothel*. The society of Hobbes and Locke exchanged for that of Sade and Genet. For a reasonable, nervous young man of our times, like myself, there's no escape. Sweet faces and sweet bodies beckon.

Look around, for example, in the berserk streets. Here in Cambridge, March is wafting its spring breezes through the frozen city, lifting the girls onto the sidewalks and toward Harvard Square, one of the city's grand display centers. A casual ten-minute walk from my apartment to the Harvard Trust Bank is filled with parading females, there for one purpose: exposure. Public and private exposure. (And if I'm driving, groups of twos and threes are spaced fifty feet apart, hitchhiking. Like packs of young wolves, they thumb in every direction, waiting to pile into your car, your pants, your life.) By the time I reach my bank—the only real competition to the brothel motif—I'm staggering, and ready to hand over my month's salary to the tall blonde bank teller, Miss Horton, if only she will invite me into her cage. Seriously ready to pay her a handsome sum to run my hand along her long leg, and other privileges, if we can do it in the cage right there. I've never seduced a girl in a bank, and wonder why I have to wait till later, in the dullness of her bedroom. In fact, it's the cage and the bank which make Miss Horton tempting. I'm mad, you say? I agree.

Made mad by the business on the streets. Monkey business. The seventeen-inch length of black leather boot and the fifteen-inch patch called skirt tempting you with thigh, thigh, acres of white thigh. The flare-bottom navy jeans that hug the apple-behinds and dare you, call you to take a bite. (And who could resist such a passion since the days of Leopold Bloom?) And what about the new liberated area, friends, the brassièreless era? The loose-haired, free-floating girls who wander about in their flimsy blouses, tantalizing in transparency, titties jiggling sweetly like pink jello? (In a hot daze, I follow every pair.) And I mean *all* the girls, not just this age group or that ethnic minority. From fourteen-year-old Brownies-turned-Lolitas, flashing thigh and leg for want of breast, to forty-year-old suburbanites, with their Heinz 57 varieties of tans and dyes. Those leather-tough Lexington and Lincoln mothers, pushed up against the wall by teenagers (their own) and affluence, are no pushovers in The Competition. In dark glasses (incognito appetites), and tight pants suits, they are professionals at advertising the right curve of belly, at perking up the aging breasts ("child stuff," a Brattle Street madame once propagandized to me derisively, as I played with hers), at accentuating the veteran crotches (true expertise). When Brownies start offering their bodies instead of their cookies, the pressure's on.

Do you see what I mean? Are you getting the gist of this?

Look, things are not as they used to be. It's in the air, in your bones, if you're alive. It's not simply a movie arcade offering a new nude, or a bikinied cowgirl shooting by in your mind (courtesy of television) every time a Dodge Coronet turns the corner. The signals are more emphatic everywhere, in that sly hippie smile, this married woman's greed, that delicious boot. The heat pours in everywhere in this Circe-Cambridge, to seduce and to transform. To suck you in. (This heat, I better admit now, affects one's prose as much as it does parts of the anatomy. In other times, this meditation might be composed with more calm, equilibrium, distance; with less attention to specific gross detail. Such detachment is impossible now. And unfaithful both to the urgency of the times and to the fever of my emotions.) An erotic Fahrenheit pressuring everything. Even history. Consider the Cambridge Common. Where three hundred years ago elections were held for the Massachusetts Bay Colony, now the kids gather to pass reefers, drop pills, rotate their hips. Where George Washington took charge of the first Continental Army in 1775, two hundred years later teen-age girls in pastel T-shirts sit curled on symbolic cannons, licking at ice-cream cones, trailing hair, titties eyeing you as you pass. By the huge Civil War monument in the center of the park, rock bands assemble to rev up the atmosphere. And by the statue of the Puritan who started the first public school in Cambridge, bare-midriff girls and bare-chested boys dance, flirt, fuck. Play dissolving work; bodies, minds.

And look at the shops along Mass. Ave. Where once was an Italian shoe repairman, a family store for half a century, now there is a record shop, slamming away for sixteen hours a day the latest in frenzied repetitiveness. Rhythms to dream of violence by. Serviced by a skinny Jewish dropout who shows you her nipples when she wraps your records, and by a pair of pretty black boys in lavender shirts, eunuchs of another age now brown gods. Social history through shoes wiped out by amplified shrieks and historyless nomads. And in place of the neighborhood drugstore, a shop specializing in skins and hair: fur caps and leather badman hats, Canadian bearskins and racks of hanging goatskin rugs, steerhide jackets and Icelandic sheepskins. The smells of killed animals. The mustached salesboy is attired in shiny leather trousers, vest, and boots, a few hundred dollars of cowboy fantasy poured into Jeremy Fishman of the Bronx. And two high-school girls swooning over the excitement of riding a fake horse and stroking his real furry mane. Making me perspire. Finally, in a leather and sandal shop, where once there was a Polish grocery, a pale blonde of twenty druggedly assents to a seventy-five-dollar leather skirt, while her tall stylish black boy friend struts in front of the mirror, deciding upon a pair of forty-dollar shoes. Fresh leather replacing fresh fish; moneyed, faceless children replacing old-world characters . . . Oh, it was jumping all right; no longer dull as it used to be with the prosaic druggists and grocers and shoe repairmen. A change signified most emphatically by the sounds ramming the new shops, as if they were all connected on one circuit. Giant speakers loomed everywhere, looking like Big Brother warning systems, announcing incessantly the hard beats of amplified drums and guitars. Smothering you in sound and din, a curious revolutionary counterpart to the bourgeois pap of Muzak. One noise counterpoised against the other. Insipid background versus intrusive foreground. Electronics interfering with talk, technology smashing observation. Noise that blurred the art of distinguishing and that jabbed your nerves with mindless anticipation. Was this the revolution—this music? this capitalism? this eroticizing?

With accompanying lyrics that matched the new décor and aura. The sexual exhortation of "Come on, baby, light my fire" and "I can't get no satisfaction" was the underlying meaning of the transformed street. The thrust of primitivism was shoving aside the dullness of utility. Mass. Ave. was dropping the M and capitalizing the A. The more primitive, the better, the motto for Ass Avenue. The more flesh exposed, the hotter. The more animal-like the Gestalt, the stronger. Of course their imaginations were dull. Picture the realization of their true desires: importing into the shops cattle, pigs, and horses, along with stalls and pens as permanent fixtures. Call a shop The Pig-Sty, which would sell expensive chic clothes. Fill it with mud, rotten apples, and grunting pigs, alongside racks of fashionable outfits for the affluent. A white high-school boy would tend the sty, while a beautiful bronze boy could handle the cash register. You would browse, spend a few hundred, feed the pigs. An agricultural fantasy to rake in the cash; pigs to spread the word and excite the senses. Enough contradictions (with the white boy serving the black proprietor) to make it fashionable.

And across the street you could house an underground

coffeehouse, bar, and dope den. Call it the Stygian Stables, with three or four horses kept in real stalls. On the pillowed floors adjacent, you could drift on your marijuana, sail on your speed, and laugh at an occasional whinny by a horse gone loony from the drugs and the smashing amplifiers. More fun: imbibing your hash, you would watch a *natural process:* a magnificent mare defecating, the shit pouring out in a liquid stream, the vile smells mingling with the oversweet aromas to produce a new pungency. Back to the land, to the soil, right there in the midst of bourgeois cities! Underground, with the shit and piss and oats and odors, dropping pills or shooting stuff, the revolving records rounding off transcendence. Who could ask for anything more? Nature and technology and chemistry in the service of revolution.

And so on down the street, until horses, cows, geese, and pigs inhabited the stores, defecating and whinnying and oinking; an Animal Farm protest in the 1970's against 1984 Man. A vision of the future based upon present realities, directions. Boys and girls joining the gander in caves of copulation, while the March of Profit continued above, unabated, by Bureaucratic Man. Id versus greed. Animals versus robots. Subversive fantasy-life versus respectable-reality. One extreme situation, state of mind, provoking their opposites. Where was discrimination, distinction? An underground world of the primitive past, of tribal rites and so-called third-world customs pitted against all that concrete folly, uptight architecture, machine progress upstairs. African dashikis and dances, Asian and Mexican drugs, Indian sitars and prayers, Navajo beads and beliefs marshaled against white Anglo-Saxon man. Assaults upon Western civilization by the savage mind and savage rites; why not savage tactics too? Lévi-Strauss versus Plato and Aristotle. Fanon rather than Lenin. Where would it lead?

Meanwhile, the brothels were here. Only the sex was free and could be had anywhere. In fact, the more public, the more thrilling. A serene blowjob under the Weeks Footbridge, with students strolling overhead; a handjob inside the Calder mobile at night in M.I.T., with a couple walking around it, a few feet away, discussing sculpture; floor-fucking in a Widener study (borrowed from a Harvard colleague to work on my Gissing), after borrowing a graduate student from the stacks. A clue to seduction could always be gotten from the latest rock lyrics: "Say the word and set me free," sang the Beatles. So with the Cambridge brothel. The female of your choice, with this season's right word substituting for the green fee: "beautiful" or "groovy" worth twenty bucks (a short time); "heavy" and "getting it all together," half a bill and a whole night's stay. (Of course, any university was a setup for a shrewd pimp.) . . . Yes, Cambridge was turning into the old Shanghai of New England: a city of sin dens and Oriental prurience, with little and big girls, daughters and mommies working the streets. All it needed to make it official was a Public Fucking Lot constructed on the Cambridge Common: partitioned spaces with four-poster beds and parking meters for short or long times . . . Was all this a prelude to revolution, American-style? Or the means of stifling and deflating revolution, also American-style? Only time would tell.

Cambridge nervousness: the result of women and the universities. A town that combined ancient Alexandria learning and Weimar culture with touches of Shanghai decadence and St. Petersburg rebellion. Exaggerated? Perhaps. But that's what you felt there. With anarchic rock concerts on Sunday replacing church services in the Cambridge Common; Eisenstein movies at the Brattle; lectures by famous scholars two or three times weekly; bulletin-board announcements of underground nihilist and terrorist movements; chamber quartets playing Mozart and Bach; marijuana, hashish, and stronger stuff (LSD, heroin, speed) available on most corners. Sex, rebellion, and learning mixing together like a massive stew. (The learning dominating to the naked eye.) In America, university towns—or universities in cities—are Einsteins amid the apes, Babbitts, and J. P. Morgans. Islets of civilization surrounded by oceans of primitivism and commercialism. Dots of sanity flashing like airstrip signals amid a terrain of irrationality and brute force.

And what better town than Cambridge for displaying the learning side of man? Dominated by our two giants of wisdom, one speaking for the past, the other for the future. Nestling in low red-brick serenity was that three-hundred-year-old Nestor of schools, Harvard. A traditional incubator for the ordinary men who lead American society—American Presidents, financial titans, newspaper publishers—as well as a sanctuary for the wilder birds of the *Homo sapiens* species, the poets, critics, thinkers. The grand house of the humanities and the classical tradition, sprawled in neat Georgian dress amid lawns and gates and courtyards. While a few miles down the Charles, plebeian M.I.T. rose skyward in its new Gothic verticals, efficient, functional, heterogeneous, unwalled. The aesthetic steeples of medieval theology transformed into the glass-and-concrete skyscrapers of the new Western religion, science. By Harvard Square, the ancient stability of classical beauty (*"Humani nil a me alienum puto"*) and Moses-Jesus ethics-religion; by Tech Square, the buzzing excitement of laser-beams, IBM computers, post $E = mc^2$ theorizing. The linear and pictorial preservation of the past versus the electronic and mathematical waves of the future. Cambridge was, in microcosm, the new crossroads of civilization. Libraries and museums collecting man's footprints; laboratories charting his future directions (to the moon and Mars and genetic immortality). Faustian force and Promethean spirit converging in pursuit of . . . a new definition of man? With those soaring steeples of M.I.T. way ahead of its obsolescent aristocratic brethren.

One had a sense that if answers to man's problem were to be found, they would be found here or nowhere. The planets and stars were observed carefully. Man's genes were broken down and reconstructed. Lunar modules were blueprinted. New theories of literature and sociology were proposed. Atoms were smashed and photographed. Pigeon brains were tested and charted. Intellectual leaders were to Cambridge what prize-fighters and baseball heroes were to the rest of America. Any day you expected to see university students flipping and matching cards with their favorites pictured on them: the acerbic DNA Englishman; the controversial Linguistics champ; the embattled King of the Behaviorists; the newly crowned successor to the psychoanalysis throne. The analogies were easy enough to construct. In sociology, for example, you had your prominent Harvard duo, the Jewish Koufax of Lonely Crowds and the Wasp Drysdale of Pluralist Models; in economics, there was the tall Scottish maverick who was as brilliant and malicious as Ty Cobb; or across town, the quiet textbook star of M.I.T., who resembled

Lou Gehrig in his indefatigable Editions; in literary criticism, the polyglot hitter from Cambridge who sprayed articles and books around like harmless singles; while his counterpart, from Back Bay, wrote polemical articles that were long-distance jobs which shook everyone up—a thin mustached Waner and a husky Russian Ruth. For any shrewd advertiser who knew his America, there was money to be made: pens and pencils could have personal signatures like Louisville Slugger bats, or typewriters could have brand names of distinction like baseball gloves. Imagine a Rahv Standard or Chomsky portable, a Riesman fountain pen or Parsons lead pencil. Fame had hit the intellectual fan; the situation needed a Saperstein or De Mille to capitalize on it.

Oh, it was humming all right. The mind. The Western mind. The north star of our universe. It had its own new imagery too, in those M.I.T.-based IBM computers that buzzed and clicked 365 days a year, nonstop, automatic. The spirit of the year 2020, some half century from now, was embodied in those sky-blue and pastel-pink vending machines of discs and tape decks that went on tabulating, memorizing, solving, thinking, talking every minute every hour every day. Absorbing man's diet of words and numbers and converting them into new solutions and languages. How odd the way in which old forms were resurrected with new functions. Those pastel upright rectangles, which in another era gave you Coca-Cola on a subway platform, or Frank Sinatra in a candy-store jukebox, now answered questions, developed theories. Clearly, IBM 360/40 or 360/20 were the new heroes; to the scientists now, but in future years, as they entered homes, to the masses. Zeus computer stores would be as abundant perhaps as Midas muffler shops. It was only a matter of time probably before man could turn to them for love, too. If not love, sex. Coupling with computers, flesh discharging its passion in metal holes, or steel surging into vaginas, would be as significant a step in altering man's patterns as flying to Mars. Someone was probably programming it now. Perhaps warming up some IBM's erotic life by feeding it, to begin with, pornographic stories.

The future of mankind was MIT Man. A whole new category perhaps. From the Neanderthals to the MIT's. Apes, men, MIT's: a progression in evolution. From Java to America; beginnings and endings. Europe in the middle. If you knew your

Cambridge, you sensed this. Living within walking distance of those sizzling fluorescent laboratories was like living beneath a volcano: eating and breathing right near where man's extinction was being computed, his transformation programmed. The thought was startling. Unnerving. It made you want to run for cover, escape. With a female. With several. Easy way out? In a way. Pathetic? Perhaps. All too human? Yes.

The pressure of the town was felt everywhere, in the gaseous air, in furtive coffee shops, in tenured and untenured bones. Academics sitting by the Charles were more interested in scholarly journals than in coeds lounging on blankets. A Wellesley professor, while getting out of her panties, told me of her latest article in *PMLA*. At a dinner party, a request for the salt and pepper brought forth a lecture on ego-formation; another time, my desire for a second helping of asparagus plunged me *in medias res* into that contemporary abyss, education theory. In short, the atmosphere of academic success and its pursuit was poisonous, impairing. Prematurely, it sifted men's hair, widened their buttocks, cursed them with hemorrhoids. To women it delivered eyeglasses, varicose veins, schoolmarm temperaments. The costs of success were high. For one, it meant alcoholism. For another, impotence, eunuchism. A third found herself a compulsive whore for short-time appointments by day (twice a week), a confused lesbian for long-term affairs. A painful double life, poor woman, endured with the aid of a permanent shrink. The hypocritical, mistaken, and insipid criteria of success—scribbling unread articles and footnotes, making up useless anthologies, writing three-hundred-page books where fifteen pages will do—all this took its toll from the flesh and the spirit. Paunchy bodies, spiritual dullards, neurotic minds it made of its clientele.

There was the pressure of the students, too. I mean more than the usual headaches of trying to deal with hordes of high-school mentalities who are permitted into college. Being a dean is no easy matter these days, even if you're young, well liked, and originally put into office by the marauders themselves. Like myself. At Cardozo College, where I teach—a liberal-arts college set on a hillside fifteen miles from Cambridge—the troubles are characteristic enough. Young boys and girls squatting overnight in corridors, like Indians, or hanging from the roofs, like chimps.

Blacks entering classrooms unannounced, to deliver propaganda and ultimatums. Anyone a Luther who has the color for it. Young guerrilla faculty preaching apocalypse from literature lecterns. Older colleagues developing ulcers and coronaries in their hatred of the students. Battles of fathers and sons, disguised beneath political rhetoric.

Our once-innocent oases were turning into bloody battle-grounds, with crass politicians, four-star generals, two-bit movie actors, and big-business magnates becoming more prominent than the poets and historians. The Id of society was the campus, exploding everywhere in rage and anger. Catching fellows like myself in the middle. Those of us who side intellectually with many of the rebel idealists—wishing the war would stop and the capitalists would ease up on profits for the sake of human decency—but who emotionally are unable to stand the new tactics. Rejecting irrationality. Believing in order and procedures. Admiring reason and excellence. Deploring violence. (For all of this, I guess, some of the students are beginning to rumble about my conservatism. But surely they know that I'm for change, serious change? In fact, if they could show me how political revolution, not theater revolution, might be achieved by certain violent means, I'd at least see more practical point to it and be able to consider the matter more seriously. But as it is?) Increasingly, I feel trapped. Which is ironically one of the main reasons why many students seem to sympathize with me (especially Pincus): they seem to like my candid admission of confusion.

Trapped. Between the two forces, armies. On one hand there are one's colleagues, decent fellows for the most part, but *tired*. Bored by wives, nagged by incomplete projects, challenged by sharp students, hounded by old ambitions. Gentle souls in English tweeds toiling quietly with little literary spades in their special-ized gardens. Bothering no one, hardly stirring up the soil. Per-forming repetitious tasks without harming anyone. And their (younger) counterparts: the burgeoning radical faculty, who discovered revolution yesterday, leaping about like bullfrogs, croaking apocalypse. Confused fellows who confuse their stu-dents, they are anxious to remake Pope (Alexander) into Mao, Shakespeare into Sorel. Growing angry when they won't fit. Ready to do away with both gentlemen because they lacked the proper radical genes! Tenured fatigue opposed by untenured confusion. And then there are the students, perhaps the cleverest, who had, out of frustration and misguidance and more confusion, been infected by the revolution-rabies. Self-acknowledged "crazy dogs," they are on the lookout for gardens to run roughshod over, for gardeners to hold hostage and kidnap and do worse things to (it was only the beginning, clearly); even though it may have nothing to do with putting a halt to the larger madness of the society.

Between the madness of that society and the chaos of campuses, between my confused and vindictive colleagues and the infected young, there seemed to be no firm ground for a sane man to stand on. No solid position to speak from.

The calm of reflection, the cornerstone of student life, has been replaced by the fury of battle, the trademark of the soldier. More and more students were becoming soldiers, cadres; but soldiers without a general, a battle plan, even at times a clear enemy. It was distressing. It meant that you never knew where you stood: one day a friend, the next—overnight—you had become the foe. Mao's China was nearer than one thought. Who knew what they might cook up for me one day? Since the chaos has started, it's been harder to think, to sleep; I seem to thrash about endlessly, my feet fidget involuntarily, students intrude upon my drowsiness, my dreams.

And they're everywhere, like ants. Putting pressure on your private life. Take the Saturday when I foolishly walked with Gwen, my black friend, and her two boys through the Commons. (The risk was serious that I would be seen by one of my other girls. Country walks are clearly the safest for a man in my situation.) My name was suddenly called, and my heart thumped. "Hello, Professor Kovell," announced a bouncy undergraduate whom I vaguely recognized. "I just wonder, sir, which novella we'll be reading for next week." (Ponytail, chewing gum, smiling.) And excited: "Did you hear the news of the new sit-in demands? Excuse me, Mrs. Kovell. I'm Carol Klein, pleased to meet you!"

What can I say to all this? Which do I answer first—novella? wife? liberation? Where am I, anyway, in Red Square, tailed by the K.B.G.? Beneath the interested gaze of Gwen, I say, "This is a friend, Mrs. Tresvant, and her two boys, Rodney and Lester."

My dark glasses return to my eyes, and I glance quickly about. Thank God, no blond hair (Angela), no convict's face (Grace), no mournful eyes (Sophie). I return to Miss Klein, mumble something cheerful about the sit-in, and announce with renewed formality Dostoevsky's *Notes from the Underground*. Smiling (why?), she runs to rejoin her friend, and the pair giggle off. From then on, the weekend is ruined. Blackmail on my brain. Will all twenty-five hundred students soon know about Gwen and the Dean? Will giant posters of us be posted on the walls, displaying me as with-it? And the blacks, how will they take it? That night, as my dark Cleopatra caresses me in bed, I pray silently for charity from Miss Klein, age nineteen, from Scarsdale, whose cunning hands also hold a piece of me now.

Pressure instead of pleasure, I suppose that's how most men live. Businessmen, politicians, these days academics. Take my old pal, Herb Bendler, with whom I had gone to grad school. Dark-haired, short, roly-poly, a smart Chicago boy full of clever irony. Look what family and university had done to that excellent third baseman, now in our history department. Take a Saturday evening outing to the Boston Garden to see the touring Russian circus. Herb had along his three children, I my usual flock of four or five—that trip, Gwen's Rodney, Sophie's Rebecca, Kate's Philip, Angela's Anthony (ages six to ten). Apart from the fact that I looked forward eagerly to my weekly or fortnightly children-tour, I had a special interest in zoos and circuses from my childhood days. A fondness for the animal kingdom which guided me into anthropology when I was an undergraduate. The differences and similarities between them and us always intrigued me.

We had barely settled in our seats, the clowns tumbling, the trapeze girls flying, when Herb's troubles began. Rosalie Bendler, age twelve, had to return to the bathroom (from which we had just come, in preparation). With a shrewish whining suddenly reminiscent of her mother, she insisted her father accompany her. Twelve years old and *insisting*. So while the marvelous acrobats flew over, under, and upon each other, Herb trudged unnecessarily the half mile, irritation mounting into controlled rage when he returned, his suit doused with beer from some corridor boor. But no sooner had the magic act begun than a battle erupted between Rosalie and her younger brother. "What I'd give to

shove her in that box!" my gentle pal hissed to no one in particular, indicating his daughter and a cardboard box into which a
Russian performer had just entered and disappeared.

I began to feel self-conscious about my good time. There
was the colorful circus (with the great clown Popov), plus my
four jacks-in-the-box, jumping up for popcorn, Cracker Jacks,
hot dogs; squealing at the elephants building blocks; questioning
with amazement the hoops of fire through which dove the daring
bareback riders; looking on with inimitable children's gravity at
the high-wire acts. All this, to be sure—their volcanic joys,
annoying troublemaking—was a joy to me precisely because I
faced it at most once a week. So that what was frequently a hell
to full-time daddies was a heaven to me, perennial part-timer. But
with Bendler next to me, pleading with his smaller son not to ruin
his newly pressed shirt (as if Marian pressed it!), what could I do
but contrive and feign similar trouble? So, to my little Philip's
amazement, I scolded him for dripping ice cream over his
trousers. Was the old reign of terror and compulsive Montessori-
ism, which I had put an end to, returning? read his perplexed
look. Herb looked at me sympathetically, however, and I felt less
bad about sacrificing Philip for the moment. In any case, the
high point of the evening, the performance of the rare Siberian
brown bears, came and went with Herb back in the bathroom,
this time with diarrhea David.

Later I had an urge to talk to Herb, to shake him loose from
baby-and-wife-sitting chains, to make him forget family tenure
for a minute and concentrate on some Ass. Ave. starlet—but it
was no good, it was naïve, I saw immediately. When I casually
suggested a drink after dropping off the kids, he looked at me as
if I had pulled a gun, and finally replied that he had been away
from home for a long time (holding up his high-school Benrus),
but why didn't I come home with him for one? Marian would
enjoy that. No good. Taking him to a discotheque, say, to
observe the bouncing asses and jiggling titties in children's ritual,
would have been nothing short of sadistic. A scene of a few
months back, in which Marian had scolded him for picking out
the wrong kettle, came back to me as we passed Cambridge
Coffee Tea and Spice, and it was too painful. Marriage and university pressure had ruined my Billy Cox third baseman. Had

made him at thirty-seven look like fifty-seven, with pallid face, shrunken cheeks, balding dome. The spirit to fight back and the spirit to have fun had vanished simultaneously. There he was, chewing Sen-Sen while Joplin sang, going on about a new essay on Disraeli in *Victorian Studies*. On Dickens he was smart (in his book), showing how hatred of authority had spurred artistic power; on Bendler and lack of authority he was dumb. And sad. When Rosalie's whine again began to accuse her father of some infraction, I called it a night and got out, saying I'd walk the rest of the way.

How many husbands were suffering such fates, I wondered. And how many of these cripples might change things by simply throwing a few punches? Or taking a few girls? Change not simply their marriages but themselves. In fact, make life tolerable again, possibly, between man and woman. A hundred? A thousand? Ten thousand in the Boston area? Punching was a language I abhorred—but with slaves like Herb and drivers like Marian, what good were words?

Not that every husband was a Herb—or wife a Marian—or every marriage a Bendler-brand. Even I myself knew a happy couple right here in Cambridge. The Freedmans were young academics (Arthur full-time, Naomi part-time) and lived on the surface like most: a pair of small daughters, a modest rented house, used Peugeot, a month on the Cape. Unlike others, however, after ten years of the same marriage—yes, ten—they were still industrious, jovial, candid, kindly, and apparently still had fun with each other. Naturally, for this, their fame was legendary. Once every few weeks or so I adjourned there, to refresh myself with domestic harmony (and challah, halvah, and other antique curiosities that one had forgotten about), and to narrate my tales of anxiety and bewilderment. It was a kind of modern version of going to the Turkish baths, from which you emerged feeling temporarily reborn. Now I suppose there's one idyllic couple in every divorce-town, just as there is one in those novels which depict unhappy marriages. And, like Joe and Biddy in *Great Expectations,* or Levin and Kitty in *Anna Karenina,* Arthur and Naomi represented the living proof of happy marriage, a kind of utopian possibility for the rest of us beleaguered ones to shoot for. Visiting the Freedmans, however, was very much like visiting a fine medieval cathedral, where the physical beauty of the place was undercut by the fact that its true meaning was a thing of the past. Irrelevant for the modern visitor. In other words, a steady diet was impossible. So the Freedmans seemed to be leftovers from some earlier age, an age more gentle, more sane, more spiritual. In our times, they were as fitting as Mont-Saint-Michel set down in the midst of Wall Street.

I suppose I felt so strongly about Bendler's fix because I remembered him when he was younger and happier, from graduate days and Stanford softball. Also, perhaps, because I saw in him some version of a future Kovell: Gulliver laid out on the ground, held there by a thousand Lilliputian strings. Unwittingly, the poor fellow had, in summoning up my own past, presented me with just a little more evidence to reinforce my current ways with girls—making sure that there were always three or four on hand simultaneously. For the health and happiness of everyone concerned. I would be a better husband by remaining a paramour, the girls better, more interesting wives by being mistresses. And playing the paramour—it should be stressed immediately, lest it be thought that the role and the situation were appropriate for every man around—came naturally and easily to me. Otherwise, obviously, it never would have worked. The sport would have been ruined by guilt. For everyone knows that excellence in one's role is a prerequisite for happiness.

Not that this excellence was easily achieved. It never is. Such achievement requires discipline, patience, curiosity, ability to observe and learn, willingness to vulnerability; in short, one must develop into a student of the subject. And, like the labor theory of value applied to the art of human relations, the real value of the product is dependent precisely upon the amount of labor expended. It is here that what appeared to be a curse proved to be a blessing: for which one of you six girls did not require labor that was Herculean and that thereby transformed me from an ordinary monogamous bachelor into a confident polygamous Atlas?

Take Melissa, Melissa Winfield Cabot. When I first met her, it was impossible for any respectable gentleman to take an interest in her, so great was her confusion and chaos. (Forgive me for putting it so bluntly, dear.) We met in the A & P supermarket, in the prosaic Dana Street branch, where professors and deans are anonymous. (I like to think of the A & P as one of the more relaxed social halls of modern times for beginning friendships. A non-cooking bachelor like myself, for example, can usually elicit sympathetic discussions in Meat and Poultry, where one inquires, from helpful lady shoppers, about taste, price, cut, and manner of cooking. The main thing to watch out for are overeager wives; either they waste one's precious minutes or, worse, start up affairs which are best forgotten.) Observing furtively the motorcycle-jacket girl's dilemma between Solid or Chunk Tuna, I finally intervened, explaining the differences by means of an analogy using Locke and Hume. Inserting an occasional question about divorced state (a timesaver these days), I noted approvingly the lack of fake makeup or too-impossible clothes (values), and surveyed with instinctive skill the surface topography (small firm breasts, slim waist, audacious legs). A straight modelly body, supporting a typical heathen face—strong jaw, clandestine nose, vague look in the eyes. She also talked, though weakly, scattered, without much purpose. Characteristic enough.

Soon, with our bundles packed into her newish yellow Porsche (signifying status or speed-neurosis and money), we had driven out to Mt. Auburn Cemetery and taken advantage of the late-autumn afternoon by strolling amid the pleasant little hills and the red and gold colors. She didn't speak much but began to point out to me the various graves, Longfellow, Lowell, a grandparent of hers. Which illness was all this, I wondered quickly, as she lit up in this peculiar Roman Forum: High-School Romanticism? Contemporary Silence? Genuine Derangement? With somberness she mentioned something about not being able to take male-female relationships any more, but I treated that like a child's prattle. After all, who could take them any more? Or any relationships?

But as we approached what looked like Grant's tomb on a gentle hillock overlooking a small pond, my new pal began to shed her vagueness and take on a sudden direction, like a race horse just released from the starting gate. Before a doughnut-shaped circle of stone supported by eight pillars about ten feet high (the pillars resting on another stone circle, planted in the center with pansies), Melissa began vibrating. "Spirit is immortal Truth, matter is mortal error," she said to the universe and, to me, "Man is not material, he is spiritual." Around the outside of the uppermost circle were engraved the words: MARY BAKER EDDY . . . SCIENCE AND HEALTH WITH A KEY TO THE SCRIPTURES. Closer to me, Melissa trembled, her hair loosened by the wind, her open jacket revealing a brief paisley dress, her face that of a fierce devotee out for a day's proselytizing. "Do you believe in bodies?" she inquired with a frightening earnestness, her own beginning to pressure mine uncomfortably, unwittingly (so I assumed). "I find them useless, repulsive, deceiving," she hissed with feeling, using hers to drive mine awkwardly against the sacred pillars. Subjectively off on her own *metaphysical thing,* objectively she caught my ear and bit lightly. And as that thin mouth whispered venomously the falseness of bodies, her lengthy knowing flesh performed its tricks upon me. Tongue whipping ear, perky breast rubbing chest (and then my hand), pelvis beginning to lock my loins. Merciless, shrewd. I could resist no longer. Leaving her spirit to ascend to Miss Eddy, I took her body down to the ground (between pond and grave). My passion for slipping beneath paisley heightened by the risk of public exposure . . . Afterward, returning to respectability, we found ourselves touring the much-less-posh Cambridge Cemetery just around the corner. Melissa's nervousness replaced by a daisy in her hand, the votary now a schoolgirl. I smiled inwardly. By chance we came upon a group of simple slate tombstones in front of a low brick wall with the name JAMES on it. Facing these was a tattered path, a dump of sorts, a gravel pit. Was this really the burial place of the great American family of William and Henry James? And this shoddy grave the country's symbol of homage? The contrast between this and the opulent vanity of the quack we had just come from was startling. Had I come upon these tombstones by chance, I wondered, or by pedagogic instinct? In any case, little Bernard Kovell did his cultural duty by lecturing angrily to his startled student—heated because of the earlier incoherent mush I had had to put up with—about the savage contradictions in American values. As if thirty minutes of reason could replace thirty years of confusion.

My first entry into Melissa's apartment the next day added

secular chaos to religious confusion. We arrived to discover that you had locked yourself out. Whereupon you calmly pulled up a garbage can and, with your white-pantied behind speared by the sun, and a Mack truck screeched to a halt for the driver to ogle, you hoisted yourself through the front window. An entry which was greeted by a rush of animals, barking, crushing. When the front door was opened, and they headed toward me, surprise withered into terror. What I made out briefly were two German shepherds, a Siberian husky, a Pekingese, three cats. Out of my dean's office, but once again up against a wall. Beaming like a prideful hostess, you said, "They just enjoy meeting my friends."

"Do they know I'm one?" I rejoined.

Amid barking, nipping, and groin-clawing, you took me by the arm and led me on another tour. A promenade of madness, which even now causes me to shudder! A white railroad flat littered with expensive Design Research furniture, teak and bamboo tables, plush club chairs, a deep blue couch, fancy air cushions. Only it was all in utter unbelievable shambles, as if the dogs and cats were hungry jungle animals. Chair legs torn apart, upholstery slashed to springs, a grand Steinway scratched mercilessly; walls, floors, rugs gnawed at, clawed, eaten away. And the air: an incredible stench of rancidness. I mean thickly rank, like a garbage dump. The consequence of milling yellow puddles on endless *New York Times* pages and piles of excrement, fresh and old, left behind doors, in closets, in cupboards, in secret niches. The flat was an endless sewer; the designer might have been Dante.

Clearing debris, we "sat" in what once was the living room, where expensive McIntosh stereo equipment, mounted firmly on high tables, blared out Berlioz, Beethoven. (Confirming my belief that, musicians apart, the mad understand music best.) Smiling, Melissa set up a chessboard, and I was given a long poem to read, written on that expensive paper which looks like paper towels. (It was tucked in between the pages of *Science and Health*.) Luckily, I didn't see the son that weekend, living amid that zoo; I'm sure it would have been too much for me. Where was I—a play from Tennessee Williams? A story of Gogol's? Who knew? The only thing that gave me any hope that day was when I insisted that the animals be sent out of the room or I'd leave, and you, after considerable cheek-twitching, consented. If I couldn't defeat shepherds and huskies right off, I diagnosed, I knew I was not the man for the case.

With the distraction eased, I was able to get a little solid information from you, though more was to come later. Like the fact that your ex-husband, a Dartmouth footballer and successful stockbroker, had deserted you at the moment you evidenced neurosis—an act which compounded your insecurity, sent you to McLean's for two years, and lost you your son, except for visiting privileges. A neurosis dating from a suicidal father (this seems to be becoming quite a problem for Gentile daughters these days, doesn't it?), and from a mother's accidental death ("A groovy chick, a crack airplane pilot till she went down too hard, in her own plane"). And you had seen enough shrinks to fill a pickle barrel, so that that antibiotic no longer took on you. Of course, you were in no condition then to realize what I had to put up with, the choice of endurance or departure. It was a momentous decision, to go against the odds that way—a history of failure with everyone.

The first thing was to eliminate the surface chaos and make sane the environment. Though you struggled fiercely, valiantly, for the rights of those animals. But what about *my* rights, *your* rights, I repeated endlessly to your tearful face, always using the boy (Billy Jr.), stored in custody with an aunt, as a blackmailing card. The dogs forced into a back-yard kennel (and reduced in number to two), the cats prohibited from certain rooms, the floors and walls washed clean, furniture repaired (Melissa's finances, another dilemma I will come to in a moment), the jungle reverted to a home. We replaced *Science and Health* with a Singer portable, poetry with cooking, chess folly with everyday discipline. (As with most of the girls, discipline and structure, sympathetically imposed, issued in health.) I can now eat a decent dinner there, have a cuff let out, or pat a cat at my—not his—disposal. It was with great pride on both our parts that at the party heralding the return of Billy Jr. to your custody, you gave him a modest lecture on never losing his front-door keys. The eighteen-month patience of a Fabius Cunctator had finally paid off, I realized, as I relaxed with the boy in the living room, to the ordered melodies of Bach.

And then there was that little problem of money. To be precise, sixteen million dollars. An American Dilemma. Money inherited from Grandfather Cabot's coal mines in Pennsylvania (now dry) and Father Cabot's land acquisitions and real estate (imagine being sued by Massachusetts Indians in 1968!). Consider: with millions dropped on one's nursery floor at age six, instead of pickup sticks, who wouldn't be crippled early?

It is one thing to hear or read about Big Money, something else to see it up close. The doorbell rings one Saturday morning, the postman (who knows me by now) asks me to sign for a registered letter for Melissa, and I return inside with a long thick brown envelope with a Florida attorney's return address. At the sunny kitchen table, Melissa opens it, and out upon the *Globe* drops a packet of stocks with an attached note from the attorney, indicating the sum of $334,465.32 (current market value), which is to be transferred to another account. Now there's something pleasant about receiving that kind of morning mail, over mundane muffins and Product 19: especially when, the day before, my own check came through from Cardozo, for $983.77 (after taxes, etc.). Clearly inheritance had something over working salary.

What could I do the rest of that day but play with that money in my little alcove study? Handling those Confederate-bill-size stocks, I couldn't help dreaming of Monopoly and buying hotels on Boardwalk and Park Place. What fine play those stocks made for an adult! Each sheet, about eight-by-five inches, made of soft paper, was colored differently; had the numerical representation on the upper right-hand corner; and, in the center, showed an individual daguerreotype picture. With colors, number, and pictures, it had to be play stuff, didn't it? Yes and no. For the pictures on the stocks signified power, though, if you looked closely, the mixture was a curious one of industrial and sexual power, as if the corporate state had been reading Marcuse. Consider the female portraits. On pale orange-trimmed Florida Power and Light, a Victorian-looking lady sat and gathered fruit; for about nine grand, the stock number of 184 indicated, you could *dominate* that pious lady. At orange Cincinnati Gas and Electric, a background of skyscraper and airplane framed a dark sexy woman gripping a globe, one leg crossed, with much thigh

49

uncovered. Marked 848 in the corner, this meant that this derisive sex-bitch would dominate you (with whips?) for about twenty-one thousand on the current market. An expensive Instructress. The next sexpot was less threatening. On the faded brown of People's(!) Gas Company, a bereaved woman sat on a marble bench, holding down her swirling robe. With her 288 shares going for 34½ (according to the newspaper), you could take advantage of her for almost ten grand. So, all told, you could get, along with your real electric power and gasoline investments, a fantasy of a domestic slave, a sex goddess/tyrant or a beaten-down woman. Not a bad lure by the New York Stock Exchange.

If you preferred men for your sex, you had a choice there, too. Upon blue-trimmed Kennecott Copper Corp. there sat, robust, half-naked, a powerful emperor type, looking down imperiously upon his copper quarry. You could own his 264 muscles and shares for twenty-four thousand or so. Or, if you wanted two Olympian beauties for your slaves, a nice powerful pair of them appeared on Goodyear Tire and Rubber, mauve-trimmed, with the world behind them. 1296 was their number, at a price of 32 per. On and on these sex and power games went—though, admittedly, some stocks were more Gilbert-and-Sullivan-like than sexy, such as Alex Graham Bell on orange A.T.&T. or bearded Richard Sears and mustached Alvah Roebuck representing their folklore firm. Oh, it was funny stuff to see such unconscious mixtures of fantasy and reality concerning women, emperors, cash, machines, American business. At one point, when I went to the bathroom to defecate, I had an urge to pretend that I was shitting stocks instead of feces. The point was, playing with that paper, trying to understand the power of three-hundred-thousand-odd dollars, was confusing and childlike. A primitive, a child, an idiot—this was what piles of A.T.&T. and General Foods Corp. stocks will reduce you to (if you're unused to wealth). No wonder my poor Lissa a few rooms down let the dogs and cats run her life, and was too confused to come! She had been forced to handle this stuff when she was born practically, and hardly toilet-trained.

Without the need to fight for what you want, or sweat to work for it, how could you be expected to develop a resilient will, a balanced personality? Why should you advance beyond that infant-woman stage—when that horrible ubiquitous jailer, Reality Principle, was bound hand and foot in dollar bills and carted off to the ghetto to perform his dirty work? No, reality was not your thing then; it was pickup sticks and cotton candy and Betty Boop dolls. Who cared or noticed if the shapes changed with the years, and the toys were called Human Beings? So long as the rules and stakes of the game remained the same: self-gratification.

Unfortunately, there was a sardonic and paradoxical side to that gratification. Poor little Wasp naïf, preyed upon by Charity Balls and Opera Benefits and Good Country-Club Causes, and pursued tenaciously by those peculiar young men (the Amos Tuck School of Business boys ilk), who courted you with their eyes fixed on their future and their penises packed away in attaché cases. Dreary days. No wonder you became a poor Schizzy, open on the outside, suspicious down deep. No wonder total gratification included paranoid fantasies and fears, and had such unhappy consequences; at the center of your honeyed valley, I discovered a frozen pond! How frustrating for me, too, those dry runs into that pond. My timid little anal-retentive—so that was the meaning of all that collected shit and piss!—my frustrated bundle of tight joylessness, what wintry nights you gave me! Those vicious green George Washingtons and Abraham Lincolns and Alexander Hamiltons and Grover Clevelands ($1,000 faces), all conspiring to make you cry instead of come. Little surprise that childish gratification helped to manufacture a frigid adulthood.

I went to work to unfreeze the pond. First, operating upon my literary imagination (Balzac, Frank Norris), I placed a bundle of money—twenties, fifties, hundreds—under Melissa's pillow, to see if I could precipitate terror or rage. When it precipitated only embarrassed bafflement, I felt like a bumpkin. Next, I heated up the bed talk. It helped somewhat. Her eyes dilated, her pallid cheeks blushed, and even, after several awkward silences, Melissa peeped forth a "fuck." Not exactly a flood of cursing, but a fuck is a fuck after two decades of systematic euphemism. (After all, her apartment was a protest in obscenity too, wasn't it?) My descending to her lower mouth brought forth much writhing and moaning, and a real college try. But still, no soap.

51

I conceived a grander plan. We would relieve Melissa of the unwholesome burden of so many millions by investing it in socially useful cooperative ventures, with admittedly little profit. And reduce her annual income considerably. The plan excited me, combining, as it did, prospects of piecemeal political utopia with piecemeal psychosexual breakthrough. All I needed was time, patience, and cooperation, I felt.

So I started researching and, after a month, came up with the town of River Falls, Montana, which was in the grip of a two-decade-old economic depression. The idea looked beautiful. We —an incorporated company—would purchase the River Falls Utilities Co., the local hotel, and the closed-down lightbulb factory, and then turn around and sell the whole kit-and-caboodle back to the townspeople by means of long-term, low-rate loans, with no money down. Depending on how quickly they could make a go of it—if at all—they could reimburse our firm, or share with us the modest profits. And if it worked, after a trial period of several years, say, River Falls could serve as a model for the resuscitation of other depressed towns (I had already sketched out three other areas: Appalachia, upstate New York, central Maine). How exciting to put the control and ownership of production into the hands of the American workers themselves! The point was to demonstrate that capitalism was not, like oxygen, a fundamental element in our universe.

All that war-machine Cabot capital was suddenly going to be transformed into Montana socialism!

And with luck and patience, all those landlocked Melissa glands were suddenly going to burst forth!

The gentlemen at Merrill Lynch Pierce Fenner & Smith, who handled Melissa's account, treated me cordially and even sympathetically. For two hours, seated around an oblong mahogany table in their Boston office, we discussed the proposal. Accompanying me were my M.I.T. friend and Melissa, looking scrubbed and Sunday-schoolish in a white dress with a yellow sash, stockings, heels, and a wide-brimmed hat. (How I longed to rape her in that outfit!) Instead of analyzing character, structure, and plot development, I found myself discussing rates of interest, annual earnings, percentiles and profits, downside risks. There was more to the world than I had imagined, I was fast learning.

The questions were put to me with courteous respectfulness. In transferring the newly acquired River Falls properties to the citizens of the town, how did we intend to make up the 3% to 5% differential on basic inflationary loss? What substitute provisions had I in mind for maintaining Miss Cabot's annual income at around its present rate (twenty-five thousand) through the years? Did they understand me correctly, that I was proposing *no* Cabot profit, only loss, for the first five years, and at best only marginal profits after that? ("Profits" and "losses" were the two words used most frequently.) As the questions came and the air conditioner whirred, I had a curious sinking sensation. For there I was, involved in quotidian facts and mundane statistics, when I had come to talk about ethical principles and ideals. Yet increasingly, it seemed to me absurd to try to bring up such matters to the three men before me (two thin-lipped statisticians, and one young fellow, Melissa's financial consultant, who reminded me of Billy Budd, so handsome and innocent and willing to help did he seem). Finally, frustrated by the questioning, I exploded with a small five-minute speech about social and economic justice, bringing up, among others, Jefferson, Robert Owen, Karl Marx. When I was finished, they were staring at me curiously, and I wondered if I had gotten through to them finally. "In other words," said one fellow, "you're proposing a permanent Cabot philanthropy fund." "No," responded the second man very softly, "I think a Cabot Foundation for Socialism is a better way of putting it." In my zeal of the moment, and what I took to be their sympathetic understanding, I said, "Yes, yes, something like that, to begin with!" "I admire you, Professor Kovell," smiled the blond Shrubbs enthusiastically. "You're a true idealist, and we don't meet many of them these days." On the way out, he shook my hand vigorously. My spirits suddenly high, I took the three of us out for a drink.

The letter arrived a week later. That is, my copy of the original, which was sent to Melissa.

Dear Miss Cabot:
    After careful consideration of your friend Professor Kovell's proposal, we feel that at the present time it would

be unwise to transfer any investment funds whatsoever from your current holdings to his project.

The main difficulty with his plan, as we understand it, is the unfortunate ratio between incoming and outgoing funds. The increasing gap between the two, at the expense of *incoming* moneys, would undoubtedly, in a short time, affect all of your holdings. As we have explained to you in the past, the over-all solvency of your total capital rests on a very delicate balance of accounts and investments, so that a relatively small shift of funds can easily have a negative effect upon the entire account.

We are grateful to Professor Kovell for taking the time to present his proposal in person to us. Clearly he is a man with many interesting ideas. We are sorry, therefore, that we cannot act more favorably toward his present project. But please remember that our first and only concern remains your personal interest and your financial welfare.

Yours truly,
James Sanderson
John Matthews
Thomas Shrubbs

Appended to my carbon copy was this handwritten message from Shrubbs, signed "Tom."

> Sorry, Bernard, that we couldn't do any better. But I want you to know that I personally admire the aim of your project and wish you well in placing it. Please stop by sometime and say hello. Or better yet, come by for lunch one afternoon.

I reread the letter three times, the euphemisms throwing me into a fury. "At the present time"—meaning, at least through our lifetime, and the lifetime of MLPFS, no funds, buddy!; "as we understand it"—meaning, as any child of seven years could see; "grateful to Professor Kovell"—for taking the time to expose himself fully and completely in person; "a man with many interesting ideas"—some of which may not be as retarded as the present one! And what about that well-meaning patronization of Shrubbs's—"Sorry, Bernard" (*Bernard* indeed!) and "wish you well in placing it" (where, down the street somewhere?).

The scene at Melissa's, a documentary on rich girls. Her face blanched with fear, her lips quivering, the tears rolling, Melissa begged me not to leave her because of the setback and her weakness. It came out that they had added a private meeting with poor Melissa, in which they explained that, if my venture were to be implemented, she could very likely, in effect, "go broke." After mumbling this phrase, she added that they had been serving her all her life, since she was a little girl, and . . . what could she do? Go broke, I repeated to myself, with twelve million and a few hundred thousand in change left after my project!

Who knows, maybe some people needed a bare minimum of twelve million to get through this life?

After a week or so, my fury wilted. Little Bernard Kovell trying to act like Trotsky in the House of Rothschild! If my innocence at age thirty-three weren't so embarrassing, I would have laughed. But it hurt too much. I imagined them talking about me for years to come at Merrill Lynch.

So what could I say to my beleaguered Melissa when she pleaded with me, on her bony knees, not to depart from her? Okay, I thought, one fool deserves another. Besides, Melissa was still the key. Obviously she was more under the sway of MLPFS than of BK. Understandable too. She had been handled by them for decades, by me for months. But what would happen if she knew me for a year, say, or two, or perhaps even five? Of course! A five-year-plan of my own—instead of collectivization of the peasants, stabilization of Melissa! The end the same—economic justice, social equality; the means would be love and trust. I would stay, and try to replace Merrill Lynch in Melissa's affective life. And why not, while planning for socialism, try also for orgasm?

Delighted as a child, Melissa sat on my lap and pecked at my face when I told her not to worry, I'd be around. Overjoyed and bursting with gratitude, she exclaimed, "And, oh, I so want to be a socialist for you, Bernard! I do, I do, and I promise to try hard!" Like a little girl promising her daddy to study her geometry. "And coming?" I asked, not being able to resist joining the two issues. Reddening deeply, Melissa bit her lips but courageously produced, "Oh, that too, you know, Bernard, that too."

And so I slowly got used to the situation, able to tolerate it because of the other girls. Thinking of Melissa as my speculative concubine in a harem where most of the other girls represented more conservative love risks. Naturally, if she were my *only* girl friend—that old-fashioned situation afflicting many men—I would have been forced to give her up, New Lanark visions or not.

Alas, there is nothing that patience, stamina, trust, and . . . and . . . being naughty won't remedy. Of course, I try to encourage this in all the girls, and at the beginning, after their lifelong training in being pious, it is difficult for them. But you must never underestimate the human capacity to learn.

One night, with Billy away, she cooked dinner for us (another immediate improvement), and I got up to put on the water for coffee. (How ironic that most of the girls drink hard black coffee—the drink of modern heroes, while I stick to my Sanka or tea, the beverages of the timid.) Anyway, when I turned around again in that flickering candlelight, I was somewhat startled. There was my Melissa, thin lips smiling uncertainly, her wool sweater pulled up, brassière gone, pearly breasts bare. *God.* Seeing those sudden white tendernesses in the midst of a salmon-pink chest and knowing how much sheer willpower it took my Lissa to work up that act, I had immediately to lean down and to kiss and attend to them. I lapped those wonderful aureoles, and she pulled at my hair. Already heady from the food and wine, I was now made wilder from that naughtiness, and sank slavishly to my knees, where I pulled down pink nylon and arranged long legs. Blissfully, I dove my face into her pale blond mound, exulting in her new-found powers. And after ten minutes of servitude that seemed like a succulent second, I felt that mound suddenly jump, heard strange cries, and had my head locked. It was happening. Edging away from safe shore on her own, and then swept farther out by me (and my tongue), now she was thrashing wildly, throwing off waters and at last swimming! It was as if an A-bomb had been set off in her own narrow placid canal.

Afterward she was a tearful grateful slave, wanting to wash my shoelaces if I so desired. However, I had other preferences.

As is the general rule, one naughty impulse leads to another. A week or so later I noticed Lissa drinking a little more than usual at dinner, but thought nothing of it and talked on about my Hum class that day. (I always give my girls a running account of the day's doings, leaving out only cumbersome details of occasional sex.) But when I turned back, there was Lissa at it again, this time more ingeniously wicked. One breast had been slipped out of its bra cup, the nipple staring innocently, while the other remained hidden away politely. My God, gone crazy. Olive Oyl trying to make like Daisy Mae, and doing it. She wanted her good times again. And soon, when she was excitedly releasing her strong moistures and quivering aromas into my devoted mouth and nose, I was proud too. Deep down. For now there really was hope for the future, and we had built that together. By turning on her naughtiness, not her goodness: by appealing to her clitoris, not her stocks and bonds.

We still had to search for ways more diverse to bring such joys—fucking still was useless—but what is life for if not searching? So long as we knew the general principle of operation—Melissa Winny coming up with the aggressive bad-girl impulse—we could certainly discover a variety of specifics. To the future!

Another sort of variety, that which citizens call the spice of life, turned from a cliché into a reality when I first met Kate. Responding to her Harvard *Crimson* advertisement to sell furniture—those one-by-two-and-a-half-inch *Crimson* rectangles are, of course, the best romance introductions you can find: a phone call, a few pertinent questions (asked with nuance, the right tone of voice), and an appointment is quickly made in the young lady's rooms to examine the merchandise; can a matchmaker do any better?—I came upon a dilapidated six-family false-brick house across the street from the Longfellow Elementary School, that affront to education and the poet's memory. (Like most American cities, Cambridge is very good at disgracing its best citizens of the past.) I had come to see a Winthrop desk and a live girl from the wilds of Wyoming. But as Kate escorted me through those sardine slum rooms, decorated bravely in orange and yellow, I sensed that I had come upon a gem, a jewel, an American rose. The signals made me weak in the knees; my subconscious understanding that I was preparing to take Kate into the harem. The Indian-red skin on her tallish, leggy body seemed from another time, another place. And that pink mouth, opening to the size of the Grand Canyon when she smiled. It awed me. And then there was her starting point; not merely Wyoming, but Cheyenne. Think of it, *a girl in the flesh from Cheyenne*. The word reverberated in my brain like Sherwood Forest or Scotland Yard, a mythical site from cowboy movies suddenly come to life. Oh, Cheyenne Kate—with pleats in your skirt at age twenty-nine, a khaki shirt for a blouse, an expression of frontier innocence and optimism on your face—how could a Manhattan boy resist you?

From the wealthy chaos of Melissa to the ordered destitution of Kate. No, as soon as I sized up the situation—a divorced Westerner on her own with two small children in the shady East—I knew that I couldn't allow her to part with those family heirlooms which she wanted to sell. Especially that high cherry-wood hutch, called a Jackson Press, which had been lugged across prairie and plain, mountain and U.S. highway, from Mother's Oklahoma to Dad's Cheyenne to your Cambridge. So I sat in the fire-red kitchen with the two small children opening their eyes sleepily from a green sleeping bag, frontier-style in the East—the furnace was out again, and the gas oven provided a warm bivouac area—and listened to yet another tale of red-blooded American tragedy. Her ancestry of an Okie mother (now a Tulsa schoolteacher) and part-Indian father (a rodeo performer and Ph.D. geologist) tantalized my curiosity, while her white boots and long legs tantalized me elsewhere. The smells of percolating coffee and oven gas blending with the rich aroma of frontier Americana dizzied me. Swallowing hard, I knew I was in for a long stay.

(Curious tangential factors enter into one's choice of mistresses. Street pickups and one-night affairs are one thing; steady romance quite another. Obviously, the former needs something special to transform it into the latter. That something special, I see now, in retrospect, as often consists of cultural ingredient as it does purely personal attribute. It's not that one consciously sets up such criteria for accepting concubines; it's what comes naturally after years and years of meeting new girls. Being a harem-keeper in a pluralistic democratic society has its advantages in this respect over maintaining one in, say, Saudi Arabia or the Sudan.)

Kate, you were quite a sight in those days, before we moved you—three times—from Longfellow school district to Central Square to Peabody district. Who would have thought that a girl who had published fiction in *The Atlantic* at age fifteen, a girl who continued to read George Eliot and Henry James, a girl who still wore pleats in her skirt while a grownup and a mother, could have gotten into such a fix? Clutched at drunkenly by the married truck driver upstairs (who supposedly was a Catholic and sculptor), pinched by the swarthy Syrian grocer at the corner (who extended credit in exchange for the feel), seized for an opportunistic lay by that forty-year-old Jewish astronomer (who hoarded his affection for the faraway planets and his mother in the Bronx). Poor squaw, you remained a sucker no matter how often you were crossed or tricked, a character trait that some gentlemen find irresistible. Like Mr. Ex-husband, a self-important fake beneath the beard and title of Artist, who married you when you were a seventeen-year-old freshman at U.C.L.A., deserted you just after the first child, returned to give you a second, then divorced you and got away without paying you regular alimony or child support (though he worked at advertising part-time, and his new wife worked full-time). Whew! And the Newton High biology teacher, the Chinese slum lord, who extracted $150 per month for his flaking-walled, cockroach-filled rooms, and was permitted to leave you without heat for three days at a time in the winter when the furnace broke down. Some artist, that husband; some teacher, that landlord; both should have had their asses hauled to court. (At age twenty-nine, in America, she still had no lawyer!) More tenacious parasites: those close girl friends permitted on the premises, who would have been better off hustling the streets than hustling you. (The hip Jewish mother always into the latest radicalism, the kook old-family Wasp girl who came around when things were going good, the shrewd Israeli neurotic who brought home her latest pickup when she had to "baby-sit.") Only Angela, whom I shall speak of momentarily, was worth having around. Poor Cheyenne girl, exploited like your ancestors by all of pluralist America! Didn't you know that no girl from the Black Hills of Cheyenne was safe in the streets of Cambridge without a tomahawk or shotgun?

A lot of good your cherrywood hutch would do!

Here in Americanized pressure-filled Cambridge, where mother competitions are as fierce as tenure pursuits, so simple an incident as picking up the children at the Peabody School is transformed into a bruising social trial. (The Peabody School is the Eton of our public elementary schools. Often whole families move, occasionally men change their occupations, or, most frequently, addresses are forged, in order to get the child into Peabody. Otherwise, it's a ten-grand bill for the little one to escape from the idiot Irish biddies who dominate the Cambridge school system. The much-heralded free-education system of our democracy turns out to be suitable for the postman's son, not the professor's.) Kate, the hick from Wyoming, waiting for the two little ones amid Cambridge mothers: those chic products of Wellesley, Smith, and Mount Holyoke, preening at noon in pants suits and swirling hairdos and fashionable minis, complaining bitterly of life in the university town after life in New York (read Larchmont), Chicago (Lake Forest), or California (San Mateo). Boasting of the nobility of their husbands, who have left successful jobs in industry to return to university life (as if Harvard Business School had some relation to the Yard). Those trim-hipped, high-tanned (Caribbean Christmases?), well-heeled Margies and Googies, what martyrs! Not to mention managers: beds made, groceries done, afternoons scheduled at eleven o'clock. No wonder, Kate, you trembled amid all that gleaming assurance and efficiency; your own apartment a mess, your mornings a drone of secretarial typing and filing, your afternoons and evenings a madness of cooking, child-caring, house-sorting. Withering there amid all that A.M. affluence, in your bangs, pleats, cotton socks, and cardigan sweater—what city fellow like myself could resist such an emblem of tenderness as that brown cardigan, especially when worn in Chez Dreyfus?—yes, of course, you had to perspire. It was your *moral duty*. Confronted by all that sociological pressure, Cheyenne girl, who wouldn't?

In sex you were limp long before you were not. At first, I was deliberately shy with you, feeling that there were already too many male sores festering on your body and hoping they would heal before I touched you. To aid the process, we talked. And talked. But then one night I accompanied you to the cellar, where, in dank darkness, amid anthracite and clanging and flames, I watched in awe as you repaired the broken coal furnace, fiddling with a thin tube of sizzling water with the courage of my high-school chemistry teacher. Then, bending over, your hips flaring outward at me like a bull's nostrils, awe drowned in desire, theory in impulse. But neither black coals nor crazy clanging nor I, your furniture-dean, could kindle aggressiveness in you that night. Sex was flat, enlivened only by perilous surroundings and our crunchy bed. Your potential, however, was obvious, as you worried humorously in my ear, "Sort of a reverse Bonnie and Clyde, huh?" Your face and arms smudged like a Hollywood Indian.

The development of faith and change in character direction are slow processes, when they occur at all. And when they do, they are felt in odd ways or small deeds, rather than through moral sermon or theological epiphany. With Kate, for example, it was the small act of getting her moved that inspired or reinforced trust. The scenes were memorable, arriving full of morning energy and, by three o'clock, dropping from battle fatigue. I came equipped with my own moving team: a pair of undergraduates to man the workhorse Ford, and I, in the open U-Haul wagon, guarding tenderly my precarious arrangement of chairs, tables, lamps, rolled rugs, chests of clothes, boxes of toys. My right hand motioning the avenue of travel (Harvard Street), waving a temporary goodbye to Kate at the door, ready to do battle with sharp turns, crooked stairwells, narrow ungrateful doors, I felt like Caesar in his chariot headed for the Gallic Wars. If only there were a Plutarch to record those Campaigns of Cambridge!

Be that as it may, furniture ordeals are less noble than military wars, the rewards and penalties less severe. I'm afraid Plutarch, out of embarrassment, would have avoided citing the wound inflicted on me. While lifting the monstrous Jackson Press up to its new third-floor home, I felt a sharp pull in my groin. The next day I was in Mass. General, chopped down from hubris. In the form of a hernia. To my surprise, after the operation and initial discomfort (including the humiliation of banal

61

afflictions visited upon noble parts), my wound turned out to be a blessing. For nearly two weeks I was tenderized by morning sunlight, vases of flowers, feet washed by nurses, the beauty of routine. Plus a well-deserved furlough from the uprising at the college and the particular joys reserved only for deans these days, the lucky ones: letters of consolation from some of my favorite (student) guerrillas.

I derived the most pleasure from the steady visits of the girls, arranged carefully so that one didn't coincide with another. To each girl I was seeing at the time—three? four?—I gave a specific chore: Melissa played Florence Nightingale and nursed me privately (mending socks, paying utilities' bills, making cakes and cookies); Sophie was Beatrice Webb, continuing my research on Gissing; Gwen consented to the part of Eleanor Roosevelt, handling all the university business (professional correspondence, rearranging conferences and schedules) and advising me. Which left Kate the job of Reader, a position of privilege because of the time spent with me. (I thought this fair because of her guilt over the Jackson Press.) So, every day for a laborious two hours, Kate would read to me from *Middlemarch* or *The Ordeal of Richard Feverel* or a new theory on the novel (those tracts were the hardest to take, reading like Puritan sermons). After an hour of "moral renunciation" and "rhetorical devices and suasions" (this decade's vocabulary), I was ready for more serious comedy, and we turned on the Nietzsche of CBS, Eric Sevareid. And after an emaciated chicken and gelatin dinner, I settled back to adventure tales, Prescott's *Conquest of Mexico and Conquest of Peru* or, more vividly, *The History of the Decline and Fall of the Roman Empire*. Listening to that marvelous elephantine prose style and compulsively ordered mind trying to come to terms with murder, madness, and degradation filled me with joy. And made me look around at my off-white hospital room and contemplate how happy Gibbon would have been there.

Also for my benefit, we brought in, twice a week, the Exotic Suzie, who performed at my bedside, ballerina pirouetting or Rolling Stone frugging—at age six already mighty competition for her mother. Kate sensed this, obliging her daughter's dancing with a Madonna's false patience. But then, like clockwork, which embarrassed even me, she would immediately—upon the tiny whore's departure with a baby-sitter—leave her chair for my bed to continue the anguished tale of the mad Carlota and the tragic Maximilian. Soon, though *I* was off-limits, I would be gliding my hand beneath Kate's woolly sweater, dropping one of her succulent pink pears into my mouth and sucking at it comfortingly, then voraciously. More joys!

I'm speaking of that special erotic tenderness between a mother and son, the kind so painfully absent when one is a fully manned attacker in the midst of sexual battle. In a way, that special sucking seemed to symbolize for me the feeling of the two weeks, in which my pleasures were of a kind not usually experienced. In part, of course, it was the tenderness of companionship without the intrusion of sexuality; but it was also that I was waited on hand and foot, served continuously and cheerfully. At first an embarrassment, it soon made me realize how very accustomed we are to accepting small annoyances, defeats, and indignities as a way of life; the accumulation amounting to nothing less than a subconscious conditioning to frustration. Must it be so, I wondered (fully aware of Mr. Reality-Principle)? Was it that way in all aspects of life? Weren't there environments where one was the assumed master, not the victim? For example, at a country inn in New England, where one didn't have to worry about crude waitresses, or leaky roofs, or pay the price of human bondage to secure a servant or cook. Or the environment of scholarly work, where one could worry simply about words on paper and not have to deal with the universities these days—student theater, administration grossness.

Friendly environments were what we wanted, those of us serious and sane, I realized. Environments of affection and respect, where services were rendered simply, effectively, and kindly—in order to get on with the serious concerns: love and work. *That* was the point of healthy surroundings. And my community of girls made that dream a reality in that hospital. We exchanged our particular talents in the service of friendship: they with services mentioned, I with my own (advice and direction about jobs, purchases, children, ex-husbands, interests). Mutual friends: I as father and son, they as daughters and mothers.

The respite from ordinary living made me happier than ever and convinced me of the desirability of annual retreats. Or, why not live in a retreat and emerge only on occasion? I was immensely refreshed when I left the hospital; and, while in it, according to the girls, my surface abrasiveness melted away. I discovered how well I *liked* my girls, beneath my passion, my vanity, my gluttony. That insight pleased me greatly. I recall the secret satisfaction I took in observing Gwen putting on her eyeglasses for dictation, or Melissa arranging the chrysanthemums to catch the sun: the small acts of graciousness done by and for a friend rather than the grand gestures made for a lover. With enormous pleasure I recalled a line from Turgenev's *Fathers and Sons*, where the elder Bazarov slips his arm around his old wife and with wise gratitude says, "My wife, my friend."

Only the simple-minded—be they lofty moralists or fashionable "activists"—will construe this speculation about a semipermanent retreat as a plea for dropping out of life, a plea for primitive regression. What jealous nonsense! It is no more than a commentary about the triviality of most of our daily doings and the reckless prostitution of our truest selves, and a private reminder to keep in touch with our strongest impulses.

The sweeping away of trivia and focus on deep concerns were obvious there in the hospital. A case in point, with Kate. She came into the room one day with tears in her eyes and, after trying to avoid the matter, explained how she had passed Sophie, just leaving, in the corridor. The green-eyed monster who had afflicted all the girls at one time or another had invaded Kate! With the tough impartiality of an analyst, and the experienced wisdom of a Vince Lombardi ("The best offense is a good defense"), I proceeded, then and later, to clarify the terms of the issue. For real problems there are no painless solutions, Kate. Any answer was only partially true; hurt and loss were inevitable. The prudent course was to choose the path least injurious and cut one's pain to a minimum. No formal contract held her, I explained; she was a free agent, free to come or go. (The precision of business terms is preferable to metaphysical nonsense in affairs of the heart.) There was no permanence in our arrangement, but contingency; nor did I wish to hold her through guilt. And so on. Weigh the issues, Kate, I advised my student: measure her past against her present, her true feelings against podium or pulpit morality, her temporary jealousy against over-all happiness. Consider it all, reasonably, I said; and excused her.

Now the experience of girls leaving because of jealousy was nothing new. Angela did this once, only to return after a short fling. To forgo modesty for accuracy, the girls had found with me too much health to put up with the neuroses or petty characters of other men. Therein was the contradiction: they were stronger women with me, but wretchedly dependent on me for that strength. But is there anyone of character whose condition is not marked by contradiction? I have to remind these women of that.

Kate returned that night, rather late, with a bag of fresh oranges (to replace Donald Duck frozen, which had been driving me mad), and I knew her decision. (Though, of course, the problem persisted for several months.) Peeling our oranges joyfully, I took the rising fragrance to be a fitting emblem of Kate's new inner peace . . . It wasn't long before the aggressiveness of jealousy was converted into bed-power. To our mutual delight. Outfitted also with a new apartment and job (after returning for an M.A.), she forced upon me, reluctantly, the family Winthrop desk. A gift she delivered all by herself up my two long flights of stairs, while I directed the operation with blushing pride. For her living room, I purchased a baby orange tree, even though I knew its life span, in our difficult climate, was limited. The orange fragrance, while it lasted, was worth it.

The turning point in matters with Kate occurred sexually, an excellent example of Freud's dictum, "The behavior of a human being in sexual matters is often a prototype for the whole of his other modes of reaction to life." I refer to Kate's general state of passivity and acquiescence. In sexual affairs, this manifested itself not merely in her uninteresting, tepid form of coupling. It also issued in a state of near frigidity, orgasm occurring only very infrequently and, at that, only after Herculean labor. Often, after a half hour or so of steady screwing, my penis felt like a bruised drill trying to stimulate steel. I half wondered if I didn't deserve a four-dollar-fifty hourly wage for such efforts, as well as a yellow helmet and union card. A Frustration Union for displaced construction workers.

And so I began to leave off sexual labors and *abstain*. A pornographic business, G. B. Shaw to the contrary.

Things changed one sunny April morning, when I awoke

drowsily and slipped my hand beneath Kate's flowered night-gown to rest on her pert breast. (I have once or twice in my life felt the profoundest sense of security and tenderness from going to sleep with my hand or cheek on a woman's breast. The transport to infant hours is immediate and overwhelming.) After a while, I stroked her breast and glided my free hand along her endless thigh. Soon Kate was twisting toward me with morning ardor. The only trouble, as I caressed and saw the sun slant, was my sense of anxiety. Anxiety about past futility in rousing Kate from her sexual doldrums. I proceeded regardless. I turned her about, to take her from behind. A view that excited me, her white ass looming like some beautiful alabaster globe cracked in the center. Holding her around the belly, I started fucking, nagged by the sense that I had been there before, to no avail. Troubled too by the time, near nine, knowing that I had a ten o'clock Victorian novel class to make. These pedestrian anxieties —anxieties of a kind which, I must admit, have always afflicted me more than any metaphysical or philosophical absurdity—ate into my vitality, my member sagging. Whereupon Kate reached to revive me, gazing at me through loosened hair with a look of helplessness and guilt. A sad sight. To my great surprise, however, that look converted my frustration into anger. Instead of repressing, I gave vent to it and, tearing away Kate's hand, started shoving my cock against her backside. To which she responded with a squeal of "Oh my God, no!" And tried to wiggle away. At seeing her so aroused, even if it was negative arousal, I grew wild with *the will to proceed* and reached over for my Gideon's Bible of sex, that I always made sure was handy, Johnson & Johnson's K-Y jelly. All the while massaging Kate's belly (her fetish), uttering calmly (though I was hardly calm), "Now you're going to be all right. It's going to be all right, darling."

I placed my penis into that upper-story parking space. Her no's continued, but as we proceeded (I gentle but decisive), they became mixed with heavyish breathing, thick groans. A dream-like scene as I observed it, and participated. To my bewilderment, for I was as delirious as she from the sudden trespass, her buttocks began to quiver wildly and relentlessly in pursuit of my prick. Her ass was ruthlessly *demanding* now (my hand in front had slipped lower to her vagina lips), the first sign of instinctive aggression let loose during our entire affair. I responded by plunging more fiercely. Her moaning—following perhaps the contours of the physical acrobatics—turned round the corner and settled into grateful plaintive whimpering, Kate's first signs of orgasm. As I came into her, I saw her tear-filled face buried nose-first into the pillow, with the memorable image of her mouth sucking fantastically upon her thumb. Afterward, she dropped into a deep sleep, which proved to be characteristic of such sessions.

The future was ripened by our joyful acts of buggering. Spinning amorously in foreplay, Kate invariably would turn to peer back at me with that peculiar glance, a glance at once inquisitive, apprehensive, and desirous. While her mouth prattled one sentimentality or another, her eyes craved mischief. Which aperture would I invade? was the question. The safe circle that broke no laws and produced no pleasure, or the taboo-slit that sent us both skyrocketing? I would start to fuck, in that familiar holy land, while she eyed me nervously, furtively. Then my journey to the wild brown wilderness would begin, my jellied stiffness encouraged by her hesitations and fears. Inward I probed, slowly deeper, as the buttocks lusted and the body lunged. The twists of our will intensified by Kate's fears bursting into obscenities (to my great pleasure, after my tutelage), a spur to my sadism. I thrust harder. And then, like a geyser gushing, she would be trembling, crying, and sucking upon that thumb. An image of regressive joy that signaled breakthrough and change in my Frontier love, and that stuck in my mind with the force of a Leonardo smile.

But what kind of breakthrough, and why? What was the meaning of the aberrant act—that delightful dirty departure from oral-genital routes—which produced final pleasure for Kate? This was not easy to discover, and I didn't, for several months. One day, however, in leafing through a childhood scrapbook of Kate's, I came across an interesting photograph. It showed Kate's father, a handsome jut-jawed man in his thirties, holding his little daughter upon his lap, while Mother sat next to him. What struck me immediately was that his hand seemed to be placed beneath the flimsy skirt of the five-year-old girl, upon her haunches. I questioned Kate and found out, after some embarrassed hedging and forgetting, that one of Daddy's fondest terms of affection was "my little fanny love," a tribute to his special feeling for that part of her anatomy. Gently I continued my probing and precipitated in Kate the memory of frequent "mock spankings" that her father administered to her. It was sort of a game between the two of them, a game to be kept secret from Mommy, for her father to pick up Kate's dress and smack her lightly on the fanny (Kate couldn't remember whether he removed her panties or not). Quite a game for John Somakah, age thirty-seven, a respectable geologist, to be playing with his five-year-old daughter.

He played more games. One night, when Kate was high from dinner wine, she began talking and associating freely about childhood (a subject I never tired of hearing about from my girls), and mentioned another routine sport. After reading her a bedtime story twice a week, he would bathe her and then tickle her furiously during the drying period. His nimble fingers roamed everywhere, Kate recalled, remembering especially a certain feathery stroke he performed in the region of the rectum, which frenzied her. (This was recounted with a mixture of ingenuousness and embarrassment; no more than usual, however, at dredging up ancient personal details.) She also recalled, though vaguely, that he managed on occasion to annoy her by a certain gesture during those sessions, but quickly converted the moment of annoyance into raucousness. When asked if she could remember what that gesture was, Kate shook her head in vain, and inhaled deeply on her cigarette, her face taut. I left the subject.

The final piece in the puzzle fell into place one night, during a back-door session. As my excitement mounted and Kate started moving her thumb toward her mouth, I suddenly grabbed it on impulse and held it, without quite knowing why. It was the right impulse. With pillow-muffled hysteria, Kate pleaded, "No, don't, Daddy, please don't, it hurts, please don't." (Was "Daddy" really uttered, or did *I* add it to the obvious child's plea? In the context, the difference is marginal.) The experience of childhood trauma suddenly breaking through adult consciousness startled me. I wanted desperately to retreat, to call Kate back from her hideous transport, her pain was so transparent; against my will, however, to get the final piece in place, I persisted. "What hurts, sweetheart?" I said low and affectionately. "What hurts, tell me." The reply was sheer anguish: "Your finger, your finger!" I released the thumb and she scooped it greedily to her mouth, the tears rolling. Her behind begged for pleasure, but I was too shocked to proceed and pulled away. Soon Kate stopped twitching and dropped into a sound sleep. I sat yogalike next to her, my mind trying to put together the facts and to construct a strategy for therapy. But it was constantly interrupted by visions of what fathers did to their daughters in real life, the photograph of Mr. Somakah and his young daughter transforming itself into various other postures. It led me to think that the removal of parents from their children, kibbutz-style, was not a bad idea for many American families.

So, even in Cheyenne, where man had all the room in the world to roam and to adventure, he found himself prey to his own fenced-in illicitness; the rodeo cowboy-turned-geologist, the Indian-turned-white-man, could not escape from a deeper and older instinct of man.

In the ensuing weeks, two patterns emerged. One was Kate's gradual, forced enlightenment—for she was all ready to block out the current event if I would let her—about the reasons for her bizarre needs. During walks by the Charles and in the Harvard Yard, amid open spaces and flowing waters and gentle courtyards, we spoke about those suffocation-origins. Wanting desperately to please her daddy when a young girl, in competition with her mother and older sister, little Kate sought to accommodate his fantasies once she learned about them; even, in all probability, learning to flaunt her small fanny and tease him with it. Which was fun except when he, roused beyond reason, violated that baby slot with his finger. And violated it vengefully, hurting you probably, out of frustration and shame, not to mention passion; and also, out of a desire to pay back the little tease—yes, that simple gesture encompassed a tangle of motives. Moreover, your subsequent protests against that illicit finger generated your own feelings of guilt and hatred, which naturally had to be repressed. So that buggering in adult life returned Kate to her daddy's finger, permitting and promoting orgasm, which, for years, she had been saving for him.

It goes without saying that this newly created autobiography of Kate's—fashioned over a period of days, but with gentle firmness, surrounding truths with compassion—was hard for her to absorb. It issued in the first sustained period of resentment toward me that she had ever displayed. Which, for the therapist-in-me, was gratifying, indicating as it did serious, painful breakthrough to repressed emotions. (To the boy friend-in-me, I will add, confronting that resentment was much harder, the specter arising of the possible end of our affair. A common dilemma in my curious affairs, where therapy always went side by side with romance. For without this added therapeutic side, I could lay no real claim to a term which I suppose describes modestly but accurately my accomplishment in the area of personal relations: Master of Intimacy. In fact, I've often toyed with the idea of awarding myself the official distinction, a kind of American Order of Merit: Bernard Kovell, Ph.D., M.I.) Weeks of uncertainty those were, in which Kate's trust in me kept fading and reappearing, like the moon going behind clouds. Or disappearing when the neurosis of withdrawal and retreat would make itself felt. The most I could do was to behave with extra concern, as if Kate were in an intensive-care unit, and hope that she would pull through. If she could accommodate her new knowledge, she would be a stronger woman and therefore better for me (although I am aware of a possible alternative motive, of creating a newer and stronger dependency in her). If not, her emotional limpness would make her a case for medicine, not love.

The second trend during that crisis period concerned *my* actions, given the new facts at my disposal. The consequences were, sexually, I came to bugger Kate less in order to inspire orgasm. Instead, with conscious purpose and dexterity, I began to explore her ass with my hand, massaging here, tickling there. It would not take long for Kate to become inflamed; soon, under the new probing, she began to orgasm during regular intercourse. And so we came to save "bowwow playing" (Kate's phrase) for special occasions only, at which point it continued to excite us tremendously. In this way, I negotiated peace between my id and superego, between natural animal greed and "civilized" renunciation. (Clearly, there is nothing so irresistible in life as hot sex. When you come across it, those few times in life, it's difficult—near impossible—to give it up. No matter what societal morality or personal conscience ordains about it, its force is overriding.)

It will be said by some that this was an unusual case, in terms of the early sexual aberrations and the severe adult consequences. Only a stranger to intimacy, a fool, a prude, a rationalist, or one hundred other self-illusionists, will think this. To anyone familiar at all, however, with girls and their histories, today or yesterday, Kate's story is rather typical. Ask your local psychiatrist, if he'll talk.

On the other hand, I obviously would not have been able to bugger Kate—and therefore not been able to penetrate the mystery of her personality—had it not been for the painful lessons of another girl friend, Gwen (lessons which I shall relate below). I am as shy as the next fellow when it comes to sexual innovations. I brood as much as any Moses about the details of hygiene. I break taboos of any kind with the greatest of difficulty. My conscience is still too thoroughly grounded in puritanical Victorian pieties, childhood Hebraic laws. A conscience which constantly scorns my yearning for sexual calisthenics, moral risk. Which derides ruthlessly my perennial polygamous pleasures. All of which is to say that it wasn't easy to move those precious few inches northward, from that arid midfield hole to that virgin zone of excremental pay dirt. A three-inch touchdown run that may have saved a life.

There's a lesson in all this: how one woman can unwittingly instruct you in helping another. The frantic erotica of Gwen, while humiliating me on one side of town, provided me with great confidence in north Cambridge. As well as a kind of guideline for action. My enforced boldness with the one (Gwen) carried over to the other (Kate), turning what looked like a mounting ordeal into a pleasurable aspect of our relations. And consider the consequences for Kate. Sexuality now had a future for her. The thought of bed sheets would now tingle her loins instead of make her heart drop. Correspondingly, the exploded glass fragments of her psyche were now uncovered and described, and even, in that one area, partially restored. How utterly bewildering was the wiring of the situation: the angry fantasies of one woman would be transmitted, through me, the catalyst, to another ill lady, with entirely beneficial results! What a curious switchboard of therapy, in which I, a confused nervous professor, served as the operator for a host of Cambridge girls whose ills and joys were working upon each other, with an

71

invisible ease, to produce spiritual prosperity and general munificence.

It may be useful to record my own impression of several of the professor's girls, the few times I came in contact with them.

Kate I met on several occasions, at the Square, the movies, and on campus. The last meeting was most interesting. Studying at Newmeyer Library on a Saturday afternoon, I took a break and saw, walking on the path nearby, Kove and Kate, the two children, and an older couple. Kove called me over and introduced me to the Somakahs, Kate's parents, in from Cheyenne for an Easter week visit. Since there happened to be a magic show for children on campus that day, an adult tour was combined with a children's outing. Kove insisted that I accompany them for a while. We toured the art museum, the theaters, the chapels, and finally headed for the snackbar in the Castle. The parents, in their late fifties, were straight Mid- or Far-western: she in a flowered dress and pillbox hat, calling the children and adults alike "guys, hey you, guys"; he a tall lean man in laundered white shirt, narrowly knotted tie, uncomfortable-looking madras sports jacket. (I'd bet he didn't buy it.) The more you saw them together, the more you saw the resemblance between father and daughter (and granddaughter): same chiseled jaw, great liquid eyes, loose-jointed amble for a walk. And all three had that fine color to the skin, though Mr. Somakah's had turned browner and more creased from years of geology-tapping.

As we ate frankfurters in the snackbar, Mr. Somakah's extreme gentleness, in the midst of the prairie handsomeness and part-Cherokee vitality, made me feel humble. His statements were obliquely put, as if he were afraid of imposing; his manner of lifting the children strong but delicate in the way that Westerners have with nature. When the sound of jazz came into the large hall, Kove asked Mr. Somakah about his collection. With halting timidity and Kovell encouragement, he narrated his early education in jazz and blues from his undergraduate days at Oklahoma University, where he played the clarinet in a jazz band. Very early, he began collecting the records of people like Blind Lemon Jefferson, Huddie Ledbetter (I had never heard that name used before for Leadbelly), Ma Rainey, Bessie Smith, Big Bill Broonzy.

"*Tell them how much you were offered for it last year, Daddy.*" Kate beamed.

Her father nodded, drinking his black coffee. "*A New York collector somehow got a hold of me and offered, well, ten thousand dollars for the whole show.*"

"*Did you take it?*" asked Kove.

He shook his head. "*No. I guess I'll just pass it along to the university sometime or other, they've asked me for it. Unless one of these young fellas gets a sudden interest in it.*" And he reached across and swung into his lap little Philip.

Soon he and Grandma took the kids off to see the magicians across the road in West Lounge.

Through it all, Kate's temperament was very much like her parents, sunny and sweet-natured, except that she was more outgoing. In fact, it had been like being at a Midwestern picnic that you saw in the movies, full of easy chat, kindly hospitality, three-generation harmony. But she was different from Kove's descriptions. First, she was attired in a mod pair of bell-bottoms and sash, the only concession to the faraway Rockies a simple white blouse. And again, unlike the total innocent of Kove's text, she possessed intelligence, charm, and irony. Much more so, it seemed, from that one occasion, than the Dean himself, who acted as if he were the Cheyenne boy. The irritable impatience and lethal wit of the classroom were nowhere in sight; not to mention the figure of the lover-autocrat he presents. On the contrary, he was terribly polite and self-effacing, hardly opening his mouth except to draw out Mr. Somakah. It was a little bit like Proust's Swann coming in contact with Daniel Boone, if you can imagine that, with Kate serving as a bridge connecting the two different breeds.

Angela, thin, breastless (lovely rosebud nipples), loose straw-color hair, alabaster body, child's voice, violent in sex. Age thirty, Radcliffe graduate, mother of two, five years of therapy. Preoccupied with her two boys and her body, to the exclusion of her apartment (makeshift furniture, scarcity of food, cats wandering loosely), her dress (skimpy and forgetful, negligent of slips, stockings, bras), her practical situation (she moves from one odd job to another, like an alcoholic seaman constantly switching ships). Has a habit of wearing on her arm, near the bicep, a metal

73

ornament shaped like a snake, which from the beginning intrigued me without my knowing why.

I met her through Kate, her good friend. Which launched the affair in guilt and wrongdoing. One night she and her children came by for dinner with us; another time Kate and I took her with us to a party. Later, when I drove her home (before returning to Kate's), she sat a little too close to me in the car. In front of her house, on a quiet tree-lined street, I mentioned what was on her mind: seeing me one evening. She blushed, and lectured me angrily on immorality, reminding me how fond Kate was of me. Her short skirt hiked six inches above her knee, her baby voice continued on about loyalty and hurt feelings, every few moments she buried her green eyes deeply into mine. Chastised and tempted, I felt released when she left.

From what? From my own illicit desires. Illicitness was fanning my passion for the girl, I knew after that night. Illicitness, and something more elusive, which I discovered only later. The *idea* of fucking Kate's friend spilled over into sexual attractiveness, like the difference between screwing in the security of one's own bedroom and in the bedroom of a woman whose daughter is a few feet away watching television with a friend. (Another memory.) To break this taboo was an erotic temptation, unwillingly present. (What taboo doesn't inspire dreams of violation in the adventurous man?) And so I tried to stay clear of Angela. But this is difficult in Cambridge, a village like Emma Bovary's Yonville. I would run into her outside Felix's, reading a magazine, or at the Russian Patisserie, taking coffee. And once the phone rang, and baby Angela was asking if I would sign a petition. The pretense amused me, the thin-shouldered body reached out to me, but I held myself in check, declining.

Until one October morning when she appeared at my downstairs door. In her electric-blue coat, voice breaking. She clacked upstairs (my heart pounding at her white pumps at 8 A.M.), as I, in T-shirt and creamy with Rise, stood baffled. I let her in, explaining that I had a nine o'clock class to make. She nodded silently in the bathroom doorway as I finished shaving. In the bedroom I dressed, and she sat on the bed, smoking. Not talking. When I got to my necktie, she began crying. I asked what was wrong, and she whimpered that her apartment had burned. Bewildered, I sat beside her. Were the boys all right? Yes. And she? Yes. The tears poured from her, and she leaned into me, so that I had to support her with my arm. The trigger. In three minutes her skirt was yanked above her pantieless pelvis, and I was undressed again. The act was brief, ferocious, unsettling. At 8:35 I left her off at the Square, promised to call her, and sped at seventy-five on the Mass. Pike. My mind tried to focus on Culture and Anarchy, my lecture for the day, but my loins interfered with that Cranach-body, my pleasure for the future.

I couldn't get enough of her. But only later did I discover the other source (besides the illicitness) of her attraction. Two days after the morning encounter, Angela called to have me to dinner. Dinner? But where? I asked, surprised. It turned out that apartment burning was only incinerator smoke, and that she wouldn't have to move after all. The little melodramatist, the liar! But when I tried to explain that to her, she grew upset and fought back: "Don't say those things to me! That's unfair of you!" (tearful). Not merely a liar, as I learned, but catty, selfish, whorish. I only sensed this at first, but it made me nervous, apprehensive. As well as attracted me in some peculiar way. I was unable to comprehend the depth of the problem or to know clearly my own responses, beyond the fact that in bed she appeared to be a paradise of passion.

Like a medieval triptych, her different panels played against each other: the talk and dress of the innocent virgin, the moralistic homilies of the leftover Catholic conscience, the stance of the brothel whore. (Ah, the irresistible combo of Catholic and whore!) I was bewildered, especially by this last pose. Understanding occurred, characteristically enough, by accident; in fact, knowledge of my desires proved them to be the exact opposite of what I had imagined. One evening, as I was removing my galoshes at Angela's closet, I discovered, off to the side, a strange pair of men's shoes. I questioned her about them; she flushed, made up some flimsy excuse, and changed the subject to a new Bergman movie. All through that dog's meal of Arabian rice and raw vegetables which she called dinner, I was nervous from Florsheim. Betrayed! Finally, still starving after dessert, I let her have it, upbraiding her with my jealousy. "What was she trying to do to me?" I wailed. To which she replied, "What about *my* jealousy!" In no mood for non sequiturs, I left.

At midnight she turned up at my place, pleading for forgiveness, telling me about the fellow (a pickup at the Brattle Street paperback shop), and promising that she would give him up immediately. The affair meant nothing, she said, nothing at all. This sounded odd to me, since my experience had suggested that casual sex was a man's sport, not a woman's. I replied that she should do as she wished, according to her feelings. With a dean's icy control, I kept my hands off her and escorted her out. And with a boy's rage, I masturbated across a lascivious photo of her bikinied body (which she had me take of her). Two nights later, I discovered that Florsheim was gone. And from her behavior (trying hard to please me, but dazed and lethargic, like a wasp after winter hibernation), I knew that the man who fitted the shoes was gone too. My baby had sacrificed him for me, I thought, taking her into my lap. *There's* pleasure for you, I mocked my juror's self. The crown was restored to its proper position (on my head), and I had visions of my Female Court once more in order, as Angela licked at my earlobe.

I was wrong. Dead wrong. Instead of more pleasure and peace from Angela's new fidelity, there was less. Less than ever. I was depressed, mystified. I couldn't figure out what I wanted— from her, from myself.

A believer in surface signs, I decided to watch her closely one evening, jot down what I saw, and work from there. She stood at the stove, in a neat little apron, peering into her new French cookbook, stirring a sauce. Dressed in blouse and skirt, her hair pinned up. As I noted all this down—mischievous little notetaker, in the guise of preparing a lecture—the changes suddenly struck me. She had become emphatically tame. *Domestic.* The word leaped at my poor brain, shaking it into revelation. Like a coach stunned by defeat who gets out the films of previous Sunday victories to understand the causes, my memory reran the films of early encounters with Angela, the ones with Kate, her, and myself. There was Kate, in bangs and simple cardigan, preparing dinner; and there Angela, hair slanting across her forehead, in a brief, flimsy dress, putting on a blues or rock LP and standing against the wall, her hips thrust out. The contrast was startling. One was a farm girl, as wicked as a daffodil; the other was a city woman, as innocent as a streetwalker. What a fool I had been! Angela recalled me to the present by asking for some thyme. I found it, but before turning it over to her, I went to her jewelry drawer in the bedroom and rummaged for another item. Once more by the stove, I placed the herb in her hands, and on her arm I fastened the old metal snake, less interested in the article's crude symbolism than in its lurid cheapness. Surprised and delighted, she ran her knee against my loin. We settled suddenly into linoleum sex, ripping her skirt and ruining the chicken. And so, that simply, the correct priorities of our affair were reasserted.

You could tell she was a pro—the word thrilled me!—by the way she went down on me. It was expert. She began by licking my scrotum, her tongue pushing inward against a testicle. Then, like an Italian tailor moving all around you on his knees in order to fix your trousers, she held up my half-hard prick and proceeded to lick it all around from root to helmet with single vigorous strokes. Bless her heart, I thought, like licking a Popsicle! My prick trembling and reddening, the veins swelling, she swathed it in her loose hair, smiling at me. Then back to serious work. Stuffing it deep into her mouth and back out, down and up, like lubricating a piston. When I moaned, she backed down between my legs and burrowed beneath my balls, her tongue flicking in, out, and reaching a foreign trench. Delirium in another sector. After a minute or two down there—two minutes there more valuable than most affairs—that Modigliani face rose and caught the helmet of my cock and sucked upon it slowly, deliberately, without moving her jaw muscles. It was maddening. I wanted to come and didn't want to come, in order to prolong the pleasure, and she sensed perfectly my ambivalence. She would release me on the edge of climax, go back to licking the side or feathering my ass. Then back to the helmet. When I did come, she stayed right there, sucking slowly, doing her job, and not coming up—I loved that not coming up, as if sperm were her oxygen and she was deep-sea diving. A furious depletion managed with expert control and mastery, and seemingly wanting to start all over again. Finally, having licked me clean as a cat, she came up, and looked as if she had just come in the door from a day's work. An exercise in hedonism performed by the professional in my harem.

It is one thing to observe a quality of degradation in a

woman and know that not for a million dollars—or, perhaps, only for a million—would she admit it. A woman's pride and willful blindness about such matters are notorious. But it was quite another matter for a man who prides himself on his self-honesty to come to terms with desires that can only be described as *low*. A man in my position, with three Degrees tagged behind his name, and who knows how many books ahead of him, drawn to the base, the primitive? Yet another contradiction, yet another blow to my desired image, yet another affront to nobility. No, it was not loyalty, proper behavior, or domesticity that I wanted from Angela; it was the girl who looked like the Circe of seduction and betrayal, the whore who had been in and out of more sheets than a chambermaid at the Waldorf Astoria. Armed with my painful knowledge (what self-knowledge isn't?), I began the campaign: the BBC French cookbook was confiscated, replaced by detective and science-fiction novels (her old favorites), the polite wardrobe of slips and suits sent to storage (Goodwill's), old torn underwear and sleazy dresses dredged up from dirty hampers. And, using all my powers of casuistry, I reversed my main position, announcing to Angela that I was wrong, she right: she should have the right to her "other" lovers, pickup or otherwise. Cupidity was making me unnecessarily high-minded, I told Angela, holding her tenderly. It was not merely her "right," I said more sternly, but her "duty" to return to her old ways! The naughty girl stared at me in absolute awe.

I persisted patiently with this theme, weaving it in and out of conversations and passions like a Persian carpetmaker, until one day I noticed a strange silver Gillette in the medicine cabinet. I smiled, relieved, pleased. And if the poor baby had little idea that she was indeed following her true interests by wandering around at night picking up her Gillettes and Florsheims, she had much less idea that her own promiscuous needs fitted my desires with powerful perfection. These thoughts were never more strongly reinforced than on those occasions when Angela would break down into tears and confess some new piece of mischief. Playing priest as well as pimp, I reassured my little whore that all was all right, admonishing her just enough to keep the act credible. On those theater-nights of multiple-role playing, I was rewarded with Angela's wildest bed-play. The entire three-hour episode of venal disguise, guilty confession, and penitential sex became a ritual, locking us together in degradation and blasphemy, like Cesare and Lucrezia Borgia performing their perversity in the bedrooms of Cambridge.

Not that Angela didn't have her problems with sex. She did. But these had less to do with her genes than with the age and the place. Poor Angie. Had she been raised in Bologna with her grandparents or mother, she would have been a suburb peasant girl, with fifteen bambinos, or grabbed up by some Antonioni and mythologized through celluloid. But here in America, especially in avant-garde Cambridge, she was just another narcissist, a breed about as rare as Sunkist. Shake any campus and dozens of these nubile oranges—ripened for narcissism by Daddy-Attention and Hollywood image-making—will fall into your hands, eager to be eaten. Self-love, but with no director to film your hang-up, only a dean to put up with it. I should have noted the symptoms immediately: the way you curled your hair into your mouth absent-mindedly, the torpid gaze that flooded your eyes when a man flattered you. But fine nuance or underlying meaning are rather hard to come by in modern courtship. It is such a dizzying business, like riding a roller-coaster: body hurtling into space (driving about everywhere), eye swamped by changing shapes and colors (rounds of dinner parties, new exotic people), stomach dropping (social anxieties, fears)—in short, experience bobbing up and down, uncontrollable, elusive, distorted. One is so busy holding on, there's no time to make sense out of it.

Who would have thought, Angela, that you really couldn't distinguish between subject and object? That your stage of development was arrested somewhere between three and seven? That your father's attention (in Hartford, Conn.) was too tactile, too Lear-ish, to give you breathing room? Which meant that you couldn't wait to get your hands on the next male, so that, by means of sex, you could transform him into an object of punishment? (That's a good girl, Gwen, hold on to Angela's hand, I know this isn't easy.) Believe me, those first few months were rough. Can you realize what kind of nightmare sex with you was then? (So different from the problems with Melissa or Kate.) Imagine what it was like, making love to someone whose only instinct and urge was, during intercourse, to be pleased. To you,

Orgasm was the be-all and end-all, a provision provided for you in the Bill of Rights and sacredly confirmed by every church in the land. Do you recall that when you didn't have orgasm in those days, you would pout and toss and, were I to murmur a word, beat me on the chest crazily? And wake me from sleep with all sorts of devices and tricks—there are certain points of intimacy which are to be experienced, not verbalized—in order to try again, or to be pleased yet again ("Just one more time," you begged, after three times already). Angela, do you realize that in those days you thought of yourself not as a human being but as a species called Sexual Orgasm?

Now this was not a state of mind easy to confront, my baby. The first thing was to get rid of your Doctors Reich and Brown (Norman), those operatic masseurs, and replace them with Doctor Freud, a less flamboyant physician, it is true, but a man of facts. Your response surprised me. You were ready to listen; that in itself was a step forward. Along with Freud, we learned some simple anatomy. Do you have any idea what metaphorical nonsense you believed about the landscape of your lower organ? What mythology, what fantasy! Your vagina was both New Jersey (in size) and the New Jerusalem (in meaning) packed into one locale.

Add to our anatomy informal therapy chats twice a week, in which you talked and I listened and directed, and the increasing trust you put in me—and now, after two long years, you're a more *whole* young lady. Certainly you still tremble and flush when someone flatters you, but at least you now have some resistance, some willpower to counteract body-power. Why, you even get ashamed now and then! (So Marx was right, it *is* a revolutionary sentiment.) Over-all, there's a proportion and variety to you now that has truly transformed you into a "new" woman. Look at yourself, a diversified girl instead of a cat in heat—involved in community projects in Roxbury, attending B.U. night school, helping to organize working-class mothers to protest exploitation by Harvard and the city. It's perfectly obvious that, since sex no longer obsesses you and dominates your thoughts, you have room for other pursuits. Why, you can think with your brain instead of your glands. Angela, do you realize you've been liberated? (Go ahead and beam, my Cambridge Monica Vitti.)

Two brief memories of Dr. Kovell's Italian girl.

The first is from the classroom. We're doing Lawrence, Women in Love. *Kove is fifteen minutes into his talk when the door opens and a slim very pretty blonde, about thirty, too overdressed to be a student, enters. Carrying a copy of the novel, she smiles briefly at Kovell and clacks in heels to a seat in the back of the room, where a boy stands and gives her his seat. Kovell is unnerved, obviously displeased. All of us turn and look at each other, suppressing smiles. Kove returns to Lawrence. After some explication, he comes down hard on the subject of Lawrence's brand of romantic mysticism, and uses as an example the famous scene in which Gudrun, the elder sister, charms the Highland cattle with a sensuous dance while younger sister Ursula sings at her command. It's just a passing reference, really, but suddenly a small voice from the back, a small and strange voice, challenges the interpretation. It's the girl. Kovell attempts to toss her off, to pass it by, with a joke. But that little voice is tenacious and proceeds to argue on behalf of the dance, Gudrun, and Lawrence. Saying something like "It's a symbolical attempt to show the basic oneness of everything alive, even the links between animals and human beings." She adds, "It's a woman's feeling which sometimes men don't understand, perhaps." Kovell lowers his text. "Mrs. Michaels," he pronounces clearly, "do you have a great desire to lie down with an animal?" We do a double take. He continues, "Mrs. Michaels, would you like to be fucked by a Highland bull? Is that what you mean by 'oneness'? That's what that cattle scene is about, dear." The girl begins screaming and crying her objections, calling Kove "a damned male chauvinist" who resents Lawrence's pro-feminism! "I take it you're not interested," he replies calmly, referring to his proposition, and continues, "Angela, you better come outside for a moment." He guides the hysterical girl by the arm into the corridor. More theater. Like ten-year-olds we crowd to the glass walls to see the performance. Kove is furious, the white-bloused girl is wiping her eyes and trying to answer. He throws her arm down angrily. Finally, she flies out of his grasp, runs into the classroom and through the spectators, retrieves her book and coat, and runs back out into the hall where she had left Kove, furious and helpless. Suddenly Angela rushes to him, throws her arms around his neck, kisses his lips and cheeks, and curves her body pro-*

fanely into his. From anger to passion to contriteness, as she lays her head upon his shoulder. Exhausted, we move away from the window, back to our seats, smiling dizzily. Thrilled. He returns in five minutes, alone, and, without apologies, begins, "Where did we leave off? Lawrence's mysticism. Okay."

Here was a professor with an interesting life! *Now how often do you find that?*

The second situation occurred at Longman Theater, when I ran into Dean Kovell during the intermission of an Oscar Wilde play. Leaning into him was Angela, wearing blue stockings, tan shoes with a pink bow, large silver triangle earrings, and a hugging white dress. Her perfume pressured from ten feet away. They were surrounded by a small academic circle, when I passed with my date. Characteristically, Kovell gestured to me, and we strolled over. The woman was clearly out of place there, talking too much, hanging on to Kovell's arm with too much intensity. The three wives kept eyeing each other with furtive amusement. Kovell handled himself with perfect equanimity, every now and then removing a part of Angela (her hair or arm) that had strayed over to his anatomy, smiling at her understandingly when she appealed to him, answering politely when he was addressed. Kove and I, off to the side, began a private conversation. Suddenly Angela was in the midst of a loud verbal battle with one of the women. "Don't you talk to me snidely! He can leave me any time he wants to, baby. All he has to do is to say the word. Can you say the same thing for your little 'Joey' there?" Looking ready to do battle with her hands or a shoe, Angela was taken in hand by Kovell. Students and other audience gathered around. "Did you hear what she said to me—did I get out often 'to see plays'? Because she lives in Newton Centre and has a maid in twice a week? Screw her!" He took it without flinching. He stayed with Angela, apologized to no one, and guided her to their seats. Out of a certain spoiled perversity, the girl put her arm around Kovell in much too amorous a fashion when they sat back down. The whole orchestra was buzzing with the incident, heads bending and straining to see the Dean and his "low" girl. Calmly he removed her arm, lifted the straw hair from his shoulder, and tolerated the embarrassing behavior as if it wasn't there. He reminded me of that circus hero in an early Bergman movie, who, in the opening scene, comes to the beach to discover his wife bathing nude in the water before dozens of laughing sailors and carries her through the cutting rocks, amid obscene mockery and humiliation. Only the sailors here were his colleagues and students. An admirable, if humorous man.

Chestnut-haired, hazel-eyed Sophie rose out of the depths of Cambridge like a dybbuk floating up from an East European shtetl. Where, in point of fact, she had newly come from. By some lust for pain, or providential joke, she had found a piece of town (north, across the tracks) that reproduced the ghetto: dark corners, secret alleys, shuttered windows, a few squalid court-yards, a sinister tavern or two. Whenever I wandered there, I half expected *Hassidim* to emerge from a doorway, instead of some Irish waitress with her unwieldy brats. Her apartment was fingerprinted with past suffering. On most shelves and mantel-pieces was a *memento mori*—photographs of parents (gentle, slender Nathan Bream and his wife, fierce dark Rose, both five-footers), a Menorah from an old synagogue, Polish sheet music on the upright piano. One quickly saw the Europe of persecu-tion, but had little inkling of contemporary perversion.

A past memorable. My holocaust girl. (Yes, we all should run into our Anne Franks. Their stories put matters into better perspective.) At thirteen, pretty, chestnut-haired, and a virgin to boot, Sophie was a special Jewish catch for the 1939 Nazis. After the relative decency of a single deflowering, she became grim sport for groups of soldiers, raped collectively several times. (All this stopped, naturally, once you hit the Camps and your female body was reduced to a bony skeleton.) Until an elder German officer noticed her in a gray gunny sack awaiting deportment from her Cracow ghetto and had her removed to become his private mistress. A very risky business, considering the punish-ment for race-mixing. Heinrich Strohmann of Lübeck, a history professor, treated her with respect and tenderness, and only made love to her after allowing her the privacy of her own room and solitude. He began to fall in love with his teenager, whom he instructed in German, cooking, Thomas Mann, among many lessons. This fifty-five-year-old humane German with a wife and three children in Berlin, and a swastika on his jacket. Who also

83

tried to do what he could for her family, keeping checks on mother and father (in Camps) and verifying that brother Benjamin (six) had probably become soap. Who held her tenderly while she cried.

Generosity is generosity, even in, and especially in, hell. And so Sophie did for elder Heinrich what he never asked from her, she went down on him to bring him pleasure. At going-on-fifteen. (Which accounts for the very special devotion she brings to that area of sex. In copulation, for example, she reaches a climax much too swiftly, and with too much guilt to be of great pleasure there. But in applying her mouth to my penis—about which I shall (inevitably) elaborate—it is as though not lust but spirit were in action. Afterward she smiles as if she were a novitiate who had just seen God. A very different sucking from Angela's solid professionalism.) When they were separated, Sophie cried. For even at the end he had remained human, and more. Their arrangement was discovered by an S.S. man; before Heinrich was shot for *Rassenschande* (race scandal), he managed to get Sophie free. Admirable to the end.

Free to move on to the concentration camps, that is. Four or five of the smaller ones—she showed me one evening a map of the area camps, as numerous as Howard Johnsons along the Mass. Pike, say—before she wound up at Auschwitz. Yes, that famous stop-point. From the human German to the normal Nazis. At A. she kept alive by her typing ability, put to work in the statistics office. And found out about her family. Her mother she ran into one afternoon in a stone-carrying line. An educated woman who insisted that her daughter carry on like a lady, dropping her foul language (which she had picked up) and washing regularly with snow (in place of soap and clean water). The habits of discipline and good upbringing must be kept up, she warned the young girl, or she wouldn't make it through. And both of them did. As for her father, a lawyer, Sophie came across him in her statistics of the victims and prisoners. His name was written on a *Totenkarte*. It seemed that he was scheduled for mine labor on 23 May 1943, but a red line had been drawn through that order, and under it was written that he had been sent to the crematorium, on the nineteenth, by mistake.

Tokens of the war, apart from those mantelpiece pictures

and Menorah, included the following: a blue number on her left forearm (A-20756), which in fact was useful in that it defined you as a definite prisoner rather than an indeterminate who might at any moment be shipped off to gas. An old fountain pen of Heinrich's. A shelf of Polish books by survivors of the Camps (none of which had been translated into English or German); and her own paper exercise-book diary, beginning in late 1939, which I urged her to translate. That nice map of the area camps. And something else, an unusual conversation piece, let's say. For as she told me this part of her story one winter night several days after our first meeting, she suddenly stood and went to the closet, in a typical act of robustness, and returned with a hanger of clothing. Actually, it was one piece, a woolen shirt of bleak blue-and-gray stripes, which had been her Auschwitz top. And around the collar of the hanger was a double-strand loop of barbed wire, which she had taken off a crematorium when the Russians liberated the camp. I stared dumbly at these remnants for a minute, then in a daze ran my fingers over the wool and the wire. They were real. Had she produced a knife or gun, a swastika or helmet, I think it would have been commonplace; the striped shirt top and the loop of wire seized my brain in a furious and indefinable way. Those paltry physical remnants of the Final Solution struck me as monumental, not banal.

And she kept them in her closet. (Too bad a photo of Sophie holding her memorable hanger couldn't be attached to her *curriculum vitae* for jobs. Under the rubric Education, where, after "1938–39, Mickiewicz Gymnasium, CRACOW, POLAND," she wrote, "1939–45 World War II, German concentration camps: AUSCHWITZ, RAVENSBRÜCK." A nice photo and nice *vitae* for some American art history department chairman.)

After the war, she emigrated to the land of butter, milk, and fresh affection. (Mother came, then went back to Cracow, and died. In restitution money, mother received about a thousand dollars, Sophie four hundred. When I asked her how that was figured out, she said for work days. The money was paid by the American government, since Germany couldn't afford it.)

College, graduate school, and marriage to an older Jewish professor followed. After eight years of patriarchal condescension and increasing boredom (on her part), she left him, with a daughter (Rebecca) and son (Daniel). Enter contemporary tragedy, American-style. She went into analysis, and, after several months, her doctor, a married man, asked her to take coffee with him. He said he liked to escape his dreary Boston basement office occasionally and enjoyed Sophie's cultured conversation. Cambridge espressos multiplied and soon changed their meaning. A full-fledged affair developed.

It is one thing to be ruined by parents, battered by husbands, or even haunted by history. None of these three agents, to be sure, promises healing or is in any way a unique phenomenon. It is quite another matter to be betrayed by one's psychiatrist, an affliction which appears peculiar to our times and to our country. A disease widespread. Stories abound of middle-aged psychiatrists who have discarded their wives and families for some fresh Wellesley coed just out of her teens. And everywhere these days one hears hints of perfidy, disguised as therapy, and shudders. A surprising kiss on the cheek from the doctor before some Marilyn is departing for a vacation is passed off (by Marilyn) as pure innocence. A free extra half hour to the regular visit, or encouragement to call the doctor at any time of day or night, is simply a manifestation of "professional concern." Or the informality of a first-name relationship, between doctor and girl, which "permits relaxation"! The story has many variations. All that immediate "super-kindness" resulting ultimately in such hard times. Patients, female patients—beware of your doctor! Don't become too helpless!

No, I'm afraid that psychoanalysis is a tenuous, delicate maneuvering between two people, and that Americans in general are not up to handling that sort of thing. Products of their own culture of fantasy, banality, and success, American doctors tend to be persons of overwhelming ordinariness, fit to be veterinarians exploring animals, not human souls, hearts. Picture them: well-trained Jack Armstrongs and well-tailored Babbitts occupying Dr. Freud's chair. If analysis were a pure science, that would be one thing. But in its essence—without the cash factor—it is as much friendship or love as it is discipline and training. Talking and recording are after all quintessentially human, and the psychiatrist is our version of Socrates—converting chatter into talk, substituting reality for illusion, hurting people's feelings to get at the truth. Preaching salvation by reason. But for such labors a Socrates or Freud is needed. In the hands of the mediocre, therapy, like art or friendship, can be a disastrous failure.

The affair itself between Sophie and the doctor was laden with bewilderment, rage, and hurt—mostly hurt—with its contradictory texture of surface reason (the doctor explaining) and submerged perversity (the doctor copulating). This last was played out in that forlorn bedroom of brass (bedstead), camphor smell, and crazy shadows (cars passing), where, at his systematic prodding, Sophie would narrate in detail her dark history. Each story of old-world violation interrupted finally by some act of contemporary cruelty, his muscular body (he lifted barbells regularly) punishing and twisting into her slim form. Clearly Dr. Newsome, owner of a fine family over in lavish Chestnut Hill, was reaching down for history when reaching for Sophie's cunt. That anvil of past collective poundings seemed to drive Newsome high, his fantasy in color with the anvil dark Semitic, the hammerings golden Aryan. Curiously, this red-blooded American (son of a Minnesota minister), so much less civilized than Heinrich of Berlin, took a particular pleasure in getting drunk orally in Sophie's southern region, so much so that the anguished girl had to punch him to a halt when pleasure spilled over into pain.

What a job getting you into shape, ancient sufferer! (And thank heavens for Dr. Kesselman, the austere Viennese psychiatrist to whom we eventually brought Sophie, and who helped in the rescue project. In schoolteacherish black shoes, bunned hair, unpainted face, she didn't bat an eyelash at Sophie's tale of European woe [the doctor had been there before]; but she did arch her eyebrow [according to Sophie] at the story of crosstown tragedy. Exhibiting *her* form of "professional concern," she initiated a campaign to have Dr. Newsome voluntarily leave the profession. He did finally leave town, she reported one day. We never again heard what happened to him, though all of us wondered sadly about the rest of the betrayers still on the loose, beneath their M.D. shingles.)

No wonder you were ready for the river basin or state hospital when I first met you. Actually, I hardly knew what I was saying when I began talking to you at that Washington Street subway station. All I remember is growing dazed at all that chestnut hair piled on your head as if you were a Caribbean woman walking to market to sell it. My eye and instinct turning out right, I discovered, since you yourself cherished every inch of those three feet, every ounce of those six or seven pounds of thick coarse fibers. What a curious thrill to watch you wash that hair, dry it with a towel, and then brush it—like watching some wild animal at a watering hole. Or I'd come for dinner and you'd have knotted it into two long braids, which hung down past your small pear-shaped breasts like wreaths, making you into a pagan virgin. (Braids on any older woman are exciting; arousing, I suppose, incest longings.) That night I realized the sexual significance of those braids when my memory suddenly recalled to mind a high-school teacher of mine, a fortyish spinster I had always been attracted to, without quite knowing why, since she was ugly. Now she came back to me perfectly, after a twenty-year absence, and I saw that it had been her braided hair, piled in coils or hanging down, that had stimulated me at age fifteen. A moment of recollection and revelation which seemed to confirm in one gesture the thoughts of those two smart Jews, Proust and Freud.

Naturally such a fetish can only be enjoyable if it's a two-way street. Which it was with Sophie, who was turned on by my special admiration as much if not more than I. Why? I discovered the reason later on (characteristically), after a month or so of our passion. At one point during her Nazi bondage (after the death of her guardian), they had brought her to a barber and had her head shaved bald, as a punishment (blocked out). The act terrified her. She was sure that it would never grow again and that she'd never be a woman again. When it did grow, it became a symbol of possibility and regeneration, and she vowed to herself always to keep it long, very long. So her hair was truly special to her, and the bestowal of it in lovemaking a special ceremony. (Though she had never done anything like what we did together, she admitted to me.) What it taught me was that the eye and instinct should not be underrated; if you noticed something just a little bit bizarre, or out of the ordinary, there was probably a good cause lurking somewhere. Every time I saw Sophie's hair wrapped high on her head, her history and her spirit were immediately signaled to me.

Lofty factors which faded when we began our antics. I loved to watch her undress and unfurl those endless intestines of hair. It would spring loose like a waterfall, and I'd have an urge to lick at it like a cat. Gradually, Sophie would lie down and spread that long thick chestnut blanket of hair upon my belly and groin. Immediately my penis would shoot up into a white bone, and she'd wind her hair around it and exert pleasing pressure; then take it—hair and prick—into her mouth and nibble like a greedy dog. Or she would throw her head forward like an excited horse and let the mane fall upon me, whereupon she'd crouch down and knead it upon me with slow subtle delicious hands. It was like going to a Bangkok massage parlor that you'd read about, where the girl specialized in hair jack-offs. For both of us, it was lovely.

But to put the emphasis on the purely sexual aspect of the massage is to pass over a further, stronger point. Sophie was only able to work upon me with such extraordinary patience and detail because of the general context of solicitude that she provided for me; the solicitude of an older woman for a younger man. In other words, the sensual delight arose from a deeper feeling, a feeling maternal. Naturally there's no experience as powerful, for a man; the more maternal, the more powerful the feeling. Until Sophie, I never realized the full force of the feeling. It was established even though there was a difference of only seven years or so separating us. I remember how peculiar I felt when she first incanted, in the midst of fucking, "My boy, my boy, my boy!" An appellation which I grew to cherish.

It was not merely age, however, which accounted for this perspective of affection. It was also the fact that Sophie remained fundamentally a European woman, or at least retained her European sensibility. The difference between that and an American sensibility as it is found in a woman is astonishingly noticeable, once one has experienced both. For love to Sophie meant a kind of selfless and egoless devotion to me that was foreign in my experience with intelligent American ladies. It was not that she abandoned her "identity"—ah, Dr. Erikson, what you've started!— or ego, but rather that the establishment of it never interfered with her love for me. Sophie's fierceness, as I've indicated, was channeled into devotion to the other (in this case, me), rather than the self. In fact, immersed in that old-style selfless devotion called love, she found herself bolstered, emotionally, intellectually. There was the beauty of her passion. And naturally, as I perceived such complete attention to my desires, I administered to her more totally and naturally, without having to think twice about doing something for her. As in work, I found myself losing myself and aggrandizing myself. It was a healthy style of loving.

You would think that Sophie would be fiercely jealous. Perhaps deep down she was. But she never complained about how often I saw her, or raged jealously the one time she saw me with another girl—Angela—in the Square. Her experience, it seems, had been too awful to her to abide by a "traditional" set of morals, or to preserve a "civilized woman's" metabolism. In a word, rules for love (bourgeois or bohemian) and conventional moral assumptions had been totally shattered by holocaust reality. She had had such precious little pleasure in her life, she explained once, lying beneath me, that nowadays when it arrived she was not going to put restrictive clauses into the contract. She simply signed on the dotted line and accepted whatever situation I shaped.

Well, not exactly. There were days when she was much "less cool," more agitated. In the beginning especially. I remember that first time I saw you out there, my holocaust girl, a furtive figure in a World War II trench coat walking in the Hancock Totground across from my front windows. Was that some television melodrama I was watching, as you circled round and round, stopping to pick up snow or to sit in a small swing and glide? My God, a man needs stamina these days! Who could bear that? Of course I had to put down my typing and rush shirt-sleeved into the wintry night and take you in my arms, right there, and plead with you not to do such things! And then beg you to come upstairs (despite your protests about interrupting my work), where I pleaded some more. Or to open the door for a 3 A.M. walk and discover somebody sitting on my stairway—it terrified me! I thought God-knows-what, a vagrant, a mugger? But it was you; and you had been curled there for hours, sitting silently in the darkness not daring to knock, but just wanting to hear me move about the apartment, "to listen to my presence" (your words). What impossible guilt! It wasn't fair, I assure you. You knew my temperament, even then. You knew I would assume the guilt of every wrong that had been done to you. Again I pleaded with you to promise not to take such horrible actions.

And for weeks afterward, seeing that face—the exquisite thin eyebrows, the perceptive hazel eyes, the small features and rosy cheeks and wonderful smile (despite crooked front teeth); and that expression of childlike faith in me despite everything!— that face followed me everywhere, in the classroom, at my typewriter, on the highway. As did that hanger with striped shirt and loop of barbed wire. It was awful, awful! I felt driven, helpless, possessed! What a nightmare! Forgive me for remembering it . . . for breaking down this way while composing a narrative . . . It's embarrassing.

Forgive me, ladies. (And readers.) You know I don't like to behave this way. I know how much you depend on me for emotional calm.

Having a Holocaust Girl was no fun in other ways. It was not, for example, like having a Miss America; you didn't call up your friends with the announcement. Moreover, the body showed signs of idiot history. Fortunately, the signs were small, furtive, easily avoided. A cigarette-butt scar above the left nipple. A curious black and violet scar, on the nape of the neck, which refused to heal in twenty-five years (checked annually by the doctors here for malignancy). Both reminders that I tried to avoid. And I tried to avoid, too, that miserable history, an obscenity that, if possible, should be removed from the memory like a skin growth or tumor. From the person, that is; not the record. Let the record show who did what, when, and to whom. But the person attacked should at least be allowed to forget. (Which Dr. Newsome wouldn't hear of. Did I mention that the curious fellow frequently recorded on tapes Sophie's history? While she talked, in the office and in her bedroom, a small Sony recorder took it all down. Tapes which, presumably, he took with him when he left the arena. Real perversity, friends, was not in your simplistic Genets, who took perversity as a way of life, a natural habitat. But rather in this shrink-poseur, this Member of the Profession of Healing, who was wandering around the country somewhere with cassettes and fantasies in his therapy-quiver.)

Why did I do it? Why not part from Sophie and all those

layers of wound? An excellent question, containing its own excellent and convincing argument. But arguments are often stronger than men; and saner. Than I, at least, I must confess. At times, anyway. Sophie was one of those times. There I was, approaching her on instinct, then knowing her suddenly, and her trusting me—all in an instant, as it were, before I could step back and away. The net was flung and I was inside it. I'd try to make it workable, I thought, before giving up on it. Why blame her for shitty luck? For monstrously unfair destiny? And desert her a priori on the basis of her type? Why not try the *person* behind the type? If it couldn't work—if my humor was unable to buoy her, and my presence unable to keep her in the present and out of the past—then I'd give it over. Abandon the case to the doctors.

But it did work. There was hardly any sinking (once we rescued her from that Newsome-clam). Mostly she bobbed on the surface, steady, impressive, gutsy. Gutsy in that she did what she was supposed to—saw people, continued pushing for her Ph.D. in art history, took care of Becky and Danny, and loved me—without lamenting or complaining or psychoanalyzing. With spirit, in fact. That's what I tried to get her to recover, the spirit. Not always a success, but good enough. She wouldn't make the moon as an astronaut, let's say, but she wouldn't burn up in space out of confusion or sink in the ocean from desperation. So, trapped by history, both of us, we didn't do badly: rejected astronaut and sympathetic control center. Not a bad retread for a discard of history.

I turn to Gwen. And I would be less than honest if I didn't admit—here in public, as I have in private many times—that I had great misgivings about our intimacy. Why? . . . It's not that you aren't a pretty girl. Certainly, in many ways, you're the most attractive of all my friends—those pitchfork breasts, those superb hips, the golden-ebony skin. Or that your personality is lacking— you have enough charm, poise, and cunning for a harem of women. And it's not that I had anything *in particular* against your color. By itself, white, brown, or olive is neither negative nor positive. It's all a matter of the concrete situation—the time, the place, the individual. Any realist knows this.

To make a long story short, in these times it's much too

complicated to have a brown girl friend. As simple as that. If I were a different sort—your *Esquire* man about town, or Playboy swinger—I should, of course, have sought you out. And paraded you around to every Cambridge coffeehouse, cocktail party, discotheque, political rally; on exhibition, as it were. (How subtly and insidiously the world of fashion invades our national life and vocabulary. The young, for example, are swamped by it. There's more ultimate danger, I would wager, in a word like "mod" than in a thousand "fucks." Go explain that to the *New York Times*'s editorial puritans!) . . . But I'm not one of those types. A recluse academic and a pressured dean, at thirty-five wondering about middle age, fond of books, purple martins, and winter birches, seeking a pastoral life in which to pursue scholarly trails. Not exactly the portrait of a man ready to replace Sinatra or Genet. Even if it is a dream.

Who needs the complications of race? Don't we have enough troubles? Isn't the serious business of everyday living sufficiently tormenting with wives, work, rents, taxes, emotions, alimony? No, Gwen, only a fool, a charlatan, or a man without serious work before him—only that kind of man will have the time to consort with a dark girl, regardless of her attractions.

In these days especially. You know what it was like, shopping in the North End on a Saturday morning—why, we were almost lynched there and then by those Italian thugs. And it was no different from Roxbury, when we went to visit relatives of yours; only then the ugliness was a different color. Even in Harvard Square, that marketplace of liberation, you're not free of abuse when you walk arm in arm. Is that necessary? Is it pleasant? Or tolerable for too long? . . . Why then should two rational adults—like ourselves—perpetuate a situation that invites scorn and threat in the most open, casual environments?

Alas, I'm weak and you're persistent, and here we are, where we shouldn't be. But your persistence only won out, I'll remind you, after you convinced me that there was a practical side to the matter. I repeat, a practical side. Your first argument was that, assaulted as you were by various noxious influences—the incessant public media and friends and colleagues alike, who never ceased for a moment to bring race into every question—that, considering this massive assault, you desperately needed a counter-influence: a moderate but hardheaded man who could serve, well, different roles. You were disgusted with the crude militants who insisted that you were essentially an African and had to adopt African manners of dress and attitude. Is that why you got an M.A. in theater at Yale, you said, to listen to that sort of nonsense? No. If you were going to play-act or masquerade, then you wanted it to be billed as such; and you expected a regular Equity salary. And you were sick and tired of being asked to participate in symposia with respectable middle-class whites and blacks, where you were told that your first allegiance was to the Cause. No again. Like Mr. Ellison, whom you quoted, you wanted a private life again; to take care of your duties as a mother, teacher, director.

That's where I came in. With so many complications challenging you at once, you needed a kind of sounding board, a counselor, a wise friend. Of course, I was not to interfere in your decisions, or to stand up and fight your battles. I was your shadow, as you so quaintly put it, in matters of morality and logic; a shadow in the wings. To give you perspective, balance. Well, that seemed fair to me. Even reasonable.

The second argument struck me as less sound, if perhaps more exotic. In fact, I doubted then and doubt today that it was an argument . . . More like a proposition, a speculation, even a tempting gambit. Since I was a professor and scholar, interested in a disinterested pursuit of ideas, concerned more with permanent truths than with the immediate passing phenomena of life— you said all this in a most disarming way, prancing back and forth in front of me in your comfortable living room, waving your gold cigarette holder, seemingly oblivious to Aretha on the stereo and to your tight miniskirt, which revealed long golden legs and full libidinous ass . . . as I was saying, since I was a scholar, remote from contemporary reality but nevertheless interested in it as an intelligent layman, why then *knowing you* would be the easiest way to experience what all this fuss about race really was. That is, you would be as pleasant as possible about the whole thing, and I would get a rounded education concerning the contemporary turmoil, without actually suffering through its agonies. (Remember, I was to be a mere shadow.) So our little *entre nous* would be mutually beneficial. I would have a tutorial program in race education, you would have your impartial rational counselor.

I should have been immediately wary of such subtle arguments. Of course, what came next was not exactly an argument, though there was certainly a vehicle used for a precise purpose of persuasion. What could I do when you casually dropped into my lap, and with one cinnamon hand slipping across my hot, beginning-to-shudder skin, you spoke of the historical precedence for such friendships (which I as a scholar could readily appreciate). You cited, among many, Antony and Cleopatra, Moses and his Egyptian mistress, Shakespeare and his dark lady. (Don't think that for a moment I wasn't blinded by the comparisons and didn't picture in my mind that sacred triumvirate—the general, the ethical leader, the towering poet, draped with their chocolate mistresses in some alabaster boudoir—welcoming a fourth arrival!) Before the pressure of that noble history (and the skill of that hand), I was no match.

But you tricked me! A shadow, eh? A "white shadow." You smiled. A cruel jest, which ceased when you ceased talking and began touching. Immediately I was a substance, a vibrating one. Which I remained. Who knew how pained your past had been? Or how complex you were? When I first saw you at that dressy dinner party, you were vivacious, charming, poised, in control. About your interior life, there was no warning! I was expecting a simple Othello, and look what I got: a black Iago!

Friends, forgive me, forgive us, for giving in to such impulses! Somehow I should have protected us from such shenanigans. Deviations. I agree. But I did try, didn't I? It wasn't my fault in toto that I failed. After all, *I* was the restraining force: the Jewish puritan, the golden-means moderate, the fatherly superego. It was you, Gwen, who was illicit. No judge who knew the facts would deny that, no matter what the strangeness of the surface. I kept reminding you of the times, of the social censure awaiting both of us from all sides, if word were to get out. And if your ex-husband, Marcellus, had found out . . . But nothing would deter you, do you remember?

But then again, to step back and try to look at this objectively, it was he who contributed to your wayward cravings. As you yourself explained, when telling me about him. The way he started to beat you whenever he was drunk, his jealousy erupting. Jealousy of your education, your work, even your lighter color —all served to fuel his sadism. How I trembled with you when you recounted those times. And the hatred with which you spit out, "He was a savage, that's all there is to it!"

Can you imagine how I felt when, walking to your apartment one evening, I was suddenly seized from a doorway by a large, unsmiling buck, and asked "How's Gwen?" Your phrase, the "savage," shooting up my spine as I looked into that coal-black face, those glowering eyes, the African dashiki. Was he going to cook and eat me, as he carried me along (his hand gripping my bicep as if it were a tennis ball)? Setting me down in a neighborhood tavern and keeping me hostage for three solid hours, drilling talk into me as if he were a dentist filling a tooth. I was terrified. "Savage," I kept thinking; "that's all there is to it," I repeated dumbly to myself. And what did he want to spiel about—cuckoldry, unfaithfulness, longing? In other words, about things really disturbing him? Not on your life! About one subject only: race relations. For three hours, race relations!

— He was mad about the colors black and white, absolutely mad, demented, as you knew so well. He raged of the horrors of white cities, white ethics, white politics, white sex. And harangued on about the new theater and arts the blacks would create, the new society they would build, the new ethics they would develop. Maddened by the excitement—the jukebox pounding and Marcellus, sporting one gold earring, booming his guttural voice like Paul Robeson—I asked him to elaborate: "A new ethic? Like what? I'm all for it. Describe it!" He clamped his hand on my wrist and in one sudden motion twisted my arm into an old-fashioned hammerlock. "Don't pull that honky stuff on me, baby!" he hissed, close to me in the booth seats. I pleaded and begged, in pain. He twisted hard. I stopped the honky stuff.

I was released when a pair of white girls waved to him. "I'm not through with you," he said, leaving me for the new action. "You'll be seeing more of me."

I did. In the street, at my apartment door, in restaurants, at the university. If he had finally one day struck me, or tried to beat me, I would have been grateful. I could have swung back or charged him with assault. But no: talk. Race talk. That's all there was. Race talk and teasing intimidation. It was getting me crazy. From every angle he would attack it. The metaphysics, the aesthetics, the geography, the genetics of race. It was incredible. And boring . . . beyond belief! It was only the implicit intimidation, in fact, which kept me from falling asleep. "What did I think I was, a simple racist?" I was more subtle and therefore more dangerous than that. George Wallace was an "honest man"; but me! I was masquerading as a "decent whitey." Masquerading to myself and to society. Precisely because I tried to be consciously decent and just—working with S.N.C.C. in Mississippi, recruiting New York City kids from my old schoolyard haunts for college—I was the more dangerous. It was *I*, Marcellus Tresvant declared, who preserved racism in the country by refusing to acknowledge my own. I countered that the capitalist system helped to foster racism and inequality, and that I was very much against it. I was all for its overthrow. Socialism was what I believed in, I started to say, when bam! I was grabbed again. Don't give him that "word-shit"! Another phony "whitey-trap." All white decency was intolerant, all white socialism a sham! So it went.

As I was coming off the subway at Harvard Square one day, Marcellus was there to meet me, by chance it seemed. Which convinced me that fate too was against me. It was enough. He had me. Enough! I'd give Gwen up, I said, dazzled by anxiety and confusion. I'd give her up. That's what he was really after all that time, wasn't he? Suddenly he was jammed in with me in the iron-barred revolving exit, stopping movement. His giant hands held my collar. "No, you don't, boy," he commanded, there being no space to move or breathe, and commuters crowding around. "You'll do nothing of the kind. You won't pull any of that honky shit on me! I'm just beginning to get into you, your real feelings, baby, and now you want to split the scene. No, baby, nooo!" It was awful. Nobody in the crowd stirred, afraid of beginning a race war right there in the MTA station. The fools! It had nothing to do with races! It had to do with my fucking his Gwen! I was being suffocated by that jammed space, that crazy situation! Finally an MTA teller, a wizened old black, arrived on the scene and ordered Marcellus to break it up, and then to beat it. "Go on, go on," he jerked his thumb when we were let out, "get out of here!" An adult admonishing a juvenile annoyance.

Written down this way, it looks unbelievable, even to me. Did I really live through that silly madness?

The ending to Marcellus has its O. Henry twist. (But then, what serious story nowadays doesn't? Name one that ends with continuity, or probability, and I'll show you incredibility.) First, a New York publisher got hold of his name and promised him a healthy advance if he wrote his autobiography. He never did, however. (Too bad, too. He had been a Chicago pimp, among other trades, before making good in college and the poverty program.) Instead, he took up a new career, repenting his militant foolishness. In fact, the letter announcing his new plans gave me a fuller sense of your own measure, Gwen, when you read it to me, interspersed with your running commentary. What wit, what uncompromising humor, in that verbal grading job: "Society reformer? He couldn't fool a goat into believing *that*." (The yellow eyes flashing victory.) "*Now* he's fulfilling his real dream—not revolution and a new society, but advertising. He's going to have his own advertising agency and be a *boss!* And on whose bread? The society girl whom he's marrying. Some radical, huh, Bernie? Believe me, he's more white than you when it comes to being bourgeois!" Removing those schoolteacher specs (she taught acting and directing at Boston University), and laughing derisively. Laughter carrying you to your knees, where you wrapped my legs around your waist, and followed your impulses, right there, in the living room, with the boys twenty feet away, sleeping.

What impulses! The crazy offspring of distorted desire, Gothic confusion. Of a secret life as bizarre as Stavrogin's. Those impulses. They came close to driving me to breakdown, ruin. How you managed to stay together in one piece having to cope with them yourself, I'll never know.

My long-stemmed yellow-brown rose, born of a West Indian diplomat and his black Chicago wife, and reared in a strict puritanical home. Father a strong, distant man, steady church-goer, sometime poet, always busy; mother a college actress and one-time model, a strict overseer. Your childhood, split between Washington and Trinidad, meant private schools and avoidance of trash, especially black trash. A daughter of black aristocracy, you were not going to be dragged back down by "some Rufus Jones" (your mother's pet phrase). So you were tucked away behind a hedge grove of respectability and sent off to Bennett College for girls in upstate New York. Where two things happened. One was you began acting in college plays. Two was you made trips to New York City. The beginning of the end of a proper girl!

Rebellion started officially when you decided to go to Yale Drama School for graduate work, instead of taking a teaching job, as your parents wished. There, two more crucial events. The first, you played the part of a black slave in an adaptation of *Benito Cereno*. Second, through one of the actors, your sex life began. Number one was a black actor, number two a white instructor, number three a black militant whom you met at a party. And for the first time in your life you were confronted openly with your color (bringing to the surface other times when you skipped by it); questions of racism and political program squeezed in upon you. Only half American, you were confused by your "political role"; black but neither exploited nor impoverished, you discovered guilt. All of which added to the earlier dilemmas created by an aloof father and a rigid competitive mother. On all fronts, there was deepening contradiction. With consequences to follow.

The mind swirled as the body dived into militancy. For good and bad. African robes striped in orange and bright yellow and vermilion converted a paisley-bloused undergraduate choirgirl into some Sudanese princess. Consciousness of black combined with newfound sensuality created a sudden pride in your body—in dance, in sex; and you discovered you were a star there. But art converted into political propaganda was a bore. And hate-whitey programs were contradicted by affairs with white men (for others as well as you). It was hard to take simple slogans instead of reflective paragraphs. And in the midst of the sudden dervish dance of your soul, your father arrived one day in New Haven (tipped off by a local dignitary?), took one look at the dashiki, Fanon, and new hairdo (natural), and told you to pack your bags. While you did that, furious and helpless, he called the registrar and arranged a leave of absence. Twenty-three years of expensive gardening was not going to be ruined by the first raccoons and woodchucks on the scene. So the Honorable Eric Masters (a supreme court justice in Trinidad), removed his fallen daughter from the contamination of American liberal schools to the sanity of their Georgetown (D.C.) townhouse. But the journey south wasn't far enough. The move designed to restore righteousness did the opposite: it fanned corruption.

For what better place than the Capital to turn into an improper girl? The opportunities were immense. At dinner parties she could make ironic racial remarks to the white diplomats, who were trapped between her lusty looks and mocking irony. The Episcopalian minister whom she was sent to see wound up—was lured into—infatuation; rejected, he left his family and his parish. She introduced the family to Marcellus Tresvant, a twenty-eight-year-old black nationalist who was currently driving a D.C. bus. When they disapproved violently, she began seeing him out of spite. (Spite: the great motivator!) On the domestic front, she pressed the attack. She took to reading books and pamphlets on the subject of black slavery, and casually leaving them everywhere about the house. Generally face down, open at some heinous white crime. So that her father would sit down to discover by his reading chair an ancient leather-bound *Report to the Commonwealth on the Progress of the Slave Trade in the West Indian Colonies* (printed 1783), open at a report of a mass hanging of twelve slaves in Kingston, for the crime of drunkenness. Or her mother—or the black cleaning lady—would find on the dining-room table a copy of Frederick Douglass's *Autobiography*, a bookmark indicating the passage where Douglass's mother was raped repeatedly by her white plantation owner. Or else, at a cocktail party, there would suddenly crop up copies of runaway-slave narratives, with passages of enforced sodomy or rape underlined in yellow Magic Marker, to the embarrassed shock of the guests.

After the first of such incidents, Eric Masters sat down with his daughter and tried to talk the mischievousness out of her. The second such incident signified clear and intolerable defiance, and not having read Spock or Freud, the equable judge lost his temper and administered a slapping-beating. (Which she mysteriously enjoyed through her tears, she explained to me. Years of analysis later, she began to see why: she was getting through to him.) It was a nasty habit, all right, hard to take for the proud and dignified Masters family. They could no longer control their daughter. Into the midst of their book-lined townhouse, tastefully civilized with objects and a maid and a fine garden, their daughter was reintroducing the jungle. It wouldn't do. So far as Gwen's personality and character were concerned, time was showing that, while she was quite ordinary as a *good girl,* she exhibited a kind of genius at being *bad.*

Everybody was pleased—except Gwen, who knew better—when she eloped with her unemployed bearded bus driver with the phony Roman name.

(This narrative told to me not in one gulp but in fits and starts. But I'm a patient and tenacious fellow who knows that everyone takes a great joy in telling and confessing. Just give the girls time and lend them an ear and poke the right question, and they'll unlock the best part of their lives: their unforeseen and unpredictable secrets.)

Skip forward some six or seven years. Marriage to Marcellus had produced two sons, endless arguments, and increasing beatings, a complete break from family and tradition. Fortunately, she had returned to finish her M.F.A. at Yale, which earned her a teaching position in the drama department at Boston University. Also, out of a survival instinct and a friend's advice, she acquired an analyst and went twice a week. Which gave her the stamina to separate from Marcellus and then divorce him. So that, by the time I entered the scene, she had, like a black moon of the times, waned through various phases of representative disintegration: pious respectability, rebellious slumming, confused militancy. And now, aided by her disinterested doctor—who was more interested in patterns of unresolved guilt and displaced anger than in color or political correctness—Gwen was trying to create or find "a new wholeness" (Dr. Ernestine Carter's term). She was ready, with her expensive experience and proved courage, to make something of the shards and stiflings and mistakes and wrong routes of her life. From now on, announced that shrewd black shrink, she (Gwen) "should give in to her impulses, allow them to flow freely and carry her where they may." For the reusing of them, like physiotherapy of the muscles, would be the starting point of her reconstitution.

A fine theory, but what about real life, Doctor? Did you

have any idea what license your words granted Gwen? Did you have any hint, seated miles away from the actual combat (Gwen's apartment), what your words would unleash? Come over here to Cambridge and play my role—I kept wanting to say in person to the doctor, through those first months—and see if you still signal green concerning impulses. "Seek self-fulfillment" was one thing if Gwen was to channel it through artistic or financial success. But when it involved another live human being in the proximity of those unleashed desires? Be reasonable, Ernestine. Please!

(Overheated, you admonish? Hear me out first and then decide!)

Not that I knew of this Byzantine history or the shape of the madness about to descend, when I first laid eyes on you at a colleague's party. The first impression of you there, your velvety brown skin and carnal curves hugged into trails of white Victorian ruffle down to your ankle, was of coming upon yet another wild leopard fitted into a dress and escorted to a party. Naturally my knees went weak. (Fortunately, most persons in our town, academics, grad students, and professionals, are poor at sighting wild animals. Instinct and experience being everything when it comes to The Cunt Hunt—the city boy's version of riding for the fox—bookish types, who have swapped instinct for tenure, are severely handicapped. Thus, those displaced wanderers from wild-game preserves who regularly come to Cambridge parties—Gwendolen Leopard, Holly Giraffe, or Rosalie Gazelle, to name three from memory—pass through virtually unnoticed, untouched. Which makes Cambridge Hunting Grounds still one of the ripest sites on the continent for the *able*, experienced Cunt Hunter. To my mind, an intact wildcunt sanctuary that rivals Nairobi National Park.)

As soon as I maneuvered us alone, I wanted to say, "Hello there, Miss Leopard, how's the jungle treating you?" And then wanted to rip off your Victorian virgin costume, designed for rape. "What do you do?" I mumbled, dreaming of licking sauce off that lusty chest, or perhaps sitting naked upon that promontory called ass and reading a paperback. Those large black gazelle-eyes reading my fantasies, you replied, "I dance. Want to see me?" Talk to a leopard and see what you get? Dance where, when? I shook my head some way. "You're young to be a dean, aren't you?" you continued, smoking from a cigarette holder. "How old and how come?" "Thirty-three and precocious," I answered, trying to absorb the color of ocher. "You come watch me dance. I do it on the sly. Moonlighting. Want to see it?" A pearly half smile of *challenge*.

In your yellow sports car (an old one from Italy), you handled the floor shift like an Indianapolis driver and shot me smiling glances, those thick lips beginning to go to my head like amphetamine. Ten minutes later, in an expensive Boston night-club, you were greeted warmly and I was escorted to a small table in front of a stage. (Gwen stopped to chat with someone and said she'd join me momentarily.) The packed mixed crowd barely watched a blond dancer go through the motions of a discotheque number. I felt awful and bewildered and out of place in the vulgar room and sudden melodramatic context. I was on the edge of leaving when a well-dressed black announced that we were in for a treat, for with us tonight was Miss Sheila Roberts, better known as the Brown Bomber. The one and only! The crowd cheered, I sat dumfounded, the name recalling to me Madison Square Garden excitement, when the girl I had come with pounced onto the stage, white ruffles abandoned for black G-string, tassels, boots. The heavyweight hero of my adolescence was now a dancer in my maturity; from jabbing lefts to feinting with elbows. Did that black-on-tan leather-on-flesh (replacing Everlast trunks) animal dancing for twenty-five minutes—eight rounds' worth—to rock rhythms really know about Joe Louis, I wondered sentimentally. In any case, Gwen Tresvant was ferocious and incredible, especially when she spotted me and played to me directly. Sitting there, I found it hard to believe that a half hour previous I was bored to tears at a fashionable Cambridge house and that now my blood was pumping furiously; and hard to believe also that that leopard of my imagination was not a squirrel in reality. No, she was the real thing, all right; slow with pelvic beauty and joyous papaya breasts, a sight to behold.

Most impressive was the ass. It was a great lovely butt, and *Gwen knew it*, which made the rites she performed with it all the more incredible. It was a high, very full ass, bursting from the body like an entire region in bloom, the twin melonlike territories glistening with rivers of perspiration. A behind with a volition and vocabulary all its own; who would have dreamed it? Facing the wall, she gyrated it slowly, looking over her shoulder at me unsmilingly; using a microphone between her legs, she slid up and down, her ass projected beyond the stage a good two feet on the descent, working all the time to the cadence of the music. Hypnotized and transported, I yearned to spend years researching the region—an academic is an academic!—and felt like an explorer about to set off for regions uncharted, drunk with adventure. (Is a serious American Cunt Hunter that much different from a great Victorian explorer? Bernard Kovell traveling up and down that black-ass region of Gwendolen very different from Sir Richard Burton exploring the Dark Continent? Personally, I don't think so. The motive of going some place new and unsettling and mapping it out unites all explorers, of land and body.) Every face turned toward Gwen in awe and desire, she was, dancing onstage, like Cleopatra coming down the Nile, a figure of unreal sensuality, a brown goddess turned to legend.

Outside in the spring night, you continued the assault with "Just to show you that we're both precocious." And handed me the keys to drive back to your place.

On the way there, you launched into a schoolmistress explanation of how you did this moonlighting to keep your "body"—how charming to hear you use that word as if you were speaking about state taxes or a vegetable garden—to keep your body in shape when you were not acting or "interpretive-dancing." Piously you chatted on about muscles, ligaments, acting theories: a leopard talking about theology. Quietly amused I drove and let you talk, seeing that your superego and Daddy Masters were getting back at you for your little adventure. And forcing you into such absurd rationalization. Misguided narcissist, how you loved it up there! All eyes riveted upon your naked body! All that concentrated rapture poured onto your ass! But you wouldn't be able to admit that, dear leopard. So talk, talk. The discrepancy between your pious and specious declarations and your true passions amazing me. And, in your affluent apartment, you went into that little song-and-dance about how you wanted someone sane around for a change. Not a father-figure, but a man your own age. And not that you were prejudiced, but you wanted it to be a white man, just now. And so on . . .

I had been through quite an evening. But as I lay on that Canadian grizzly rug, I began to understand the attraction which had gripped me earlier at the party, and which had continued. The discovery surprised me as I named it: your *color*. The blackness. The bronze-pecan of your arms. The well-made chocolate legs. The ocher and walnut face. The pink slivers of lip mobbed by mahogany. The pale brown forehead set off by coal-black eyes, hair. Black-brownness was flooding my senses, and I felt *helpless* before it. It was idiotic. Senseless. Probably racist, I thought. But there was no time for thought. There was only sensation. *The sensation of a new color.* I had been so used to whiteness in women over these years that the sudden shift was startling, provocative. And sexual. Uncertain of this last, I knew it for sure when your cinnamon hand reached down and caressed my face. I was wild for the brownness of you.

Helpless before your color, I was helpless too before your desires. Lured into their dark depths, I was Conrad going into the Congo and discovering life for the first time. Life defined as new and dangerous experience which upset one's view of the world and self. Once we got beyond those first nights of innocent lovemaking, you started in. With requests that were illicit, requests that would soon turn into *demands*. Sexually non-negotiable. How horrible it was to begin to give in to you. To begin to experience those waves of guilt and shame—mainly shame—that kept mounting and increasing. To experience them, moreover, at exactly those moments when you were most glutted with pleasure, and when I was explicitly prohibited from expressing my own displeasure. An added insult.

But it was only fun, you explained, if I was your complete master and you were the complete victim: the slave. I remember the first time you used that equation, those words! It was the middle of the night and you were whispering; I thought for sure they were nightmare words, and I shook your shoulders. But when I put the light on, you were wide awake, your teeth set and smiling terrifically. "I want you for a master," you said. I was terrified. You let it sink in, whispered it to me again, another night. And again. "I want you for a master." I knew you were crazy and that I should escape, before . . . it was too late.

The Hegel equation began to be dramatized. One morning I awoke to find you curled at the bottom of the bed, having slept by my feet like a dog, a servant. You opened your eyes at my movement, kissed my feet, and smiled angelically. I was startled. Patiently, on your knees, you tried to explain to your pupil. You realized it was hard on me, going against my feelings, the grain of the culture, romantic notions. "But doesn't my pleasure come first?" you asked, simply. Another word turned upside down! That night the speech continued. If I was to be kind to you, truly kind, then I must forget newspaper clichés, Black Power slogans, religious pieties, sociological explanations, and attend to your real desires. Your deepest personal needs. Two mornings later you were back at my feet when I awoke, your face shining with joy. My shock was less. In fact, as I lay propped against my bamboo headboard, I rather liked seeing you there curled sideways in your pink nightie at the bottom of the bed, the frizzy hair and walnut face next to my white feet. The scene was very Oriental. It afforded me a curious pleasure.

That was the beginning. But letting you lie there was quite another matter from giving in to other needs by active participation. Another night. More talk: Didn't you have a right to be *human*, you asked, hands on lace-pantied hips? Didn't you have a right to your illicit drives like everyone else? *What did I want to do, treat you like a black?* Well, you weren't going to take that. You were going to have the right to be as "licentiously human"— delicious phrase!—as anyone else. Unless, of course—your half West Indian singsong and half-actressy exaggeration dropping into street inflection—I really was a bigot beneath the rhetoric? My God, only the most ingenious lawyer would have dreamed of such an argument! But you? It scandalized my understanding, scrambled my emotions. I perspired. You persisted. To be Gwen Tresvant first and foremost, and to hell with Humanity-at-Large and Black-Is-Beautiful slogans. "Self-fulfillment first," you tapped your black bra, the analyst speaking through your mouth. That was the real test for me, the lust in your eye as you swung toward me to the tune of Dionne Warwick, not whether I'd sign another advertisement for black rights. Those hips jutting rhythmically a foot to either side, I was stupefied. Imagine Clarence Darrow summing up with those brilliant hips! It was not easy to remain an impartial juror. I was lost.

The rest is history, painful memory. All downhill. It was not easy giving in. No matter what you said about personal unhappiness, or how much you reassured me, or how often you undercut my feelings with your logic. But what patience, stamina, shrewdness! What single-mindedness of purpose! What strategic brilliance! Headway was made. Awakening one night at 3:30 A.M. (by luminous dials) to find you mumbling and pleading inaudibly, and turning over, hoping you'd return to sleep. Moments later, feeling myself being lifted, my pajama bottoms slid down, a pillow eased under me, and suddenly a feathery sensation scudding downward from my belly button. Somnolently I sensed a wet heaven lapping back and forth somewhere beneath my scrotum, fingernails stroking my thighs in sharp counterpoint. Was it real, I remember thinking, too pleased to want to wake fully, those brown limbs curved into a servile "C" beneath me, an apparent one hundred tongues lapping and nipping, a creature moaning pleasure in devotion to its task? At one moment I was an infant being changed and diapered, at another a helpless fleshy morsel being sucked upon and squeezed by some hungry sea squid. I split my pleasure between shifting dreams and tantalizing tongues and fingers. The feeling of Caribbean water pleasure billowed everywhere, including my soon spouting spermatozoic self. Then the brown shark wrestled upon me—after twenty minutes, a half hour, an hour *down there?*—a mother-of-pearl smile, lustrous brown limbs and pungent smell of excrement engulfing me. It went on and on, surrounding and mesmerizing, through the night, leaving me limp, sated, exhausted, a windless bag of glutted sensations.

Still, a man's basic instincts are not easily overcome, guarded and reinforced as they are by the standards of society and rearing of family. I recall the next seminal night when your demon went to work on those instincts. (During those weeks, I was again this close to leaving, afraid that I was getting in over my head. Controlling my girls, remember, is a matter of necessity.) You began that A.M. escapade whispering in my ear until I awoke to crazy charges. "Jew racist," she said. "You're a Jew racist!" I smiled, said go back to sleep. No soap. I had to talk about it, then, there. In my mind deciding this was it, I would leave, no more madness for me, I told her to fuck off and buried my head on the other side of the bed. The next assault was spit out: I was shitty in the sack.

That's right, boy, *shitty*. Finally, as the tempo continued in this vein, I turned over and slapped her with my open hand across the face. Her head jumped away and then back, like a cobra. Once more my hand went out, hard. For a minute or so it felt exhilarating, before I realized what I had done. But just as my guilt set in, Gwen began smiling. Idiotically, I thought. Angered wildly, I shot out my hand again against that soft cheek. "Stop grinning, will you. Stop it!" Yes, she had her man. Infuriated, I held her by her pink frilly nightgown, splitting with anger. The glow on her face was of triumphant joy; a general suffering, a temporary loss in the service of ultimate victory. I began cursing and reviling her, using phrases that I had never used before but that had been insidiously taught to me by her sleepy whisperings of smut, like some sleep-machine of obscenity. I found myself adding the word "black" to almost every swear.

A god-awful night that I tried to put out of my mind, but which, I'm afraid to say, was repeated on future nights with variations on the same impulse: her impulse to be dominated.

I skip to the next step of outrage. (Were I to go into detail about the whole design and momentum of Gwen's strategy, I should wind up writing an article for the Encyclopedia of Perversity. Suffice to say, this was not your ordinary masochist. This was a girl of inestimable guerrilla nuance and dirty strategic brilliance. The timing of her gestures, the build-up of provocation, the calculated gradualness of pleasure-giving—in such matters Gwen Tresvant was an artist.) The final outrage. We had come back from one of the "new plays"—another one of those primitive exercises of heehawing and simulated copulation that Gwen called the avant-garde theater and I the retarded theater— when you suggested some hashish to round off the evening. Suggested it casually, as if I—who barely touched liquor—took drugs regularly. My "no" turned to acquiescence in the face of your lying diatribe about my infantile fears and your boredom at pampering me.

Tricked again, I having no idea that the whole thing was yet another guerrilla ambush on my morals. In your bedroom I puffed against my will on the small silver pipe you handed me, passing it back and forth, back and forth. After some twenty minutes, you wavered as you came toward me, and when I reached out for the pipe and missed, the signal was clear for you. Without the deception of hashish, what happened next never would have happened. That goes without saying. And without a first time, there never would have been a second, a third. After all, there are certain limits beyond which even a driven man won't proceed, held in check—fortunately—by ancient codes and learned taboos. I don't remember all the sordid details. We were undressed, you were on your knees, I was being caressed, the odor was acrid, the walls were swimming . . . Can you imagine what it was like for me, Gwen, as you writhed and moaned with pleasure while that hot yellow stream poured upon those black papayas, the long neck, your lovely face? How I tried to turn away, do you recall, Gwen? Out of pain . . . humiliation . . . fear. Mostly fear. But you grabbed my hand and made such a love-sick call that I had to turn back. Half your pleasure, it was clear, was for me to view you in that position, basking in that unholy shower of thick yellow. Was I crazy in thinking that you were crying? (The fluids indistinguishable.) Who knew? But I was surely made crazy by your gesture of gratitude (kissing my hand). It was insane.

There, another secret let go of. Sophie and Grace, Melissa and Kate, Angela, all the children: *forgive me*.

When it occurred again, it was without the aid of hashish. I despised and adored it. Citizens of the world, respectable people of Cambridge, colleagues and students, do not think too badly of me for saying, I came to despise and adore it. For the self who disliked it I knew well: he was like yourselves—civilized, moral, society-reared and -geared, a fellow of *straightforward* decency. The self who enjoyed it was, be assured, *a stranger to me*. Some primitive outlaw who had never heard of democracy, justice, laws, unbreakable codes. Clearly my immoral stream summed up in dramatic fashion all of Gwen's strivings for a relationship based on inequality. For me—the straightforward me—the message was startling. For him—the warped stranger—the feeling communicated was familiar and becoming. (That startled me even more!) *He* seemed to bask in the idea of inequality, with him the master. The power intoxicated and attracted him; he felt it was his due, almost. Having total control of another human being—though perhaps he would have preferred it if the other party didn't wish it that way but was forced against her will into that position—was enormously gratifying. Being a master seemed to make him more of a man. Moreover, that stranger in me agreed, the naked exposure of power between people seemed healthy and even therapeutic. In two senses. The first was that it cleared things up about how people stood with each other, a matter badly needing clearing up in these days of confused positions. The second was that it brought to the surface what was known all along by intelligent men to be a truth, a reality, about human affairs. That is, one person bossing another around, or being bossed, was at the bottom of most if not all dealings between two persons, though there had been through the centuries an overwhelming amount of propaganda to whitewash and euphemize the brute fact. The religions, morals, and customs of middle-class society had sought, rhetorically at least, to establish an all-embracing utopia of democratic cooperation and universal benevolence among human beings. It was a system of morality based upon self-serving myth (the preservation of Christianity), not upon human psychology. Furthermore, it was a Sunday myth contradicted every working day by the system of capitalism, where some of your best Christians were frequently your most brutal masters. Throwing off its shackles, a task fitted for certain men, was a great liberating moment of truth. Or so the stranger in me argued, with delight in his eye when thinking of his Gwen-sessions.

Of course, I paid dearly for such theories, such gratifications. Outside, in the streets, at the campus, in the classroom, I was agonized by the split in my life between my role as professor and my relations with Gwen. More and more, I felt like a criminal. Whenever I passed a black student on campus, I shuddered; the company of my liberal friends unnerved me; student radicals—well, no need to comment on their effect upon me. If the situation ever leaked, given today's racial climate, it would surely be misinterpreted. Misinterpreted? What a colossal euphemism for the real consequences! Public disgrace, near-lynching, and Canadian exile! So while my colleagues, students, and ordinary citizens slept, their consciences untroubled, I walked the streets; while they cheerily went to work in the morning, ready to correct wrongs, to bolster themselves in the world, I went around less energetically, less free . . . in shame.

And then there was my role. Could it be true—was I in fact evolving into a loathsome, perverted sadist? Would I soon be one of those *National Enquirer* moles who burrowed through magazine racks for hints of "strict Swedish governesses" and "communal Leather Clubs"? After all, perversion was sweeping the nation, whipping it into a frenzy, from eulogies of Sade in literary quarterlies that used to admire Trotsky to *Daily News* features now appearing regularly in the *Times*. At the Harvard Square kiosk, Radcliffe girls in dark stockings giggled with their Yard boy friends over pulp like "Slash and Scream." A step up, at the austere Coop, the likes of Genet and *Story of O* had become continuous best-sellers to distinguished professors in tweeds. At the university theaters (Kresge Auditorium, the Loeb Theater), well-dressed suburbanites joined the flocking students to see the new plays, those concoctions of sex and shock that had about as much to do with Brecht—as many claimed—as red borscht had to do with Lenin (and his revolution). Even at Cambridge parties, I occasionally felt my innocence. (At one of these, for example, a forty-year-old, miniskirted, Lauren Bacall-ish wife of a well-known biochemist invited me to spend a long weekend with them in the countryside nearby. "I think you'll enjoy Lincoln croquet," she smiled thinly. "The mallets and wickets are rather novel. So are the rewards and punishments." Was that how DNA geniuses were made, I thought, awed.) Yet, despite the waves of pornography crashing through the culture more and more, a counterpart perhaps to the primitivism and brutality of the political life, the prospect of my own (unwitting) participation unnerved me. On certain mornings, I looked with fear in the bathroom mirror. Over there, I noticed, beneath my left eye . . . was that the yellow circle of the sadist? And I would wear my dark prescription glasses throughout the day.

For the first time in my life, I resorted to Librium, Miltown. I stocked up on Reik (Theodor), Sade, various writings of black psychiatrists. My fears for Gwen and myself seemed confirmed; we were in for a lifetime of sadomasochism. But that didn't solve the immediate problem. Desperate, I visited the legendary Ernestine, Gwen's shrink. A small homely lady wearing rhinestone-studded eyeglasses, the genial doctor asked me to be seated. Nervous and stumbling, I tried to explain who I was and what the situation was from my point of view. Was there hope for Gwen,

I wondered. Should I get out and leave her alone? The doctor smiled compassionately and said something about an "important transference phase" which would run its course. "Just bear with it, Bernard." (The familiarity reducing me to seven years old.) "Now," pursued the lyrical Barbadian voice, the eyeglasses dropping to her skinny chest, where they hung on a black strap, "what doctor are you seeing? And how long have you been in analysis?" More humiliation. "No doctor," I said, "no analysis." After a moment of eye-widening surprise, Ernestine adjusted her glasses like a pilot, took out a fountain pen, and wrote on a slip of paper the names of two doctors. She thanked me for coming, advised me to seek consultation immediately, and said the hour was up. In the reception office, her pert white secretary wondered if I wanted to pay now or be billed? Now *my* eyes widened. Transference phase and an announcement that I needed consultation had cost me forty bucks. And all I wanted to know was whether to allow that fiend to continue reaming my asshole!

(Admittedly, Gwen's consolations were cheaper, in every way. Smiling at me as though I were a nervous parole officer, she dismissed my anxieties with "Don't worry, there are no *laws* broken.")

Matters began to change more from accident than from purpose. One night, watching Gwen turn into the Brown Bomber—like Mary Batson turning into Mary Marvel—and gyrate onstage, I was crazed by that sumptuous behind. Later, in her bedroom, I went to work on it, showering it with kisses and caresses. To be truthful, I sort of got carried away and stayed down there for quite a wild while, my nose and fingers burrowing into moist dark openings, my lips sucking up juices, perspiration, and God-knows-what-else, my tongue finding transport and delight in eliciting moans miles north. And when legs wrapped around me like an excited boa constrictor, I was delirious. To be gripped in a vise of pleasure is strong stuff. With soft moans and imperious commands tossed down from above—and there exists, from down there, a dizzying sense of distances and heights—I stayed on duty below, pursuing plateaus of smooth brown, a mound of stiff black bristles, a long dark crack that continued on and on like some San Andreas Fault. It was grand in more ways than the surface would indicate. I had suddenly come upon a task that removed me from my exploiter's role. And I discovered that I took to the task like a professional coal miner, with pride and skill and a sense of daring. Moreover, to be thrown amid an underground of brown interiors fulfilled my early fascination with the strange new color of this girl. As I surfaced, my chin running with viscous juices from exotic regions, I was greeted with a great hug and satisfaction-smile. Obviously, I had made an excellent slave.

(It will be observed that I have a penchant for looking at reality in a picturesque way; or, more precisely, a habit of speaking about simple phenomena in elaborate or metaphorical terms. I believe this is the inevitable result of a lifetime of literary affliction, reading and teaching and thinking about printed words the way another man breathes oxygen, so that even the most base object or low activity can be imaginatively perceived, decoratively understood. The danger here, of course, is blurring distinctions and confusing the real-life object with the literary description. For protection, one keeps a sane and impartial mind, realizing that, while both have their advantages, the two are separate. Obviously, the minute investigations of Gwen's private parts are very different indeed from coal mining or great land explorations. Without my overexcited imagination, however, which conceives of cunts in terms of foreign lands and adventures, I doubt whether I should ever take part, let alone write about my delvings into women.)

It was a curious relief to discover that acting a role of servility was not for me odious. And that, on the contrary, it had its own system of compensations and rewards, which were almost as great as that of the master's role. (The great pleasure of each was that it placed you squarely: you knew where you were, what your station was. Ambiguity and ambivalence, those assassins of pleasure, were gone.) And it was useful, too, to know that my inner feelings, my psychosexual needs, fitted in rather neatly with the politics of the situation. That is, I enjoyed playing at sexual servility, rather than just going through the motions for the sake of those obscene emotion directors, guilt-relief and pseudo-justice. Naturally, Gwen enjoyed it too. But not as much as she savored the part of debased servant, which she stuck to, in the main. (This bewildered me a bit, but I chose to let her have her

113

way, her dubious explanations beside the point.) And having seen the other end of the matter, so to speak, I felt much less badly about the positions we assumed sexually. I saw clearly that pleasure began at the far end of morality, where needs took over; if this meant unusual positionings, like radical shifts in offensive lines before the hike, so be it. Moreover, as I began to descend with a certain regularity to a slave's quarters below—though I must add here, for the sake of accuracy, that when I discovered that my Brown Bomber had piles, I was put off psychologically from such descents; who ever heard of a leopard with piles?—as I say, as I was ready to leave off the master and play the slave, so simultaneously Gwen's desires for the extremities of domination gradually eased. Sadomasochism was modified to a reasonable perversity level.

Another decided change took place less gradually, and concerned a specific evening. It was late October 1967, I recall, for we had watched Miss Louise Day Hicks campaign for mayor of Boston. While in the shower, Gwen called out for a nightie, suggesting that Sarah Caldwell, the Boston opera producer, could make a million redoing the Laurel and Hardy films, using Miss Hicks for Hardy. Smiling at the project, I went to her bureau and looked through the drawers, coming upon, by chance, a pile of cheap pocketbooks tucked amid layers of frilly panties. I couldn't resist removing them. They were the kind of cheap pocketbook printed years ago, selling for thirty-five, fifty, seventy-five cents; a typical title was *Mandingo*, which had a cover picture of a white plantation owner and his mulatto mistress-slave. The remaining bunch were similar, cheap lurid thrillers of naughty miscegenation. A little dazed, I brought Gwen her nightgown and returned to the bedroom. The small pile of her dirty books was bizarre, scary. Uncertain of what to do, I put them back and pondered. Soon Gwen appeared, a pale brown daffodil in her yellow nightie, and, pecking me, said she was going to write some letters. When she departed, I returned to my cache. Leafing through them, I saw that they had been systematically marked at points of sexual abuse by the white men. Disturbed, nervous, I began to browse through the line of books on the headboard shelf. An anonymous book in plain yellow wrapper interested me. It turned out to be a very old *History of the West Indies,* bound in cracking leather, published by a respectable English press. The clandestine wrapper, used to clothe hard-core pornography, therefore surprised me. The book opened to a well-read and well-marked section covering the colonial reign, in the nineteenth century, of an infamous English colonel who served as the island's governor. The narrative of his imperial rule seemed to be the usual colonial politics, though a bit more ordered and just. A long footnote, however, was starred in red; it ran across two pages. In infinitesimal print, it was suggested that the colonel's private life had a certain apocryphal reputation for bizarreness, including the tale of a fifteen-year-old native slave girl who served as his mistress. "Mistress," however, included flagellation and other torture techniques, which supposedly went on for a period of two years in open view of the government. In all likelihood, continued the author, the tale was one of "wicked fancy" (marvelous phrase!), since the evidence upon which it was based —"handed-down oral testimony of a *native* servant"—was itself open to serious question. I tried to correlate the grisly footnote to our own relations. "How dare you!" Gwen screamed, suddenly appearing. "How dare you go into my private things!" Grabbing the book from my hands, she whacked me across the head with it. I snatched it from her, and she turned to the spread-out pocketbooks on the bed, flinging them at me, her face distorted by fury and pain as she tossed those secret texts. I got out of the room and the apartment as fast as I could.

I walked in the cool night, pondering the future with Gwen. The dirty-book find revealed only too clearly that her layers of political-sexual confusion were endless. Who could tell how much her desires for humiliation and injury were sincerely (neurotically) felt and how much manufactured through her crazy political misconceptions? Did Gwen herself know? And how in the world could I ever infiltrate that camouflage of political and racial dilemmas to her true personal needs? In other words, how could I instill in her trust if she in fact blamed me personally for my color heritage? In the streets and by the Charles, and finally amid those career-and-children-watchers drinking in the Wursthaus, I agonized. Finally, all that Harvard comfort and middle-class sanity forced me up and out. Unable to act upon the logical conclusion to my deliberations (departure from the affair), I found myself wandering back to Gwen's. To the problem of black and white I had no answer, except proximity and endurance with compassion. (Shivering past a group of three bebopping black teenagers, by Holyoke Center.) Each of us had a psychological plight, a collective burden (hers anger; mine bewilderment, guilt). If our skins were a collision of pigments—three motorcyclists roared across my thought—we had to hope that our spirits would meet. And compensate for the twists of our bodies, our reflex selves. (From the Orson Welles Cinema spilled forth a crowd of moviegoers—underground squaws, Godard-lovers, pug-nosed Irish girls with twitching behinds, forty-year-old hairy-chested hipsters. Who could reflect quietly any more on the streets of American cities?) Despite my self-serving attempts at understanding, I found myself breathing hard as I pushed the elevator button and watched Gwen's number 8 light up orange. And as I was propelled upward, I was seized with a dissolving fear that I was in a moving coffin.

Gwen was sitting in a stuffed chair in the unlit study, a drink at her side, smoking, staring out at the darkened city. As I came closer, I saw that she had tied her hair into two pigtails and bound them with ribbon. She looked like a lost pickaninny. It moved me. "I'm pretty messed up, baby," she began matter-of-factly, without looking at me. "And I'm not doing the kids any good, am I?" I sat near her and in a quiet voice asked about the books. Had she said to forget it, or tried to avoid the subject, it doubtless would have been the end. Instead, it was the beginning. Her reply was a two-hour narrative of her life (which I've related before); including the use of that pocketbook arsenal as blackmail and vengeance in Washington, D.C. In a neutral voice, as if speaking of someone else's life, she chronicled the interruption of her innocence, her routes of confusion, some gory details of marriage, her increasing resignation and defeat. And revealed, too, how her early desires for me to rape and abuse her were conceived of as "political acts." But since they filled her with pleasure, she was left with a hangover of guilt. Soon she was too confused to separate the two meanings. Finally, I left the study and went to bed; she was surprised to see me there when she came in. And through that night she did something which changed the course of the relationship: she kissed me repeatedly, thinking me asleep. Kissed my hands and the length of my fingers, my shoulders and forearms. Little gestures of love and gratitude which washed upon my drowsy consciousness and penetrated deeper, soothing backward through our entire affair of four months, like ointment upon sore wounds. In the morning, my heart overflowed with forgiveness, humility, love. All told, it was an eight-hour period of unusually powerful and tender feelings.

The night and morning were a kind of turning point, a trial whereby I had experienced the full depth of her chaos, the full explosion of her anger, the deep extent of her infirmity. And where she, in turn, recognized—to herself, unconsciously—in my endurance a force for psychic good. So the affair grew calmer, more intimate, rich with that sweet rhythm which romance can turn life into when it's flowing right. In retrospect, why did I decide to go back and endure a madwoman? Out of the knowledge taken from humanities lectures that only from suffering can wisdom come? Possibly; though too often this high-minded formula proved at odds with one's experience, where dumb animal pain was the only consequence. Out of one's hope that there's something salvageable from a particular wreck? Possibly; though such romantic optimism was frequently no more than a mask for a lower impulse. Out of the knowledge that, among the many contemporary claims to illness and agony, Gwen's application was more worthy than most, considering the times, her experience, her color? Yes; though again, the role of Red Cross Knight or Humanity Aide was inimical to me. No, endurance for me, I realized, had to come from something else, a source deeper than moralistic ordinance or social piety. From some sort of attraction . . . or gratification.

I was back to gratification. Beyond the shame, bewilderment, and humiliation, there was *that*. A thought not pleasing. And a further unpleasant notion: that the affair and Gwen were teaching me something which I only dimly perceived; some kind of instruction concerning the emotions. My intuition suggested that the experience was important, perhaps liberating. An intuition which violated my morals and therefore disturbed me.

A small thing happened one night which answered my puzzlement and signaled a larger emotion. At a dinner party,

Gwen flirted outrageously with a colleague of mine; afterward, in the car, when I accused her, she tossed the whole thing off as a figment of my imagination and continued to apply her Revlon. In one easy motion, I threw aside her lipstick and slapped her. For the first time, a slap of deliberation, delivered without hesitation or guilt. I began driving, relieved. To my surprise, Gwen leaned her head onto my arm, squeezed my hand, nuzzled. She added softly, "I *so* like being obedient to you." The air was cleared.

How simple it seemed, as I drove, Gwen purring like a cat. Scarred by the lack of a father's closeness and by the confusions of her past, poor Gwen craved intelligent but decisive authority in a man. I had been intelligent enough, but not strong enough, in the beginning. So that, among her *meshuggaas* (madness), there was also her "project": *to educate me in the ways of authority, domination.* It was months before I was able to deliver that first conscienceless blow. Others, however, followed more easily, when there were no other means of reestablishing order and sanity. An endless argument in which hysteria rose faster than logic? Boom! Order. An obsessive provocation concerning race that arose from her demon self? Smack! Sanity. In both cases Gwen calmed down immediately, the situation was angry but controllable, we could talk reasonably again.

It was a pleasure to assume authority so swiftly and emphatically. With derisiveness, I saw how my earlier ambivalence about assuming authority had made us both weary, frustrated. And physical symbolism, that simple sure signal, had been out of the question. A weakness nurtured by the culture and by my own attenuated Jewish heritage. Who ever heard of a Jew beating his wife? Usually it was the other way around.

The lesson of Gwen stayed with me, and I found myself, when the situation called for it, applying it to my other women. The results were surprising. One evening Angela showed up at my apartment, against my precise telephone wishes two hours earlier. On the pretense of narrating some new woe, she was soon curled into my lap, her body beckoning other matters. I lifted her off (embarrassed by my stupid stiff member) and told her to get out. "How could you behave this way to me?" she wailed. "How could you be this unfeeling?" I told her, once again, that she was not to come over when I advised her not to. More tears and anguish. I didn't care for her at all, she complained, I was selfish, selfish! I moved forward a step and, for the first time, smacked her twice. She held her hand to her cheek, amazed. I was calm. "Now out," I repeated, and helped her along. The next day I received a note of apology, on pink perfumed paper, with this memorable admission and reminder: "Of course you were right to slap me. I certainly deserve it when I turn hysterical that way." The eager plea for future chastisement caused me to sink in my chair, enlightened. How little we know ourselves, or others.

A similar instance occurred one night in bed; I finally stopped Kate's endless whine about permanence with the palm of my hand. I surprised both of us. Whereupon she tucked her head into my chest and squeezed me. Before I realized what was happening, the tearful girl had slipped down on me, sucking upon me with a devotion and craft that I had never seen in her before. Afterward, I couldn't resist remarking, "You know, dear, you were pretty delicious. Those slaps seemed to do wonders for your spirit." She blushed deeply. But when she looked up, it seemed to me that her eyes were not without a measure of pride.

As I was reading Wittgenstein one evening, my mind wandered to my recent tactics and the responses they elicited. One fact was unmistakable: my spurts of truck-driver muscle pleased and excited the girls (three at least). The experience was new to me; it was a role that I had stumbled into or, more exactly, had been coerced into. Clearly, my Gwen was shrewder in her madness than I had allowed for. She knew far better than I did what certain women desired from their mates. I recalled Kate's joyful cry after a brief show of force one day, "God, how long I've waited for a man!" What that all-inclusive term really meant, of course, was boss, or more specifically, father. That is, the return of *a male with authority*.

Now the handling of women (wives, mistresses) with such physical decisiveness is looked upon in our culture with great disdain. It is regarded as something primitive and therefore degrading, and any man who commits such dastardly acts hostages himself to societal condemnation and punishment (in divorce situations, the term, I believe, is "alimony"). But how easily we are persuaded to take cultural judgments for universal truths, social customs for existential realities. How few there are who have the time or brains to look with perspective, with a historical eye, and to see morals—I'm tempted to say, hitting girls, but it will be construed wrongly—as something historical and dynamic, not abstract and static. Certainly not your ordinary grocer, academician, journalist, or surgeon. In any case, an afternoon's research at the Widener taught me a few simple facts: namely, a good part of the rest of the world still lived according to patriarchal rules and pleasures. Item: a Tatar from the Caucasus who doesn't beat his wife is considered an inferior type and is treated accordingly. Item: in most Arab countries, to be beaten by male royalty remains a high privilege for a female. (Not to mention the widespread non-European, non-American practice of lending your wife to a guest, as an act of hospitality. Imagine the joy of that obedience!) The point was, once the reign of authority was weakened at the top, the entire fabric of the society was threatened. Everyone suffered—the man, the woman, the culture. And authority began with the family and the figure who sustained them: the man. I went back to my favorite novelists, the Russians, and discovered in a slim volume of Dostoevsky's (*Winter Notes on Summer Impressions*) his great amusement with the European notion that the beating of women was an uncivilized act. As with other European ideas of progress, this one, too—according to that shrewd psychopath—depended more on self-serving piety than it did on human psychology.

The years and years, I realized, in which male authority had been on the decline in Western civilization, in America! Who ever dreamed that, by repressing my impulse to slap Angie or Kate when they turned uncontrollably foolish, I was in fact undercutting the full intensity of our relationship, and undercutting my own energies? That, in my tacit assumption concerning the fairer sex, I was aping the absurd image of refined gentility propagated by Victorian novels and perpetuated by life in academy-land, which before my eyes turned out specimens of human nature called men, who, when it came to dealing with women, were much closer to terrified mice or earnest mules? Who ever thought that a serious source of my general uncertainty was my unconscious acceptance of the sentimental myths enervating the culture, stemming from television melodrama, romantic pieties, social-science humanitarianism? Or that I, a non-Jewish Jew, had suffered in my own way from the image of the Jew as humble scholar or defeated sufferer, which had seeped down to me through the years? Oh, I knew well enough about the wisdom of Maimonides, the sacred obedience of Abraham. But what about Moses smashing the Tablets in anger? Or David violating Bathsheba and transgressing the Laws? Couldn't I preserve those images of aggressiveness along with the traditional ones of passivity and submissiveness?

These heretical thoughts, however, were in no way to be confused with a credo of primitivism, or with a desire to forgo deserved virtues like compassion, charity, tenderness. These remained for me the lubricants that sweetened life, that fueled the precarious human journey with an appeal that the smooth Apollo shots lacked. And never for a moment did I wish to abandon my moral sense for truck-driver power. If I smacked Angela, this did not grant me license to hit her whenever I wished, or to behave badly toward her outside the moment. It meant rather that there were times when the situation called for it, or times when she (and I, I suppose) demanded a tangible reminder of our different roles. There were occasions, moreover, in which Kate's attraction for dominance would spill over into a frenzy of masochism, and she would itch and plead for wholesale beating (after a slap, "Do it again, will you? Again!" and, while edging into passion, "Pull my hair hard, please! Harder, harder!"). But for this task I was not equal, nor did I wish to be; I had had enough nightmare episodes with Gwen. And finally, I was neither foolish nor pompous enough to act upon the simplistic assumption that all women were the same and demanded equal treatment. Not with all the girls was my new behavior desirable or pleasurable. With Sophie, for example, the urge to strike her never once arose. Why? Because she was Sophie. For us, words were always sufficient. And the one time that I slapped Melissa she dropped into such a fit of depression that it took me two whole visits to bring her back to herself. She was like a small dog who, in memory of a former master's brutal care, suddenly hid under the bed, paralyzed with fear, at the slightest threat. With these two women, then, my authority was clearly defined by the structures of reason and solicitude. But with the others, occasional physical force was of enormous value for sustaining our mutual happiness.

Back in his *Blue and Brown Books*, Wittgenstein was once

more emphasizing our need to examine language with more precision. And I thought of the way that our own culture had distorted and abused the word "civilized" in relation to men and women. Just look around; how weak and unmanly the men had become, how aggressive and unfeminine the women. Why not? Did anyone of experience and honesty really believe, for example, that a real, live woman—Our Gal Sundays to the contrary—could find happiness and satisfaction with, say, a Princeton Ph.D. in English? How could that graduate cope with her? Would his school tie be as useful upon her thigh as another fellow's tongue? Would her hips and ass arouse him as much as a solid heroic couplet would? And how in the world would he be able to *take charge* of a woman, tame her? When she growled at him like a lioness in heat, and reached for his flesh with a nail-polished paw, what was he to do, recite *The Rape of the Lock*? Remember, these impressionable young men spent their youths not between the thighs of Harlem whores but between the covers of Henry James's novels. Syphilis is not merely educational—it has a strong literary tradition behind it—but also curable. But an early passion for *The Golden Bowl*? How can you hope to recover?

I thought of Herb Bendler, having to account for his every "missing" hour to his wife. In response to such indignities, was he a *gentleman* for not socking Marian, or, more honestly, something less than a whole man? Instead of those TV commercials inspired by Hollywood fantasy, couldn't we have some down-to-earth reality? Rather than watching some Marlboro caricature of a man prancing across a Montana plain with his smoke, couldn't we observe some ordinary Bendler removing by force a nagging wife from his own living room, so that he can enjoy a cigarette in peace? *There's* a scene that would be truly inspirational—and therapeutic—for the thousands of beleaguered husbands across the land, in Cambridge *and* Montana.

My mind was a projector, running two films side by side. In one, Bendler was in the kitchen, an apron for a loincloth, drying the dishes for Marian, who was badgering him about a new Maytag. In the second, a pleasant Neanderthal fellow was dragging his spouse by the hair and beating her for saying that she preferred hippo meat for supper instead of the deer he had just brought home. Which man was preferable, I wondered, Bendler the Civilized, or Tumac the Primitive? All right, neither. Something in between. Someone who had preserved stubbornly both sides of his nature, the higher and the lower. How could the students, for example, respect Herb if they ever saw him in action, with the cameras shooting—with his apron tied, his ego drowning in lemon-fresh Joy? Doubtlessly a woman like Gwen would drive the poor fellow either to McLean's for treatment and rest, or back to his Good Humor ice-cream bicycle. Without authority at home, how could he provide students with the proper authority in school? No wonder the students nowadays were like the Red Guard, after their professors' scalps—many of these fellows were enfeebled beyond recall by domestic harassment. If they couldn't handle their middle-aged wives, how could they be expected to handle young revolutionaries?

Thinking of poor Herb being made mincemeat out of in the classroom, I shut my Wittgenstein in a fury (can you imagine what Marian would have done to poor Ludwig?). For solace, I turned to a desk photograph of Gwen and myself. Taken by a wandering old man with a box camera along Mass. Ave., the photo showed the two of us poised for combat, fists bared. On the spur of the moment, Gwen had struck a boxing pose, and when I attempted to shrug it off, she jabbed me into combativeness. It was a fine funny photo and I smiled, thanking Gwen to myself for her madness. It had revived something in me which was on the brink of being lost forever. Something like my boyhood bow and arrow that had given me so much pleasure, transformed now into precise emotional instruments.

I'm forced to intrude here to note the strong objections voiced by my colleagues to the uncensored inclusion of the Gwen tale. They have argued that such open bigotry, in the form of a rascist fantasy, is tantamount to fascist propaganda and does not belong in a revolutionary text. I dispute these claims. Our society, pathological and reckless, plus nature, wild too, produces all sorts of disabilities, regardless of color. And certainly all confused lives deserve their place in our history. To do otherwise, or to turn unpleasant fact immediately into fiction, would be to miss Mrs. Tresvant's own useful argument. I leave it to the intelligent reader to sort out and measure the varieties of educational experience given here.

And now, allow me to introduce (yes, yet one more) by means of a letter, Grace. The dilemma she raises is not an uncommon one. In one way or another, all the girls have touched upon it; some early on, some later.

Dear Bern,
Your seeing me twice a week is in many ways more painful than if you didn't see me at all. I've come to love you so much that to do without you, when you are ten minutes away, is awful. Awful. Why did you bring hope back to me, if only to frustrate me this way? I know you haven't meant it to happen like this, but it is. It is.
Can't you stay on with me for a while, anyway—say, a year or so? I wouldn't hold you to any firm commitment of time. I wouldn't badger you with talk of marriage. Those things are not immediate needs of mine. But having you around for more than two consecutive nights is a need.
I wouldn't stop you from going out when you wished, either. You would be free. But I would have some permanence with you.
Don't be angry with me for behaving weakly like this.

Now there's a little more about Naaron, the boy, expecting me to . . . but that's not relevant just now. (A curious little man, Naaron. He would get on marvelously well with Sophie's Becky. They're both progressing very nicely with their chess lessons.) But a touching epistle, is it not?

A little background is perhaps in order, so that there is a context for Grace's interesting, let us say, "charge." I refer to the sentence "Why did you bring hope back to me, if only to frustrate me this way?"

Now hope was not an easy thing to recover for Grace. Not at all. When I first met her, she was (yes, yet one more) a bag of bones, consumed, utterly consumed, by hostility and *resentment*. A bag of bones except for her belly, which was bloated with another baby. And the husband, or father? He had departed, so far as responsibility was concerned; of course, it was all done very quietly, for he worked at the same Boston television station as she, was well known, and already possessed one complete family in the suburbs. The moral principle upon which a course of action was based was simple enough: propriety was to be served. Thus it was decided that Grace would receive a reasonable stipend, have an abortion, find new employment. All very tidy, efficient. The only catch was the obstinacy of our Grace, who elected instead to go through with the birth and, furthermore, to keep the child. Now since she already had one child by an annulled first marriage (annulled by the boy's father, who assured his stalwart scion—of Choate and Harvard, you understand—that if he persisted in his ways and remained married to the impoverished daughter of a suicide, the legal firm of Jenkins, Chase and Jenkins would have no further use for him, and he would no longer exist as the prospective heir to a modest estate. Under such circumstances, what could that young lawyer-lion do?)—as I was saying, as she had had one unpleasant experience involving cash, children, and respectability, she was used to them. And since her one joy in the past few years had been her young son Naaron, it was natural enough that her already baffled ego—in the midst of such pervasive male rectitude and valor—would cry out unrestrainedly and act imprudently. This, in spite of the tons of paperback advice and personal homilies by some very well-trained people and lifelong professionals in that area. Data, statistics, charts, graphs—a Great Wall of Knowledge, surely, to try to overcome!

Why make the attempt then? Was it wise? Or practical? Neither. It was simply a way of saying no. An existential breath. A rage of irrationality against a wave of rational oppressors. Most important: a result of the instinct to survive. If she had allowed herself to be bought off, and the stain to be euphemized (the punishment eased), she might have used the same prosaic .38-caliber that brought a lasting consolation to her father's life—and a lasting nightmare, need it be added, to Grace's. But are these justifications for such action, you ask, thumbing through Grace's *curriculum vitae?* I leave that to wiser judgment.

So: distended and abandoned, already saddled with one little hostage to fortune. Not too comforting a picture. Especially when your background is Boston Brahmin, your schools Buckingham Day and Smith College, and your friends are debutantes who wind up in the Vincent Club, Junior Assemblies, etc. Or when your father turned renegade from ancestral gentility and died a helpless, penniless painter. No, no, there would be little help for girls like you, Grace, who meander off into errant paths and refuse conciliation.

Obviously, the rest of the family wanted nothing to do with you. Neither mother, who was married again (a paunchy, reasonable stockbroker after that crazy undernourished failure), nor sister, tucking in her three children in her nice new split-level in Lexington. Nor, if the truth be known, Uncle John, Dad's one brother and, incidentally, owner of a prominent Cambridge bank, to whom you appealed for help (a loan, no less): "You made your trough, now collapse in it" was his response, adding a touch of poetry to his sadism. "Commit any sin" continued his countenance (as you recalled), "but you can't dirty the name of Lawrence and be forgiven!" To which you responded, in a more valiant, contemporary manner than he had perhaps expected, "Fuck you, Uncle John." And stared. A high point in your wars against the Brahmins.

And an incident which added to your special feelings about men in general, no doubt.

You were a wild animal in those days. Always ill with a virus or dysentery, a perennial cougher, anemic as a mannequin . . . as if the venom had entered your bloodstream. A rattler, ready to spring if a male footstep approached. There were no jokes about this girl then, no occasional easy laughter, no small talk or gossip, not even solemnity or petty hates—Grace was beyond those forgivable habits of prosaic mortals. Just rage and fury. My bony, blunt-featured Episcopalian, displaced from the gracious mansions of Beacon Hill to the grimy graffiti of east Cambridge; my well-bred Brahmin lady exiled among the *Lumpenproletariat* of the lower depths (beer-swigging, cursing Irish; beaten-down, militantless blacks; jabbering, factory-working Puerto Ricans— yes, right there in the same city with those twin citadels of knowledge and truth—a strange city of bedfellows!). So, while others of your generation and class were out at discotheques, jet airports, Paraphernalia shops—making like that international First

Lady riding the waves of the new opulence—my Grace was hardening into a Niobe of Pain and a Clytemnestra of Revenge—all at age twenty-six and without a crown.

I had to force myself upon her, almost literally. I only heard of her in the first place because a cousin of hers, a graduate student who was scared to death of and for her, told me she knew of someone who could badly use any typing work I might have. The girl needed money desperately, but wouldn't accept anything like a handout or loan. So I rang her up—her gravelly voice jumpy and skeptical on the phone—and brought her some Gissing manuscript to type. She lived in three or four rooms over a garage, overlooking Ken's Junk Yard in east Cambridge. Walls flaking, beds unmade, bare lightbulbs, an ironing board out with clothes tossed on it, sparse, second-hand furniture. And the girl herself: in denim shirt and a boy's haircut, looking like a female convict out on parole. The plain American face showing the sort of blind hopelessness and deranged anger which you associate with ten years in prison. Frightened, I left the typing and got out, wondering what I had let myself in for.

On the pretense that she might be finished with it early, I sneaked back later in the day. She was in the middle of making dinner (corned-beef hash, chili beans, Tip-Top bread, and water —yes, two glasses of water—in 1969!). Naaron, four years old, with blond hair cut in Beatles' bangs, smiled at me while drawing with crayons and watching television (the picture almost black). Immediately I sat down with him, in that twelve-by-eight alcove called a living room, and started chatting, before she could say anything. She looked doubly suspicious and angry when I announced that I had brought something for him and would get it from the car. In one hand I managed the handsome fire engine that I had bought at Sears toy shop; in the other, two bags of groceries.

It was a moment not to be forgotten. While Naaron's face lit up with delight and curiosity, his mother's lips began quivering when I placed the groceries, as if by chance, upon the kitchen table. The hopelessness in her face gave way completely to anger, and I'm sure that if she had had a knife handy she would have thrown it. Nobody was going to bribe that Brahmin con so easily! She swung at me wildly, punching, slapping, scratching.

127

When her nails dug into my forearm, I had to push her aside. Almost falling, she grabbed the brown paper bags I had brought upstairs and began heaving the contents at me—tin cans, lettuce and tomatoes, cartons of milk and juice. Finally, she flung a bottle of wine, which missed my head as I ducked, and cracked against the kitchen wall, splattering wine everywhere. Screaming, she tried to grab Naaron to her, but he was frightened and crying, and ran to me. That betrayal, plus her sudden burst of fury, was too much for her, and she dropped on her knees to the floor, like a deer stunned by a shot.

I don't think I had ever heard anybody truly *wail* before, but Grace was wailing. It's an awful sound, much more sustained and full-bodied than a scream or shriek, much more horrible because it seems to have the air of predetermination about it. Terrified, I moved toward her, and she looked up at me, her face clammy and pallid, her gray eyes bulging, as if I had a shotgun and had come to finish her off. She wore an expression of joy and fear. She looked just barely conscious, frenzied in a religious way, perspiring; her exhausted fury seemed to bring out all the fragility of her body, a fleshy geometry of bones and angles with a hump in the center. As I kneeled by her, I was sure she had lost her child. She, too, just about that time, must have sensed that, for she reached down with one hand to feel her stomach, as if it wasn't exactly hers. For some reason, out of fear or helplessness I suppose, I reached out my hand and covered hers gently. Her eyelids closed slowly at that gesture, and she slipped her own hand away so that mine felt her belly directly. She pressed down upon my hand, her eyes closed. For comfort? For more pain? Soon I felt the baby jerk or kick. Her gray eyes, now more green, opened and stared at me. Ah, what a look—incredulity, wonder, innocent perplexity. Neither of us spoke. Had I been able to speak, I would have told her that I'd do anything for her, then and later, and that she must let me! Perhaps my look said as much, I'm unsure.

Finally, like a child drowsy with satisfaction, she reached out and with long thin fingers began to play absent-mindedly with the end of my tie. That gesture did it. The sudden breakthrough to trust and intimacy, after so much resentment, was unbearable, incomprehensible, unfair. Unfair to herself! Tears began rolling down my cheeks. Totally lost—to the moment, to hidden forces in myself, to the battered creature lying before me—I found myself leaning forward and taking her hand to my lips, again and again, weeping like a child myself . . . Scenes from Dostoevsky and St. Petersburg, right here in Cambridge . . .

Why? Who knows why? Obviously her suffering and depth of insult—and remember, I had only accidentally brushed against the barest surface—had overwhelmed me. Who wouldn't lose self-control, when a young woman's deserved anger at the world suddenly lets up, only to reveal endless depths of self-mortification and self-abuse? All right, this much is obvious. But what was impossible to cope with was her readiness—no, more than that—her fervent desire—to give herself over to my hands, the hands of a perfect stranger! Do you see how much she *yearned to be judged?* There I was, an ordinary fellow, who moves through life as casually and obliviously as the next shoestore clerk, dentist, or academic, suddenly propelled into an orbit of intensity and deep feeling! It was extraordinary. An astronaut of the emotions? A professor of compassion and judgment? Where was I to get the training for such roles? Didn't the girl lying there, waiting for me to make the next move—to shoot her or redeem her or leave her—didn't she know that my degrees came from schools, colleges, universities, not Life?

After a few timeless, pulsating minutes, I lifted her into my arms and carried her hundred pounds to the bedroom. Not a word between us, while we stared at each other. I remember focusing on the delicacy of her eyebrows in the midst of that swollen distress. I laid her in the double bed, not having time to change the soiled sheets. I asked her if she was all right. No answer. I was about to leave the room when I noticed a darting movement a few feet above her head. It was a cockroach, a fat one. It stopped, as if it sensed my having observed it. It was pointed in the direction of Grace's head. Its ugliness transfixed me. I looked around for something to hit it with, but seeing nothing, and curiously afraid of leaving Grace a helpless target, I squashed it with the palm of my hand, feeling its squishy death on my skin. What at other times would have been a revolting vileness was now simply another duty.

Back in the kitchen, I washed my hands and got to work

cleaning up the litter and splatter of the Grace-earthquake. And broiled the steaks I had brought, cooked the asparagus. During this half hour, Naaron stayed by me in the kitchen, playing with his new fire engine while helping me with mundane problems. He was especially awed by the automated extension ladder, which, when fully elongated, stretched higher than his own two and a half feet. I don't think I ever knew the enormous pleasure, or, better, restorative power, that such small creatures were capable of inspiring in adults until that half hour. When the meal was ready, I brought his little table—the miniature size of everything connected with Naaron, and his own coherence and dexterity at that diminutive size, amazing me—into his mother's nine-by-twelve bedroom cell, and he ate cheerfully while I fed Grace. (That is, I forced some bites down her throat. Months later she said that it had been years since she had permitted herself steak.) While Naaron and I talked, Grace nodded or shook her head or gestured weakly. She had given in totally to my presence in the rooms.

Afterward I cleaned up once more, told Naaron a bear story, and watched him get into his flannel pajamas with blue clowns tumbling and daisies sprouting. When we went in to kiss his mother good night, she was fast asleep. We took a teaspoon from her hand and left her. Bearing his fire engine in his arms, handing me his Babar book and astronaut book to carry, Naaron retired to his room for the evening. I observed his little ritual of getting under the covers after first securing the gleaming-red engine by his side. He opened his book beneath the hurricane lamp. Before I left, he said to me, matter-of-factly speaking and glancing up from his page-turning, that he sure wished I would come again.

It is impossible to describe the effect on me of those few hours, as I left the house. Aimless and dazed, I wandered about in those desolate grimy junkyard-ridden streets, stupefied—by the pain of Grace, by the surface serenity of Naaron (what was it costing him?), by the sheer incongruousness of one set of lives next to another in the same city. Oppressed finally by those east Cambridge Gogol-depths, I got into my car, found a highway, and drove. Clearly the truth of real lives was much more bizarre and amazing than any fiction or lie that could be made up or invented about them! That single notion pumped itself into my head. Finally I was lost, not knowing which way the receding white dashes were taking me; that unnerved me more. Lost. For ten minutes or so, until I located myself heading north on 128, I was desperate. I returned on the opposite side of the dividing embankment and drove to a friend's apartment not far from the Square. Shaking, I had a few drinks, keeping my adventure secret, trying to immerse myself in the cheerful living room, in the baroque songs piped through tall speakers, in the pleasant talk about books, movies. Gradually I was released back into the dull protectiveness of routine life, allowed to leave that stage of pain and settle back into my comfortable spectator's seat. Yet I couldn't entirely rid myself of fleeting images, the sight of that blond boy awed by the ascending ladder, the experience of his mother's fingers playing with my tie . . . You can see that Naaron was going to have his wish fulfilled.

Well, there is no point in prolonging this. You can gather what my days with Grace were like, those first few months. Moments of trust followed by relapses into a shell of self-anger and catatonic bewilderment. When you tried to break through, she fought savagely, often physically. What eased the situation was the new baby (a second boy). Another trick of the world: by incapacitating her further, it forced her to accept my help, my presence. Without the addition of little Sam, I doubt that I would have gotten through to her in a permanent fashion. From the old school of moral right and wrong rather than personality states, Grace wouldn't hear of a psychiatrist, even if she had had the time or money. Obstinate certainly, but an obstinacy of pride, a tenacity of necessity. How odd to think that a visit to a shrink often reduced pride severely, creating, on top of the psychic problem, a gut-feeling of cynicism and futility. It was a good six months before our tough Brahmin convict was able to set foot into ordinary life again (parties, restaurants, people). Now there are those who might argue that this is not such a wonderful thing in itself, and that there was something special in that earlier sufferer which would now be lost. To such supreme judges of others' lives, I recommend the tales of fiction writers to fulfill their social-gossip voyeurism and misguided idea of glamour. In person, suffering is neither a pleasant nor a therapeutic sight.

131

Such a heart-rending history only adds poignancy to the appeal in Grace's letter for some sort of temporary permanence. From this history and from my own part in it, it will be obvious to the sensitive observer how difficult it is for me to respond negatively to it, as I must. On the other hand, it is useful that Grace's situation has been presented within the context of my family life as a whole, that is, against the background of harem life; thus the full delicacy and appropriateness of that negative response is self-evident. Such a negativism, to my mind, is the true begetter of affirmation and good deeds.

Naturally, I hope that dear Grace will see the impossibility of her request, as she and the other girls always have, in one way or another. Underlying such pleas, I believe, is a perpetual flickering of uncertainty regarding our new style of affair, in contrast to the old-style families. This is plainly understandable. Old patterns of loving, old structures of emotion, the sheer force of habit—these don't die easily. Certainly, furthermore, ours is a unique circle of friends, and its unity and survival rest on very delicate threads indeed, all of which need constant looking after. You girls present a rich diversity, I stress again, and whether it is as priest or psychiatrist, doctor or porter, financial consultant or teacher, I must be free to maneuver, to be at the beck and call of the collective whole. (It is worth noting that, just as the girls live in different parts of Cambridge, so they come from very different backgrounds and possess very varied life-styles and personalities. Not for me is the joyless mechanicalness of Xeroxing my experience six times over!) It is obvious by now, is it not, that a purely monogamous situation—to use that frigid term—would indeed in our case be more injurious and painful than beneficial? I know, after all, that you girls are nothing if you are not logical and moral, and that therefore appeals on my part to your sense of collective or universal justice will evoke a more favorable response from you than if I made a crude appeal to your emotions only.

So that, dear Grace, it has not at all been my intention "to frustrate you." For what I wish to make most clear to you is, first, the high moral enterprise that we are embarked upon and, second, the enlarged concept of family that we have been enacting. I ask you, Grace: what is jealousy next to such high attributes and lofty creations? Remember that when next the green-eyed monster appears!

We have effected this richer family life, I must add, not by histrionics or fanciful schemes, but by avoiding extremes: both the quaint, simianlike structure of the feudal and bourgeois eras (monogamous marriage), and the abrasive, simple-minded structures of today's avant-garde. I speak now of such false salvations as indiscriminate communal sexuality or those cheerless variations of group therapy. The first is offensively primitive, vulgarly simple-minded, an insult to civilized dignity; the second is painfully pathetic (look in on an encounter group one day, and you'll want to cry), painfully medical, artificial; both smack of the contemporary urge for instant joy, short-cut solutions, and, perhaps the most despairing, the mechanization of spontaneity. No, on no condition will I allow my ladies—my very heartbeats and inspirations!—to slip back into the ugly computer slots of modern life. I pulled you out once, and out I shall keep you!

(I blush, girls, at my fervor. Forgive me. As you all know, I am by nature a practical man, not an emotional one. Otherwise, God knows, it is I who should have to be rescued.)

Let us proceed then with fraternal care, with artistic delicacy, with large sympathies. I realize that to do so is no simple matter. Especially these days. The times call for dissonances and destructions, and I make a plea for continuity, harmony. The times preach the principle of selfhood first and foremost; and here I am reminding you of selflessness, community. The age flaunts its violent self-abandon and narcissistic bravado, and I appeal to you with a plea for a high moral and ethical code. Forgive me if I sound at times like a Moses demanding, above all else, allegiance to the Tablets and to our small tribe. But what must be uttered shall be uttered, no matter what the consequences. As you can imagine, it's not easy being Moses, living in the heart of Sodom and Gomorrah.

Obviously, too, this over-all arrangement and this philosophy will not endear me, or you, to many individuals in our culture. For some, I am merely a child and you innocents. For others, I am a scoundrel and you victims of wickedness. One says, Diaper him, give him a rattle, and if he's still not content, give him a good spanking. The other asserts, Put him in prison stripes,

133

attach a black lead ball for each mistress to his ankle, and force him to the fields for hard labor. And let him stay there until he's built with his own hands an altar to respectability, so that he appreciates what it is. The syllogism is simple enough: pleasure equals infantile, infantile equals immoral, immoral equals dangerous. So he wants pleasure, does he? An irredeemable child! So he needs mistresses? A swinging immoralist! *Six* mistresses, no less? A *chazah* too! (an "ethnic" phrase meaning pig). In either case, child or immoralist, he's a dangerous sort and ought to be punished! What? You say it's not exactly adultery, then what's the charge? Corrupting morals, you fool! You say he's not injuring anyone, the girls accept the arrangement? Setting a dangerous example, blockhead! What? The girls will not testify against him . . . but side with him? Then they've grown mad, possessed. He's doped them somehow. Charge them with societal irresponsibility and pack them off to a Morals Rehabilitation Center. But under no circumstances permit the situation to continue! Or the fellow to go loose!

I'm sure you'll laugh at this, ladies—at the preposterous twisting and juggling that the self-appointed moralists can manage. But allow me, for the moment, to treat their tendentious hyperbole as serious argument. That is, we shall grant that our particular form of family happiness is in reality dangerous—on moral, psychological, and societal grounds—because of its strain of, let us say, youthful abandon, primal horde primitivism. (What amusing fellows, really!) Now, I address these venerable gentlemen. Sirs, allow me to inquire: what good is childhood if the major lesson to be gleaned from it is that we must totally and eternally abandon it? A time of life so powerful, so intense, so very bracing. A period so fecund for pleasure, and, in later years, so fecund for knowledge. Give it all up? Does that make sense? You mean, that which is most powerful is also most dangerous—without qualifications, distinctions . . . throw it *all* overboard?

Friends, is this reasonable? *All?* Can't *something* be saved? A portion? Some aspects?

You mustn't misunderstand me. I realize perfectly that we must give childhood over, if we are to grow; that youth, like everything else made of substantive matter, must pass; that the pleasure-principle by itself is self-defeating and societally destructive; and so on. All this is obvious enough to any reasonable man. But why must you push it a step farther and insist on total surrender? There's the difficulty. You see, gentlemen, all that I'm arguing for is—*compromise*. Nothing more. Not mindless "regression," but reasonable compromise—a deal, if you will—you know, something *moderate*. Don't you think that's fair? Just? And especially appealing, compromise in an age of extremities?

It will be understood clearly by now, I hope, that I myself have doubts about the role. At times it is very difficult playing Moses the Lawgiver, David the King, Freud the Doctor. I too am overwhelmed by the emphasis on eroticism: the need for carnal play, the urges to fondle flesh, to pursue new secretions and odors. How tiring it is for me too by now—though always momentarily exciting—to examine girls' panties and bras, to look at cup shapes, at new floral designs, at the transparency of the new tricots, at brown and yellow and red stains, to pursue all this *erotic trivia* the way a naturalist seeks out his flora and fauna, making distinctions and classifications with loving care and gentleness. I find that I can't help myself. Panties, brassières, stockings, slips, nighties are as precious to me as zinnias, lady's-slippers, daisies, orchids, marigolds. My heart flutters with excitement when my fingers find a new texture or my eye locates a new girlish habit. Is there a word like ornithologist or naturalist to describe my passion? Eroticist? Pornographer? Voyeur? All too simple, narrow, misleading. Perhaps gyneologist. A Charles Darwin collector of girls: to study, to love, to explain.

It embarrasses me the way attempts at good cheer and fraternity frequently get out of hand and turn into . . . situations I never wanted or imagined. Take the night I decided to try to bring two of the girls together, a sort of celebration dinner commemorating the second anniversary of knowing Gwen and Angela. We ate in the Parthenon, a modest Greek restaurant around the corner from my apartment; quiet, uncrowded, the food decent, one of the Greek waiters a friend. "Gwen, this is Angela, whom I may have mentioned to you" was the way I introduced the girls. Taramasalata, shish kebab, ouzo, Pendeli wine, grape leaves, Turkish coffee mingled and flowed, while we chatted about students, education, ecology—the usual nonsense. At first I was quite nervous, uncertain about the direction of the event or my motive in arranging it. But as the evening progressed, I settled in and enjoyed matters; in fact, it became exhilarating. There really is nothing like entertaining two mistresses simultaneously; it inspires a pleasure as unique in feeling perhaps as scuba diving for swimmers. As I sipped wine, I had visions of more dinner occasions like the present one; and why not larger ones, I pondered, a King Bernard of the Round Table, with three or four girls? Meanwhile, at the dinner table, Angela and Gwen were chatting away. The little darlings—one a civilized black leopard in a lovely spring (yellow flowered) dress, the other a Via Veneto prospect in a body-hugging shiny red pants suit and matching red pumps!—pretending to "discuss" children. Beneath the surface, however, they were a pair of cagey boxers in the first rounds of an important bout, feeling each other out, jabbing and feinting, circling and observing, searching for weaknesses and openings to exploit later on. The slips and the reactions were delightful, even if one-sided. Poor Angie! Stretching across the table for salt brought a lighthearted glint to Gwen's gaze; removing with petulance her loose blond hair from her eating periphery inspired a furtive Gwen smile; and finally, Angela's teenybopper-sexy walk to the ladies' room raised Gwen's eyebrows gloriously. "She does have her own *style*, baby," Gwen said graciously. "I'll grant her *that*. And that outfit—too much!" Giddy with secret delight, I spoke soberly about an upcoming dinner engagement for Gwen and me. When Angela returned, however, dear Gwen couldn't resist turning the moment into an open contest. With her great panther poise, splendid voluptuousness, and unmistakable color haughtiness, she retraced Angie's path to the ladies' room. Well, the show put on by the two girls, first the hustler and then the panther, dazzled me. (So much so that I was inattentive to the signals about the future of the evening.) Anyway, it was Angela's turn for private appraisal. Her baby voice giggled admiration: "She really has it, doesn't she? *Ma-don!*" The flare of generosity from that little narcissist's heart touched me.

Preparing to leave, I noticed the crowd of turned faces following us. Did that monogamous audience sense the truth behind the Dean's floor show?

Outside in the pleasant April evening each girl took an arm,

Angie possessively, Gwen coolly. We walked toward the Square, an owner walking his two thoroughbreds in the paddock, to the admiring eyes of the passing bettors. (Don't Harvard Square walkers wager on the people they see? I certainly do.) Or better, a Cambridge pimp walking with two of his stable? *What respectable man can resist the image of a part-time pimp?* Puffed by the splendid amusement of the evening, and the delicious preening of the promenade, I suggested a nightcap in my apartment. My eleven o'clock high shifting into a near-midnight hubris.

Perfect little baroque dances of Praetorious and Gastoldi cheered the living room, while a round of vodka tonics came and went. Gwen, legs crossed demurely on the Morris chair, and Angela, sprawled languorously on the sofa, chatted about careers and roles for women. The circumstances turning the little boring talk into yet another charming, ironic episode! (Those circumstances! I couldn't stop enjoying them in my mind, like a boy crayoning all the pictures in his new coloring book the first day he receives it.) In the midst of the second drink, Gwen casually went to the record rack and bending low—that brown behind a pedestal of beauty—selected two records to replace the completed baroque. Listening to the infant prattle of Angie, I was taken by surprise by the full-throated sweetness of Aretha Franklin (a gift from Gwen). Which was nothing next to Gwen suddenly "moving" to the rhythms of Aretha, her hips and arms undulating, turning the room space into an aquarium, herself into a fish. The talk stopped as Gwen began to hypnotize both of us. And when Aretha stopped, Gwen, smiling fully, gulping vodka tonic, unzipped her dress from her body and continued dancing in frilly black panties, floral black bra, stockings, and high heels. Now, to the rocking voice of Otis Redding, she swam about more lavishly, seductively. Well, it was breathtaking, the headiness of the atmosphere heated by the presence of a third party.

The evening expanded—blurred, diffuse, sensual. When the rock stopped, baby Angela rose, kicked off her shoes, and went to the records. While the Scott changer maneuvered, Angela unbuttoned her blouse, removed it, giggled, dropped her trousers to her ankles, and, like a little girl, sat on the floor and pulled them off. To the exotic Greek and Turkish music, in bare feet and brightly flowered bikini underwear, the slim boyish figure

began her "thing," the belly dance. (During this unrobing process, Gwen had begun to tug at my shirt and more, so that I found
myself watching the performance clothed in my Jockey briefs
only.) Well, that whorish wop didn't embarrass me before the
professional Gwen, not at all. Very suavely that belly gyrated
round, pulsed in and out, teased up and down; that belly button
eyeing us. Not bad at all—that amateur was giving the Brown
Bomber a ride for the prize all right. And with that great sex
instinct of hers—no amateur when it came to smelling *that odor*
in the air—she edged to within a foot of myself and Gwen.
Fixing our gaze, she rotated that white belly with slow expert
provocativeness.

The next steps were both inevitable and surprising. As I
leaned forward in a daze of sound and desire toward that pulsing
body, a pair of brown hands reached out to rip away the bikini
bottom. For four or five minutes, I was then tormented and
tantalized, as that belly was joined by the naked mound of blond
hair, to rub my nose and tongue, and then back off, rub, tantalize,
and dance off. Meanwhile, hands were soothing my neck,
urging me on. The three of us were then on the rug, caressing
like calves. My briefs were slid away by brown hands, while
black panties were removed by girlish hands. Certain things stood
out amid that tangle of bodies. Immediately apparent was
Angela's desire for Gwen; she was all over her, kissing her
wildly, a thin white cub climbing upon the dark mature lioness.
The passion was so devoted and total that I sat on my haunches
and observed, like a wrestling referee on his knees, trying to
assess a shoulder pinning. I was transfixed as that swooning
Angela trailed her pink tongue down Gwen's luscious curves,
Gwen taking her in and encouraging her and saying, of all things,
"It's all right, baby, that's all right," before she started saying,
"That's good, baby, that's good." To tell the truth, I could have
stayed content in that spectator role, exulting in their lesbian
lesson, except that Gwen lured me to her with her hands and
engulfed my prick with her mouth. My thighs sandwiching
Gwen's swollen upside-down face, I was able now from another
view to watch the avid Angela sucking pleasure from and into
Gwen's lower openings. Terrific stuff. I was dying to get hold of
Angie, despite the other joys (watching and being swallowed).

Finally I reached out, tugged Angie's hair, and managed to turn her around, so that I could go to work on her own bottom. With elbows, lips, and limbs mixing, and positions bizarre, it was like some European acrobatic team rehearsing for the Ed Sullivan show. Where were the CBS cameras?

The climax embarrassed me as much as it thrilled me. With moans and shrieks and body English growing more frenzied, I began finally coming into Gwen's mouth. But suddenly she maneuvered away so that I was lathering her face with the white sperm. Whereupon Angie, bellowing like a cow in heat, suddenly dove down upon that face and began lapping it up. Incredible. The denseness of appetites was so thick by then, the flow of juices and secretions and passions so rich, that it was like being at a feast of cannibals. I tell you, those girls would have eaten anything, anything!

We lay upon each other, three spent animals. Minutes followed of panting leisure, body odor, sated feeling, curious relief. We smoked and talked on the rug, Angela cupping a brown breast, Gwen covering my penis tenderly with her hand. Angie began asking us about our astrology charts, and gave a little spiel about the conjunction of my moon and Mercury. Was she demented? I wondered. And then we were going at it again, with Gwen and I fixing that wop's wagon—"You dirty little guinea!" I remember saying, picking up Gwen's hints—and glutting ourselves again. This time, thoroughly exhausted afterward, we simply lay in our perspiration and breathing: no talk, no touching, no anything. Glutted. Then we started to recoup and dress, the girls having to return home to release their baby-sitters.

I'm unsure how the fight started. I know the girls were three-quarters dressed, when some words were exchanged, looks grew harsh, and the atmosphere of sweet cordiality of ten minutes previous was suddenly shattered. Why do these girls do these things, tell me? Why must they always everywhere cause *some* trouble? (Angie says that Gwen suddenly grew jealous because she suddenly wanted to play more. Gwen says Angie just grew crazy and insulting. Naturally I trust Gwen more—but in such circumstances, who could tell?) In any case, Angie was suddenly pulling upon Gwen (screaming her non sequitur, "Get away from him, you!"), who, half laughing, was trying to comfort her. But then they were going at it, full steam ahead. Pocketbooks swinging, hair pulled hard, crazy tumbling over. Gwen bitten on the side, screaming, and belting Angela in the jaw. After a futile attempt to separate them (getting scratched in the process), I stood aside and looked on. If the trio-sex was special, the fight was extra-special. What enormous joy in watching two women go at each other violently! How different from the fear when watching two men break each other's bones. Here there was perspiration, loose hair, girlish holds, bitchy swearing, and no real damage. A pair of alley cats screeching and scratching. And over me! I restrained my laughter and joy.

It was over as suddenly as it had started. It simply ceased, the winner Gwen rising from the vanquished Angela. As soon as Angie was on her feet and I saw her crying lightly, I knew that she had gotten exactly what she had wanted from the evening: a split lip, ripped blouse and underwear, lots of sex and fighting, melodrama, whimpering tears, childish breakthroughs. What a whore! Delicious. Watching her phony feeble attempts to make herself presentable for the world again made me smile openly; even smirk, I'm afraid. Well, it was an error. Out of a sudden sympathy with her defeated enemy, Gwen walked toward me, saying, "Don't you laugh, buster!" And smacked me hard across my face. Me, an innocent bystander! Before I had time to recover, the two of them were upon me, clawing, wrestling, slapping. And cursing me: "You pervert!" cried the demented Angela, digging into my wrists with frantic fingernails. "You pervert! You brought us here to humiliate us! That's what you are, a pervert!" Weakened by drink, sex, laughter, I was no match for the pair of them. Tearing my robe from me, then ripping my Jockey briefs (a symbolical gesture, in place of castration?), they left me on the floor, naked, dazed, hurt. Her arm around her new pal's waist, Gwen led the whimpering Angela out of the room and the apartment. Lying there, near tears, I was in a state of shock from the turn of events and from the thought that I had messed up irreparably.

That's what hurt most, then, and in the next few days—that I had lost one or both of the girls. It was horrible. From greed, and overweening pride (that nightcap), I had bungled it all! I never knew how much I needed those girls until I was faced with the prospect of losing them. To do without Angela's sluttishness?

Gwen's blackness? I would go crazy, absolutely crazy from my fantasies if I lost them! The jingle of Humpty Dumpty not being able to be put back together again kept running through my head. And apart from my need and desire, what about the *waste?* Two years of training, almost twenty-four months of work, down the drain! It killed me. After two or three days, I got up my perseverance and went around to beg and plead. What else could I do, suffer endlessly?

I was wrong again. I had misjudged once more. It took one (Angie) to three (Gwen) weeks to overcome anger, retribution, petulance, hypocrisy, but I did it. And I mean solid weeks, employing my entire assortment of endearments—country picnics, canoeing, trips to museums and ballets with the children, talk, cajoling, apology, tenderness, flowers, proximity; God, that dull proximity! But I put the time in, like punching a clock. Yes, I retrieved them. Back to the fold. And why? Because of my charm? Nonsense. Save that for your braggadocios or romantic biographies. Because of their *hypocrisy*, I had underestimated how much they had enjoyed the little orgy. I had forgotten the joy and hunger that I had witnessed with my own eyes, replacing that truth with moral platitudes and pieties. Not only enjoyed it, but wallowed and luxuriated in it. That's why they returned to me. *They had loved it.* Of course, given the circumstances and the culture, they wouldn't admit such a thing. The hypocrites! (In the same way that neither one would divulge to me the true meaning of their continuing quaint friendship. Why else, except for lesbian delvings, did the two girls still occasionally see each other? They were as opposed as could be; Gwen could never take Angela's disorder or frivolous life. The little liars! I know they go at it on occasion. I'll bet half their desire is to make me jealous. Out of spite!) Is there any doubt that the female species is infinitely more wanton and more perverse than the male? After all, biologically, able to come three, four, five times to a man's one, she is more fitted for sexual sport; and culturally and psychologically, living a restricted, conventish life within a male society, she is more fit for perverse thrills. Logic and history are simply on her side when it comes to wantonness.

Yet, no matter how much I understood the truth, or thought on my own part of more orgies—once you've had them, they're unforgettable; oh, how you yearn for three people instead of two, and fantasize about it!—still, I couldn't or wouldn't do it again. Too much risk involved. As simple as that. It could get out of hand too easily, a girl would get seriously angry, and I'd be risking the loss of one, and perhaps both. It was unthinkable. The pain of lying on that floor and thinking of my blunder, and loss, was too much. Harems are not easy to construct. Like good basketball teams, it takes time to recruit the right elements, to find the right combination to make a workable, cohesive unit. Yes, there's a reality-principle in harem-life too. The sad truth of the matter is that I'm very conservative when it comes to a harem girl. (Now, an outsider . . .) The training and effort to have her fit in appropriately, as I have described, is enormous. Sometimes it takes three or four months for me to see that I've started on the wrong trail. By the time I'm through with them, they're no longer loose vague purposeless mongrels but thoroughbreds, with definition and purpose. The risk was too great. So that, for trio pleasure, I had to turn to Piatigorsky, Heifetz, and Rubinstein, or else replay my memory for the seventy-fifth time of that singular scene. Regular orgies were out, forbidden. (And occasional lapses? . . . No!) One of the limitations of the harem trade, you might say.

Does it seem harsh to admit that I'm fond of describing my girls as racing thoroughbreds? Or my admission that I've also thought of a tout sheet for personal purposes? I hope not. For the sheet provides me with an immediate bird's-eye look at each girl's capacity and essence; in other words, a reminder of what they're like. Look, it's no different from the kind of index cards the shrinks file on their patients in order to keep them in health and working order. That's the way to perceive this listing, as a guide to therapy:

Entry	Forecast
1. (Melissa)	
RICH SCHIZZY	Leggy, meek, downtrodden
	Slow to pick up (lousy finisher); slower to lay 'em down
	Very long shot for pleasure
	Deserves compassion

2. (Kate)

GOODHEARTED SQUAW   A redskinned horse; sire troubles
Needs experienced backside rider to go
at top speed
Good obedience; craves discipline
Worth a nostalgic bet

3. (Angela)

WHITE TRASH   Strong in mud, dirt; weak will; titless
Splashy melodramatic filly, loves atten-
tion
Endless comer, climaxer
No integrity whatsoever
A favorite on cheap tracks

4. (Sophie)

HOLOCAUST GAL   Older nag, but steady, reliable
Gutsy sprinter
Terrific mane, mouth, will drive you
crazy
Devoted and loyal. Shtetl blood
Perhaps too many races?
Better than you would think

5. (Gwen)

PLANTATION THRILLS   Needs firm jockey, otherwise forget it
Excellent competitor, plenty of poise
Beautiful brown-black mare, lots of ani-
mal savvy
Demanding horse, exciting to watch and
handle
Best lay

6. (Grace)

BRAHMIN CONVICT   Angry miler; handle with kid gloves
Sure trouble always
Unpredictable, unreliable, hysterical
Thoroughbred parents meaningless
Loose-jointed angular nag, nice to look
at in the old-fashioned slips
Will break your heart

143

I know this looks, at first glance, absurdly arrogant, childish, managerial, grotesquely narcissistic. But don't be misled by appearances. Look into your own heart. What man has not wished to own a stable of girls?

And then again, don't forget, I have a Moses side too. A Moses heart and Spinoza mind and Freudian touch right next to the horse-owner instinct. In other words, I'm not very different from most nervous intellectuals of our day—except perhaps that my life forms the substance of their dreams.

But I have spoken too long. And perhaps too much on behalf of myself, my position. When it comes to words, I'm helpless, that's clear. I can't stop. But I will. And let the other side of the ledger speak, the girls themselves. From letters. Ah, those letters. How they love to write 'em.

Let me begin with this nicely written letter from Sophie. Still working on that dissertation, and a part-time textbook editor, she does have a style of her own.

My dearest,

Do you know why you're different? Or special? . . . Because of your intelligence? There are probably dozens more intelligent in this town. Your strong sense of responsibility? I've had that line before. Your well-celebrated (by me) capacity for patience? By itself there's no more deadly virtue.

Because of your *boyishness*.

Surprised? I'll explain. Your boyishness, in the midst of all those loftier qualities, is precisely what makes them authentic. Is there anything more potent than the sense of *play* in an adult man (or woman)? I don't think so. It means that he's still capable of experiencing pleasure. And, therefore, that his saintly deeds derive from real needs. He helps others because *that* helps him; involvement, difficult as it may be, is psychologically satisfying.

The problem is particularly tangled when academics are involved. (I had one before you, remember?) You know as well as I the embarrassing drawbacks of the second-rate: those who pursue their careers feverishly, or those who hide their thin emotions behind the façade of ideas. (Is this too simple?) They deeply distrust pleasure. They learn to turn against their instincts. They ward off involvement by being husbands or scholars, moralists or swingers. (Any one of the four may be a common cop-out. The first three refuse to unlock the door to their personality, to let someone in or themselves out. In drab uniform they stand guard outside the door, totalitarians of the self. In the service of rationality, of course. How often have we heard that tune! . . . On the other hand, the contemporary version of swinger believes that the door to the self should be a revolving glass one, in constant, indiscriminate use. Traffic always, and both ways. After all these years, I prefer privacy and selection.) It's all very sad. Self-betrayed, distrustful of themselves, they make me distrustful. Like my ex. (Or the Healer, whom we've spoken of at length.) Every face of goodness was a mask for manipulation; pumping his ego meant crushing mine. Poor fellow, pathetic unto himself, painful unto me. No worse tyranny than that of the perennial altruist. Imagine such a deception these days.

Do you think for a moment that I would have let you into my life so easily, so immediately, if you had not exposed very early your own flaws and scars? (Now don't get alarmed.) Perhaps not in words, where you are a master at protecting yourself, with all your avuncular wisdom and analytical patience. (At thirty-five yet!) Do you treat all your girls as patients? No, I never get anywhere near your hurts that way. You're a regular little Goethe, in relation to yourself and women.

Had we met at an ordinary dinner party, or through another polite channel, I would have surely kept my distance. Not that I wasn't confused beyond belief then, but I still had *some* pride about my pain. Oh, you could have laid me all right. No problem about that. But *know* me? No.

But the way you came on! Clearly you were as mad or madder than I. Cornering me at the MTA underground station at night; talking to me so suddenly about my personal life on the subway car; and then, to my amazement, grabbing me off to the side at Harvard Square, and right there at the platform, kissing and touching me. And worse, I responding! And not letting me go until I had sworn that I would see you later that night, after my date. That you were crazy, I was convinced. Absolutely convinced.

It tormented me all through my dinner engagement, wondering what I had gotten myself into. Had you never forced your way into the apartment, after I told you on the phone to forget it, I changed my mind, I'm sure I wouldn't have allowed you to see me again. Or called the police if you tried. But there you were, suddenly at my door! And all the while passing yourself off as an academic at a respectable university! That was what made the whole thing extra-suspicious. I could understand an associate professor who was a Tim Leary type behaving like that. But one who dressed and looked like Sartre, showing such odd behavior? It didn't fit anything *I* knew about. (And your shrewd intuition to arrive at the door, with a copy of the university catalogue, and simply hand it to me to prove your story. I knew I had my hands full as I weakly took that blue booklet in my hands. Who ever came courting carrying a catalogue instead of flowers—and in the middle of the night?)

But as things turned out, the madness was not the kind I had feared, the uncontrollable egotism of the maniac, but the kind I had never known, the helpless, humorous (excuse me) egotism of the little boy. This was new to me. I knew first-hand about the children-boys. But the men-boys? A new genre. I had no idea that a little child could live secretly inside an adult man; or the strangely satisfying returns it could have for a woman. Of course, the boy without the man is an impossible burden; for that, one gives birth; but the latter without the former is another kind of burden: dullness. There's a trial known only to a woman, having children by one of those kind. But the combination of the two, man and boy, a consummation not to be missed! Like Hamlet or Prince Hal, those manly boys (not the silly child Romeo). It's near-irresistible.

And what is that boyishness? The kind of childishness, really, you find in any young boy of seven or eight. The urge to break rules, the inclination toward mischief, the passion for coming home with dirty clothes, bruised knees, and all sorts of foreign objects in your pocket. Let me translate freely: arriving unannounced at 1 A.M. and surprising me right there on my Sealy with your lovely loving; playing baseball inside the apartment with the children, not out of obligation but out of sheer madness. (And, when rounding third base—the chair—crashing into the bookshelves, and sitting like a guilty mutt.) Or slipping in one morning at dawn or something and preparing wheatcakes for me and the kids; then hustling us off to New Hampshire for swimming, rowing, and kite-flying. Unpredictable, wild, pleasurable, at times a great pain in the ass.

And, of course, the curious boyish greed for the special love of a mother: totally protective and devoted, a universe of security. Making me into a tom-girl (kites and baseball and tree-climbing, on Cambridge Common, no less) and a mother (wrapping yourself in a cocoon of my arms and legs and breasts minutes after flooding me) at first disoriented me, but then made me feel stronger. I can't tell you what strange feeling you aroused in me, God knows! So incestuous. So strong. I grew as lustful to hold you that way as to have you ride me to heights of pleasure. What desires you uncarthed in me, what capacities for feeling that I never knew about. Until your fucking me and needing me in your curious way.

I thought I should go mad from your alternating desires and impulses. I did. With wild joy. And exhilaration. Which I never knew before. Never.

That, my friend, is a definition.

Not a bad letter, is it? Despite the literary allusions. A little too intimate, but then these days we are all a little more intimate with each other. (Though even Sophie would rather speak of intercourse joys than those hair-penis massages she loves to employ. What self-deluders these girls are!)

Not that Sophie's interpretation of things is exactly sound. Yes, I do enjoy an occasional game with the children, but it is going a bit far to describe me as "childish." I should think "exuberant" more just. Frankly, I am not all that "youthful." For

147

how will one ever get books written if one spends all one's time amusing the girls. One won't.

The business about that little MTA meeting and its aftermath has its embarrassing side, admittedly. But again, Sophie exaggerates. There was a small kiss, on the cheek, as I recall; not much more. True, I did show up later at her apartment, but there was much more decorum to the late-evening call than Sophie's account suggests. The important thing is, girls, as I've often said, that such doings must remain between us, and between us only. Please. Remember, Cambridge is a small town, with Very Large Ears. If certain occurrences were to get out and be whispered about at espresso shops and dining rooms, it would not win me any honorary degree. It would, in fact, tarnish my reputation, as much as I hate the word. With students, friends, colleagues, even with shopkeepers who know me. No, the exposure of one's private life is not my idea of fun. Reputations are not so easily come by that you can afford to lose one overnight. I move on. And, to be perfectly fair to the girls, let me select passages from other letters which show me in a different light. In fact, passages which are actually critical of the girls' beloved benefactor.

It is worth noting, in passing, an interesting coincidence concerning these critical letters: they are generally composed during menstruation time. Whenever the postman deposits one of these paper knives, I can pretty well assume that it's a product of blood. Is there any reason behind this coincidence? Certainly pain and annoyance are likely to produce a period of burdensome morbidity. And if the connection be made for a moment between a woman's attacks and the cycles of the moon, we might say that a woman seems to express herself most critically when she is at the edge of siege. No wonder then that lunacy often in the past was defined as "intermittent insanity." It is my opinion that by "insanity" here (in relation to women), we mean "different from men," and that the phrase is, at bottom, a form of male jealousy; we are jealous that the dears are so naturally in touch with the elements. All this would suggest a theory I have often pondered: namely, that women are a different species from us, who happen by chance to fit our chromosome makeup. They seem to me to be a far older lot, too. (One would do well here to reach for our anthropological sources.) Hence the phrase, so often used with irony, "They think with their intuition," not to mention a specific part of their anatomy, may in fact be deeply complimentary, implying that they carry their wisdom far more easily and naturally than we.

For my part—to cut through this thicket of abstractions—I have never failed to note that there arrives that moment in every affair with a female when I'm flabbergasted beyond speech or reason by something she says or does. "What in the world is she up to?" flashes through my mind. "What form of species is this creature? They use the same words, but the meanings are so different!" Exclamations not so much of anger as of total bewilderment and wonder. Please, is there a Margaret Mead in the house to diagnose this?

Perhaps the truth of the situation is seen most visibly not in life but in movies. I mean those movies remade every few years about the great gorilla King Kong and his dumb, endless fascination with the females of our species. In that child's delight, we see that the gorilla is attracted by some sort of pull and knows just enough to carry off the girl; he does not know enough—and perhaps this is where we might learn—to "speak" to her: about his "feelings," about his hopes and ideals, about a possible "relationship." That part of the affair is hopeless. The erotic pull is what counts for old Kong.

Now, is it possible that the movie myth is right and social reality wrong? (We are constantly finding out, from Piaget to Lévi-Strauss, how much we can learn from children and primitives, yes?) And that surface similarity of words and bodies which draws men and women together, deceptive? Hasn't every man, at one point or another, felt himself transformed morally and physically into some primitive animal by his tender partner? How often have we been stung to the core by appellations like "You ape!" when we seek to rise from our puniness? Wouldn't it, therefore, seem to be more consistent with internal truths if we males returned somehow to ape shape, grew out our hair, developed a better set of molars, and grunted instead of spoke? (And who is to say that in our new form we wouldn't be more attractive to the girls too?) Thus, the crazy accident of nature, whereby the two species were curiously suited biologically, would be exposed for the humorous trick that nature has played on us, and the proper relation between the two parties could be run with a little more common sense and sanity.

These idle philosophical speculations stem in part from my long-time interest in the philosophy of environments. I have always found it a matter of great interest how man has been able to master the animal and vegetable kingdoms, so to speak, but not the woman kingdom. The environment of women remains a perpetual bewilderment, whether one is domesticated or not. And so, in trying to speculate about this profound gap between the species, I have at times tried to investigate beneath the surface of common anecdotes, popular tales, and myths, to see if clues to the mystery could be found.

I recall speculating about this matter one dinner hour to Grace, who was fixing food for myself and little Sam, her new boy, perched in his high-chair. (Naaron was out, at a new pal's place.) Throughout my rising excitement, I was careful to pause, to repeat that I was not trying to be polemical about this possible "species gap," merely analytical, descriptive. Suddenly struck with a brainstorm, I rushed into my converted study-alcove— yes, I had done several conversions around town—and found, amid Grace's and my books, some appropriate sources to make my particular point. Armed with Graves and Fraser, I hurried back to the kitchen. I was met with jars of Gerber's baby food whizzing by that heretical brain of mine and smashing into the wall. Some response to erudition, I thought, crouching under the table until the physical assault was finished, meanwhile suffering the verbal artillery ("Screw you and your differences! Don't give me that crap! Nobody's bugging you, mate, about marriage, so don't give me your bullshit theories about why it won't work!"). Meanwhile, too, little Sam was screaming his boy-head off and, to add irony to pathos (mine), looking at me with vicious hate, as if it were my stupid philosophy that had robbed him of his lousy apple sauce, rather than his mother's illogical anger! Such is the reward from male comrades for showing courage. Finally, with minimal calm restored, I crept out from my safety cave, eyeing volume X of *The Golden Bough* facing downward, *The White Goddess* up against the wall haphazardly, and the broken Gerber's jars with their horrible goo spread on the floor. Out of guilt and penitence, I got down on all fours to clean the mess up, noting to myself that the rest of the family had somehow missed my point.

To the letters!

From Gwen, typed out; as always, the professional:

Oh, baby, you're too much. Watching you squirm and wiggle like a worm when I get around to asking you to play daddy with me. It turns me on, honestly, just to watch the color drain from your face. I never knew a man could be as *timid* as you! How did you get that way? From reading all those books? I've never in my life had a man, baby, who's as frightened of me as you seem to be. I just wink my eye and you tremble, like you were going to shit. From the time I was that high, men have taken their belt or hand to my skin; it's as natural as sucking tit. But with you, it's like pulling teeth.

And your habits, they're too much. You're a thousand times worse than Rodney, who's six. I've never met a man who doesn't smoke or drink but insists instead that I stock up with skim milk and Johnson's Band-Aid gauze. I thought you were kidding me at first, until the other night when your nose began to bleed and you were about ready to kill me because I was without your gauze! Honest, the way you acted, as if you had just come out of major surgery—"Now don't touch me! No, the cotton is too wet, too soggy! I told you it wouldn't work. And stop laughing, it's not funny. I can bleed to death here!" Too much. That was the funniest act I've ever seen. I must have laughed ten times since then thinking of it. Do you know, you're a *hypochondriac?* And a neurasthenic!

What can I say to this? The girl has a right to her interpretation of things. But not every nosebleed is the same, surely. For some men, I agree, there is nothing to it. A little spurt of blood, they blow their nose hard, and it's disappeared. Ordinary life returns. With me, things are not so easy. When I was eight or nine, for refusing to cite my allegiance to the Brooklyn Dodgers, my nose was banged against city concrete, which impaired forever the strength of the blood vessels. I had to go around with dissolvent gauze up my nose for some ten days, and not dare to sneeze during that time. It was very embarrassing, making sure the gauze was tucked securely up there. (Mrs. Leonard, my third-grade teacher, looked at my forefinger askance every time it ascended in that direction.) Ever since then, I have to be very careful, making sure I sneeze lightly (and never in the morning), and that Johnson's gauze is on hand most everywhere. I am especially careful after the first nosebleed, which can easily, without the proper safeguards, turn into a daily bloodfall. Does this sound like hypochondria? And as for neurasthenia, where's the *proof?* Will they never learn to back up their assertions with concrete evidence!

And look at this surprising little section of a note from Angela:

Pompous? That isn't the word for you, my dear professor. Do you realize how often you use the phrase "That goes without saying" or "Obviously, obviously," when I begin speaking? Or what it's like to go to a movie with you and come away with a different opinion? You act like a madman, a CP member during the days of Stalin. I happen to think that Bergman is terrific and not "melodramatic" or "pretentious." So what if "psychological investigation can be better studied in a novel"? I still think *Persona* was great. What pisses me no end about Tuesday evening is that you treated my opinion as if some Black Angus calf or cactus plant had given it. Come off it, will you?

Happily, things change when we screw. Despite your admonitions about my "neurotic" sexuality, Prof, you're as kooky as I am. No need to pretend otherwise. Do you really think that you have me belly dance and then pull me to the floor for my sake only? I know very well that I told you that that's what my former husband used to enjoy. But still, love, no one *forces you* to continue such operations (as Arnold keeps reminding me). And you do seem to enjoy those bouts with my "handful of wop behind" that I go through for your pleasure. Analyst also has a few things to say about *that*, love—though we both know what a sap Arnold is. So don't let's overemphasize *my* queer desires, okay? Let's spread the blame—or credit—around evenly.

And this choice paragraph:

> I chalk off your pomposity to (1) life in academe and (2) the endemic disease of males when in contact with females: superiority complex. The attitude is insufferable. Why do we put up with it? You have the curious habit of wanting us to be sex-machines. But when we conform, to satisfy *you*, you make fun of us. You want to have it both ways. So into the sack we climb several times a day, and fidget with new ideas of your origin, and then suddenly we're the neurotics with sex on our brains! The whole thing is a trap to turn us into the inferior creatures you imagine and want us to be. Whenever you want to stop the sex game, love, tell me. Then we'll see who's neurotic. Or perhaps I should Lysistrata you, lock my darling box away—not to stop any war, just to purge your prejudices. What do you think of the idea?

Fantasy-ridden and self-deluded, yet not at all bad for an Italian sexpot. Of course, Radcliffe will get you to write correct sentences. But can they ever train girls to think clearly, instead of chattering and confusing things? Why is the girl so afraid to admit her terrible sensual needs, and want even at this point of intimacy to be thought of for her *ideas*? For example, note her evasive and distorting remark concerning the pleasures of the backside. The poor thing can't get enough of it that way, once we get going. It's she who turned me on to such doings, with coy statements like "You wouldn't dare to do such a thing to me." But when I did dare, *I* was the culprit. Similarly, when she repeated to me how her husband used to rape her. What could be a more direct invitation than for me to buy the Turkish music and perform the ritual? About Arnold (the shrink) with his theories, he's dying to lay his hands on her, though Angela would never admit such a thing. But what the "sap" can't figure out, though he's spent three years at it and taken a few thousand from her, is the source of her crazed sexuality—the fact that with two small

153

bumps for breasts, she had to compensate somehow (to win her father and the rest of us men). Poor Angela still doesn't have the slightest notion who she is, though now she's calm about it. And even assertive.

Onward to Kate:

> Hey Bernie, do think about *my* feelings a bit. You can love my daughter, the sweet child, but does it have to be at my expense? As Angela said the other night when you called, "It's Kovell, he probably wants to talk to Suzie." Was she ever right!—fifteen minutes with a six-year-old girl? Darling, that's an awful lot. The sweet child is getting the wrong idea of things. She thinks you're *her* boy friend, not mine. I have enough competition hours with her as it is. Must I fight with her over you too? And lose?
>
> The phone calls are just one item. What about when you come over to take me out and I stand at the door with my coat on while you say good night to the child? Even those Leslie College baby-sitters look at me strangely. Or when you read the children a bedtime story and then, after Philip is off to bed, you spend another half hour on Suzie's bed, playing all sorts of games with her? The scene is very endearing, agreed, with the little tyke's head lying on your arm, listening away. But why don't you ever hold me with such concentration and tenderness? I'd like it! And, dear heart, to have my little friend surprise me in the morning with the new ring or bracelet you've left for her the night before, and she asks me, "What did you get?" and I have to say, "Zilch, zero, nothing," well, it gets me a little uptight.
>
> I'm jealous. JEALOUS. Need I say more?

A common predicament among young mothers with daughters, when there's no man around the house. The man naturally is going to be fought over vigorously, when he finally does show up and tries to play *father and husband*. Obviously—that word! sorry, Angela—obviously Kate exaggerates the matter. But it's understandable. I do like Suzie, she is a charmer, as I've said, with her wild eyes and gypsy skin. But I like the mother too. Kate is a very different type, much longer and larger, less exotic

154

but nevertheless lovely. Surely it would be senseless for me to try to explain to Kate that at age six her daughter is not all that innocent; or that at times her pursuit of me reaches embarrassing proportions. Can I explain, for example, those afternoon phone calls that she makes to me while being baby-sat (on the pretense that she wants to tell me what school was like that day)? Or when she cons her mother into getting me to take her along to a Red Sox game, where she will sit only on my lap and continually play with my ears and hair? No, in certain situations, the wise man is he who keeps his wisdom secret, rather than blabbering it around. An embarrassing situation is an embarrassing situation.

And what would the world of my mailbox be like without the touching notes of Melissa, who had never before written a letter longer than three sentences.

> Forgive me for writing this, Bernard, but must you push me so hard about neatness and order? You know I respect and listen to everything you say, but it will take me a while to change completely for you. Meanwhile, I do think—please forgive this, you will, won't you?—that you are somewhat rigid yourself about these qualities. I've never seen anybody worry so about punctility [sic]. Everything must be just so, and not any different. If I wash your socks, they must be done by hand and then rolled in a towel before hung over the stand. If I boil eggs and they're loose, you refuse to eat them. If I leave dishes in the sink overnight, you wake me up in the middle of the night to tell me about them. It gets so that I'm afraid to do anything with you around, for fear of making a mistake.
>
> And your punctility about your routine is very difficult to get used to. I'm just not made, dear Bernard, to fix dinner at exactly seven-thirty, or to survive evenings with as much silence as you seem to need. Or to answer correspondence as quickly as you think I ought to. Couldn't you compromise somewhat? Meanwhile, I am practicing very hard my handwriting lessons, so that it won't look like a left-handed chimp's, as you call it. Do try to understand that I am making a serious effort in all these things, but that there are very many (things). It is very difficult to keep them all in

mind. Forgive me for not making myself too clear. I hope you will understand.

Yes, I do have a few habits and eccentricities, like all men, all women. But it must be recalled that, for a chaotic like Melissa, the retention of a front-door key requires a major effort of the memory. Another missive by this same girl is perhaps more interesting.

> Dear One:
> You asked me always to be as truthful as possible. Furthermore, you said that the hardest thing to be truthful about was sex. You're right (as usual). It *is* hard. But I shall try.
> Bernard, why are you occasionally impotent? Has this happened before, dearest? With any other girls? Or does it have specifically to do with me? If this is so, could you go into details?
> I so wanted to have you inside of me last Sunday night. At the dinner table you were so cheerful and witty and attractive. Charming my girl friends that way! It made me jealous, honest; and I wanted to get you back. And then, when you drooped that way in bed, I didn't know what to do. I was disappointed. And guilty. Forgive me for putting it this way. So bluntly, I mean. *I am merely following orders.*
> Do you think it will recur? If so, can I help?
> Need I add, dear one, that even if you *had none at all*, like Jake Barnes, I still would love you and hug you and serve you, my sweet.

Downtrodden Melissa composing a letter of such frankness. Unthinkable, but there it is.

Impotency: next to cuckoldry, a man's greatest fear. Why not? Incompetence of any kind is hard to take, especially one's own. Sexual even more, perhaps, in today's climate of exaggerated virility. Nevertheless, it rises (the problem) and therefore must be confronted. Reality won't go away if one closes one's eyes.

To begin with, it's true that every so often, with Melissa, I fail to perform. My penis fails to stand and serve. Now there may be a host of reasons for this—childhood fears, present anxieties, or whatever—but what is more relevant is the fact that my little pal does perform regularly with the other girls. *There* is the great benefit of having a harem family: it tests propositions and prevents hasty conclusions. Instead of hanging my head in shame for having loved my mother or ceasing all functioning because of self-doubt, I made swift arrangements to go across town to see another friend, after the first signs of decay. A kind of love-checkup. Sure enough, in Angela's Harvard Frame bed, I was just fine. Straight and sturdy as an arrow. With a perfectly timed splashdown. Afterward, lying beside my sex-nurse, I breathed easier, smoking carelessly. And considered matters.

But wait, I've moved too fast. Something important happened at Angela's. Let me describe it. When I got there, I was tense and rageful. She started to play kittenish, but saw my mood and shifted into sex gear. She began by playing with my penis—after pulling down my briefs to just below my groin—stroking it lightly from the balls upward in thumb, forefinger, and index. A lovely feather stroke. Immediately I stood stiff. Leaning forward, she put the helmet in her mouth and tongued it, holding me with one hand, occasionally smiling up at me like a dutiful child. But I had come for something else and spun her over and around. I put it into her dog-fashion, one hand around the front upon her clitoris. That skinny white ass wiggled and jerked in joy, pumping my blood. I fucked first in a slow gyration. Second, straight ahead with pistonlike regularity. Third, long slow deep strokes slowly sunk in and more slowly drawn out. She urged me on with "You fucker, oh, you fucker!" She moaned, cursed, hissed, perspired, tried to twirl her ass on my prick like a top. She began to orgasm and cried more violently, "Fuck me! Hurt me! Till I bleed, please."

Well, it drove me wild. At first I was a vengeful rider taking out my pent-up frustration and anger with Melissa on Angela. But as I stayed inside there, moving in that liquefied orifice, I began to achieve some control, some organization; which affords terrific confidence. It made me a momentary power station, just wanting to keep it going, keep it going, keep it going. Laps in a pool. Push-ups. Firing fastballs. So we went on, bull and cow, fish

157

and bait. Furious lubricant interlockings. From vengeance to poised control, I found myself leaping into a state of madness, a quicksand of animal excess. I clasped her ass closer, pressed her flat belly with my hand, and started to orgasm. An image crossed my mind of tossing out a long rope and lassoing a steer and jerking powerfully, controlling the neck and force of an animal three times your weight and strength. The momentary illusion of omnipotence, but a grand illusion. Total dominance.

Only dimly during it, but emphatically afterward, lying depleted and gorged, did I grant to myself the absolute validity of hierarchies of orgasms. For the first time I thought about it, and categorized. Grace brought to mind the Mechanical Service types, as routine as pumping Esso into a Chevy. Melissa recalled the puny spill that came after too much hard work, in which you were too tired to enjoy anything; the task as pleasurable as emptying a latrine basin. Kate inspired memories of those brutal jolts of buggering, the thrusts of fury, as interesting as the monotone of hammering an anvil, an orgasm not nearly as complicated or various as vagina-mining. Then I thought of the quick hard emission, too brief to be really memorable or to rate a *Consumer Guide* check-rating; the unfortunate result of too effective an alternative pleasure, like Sophie's masterpieces of sucking. Which left me with Angela and Gwen. A pair of super cunt-owners, orgasm-entrepreneurs. Angela inspired the Grand O partly out of the context of impotence and frustration I've described, partly out of her whorish carryings-on, enough to drive any man to Xanadu. And with crazy Gwen and her black naughtiness, again you grew wild and angry and loose enough to make the breakaway orgasm, not the five- or seven-yard gainer, but the sixty- and seventy-yard open field run, full of glamour and surprise, scares and traps, missed blocks, frantic escapes and hurdles, the sudden cuts and hip nuances, and finally the sheer animal joy of explosive speed, blinding speed, breaking away from everyone in sight and running free.

The special orgasm. Something you've had to experience to appreciate. Pleasure-lasting and strung out in varying rhythms, tearing away puny restraints and cutting you loose from social fibers. Opening farther and farther out, like the sweet smash of morphine, so that it's no longer a Webster-bound definition, an advertising formula, a State Goal. Pleasure, beyond the vocabulary and domain of the tight-lipped, winter-reared New England Puritan, the bleary-eyed, Bible-fanatic Southern Baptist, the waterless mountainless corn-and-wheat-field-filled Midwestern Babbitt preacher, the yarmulke-capped, scraggly bearded moralist-minded Jewish Yahweh rabbi. Pleasure beyond the grease-slick-coated commodity packaged by the Madison Avenue hucksters, the dumb viciousness practiced by the professional murderers of society (the hunters and soldiers), and beyond the thin-blooded anal-haunted abstraction squeezed out in print by the intellectuals, or the constipated conception of the genteel academicians. Strong fucking came finally from the gut; you knew you were risking it as the heart-ticker speeded up violently, and the tragic race between danger and pleasure was not unlike a microcosm of your whole life as you pursued an evanescent prize. Sudden lightning from the interior, it was beyond the limits or the law, a momentary fulfillment of utopia.

Hot sex. It was a deluge of power. It dissolved reason, culture, civilization. A fluid which reduced you from a complicated organism, possessing attitudes, needs, and levels, to a single point of white-hot desire. Paradoxically, it performed the religious task of release from body-boundness, spinning you into a brief orbit of transcendence. The catalyst was not catechism, however, but pleasure. Odors, furs, secretions, holes, frictions—they turned you and turned you, until madness. Pleasure: the enemy of the State; of the Mind; of Morals. It brought down order, work, concentration. Once you got hooked on it, you were finished. Thirty, twenty, ten, five, even three minutes of delicious sex was enough to make men betray, steal, murder. Five minutes of the real thing, say two or three times a day, stole husbands of twenty-five years and transformed responsible citizens into lust-driven fools. A playful knowing cunt—a pair of agile lips that could expand and contract, bite and nip, plus a little protrusion of flesh, all set like a guerrilla hideout into a camouflaged mound and firing off special salivas and smells—this infinitesimal house of pleasure had toppled kings, altered history. Not bad for a body circumference of a few inches. Shakespeare, who appreciated this point in his work with some devotion, might have revised his famous Richard III plea to: "A cunt! A cunt! My kingdom for a cunt!" No wonder they wanted you to remain virginal until marriage, and monogamous afterward. To keep sane. And to marry early, to get your freedom over with as soon as possible, without your dipping into a variety of holes. Like other maddening pursuits—those for alcohol, opium, or gambling—the lust for cunt had to be curbed; otherwise, civilization would return to water and sand.

I had come to Angela's to check up on a defective part. I had gotten more than I had hoped for. (And was sorry for the previous lectures I had given to Angela on her orgasm obsession.) I had fallen into a passionate dream, a sexual Kubla Khan, where only a few had happened to travel. Naturally most people wouldn't understand, or believe. Would resent. Would accuse me of exaggerated *machismo*, meaningless language, and laugh it off. Fair enough. Not a Christian proselytizer, I wasn't about to be one for the heresy of orgasm.

Back to not getting it up.

My detumescent pal was not a total betrayer after all, just capricious. His resistance was clearly a local matter, relating to Melissa. A consoling thought. (I stopped Angie's hand from straying southerly, since I was thinking now and had proven my point.) Immediately my universalist impulse stirred and my heart flowed with sympathy for those hundreds of boys and men around town who, confined to one woman, suffered a similar ignominious setback. For where could a beleaguered monogamist go in order to check the real source of the failure? What laboratory other than a shrink's office—the four-to-five-year class costing about twenty-five grand in tuition—would accept him? Could he look up Harem Enterprises in the Yellow Pages? Or Beacon Hill Brothels? Monogamy usually was merely dull and monotonous. Consider it amid the climate of impotency: *a dog's life.*

Not that it was all Melissa's fault. After all, I did manage intercourse with her with a modest regularity (once every few weeks or so). But was I, or any man, to be judged like a Kenmore or Westinghouse and sold at Lechmere Sales, a kind of automatic hard-on machine stiffening to attention at the drop of a bra or the exposure of hair? Such habit-forming can be a hazardous, not to mention comic, occupation. Imagine a piece of one's anatomy growing rigid at the sight of baby-bottle nipples or a scampering mink? Or suddenly bulging in the trousers at a cocktail party just because an attractive woman wears a strip of fur about her neck, or a patch of decorative hair upon her breast? Of course many Americans—myself not totally excluded, sadly enough—have been programmed this way. Not to mention the ten thousand husbands across the land who couple with sheep or dream of pigs because of boredom with wives, marriage. In any case, I've given up judging the next fellow's "aberrations," or the apparent quirks in his life. Without knowing the private life (sexual) of a man or woman, you know nothing about him or her. For my part, what I wish to caution against is the danger of internal automation, in sexuality as in attitudes. A little failure now and then, so long as it is not permanently disabling, is good for the ego. A red signal in this green-light country, it brings to a halt (if only for three minutes) speeding narcissism. Detours from success return one to reality in America.

Finally, it is not all that easy, waxing excited with girls who don't really have a taste for sex. Not after you've experienced in your life a true sexmobile: a girl who exists for sex. Try as we might, there's no altering certain constitutional traits. About such matters, Gertrude Stein's rhetoric is more useful than psycho-analytical jargon. A bad comer is a bad comer. A lousy blowjob (after training) is a lousy blowjob. A dead lay is a dead lay. Melissa remained basically unequipped, constitutionally uninter-ested. Am I supposed to get hot with a log simply because it has tits? Melissa in fucking was wood, and wood—be it pine or western hemlock—just doesn't turn me on.

But try saying all this to that log, and see if it'll get you a veal paprika dinner! Which my Melissa prepared for me the night I "explained" matters (overwork, exhaustion, etc., were the words I used, not sexual boredom).

Sexual boredom: the description of most marriages. It's what drives healthy men to ignominious cheating or to a painfully false life of sexual fantasy. I remember Melissa asking me once, when I had just finished upon her, what I had been thinking about. She couldn't help feeling, she murmured, that I wasn't *quite there*. Shrewd as a cow, my pal. You bet your life I wasn't *there*, who would be? In my mind, I was out banging Gwen. And another time, I'll admit, I was wondering whether it would be very different if a goat were beneath me. Honest. Or again, out of a kind of perverse amusement, I tried to plan a lecture on Conrad's "Secret Sharer" in the midst of intercourse. (Shifting between my ideas and my perversity, I enjoyed Melissa greatly that evening.) The point was, concentration on that fleshy "driftwood" —that word kept floating in my consciousness—was not exactly turning me on. Often, in fact, it turned me off . . . Can you imagine what men think of when they're in the saddle with a dull lay of twenty years, or with the prospect of twenty years ahead of them? Think of that cruel fate! Wiretap them at such moments and you get, I imagine, a range from unbridled sadism to careful business planning to schemes for murder.

The prospect of a lifetime of dull but necessary sex should be grounds for divorce in any rational state.

And finally, this one heady paragraph from Grace:

> You're the moodiest sonofabitch I've ever met. And the most impolite. One minute you're all lovey-dovey, the next you're as abrasive as sandpaper. (Like that goddamned stubble on your cheek, which you refuse to remove, though I tell you every time that it makes my face sore for days. D-a-y-s.) Take dinner with the Blockmans the other night. I know they're not scintillating company, but they're my friends. For the first hour you were perfectly decent, then crash! All of a sudden you were insulting and caustic about everything they said. You didn't let a word pass. Don't think you didn't embarrass me deeply, you did. What gets into you? Why are you so unpredictable? I have moods too, but at least I try to control them. The Blockmans were perfectly decent, and you ruined the evening!

First, concerning the "stubble." I've explained to Grace a dozen times that my skin is tender and therefore I can shave only with downward strokes. I realize this is inconvenient for her, but the alternative is to come to her with a face bandaged like some Civil War veteran. The second point, the Blockmans. How can you behave with this type, except with irony? A pair of young marrieds, in the teaching business, going on endlessly about their search for a house to buy. Did I know Lexington? And what did I think of the Montessori schools? Or Shady Hill? I told them that I preferred zoos to schools, Proconsul apes to Montessori teachers. And why didn't they split up, I suggested, before they became a pair of His and Her towels? That didn't go over well. Grace is perfectly right, I was impolite. I'll apologize too one day, I suppose, if I ever see them again. Why take out my anger at the whole class of pusillanimous Young Marrieds on the poor Blockmans? But the point is, so far as moods are concerned, any civilized person is vulnerable to them. Show me a moodless man, and I'll show you a boob. A person not subject to moods is the same person who is asleep three minutes after his head hits the pillow at night: a spiritless man. Besides, a mood is a mood. What would she have me do, pop a tranquilizer every time one assaults me?

The important thing to note about all these little criticisms, however, is that the girls are able to make them in the first place. There is the crucial fact of it all: a signal to what's happened to them under my tutelage. Two or three years ago, it would have been near-impossible for girls like Grace or Angela *to focus* on a single point of disturbance, let alone put it down on paper. The articulation of grievances, no matter how half true these may be, is the surest evidence of the direction my girls are headed in: forward. (Not to mention the improvements in penmanship! Melissa's chicken scrawl of tiny illegible letters, the handwriting of fear, has been replaced by a schoolgirl neatness. The result of an hour's practice daily. And Angela no longer misspells monosyllables or skips words—too often—her drastic plea for attention heeded by discipline. Actually, no therapy has been stronger for these girls than discipline. As they understand, it's a sure sign of care . . . And if they're afraid sometimes, that's good too. Mostly their fear is a product of uncertainty about themselves; and so they're afraid of being found out. *Of being known.* Which is why they stick with me, to put the matter crudely. I *know* them.)

Like brave camels, the girls have come a long way through the American desert. Having been victims of contemporary wars (marriage, friendship, affairs) and captives of today's camps (conjugal bedrooms, divorce courts, shrinks' offices), they are

163

now walking upright again, smiling, pushing prams, working on books, functioning with spirit. Beginning to know their own desires again. Self-believers. Ambassadors of hope. Need it be said that such transformations cannot be achieved by the principles of abandon or excess, but rather by disciplined labor, patience, devotion to an ideal? In a word, the marks of maturity.

And there is a remarkable thing about all this, I believe. The girls now have a real feeling for life. A curiosity. An aliveness. A sense of humor. Their eyes follow alertly. They interrupt with intelligent questions, reactions. All this was so conspicuously missing when I first knew them, typical psychic cripples of the time, computed and coerced into defeat. This new feeling is really so curious because it is tantamount to a kind of spiritual faith. How odd a phrase, a feeling, in these coarse secular days. A faith in their own spirits, in living. Now where are you going to find that nowadays? I call it a revolution of sorts. Well, better a miracle.

So, girls, I toast our little community. To our health and spirits! May we soon celebrate yet another season of family happiness! And let us conclude this affectionate memoir by recalling the words of the wise Spinoza, who, with his eyes turned toward heaven, wrote,

"All things excellent are as difficult as they are rare."

2: BARRICADE ANXIETY

Now that you have a sense of the Dean's curious personal life, I'd like you to observe him at work, as a man of official authority. From his intimate circus to our barricades. For this reason and because of the notoriety of the events concerning the Berg Art Museum Uprising on the ninth and tenth of last June, I present here selections from the Dean's famous four-hour-plus speech, given on that fateful June 10, to the students occupying the museum.

Briefly, the setting was this. A few days before regular graduation proceedings, we, the student rebels at Cardozo College, decided to hold a counter-graduation—a protest against the war, the government, the approaching elections. Against our approaching fate in the society, that of grown-up Americans. So we decided to seize several buildings—as to why the museum and library, I shall explain later—to use as sites of occupation, for whatever ceremonies we were going to create. As for the remaining details of the affair, they can come afterward, in chronological order, following the Dean's speech. For it was that speech which helped to inspire the later shenanigans, and which provided, unwittingly, impetus to action.

167

Let me say right off that Barricade Anxiety is optional reading. I've had my own doubts about including it here, being as it is a defense of a way of life that is, to describe it kindly, a way of the past. Optional then, because it is one thing to listen to a Fidel elaborate for five or six hours on his new society; to listen for a similar length of time to a university Romanov harangue his obsolete philosophy is close to intolerable. Why print these selections then? First, because there are intelligent citizens in America in the 1970's who would agree with the Dean's thoughts; they represent a point of view that is still widespread, I fear. Therefore, to cite these beliefs is to show the world what we are up against and what we must not merely smile at but overthrow. Second, the speech will show most clearly why we took the actions we did that day in the museum, and later, in society. Actions which seem to have touched central nerve cords in the nation. The final reason is, as I have indicated, to show the public side of the Dean, after you have seen his personal life. As you listen to these words, keep in mind that personal life; in that way, the full rich humor of his position will not be lost.

My own concern here is with the moral and intellectual content of the speech rather than with the narrative element of the story—the events leading to the uprising, the Dean's role, the disturbance itself, the general consequences which were to follow. As I've said, I have placed that interesting narrative in the section following the speech; certainly some readers will want to turn there out of . . . embarrassment, rage, boredom. But perhaps this last is unfair to the Dean and to men who think like him. To solid American citizens who call themselves liberal and enlightened thinkers.

To the Dean's remarks I have added a general title, a necessary footnote here and there, and small critical appendages after each Dean-selection. To be perfectly honest, I had no intention of adding these comments when I first began the project, but as I got into the actual process of editing and selecting the taped words, I couldn't resist some counterpunching. The passages begged for it. At least they were so full of direct questions and challenges to myself and my friends that I felt I was being true to the spirit of the talk by answering them; or by turning the monologue into a dialogue of sorts. Isn't that what Kovell and men like him are after—to get boys like myself, apprentice troublemakers, to respond to them?

It is 10:30 P.M. on a cool June evening when the Dean begins. The students have been inside the museum for almost two days and nights, and the Dean has interrupted his weekend in New Hampshire to appear—a kind of high-school halfback addressing a school rally. Begged to come, in fact, by Dr. Schlossberg, the college president, who had urged the students earlier that Saturday to give up the occupation and negotiate, to no avail. Arriving with the Dean is one of the legendary mistresses, Grace, along with her son Naaron. The willowy dirty-blond woman, in her late twenties, sits on the floor among the students, while Naaron, age six, egged on by cheering fans, is placed upon a blackboard atop the improvised barricade at the front entrance. There the boy sits, swinging his legs, giggling, before he finally falls off to sleep. By his side, braced precariously on a wedged desk top with a broken bannister for a railing, and leaning for support on a standing lectern, is Dean Kovell. Wearing a thin windbreaker over a red pullover, tan dungarees, and fidgeting with his wrist-supporter, he talks in a rapid city-style rhythm, a new thought jumping out before the first is quite finished. Although he has various bits of paper—an index card or two, a notepad, backs of envelopes—to which he occasionally refers, mostly he improvises. You can tell this is about to occur when his hand goes to his thick hair and scratches aimlessly. The barricades and we students seem to have made an already nervous man that much more itchy.

Good evening, boys and girls, nice to see such a good late-evening attendance. [*Laughter, cheers.*] Let me tell you that it's probably a little more comfortable where you're sitting than up here. I find it sort of interesting that you construct a barricade and then put me on it. It's not quite "up against the wall," but . . .

Let me begin by making use of this curious angle; philosophical or moral use. That is, my extreme position on this risky, uh, barricade, having to be careful not to upset the balance while I talk, so that the whole contraption doesn't fall and take me with

169

it. As you know, I can think of better ways of returning to the hospital.* [*Laughter and a modest ovation.*]

Being careful to keep my "balance." It's a word, a term, a feeling, that's gone out of fashion these days, I think. And been replaced by a vogue for distortion, for imbalance, for . . . fragmentation. All the elements that make for dissonance, disharmony. Why? Are there good reasons for this? And, furthermore, does the old term have any virtue for us or is it truly antiquated?

The desire for balance replaced by the urge, the compulsive urge for derangement, for extremity, for disturbance. Yes, an infatuation with that prefix, "dis." Those simple three letters that provide the force of the negative upon a word. You admire that, perhaps unawares. A fondness for the underground God, for the Roman Dis. But I'm sounding like a professor now. [*Mock jeers.*] And that other word, extremity. To be extreme is to be With-it; extremity is In. Without a position of extremity, you're considered dull, useless, and worse—counter-revolutionary. Boys and girls, I reject this notion, reject it wholeheartedly, and reject it on many levels.†

You see, balance is the cornerstone of society, of individual man and accomplishment, of what we mean by civilization. What is so hard to convey to you, and yet what I think is so crucial, are

---

* This is a reference to the nervous breakdown of the Dean, during the 1970 crisis, at the university, when Kove spent two weeks at McLean's Hospital. The story of the well-known collapse, which made him a favorite with us, is told later on.

† "Levels"—or "aspects"—a favorite word and concept of Professor Kovell and others like him. It is symptomatic of a certain disease that afflicts very smart men of our society. It is a disease of the nerve, the moral nerve, which suddenly finds itself paralyzed and unable to exert itself. Men who have it, embarrassed as if they had chicken pox, try to cover it up by naming it "complexity." Just as chicken pox affects one group primarily, children, so complexity pox strikes at enlightened men primarily, especially those intellectuals who once upon a time manifested revolutionary symptoms. In its more virulent form, which may be seen farther along in the Dean's speech, the nerve begins jerking again, only in a new and perverse manner. Now it proceeds to go after its own earlier directions and symptoms in the form of younger persons showing similar radical disorders. Once this later stage sets in, there is little hope for the sick man, except strict quarantine and intensive re-education. A therapy currently being tried on the Dean.

the premises upon which man comes together to emerge from the jungle and to create clearings; up from primitivism and into communities, societies. This act is based upon factors which I'm sure you know about once they're spelled out, but which perhaps you've forgotten. I'm talking about the need to survive and the subsequent knowledge that in order to do so, you cannot give free rein to every emotion, every sudden whim or impulse that strikes you. We know that nowadays the air is poisoned in more ways than the physical, that, in fact, for intelligent persons, the pollution of the intellectual climate by maniacal ideas is just as dangerous in its way as automobile and gaseous pollutions for the general public. We live in an environment in which we are daily and weekly assaulted, by means of radio, television, newspaper and magazine, by every nutty idea, every half-baked notion, every fallacious argument, every slippery offer that the charlatans, lunatics, and shysters can think up. It's a horrible disease, what I'll call media-itis. And it grows worse, because every one of these lunatics with his dangerous idea is a potential money-maker in our culture. There's the crucial fact, that our culture rewards criminals, fools, and madmen much better than it does sane men. A stupid criminal who calls himself a revolutionary, or a revolutionary who calls himself a criminal, will earn ten times as much cash as an ordinary professor. Think of that. Just think of that.

Why? Why are pathology and extremity so popular? As valuable as U.S. Savings Bonds for future dividends. Why does Mailer [*cheers*] yes, I know you like him—why does he command a million bucks from *Life* magazine, or Genet a hundred thousand from Grove? While I earn eighteen? [*Jeers.*] Thank you, I appreciate that, and hope that Dr. Schlossberg is listening. [*Cheers.*]

Because boys and girls, members of the middle class, many of your own parents, in fact, are befuddled. They've become unsure of themselves. Unsure of their values, of their accomplishments. Like yourselves, really. You're bewildered too, aren't you? Be honest with yourselves, and consider. Bewildered as to *what's right, what's good, how to act to fulfill your ideals*. All right, fair enough. Everyone who leads an honest life will realize that living is confusing, that it is tragic, that it is problematic, that it offers

171

no easy or comforting answers, that it instead grows harder and harder, more and more tragic as we get on, as we get older . . . as our bodies wear down, our friends die. Death, boys and girls, is finally very bewildering, to a terrifying degree; in fact it begins to make life that way too.

But to admit this is not to opt for the next salvationist who appears on the scene, the next apocalypse-man who says, This is the way that will save. The horrible brute ugly fact is, there's no saving oneself from the ultimate tragedy of a *life that suddenly stops.* We all suffer beneath it. Just watch one man or woman die, watch the clots develop through the skin and the eyes change to terror and anger, and you'll understand what I mean. Visit a morgue instead of your next rock festival, and it might change you . . .

[*A drink of water.*]

Balance. (And forgive me if I ramble on here, I'm speaking more from ideas that have been in my head for a long time now, simply gathering steam, ideas that I've wanted to say to you, rather than from these notes only.) It all depends on the attempt at balance. Take a man and a woman. The amount of consideration and forbearance that goes into a relationship between two adult persons is astonishing. It's not simply that you love someone all the time, or that the first time you stop loving him or her it's all over. The emotions are not black and white that way, as sometimes you're fond of urging when you urge "love" upon us, the world. In fact, so-called love is full of stretches of dullness, moments of irritation, small miscues and miscalculations, periods of great loneliness, a hundred and one nuances of feeling throughout a single day, let alone the affair. [*Cheers.*] You like that word, huh? [*More cheers.*] But if the balance is there, it will work. Your tenderness for each other will stay alive; thrive even. For you'll know that there's a deeper understanding between you that can support temporary folly, anger, crudeness, selfishness— yes, all those nasty things that we all have in us. With the balance of consideration, these ugly features, which are in all of us, can be held back, starved of sustenance, diminished. More and more, the best parts of ourselves can emerge as consistent character features.

Now, what makes up this balance that I've been praising? At

172

least two things come to mind immediately. The first is reason, the power to reason. It's our single outstanding capacity, say what you want for the others. Any monkey or dog can work up anger, lust, or devotion, but only a man can be ironic, humorous, *seriously* reasoning. And by this I include symbol-making, language development, etc. Need it be said yet again that the only quality which makes us unique on this earth is reason? That our capacity to build bridges and airplanes, to cure people from tuberculosis and to invent polio vaccines, or to make great cities on desert lands—all that we take for granted in other words—is based simply on our power to reason. Reason has been the catalyst in the growth of civilization; and if there are those of you who believe that there is no "growth," that it's a mythological concept invented by white Westerners, then I suggest two things. First, that it contradicts your own policies protesting financial inequity, social justice, racism—all of which presuppose a more progressive and less progressive state of society. And second, since seeing and experiencing are the best teachers, I suggest you visit the mountains of Peru, the jungles of Brazil, the deserts of Africa, the streets of Calcutta—and see whether you do or don't believe that there is such a thing as "progress." See for yourselves if there are differences, besides cultural ones, in human society. See whether you'd prefer to live in this or that society. Don't be misled by interpretations by Mr. Lévi-Strauss, or by me, friends. Try out countries and places for yourselves and see if there are differences. And then let me know.

Along with reason, there's the second quality, made up of two parts, one of which I've already mentioned. I mean forbearance. The quality of patient, forgiving endurance. Be a little easy on other people who disagree with you, on other ideas, on society. You're not the only ones who have lived in human history or suffered through trying times. Your parents [*hissing*], for example, at your age or younger, lived through a difficult time in this country, a time of material privation and scarcity which you've never known, and they came through. Now they may not have had the good luck or time to go to a university, the leisure to read books "exposing the capitalist system," the money to buy hashish, and so on. Instead they were working, or trying to find work, in order to survive. So their ideas and their attitudes were formed by experience, not by books or slogans. Now don't hold that against them. On the contrary, try to learn from it. To my mind, for example, a university education is much narrower in scope and thinner in feeling than what one learns from experience. But that's another matter.* The point is, try to understand—no, give them some credit for pulling through, for accomplishing things.

Which leads me to humility. That very old-fashioned Greek and Judeo-Christian virtue. Socrates practiced it, Jehovah demanded it, Jesus built a philosophy upon it. Along with curiosity, it's the single greatest educational principle. To act from the assumption of ignorance—that you don't know and that others are capable of teaching you—is the way to begin to know. I'll tell you something, pals: I don't think you have nearly enough of this attitude toward life. Somewhere along the line, you've short-changed yourselves on this. Too easily and too frequently you connect humility with blind subservience, with bullied passivity; you make it over into a psychoanalytical principle of domination by the superego or father. It's not any of these things. It means rather that you're always on the alert to learn, on the lookout for that something different and unique about experiences. You've got to learn *to listen* if you wish to push your mind forward. Otherwise you're doomed to your own perspective, a perspective which, when you're young, suffers inevitably from provincialism, from prejudice, from stupid pride and lack of refinement and shortage of charity, and a dozen other myopic defects. Boys and girls, believe me when I say, you never stop trying to escape the boundaries of your own ego. Like stone walls, they're limiting and diminishing. One of the hardest things to preserve in life is the quality I'm speaking of, humility. And, to be frank, most people don't. Most of my colleagues are as locked into the arrogance of their own worlds as I'm suggesting you are now. Well, do something about it, escape it, and keep escaping it, and keep reminding yourselves of the necessity to do so.

[*Putting a jacket over the sleeping Naaron.*]

Rome wasn't built in a day, and civilization wasn't built in a

---

* It is too bad that the Dean doesn't explore this point any further, as far as his own somewhat singular personal experience is concerned. It would have been amusing, and made more convincing his present words.

lifetime. But it can be destroyed nowadays in quick time, quicker than it took to build. And there you have an irony of existence—how much longer it takes to build than to destroy. And the more complex the organism, the more time, the more patience, the more labor, the more care it takes to bring it to life. Although you would think that civilization is a permanent fact of life, like our galaxy perhaps, it's not. It's much shakier than that galaxy, which is itself not permanent. It's here—civilization—basically because of *consent*, the implicit consent of all of us to come together to preserve life. In fact, in certain ways, you should think of it as a house of playing cards, where one false move will bring it all down. Now I'm not saying that you have the power to bring it all down, though you certainly have the power to bring yourself down with a false move, a move by yourself against one other person. Just that single destruction is enough to cause your own. But to return to that larger house, of civilization; the power to bring that down does these days exist in the world, and what you do may very well have a serious influence on that power. So you're really involved in a continuous chain of responsibility, beginning with yourself and your family, extending to the society here at Cardozo and then to the nation, and finally to the world. For the first time in human history, you're truly a citizen of the world, your responsibility extends *that* far. Whether you think this or not, it's so. And it's up to you to imagine that responsibility when you act, in the same way that you do when you try to imagine yourself a Vietnamese peasant, or a poor black. For that attempt at empathy, you're to be congratulated. The gesture is an impressive one.

Forbearance, humility, reason. These are the virtues. Their opposites are qualities like impatience, arrogance, irrationality. For what I've been speaking about finally, although you wouldn't know it perhaps from the way I've rambled, is the kind of training you should be acquiring here at Cardozo. It's not a training in facticity—in numbers, statistics, names, places, or dates. Rather, it's a development of a method of reasoning and feeling about the world that deepens your appreciation of the value of life. A method. It's really as simple as that in an important way. The value of life. The sheer value of existence, of plenitude. Something that you may perhaps take lightly, or take for granted.

Method. And that method is nothing without the qualities I've mentioned. But once you're imbued with them, you will begin to see, to intuit, the tremendous fragility of this whole project called civilization, and the indescribable cost and effort that it's taken to construct it. Look, think for a moment of a spider weaving his web—and to those of you who have never witnessed this common but delicate task, I recommend it, especially with the aid of a magnifying glass—consider the delicacy and the patience of his labor, to construct that gossamer complexity of great design and beauty. And imagine this tiny but miraculous result in relation to what we've built here, just in a small town, say. What you might also do, for example, is take a drive into the New England countryside, to New Hampshire or Vermont, and look at some of the old existing villages there that date back to the founding of this country. Drive to a little town called Harrisville, population a few hundred, in southern New Hampshire and walk around there. What you'll see is a one-story library, a general store, a post office, a one-floor schoolhouse, and a textile mill, still operating—all of this set side by side, colored the same weathered red-brick, and built along a pair of connecting ponds. I think that the simple harmony and lovely sanity of the place might surprise you. And right there, the whole idea of cities is presented, in embryo, like a perfect biological specimen. And then work your way up, to the capital, Concord, a town of about ten thousand, and finally to a big city like Boston. And what you should be following and tracing is the idea of growth, development. The beauty of process. How things are made, put together, so that they work efficiently. That's all, an interest in the *how* of things. You'll appreciate the *end* more.

This is not to make it all glamorous. It's not. There are hazards and costs as well as benefits and beauty. And when you get to a city like New York today, the costs will be only too apparent. But don't be so naïve as to believe that you can purchase anything in this life without paying a price for it. You can't. It's the lesson of any serious thinker, from Sophocles to Nietzsche to Freud. [*Jeers.*] A price for all things worth having. For love, for friendship, for industrial development, for self-improvement, for wisdom. It all *costs*. It's a hard but necessary lesson to learn, which I'm not sure many of you understand yet . . .

An interest in development, in process, in how things work, in cause and effect. This takes observation, experimenting, reflection. You can't do without reflection, it's a habit you had better get hold of early in life, now when you're a student, or you'll never acquire it and miss something crucial in life. It's what a year of graduate school, with all its boredom, sometime forces upon you. For without reflection you might as well be a monkey or guinea pig, responding to a variety of stimuli in the laboratory called the American environment. That's how most people act, don't they? Responding to this commercial for soap or deodorant, to that appeal for racist victory or philistine prejudice, to this call to despair or that one for instant joy, to this exhortation to rise up and smash the state or that one to band together to beat the shit out of the students. Responding to the collective call to whatever is fashionable at the moment—as if your attitudes toward society and toward your fellow man can be shifted as easily as changing from minis to maxis, narrow to wide ties. Forget the fashions, those external summonses of how to live your life. Resist them, my friends. Learn to *determine for yourself* how you want to live and how you can live. I suggest that you don't sacrifice that choice for the sake of any cheap demagogue, be he political or commercial, reactionary or revolutionary. In other words, *reflect* rather than respond immediately. Reflect on your alternatives, on the possibilities. *Discriminate* among appeals. Discern differences. Make *distinctions*. Get into the habit of reflection and you'll be stronger, your decisions will have more quality, regardless of what they are.

You see, there's more to life than the pleasure of the moment. There's also the pleasure of memory, of historical recall; and a pleasure in contemplating the future. In other words, by means of reflection you can bring into play more dimensions to life than what the mere *present alone* can offer. And I say this because I think you're in danger of fetishizing the present and making a habit out of it. Don't. Avoid it. Don't close off the past so easily or give up considering the future for the sake of *now*. Give the past and the future their full due, let them operate freely and justly upon your sensibility, your imagination, and the present will be all the more enhanced, made all the more substantial, all the more complex and rich. Instead of playing only the infantryman, marching into every battle directly upon the blowing of the bugle, also play the part of the general, who considers the whole battlefield, and the statesman, for whom war is only one alternative and that the last one. Why limit yourself, your variety, your horizons?

[*A pause.*]

And don't think for a moment that reflection, or the habit of reflection, is easy. It's not. It's like reading, there are many more "fun" things that I can think of. Forget your high-school sermons about how much *fun* it all is, reading Shakespeare or working on a paper. It's not. But so what? Give up, too, the notion that everything that's pleasurable is fun, or must be fun. It's a dangerous untruth. Writing a paper is hard work, and there's no getting around the matter. And the grander the work, the project, the harder it is. Learn that too. Which is not to say that there's no pleasure in it ultimately. On the contrary, it generates, finally, the highest pleasure. But only of a very special and carefully defined kind. Not the pleasure of happiness or self-congratulation. No. More of a unique, elite pleasure, not open to everyone. A pleasure in the habit itself of work, of reflection, of reading. A pleasure in being able to think. A pleasure in ideas. A pleasure in the life of the mind, in the same way that many of you tonight believe in the pleasure of sheer action. Perhaps that's a blunt way of putting the matter: learn to reflect and to get pleasure from reflection in the same way that you take pleasure in political activism or a rock concert. I'm not saying that you ought to give up one for the other—although occupying buildings and political activism are not necessarily the same activity—but rather, let the other shop get some business too. Let reflection make a living also. [*Light laughing.*] Activism has grown wealthy and overabundant with your business lately, it's become a supermarket, a Grand Union of activity. Well, give the corner grocer a chance. *Take your time and think matters over before you rush to buy.*

Let me close these general remarks with a quotation from Freud, who, I can see, is not your favorite philosopher. "The voice of the intellect," he wrote in 1928, "is a soft one, but it does not rest until it has gained a hearing. Ultimately, after endlessly repeated rebuffs, it succeeds. This is one of the few points in which one may be optimistic about the future of mankind." So that all I'm asking now is for all of you to listen to that voice during these proceedings here, and during the next shrill speech that comes your way.

And now, let me turn to more mundane matters, the occupation of this museum . . .

The beginning of an amusing and disappointing sermon. I've allowed it to go on at length simply because it's the Dean's opening words, and you can get a good idea of both his general allegiances as well as his curious public tone. I call your attention in particular to remarks like "It's a hard but necessary lesson to learn, which I'm not sure many of you understand yet." The pomposity is staggering. And those Victorian images, such as that of infantryman, general, and statesman, are heartwarming in a kind of Kiplingesque manner. Not to mention the fragments of Jamesian exquisiteness—the past operating "freely" upon one's "sensibility" and "imagination," or "gossamer complexity" and the spider stuff. Clearly the role of public office can do strange things to a man.

It's rather surprising, isn't it, that he wasn't cut off abruptly in the midst of these remarks. Which shows you how mistaken he was, to begin with, concerning forbearance. What honest boy could take such warmed-over pap nowadays and not either walk out or else remove the speaker to some hospital or monastery? To talk about the Western enterprise of "building bridges and cities" here just when we're in the midst of destroying them over there, in Nam, is not exactly uplifting or wise. And that vocabulary, "forbearance," "responsibility"—that's pulpit talk.

Victorian terminology, Jamesian feeling, pulpit morality—a triumvirate of qualities not usually associated with the Dean's personal life. Consider the discrepancy.

For "humility," I advise the reader to look back at those pages of Family Talk, where the Dean narrates his lesson on slapping women in order to control them. Concerning "curiosity," that "great principle of education," see the section where Dean Kovell explores the entire lower regions of Gwen Tresvant's brown body, fascinated by every nook, cranny, and crevice. Regarding the awesome power of "reason," the reader can observe throughout Family Talk how this "power" influ-

ences his relations with his six mistresses, or with his own emotions. And finally that wonderful opening about "balance." A remarkable virtue, declares Mr. Kovell. One which his life is emphatically lacking, and which, therefore, he urges upon the rest of us with great fervor. Consider the extremities of emotion, the plunges into moods, the endless street pickups, the incredible egotism of that life. It is always enlightening to witness the calls to law, order, and balance by the cripples of the world. No, for "balance" what the Dean must have in mind is better understood from a little scene from his life, where the Dean takes not one but two girls for his night pleasure. The sexual orgy with Gwen and Angela is about the closest thing to balance in the Dean's life.

Can there be some insidious tie-up between the Dean's present rage for order and balance and his recent experiment with monogamy, which had been rumored? A speculation worth considering. Too bad Kovell doesn't look into it himself. Even his delivery seems more formal and more stiff than usual.

And to try to apply Kove's "virtues" to our government's behavior in the past decade would be to insult the reader's intelligence. Look in on the evening news any day of the week and see if you can find, in our government's policies, any trace of forbearance, patience, humility, or reason. Whenever I try to tune into Freud's "soft voice of the intellect," it is blocked out by the "voices" of our national leaders. The Voice of America, over there and here, is not exactly a voice that would have pleased the reasonable and intelligent doctor from Vienna.

A moment ago I spoke of the decline of excellence in our society, its decline as fact and value, and I think that you too have succumbed to the fashion. You seem to be fond of disregarding excellence altogether, writing it off as a puritanical goal of the older generation, or else, downgrading it, mocking it. This is disheartening. And I think one probable reason for this last has to do with your mistaken and misguided attitude toward the poor and the downtrodden. Instead of trying to pull them up to aspire toward excellence, you've fallen into the familiar trap of letting some of them call their own shots regarding excellence and culture. This amounts, in fact, to no more than the old reactionary policy of racist segregation, of permitting them to stew in their own ignorance, and by that, proving that they are in fact inferior. Of course, that is not your intended result, but that is the real consequence. As I say, this is misguided idealism and dangerous sentimentality. You do black people no good at all by renaming their backwardness and their ignorance "culture," and pretending that this is every bit as valuable as real culture. This is painfully false.

But this is just one aspect. There is also the manner in which you treat excellence right here, in your own back yard as it were, in the universities. Specifically, take the manner in which you honor your teachers—whether it be praising them in the student handbook, setting attendance records in their classrooms, or giving a Teacher of the Year award. (And by the way, concerning that award, don't you think a very fine set of books or perhaps a handsome desk would be a more appropriate award than a thousand-dollar check? Why use money as a token of your esteem?) Anyway, in honoring them, do you really know what it is that you should look for in a professor? Or what attracts you? Have you thought seriously about this? I think it's rather interesting.

Take last year, for instance, when you voted Professor Eric Asarnow, then a colleague in my department, the Teacher of the Year. All right, it was your choice, and I'm not interested in taking that prerogative away from you. But now that Professor Asarnow has left us, for a more "exciting" existence outside university life, I want to give you my assessment of your choice. Because, friends, again I think you made a mistake. A *representative* mistake.

An assessment really of a professor's "evolution," for Professor Asarnow changed profoundly in the time I knew him. When he first came here—and I had known him briefly as a graduate student comrade on the West Coast—he was a quiet fellow, with a small mustache, neatly cut hair, fond of Harris tweeds and good pipes, a kind of Edwardian gentleman via the Bronx. A typical enough journey. Now he was not a first-rate mind to begin with, but that's all right; in many cases that's very good, since frequently the best teachers of undergraduates are not the smartest of men. Real first-raters, you see, are too busy with themselves and with their own ideas and projects to be interested in teaching others. It affords them too little intellectual return, and essentially they're too selfish to do without that. Their own education comes first. (Scientists are another matter.) But what Asarnow did possess was both a knowledge of his subject and a fondness for literature, a kind of implicit belief in its possibilities for refining the sensibility. Most important, for certain authors, such as Chaucer, he had a real love. Now Chaucer is not a bad author to read, to teach, or to love. There's an awful lot of wit and humor and psychological insight that holds up well there, which is pretty impressive for a six-hundred-year-old writer. That's about the best endurance record around. In fact, there's enough real obscenity . . . scatalogical humor and sexual farce to make him a very contemporary figure, a kind of Philip Roth of the fourteenth century [*cheers*] among other things. All right, now Professor Asarnow taught Chaucer, and got his thirty kids or so to come, and two-thirds of them would be bored stiff, about the usual percentage—but about ten students would be surprised to find that Chaucer was pretty good reading, and two or three would even go so far as to take a real interest in Middle English because of him. And so two or three innocents would be "turned on" to literature, while the rest would get by, by cramming the night before for their exams and by producing those dreary useless pages called term papers. And Asarnow would have accomplished his job, without too much fanfare or too much credit; with no interference from awards committees or student ratings. It's a very undramatic profession, remember—not like movie-directing or heart-transplanting. Bernard Kovell is less well known than Christiaan Barnard. [*Shouts of No, No!*]

Thank you.

Now let me overstep my bounds [*cheers*]—you love that, don't you? [*more cheers*]—and say a few words about the professor's personal life, because that has an important place in this story. Asarnow was married, not very happily, was the father of a young daughter whom he loved, and was also in analysis. He had already published a book, a very scholarly and somewhat original work on Chaucer, showing a newly found German influence on his work, beside that of Jean de Meung and the French. It had been his doctoral thesis. And he had begun work on a second book, something pertaining to his great love of classical music, a study of the masque in Renaissance plays. Again, nothing to change the world, but interesting in a minor key. And scholarship has other functions than the political or polemical.

So what you have is a rather typical professor, very unspectacular, a little gardener toiling on his own small plot of ground. Dull perhaps in the eyes of the world, but knowledgeable and interested in his subjects—literature, music. With a certain kernel of integrity—another vanishing virtue to keep an eye out for—which usually exists at the heart of a teacher's life.

Enter the changes, for good and bad. After years of analysis, Professor Asarnow entered group therapy and became a "new man." Or liberated. Without questioning the full validity of that term, let me recall to you some of those changes. First, he stopped being a properly married man and became instead a free-wheeling bachelor. Second, he stopped being a proper academician and turned into . . . well, a man pursuing his own new interests and self-expression. The big change was his loss of interest in high or serious culture, and its replacement with popular culture. Rock groups became more interesting than Beethoven sonatas, the phenomenon of Joplin or The Who more intriguing than Chaucer or Shakespeare. And so he inaugurated a course in pop culture, which, as you well know, became the hit of the college. From thirty kids trying to read Chaucer's Middle English, three hundred showed up regularly to hear the Beatles or to watch a Bergman movie. Not only the class but Mr. Asarnow, with his new style, was an attraction. No longer was he a safe, proper, dull academician imparting a body of learned knowledge to a note-taking class, but he was a challenging, humorous, even dangerous man, whose classes occasionally turned into fierce and filthy encounter sessions.

All right, you get the drift of this. And you remember Professor Asarnow yourselves. But the question is, Was he the best teacher of the year?

I would say No, definitely No. Not the best teacher, if that term means great intellectual stimulation or exciting exercises in how to think or examine a subject. No, he wasn't that. Which is not to say, however, that he wasn't other things.

For example, apart from the obvious distinction of "the most changed teacher," I would have voted for him for the most

183

"gutsy" teacher and probably the most "entertaining" teacher. Both of which have their place. It takes guts to change over completely from one kind of teacher to another, after you've been doing it for a decade or more. And it takes guts to be impolite in a classroom today, even when the situation demands it. As some of you know, I move in that area occasionally myself. [*Cheers.*] Yes, it takes a man to say to a phony student who's offering you absolutely slipshod work, "Don't hand me that shit! Save it for the coffeehouse." Now, I'm unsure whether I'm quoting Mr. Asarnow or myself, but we're a pretty polite profession generally, and we could use some more *valid* impoliteness. Because of its absence, I'd say we have many frustrated and bored teachers, as well as an immense amount of dead weight that floats through college. Too bad. Well, good schools shouldn't put up with it, it's unfair to the real students and real teachers. And since Asarnow had become an enemy of that classroom piety, I admired him.

He also became quite an entertainer, and that too can have its positive side. After an hour with Hegel's dialectic or Tolstoy on Art, some good entertainment—built on knowledge and developed with a sense of humor—is a fine way of learning. And Asarnow had become in his own way very good in talking about popular culture, especially about rock and jazz. There was no one like him for accompanying a jazz solo verbally! Furthermore, too few intelligent people look at that culture, and as a result it's left in the hands of second-rate minds, who simply enforce it. Whereas Asarnow, with his musical training and knowledge, was able to discern differences between rock drummers, say, and to describe intelligently the evolution of jazz, and he was also shrewd enough to see when the sociology of a commercial phenomenon was more important than the product itself. In other words, he was a very useful critic here.

All this is to show that there were benefits from his changes, which I too acknowledge, as well as shortcomings. The latter he recognized, too, with refreshing candor. He was the first to admit that his course attracted too many heads and freaks rather than real students; that it was considered, rightfully, a gut and fun course; that his long hair and black cape and wild humor made him the subject of the course as much as anything. And he could be pretty ironic about all this, as when he received the teacher award, smiled, and said something like, "So I'm the guru of the year?—okay, pops, that's fine with me. Just give me the loot!" [*Jeers.*] I know, my imitation is not very good.

There's an ironic story here, which I'll let you in on. [*Cheers.*] At the same time that he was a great hit here, he was asked to another school, a much more prestigious one than Cardozo, where they were considering Harry to head up a new interdisciplinary department. Do you know what happened? He was turned down. And do you know by whom? By the students. And why? Because he was too honest for them finally, at least according to the report I heard. Of course *the students* did the interviewing—the school is very progressive Ivy, you see—and when they asked a silly question, he laid into them. *And they couldn't take that.* Interesting. Just as many colleagues here were upset by his impious ways, so the kids there were too uptight when he laid it to them. You see, friends, the sons are not very different from the fathers frequently.

Now what I've described here is a kind of defense of the new Professor Asarnow, to show you that when I say that despite his attributes, he still didn't merit a teacher-of-the-year award, I'm trying to make an impartial point. Pop culture and the Beatles still are not Chaucer or Shakespeare in terms of long-range importance. And Harry's new style is finally not a style fit to epitomize classroom instruction. It's fit for other things, as I've indicated. So all I'm asking is for you to be more accurate in your voting. More precise. To make more distinctions. That's all.

[*A pause and drink of water.*]

Let me mention another case and describe another teacher whom you've followed avidly. One who is here tonight, I believe, taking part and sponsoring this illegal occupation—though for the moment I can't spot him. Now you've liked me too [*cheers*] and so I'm not speaking from jealousy here. But your affection for Professor Goodspeed is based upon a deception too, though here it's much more a case of political rather than cultural radicalism. Yet not even really political, since Mr. Goodspeed doesn't know the first thing about real leftism, political process, or revolution. But he uses all the phrases and words and intonations—the truth is, there's a rabbi hiding beneath the

185

guerrilla-mask—phrases that identify him nowadays with an In political position. I mean, the prophecy of apocalypse just around the corner, the cry of American fascism here and now, the mindless defense of everything demanded and done by blacks, browns, and the poor, a total dismissal of everything middle-class American, from installment plans to public schools to voting in presidential elections. This son of a very affluent Midwestern family has just made the astounding discovery that he is a "bourgeois professor," and walks around as if he had just been informed that he had cancer. Boys and girls, it's not that bad being a "bourgeois professor." I'm one, and have been one for quite a while, and I've managed to survive. After all, the bourgeoisie, apart from having a philistine and material side, has another side, which has produced, in recent history, the likes of Marx and Lenin, Shakespeare and Dostoevsky, Darwin and Nietzsche. In fact, most of the important artists and thinkers whom you and I read and rely on have been reared from that horrible "bourgeois" womb. So don't be too ashamed of your middle-class background; it's really all that there is, except for a poor prince and queen here and there, who'd much rather have been born bourgeois, if they could have had their way.

Now my only question to you is why you fall for the kind of corn flakes that Professor Goodspeed feeds you? All right, I understand why you are crazy about his literature classes—they're exercises in religious belief, decorated with mystical intonations, metaphysical warnings, esoteric biblical references, all the trimmings that students too frequently prefer to true substance. Now, apart from the fact that religious belief is easier to get than literary understanding, there's also the "show" that Goodspeed puts on up there. But a very different sort of show from Asarnow's. This one is somber, pontifical, humorless, and full of "dark" portentousness. Exhorting the heavens with those mandatory figures like Blake and Yeats, Goodspeed is that rare breed, a literary cosmologist. Fine, let him preach to you about madness and mystery and the universe. But must you pay the same attention when he switches to the university and claims that it is degenerate and poisonous and must be done away with? [*Cheers.*] In other words, when he's talking about something that you do know about, that's tangible and at your fingertips, can't you think for yourself? Is it really such an awful place? God knows, Pincus, you've told me twice what you think of the fellow—then why do you allow him in here in the first place? [*Heavy jeering at the Dean.*] Good, I feel better.

If you're students, why be sheep? You're not out in society yet, you don't have to start behaving like the majority of citizens. Consider matters. Reflect on what a teacher tells you. On what his class finally has given to you. Think about what you're learning. I'm not saying that there's only one kind, or that you can't get different things from different teachers. But look, when you write in your student critique that Goodspeed is a "fantastic experience, unforgettable," when at the same time you judge that Professor Truscott is "dull" and "not exciting enough," then I know that something's wrong, seriously wrong. Sure, Truscott is not a Dr. Metaphysics in class, but then his concern is with literary judgment and literary taste. Forget about his "personality." So what if he is shy, uncertain at times, quiet, understated. If we're considering the life of the mind and literary matters, which I think you should be considering wholly and essentially, then he's as exciting a teacher as has ever entered a Cardozo classroom in literature. Furthermore, not being notorious, like Goodspeed, he doesn't have to live up to that burden. And so, what you get in a class with him is not some foolish adulation of a Whitman or Ginsberg, but an exercise in logic and literary judgment, and an example of how serious taste is formed and articulated. You learn that most difficult of lessons, *how to read a book.* It's something you'd never get in a hundred sessions with Goodspeed! Boys and girls, the life of the mind may appear to you dull, and it is, in the sense that it does not provide sensational or instant gratification. But if you see it through, if you read to the point where you can't do without your two or three hours of reading a day, literally can't, or you feel depressed—well, when written words come to be a passion and a necessity with you, then you'll appreciate the real thing, a Truscott.

Forget the charmers, the charlatans, the mystics, the declaimers, the prophets, the preachers, the rabbis, the metaphysicians. And give up idolatry. *Learn how to read a book; acquire the habit of reading and you'll have gotten an education.*

I like that "life of the mind" stuff. Pretty heady. Recalls my sophomore classics teacher celebrating the glory of ancient

Greece, omitting the Slave-State details. The sad humor here is that the Dean is sincere, he believes it all. As if those "values" had anything to do with his real life. What self-delusion a man can live with, even the most sophisticated!

It is also amusing that he expects us to believe it too. Well, we don't. And happily, down deep, where it counts, neither does the Dean.

He asks what we look for in a teacher, his attractive qualities. Consider an incident with Kove himself—which, though I promised silence, it is now necessary to disclose. In brief. Apart from his official office in the administration building, the Dean maintained his old office in the English Department, in Tanner Hall, where he would see his own class students. One day, about 5:30 or so, when everybody else was gone, I thought I'd stop by and see if he was in, as he was occasionally. Well, the door was closed but I heard some faint movement and perhaps a voice, and knocked. No answer. Again I knocked, again silence, no answer. I could have been mistaken, and left. I was opening the glass exit door to leave the building when I had another impulse and re-traced my steps. In the corner of the small landing outside room 238, I sat and took out a paperback, trying to concentrate but staying alert. Feeling silly. But sure enough, about ten minutes later, the door opened and a girl emerged, her hand adjusting her long hair. A slim dark girl in boots and miniskirt, she seemed surprised when she saw me, then asked if I was waiting to see her. She had a pleasant smile, I recall, and wore thin silver glasses. By then Kove was at the door and said, no, I was probably waiting to see him. He gave a little goodbye wave to "Miss Lowenfeld" and said something about revising the outline and showing it to him again. The girl, obviously a teaching assistant, opened the door to the next room, really a cubicle, and disappeared inside. In his brick-walled office, Kovell asked what I wanted, his face slightly pale. My eye caught sight of a small object on the floor, and, for some reason, I leaned over and picked it up. A bobby pin. I handed it to him. "What happened?" I smiled. "I ate her," he answered. And told me in a sentence how a dissertation proposal and exposed thigh had led him to sexual wildness. We went on to talk about The Possessed, *the reason for my visit.*

That's why we loved him. He took chances. Crazy risks.

Was willing to face shame. Was ruled by his passions. Was not in control of his personal life. These things impressed me. The Dean was a man; crazy perhaps when it came to sex, but that was fine too. He was a man whom we might one day convince to join with us in our own logical madness. The incident convinced me.

(And when I found out later that he was carrying on an affair with a dark-haired senior—those things never stay hidden if you're alert—I made a private mental note and doubled my efforts to win him over to my extreme ideas. Interestingly enough, neither the office incident nor the undergraduate affair found their way into Family Talk. Which just proves that there are probably many more girls, many more embarrassing details, in that already erotic-heavy life.) I still believe strongly in Kove's potential for our cause.

In sum, we are no longer interested in teachers who mine their specialty, this plot of literature or that ground of history. Or who are considered profound thinkers or excellent lecturers. All those criteria are obsolete, gone out with knickers, bowler hats, colonial rule, Victorian authority. Lingering here in English departments like genteel skirts. No, we are attracted to men, not complacent professors who received the stamp of permanency long ago and have gone on unchallenged, teaching the same books, the same courses, year after year. Men, not tenured bureaucrats, respectable fossils, professor-hens. Men who will think for themselves and not be slaves of tradition and lackeys of convention. We are attracted to men and women who welcome uncertainty, court disaster. Who have been defeated and shamed. Who smile oddly. Excellence is empty without a background of degradation, struggle.

As for the teachers cited by the Dean, it's obvious that he has a mistaken idea of what we really thought about them. Truscott, everyone knew, was intelligent, but he was too timid, too beaten down, to amount to anything. How could he understand Dostoevsky, let alone be useful to us, if he was frightened off by the first grad student who tried to have an affair with him? (How do we know this? The girls. They talk. Especially when they've just conquered some older mind with their young bodies.) And terrified of his colleagues' judgment. The other two professors present different situations. Asarnow was an honest fellow going

189

through changes, so why not encourage him for that? His capacity for wild humor was an inventive quality. It's to our credit, I think, that a man whose politics are essentially conservative, as his were, should nevertheless earn our esteem. He was the rock representative on campus, no more, no less; the professor who made a significant popular phenomenon a subject of study. His achievement was not very different from his earlier work on Chaucer, as Kove describes it. I'm afraid Kovell criticizes from jealousy here. He doesn't have to. Asarnow was simply a modern Ariel, a charming spirit, next to Kovell's Prospero/Caliban role. Goodspeed is a perennial favorite, and shouldn't be underestimated. It is not so much literary sense that he delivers (who needs that?), but in his great guttural voice, provocation, warning, lament. His lectures serve as inspirational prophecies, rivers of poetry amid landlocked arid prose. What's wrong with a mystic, a preacher, a wounded prophet in an age of dry technocrats and social scientists? No one thinks of Goodspeed as Jehovah or Lenin, but rather as Isaiah, a mighty prophet demanding holiness, and warning of the approaching scourge. Those who think differently had better reread their texts.

Concerning reading and the written word: why transmit a dead value by means of a dying system? Why prolong the agony? Films, tapes, and recorded sound represent the future, not writing, not literature. If fetishism of the present is bad, what about fetishism of the past? A worse malady, I should say.

So much for the "life of the mind."

What's that, do I want a smoke? Some hash? No, boys and girls, I'll do without that, thank you. But what I wonder is, would you like some milk and cookies with your hashish? Grace there has some brownies, and we could probably rustle up some Oreos from my office. What do you say, how many hands do I see? I see you're giggling. Well, perhaps it's late. It's almost 1 A.M., you know. Don't any of you believe in your eight hours of sleep any more? Come now, you can't all be radical about sleep and milk, can you? Or are you planning to "rip-off" the cookies when I take a nap? Yeah, that's probably it, I could tell from your faces. They're too innocent and sleepy-looking to be planning anything but small heists.

In fact, I was thinking of telling you somewhere along the line a little bedtime story. Do you think this is the moment? What is it about, did someone ask? It's a children's bedtime story, what could it be about but a bear settlement in the Adirondacks and some of the bears' dilemmas? How else to put little children to sleep if not to tell of the adventures of animals? Now, you just put your heads down on the blanket rolls, or on some comfy lap, finish up your hash and your grass like good little boys and girls, and I'll tell you how Adrian, a fine female bear in her teens, met Maxwell, a very young Boy Scout who had strayed from his group during an overnight trip. That's it, that looks fine right there. Just like that. Now you just be still for a while and listen. You see, Maxwell had come up from the Bronx with troop number 232 . . .

This cute interlude went on for almost ten minutes. To my surprise I saw several students who had obeyed the Dean's instructions and fallen off to sleep on laps. Even Linda Sperling, our Jane Fonda, with a copy of Lenin's State and Revolution *in her dungaree pocket at all times, fell under the spell and was gone. For that's what that tale was, a becalming spell cast over the audience. Kove could turn on the Words when he wanted to, that shrewd bedtime storyteller.*

Good. Some of you were tired after all, see? Now let me go on, there are points I wish to make to those of you who are still awake.

I want to warn you against two tendencies in your political style. The first concerns the use of political confrontation for purposes of personal therapy. The conversion of political acts into psychodramas, acted-out fantasies, wish-fulfillments, is a hazardous undertaking. Don't confuse one with the other. Now, of course, I'm talking to a minority of you when I say this, but you're a significant minority. It is you who frequently make the decisions. It is you—let's face it—who frequently are the leaders, the smartest few. The wide-awake.

And why do you do this? In part, because you believe your own press notices, which say that you're causing a lot of trouble and which also say that you're introducing a "new consciousness" into society. Boys and girls, I'll be perfectly honest with you. You're *not* causing any *real* trouble, you're just *annoying* a lot of people. And as for "new consciousness," that's *Village Voice* or *New Yorker* magazine wisdom. It's hokum. Pure baloney. Your new consciousness, which advocates "love" and "feeling" and "community," has been proclaimed before, by Jesus and his followers. That's right, what you're asking for, those that speak for the new consciousness, is a change of heart by your fellow citizens, a conversion to Christian ways. Now there's nothing wrong with that, please understand me, except that, so far, it's not worked too well. The Christians have been trying it for several thousand years now, and do you see where it's gotten the world? There's still capitalism, corruption, exploitation, there're still brutal political systems, there's still a fair share of malignant persons. The so-called new consciousness is a way of avoiding very important issues, a very old and very naïve cop-out. It is also anything but *new;* in fact, it is ancient.

Another thing is that I believe you've been infected by certain poisonous ideas which have been infecting the entire intellectual climate lately. I'm speaking about the philosophy of apocalypse and extremity which has implicitly taken hold in certain fashionable circles. Thus you believe that change must be effected *now or never*; that fulfillment of your "demands" must occur instantaneously; that the way we're living now is intolerable and can't be permitted to go on. Such thinking, I'll tell you, strikes me as melodramatic and exaggerated, rather than accurate or thoughtful; it's propaganda not analysis. At the risk of repeating myself—as I probably have more than once this evening—organized society wasn't built in a day, don't expect it to change overnight. Give it time, have some patience. This is not to deter you from criticizing seriously the conditions here; any good citizen has it as his duty to perform such criticism. But before you write it off as a means for changing things, give it some time. As for calling it "intolerable," that's going a bit far. Just look around you, at your own life, before you take the word of some radical ideologue who's all ready to explain that your eyes and ears are deceiving you. Then, too, I advise some reading and some general observation. See if life here and now is more miserable than it was a hundred years ago in England, six hundred years ago in China, two thousand years ago in Rome. See what life was like in the so-called great regimes of the past. And now, too, look at the Russian way of life today, or the Chinese. Better yet, visit them for yourselves, if you can. If you're serious about believing stories about the wonders of the Chairman, then go there and live. Try it out for yourself. My point is not to rely on anyone's stories or propaganda finally, but to see for yourself. *Experience.* Then judge whether life here is "intolerable." Or even truly awful.

But I started by talking about therapy and politics. Look, it's very simple—if you're unhappy, if you're disturbed personally, become *a patient not a radical.* See a psychiatrist, not an ideologue or demagogue. Don't look to the revolution to save you, it won't. It's not meant to do that, or equipped for it. *Its aims are to change political and economic systems, not salvation.* And stop mixing up the two, you're doing neither any good—yourself or radicalism. I repeat, if you want to be saved or uplifted, see your local priest or shrink. But forget politics.

Now I think this is necessary to say because, unfortunately, too many of you are involved today out of neurotic or missionary impulses, and what's happened is that it has affected seriously the content, style, and tone of radical politics. And this influence —of the neurotic and the missionary—is ruining and degrading serious leftism as much as it is impairing ordinary liberal decency. You're in the midst of turning leftist thinking into absolute child's play, with squealing, sandbox demanding, and shrill self-righteousness. And it's going to lead to a lot worse if you keep it up, as the signs already indicate. I mean that if a child doesn't get his way, doesn't obtain instant gratification, he immediately goes into a temper tantrum, to see if that will get him anywhere. Well, I'm seriously afraid that more and more you're heading in that direction, with tantrums replacing programs in your thinking and action.

This has already led, in certain circles, as you know, to out-and-out terrorism as a principle of behavior. Need I tell you at this late date that there is no more futile and self-destructive politics than a bomb here, a bullet there? Surely you know, the serious ones among you at least, that every serious revolutionary, from Marx to Lenin, rejected outright and rejected vigorously all nihilist terrorists and all violent anarchists as true revolutionaries? Putting a bomb in a Standard Oil building will destroy some brick and mortar along with some innocent paperwork and innocent persons; and blowing up this or that C.I.A. center might destroy a counter-revolutionary paper or two; but neither act will bring down any regime, change any system, or make any fundamental difference in the society. But it will have the disastrous consequence of bringing down upon the necks of all leftists the police and the F.B.I., and destroying whatever organization may have been built up. Furthermore, it will alienate forever good citizens, whom you will want on your side. If you're serious about one day overthrowing the capitalist state, then, like Marx and Lenin, you won't for a moment stand such childish and dangerous nonsense. That's why mad anarchists like Bakunin, not to mention crazy terrorists like Nechaev, were complete anathema to them. All that the terrorists ever did was cause great mischief to everyone and some senseless deaths. Look, real revolutionaries are not interested in children's games, they're interested in how men live and in those economic and political systems that dictate the everyday living conditions of those lives. To kill the President of the country will only mean that another President will take over. To kill an innocent bystander in a building is doubly senseless and criminal. And both acts will provoke hatred in the very people you'll want one day to convert. In other words, in political terms, there's nothing more stupid or immoral. Need such commonplace warnings about terrorism be repeated, after so much history? Haven't you done your homework?

My friends, I hate to lecture you this way, but if *I* don't, who will?

Tantrums and terrorism lead me to my second warning, and this has to do with your increasing adoration of criminal elements in our society and in the world. More and more, you're making criminals over into heroes; in fact precisely *because* of their criminality, they take on heroic dimensions. This is terrible. You're playing with matches, bound to go up in your hands, as they already have, in the hands of some of your colleagues. Now I certainly don't hold you responsible entirely for this kind of perverse hero-worship. Certainly the trend has been set among fashionable adults nowadays. That famous French homosexual is praised to the skies for his glorification of crime and perversity. Our famous New York writer/promoter is considered magnificent because his life and his books hold up to us images of violence, sadism, murder as goals of aspiration. And look at the publicity given to that exiled American black ever since he described his rape of white girls and his days in jail. Now why should a thief like Genet, an entrepreneur and near killer like Mailer, a rapist like Cleaver become heroes to you? Just because publishers pay them glorious sums and chic crowds pay them homage? You know why these creatures appeal to these adults, don't you?—They appeal to their middle-class provincialism and boredom. These criminal types appear, to the dull monotony of their lives, as figures of romantic bohemianism. Well, let me tell you, there is nothing romantic or bohemian about having a knife shoved in your back or having your head cracked open. It's just brutal and painful. And don't underestimate physical pain when it comes to naming the worst single punishment in life. On my list it's the worst. Let's not romanticize it. Your lives are not that dull yet, you don't need criminals to fill the bill for entertainment and heroism. Believe me, it's much less fun than rooting for your local high-school halfback. [*Cheers.*]

But not only do you seem to me more and more infatuated with these cheap crooks, but anyone and everyone who breaks the law gains your esteem these days! For example, all a foreigner has to do is to wear a bandolier, brandish a rifle, and call himself a guerrilla fighting for social justice, and you adore him as if he were John Wayne. Now, boys and girls, that's not sound thinking. Or careful observation. Or shrewd strategy. You're confusing gangster movies with real life. It's not a matter of who's colorful or dramatic as to whom you're going to root for; it's a matter of who's legitimate and who's not, when he says he's working for social justice. The Vietcong are one group, the Red Guard another, blacks in this country a third, El Fatah yet a fourth, and so on. Israel is *not* Vietnam, where a civil war has been going on; America is *not* Nazi Germany, where political rights and civil liberties were *legally* suspended for a specific ethnic group. I repeat, *Make distinctions.* To be a guerrilla in Vietnam has some strategic and moral purpose; to be a guerrilla

195

in America is to be a g-o-r-i-l-l-a, an ape, not a shrewd fighter forced into his role and struggling for real political freedom. Nor are all guerrillas the same in terms of rightness. Perhaps El Fatah, objectively speaking, has as much or more moral right to attack regimes like Syria's, Iraq's, or Egypt's as it does Israel's. For those countries, not Israel, claim to be its brothers, yet have never admitted their fraternal brothers to be full citizens in their own countries. [*Assorted jeers.*] Yes, I know your sentiments here, those of you booing now. But you won't bully me, the way you do some of your pals, with your confused romanticism.

Friends, students, young citizens: because degradation is fashionable in adult society today, there's no need for you to follow the pattern. Resist it. Show them you're better. And tougher. And smarter. Go your own way. Be your own men. Leave your bored and tired elders to worship excrement and degradation. *Be better than they.*

But you're no better when you do things like pasting on the front doors that set of posters. What do you mean, "Prometheus NO, Nechaev YES"? Oh, it's ingenious whoever thought of it. [*Looking at me.*] But tell me, why do you prefer that crazy assassin to that ancient symbol of light and moral suffering? Tell me, whoever put it up. And what in the world do you mean by that other poster, with that young girl on that older man's lap, and the words STAVROGIN LIVES? Is that some kind of perverse joke? I find it devoid of humor, if it is. Lives? Lives where? He doesn't deserve to live, that demented, vicious criminal madman! Let Stavrogin step up here and I'll personally take care of him! [*Cheers.*]

I'm sorry, forgive me for that kind of talk.

But why promote assassins and madmen? Why not post up men who stand for something positive, for real values? Why not Freud or Einstein? And even if Stavrogin's a joke, there are consequences. That's what's so disturbing about you frequently, the way you forget that acts have *consequences*, which are accountable for.

Finally, there are those among you who know better, much better; that's what makes such deeds so thoroughly ghastly and incomprehensible. Why, Pincus, why does an intelligent young man like yourself get involved in degrading, irrational deeds? Oh,

I know you hate me to single you out this way—you so value your privacy and anonymity—but you know that you're the cause of so much of this—why shouldn't you be singled out and put up against the wall? You've done it enough to me. Explain yourself sometime, if you can. To me, or to yourself. You used to have a certain fondness for the *examined life*. I wonder if you still do. I can't believe it when I see characters like Stavrogin flaunted around the place! Some heroes.

The Dean is angry. Good. He could use some more of that emotion.

He is also naïve, painfully so. That Nechaev and Stavrogin are used on cardboard posters doesn't make them "heroes." Does he really want me to paste up Sigmund Freud? What's that supposed to mean, except a perverse joke? Posters are for simple propaganda, for eye-catching symbols; they're not moral or political essays, and nobody says they are.

The whole idea of "heroes" belongs more to high-school seniors with their halfbacks, and college professors with their Hemingways, than to myself. It's silly. There are certain men I admire, others I don't, who may nevertheless teach me something, others whose writings are interesting but not their lives, and vice versa. It's not a matter of heroes and villains, that's out of the movies. Stavrogin's joining of extreme sexual and moral and political ideas seems to me interesting, contemporary. "Where does he live?" Inside all interesting men. More: it was my opinion that, knowing a little about the Dean, he especially would appreciate a picture of Stavrogin holding the eleven-year-old Matryosha on his lap, preparing her with his hands. In a sense, a twentieth-century American cripple looking at his nineteenth-century Russian counterpart. But perhaps this is why Kove seems so unnerved by the poster? Poor Kovell, doesn't he know the basic fact about American life: that every intelligent man must have his secret sexual life, otherwise he'll go crazy?

Now you tell me who's more criminal, poor literary characters like Nikolai Stavrogin, or flesh-and-blood planners of technological murder like Rostow and Rusk? And from whom does the Dean think he can learn more, or would rather spend an hour with, Mr. Stavrogin or our esteemed President? As for X-ing out

Prometheus and inserting Nechaev, all I wished to do was replace mythology with realism when it came to suffering. And a special suffering, as may be seen in this eye-witness description:

Of all the inmates kept in the Fortress since 1825 [Shchego-lev records] Nechaev alone displayed such an indomitable opposition to, and contempt for, the Tsarist order as to be considered by the authorities in a category of his own. His hands and feet were put in heavy irons, and the chain connecting the shackles was made especially short, so that the prisoner was compelled to remain continually in a crouching position, unable ever to get up. Open wounds which never healed covered his hands and legs. For two years he sat like this chained to the wall and chained to himself. From time to time (during the trial, at which he behaved with dignity and defiance) instructions were issued to flog him. Yet even then and throughout his imprisonment he continued to preach revolution to the soldiers who guarded him. They called him "our eagle," "our own intercessor," a "man not of this world."

Nechaev died in jail, of scurvy and exhaustion, about a year after the assassination of Alexander II was carried out, after advising a comrade to forget his (Nechaev's) liberation and carry out plans for the assassination. It is this determination that interests us. This pain. The rest of the man, his ideas and terrorist acts, mean little to me.

As for the three sensational figures mentioned by Kovell, they are useful as verbal terrorists, high-priced camouflage. Of course, two of them are ultimately boring. It's the Dean who seems taken with them, not I. Mailer is a more complicated case, I admit. About therapy. One would think that a white professor who can humiliate a black woman in the year 1969 might want some of that therapy himself. Point number one. Number two, I would think that those men who discuss ways of defoliating lands with chemical gases, of tearing apart human limbs, of disrupting cultures which have taken thousands of years to construct—I would think that those men are in desperate need of "therapy." Like most of our leaders in the White House, the Pentagon, the House and the Senate. Number three, yes, there are those who come to our side out of "neurotic and missionary impulses." But so what? It seems a very fitting description of the Dean himself. And one can also say that most professors and college deans are authoritarian personalities, while most of the great artists who have ever lived have been deep neurotics. But where does that get us? The question is what deeds are accomplished by what people, not their motives. To turn political events into a psychoanalytical session is a typical bourgeois ploy.

I find it amusing when Kove says that neurosis has affected "the content, style, and tone" of our politics. Is he analyzing politics or a novella? There's nothing more spurious than literary men writing about political situations. They are forever embroidering reality, decorating it this way with fine turns of phrase and that way with aesthetic aperçus, until you don't know what you're reading any more, a piece of fiction or an accurate report. When I want my fiction, I'll go to Mann, not to Kovell.

I gather from some of your smiles that you think I've been exaggerating the matter. Do you really? Well, let me be concrete. And deal with details, unpleasant details. We all know about the events of a year or so ago that shook this college to its heels. I mean the crazy bank robbery and murder that sent four people to prison for the rest of their lives, and that almost resulted in the closing of this university.* Even now, look—those few persons clapping and whistling, as if the whole thing were a camp joke! It wasn't and isn't. If you don't believe me, pay a visit to Miss Lefler in the penitentiary, the way I have, or speak to her father. See how funny it is then.

I remember those days well, the F.B.I. in every day, the newsmen taking up more space than the students, and those endless headlines about Nasser and Steele, Nasser and Steele, Nasser and Steele, until I wasn't sure just who had died of a heart attack and just who had held up a bank and killed a policeman. And then, finally, the capture of those coeds, and the visit to Helen

* The Dean is alluding here to a Boston bank robbery, in which two coeds were involved with several ex-cons, one of them a student parolee at the college.

199

Lefler, who three months previous had been showing me her short stories—unfinished stories about disappointing love affairs—now she was crying like a baby, about to be sent to prison on nine counts for a total of eighty years. It was pretty hard, I can tell you, to sit and hear this girl who a short time ago had argued so articulately about character development and plot structure in the classroom, now wondering over and over in a broken voice— the kerchief gone from her hair, a gray gunny sack replacing her smart pants suits and miniskirts—wondering if all this was really happening to her. As if she had been found holding some lottery ticket of disaster, which by chance had been shoved into her hand. Well, friends, if you still believe in the Billy Steele character of your invention, a contemporary version of Robin Hood, instead of the reality, a dangerous shrewd crook, then I recommend that you visit Helen one day at this Framingham State Prison for Women.

Excuse me. [*Wiping his eyes.*]

Oh, I knew Steele all right, knew him pretty well, and I can tell you that were it not for the climate of violence permeating the campus these days, he would never have had a chance at any influence and might very well have learned something about being a decent citizen. But it was the whole lousy climate that "coerced" undergraduates to go along with him, to lionize him, to turn him into something he was not. You see, I believe that the one pathology fed the other, the new violence of campus radicalism nourishing the violence of the criminal, and, vice versa, the madness of the criminal spurring on all sorts of ideological fantasies in the students. That's what made it all so terrifyingly Dostoevskyan. (Although, God knows, you're not trying to connect Stavrogin, a man of ideas, with Steele?) There seemed to be no clear way of distinguishing between the two pathologies after a while. Where did the psychological passion end and the ideological obsession begin?

Certainly, when Steele came around to talk to me, he sounded like a sophomore bubbling over with a thousand newly discovered but undigested ideas, a crazy Mixmaster spinning everything together indiscriminately to form a concoction of half-baked notions and understandings. Camus and personal dignity got mixed in with Fanon and manhood of violence; Mar-

200

cuse's idea of repressive tolerance was trotted out alongside Genet's freedom from bourgeois life by means of crime; even Mailer's Rojack, that cardboard fake, was treated as if he were the personification of some significant ideas. Around and around it went, and it was all right insofar as Billy was trying to understand these ideas; but to try to understand his own life in terms of these figures, that was another matter, one much more foolish. But after all, he did have a psychiatrist, who, I assumed, would see to it that he could keep in mind the boundary between life and literature, that sharp boundary.

I want to tell you that his failure was in part *your* failure, *your* responsibility. For, more and more, I could see you becoming infatuated with Steele—and infatuation is precisely the attitude, the word—an infatuation which was becoming an increasing problem for him to cope with. Since, in part, he never really believed in himself—why else does a man commit crime or gamble, except to punish himself for his belief in his own worthlessness?—and since he believed *only* in himself, what he had to do was to live up to the role of mythical hero that you and the present climate of ideas were helping to construct for him. It was that infatuation, stemming, again, from an overdose of gangster movies and gangster ideas, that led to his and the others' destruction, to my mind. It was an awful cycle to observe. And when I touched upon it in our conversation, warned him to stay out of things, he responded angrily with charges of my bourgeois instincts and counter-revolutionary beliefs. In other words, I was trying to persecute him for political reasons. Not so. Not so at all. I was simply trying to keep him from returning to crime, out of panic and confusion.

Again, I don't blame you entirely. The newspapers, magazines, and television stations didn't leave it alone. The *Globe*, for example, had a headline story on the criminals practically every day for a solid month, full of the most insipid and most venal pseudo-psychology, passing for journalism. And once the trial began, it all started up again, like a forest fire. And then the crowning irony, the typical American syllogism—our Vice President gets into the act with his paranoid and political version of conspiracies and undergrounds, and a New York publishing house responds by offering Steele thousands of dollars to write his autobiography. It pays well to be a criminal-radical, I repeat. The complete American circus, in which Steele was being turned into a culture hero. How often must we do this to our madmen? See, right here we have idiots who clap! As if it were all great fun! You few ought to be lined up and put away, I'll tell you that!

Where was I?

Movies. That's what it all comes to, I'm afraid. You prefer them to reality. I implore you, STOP TAKING THOSE SILLY FILMS FOR TRUTH. I plead with you, STOP THROWING YOUR LIVES AWAY ON THE ADVICE OF MONSIEUR GODARD. Please, I beg you, grow up. CELLULOID IS NOT A MODEL FOR LIFE. If you want to keep movie heroes, hold on to John Wayne and forget the phony revolutionaries who've just read their little red books! Forgive me for yelling at you like this, but it's the only way to get through to some of you. Continue to play with matches and you're going to have to be taken in hand. Otherwise you'll burn us all up with you. If you want to make real changes around here, stop playing cops and robbers against the F.B.I., the police, and the United States Army. You don't know how foolish you look, and how severe the consequences can be!

Look, Helen Lefler writes me once a month from jail, telling me what it's like, along with telling me about her reading. And I hear occasionally from Billy Steele too. Next time you have the impulse to commit a crime in the name of the revolution, come in and read a letter. *Do.* It'll put you in touch with reality. You could use that. Helen Lefler and Billy Steele in jail are more real than Bonnie and Clyde on the screen, and that's what you better understand before it's too late.

I suppose it is a commonplace to remark that men's blind spots are directly related to their inner lives, especially to areas of sensitivity and humiliation. For example, the secrets of sex. Otherwise, how account for this schoolboy interpretation by a sophisticated man of Billy Steele and his notorious bank robbery? The Dean's account reads like a Time *magazine version, in terms of its sentimental rhetoric and cheap insight. Exactly the kind of romantic portrait and missionary impulse—"I was simply trying to keep him from returning to crime"—that he blames the media for producing. The simple-mindedness is overwhelming, as when Kovell pontificates on why people commit crimes—they're unsure of themselves, he claims, and they wish to punish themselves. But what about the opposite impulse, self-aggrandizement? Or even the logic of playing the perfect capitalist, stealing money from a bank that itself steals, only legally? (This was not Steele's argument.) Or committing a crime out of great and urgent economic need—someone dying and needing the money to keep himself alive in this just and humane society? Kovell's pontifical simplism on a subject of great complexity—the motivation for crime—is especially boorish because it comes armed with a deliberate political prejudice.*

I'll elaborate.

Billy Steele was a cunning but obviously schizophrenic criminal who never should have been allowed to leave jail. But if he was, putting him in among young students was even more irresponsible, like setting a fox in a chicken coop. One side of him was normal enough, capable of performing schoolwork and other tasks satisfactorily. But the other side was destructive and out of control; you didn't have to talk with him more than a half hour to have some topic arise which would cause his eyes to look odd, his face to tighten perceptibly, and to see his whole bearing change, from casual wit and irony to vindictive and barely contained anger. The sudden change was frightening. As I've said, a fox set among the chickens. For this serious misreading and misplacing, his psychiatrist, his parole board, and various Cardozo administrators are to blame. Not the students, Billy's victims.

A Vietnam veteran and inveterate thief (local banks and Western Union offices), Steele had had about nine television lives' worth of violence, brutality, and crime. Nine lives' worth at age twenty-six. Obviously, this real-life criminal was no match for children whose notions of crime came from comic books, and possibly some literature. Combining animal savvy with tough good looks, glamorous mod clothes with a cynical insulting manner, he was especially attractive to certain types of girls—the weak, the neurotic, the romantic, the innocent. In other words, most. And with professors, he had a clever instinct for weakness and vulnerablity, which he would locate and file away and draw upon when necessary. Furthermore, to show his diabolical in-

203

stinct, he had a habit of charming people—through his situation as an ex-con, his desire to reform himself, and his apparent interest in finding out why he had turned to crime in the first place—charming them, and then holding them in complete contempt for their stupid folly. For how smart could they be if they liked him? If all this sounds Hollywoodish, it was, but as is obvious, not in the sense that Kovell intended. Do you see the great irony?—A man like Kovell who could interpret Dostoevsky but not Hitchcock? Hitchcock with sex in it, which was an added blind spot for this sex-haunted professor.

So far as revolution was concerned, Steele had heard the word, saw that it was magical like the Bible, and began to use it; in this respect, I agree with the Dean about his earlier warnings. But he does, here, fail to take note that I and several others immediately understood this about Steele. He omits to mention the crucial fact that when Steele came around to our meetings and attempted to break them up by accusations and physical threats—after being permitted to jab away senselessly and incomprehensibly about giving him an "armed cadre" to work with—I told him to get his ass out of there or I'd have him thrown out of the room and out of the school. He threatened me personally several times for this—once shoving me up against the wall when he was drunk—he was a crazy drinker—but I knew he was too smart to carry anything like that through. After all, what could he get from pushing me around—except a sure return to jail? I was no romantic professor whom he could charm, threaten, or cow. He knew that, should he lay a hand on me, I'd swear out a warrant for assault as soon as I could reach a lawyer. And get him back behind bars where he belonged.

No, he couldn't use me, since his objectives had nothing to do with me—these were money and power. For these, he'd use women. And as much radical rhetoric as could further his crude and obvious ambitions. As far as I could tell, from reading his letters from jail and recent book, this consisted of four or five political words and never more than a single coherent sentence concerning political philosophy. The only person who could take an idiot like that for a serious revolutionary is a local police chief, ambitious for higher office. Like the one in Boston.

Sex and sentimentality got him places. The reason he got out of jail in the first place was a woman, the wife of a professor on campus who had started a tutorial program in the prison. Thanks to the same woman, Steele was given a try at Cardozo; the first time they had ever tried such an experiment. Needless to say, he was probably fucking her when he came out on parole, since it could be useful for him as possible future blackmail. For he regarded sex by the same criterion of worth he regarded everything else: utility to Billy Steele. Self-interest. (Some revolutionary.) It was child's play for him to take on the undergraduate coeds. He'd flash that boyish Hollywood smile, tell a girl she suited him, and ask her out; if she refused, his manner would change abruptly. She was afraid of dating an ex-con, he'd start, and begin to attack her middle-class background. "You frigid little Jewish cunt!" or some other little phrase he'd send at her, for a beginning, especially if he were drinking. Perhaps slap a girl right there in the dorm, just like on the Late Show. It wasn't long before he built up quite a reputation on campus as a lady's man. (One wonders if this is a reason why Kovell didn't really step in and warn Steele about what he was doing. Could jealousy have prompted the Dean, himself a cunthound, to take pleasure in Billy's increasing problems? Who knows. Stranger things have happened.) If it seemed like the reputation of a shrewd tough-guy ex-con in a forties melodrama, it was. The difference was that the scene took place on campus now, not in some roadside shack or gambling house.

I was not Steele's shrink—though how could I do worse?— but one obvious source of all this trouble was one Mrs. Julian, a tall fortyish blonde, just this side of cheaply glamorous, good-looking in a tough, fading way. At one time she might have been an Oklahoma beauty queen, but now she was a woman you wouldn't want angry at you, although she had probably been so with several men, having been married four or five times. I saw her come into the snack bar once, on Billy's arm, and figured here was his perfect match. You couldn't tell whether she hashed potatoes or danced in a chorus or was simply someone's moll. She was, in a way. Billy's. The lady, in from Chicago for a campus visit, and staying with Billy in a nearby motel, turned out to be his mother.

No wonder it was difficult for Billy Steele to "give himself"

205

to ladies, to ponder his masculinity and his freedom, and so on. The pull of that mother seemed to me powerful and paralyzing; Billy, a man on the outside, was very much a fiercely ambivalent and frightened son on the inside.

As for Helen Lefler, she was not really worth all that tearful emotion and lofty concern by Kovell. She was one of those instant radicals who, a year previous, would walk by an ABM protest and throw out some condescending jibe to a friend, loud enough for protesters to hear. Her shift to radicalism was about as difficult as turning on with grass; a movement of the moment, not real conviction. What was real, however, was her affair with Steele; she was hooked on him. (Remember what Professor Kovell said about her stories of unsatisfied affairs.) And Steele knew it and exploited it. He used the fucking to secure the so-called emotional bond—he was incapable of sustaining any positive emotion, his energy was always negative, in anger, seduction, betrayal—and exploited the radical rhetoric to introduce the crime pact. The undoing of Helen Lefler then was fashion and sex, to a great extent. It was a mistake to think of her downfall as brought about by misguided idealism and passionate devotion to a cause. The only cause in this case was a hard penis, and the only real lure the glamour of an ex-con. That's the sad truth.

Does all this make for evidence, as the media and the Dean would have it, that radical politics was responsible for Steele, Helen, and the bank robbery? Or does it rather suggest that old-fashioned do-goodism and zealous innocence on the part of liberals—the shrink, university officials, the seduced wife, the suburb coed-radical—were the main engineers of those wretched events? You be the judge.

I can't help thinking that a great part of your difficulties stems from your casual misuse and determined abuse of the language. I wonder if you're conscious of this? If you've never read George Orwell on the subject, you certainly ought to. *Nineteen Eighty-four*, for example, and the appendix on the language of Newspeak. Better yet, for a starter, his essay "Politics and the English Language." It's mandatory reading for any freshman English course that I've taught, because it's the best single introduction to clear thinking by means of clear and effective use of language. And it is brilliant on the political dangers of imprecise language. In fact, a study of Orwell would make a very useful semester course these days, for any number of subjects—politics, English, humanities. He was just the kind of tough-minded humanist and authentic socialist who is a perfect antidote to the muddle-headed and charlatan philosophers on the left today. Best of all, he was a pretty tough man to bully, and we need more of that kind. Men on the democratic left, with guts and savvy and talent, who can stand up to the roughnecks and bullies on the left and the right.

Abuse of language, I said. Let me illustrate. Take that notorious word of yours to designate policemen, "pigs." Oh, it's colorful and new, but does it really work? Does it serve a progressive purpose? I suppose the argument goes that policemen are the ugly oppressors of the "people"—of course, to stop right here for a moment, you don't really mean the people, all the people, you mean an elite, specifically the blacks, which makes me wonder about a phrase like "power to the people"—as I was saying, "pigs" is used to designate these vicious creatures in the eyes of the oppressed. But to begin with, if the police are considered "vicious," why choose a pig as their animal representative? If you want viciousness and dread and curling fear, why not "rats"? Or, take oppressiveness: are pigs really oppressive? Not the pigs I've seen. Not in any sense. Which means that both vicious and oppressive are not at all implied by the use of your epithet. But there's yet another aspect to the lack of consistency here, when the term "panther" is brought into play. If the oppressed are panthers and the oppressors pigs, why then, there should be no problem at all for the oppressed to rise and conquer the pigs. One is a powerful and cunning wild fighter, the other a shrewd but helpless domestic animal. But of course, such is not at all the case in reality. If the panther were to take his name seriously and spring upon the pig, he would find a very well-armed pig, with squad cars, guns, ammo, tear gas; Las Vegas will give you very strong odds against the panther in such a battle. But take the arms away, and still you have a pig with two hands and legs and every bit as much strength as a panther. So where's the substance to this imagery? Which is to say, you can't have it both ways—ugly feeble pigs as real-life oppressors, fantasy panthers as real-life victims. It doesn't hold up.

But besides the linguistic inaccuracy, it fails as political imagery. To designate policemen as the enemy, rather than as the victim, is to convert a potential ally into a permanent enemy. For it is to miss the crucial point that social revolution is in the policeman's self-interest too, if only he could be made to see the real situation. He is, after all, a mere worker too, not a capitalist. So why turn him into an enemy by abusing him? You don't, unless you're confused theoretically, or permit yourself to turn a ghetto emotion into a wholesale political strategy. Not to mention the desire for sensational publicity. These are the hard truths, I'm afraid.

That doesn't mean that you can't call him a name which will be of some use. "Puppet," for example, or "sucker." Yes, that good old-fashioned native term, "sucker." Isn't that what he is, a gullible dupe of the system? Suppose you dropped "pig" and started referring to him as "sucker." Don't you think that might make some policeman reflect rather than react? Him, a sucker? How? What does it mean? And instead of pure hatred, you're throwing out provocation and, hopefully, the beginning of education. You might even take to giving policemen lollipops whenever you see them. A playful symbol of their new designation. Two-cent lollipops instead of hostile and stupid epithets might stir in him a desire to learn a little about why you think of him as a Sucker. And right at that point, where he's asking himself if he *is* a Sucker, the business of revolution becomes serious. For it's the beginning of his education.

An education on at least two levels. [*!!!*] The first being the most pressing, namely, that he must act decently as a policeman and not lose his personal humanity, which the role and the uniform are constantly threatening. This involves the incredibly difficult and delicate task of preserving a certain sympathy for the wretched of the cities, at the same time that he has to cope with the higher crime rate existing there. It's a balancing act not to be underestimated. Put yourself in his place when he enters a depressed area these days. It's pretty rough.

The second level concerns the gradual awakening of his class consciousness, beginning with the immediate realities of his situation—his wages and living conditions in comparison with the rich in society, and in comparison with policemen in *other* societies. And leading to an understanding of his deeper role within the structure of capitalist class society, as a member of a real brother-hood called the working class. In other words, you show him that the present system exploits him as much as it does other workers, black and brown and Spanish. Out of *self-interest* he belongs on *their* side, not out of sentiment. That's the goal to strive for. Admittedly, this is long-range, in view of the present level of antagonism which he feels for many of you—with very good reason; but at least it gives back to the policeman a moral standing in your own rhetoric about social change. Furthermore, this kind of education puts into practice what I thought your Movement was about in the first place, humanizing people who live in a dehumanized environment. Now, do you think for a moment that you are helping to humanize him by calling him a pig? Or are you doing just the opposite? To me, this is a perfect example of Doublethink.

No, names like "pigs" and "panthers" are better suited to base-ball and football teams, or to certain male fraternities, than they are to political understanding or serious social progress.

In all of this I also get the strong suspicion that you're hostile to the whole idea of a police force, as if society could and should operate without one. And in its place there might be self-protect-ing vigilante groups, each protecting its own small territory, which would give the community in question both protection and some form of self-rule. Children, the basic impulse here is an anarchist fantasy of the most primitive and naïve sort. Any organized society needs a police force to ensure that the game of society runs smoothly; the police are simply the referees and umpires who see to it that those who commit fouls—the crimi-nals—are curbed and penalized. As to whether I'd want a local vigilante group protecting myself and my store, if I were a black citizen, I'd think twice. But I'll tell you that my main yardstick would not be color, but competence; and not neighborhood partiality, but true impartiality. If I call a cop to arrest a hoodlum for mugging my mother, I'm not interested in that criminal being "sympathized with" because everyone knows that he was an orphan. What do I give a shit? There are also orphans who don't hit women in the head and run off with their pocketbooks! . . . But again, to return to the main point here, you don't think or imagine that a revolution means the end of organized society?

You can't. It means simply that the game is played with new rules, but with pretty much the same arbiters—leaders of parties, the police, and the army, et cetera. Police are as crucial to a society run by Lenin as they are to a society run by Eisenhower. You can't have criminals running around just because the dawn of socialism has arrived! For by that same evening you'll have chaos, and then where's your new society? *A criminal is a criminal is a criminal.* There's no use pretending he's something else. He's as liable to knock off a good socialist revolutionary as he is the next capitalist reactionary, if the socialist has enough cash. Muggers and thieves and murderers have a very, very simple ideology, my friends, and it doesn't include the class struggle . . .

"Pigs" is just one example, but you abuse other words just as casually. "Right on!" Right on where? What kind of slogan is that? At least with "Workers of the World, Unite!" workers are told what to do, given a task. A more serious abuse, involving historical accuracy, concerns the word "ghetto." This is worth exploring for a minute . . .

We can skip this lecture on European/Jewish versus American/black ghettos, with its simple interpretation of racism, stemming from the Dean's boyhood basketball games.

Apart from political mythologies, this imprecise and manipulative use of language is also responsible for creating a world of political fantasy. It's dangerous. Consider everyone's favorite word these days, "revolution." Dress designers, automobile makers, rock groups, hair stylists, people who have intercourse with each other—everyone is in the midst of making a revolution. How odd. All those activities that have gone on for centuries are suddenly called revolutionary. Pals, it's not true. All that's going on is that the "business" of revolution has become a *real* business, raking in the cash; the idea of social and political change has been converted into a huge moneymaking operation by means of Madison Avenue and you people.

I know this is unpleasant, but hear me out. Just wait. Just sit down there and wait! Good.

Now, how many of you really have something clear and definite in mind when you use that word? Or is it really a catch-all phrase that means a hundred and one different things to you, from a new exciting life, to poor people suddenly being rich, to everyone suddenly loving each other? Boys and girls, you mustn't use a word unless you know its precise meaning. You mustn't. And especially a word that stands for a whole complex of actions on your part and around which you propose to base an ethic of behavior. You saw what happened to the girls and Steele. So what I'd like to see is a moratorium on the use of the word, for an indefinite period. Try something else. In fact, what you'll find is that by *not* using the word, you'll find out what you really mean, you'll be forced to. Instead of a maze called revolution, you'll begin to make real inroads—whether they be reform, liberalism, ordinary human decency. Which are hard enough to accomplish, my God; just look at the great struggles and failings in recent years.

So give up the fantasy of revolution and pay attention to the harder job of changing America. You'll find that you're talking about a very long-term commitment, longer than mine or your lifetime. It'll be more realistic. For anyone who knows the slightest thing about societies can tell you that profound change in our country is a difficult enough goal; full-scale upheaval, which will overthrow the capitalist system, is out of the question. There's no chance. The majority of Americans are not alienated from their country, they're hugely satisfied with it. Most people who work for a living are doing well enough. Not wonderfully, but decently. For you to arm yourselves to the teeth and believe that you can topple the government is like tribes of Iroquois marching on the Pentagon with bows and arrows. It's a scene directed by Stanley Kramer, not Volodya Lenin.

Even revolutions, do you know, are old-hat to the civilized man. He knows too much about them, knows how easily they are corrupted and betrayed. He knows, from history, that they can be made only by small groups of leaders—the Party, say—which, ironically, can lead only to oligarchies and dictatorships. And not dictatorships of the proletariat, which was the hope and promise, but dictatorships of the Party leaders. So that while you may get a Lenin to make a revolution, the chances are equally as likely that you'll get a Stalin to follow him, at one point or another. In other words, it's utopian to believe that one Lenin will follow another Lenin, and so on. That is one of the dilemmas.

There's another. Knowing the history of disgrace of this

century's revolutions, how many of you are willing to shoulder the burden of the morality of revolution? An absolute morality which demands severe obedience and which can lead to severe consequences. Remember: for the sake of some future millennium, some twenty, ten, or one may have to be killed, *now*. The commandment is as strong as any of the Big Ten: the only moral action is that which furthers the revolution, the only immoral one that which delays it. Are you strong enough for that? [*Looking at me.*] Think of it, consider. As those of you who've read Dostoevsky will know, the responsibility for a single suffering, a single dead life, can be very great. Overwhelming. Are you ready and willing and capable of taking on such a burden?

In this clumsy roundabout fashion, what I'm saying to you is simple: watch your words, use language precisely. It'll keep you out of mischief and fantasy, the kind created by empty and mistaken rhetoric. And listen closely to words being used on you. Just because some criminal tells you that on account of his thefts he's a radical, or some demagogue, that on account of his color he's a revolutionary, don't be hypnotized. *Think*. The more you're lackadaisical, sloppy, and irresponsible with words, the more they will become your jailer; the more you know how to use them properly and expertly, the more potent will become your ideas, the more effective your acts. Don't become verbal Arabs, relying on others for the use of valuable equipment; for you'll remain then, at best a parasite, at worst a victim. A victim of others' manipulations and a victim of your own fantasies.

That talk. That tone. They're murder.

Yes, I've read Orwell. Though smart and tough enough to make him the darling of the social democrats, for me he's a clever also-ran. His novels, when successful, are clever and tendentious constructions; he's not in any danger of being considered in the first rank there. His political journalism, his mainstay, gathers its strongest impetus from its anti-Stalinism; this is quite different from a man with a theory of a new society, or a wholesale critique of the old. No one is naïve enough to call Orwell an original thinker. He was a man very much of his time, of a certain epoch, but not beyond that: therein lies his limitation. A severe one. As a man, he was narrow of emotion, puritanical by temperament, acerbic rather than passionate. His asceticism pales before that of a Gandhi. His courage, when compared to the cowardice of many of his peers, is impressive; when held up against that of truly courageous individuals, is only modest. In sum, I can think of more impressive figures to study for a semester.

Interestingly, the only names I can think of are the artists, Picasso, Stravinsky, Kafka, and possibly scientists like Oppenheimer. (A course in Oppenheimer would be rather interesting, wouldn't it?) Isn't that one of the age's serious problems, the absence of interesting public leaders—the Disraelis, Lincolns, or Trotskys?

The Dean is certainly right about our difficulties with language. But he is wrong in his analysis of the source. As we are looking for new ways to organize society, for new norms of dignity and new dimensions of ethics, so we are searching for a new language. Words like "pigs" and "ghetto" may be used loosely, but they should be understood as transition words, not permanent additions. Furthermore, words like "pigs" are not the products of classrooms, salons, conferences, textbooks, dictionaries; instead they come from the streets and express the spontaneous feelings of overwhelming visceral hatred on the part of a victim of an unnecessary and/or brutal shakedown. Street words recalled instinctively from childhood aversions to swine, they have a powerful resonance because of their unmediated and direct form. They are less unreasonable, it should be remembered, than the unreasonable acts which provoke them. In political terms, Kove is once more naïve when he fails to recognize these words as small movements in an over-all strategy; they are the movements of pawns, not heavy artillery like bishops or rooks. Their aim is to provoke, to test, to unnerve marginally, not to land crushing blows. If crushed and inarticulate persons are to be prohibited rough words as well as firearms, what are they permitted to use to express their anger?

Phrases like " . . . you mustn't use a word unless you know its precise meaning. You mustn't . . ." are the embarrassing consequences of a lifetime spent amid "theme-grading," a fate as punishing as Siberian exile (as the Dean himself once remarked to me).

Concerning racism. Whenever an orator gets going good, gets preachy and hot, you can bet the reasons have little to do with the occasion and more to do with the interior life. Specifically, the sexual life. Thus, for the motive for Kove's self-righteous sermon about racism, I refer the reader back, once again, to the Gwen Tresvant tale in Family Talk. Shame on Dean Kovell!

The dead Jews of Europe and living blacks in America are not as far apart as Kove would have it. Both have had mingled histories and bent bodies before the wills of white Christians. They are related by their history of suffering and their forced exiles. The Jew has had a cultural tradition to uplift him, the black has had an Edenic soul to redeem him. The brown skin and the long nose mark their brotherhoods, the one belonging to the most innocent race on earth, the other to the most sophisticated. It is natural that they should develop a special, intense, and ambivalent feeling for each other.

While some of my friends may suffer from the disease of political fantasying, I don't think I am overly afflicted with it. Dean Kovell speaks accurately, if platitudinously, when he describes the powerful entrenchment of the capitalist system. I have little hope of dismantling it in my lifetime. My much more modest hope is to put certain persons, like Kovell, up against the wall in relation to their own lives and the future of civilization. I want to make it hot for them, to narrow the distance between that larger future and their own, so that they can join me in anger. That's all. My main problem with the Dean is how to unplug him from his own fantasies, the sexual sort, in order to introduce him to political reality.

I would be glad for a moratorium on revolution if the government would reciprocate and call a moratorium on governing. This is another small aim of mine. Assuredly, their moratorium would affect more human beings than mine. Why not give the citizens a brief letup from insanity?

Yes, the word is overused and I'm for a new one myself. But the activity is hardly beginning.

I'm also for long-range education, but looking realistically about, the only things that are long range these days are MIRV, *Atlas, and Polaris. General ideas have lost out, I think, to rockets and missiles in the long-range category.*

You can see for yourself that when the web of charges, accusations, and warnings is broken down and analyzed, there's not much substance or stimulation in this section. Nor is there the rather charming humor that is apparent in Family Talk or in the Dean's classes. It is too bad that Mr. Kovell is turned on by racy matters only, for much is lost of his considerable attractiveness when he sermonizes.

The Dean continued on. And on. And on. Drinking water, attending to Naaron, referring to notecards. His Fidel-like speech covered an awesome variety of topics: the danger of drugs and a drug culture; the meaning of education; the problems of decision-making; the fineness and slowness of democratic procedures; the fallacies of the women's movement; a thumbnail history of the Left in this country; the lessons of history. As the reader will see, I've spared him a long-playing record on six or seven of the dullest subjects in contemporary conversation. Suffice to say that there was the usual mixture of severe chiding of students, faint criticism of the society, and steady plea for "basic decencies" and for the "best of the past" or the "noble heritage of the past." Other lofty phrases too. He closed, or rather, was closed off— thankfully—during this next rambling benediction.

I wouldn't say these things to you, be so openly critical, if I weren't . . . very fond of you. If I didn't love some of you as if you were my own, my very own children. Do you understand? And I mean some of the leading troublemakers too. [*Cheers.*] That's why it upsets me so to watch you ruining things, acting so crudely with your lives, turning nasty and thoughtless with people older than yourselves, your families . . . You, Pincus, what's happening to you? . . . [*Wiping his eyes with his handkerchief.*] Excuse me . . . breaking down here . . . this way . . .

You must understand it's my affection for you that is at the bottom of my disturbance with you. Isn't the nation in bad enough shape without your adding to it? Don't we have enough hatred and divisiveness? Enough name calling and political labeling? Double talk and violence? Hasn't there been enough of this? That's why it's up to you to change things. Please, boys and girls, you *must* do something. But it must be *positive* not negative; it can't come from the same sources of disdain and disregard and negativism that you've been trying to attack in the first place. It can't, or it won't work. It's up to you to build, to plan, to create, not to disrupt and to *annihilate*. You simply can't act that way and shouldn't be allowed to! This is not the first time that government officials are demagogues and callous hypocrites, nor will it be the last. But we must weather it. Weather them. *Together*. It's up to you, the sons and daughters, to help the fathers in this fight. *We're on the same side as you*. Don't you get that? Not to disregard your fathers, but to aid them, to join with them—that's the task!

Look at history, again I plead with you, to see that annihilation has begat only more annihilation, more misery. In one great country of revolution, the heirs created a society of purges and police terror, of constant surveillance and lifeless uniformity. In another, a dictatorial chairman has sacrificed millions of people to his own fanatical ideas and his own personal megalomania. Do those millions of tin soldiers or little red robots fit your own aspirations as human beings? Do those societies present a healthy alternative to ours? How would you like to be forced into "toiling the earth" when you'd rather be out on a date or reading a book? Or forced to recite political catechism every morning before you're allowed to study your physics? Or, if you protest Vietnam, let's say, risk being sent to northern Montana for three years of forced labor? Or play *informer* on your mother if she says something counter-revolutionary? Think of the special police leading your mother away, on your say-so, and you held up for citizen-acclaim because of it? Is this what you hope to replace America with? If not, then you better say so; and say it *now*, before you go about trying to tear it all apart. What kind of society do you want to replace this one? Tell me, tell all of us, for godsakes!

What I'm saying and repeating in a variety of ways is that you must begin with some belief, some positive belief—if it's a god or a new society. But you can't begin with nothingness, with nihilism, with no vision except destruction. You must have some measuring stick of virtue, decency, and quality by which to judge human events and men's actions. Without it, why, you're lost, absolutely given over to a morass of cheap slogans and instant

strategies, plans. Lost in a desert where there's no values whatsoever and you're *free to do anything*—to steal, to kill, to
slaughter. Is that the kind of freedom you want? . . . *Belief.* Is it
so hard? Haven't we—the human race—*earned this belief?*
Again, I implore you to look around, to open your eyes to what
we've created and accomplished, to the sheer magnitude of the
accomplishment. OF COURSE I KNOW THAT THERE ARE DEFECTS AND
PROBLEMS AND DILEMMAS AND LOUSY UNTRUSTWORTHY SOULS, but
that's in the cards. It's part of the human setup. One serves the
other—obstacles are created and men overcome them and become tougher for it. Without some pain and sacrifice, how can
you expect serious improvement, serious change?

But if you simply kill the fathers—give up on your elders—
you cut yourselves off: from continuity, from paternal feeling,
from history. You can't, you simply can't. Replace them yes, but
destroy them no. By yourselves and unto yourselves is not a
human existence. I know that my colleagues, my peers, and what-
have-you are full of weakness, timidity, error. But instead of
doing them in for this, why not show some compassion? Pity.
Where is your pity? That's what I want to know, where is your
sense of pity for human weakness? Must it be all pride and
prejudice on your part? Don't we as teachers have sympathy for
you when you commit errors? Don't we try and make you better
instead of dismissing you? Don't we? It's that we want you to be
better. The whole notion of teaching is that one person can help
another move from the tunnel to some light. I don't have you
come to me so I can say, All right, you're through, you've made
an error. There's sympathy on my part. And there's belief in the
species. You don't move ahead by destroying! . . .

Boys and girls, Pincus, if you don't end this occupation . . .
these uncivilized demands . . . your irrational ways . . . Forgive me, I'm at it again . . . like a little boy . . . excuse me.
[*Crying.*]

But without some sort of love, you—what? what was that?
say that again, did I hear you right? What! Where do you think
you are using that language, in the streets! Who are you? This is
just what I mean, a perfect example of the ugly behavior—what?
Do you think I'm going to let you get away with that? Look
you!—just look here!—

"Fuck off, Dean" were the words that the Dean objected to in disbelief, and soon after *"That's right, baby, fuck off—you and your jive."* It was the beginning of the unceremonious halt to the Dean's lecture, although there followed some give and take, and more Dean-talk, before full chaos broke loose.

"Belief." "Values." "Pity." "Love." Humiliating words. Double talk. In America today, these words are sham and hypocrisy, masking greed and murder. Our napalm has no pity. Our MIRV's have no belief. Our wiretapping has no conscience. Most congressmen and senators have never heard of Kovell's values. And love was replaced long ago in America by dollar bills. Like a bad garden, it all has to be uprooted and replanted, which is the aim of our camp.

The men who have ruled us in these recent years are better understood as animals, not human beings acting with reason. This is self-evident from their year-in, year-out major decisions. To try to reason with them—and it has been tried and tried and overtried, even by their own commissions—is silly. It has as much sense as trying to reason with dinosaurs, cattle, insects. Only these creatures look like you and me, they speak the same language, wear the same clothes (roughly), digest and shit the same. But they also have the power to push THE buttons, make THE telephone calls. That's why they can't be shoved under some rock and ignored.

Come now, do you really expect a civilized man to reason with our attorney general, that paunchy perverter of justice? And what about that dinosaur who heads our secret service, covering as a patriot, but really Public Enemy No. *1* of democracy? Or the cow who grazes in the vice presidency, and runs the Bureau of Lying and Distorting? One can go on, but reasonable men know all this. The point to be emphasized, so that the Dean Kovells will understand it, is that it is a contradiction in terms to expect civilized men to reason with dumb creatures. It can't be done. And, if I may say so, it is also somewhat unfair to the creatures. How one cringes in embarrassment when they use those words—the cow talking about preserving civilized society, the insect about law and justice, the dinosaur about beliefs and values, or the plastic reptile who is President about pity and peace. Obviously these words will not do any longer, having been *contaminated beyond cure, distorted beyond meaning. But what can you expect when animals get hold of words?*

The talk of annihilation from us is silly, the historical examples propaganda. It is not we who have the capacity for annihilation, but our government. And there was no mass slaughter or purposeless murder when the Bolsheviks took power. The American murders at Jackson State and Kent State were much more savage, and the attempts to whitewash them much more reprehensible, than anything that went on at Petrograd. Why is it that enlightened citizens are so ready to vilify when it comes to this century's greatest political event, and so ready to whitewash and to justify when it comes to our own history of political banality, greed, and, lately, international murder?

Regarding a new society: there is no blueprint for this or that reform, and to ask for such is either naïveté or radical-baiting. What we do have are some general principles upon which a new society can be constructed. Naturally, the specific implementation of these ideas will have to wait until the new government is here and matters are studied by qualified persons. But decisions will be made within the light of the new values and the new principles. These are so obvious that they hardly need stating. But for the sake of the truly innocent, here is a list I composed for a liberal professor I once met on the MTA, who kept challenging me on what we wanted. His hazel eyes and gentle seriousness were attractive, and so I sat with him on a bench by the Square kiosk facing the taxis and Harvard, and wrote my list on a loose-leaf page. Afterward I thought it was useful and Xeroxed it to carry around with me. As you can see, it's piecemeal, disorderly, and rather simple, but it'll do.

A more equal redistribution of wealth
Just guidelines on business profits
Curbs on private property
Public park and building laws (a public park for every city skyscraper?)
More public ownership and control of radio, television, and newspaper media (to include open hearings on programming, equal opportunity for private individuals to answer political hacks and dangerous fossils in office, and so on)

219

Breakup of obsolete bureaucracies (government, education, labor)

Establishment of revolving roles of authority in public domain (bosses become workers, private citizens political leaders, etc.)

New and severe punishments for public officials, elected or appointed, who lie or deceive the people

Abolition of residential landlords

Land and population redistribution (no more New York Cities; people in cities sent to depressed rural areas to work; adult citizens given a piece of America to cultivate as they wish, on experimental basis)

Rehumanization of city life

Dismantling of war nation and conversion into peace state (e.g., destruction and death factories producing bombs and bacteria warfare converted into life research—human genetics, cancer studies)

Establishment of non-partisan boards of scientists and distinguished citizens to report facts and alternatives to the people on a regular basis

Public explanations of mystical, emotive, and biased political terms (e.g., patriotism, free world, anarchism, socialism, democracy, Reds)

Compulsory adult education: required four hours a week of learning about our open plans and secret workings for annihilation (e.g., the number of nuclear missiles and warheads made that month, the new projects for biochemical ravage, the incessant and disproportionate befouling of the planet by native technology and capitalism). Free subscriptions to a new *Bulletin of Atomic Scientists* and a new *Reader's Digest of Destructive Science.*

Human sympathy. (Most difficult category. Some proposals: one year of work in another country before age twenty-one and another year in one's forties. No higher education *before* the age of twenty-five; *after* twenty-five, constant education of one sort or another until death. Contact with foreigners and foreign places mandatory. Regular work visits to China and Brownsville, Cuba and Mississippi, Russia and Roxbury; people to replace isms)

Not profundities, just jottings, as I explained to Dr. Zinder. Long-range notions to be tested out in reality before some were jettisoned, others improved.

Once you replaced profitmaking and deception with citizen needs and social justice as guiding principles of society, it was not difficult to make most specific decisions, I explained. But to declare now that this utility or that industry should be nationalized would be premature. Such thinking would have to wait until citizens with the new moral idea took political power.

But for now, the interim, I continued, excited, certain words will have to go. Like "truth," "freedom," "democracy." In the mouths of our leaders, these words have become contaminated, so that they mean nothing, or their exact opposites. We'll start perhaps by substituting "shit" for "truth," taking our cue from our nation's officials, who are constantly using one word but really meaning the other. Language will be less deceiving that way. Dr. Zinder said shit was shit in anyone's language and he preferred other terms for human intercourse. He took my list and said he'd try to answer it sometime.

As interesting as Kovell was when exclaiming about women and sex, so, when he comes to morals and politics, he is over-whelmingly dull. Or routine. The only moments when his face truly lit up during this talk, in fact, concerned that hidden life, as when racism was discussed. With women he is a philosopher-king and Talmudic hedonist (distinguishing among his pleasures); with morals he is a pulpit theologian, a stiff-necked servant of a self-righteous Lord. Only now, instead of God, Dean Kovell's ego is the Lord. Or better, superego. A theologian of the superego is what we have in these public utterances. I prefer the Talmudic hedonist.

It is in the last few pages, however, that the first real signs of health appear in Kovell. I refer to the tears, the plea for forgiveness, the bewilderment and near breakdown. All this is honest. True. Therapeutic. It signifies that the Dean himself is ready for the interruptions to follow—the uprising, the chaos, his removal. More than ready; desirous, needing.

Finally, the contradiction of his life breaks the smooth surface of his exterior. The chaos of his emotions more and more shatters the formal mask of preacher, teacher, and authority. It is a contradiction that represents what is most fine and most hopeful in Professor Kovell; it shows that his strongest impulses can no longer cohabit with his public manner, his hysterical moralism, his false flag of hope. A contradiction between the way he acted and the way he spoke, between his verbal hypocrisy ("respect, dignity, values, pity") and his authentic nervousness.

It is little wonder that one side of Professor Kovell welcomed with open arms his change of air, his new dress, the new ways. But that is another story.

A new language, I said a moment ago. And new values. All grounded in hopes for a new man, a new sort of American, let's say; or at least a new Kovell. For the man you have witnessed here, and in Family Talk, is a cripple, an emotional and spiritual cripple. That much is obvious. He is a representative of a culture of hysteria, greed, and self-righteous authoritarianism, which has itself been created by increasing guilt, shame, and self-doubt. We hope to change some of that. To change Kovell. "All wickedness comes from weakness," wrote Rousseau. "Make man strong and he will be good." We hope to straighten out Kovell the Cripple— and in his lifetime, if this is possible and not overambitious.

3: GORILLA TALK

When I claimed a moment ago that Kovell represented a culture, it was true and not true. To say that he represents all or most Americans would be a compliment to the life-styles and imaginations of the natives. Democratic Vistas does not yet, for most, include sex. What Kovell is is an intelligent man, perplexed and unhappy about his life, trying to find a woman-arrangement that fits his various emotions and complicated tastes. Now to me you can learn more that's significant about a culture from a specific interesting life than you can from a thousand common case studies. For it is generally in the minds and gestures of those few persons of genuine intelligence that a culture throbs in all its rhythms; and certainly the more interesting the person, the more discordant that rhythm, at least here in the West.

All interesting men are rebels, and Kove's no different. What makes his sexual radicalism so appealing perhaps—apart from the earthy level of humorous details which his girls so readily detect —is that it is constantly fighting against old emotions and old traditions in order to sustain itself. If Kovell is not a Babbitt, neither is he a modern Playboy, a witless one-dimensional penis.

His plunge toward hedonism is serious, complicated, of the historical moment. What I'm talking about may be seen most clearly in his relations with Gwen ("Plantation Thrills"), in which the Dean is constantly at odds with himself, one foot (or hand) in saucy hot holes, the other on safer, cooler ground. His problem is in part that the cooler ground is dull, deadly dull (the old emotions, say), while the hot holes are sweet but risky and confusing (the new color, the new demands). He seems to be as afraid of *discovering* as he is of being *found out*.

At odds with himself—is it possible to live an interesting life otherwise? Has it ever been possible at any time, anywhere? Not in harmonious, ancient Greece, if we are to take seriously Socrates jailed and killed, or among the biblical Jews, where David the great king found himself a robber, killer, homosexual, incorrigible lecher. Not now in America, where man has what he wants of *plenty* and still is profoundly unsatisfied, even exhausted. Even as the Dean pursues his fleshy apertures, he knows that it is no answer to the dilemma of his spirit.

Can we do something with a Kovell? Can he change? Would he be reduced or enlarged? Take away women and what becomes of him? Will he conquer states and bring a new twist to political power? Run a new type of state (with bordellos replacing legislatures perhaps)? These questions are intriguing, especially in the longer run; and especially to a boy who himself is finding out how difficult it is to become or want to become an American adult, and who more and more wants no part of it. Yes, I'm against adulthood nowadays, and therefore a maverick like Kovell, who uses polygamy to hold out against modern adulthood, possesses a certain charm for me, at the same time that I recognize his dilemmas and his confusions. After all, I have a few of my own.

1. The Berg Museum Uprising

If you're thrown into battle against a powerful enemy without proper training, suitable armor, or experienced generals, there's bound to be mistakes and chaos, crazy comrades and weak strategies, needless blood and fatal accidents. And of course losses. One can surrender at the very prospect, or go ahead against the odds. To make trouble in America, one has to be a combination of gambler and sucker. It is a combination which doesn't inspire trust. But the days of rational rebellions in the West are over. Our fathers, philosophical and real, don't seem to understand this. But I didn't at first either. I guess we could all use some combat experience.

Contrary to my press notices, I'm not a Karl Marx, able to produce an "Eighteenth Brumaire" analyzing the Berg Art Museum Uprising within the perspective of a full-fledged theory. I remain basically an American boy, a student of literature, who is constantly amazed at the surprises and turnabouts created by men and chance. I come armed with a spiral pad and pencil, a camera and my own eye, memory and curiosity. And an instinct for not abandoning my feelings for the sake of an *idée fixe* or formula truth. It amuses me the way human beings constantly, and almost against their will, dodge a theory meant to hold them or elude a role for which they are supposedly fitted perfectly. I myself take a certain pride in stepping out of my prescribed lane of radical behavior, if only for the sake of spite against general systems and airtight theories. Naturally, this offends many on my own side—as will become evident—who prefer, like most men, the simplicity of black-and-white alternatives to the difficulty of finding too many alternatives, or none. But this is getting ahead of myself.

To those fatal days and nights of June 9 and June 10, 1972.

As I've indicated, a few days before the regular graduation, scheduled for Sunday, June 11, we decided to hold our counter-graduation. Apart from the obvious point of protesting the war, the government, the coming elections, there was also the unconscious need to stir things up in general. It had become so quiet lately. (In fact, if it were not for the blanket of stillness that had recently covered the campuses, I doubt that we would have gone as far as we did. In other words, boredom was probably as important as monopoly capitalism in spurring on our crazy and foolish acts—a motivation that I personally admired, it being so universal.) For several reasons I chose the art museum and the library for our sites of occupation. Since Cardozo was a liberal-arts school primarily, those sites seemed more appropriate than

227

more innocuous ones, like administration buildings, auditoriums, or lawns. I knew too that visiting parents generally were given tours through the museum and library, and I thought it would be nice for them to see what students were up to, if they did come around. These were my thoughts. At no point, it should be said, did I plan or imagine the events to follow. This is worth stating, not so much to proclaim my innocence, let's say—you'll see enough of that, I think—as not to deprive others of their full due. For it is only later that my own efforts on behalf of troublemaking deserve some credit.

Securing the museum was easy enough. An art major named Ronald Neigler, a familiar face there, hid in the bathroom until the building was locked for the night. At the appointed 7:30 hour, he opened the back doors to the student cadres, who slipped in quietly by twos and threes. (About midnight, the same was accomplished in the library, where a much smaller contingent did the job.) A janitor was held temporary hostage until we were all in, and then released. Immediately a barricade of desks, chairs, blackboards was roped and wedged together by the front doors. Supplies of food were laid in and two picnic tables set up; blankets, pillows, sleeping bags were brought in along with phonographs and transistor radios. A communications system of walkie-talkies was established between the two buildings, though for some reason this broke down and we only found out later what happened at the library. A Politburo committee of twelve was elected, four permanent members (including myself), eight revolving. Sergeants and marshals were appointed. Our bivouac occupation had begun.

With about a hundred to two hundred kids, the museum was pretty packed. Set on a gentle elevation on the northern tip of the ninety-acre campus, the Berg Art Museum is a small tasteful building of two levels (one beneath the ground), built of modern glass-and-concrete design. The only structures very near it are a series of sloping art studios, some two hundred yards away. Otherwise, its back and sides are engulfed by deep-set pine woods, a fact of some logistical importance both for entrances and escapes. On a lawn in front are set curious pieces of metal, bronze, and wood sculptures, shapes from dreams and the primitive past by Smith, Nevelson, Lipchitz. I know nothing about art, let me say immediately, except what I've picked up in some paperbacks, an occasional art history class, some Hilton Kramer articles in the *Times*. But those wooden totems and giant metal swoopings outside the museum always gave me a chill if I came by them at night. I mention this because what came later seemed, afterward, a fitting fulfillment of my eerie feelings. Also, more relevantly, those sculptures, according to a Cardozo art historian, gave a fair idea of the quality of the art inside. It was excellent. By means of the luck, energy, and donations that a new school can sometimes obtain—Cardozo was not yet twenty-five years old, and the smallest university in the nation—it had slowly built up a fine permanent collection. This included European masters from Impressionism on, New York abstract expressionists, supposedly high-quality American works. And because its director had been recently associated with the Boston Museum of Fine Arts, it was assured of interesting shows throughout the year. At the time of our occupation, in fact, the Theodore Sloan collection was on exhibition. A collection of what I took to be cubist and post-cubist greats, including several Picassos and Matisses, a Miro, a Kandinsky, some Giacometti sculpture. But there were also other works (by someone named Schwitters, by Cézanne), and I remember being especially impressed by the lonely landscapes, city and country, of an American I had heard of but never seen, Edward Hopper. To my amateur eye, they seemed the most accessible and most moving.

From the outside, the museum never looked more enchanting than it did that night, lit up like a glass chandelier in the darkness, students strolling—you could see this through the floor-to-ceiling windowed front—and talking and lying on the floors like Boy Scouts billeted for the evening. Looking at it, I felt more convinced than ever that it was a good choice for a symbolic gesture of protest. After all, wasn't the world of art—painting, literature, music—the one sure bastion of truth throughout history's fluctuations? Wasn't great art essentially immune to political ideology and propaganda? Therefore, by definition, wasn't it the one sure *institutional* enemy of what was going on in our country's political life? I thought so, at least. And I thought it was fitting then that we, the *moral* opposition, should use that site of art to express our dissatisfaction and anger.

The scene and the sociology inside were familiar enough, as I walked about, occasionally shooting newsreel with my 8-millimeter hand camera. Around a few desks by the side of the stairway leading to the basement floor, the small hard core of radical theorists conducted seminars for themselves and for novitiates to the cause. Dressed in the main like Soviet bureaucrats or Chinese peasants, they sat in circles discussing a particular text like *The Wretched of the Earth*, or a leader lectured on "Repressive Tolerance," the Marcuse essay. Although these comrades looked with disdain upon the majority of students, if they looked upon them at all, some were not above accepting help. I have in mind one very stern sociology graduate, a beard named Graff, who, sitting on a corner of the stairs, was permitting a red star to be sewn upon his sleeve by a lovely long-haired hippie—a rather touching modern scene as the boy looked about nervously. Indeed, the hippies, wearing their obligatory costumes (sandals, animal skins, Goodwill rags and hand-me-downs, army surplus), were a constant annoyance to the more severe political types. For example, by the running-water fountain downstairs, a made-up Indian girl from Long Island, Rebecca Price, kept wandering over to Mark Levinsky, a pipe-smoking Sovietologist engaged in a seminar, to smile at him and ask him to turn on with her. Mark was furious and flabbergasted as he tried to proceed with his talk on the radical elements in the first Russian Duma in 1905. Comrades smiled or looked stern. Dope and passion were emphatically *bourgeois* to them. Levinsky, the poor displaced Menshevik, trying hard to transform himself into a Bolshevik, pleaded on the side with his Jewish Indian to leave him be.

The blacks stayed mostly to themselves, either on one side of the fountain or upstairs in a corner, with a stray here and there. In colored dashikis, natural cuts, and an occasional fez, they looked very exotic, a group of dark-skinned Bedouins just in from the desert. They tapped drums, sang and chanted, moved to soul music, self-segregated. There remained the majority, ordinary college liberals, children of affluence and Eugene McCarthy, scrubbed with Dial soap and smelling of Arrid, rubbing their eyes tiredly, brushing their hair, trying to look brave and cheerful. Sweethearts mostly. They huddled to listen to Dylan, Seeger, Baez; read *Growing Up Absurd*, Vonnegut, *Trout Fishing in*

America, and the *Siddartha* (the last three their Bibles of simplicity and mysticism); and worked on course incompletes, in English ("The Imagery of Doors and Windows in *Wuthering Heights*"); abnormal psychology ("The Authoritarian Personality in Times of Stress"); British history ("The Victorian Landed Gentry: Class or Caste?"). Sitting lotus-style, chewing gum, taking notes: the charm of it! Of course, the groups occasionally crossed swords, or pencils. A pair of staunch radicals mocking a young boy and girl in Wranglers, much more interested in "Hey Jude" by the Beatles than in Corporation Elites, the seminar topic. The frivolous English majors and the somber social-science pair, a contrast to behold; as Kove might have said, Like the difference between rival tuna-fish brands.

A happening, not an uprising, in other words, was the way it began. More innocent than a happening really. A get-together before school let out for the summer. A Revolution Prom, you might call it. A combination of radical rhetoric, prom-night poignancy, and very earnest sentimentality. Not only was there no mention of a "museum uprising" (see the mistaken *Times* report, June 12, in *The Week in Review*), but there was barely notice of what turned out to be an important factor, the Sloan art collection on loan to the university. Barely, I say, because at one point an art major named Mickey Klein, a thin intense mustached painter of twenty, who really couldn't care less about rebellion except artistic, insisted that I come with him to see a painting. Not that I knew the first thing about art, as I've said, but Mickey knew I was interested in literature and the movies, and we had worked together on the literary magazine. He was crazy—nervous as a squirrel, never able to sit for more than two minutes, and obsessed by the idea of success, a problem created by a successful symphony-conductor father—but interesting. Before a 3-by-3 Matisse, he began to explode with glee, explaining the "use of color to transform inanimate objects into a dynamic subject"; elaborating upon the open violin case resting on the chair and the open shutters to the window, which created such "dramatic space" in the picture; praising the "sheer formal genius" in perspective and line, so that finally what was most impressive about the "apparent representation was its abstract painterly qualities." To me, the picture had looked nice if dull, but by the time he

231

was finished, I was convinced of my ignorance. Suddenly his expression changed. "Shouldn't we be pretty careful while we're here," he said, "with this kind of stuff around?" His voice grainy, and periodic giggles giving away his adolescent uncertainty. "I mean, maybe you ought to say something about being careful with all this here." I agreed, and told him not to worry, and soon arranged for Mickey and three others to rope off valuable and vulnerable areas. Also, during our next round of announcements, I included a word of warning about where you walked and danced. It was greeted by a cheer.

Details of the setting: beneath a blue-period Picasso, two girls munching chopped-liver sandwiches (from the student center), turning pages of *Life*. Alongside three Kurt Schwitters collages, two black couples moving to the Supremes, from a transistor. By an Edward Hopper interior (a girl alone in a Manhattan hotel room), several Cardozo-style Buddhists, head-shaven boys and ascetic-faced girls, all in orange saris (the effect marred by torn tennis sneakers), chanting in a circle, "Hare Krishna, Hare Krishna." One of them, the daughter of a Duke physics professor whom I had known from a Hum class with Kovell, nodded to me meaningfully. I guess they, too, considered themselves revolutionists. Just by the side of a glass case of Giacometti figures, that attractive Talmudic English professor— the Goodspeed of Kovell's critique—was conducting a seminar on Culture in the Third World. Finally, in front of a very long and very narrow Jackson Pollock painting (15 by 3?) and a black-and-white Rorschach Kline, skits were going on about racism and war, upon one of the barricades made into a stage. And drifting through the museum was the sweet aroma of marijuana, the counter-air to the polluted oxygen breathed by capitalist society. How proms have changed in recent years.

At 10:30 P.M. the first pleas arrived to negotiate us out of the place. They kept coming through the night: pleas by faculty members; compromises offered by concerned administrators (most didn't want to deal with us at all); warnings by university police; a heartfelt note from a Concerned-Parent group. About two the next afternoon, the president of the school appeared. A smallish, bespectacled man in his sixties, a prize-winning bio-chemist with rabbinical voice and old-fashioned urges to dominate and to love, Dr. Schlossberg explained that he didn't wish to call in the police but would have to if we persisted. Besides, he asked, hands outstretched, his best patriarchal smile flashing, what did we want? "Just what we're doing," responded some Levi jacket dully. If we weren't bothering anybody, why was he speaking about calling in "fuzz"? Because first, he answered, what we were doing was illegal. And second, we happened to be sitting in the midst of a valuable art collection, whether we knew it or not, and the museum director and the Sloan people were growing very anxious. He avoided mentioning the effects upon the parents. "Now look," he turned warm and fatherly again, "if you want an area to stage a counter-graduation or protest, take the gymnasium . . . the baseball field." He shook his head. "The Longman Theater, it would be perfect." But buildings like the museum or library were simply off-limits; they were the property of everyone. "Then they're ours to use, like a commons," came an answer. Dr. Schlossberg then made a mistake: he issued an ultimatum, saying we would have to be out of there by six o'clock or he couldn't be responsible for the consequences. "Remember," he finished, "you're not the only ones with a right wing to contend with." A half-serious, half-humorous finale which I rather liked. After the laughter, a braided brunette stood up, hands on hips. "Where's Dean Kovell?" Schlossberg said that he wondered the same thing (more laughter, girl-whistling), but that he wasn't answering his phone and must have gone out of town. "Not everyone stays around on Saturdays waiting for sit-ins." He smiled. "I need him more than you want him, I assure you." And then, as a shrewd rebuff, a chant spontaneously started up, "We want Kove, we want Kove, we want Kove!" Dr. Schlossberg at first smiled, but when he held his hand up and tried to speak, the chant continued. Set back in this peculiar way, like a father's favors rejected for love of an uncle or older brother, Dr. Schlossberg walked out, clearly angry. Personally, I liked his jealousy very much. It was very human.

A debate followed about whether to evacuate or not. The ultimatum worked against Schlossy. It was also argued that the chances of calling in the police were slim, since parents would be around and it was the last few days of university session. "And we can always fake them out," announced one fellow, jerking his thumb, "by threatening their sacred pictures if they threaten to use force." A decisive point. Inadvertently planting an idea of combat amid the garden of fun. Sure enough, six o'clock, ultimatum hour, came and passed quietly. Someone got up and announced with bravado, "Schlossy chickened out." To celebrate our first victory, transistors were turned up and dancing broke out.

And so we sat, dozed, snacked, rapped, watched skits, danced, read, discussed strategy, got to know each other. The occupation had its retreat aspect. Family feeling developed, which was nice, though I always found that hard to enjoy. I preferred my privacy and less large groups to invest feeling in. A communitarian in theory and desire, I seemed to be a loner in practice.

Early in the evening, I slipped outside for a smoke, just on the edge of the pine forest behind the museum. Periodically, you could hear the voices of the university patrol guards, from around the building. It was a pleasant spring evening, clouded over, a star appearing now and then; a perfect time for naughty plans. The scent of pine was dizzying, and I barely heard the girl move at my elbow. Ponytailed beneath a floppy blue felt hat, she was carrying a copy of *Dylan Thomas's Poems*, and shook her head with enthusiasm when I asked her how she liked it. We had known each other from around campus, having attended meetings together and sat at the same table in the Student Union occasionally. Now, as we talked—she asking me what I thought would happen that night—I saw that she was attracted. I suppose that my reputation as a loner and my position in the Movement didn't hurt. Her name was Lauri Pearlman, later to be Comrade Pearlman. But just then she was just Lauri from Shaker Heights, Ohio, a half-peasant, half-hippie type with apple cheeks, peasant blouse, and white Wranglers, and a child's laugh that was infectious.

We sat on the ground about a hundred feet from the museum, and I could see that Lauri's brown eyes were watery from contact lenses. I told her to take them out if she wished, and she nodded, relieved. Mostly she wore her glasses, she said, especially when she was drawing or etching, her work. Distracted by the fragrant relief from politics and slogans, I must have asked her a question about her past, because suddenly she was talking about her life. What came out in the course of forty-five minutes or so was a history of bad times and scars, unusually scary it seemed to me for someone so young (twenty-one); what re-deemed it—if that's the word—was Lauri's persistent innocence or feeling of goodness in the face of it all. Bad times began with Mother, who interfered with Dad in his import-export business, and ran the household with icy efficiency. Dear Mother made Lauri's two sisters anxious very early on, so that they developed a premature fondness for cunning play-acting and vicious rivalry (for success and for Daddy's love). Lauri retreated to art, making her first serious drawings at age seven. Men began seriously at age fifteen, when a forty-year-old painter broke through her vir-ginity in a Vermont art colony. Ben A. was the next boy friend, at Syracuse U., her first school; he was a crazy impotent boy who alternately beat her and then pleaded desperately for forgiveness. Onward, to a New York City summer, teaching art in East Harlem and being the mistress of a married Moroccan architect who, between hash, tea, and defaming America, was keen on buggering (the cause of her piles, she believed). Finally to San Francisco (and the second college, S.F. State), and a mountain retreat by Point Reyes; this time a chemistry professor took her up, said, "she made him young all over" (body and mind), but wouldn't leave his family. She related these tales without ven-geance or pent-up scorn; rather with a kind of sympathy for all concerned. Meanwhile, she had continued to draw, paint, and etch, until the accident. After a period of sudden depression—awaking one morning and finding no desire to leave her bed, which she didn't for three days—she went to San Francisco Hospital, but was released after two days by a young psychiatrist who said she shouldn't be afraid, she wasn't suicidal. Two days later, taking an early-morning drive, she found herself missing a hairpin turn and surging forward into space, over a cliff. When the Chevy landed, she whispered to herself, "I'm alive, I'm alive." But she couldn't move and barely believed her own message. Until she was pulled from the mangled steel by a couple who happened to be driving by in the opposite direction and had just caught sight of the flying descent. Otherwise, the whisperings in the canyon would have gradually been stilled. The result was severe concussions and headaches for a month, multiple bone breaks; and small bruises and cuts that covered her body like roads on a map; a permanently misshapen shoulder. Mother, by letter, told her she wanted nothing more to do with her. Daddy, however, remained loving and came to the Coast and stayed with her for two weeks. And when a friend there mentioned that a well-known etcher was coming to Cardozo as an artist-in-residence, Daddy immediately encouraged her to apply and helped get her portfolio together. The work was good and gained her entrance, despite her two previous failures to stick. But here she had been, these past two years; and now she was about to graduate. She smiled, her teeth attractively crooked, her brown skin animated by the talk and life-exposure, her chin from Jeanne Moreau. I leaned over and embraced her.

She asked me about myself. I didn't know where to begin or what to say. After bumbling around, I settled on draft resistance and my days in jail.

"The first couple of weeks were the hardest to take. You're not used to regimented madness and suddenly you're thrown into it. It's difficult to describe to someone who hasn't experienced it. To be closed in by walls and bars and confined to a tiny space suddenly, just like that, is a form of madness. And, when you think you have to go out or you'll die, absolutely go crazy, the guard says, 'Take it easy, buddy, or you'll wind up worse.' You lie back on your cot and pray, literally pray, that claustrophobia will leave you." I paused and tried to remember as closely as possible back to those days. "Especially when you're not consumed by guilt for any crime. It's easier in that condition, I would think. At least there'll be some desire for the punishment then, deep down somewhere. The worse the better, in a way. You see, there's a rationale there, some validity and meaning to it all. But if you've just broken a legal law, and for the sake of something you think is *right*—then the whole thing is absurd and hurts. There's not a shred of inward or outward sense in it. So jail, which I suppose can have its therapeutic side, becomes like an insane asylum. A *Ward Number 6*." Lauri looked at me, and I described briefly the Chekhov story (from Kove's class). She remained quiet, her brown eyes beckoning me to go on.

"I was a federal prisoner, but they were holding me in a

county jail. Which was illegal to begin with. It's hard to find
your local A.C.L.U. man when you're not allowed near a telephone. Anyway, a sergeant placed a legal document before me
and told me to sign it. When I asked what it was, he told me I
didn't have to know. I refused. So they put me into a place
reserved for delinquent prisoners, the hole." The word chilled me
and I stopped. Lauri touched my arm, which I hated. "The hole
was a 5-by-8 room, made of concrete," I continued in a flat voice,
"covered with a putrid-smelling thin yellow rubber. There was
no bed, blanket, or water. My shoes were taken away from me.
The toilet was a hole in the floor, covered by a brass grating.

"In the hole when I arrived was Luther Jackson, a six-foot-
six black from Louisiana, there for hitting a guard. He glanced at
me without speaking. Next door, a young guy was whimpering
without letup, and every so often Luther would shout at him,
'Shut up, you mother-fucker!' By way of explanation, he told
me that the boy wasn't scared at all, but just pretending madness
in order to get shipped out to a loony bin, where conditions were
better. That's why, Luther said, they had sent him down here in
the first place. That evening, a prisoner named Bull, in jail for
second-degree murder of a hippie for his boots, was let loose on
the boy. It seems that Bull had been given unofficial permission to
take care of any prisoners who were making a nuisance down in
the hole. From my cell, it was easy enough to hear Bull taking
care of the boy. He beat and raped him, cursing with joy. Afterward, he was released and set into our cell, where he rejoined his
old buddy, Luther.

"I had always thought that the hole was for one person,
alone. Which it was, except when they wanted to show you
something.

"Bull looked like his name: no neck, smallish head, enormous
chest. A white guy. With a scar running down along one ear and
stubby crushed fingers, from when he used to catch in his Class B
baseball days. With the boy next door moaning steadily, Bull and
Luther began recounting old times together. Mostly this meant
remembering and detailing jail brutalities they shared. For example, a gang assault on a boy in a Pennsylvania prison where
homosexuality was pretty much accepted in certain dormitories."
I nodded in appreciation. "It was terrific the way they told the

237

story, like a couple of advertising men having a drink together and recalling their salad days. The assault was like some great gang-bang, except that the boy who was the receiver didn't want any of it. Making him do it added to their fun. I listened in my corner, not budging, trying to cringe out of sight and trying not to cry. Oh, they were half playing with me, I'm sure. It worked. I was terrified. Whenever one of them so much as shifted his weight, I jumped like a guinea pig prodded. Through the night it went that way. Once Luther got up, and I couldn't keep from shitting. It just came out. But he only pissed and returned to sleep. For seven or eight hours, until dawn, it was like that."

Lauri wanted to say or gesture something sympathetically, but I held my hand up to stop her. I was too tense with the memory.

"In the morning Luther and Bull were released from the hole first thing, but I was kept there. A guard from the outside pressed a button and flushed the latrine hole. It overflowed and ran everywhere, at a low level. Over me too. After an hour of the stench and the touch, they let me come out. They gave me a new pair of trousers and undershorts, but no bath or shower. I was allowed lye soap for my face, no toothbrush, and was put back in the hole. Bull was gone, Luther remained. I spent four or five nights there . . . But that first night was the hardest, I think. Although maybe some worse things happened to me later on. But the first night was pure shock. What it did to your body was less important finally than what it did to your mind. . . ."

I don't know how long I talked, or the rest of what I said. I know that when I stopped, my head was swimming, my heart pounding. The girl and the trees seemed strange to me, that prison regression having been so intense. After a moment, she tried to console me. At first I was resistant, angered that she had seduced me into revealing something awful and private. But she persisted, her hand touching me, and I soon gave way, melting in her arms and breaking into tears. I cried like a baby. She caressed my neck and head maternally, at length. Finally, I regained some presence and returned to normalcy, after the five minutes of letting go. My heart filled with the girl before me. Her hair was disarrayed and she looked fatigued, as if she had told the story, not I. But those small brown pupils fixed me firmly, and with one hand she

238

rubbed my forehead. They were special moments. For her compassion, I was very moved and grateful.

Back in the museum, I told her we'd see each other again during the occupation, and she nodded and walked off. Curiously, I felt renewed. It was terrific to have relief from the dry politics of the sit-in, like a short furlough of feeling after months of abstinence. Strategy-huddling, the endless rhetoric, the collective life were making me stale, worn. (Not to mention my own capacity for stiffness and coiled emotions.) To have those moments of privacy and confession made me feel more relaxed and more generous toward students and comrades. And I realized how much private (or sexual) energy was being deflected into political posturing in that museum bivouac.

About 10:30 P.M. there was a disturbance at the back entrance, and word spread quickly that Dean Kovell had arrived. People stood and turned. The effect on us—a youthful audience in search of an adult hero—was electrifying, and students began clapping and whistling and stomping, like a high-school cheering section greeting its star quarterback. Only this quarterback, in a cream-colored windbreaker and pullover sweater, was accompanied by a willowy blonde in turtleneck and slacks, and a young boy, about five. Wilder cheering rose when Grace and Naaron were spotted and associated with Kovell. From legend to reality, there they were—Kove and another mistress. While room was made for Grace and the beaming Naaron on a sleeping bag, Kove saw me and pulled me aside. "What's up? What's the point?" he asked, unsmiling. "Schlossberg is making no sense whatsoever." I shrugged my shoulders, not knowing really what to say, restraining my sympathy. "I don't really know," I answered honestly. He looked at me, suspicious, angry. "You kids are a pain in the ass," he said deliberately. "So are you adults," I found myself answering. We exchanged a look, then Kove walked off, toward the barricade stage.

Things were changing all right. Kove's anger and my retort had hit home. The first moment of cutting out on my own?

Earlier I have presented and analyzed the content—that anachronistic content—of the Dean's speech. Just now I want to speak more personally and to provide a straightforward narrative of events, for historical accuracy.

239

Having Grace and Naaron there, along with Kovell, light-ened the mood. A version of family day in the Sierra Maestra Mountains, with Kove as Che and the museum as the mountains. Our hero Dean, standing uncertainly on a desk turned on its side and held in place by rope and wedged chairs, began speaking. He hadn't gone two sentences before Naaron ran up to the barricade stage and pleaded with Kovell to lift him up. Kove nervously called to Grace to retrieve him, with a look that said, "For godsakes, this is no time for children's games!" But we loved it and screamed, "Naaron, Naaron, Naaron!" (How in the world did the kids learn his name so fast?) Amazed, Kove looked at Grace, who, like Lauren Bacall returning the hot potato to Humphrey B., held her hands in the air. With reluctance, almost slipping, the Dean lifted Naaron over the rope, but could find no place to settle him. An ingenious student ran up with a portable blackboard and, placing it over two armrest chairs, made a safari-type seat for the boy, atop the barricade. And so Naaron, like Sabu atop an elephant, a Red Sox cap his turban, sat swinging his legs. In such a carefree and curious atmosphere, so alien to the decorum and order which Kovell preferred, did the Dean begin his curious speech.

Did this casual environment affect what the Dean had to say? How upset was he at the fact of having to leave his New Hamp-shire house in the middle of his cherished weekend retreat to confront yet another Cardozo rebellion? Certainly, he couldn't have been pleased about the absence of decorum and the inter-ruption of his country work. Nor could it be pleasing to be forced to bring his personal life right there into the museum arena. Pleasure and official duty weren't joined easily in that man.

What did we expect that night from the Dean? It's hard to say. Obviously we were very fond of him; I suppose we felt that, no matter what he said, he wouldn't betray that affection. He had been our choice for dean, remember—radicals and moderates alike—against the administration's will, and against his will. And for the past two years or so, there was no one figure on campus who commanded more respect or good feeling from us than Kove. For being tough-minded and his own man, as I've said. Neither youth-panderer nor youth-hater, like so many of his weak and confused colleagues. And he presided without a fixed politics to the right or left, preferring to render judgments according to the specifics of the situation.

A demonstration of good faith, not words—once again those "foes of reality" come into play—was what we wanted. It was a quality that Kove was always providing. Interestingly enough, in the sense of what it tells about the times, one of the crucial acts of such faith had occurred during another occupation crisis, about two years previously. In the midst of a two-week ordeal of trying to learn facts (the students claimed unofficial trustee promises had been made and broken), the Dean broke down. With a female friend I was sitting in his office, counseling and consulting, when he left his seat and began pacing, talking. But talking not to us. Up and back, in front of the plate-glass window, with students passing. Talking non-stop about all kinds of things—the war, the crazy society, the girls in his life—switching back and forth, without connections . . . (Picking up the newspaper.) "Why should I advocate sanity if they're going to pass their fucking ABM bills? . . . What do I know about 'settling problems,' 'making compromises,' 'adjusting matters'? . . . Students are a pain in my neck. Let my colleagues deal with them . . . What does Gwen want from me, what? She'll drive me out of my mind! . . ." Suddenly he swayed sideways, knocking into his rubber plant. We lunged for him before he fell and helped him to the sofa. We asked him for the number of his doctor, and he stared at us as if we were total strangers. So, instead, we called the university psychiatrist, who came over. In ten minutes, we were driving Kove to McLean's, where he spent the next two weeks. A case of complete exhaustion. As Kove read to me, amused, from the shrink's assessment—"an unhealthily intense involvement with students and their present crisis." (This was too good to resist. I had this diagnosis printed on a thirty-five-foot banner, Chinese-style, and hung it in the student cafeteria. It was a great success.)

The news of the breakdown spread quickly. We made him an enormous get-well card, an amusing drawing of student guerrillas in football uniforms hoisting their coach, Kovell, off the field after victory. There were three hundred fifty signatures (no room for more). He laughed heartily when I brought it along during my first visit. We had a good walk and talk, during which

I informed him of school events, and he told me of the famous novelist residing there and the frenzied antics his presence generated in his friends and admirers. Amusing stuff. On the way out, I ran into Gwen Tresvant, who surprised me with an embrace. "He's doing much better, don't you think?" she said. I agreed. "Now if only you kids would stop breaking his balls," she added seriously. I reddened and felt responsible.

To us, the actual breakdown suggested Dean Kovell's health, his personal integrity. No decent man, we felt, could stay in a position of authority in America today without suffering nervous collapse from the lies and hypocrisies he had to pronounce and put up with. So struck were we, in fact, with the Dean's dilemma that we got to work and began a seminar on the topic in his honor. It began the third day he was away and continued on, once a month, through that spring term. We called it the Kovell-Kondition. We defined it, in a leaflet announcing the seminar, as:

> The periodic and inevitable breakdowns suffered by men of healthy morals who live and work in America of the 1960's to the 1970's. The cost of honesty has risen in the country in the past decade. For the young, it means jail, underground exile, the F.B.I. on your tail; for adults, hospitals, clinics, shrinks.

Unfortunately, in those sessions we were without the great clinical benefit that Family Talk could have provided us. That confessional brief of personal confusion. In any case, when he returned two weeks later, himself again, we felt more intimate with him. *Connected.* As if we had X-rayed him morally while he was away and found him not only well but thriving. It was strange, that subtle shift in our affections.

This was one of the ways he had captured our hearts, the man who spoke to us that night.

The events. Which may be familiar in a general way but without details, tonalities.

So Kovell began, referring here and there to notes, mostly improvising. Twirling a rubber band nervously in his hand, smoking, looking odd up there in his windbreaker, like standing on top of a tank. Our Dayan. Somebody offered him a pipe of hash, but he refused. The words flowed, the pot drifted, rock-and-roll drummed occasionally in the background. While a Jeffersonian Romanov addressed the American kindergarten. Naaron finally fell off to sleep in his seat, covered with a pullover. The captive students listened and dozed, having been there almost two days, awakening to hear the words still coming. And when you looked up and around, you saw a Klee boatman, a Braque still life, a Giacometti man—not reproductions but the real things. It felt odd, eerie. Meanwhile, throughout the evening, outsiders appeared, coming, going, lounging. A strange black or two, a familiar Cambridge leftist, a man with a cape who was associated with the Action Theater Repertoire, a group performing that weekend at Longman Theater. You barely knew these people were around, really; you saw one or two floaters out of the corner of your eye and then forgot about them. It was only later that their presence was keenly felt.

It was 2:45 A.M., several hours after the talk began, that the first interruption occurred. A leather-jacketed stranger leaning against a wall yelled aloud to the Dean. Kove stared at him in amazement and asked him to repeat his words. Through cupped hands, the fellow yelled, "Fuck off! And stop this shit!" The Dean stood stunned, but several students rose up angrily at the heckler. From across the way, a woman with long hair and heavy makeup, obviously an actress, took up a bullhorn. "You've had it, baby! You heard the man, fuck you! This is the revolution!" I myself was furious at the interruption, and was pleased when Kove demanded to know the identity and purpose of the intruders. Immediately marshals and captains encircled the newcomers and told them to cool it, or else leave. The first inkling of confrontation, won by the kids. The heckling ceased. But the air was different when the Dean resumed talking. Even he was visibly shaken. The warmth of the student get-together, the charm of a high-school football rally were dissolved. The prom was over. Instead there was uncertainty in the air. Strangers were in our midst, and no one quite knew what to do with them. Or what they were up to. I myself looked for the other Committee members, but they were scattered everywhere. The familiar was becoming unfamiliar.

As Kovell talked, small arguments arose about whether or

243

not to throw the new people out. After all, as someone pointed out, they could be police or administration plants. Finally, Kove moderated. When one student insisted that the protest be open to anyone against "the war and racism," a gangling basketball star, who had surprised everyone by being there in the first place, stood to answer him. "Is it open to anyone whose only purpose is to disrupt us and destroy what we've done so far? To anyone who has nothing positive to contribute?" His six-foot-seven frame shaking from anger and embarrassment. "This is a United Front," rejoined a bearded grad student and seminar leader. "We have no time for bourgeois subjectivizing." The basketballer began to answer, but was cut off with "Sit down, jock, or we'll think you're the F.B.I.!" The derisive joke, "jock," cutting more than agent, humiliated the hook-shot artist, who sat, amid cries of "Down, jock, down!" Kovell returned to his criticism of disruptive tactics. But no longer was anyone smiling or dozing or dancing. The girls sat closer to their boys, and everyone was waiting for the next act in the drama. Kovell looked over to me with renewed appeal. But strangely, as much as I abhorred the imminent threat, I realized that our protest was itself futile as it stood. It sought to change nothing fundamentally, and was getting bogged down in rhetoric, in words. Perhaps the new element was the right catalyst. So I followed my intuition to let things flow, without trying to impose order or reconciliation. I turned away.

Some twenty minutes more of Kovell-talk before all illusions of a return to normalcy were smashed. Standing by a partition on the side, a cadaverous, bald, fortyish man in a black cape spoke from a bullhorn: "This is cop-out shit! This must be halted! This is counter-revolutionary!" A British accent, like a man announcing a bombing raid over London. (That's Horner, someone said, the director-producer of ATR.) From the opposite direction came the shrill counterpoint of the actress in her leotard, Horner's wife, "Fuck you, Dean! Fuck you, Cardozo! Fuck you, little Jews! And you too, little black Toms!" The theatrical slogans sprang students to their feet—wild with anger but bewildered what to do with it. Kovell pleaded for order, called for the marshals to close ranks to prevent violence, and invited the agitators to make their case from the platform. "Case?" mocked a tall handsome black, at a side mike, a stranger in an expensive ribbed sweater and shades. "Case? The cat there is right—the Dean's been jiving us with honky-talk!" Pointing at Kovell, his deep bass voice boomed, "This man has GOT TO GO!"

Bedlam, the beginnings. The fantastic terrifying magnetism of violent events, which is so hard to capture in words.

When three kids charged the wild-eyed producer, his face lit up with excitement. "Yes, that's it, come on now, come at me!" he urged the boys, who suddenly were cordoned off by marshals. "Come on, don't let these fascist guards stop you! Unless you're faggots." And suddenly the three students were swinging wildly at the marshals. An electric signal, it seemed. For simultaneously, on the opposite side, kids had broken into small gangs and were slugging at each other, at marshals, at strangers, using fists, belts, boots. "Now you're getting it all together," cried the actress with hysterical glee. "Beautiful! You're beautiful!" And just by the natty spade, three blacks were beating the shit out of a white boy. "Now you're acting *black*, baby, now you're doing it!" he called out, grinning. "Let's break up this ofay Mew-zeem!"

My response to the spectacle was fear and shock. Inured to television, movie, and newspaper violence, I was jolted by the intrusion of real-life punching and blood. Awful, just awful. All my past theorizing about violence was just so much cheap talk next to the real thing. How much more convulsive and painful the reality! On one hand, I wanted desperately to separate the fighters, evict the troublemakers, restore order. On the other, I had learned to float with an experience, to feel it out before squashing it immediately, to try to get at its underlying meaning. My head and stomach pumping away, I found myself craving a machine gun instead of a camera. That's what violence does to you, or at least it did to me—provoke fear, unleash animal feelings.

Until I was suddenly caught from behind, my camera grabbed. "Leave it go, Lenny," warned Cecil Daws, a black friend. "It's a new ball game now. We'll take the pictures." Another pair of arms (white) wound about my neck. "Give it over, sweetheart." For some reason, the camera suddenly meant a lot to me, and I fought furiously, an elbow in the stomach of sweetheart giving me temporary release. But then Cecil rapped me on my temple, someone else banged my ribs, and I was out of air, falling. I must have been out for a minute or so, for what I remember next is lying on the ground, my ear ringing, my lungs gasping for oxygen. My camera lay against the wall, smashed.

The assault had taken a minute or two. I crawled to the camera, got the magazine open and the film out, hoping for the best. And lay against the wall, watching stage two. Numb with hurt and anger. By the stairwell, a pair of blacks were methodically raping that tall blonde in Buddhist sari, the professor's daughter —one sitting astride her shoulders while the other pried open her clenched legs. Two actors in black turtlenecks had pushed the basketball center up against a wall and were forcibly embracing him, feeling his ass and groin. Blood spurted brilliantly from the black head of Harold Ussery, '72, a classical pianist. Shrieks from Lloyd Kapsack, a pre-med senior, whose leg was crushed beneath a tangle of bodies. A sophomore girl in braids, up from Atlanta to obtain a Cardozo education, held her boy friend's cut head in her arms and moaned like a Vietnamese mother. Kovell had been dragged from the barricade and was held prisoner. And above the screams, moans, curses, rock music, soared the panting frenzy of Helena Horner. "Do it! Do it! Do it!" Familiar enough from hearsay, perhaps, it was fantastic and unbelievable up close.

The next stage was the turning point. New. A tragic scene concocted by Artaud and Fanon rather than Aristotle or Marx. Three blacks, two of whom I knew, had climbed upon a chair and had taken down the lengthy Jackson Pollock painting. Holding it aloft horizontally, one of them wrote on the wall in lipstick, DOWN WITH WHITE ART. Then they began winding through the exhausted, bleeding battlefield, like a group of Red Sox fans carrying a Yastrzemski banner through the stands at Fenway. After jabbing and slicing it with a knife, they stopped to invite friends to join in. They grabbed another painting, the Braque, and wrote in its place, HONKY CULTURE INSULTS THE REVOLUTION. And began shredding it apart, as they ran and chanted their graffiti. The human battle began to be upstaged by the destruction of the art works. It really excited Horner, who directed from the sidelines like a boxing manager. "Out of sight, baby, out of sight! You're into it now, you're creating the revolution. This is it!" The voice and phrasing were just right, turning on whole groups of kids who had simply looked on in dumb fear and awe until then.

Now they got into the action, joining the blacks. When Howie Gross, a talented poet and editor of the literary magazine, cracked open a glass case and flung a Picasso sculpture against the wall, smashing it into pieces, he was cheered wildly by onlookers. Or when Cecil Daws shattered the glass containing two small Kurt Schwitters collages and squashed them like putting out cigarettes, he was kissed on the cheek by a blond girl and had his arm raised by a white boy. On the wall in its place, he wrote with black chalk, NO MORE IMPERIALIST ART.

So the children's games proceeded, art works broken apart like cartons in the supermarket—wooden frames torn loose, Klees and Picassos ripped apart and tossed away like Del Monte flaps. The Berg Art Museum had become a Chicago slaughterhouse, with culture replacing cattle.

Two incidents haunt me still. First, I see skinny Mickey Klein running wildly, his shirt out of his trousers, and shouting toward a crew of boys approaching his beloved Matisse interior. At the wrecking crew, he is tripped by a grinning actor and pinned to the floor by two white boys. There he watches as a black unzips his (own) fly and proceeds to pee across the canvas. The jest is complete when the sopping mutilated colored picture is flung onto Mickey's lap.

Second, I'm recognized by one of the roving bands. "C'mon, Pincus!" orders Marty Gold, a newcomer leftist and my enemy, "get your hands dirty!" Thick black arms grip my neck, while Luis Rodriguez pins my arms (smiling). A push-button knife is fitted into my fist, while a de Kooning woman, a 4-by-5 canvas, is placed before me. "Cut her open, baby," whispers the black. "They're right, Lenny," explains curly-headed Marty, headed to Harvard Medical School before the Red Book popped up. "The whole structure has got to go, and it's beginning here." He nods at the pair holding the painting. "The natives are the new vanguard, Pincus, whether you like it or not." I want to tell him to ditch the Fanon and look at America, as I've told him before, but pressure is applied to my windpipe, and I well up with impotent fury, loss of oxygen. Finally, I jab out at de Kooning, and the hold on my neck is relaxed somewhat. I let out my anger at the primitives and idiots by slashing away at the distorted pink belly and the split face of the woman. Laughter and words of encouragement provoke me to an orgy of jabbing and ripping and cutting and slashing. When it's over, I'm kissed on the head by Cecil Daws and patted by Luis. They leave me alone with the debris. My brain spins like a wheel in mud.

A half hour, an hour? I lose track of the time . . . Around me there is whimpering, low moans, occasional shrieks, a periodic tapping of bongos. And the stench of urine and feces rises. A couple here and there are still wriggling, skirt up, pants down, arching for release. A lovely dark-haired sophomore named Karen sits yoga-style near me and cries hysterically, bloodstains on her navy Cardozo sweatshirt. A white sociology professor, competing for publicity and favor with the blacks, squats over a painting, his trousers at his ankles, and shits. To add to the piles of excrement which lie scattered upon canvases. His signature.

Fragments of a speech by Marty Gold filter through the chaos. "We are in the throes . . . our cultural revolution . . . our counterpart to the Chairman's Hundred Flowers . . . welcome the forces of progress at work tonight . . . the peasants once more showing the intellectuals the road to revolution . . . salute our peasants, the blacks!" Assorted cheers and fist-waving are dampened, however, by two "peasants" jumping on the stage and twisting Marty's arm in a hammerlock, leading him back to the mike. He apologizes publicly for his mistaken racist terminology.

He is interrupted by the news that someone has gotten loose from the museum and that the "regular pigs" had finally been called onto the campus. Thank God for patient academics in situations of crisis, so that we could get our work done!

Commotion, disorder, evacuation.

I raise myself, dazed. Lauri Pearlman is at my side. A Politburo member touches my arm and shoves a makeshift parcel under it. Like refugees, we file out the back door, carrying blankets, sleeping bags, transistors. As we move down the sloping hill toward the chapels and then begin to climb the Cyclone fences separating university grounds from the town, the image changes from refugees to parachuted soldiers dropped behind enemy lines. Wary and fatigued, I climb the fence, squeezing the wire fiercely with my hands, summoning up childhood entries into schoolyards. Lauri calls out for me to wait for her as I jump down, on suburb woodlands. The two of us wander through the moonlit woods, not talking. A woodland of pines and oaks, neat houses some two hundred yards off. Finally, I motion to a darkened spot, and Lauri spreads her blanket by the side of a tree trunk. The ground is soggy from a drizzle, but fortunately it is not cold. In a few minutes, the girl is sleeping on my arm. Smoking, I open my parcel. A piece of paper is tied by a rubber band covering a small sculpture. A brief message announcing an emergency meeting the following Monday night at a Cambridge address. The sculpture is that of a bronze man, about a foot high, walking into the wind. A Giacometti man, the torso emaciated, the cheeks shrunken, the eyesockets deep and empty. He looks at me and I look at him, and I don't get it. I set it aside and try to sleep. The temple above my left ear, the damaged one, is ringing . . . A sudden light movement across my chest, and my eyes open upon an eight-inch rodent, brown, furry, the small head jerking about nervously. The beady eyes fix mine momentarily. I have no desire to chase him away. He passes on to inspect Lauri's face. When his fine teeth probe, she awakens, but I cut off her scream with my hand. The field rat or whatever flees.

Lauri looks at me with horror-filled eyes as I release her mouth. Still I don't speak. Suddenly she moves upon my frozen face, nipping and kissing, her hand massaging my stomach beneath my shirt. Her hand finds what she wants, she smiles. Soon her Wranglers are down and she is above me, moving up and down, circular; making love while I still see the museum. Afterward, her head is upon my chest. I look out through the trees at the black sky and gray clouds and wonder where I am suddenly. Lauri talks, stares at me; the words seem strange to me. When I look at her eyes, I see the paintings slashed and shat upon. Slowly she senses something, backs off, and asks what's wrong? Dressing herself, she asks the question again, touching my shoulders, trying to revive me. But it's like reviving stone. She runs off in tears. The wetness meanwhile seeps through the blanket, and I find myself saying over and over, "Waltham, Massachusetts, 1972; Waltham, Massachusetts, 1972." But I don't believe it. Perhaps the Sierra Maestra Mountains? Or a stopover on the way to

Shensi? . . . Something stirs at my leg, and I get up and start moving, running.

I spent the next several days in assorted hideouts—in a vacant bus in the Riverside Station, on the floor in a Littauer building office, in a friend's Somerville apartment. And walked around Boston and Cambridge, trying to make sense of the museum actions and to feel out their implications for the future. But it was hard to get beyond a certain shock and disbelief at what had occurred. Civilized Lenny in the midst of barbaric destructiveness. I walked and rewalked my old territory— the narrow winding cobblestone streets of Green and Franklin and Howard, where *lumpenfolk* and students and freaks mixed uneasily, and cats prowled for garbage in a bit of Venice; or to the protective green patches off Kirkland, where Harvard wives pushed prams and swung tennis rackets, and large Victorian mansions offered solidity and history, perhaps a bit of England—but neither helped. I still felt this new surge of pressure in my head, like being carried out to sea by a whirlpool. And the more I fought to resist it, the more it seemed to hurl me in its grip, toward some unknown but frightening destination.

> *As for Doing good, that is one of the professions which are full. Moreover, I have tried it fairly, and, strange as it may seem, am satisfied that it does not agree with my constitution.*
>
> (*Did Thoreau ever utter more attractive words in* Walden?)

2. Lenny Gets Busy

Pressure didn't seem to let up in those warm summer months, before the siege started in September 1972. In fact, two events occurred which intensified it. With the first, many of you are already familiar, I imagine. On August 5, a steamy Friday night at approximately 1:43 A.M., a man was murdered in Cambridge, a well-known figure from the world of culture. But behind that notorious public story lie some interesting details of private motive and deed. To rephrase a famous first line, every murder, unlike every marriage, is uniquely interesting.

About the second event, my relations with the young teenage girl from—but wait, I'm getting ahead of myself.

Again, in the days following the Uprising, I walked around disturbed and confused. No matter how I understood intellectually or rationalized what had gone on, I couldn't get it through my bones. My instincts remained repelled. Destroying pictures, ripping up a museum, rape, damaging books—comrades in the Newmeyer Library tore and mutilated hundreds of books when they found out what we were up to in the art museum—all this went against my thinking and my nature. What to do? Get a new nature perhaps. Easier said than done. For others, I might add, things were easier. For Luis Rodriguez, for example, a Puerto Rican on scholarship at Cardozo who had held my arms at one point in the museum, I simply worried excessively. "Just take it easy, brother," Luis cautioned one day, with his usual mixture of sincerity and derisiveness. "You seem all wound up, tight. Maybe it's all too much for you."

Maybe Luis from San Juan via Spanish Harlem was right. A thin taupe-skinned senior, with a pencil mustache, long sideburns, ambiguous smile, who, when I first met him, greeted me with, "I'm Rodriguez, spic. Pleased to meet you." I responded in kind, "Pincus, kike. Likewise, I'm sure." I think we got on, as well as you could with Luis. He had a habit of cleaning his teeth with matches, and, one day when telling me about an adolescent skirmish, he casually held his palm out to show me that his innocent pack of matches contained a narrow single-edged razor blade which had been his childhood arsenal. (Along with special sharpened taps on his black shoes, which revolved outward and acted as a small blade to the shins.) Next to Luis's homemade instrument, my own .38 Smith & Wesson seemed tame, clean, and correct. As *I* felt, next to him. I probably did have too much of the "bourgeois" and "white boy's instinct"—as Luis always seemed to be hinting, without ever saying, he was not much for slogans himself—to be a model guerrilla in the new wars. The museum shock reminded me sharply of my intermediary condition, of the long way I had to go yet in my evolution into a primitive rebel; an anxiety reinforced whenever I was in the presence of Luis and

251

certain other comrades, whose purpose and anger seemed straight as a bullet.

But what could you do with your own flesh and instincts, treat them as you might an automobile? Paint over one, and, for the other, change your emotions and fix your reason, as if you were inserting new points and plugs and adjusting your idler?

If not that, then how?

I picked her up on Massachusetts Avenue, at the edge of M.I.T., heading toward Harvard Square. She was standing demurely between two parked cars, thumb protruding. It was a renowned Cambridge pastime, for girls especially. They lined up on the streets, to use a Kovellian image, like girls in a brothel, parading their wares to attract you. In Cambridge, a key resort town for the new tribes of teen-age nomads. Since I rarely had a car, I rarely picked one up; and when I did, I usually was busy with other things. But now, feeling low and driving Kovell's second car, the Ford, I pulled over—or was it the Ford moseying over to the curb from its own habits?—to the girl who looked so unlike the typical hitchhiker freak in army surplus. This girl was entirely the opposite. Her light brown and blond hair was tied neatly in back with a blue-and-white silk kerchief, and she wore a smart matching miniskirt and British Army officer's shirt-jacket (from Bonwit, not Goodwill), complete with epaulets. She was also rubbing one eye, a tender gesture.

When she got into the front seat, she brought with her a small suitcase with a TWA baggage claim attached. I hadn't noticed this before, and it aroused my interest. She sat in the front seat very shyly, hands clasped in lap, looking down or out her window. I said something briefly about the weather to reassure her; then, seeing a paperback peek out of her straw tote bag, I asked her what it was. *Trout Fishing in America*, by Richard Brautigan. Did she like it? She nodded, blushing. Another child, I thought. It was only when I asked her how old she was that she looked at me straight on, and then only momentarily; but it was enough for me to be slightly thrilled at the perfect pink youth of her face and her clear green eyes. "Going on nineteen," she said in a low thin voice. Fair enough.

Toward Central Square, I tried to get her to say a few words about her paperback, but what she produced was "I really like him." She remained reticent, contained, upright in posture. Where was she headed for? I asked. She shrugged small shoulders. "Shall I drop you at the Square?" "Uh, okay." I paused, then asked, "Have you been here long?" A pause. "Not really." "Do you know people here?" "Not many." When we got near the Square, I asked her how long she had in fact been here. Her lower lip moved forward, and she emitted, so low that I only heard it after replaying her answer, "This morning." And I saw tears running down her cheeks.

I gave her Kleenex from the dash and said a few words about the Harvard buildings along Mass. Ave., which we were passing. She blew her nose and nodded, and I kept talking, noticing the modest ring she was wearing, with a series of small turquoise stones. Driving slowly, I asked her if she had a place to stay. She shook her head slowly, Kleenex at small sharp nose, that lovely lip moving again. I said very matter of factly that I knew a commune in the area, where I sometimes stayed; would she want to stay there a few days until she found a place? "I better not" was her small utterance, while her small will—for that much was apparent already—struggled with the question. And suddenly she looked at me again, full of brave innocence and great shyness. I smiled easily and pulled up to the curb by the kiosk in the center of the Square and told her to get some magazines. She stared at me, confused. I got out and waved her outside, and she followed. She didn't know where she was or what to do when I brought her to the vast magazine racks there, but I left her to herself while I went to the other side to buy a *New York Review of Books*. After paying for it, I noticed that she had a copy of *Seventeen* in her hand and that her white stockings encased perfect young legs. And black Pilgrim shoes with buckles, which touched me. I took her elbow, paid for *Seventeen* (which I had never seen anyone read before), and took her back to the idling Ford. It was tacitly settled.

Driving the hot Cambridge streets, I asked her name. Nugget. Amused privately, I pursued her real name. Joan. Joan Cummings. And "Nugget"? A childhood nickname, dating from her first spoken syllable ("nug") and officially affixed by her six-year-old sister. A pause. Was that a high-school graduation ring?

She nodded, this Nugget, and looked away. I commented on the spread of fashion stores into the Putnam Avenue area and asked where she had come from this morning. Washington, D.C. . . . We pulled up in front of the commune on Western Avenue, a huge Victorian monster of wooden gingerbread and latticed balconies. "Gosh," Nugget said, gazing. I said something about John Ruskin turning over in his grave, but she stared blankly at me. I switched to Hansel and Gretel, and she giggled. A real giggle. Carrying her suitcase up the wooden stairs, she pulled my sleeve. "I lied to you." "What do you mean?" "About my age," looking down, fingering her shirt button. "I'm not eighteen." I waited. "I'm . . . going on fifteen." I nodded, restraining surprise. "You won't tell anyone?" "Not if you don't want me to," I said. She shook her head. "I wanted *you* to know the truth, that's all." The disclosure and the timidity made my heart thump strangely as we went inside.

I installed Nugget in a third-floor "road" room—shingled so— used for outsiders and needy friends. A plain room (down the hall from mine), with single bed, student desk and chair, chest of drawers and bookcase, small closet. I left her staring at the Kokoschka reproduction of a gorilla and went downstairs to make her a sandwich. The commune, which I would use periodically over a three-month period, then not at all, housed a nice variety of family-people, students, children (real), dropouts. Although I knew everyone, I kept to myself mostly, in my room upstairs, hardly ever using the commons room to read mags, listen to music, or participate in discussions. Occasionally, I ate dinner there (the cooking depended on the cook, a rotating role). In general, there was a decent feeling about the place, with no one asking any questions and a temporary resident like myself paying what he could. And, as I've said, the variety compensated for ordinariness—academic families from Wellesley and M.I.T., a Harvard professor (sociology) and two grad students, an undergraduate pair from Cardozo (gentle Maoists), B.U. filmmaker hippies, dropout macrobiotics (who could ruin brown rice). It was a good place to be a monk or murderer, so steady were the long-winded discussions, so uniform and settling the tame atmosphere and seedy furniture. Furthermore, because of the three professors who lived there, and their two good lawyer friends from Harvard Law, cops didn't just barge through the front doors. I closed the refrigerator door and smiled at the long anarchist calendar next to it, with a photo of Sitting Bull above July. Even fifty-year-old authors of "Good-Ought" ethics theories couldn't shake their Cowboy-and-Indian upbringings.

Nugget ate the ham sandwich on the bed, knees together, while I sat across from her on a chair. She had already arranged herself neatly in the room, a suède vest and buckskin blouse on a door hanger, toilet articles on the bureau. Already I longed to see her jammies and pigtails—thoughts I immediately dismissed as I questioned her softly about home. (I still didn't know what I was doing there, you see.) Her family lived in the Georgetown section of D.C. and on a farm in Virginia. Mummy was silly—not her real mother, who died when she was seven—but okay and spent most of her time with her friends; but Daddy, who was an OEO director, was "well, really strict" and it made it hard to stay home all summer. He always "bugged" her about hours to be in, guys she could see, concerts she could go to. Things were much better during the year, she continued in a small voice, gulping milk, tiny skirt hiked high, when she went away to school, at Milton. That's how come she came to Cambridge (she had visited it a few times during the year); also the fact that Sis lived in Boston. But "she and me don't get on too well. She's kinda hung up on herself too much." She cleaned crumbs from her napkin with her slender fingers. Her dark blond hair was parted down the center, and her fair pink face, when she smiled, lit up with childlike luminosity. Did she just run off? "Not really. I left a note saying I'd contact 'em in a few days. I will, I guess. I said I had a job lined up in Boston." There was a pair of modest dimples when she smiled.

I didn't know what to make of it all. I liked her, and yet felt curiously unnerved by her, though ever so slightly and without any clear reason. She was so incredibly reticent and shy, except when speaking about her father; then confused fear wrinkled that small forehead. For the first time, she spoke up on her own, saying, "I don't have much money, and this room . . ." I told her she could pay what she could afford, or nothing if she was really low. Then, on an impulse, I added, "I'll take care of it." But all I meant by that, in fact, was to tell Bob H. of her financial status—why then did my sentence imply something more, as if possibly I'd pay for it, if need be? I felt strange suddenly, while she, head bowed, said, "Thank you." She sat back down, her legs parting slightly. It made me uncomfortable, and I stood to go. She followed me to the door. Standing close to me, her pink skin dazzling young, she said, "I . . . I hope I'll see you again. Soon." I nodded, and told her I was down the hall in case she needed anything. I wished her luck, left the room, and went into my own. Similar, except for a sloping ceiling and a modest view of a patch of dreary garden below. Picking up Nietzsche, I tried to concentrate on "The Spirit of Modernity" in my Mentor anthology. But that angelic face and certain phrases ("going on fifteen"—in eleven more months, it turned out!) roamed my mind.

Skip two or three days. I had been away from the house for a few nights, sleeping in a friend's apartment, and when I reappeared now, in the late afternoon, the place was a hive of activity and dust. The dining and commons rooms were having their floors sanded, and everyone was pitching in to help. In the dining room, two girls with handkerchiefs over their mouths were on their knees, wiping up dust. One was Nugget, her little behind arched high. She looked like Zola's Gervaise, perhaps; it was charming. I was glad to see that she had fit in so quickly, and felt relieved as I climbed the stairs to gather a few things, shave, and be off. Relieved.

I was shaving in the bathroom when there came a knock at the door, and before I finished saying come in, it opened.

"Gimme a hand, will ya? I got a little problem." She was short, dark, in Eisenhower jacket and bellbottoms. I had never seen her before. "Don't give me any shit now, will ya? I'm in a bad way. Gimme a break, huh?"

The next thing I knew, I was following her down the dark vestibule, razor in hand, and wiping shaving cream from my face.

In the second spare room on the third floor, she closed the door, threw off her jacket, and, wearing only a black bra on top, said, "Just hold this tight, will ya, buddy? I'm in a bad groove and really need an upper." She handed me a thick leather belt and held out her arm, to the bicep. "Wrap it tight, go ahead. Don't *stare*, for crapsake, just *do*. Please, buddy, huh?"

Mesmerized by the grotesque pathos and eeriness, I did as I was told, wrapping the belt.

"Tighter . . . tighter. That's it . . . there, a little more, a little—good, good. Let's try that." The flesh was pulled taut, so that the veins were emphatic. Several tiny holes marked the vicinity. With her free hand she reached over to a white basin of water and took out a syringe. "Wanna do it for me?" Her black eyes looked at me with cold venom, and I couldn't have told you if she was thirty or ten. "It's not hard, honest," she pursued, and, suddenly, I felt this curious metal in my hands. It was like holding a nineteen-cent ball-point pen. Nail-bitten yellowish fingers pressed olive skin. "There, right there, let's try that. Just put it in, go ahead . . . there, and press slowly . . . slowly. Yeah . . . that's it, slowly." Her eyes closed peacefully. And then opened, more relaxed. "Good." She pulled the syringe out and placed it back in the basin. She took my face in her hands swiftly and pecked my cheek. "Thanks, pal."

I turned to go, shaky.

"Stay a minute, will ya. Just a minute till I get straightened out. Flying. It won't take long . . . here, would you like some shit? I've got some speed if you'd like, or acid." I shook my head at the small narrow box she had opened. Instead I took a cigarette from a pack of Luckies, checking first to make sure they were cigarettes.

She sat in an old wing chair that fit a darkened alcove and held her like a maroon throne. "Some gig, huh?" I shook my head. "What?" "*That* shit. She's always pulling it." I looked to the object of her pointed scorn, a copy of the *New York Post*. I took it off the bureau, and it was opened to a page 5 photo (UPI) of a young girl dressed in an expensive fur coat and hair style, and a handsome middle-aged lady, elegant with coiffure and pearls. The blurb ran, *Thirteen-year-old heiress runs away for second time in three months.* Mrs. Helena Forbes of 1090 Park Avenue had put up a ten-thousand-dollar reward for the return of her daughter Elizabeth, saying, "This will never happen again. As soon as Betsy returns, I'm taking her out of this crazy country and returning to Europe for good. It's quite impossible to bring up children here anymore."

"That *cunt*," she hissed, "with that Betsy stuff! I'd love to

257

shove that ten thousand right up her gazoo!" Her olive face
jumped, then relaxed. "God, what shit. The best scag in New
York, and that's saying something. Fifty bucks a hit. But man it's
groovy . . ." She motioned to a wooden chair and I moved it to
her. It was as if I were watching a TV documentary, it was that
strange. Her legs upon the chair, she moved back into her tone of
plea. "Do me a favor, pal? Could you pull these leggings off? It
gets pretty cozy when the horse starts travelin' across your
body." She was not talking to me directly, but through a cloud,
hoping the words would reach their destination. "C'mon, sweetheart, don't get uptight now. You been a doll and I feel too good.
Okay?" Opening her top buttons, she arched her back and
reached out her hands. "That's a love," she said, as my hands
found themselves beneath her haunches, pulling the striped
trousers from her legs. I too felt caught up in some drug, a non-
chemical sort. She wriggled her toes loose from the bottoms and
smiled widely (which was grotesque, for she had a tiny face).
Her body was narrow, dark, and firm, an Arab in black bra and
black nylon panties. "C'mon, doll, wanna ball me? Want me to
suck you off? Anything goes when I'm feeling good like this. I
tell you what," she said, her voice fading in and then coming
back, like a bad radio connection. "I got a betta idea. Like Ford."
She giggled heartily. "Put some sound on first, huh? Anything
over there, I tote my own when I'm moving. And I've been
moving on and off for two years now. You shoulda seen me when
I was ten and first turning on. My horse and my sound, yeah." I
took the first two records—trying to picture her at ten—and
placed them on the machine. Joplin and Jefferson Airplane. "Oh,
it *feels* good. Oh, you're missing something cool. God, how I *dig*
it. *God*. I only wish *Mother* could catch me now. That'd be
cozy, wouldn't it? For her to catch me at it, right here, and then
for me to turn her on. *Cheesus*, I'd love to see her go up on that
stuff. All that pain and grossing she hands me . . . all that
fucking *Park Avenue shit*." She shook her head, dreaming.
"Yeah, to bring the horse to her . . . hey, my idea, I almost
forgot." She giggled, and for the first time I got a sense of a
young teenager. "In that bag there, baby, hand me it . . .
thanks." She reached down, rummaged, and brought out a bristle
hairbrush. She smiled and brushed her hair. Then she dangled the

brush in the air. "Pretty nice, huh? Here, do it just a time or two. C'mon, here." She gave me the brush, and again I was doing her bidding, brushing the stringy black hair. "A little harder, just a little . . . yeah, that's it. That's nice, make me feel it." As she panted, I stopped abruptly, in terror. I moved back from her, and she drew open those large lids. "What's your bag, baby, what turns you on? Don't tell me you're still wet behind the ears? Do you want to use this"—she had taken the brush from me—"on old Lizzie a little, huh? Right on her little butt? It's a nice one, baby, look—" With an effort she got up, smiled, ran the brush down my cheek lightly, then, in an efficient daze, piled two pillows on the single brass bed and lay upon them, belly down. "How is it, baby, how's it look?" she inquired, in reference to that jut of flesh propped in the air, covered by thin nylon. My head spun as Joplin screamed and Elizabeth continued directions and cajoling. "Pull the panties down, baby, go ahead. Give yourself a break. One good turn deserves another, they say," and she giggled before resuming her sultry voice. "C'mon, baby, it'll be sweet. For both of us. Take the brush . . . atta boy, and pull the panties down. Just touch it first, try it. And then take Momma's brush to little Liz's ass. It'll give us both a gas." I couldn't resist touching that behind with my fingertips, mesmerized. The girl moaned, half-theatrically, half-real. I pulled slowly at the panty, and that behind wiggled. "Go 'head, hit Lizzie a little. Try it, just try it, baby. Momma'd love it, use her hairbrush, baby. Go 'head." Somebody in me obeyed what she said, lightly tapping her teen-age buttocks with the brush and observing the little red consequences. Fascinated and terrified, I had no strength in my limbs. "Harder, doll. Make Lizzie jump. Make me scream. *Please.*" Just then the record went off, and the brush dropped out of my hand. I bent to pick it up and saw a spider nearby on the floor, hesitating. Gangling, black, and grotesque. "Hey, hey, lover, what about me?" came the voice from above. I backed away, dazed. "Hey, baby, where are you, huh?"

Walking in the hall corridor like a drunk, I made the bathroom and poured cold water on my face and neck. Smudges of shaving cream had remained, absurdly. More cold water; then I changed to hot and shaved all over again. The sound of the Airplane came through the doors. I was almost done when there was

another knock at the door. I froze. It came again. I jerked it open
and grabbed the fiend by the arm—"

"Len, Len, what is it?" came the frightened voice of Nugget
Cummings, whose wrist I was holding harshly.

Near tears from tension, I released her wrist and gazed at the
girl. It took me a few moments to realize who she was.

"I thought I saw you before, downstairs, but—Where are
you going? Are you leaving? But you just came back. I don't
understand. I've heard from the others—"

"Heard what?" I suddenly turned on her, inside my room.

"Just heard that you like to be alone, that's all. They all
respect you very much and say you're doing very important
work . . ."

I didn't listen, but saw the loose brown-blond hair and the
bare midriff revealed beneath the tied shirtwaist.

"I'm getting along real nice here." She smiled. "But I
thought you'd be—"

I was taking her face in my hands and kissing her softly. To
my surprise and confusion, that virginal body openly sought me.
With a strange determination I pursued her neck, lips, and ears,
and she kissed me back, although (in a curious way) I was barely
conscious of this. I was being driven by more than that slim body
I was squeezing.

I removed her denim blouse, opening the buttons as she
looked down, and then unhinging her white brassière. Her teen-
age breasts were little buds of pink, with dark brown protrusions
for nipples. The skin was fragrant and indescribably smooth. I sat
her on my lap, facing me, and she turned scarlet and blissful as I
caressed those small blossoms. She barely looked at me while this
play went on, either looking down or leaning forward against my
cheek. Because of this, I enjoyed lifting her chin to face me.

My stroking had aroused her strongly, and I placed her hand
on my penis. At first she resisted, but I put it back and held her
hand there. I told her to unzip my fly and take it out. Slowly, I
repeated the instruction, and she did it, gazing at my prick,
which sprouted as she held it, as if it were the strangest thing she
had ever seen. Her face was scarlet. When I saw she had grown
relaxed (pushing down on the helmet and watching it jump up
straighter and taller, and then giggling), I said, "Come." And

raised her up kindly in order to lower her skirt and white panties. She touched my hair childishly and said, "Should we? I'm . . . afraid . . . I'm a virgin. You probably didn't think that, did you?" Her flushed face was deliciously somber. "I thought that," I answered. Naked, she showed herself more delicate and more teen-age, remarkably white-skinned (with touches of pink bloom), smooth as mother-of-pearl. And fragrant, like a young tree in blossom. She smiled awkwardly (for I had been staring), and I returned her to my lap (my trousers gone), her back to me. As I began to feel her from beneath and under, she turned back her head to mine in a striking and moving pose. I was caressing from her anus to clitoris with my thumb and forefinger, and massaging that blocked vagina. It was barely a minute or two before she was breathing deeply and groaning. "Oh God, oh God, I didn't know, Len . . ."

It was quite touching.

I lifted her easily (she weighed ninety-eight pounds, which thrilled me!), laid her across the bed, and got out of my shorts. Rising to her knees on the bed, she said, "I'm frightened, Len. I am. Maybe I shouldn't now. I'm . . . not yet fifteen and . . . Oh, I want to be with you, but I'm frightened. And we only know each other two times, not even that . . ." Her face was a mixture of appeal, innocence, and excitement. Now a curious thing occurred. When I saw her appeal to me to wait and hold off, when for the first time *I saw that youthful will trying to exert itself,* a tide of new emotions swept me. Anger. Spite. Possibly vengeance. Until then, I had felt wholly kindly and loving toward her, and suddenly these emotions were swept away. That slim waist and teen-age pubic hair and unviolated opening, all now turned into a fourteen-year-old trying to exert her will. It amused me perversely—I even think that for a split second the thought ran through my mind of dragging that fiend from down the hall into the room—but I didn't say a word. My heart pumped, madly. It was perversity that I had sworn myself to, it ricocheted in my head, and now I had to pursue it.

"Oh, Lenny, please, I'm unsure—no—Len, Len—"

I had pushed her roughly onto her back. Her face wore a new expression now—how many *new ones* I had already inspired—and she began to struggle, which I enjoyed even more.

261

Our bodies grappling, I also was fingering her clit again with broad strokes, until her struggle became mingled with desire. Dominating her physically at the same time that I titillated her, and sensing her oscillate between desire and revolt, were delicious. My prick was rubbing at her vagina and as it met resistance, pushed harder, making Nugget yield and yield—to it, to her desire, to me. It was keenly pleasurable to defeat her that way inch by inch—how marvelously right the Sartrean notion of politics in sex—having her come round to total desire and my will. More and more, she moaned and panted and pulled on me. Finally, I pushed very hard, and she screamed and bit me somewhere, and there were tears in her eyes and down her cheeks, and she was holding me desperately close, and I was locked inside of her in a vise of bliss, not very deep but held tight as a fist, and it wasn't too much longer (a few seconds) before I came, although before that, each rotation and each movement were a combination to her of excruciating pain and thrill. As she was saying softly, "I love you, I love you, I love . . ." I disentangled myself and got off her.

I dressed with indifference.

Yet, when I saw the smear of blood on her and the sheet, indifference gave way to confusion. I told her I'd run a bath for her, and she could wash herself. Her lower lip protruded and she asked, in a tearful voice, "Will I be pregnant for sure?" I asked her when her period was due, and when she said in a few days, I said probably not at all. "Come on," I said, "we'll run a bath," and, putting a shirt of mine over her, I did so. She tried to be warm toward me in the bathroom, while the water ran, but I wouldn't have it and left her in there alone. All I wanted was to get away from her (and, although I possibly didn't recognize it then, get away from myself too). I lay down on the bed, listening to the rhythm of Airplane mingle with the running water.

I must have dozed off, into a grim dream of the two girls pleading and demanding, when suddenly Nugget was calling for me. I ran to the bathroom, where Elizabeth Forbes was just hitching up her trousers (wearing only the black bra), and the toilet was flushing. "Your puss is afraid, huh?" she said to me, indicating the terrified girl standing in the bathtub, who was covering herself with a towel. "Don't worry, chickie," she said to Nugget,

"Lizzie's not going to hurt you. You're too tender." She moved past me and out, down the corridor.

Nugget leaned on me, wet and trembling. "She just walked in, Len, without knocking or anything, and I guess my eyes were closed, for she was suddenly standing right here above me, touching my hair. It gave me the creeps! And then she sat down and, and—started going to the bathroom right in front of me! Who is she, Len? Does she live here? It was so creepy, I—"

Just some runaway, I said, and helped Nugget out of the bath. I dried her with a huge navy bath towel, marveling again at the girlish breasts and hips, and the glistening smooth skin. Her shy smile contrasted with the new rich glow on her face, and she shone with innocence again. I held her close. As she whimpered her love chatter and I looked over her shoulder at the emptying bathtub, that other dark face seemed to float toward me for a moment and then disappear. It was grisly. Nugget continued to snuggle with an empty shell.

I left her in her room and went out. It was late afternoon, almost twilight by the time I got to the river. Red and violet were beginning to agitate the placid sky. It was warm. Summer-school students walked past in couples or lay in clusters on the grassy riverbank. I tried to concentrate on Nietzsche.

> THE NEW PASSION. Why do we feel and dread a possible return to barbarism? Is it because it would make people less happy than they are now? Certainly not! The barbarians of all ages possessed more happiness than we do—let us not deceive ourselves on this point!—but our impulse towards knowledge is too widely developed to allow us to value happiness without knowledge, or the happiness of a strong and fixed delusion: it is painful to us even to imagine such a state of things! Our restless pursuit of discoveries and divinations has become for us as attractive and indispensable as hapless love to the lover. . . .

It meant little to go on. Next to my tumulting emotions, it was a word-exercise. Sterile. I closed the pages and stood and walked.

Sickly and torn. My idea had been to wipe the value-slate clean and begin again. An idea simple enough. But in real life it was harder, all of it was *so much harder.* To oppose society and the state was one thing, with only jail and obloquy to face; to oppose myself was grim going. An abyss of loneliness and strangeness, hard to convey to anyone who's not been through it. Suddenly I was asking myself to go against lifelong habits and directions that had given me equilibrium. I was being asked not merely to dredge up desires from the muddy bottom of fantasy and nightmare, but instead of throwing them back after realizing their noxiousness, to go a step further and act upon them. It was horrible and unlivable, no matter what sort of instruction I handed myself about "necessary stages." In fact, the very re-minder itself—that pompous absurd slogan out of some Marxist primer or nineteenth-century novel—only served to intensify my self-loathing.

A few days later, I found myself back at 17 Western Avenue, telling Nugget to dress up and we'd go out to dinner. She was thrilled. We went to the Mexican café on Mt. Auburn street, where, amid the local fakery of guitar strumming and student play-acting, my girl stood out like a fine jewel. Those girlish hips hugged by corduroy, the teen-age chest swathed in lavender, with a frilly lapel and balloon sleeves (and a fiery orange sash tied at the waist); that soft brown hair piled up and up—it suggested a modern Natasha coming out for her first ball. But best of all were the color and fragrance of her skin, pink and fresh as a pale rose. She was especially impressive by way of contrast with the style of trash and sloppiness worn by the majority of the customers. Jewel, rose, and Natasha enjoyed immensely the noisy dinner of enchiladas and beans, delighted by the playful glamour, and later by our evening walk by the Charles; holding on to my arm with feathery glee, giggling joyously at every joke (simple ones), attending to my every word and whim. It was clear that Nugget was becoming devoted to me. More: *she was grateful that I allowed her to be devoted,* loved me all the more for it, thought me all the more perfect because of it. My vanity she called magnanimity. And, read her actions, she was anxious and ready to place her will in my safekeeping. All this at fourteen!

For my part, during that walk and dinner, I was charmed, amused, and delighted. The enormous inequality between us, a fact that would set my passions swirling uncontrollably, was absent here, and I was able to relax and enjoy her . . . Did we have to return to that house?

When we did arrive at Western Avenue, however, I felt fresher and freer than I had in weeks, as if that other self (or my disturbance) had released me. Filled with this new-found cheer, I took Nugget to my room, where we quickly began to make love. How I exulted in removing that blouse and brassière, while my girl blushed like a child, and she loosened those coils of young hair, which dropped almost to her navel. That young body all at once overwhelmed me again, like returning to one's favorite spot on earth, a paradise of fragrances and sights, after forgetting how powerful it is. (That's how ironic the whole thing was, for she made me happier than I had been in months; at the same time that I gave in to low desires, I was never more hopeful or exultant.) I touched those pinkish buds with my fingertips, lapped them with my tongue, tickled them slowly with her own hair, slow gestures which drove her wild. (It is painful to remember and record all this.) Beside herself with joy, she took my hand to her mouth and kissed it gratefully. I pulled down the corduroy pants and put my face against that white-pantied bottom; then I slowly lowered the panty and buried my nose, cheeks, and lips against that cheerleader's bottom. It was fantastic, and I couldn't resist running my tongue along her assline, my head sideways, which brought forth groans and involuntary childish urging (with her hand feeling my head in back) for me to continue it.

That urging, which I adored, unnerved me. I tried to put it out of my mind. And did until she went to her knees, soon afterward, to kiss my hands and open my trousers with a playful loving smile on her face. *More devotion, more inequality*. I tried to contain myself. Standing, and extricating myself from her hands, my eye caught sight of a new paperback next to *Trout Fishing* and *Astrology Manual*. I picked it up—*Cat's Cradle*, by Vonnegut. "Oh," said Nugget, seeing my attention, "Liz loaned that to me today. She said it was groovy, and I should read it. He's her favorite writer." I stared at the red cover, with the slick tetraptych of nuclear apocalypse and children's demonology, feeling new pressure in my chest at the source. Nugget continued, saying that she had gotten to know "Lizzie" in the last few days, and she was "really neat." I kept my eye upon the book. "Are you disturbed? Is something wrong? Why aren't you talking? Shouldn't I know her? Tell me, and I won't, I promise!" She had crawled closer to hug my feet. I told her that her friends were her business. I didn't really know the girl well at all. And realized that, in the distance, the sound of Jimi Hendrix had started up. Giggling, on her knees, she urged me back to love play. I returned to it, but with a new determination. I removed my underwear and, when Nugget sought to rise to climb upon me, I kept her down. With words and hands, I urged her to my penis. She shook her head vaguely, in indecision and fear. Which I cherished. Holding her neck, I moved her back between my thighs, and she took my soft cock into her mouth. I told her to suck upon it until it grew large; she did it briefly, then looked up at me, bewildered and hot. Again I moved her mouth back to the task, like a game of resistance. After her initial timidity, she found it wasn't so bad and began to discover variety. She experimented by lapping at the sides as if it were a fudgicle. (Shades of Kovell.) This show of interest infuriated me, and I stuffed myself deeper in her mouth, which made her choke. But she accommodated herself to it, tucking her knees under her and resting on her haunches in a child's position. At one point, her face terribly flushed and shaken, she looked up and asked timidly, "Is . . . is that enough?" I shook my head, gave her mechanical instructions for improvements, and directed her back to work. Finally, after ten or fifteen minutes, I began to come. She gagged at first, but I held her head steady, only allowing her to pull away momentarily to smear her face with sperm. Afterward she looked at me with abject humiliation, her angelic face flushed and dripping. It was revolting but powerful.

The door opened, Nugget screamed, and like a dog crept behind me; and Elizabeth Forbes, dressed and wearing high boots, said, "Oh, shit, sorry, fellas. I came to ask if anyone wanted to come out, but I guess no one does." She turned around and casually walked back out, leaving the door ajar.

Bewildered and incredulous, I stood and closed it.

Nugget was whimpering and clinging. Looking down at her, I suddenly had a rush of sympathy and, sitting on the bed, held her to me. Rocking her in my arms, I said, "It's okay, darling, it's okay." My curled darling continued to whimper, like a spaniel lost and then found again but still shaking; soon, however, her thin fingers stroked me with affection. I held her face up in both hands—it was odd the way the sperm stayed on, in milky blobs, but it was better than napalm I immediately thought—and suddenly kissed her forehead and mouth with deep feeling. She broke out crying and squeezed me with all her thin might, as if she were the naughty one! Those green eyes looking at me for guidance, approval, instruction. Suffering was impressive on that youthful face, turning the little girl into a Joan of Arc trying to communicate her "voices." The moment drenched me in emotion.

I changed the subject, got her to chatter, and went through her high-school magazine, reading her published poetry. ("Moon Lover" showed the power of night upon a girl's imagination, in which a lover is conjured up and disappears with dawn. "Jesus Doesn't Save" was a prayer for someone to "relate to her better," who doesn't.) Harmless thoughts expressing a yearning for Daddy, I interpreted privately. I appreciated much more her cheerleader's photo, and then left.

Nugget grew more attached than ever. In the ensuing days, the more I proceeded to lose control with her—which came rather regularly in the next week or two—the more devoted she became. The cycle was horrible—my sudden bursts of cruelty, her resistance and then yielding, leading to humiliation and devotion, then my wilder insolence. I couldn't resist nudging her will into existence and then *crushing it*. Just as I couldn't, during those ten airless and frantic days, control my own impulses or scorn. Occasionally, I saw Lizzie around, but not much. With the exception of one incident. A memorable one.

One night I arrived at the house, after yet another afternoon of dirty political talk—that's what it was, our talk—and found on my door a scribbled note from Nugget, saying that she was down the hall in L's room, should I come in. I tried to forget the situation by concentrating on Che's Bolivia diary, beneath my slanted ceiling. But the faint sound of rock drew me back to that child's scrawl, with her cute cartoon of a dottering old man with a cane chasing after a seven-year-old in miniskirt. The new humor was charming, as was that absurd signature, "Nug." Che didn't stand a chance next to that pretty appeal. I got up and, in my socks, made my way down the hall.

The door was slightly ajar, and the two of them were talking. Elizabeth talking, that is—or rather, doing imitations of her mother, French accent and all—and Nugget listening and laughing. It was amusing, the two young girls together, play-acting and being silly, and I felt relieved. As I was about to leave, however, Lizzie shifted tone and said, "Look, why doncha try some a this shit, huh? Nothing addictive, see? Just an upper. I'm about ready for one myself, and I hate to turn on by myself. We'll shoot one and that's it. And when your man comes, split." That trashy seductive voice enraged and pleased me. I waited. Little angel begged off shyly, scared. But Lizzie pursued, a shrewd hustler at thirteen, answering calmly, cajoling. I began to perspire and feel that familiar pumping excitement of the last few weeks. It was like being at a special brothel in Fez, where I paid to watch a city teenager hustle her country counterpart into prostitution. Inching closer, I watched, through the crack of light, little angel against the wall, demure in her denim skirt, looking sideways, confused, as that bell-bottomed dark mouse moved closer, talking softly, pitch black hair shielding her tiny face. "Oh, go ahead, chickie, try it. It won't hurt you, baby. You'll dig it. If you don't, don't do it again. As simple as that. Okay?" Her palms out, she retreated to pour water from a pitcher into a glass. Nugget looked on with hesitant curiosity as her dark pal smiled sweetly, then threw her head back and swallowed, and came down grinning triumphantly. "Just an upper, see? It'll move your head until your man comes." Nugget smiled out of confusion, and I suddenly saw her out of that suffocating room and on the sidelines, leading a cheer in her white tassled outfit. She tried desperately—for I could tell by now the meaning of her every gesture, the repertoire was so small—to avoid taking the step; and I, on my part, dug my nails in my palm to keep myself from entering. "Atta girl, just relax," said the little monster, placing the pill in Nugget's hand; slowly—so slowly that I could have sworn the gesture took close to a half hour— she raised it to her mouth. She threw her head back (in imitation), drank, gulped, and giggled slightly. "Sit right down here, baby, and when it comes over and smashes you, I'll be right here, flying right with you." Nugget was settled in the armchair by her powerful friend, who proceeded to put more records on. I walked away slowly.

Back in my room, I turned on the radio and smoked on the bed, in the darkness. *On junk.* I felt relieved somehow, as if a final decision had been made. I remember thinking, It'll be better this way in the long run. That's what I must keep my eye on. The long run. (What did I mean by this? Political values? Myself? Nugget and me? The rhetoric one uses to cover up confusion and pain, is incredible. And humorous.) *On junk.* Terrific. (I had a fantastic vision of her daddy coming to Cambridge to search for his daughter, last seen at age fourteen in trim skirt and blouse, now age one hundred and fourteen, with a needle hanging from her arm . . . Let *him* go figure out the times.) *On junk.* The thought excited me.

"Oh, God, my head's coming off, just off—why didn't you tell me you had come in? I saw the note missing and knew you were here." A giggle and a wet kiss. "I took an 'upper' from Betsy—oops, I'm not supposed to call her that, but I can here" (she giggled dreamily)—"and I guess it's taken hold—wooooooh!" She ran her hands into space, modern dancing, and continued to move to the slow tune on BCN, her hips swaying in the tiny skirt, her hands drawing circles above her head. My junky showoff. Smiling sweetly, she rocked closer, leaning her fragrance into my senses and touching my thigh shrewdly. Pretty good for ten days' experience. Mrs. Forbes, you were right, bless your Francophile heart, America is a rough place to grow up. Especially with mothers like you and fathers like Claude Cummings. Perhaps you and the director could get together afterward?

When she tried for the bed, I took her to the floor. "Owww, that hurt . . ." she moaned, "but it's better now . . . ooohh. Please fuck me now, will you? That would be so nice. Whatever you want to do, sweetins, would be *so* nice now. Whatever." Do you see what she had become? And how quickly? With no ambivalence, no second thoughts, I took deliberate time in raping her, although it was hardly that, given her encouragement and receptivity. The way she curled her legs around me perfectly, reached beneath us with a free hand to fondle my testicles, nipped at me with her cunt—fourteen and using her cunt that way!—all these gestures were the mark of the journeyman, not the amateur, in the sex trade. Yet, curiously, it was frustrating for

269

me in the sense that no matter how much I pushed her beyond respectable sex and into something more violent, she simply moaned momentarily and said, "That hurts a little, Len," and went right back to loving. Absent was the extra charge derived from cruel domination.

Afterward was the best. Despite her protests and pleas to stay, I forced her out into the hallway, throwing her clothes after her. Forlorn even in her high, she stood there naked, saying, "Please," picking up her things, trying to cover herself. *Please, Len.* Trying to understand. Drugged.

I was insomniac and walked about until very late, when I came back to sleep. A sleep of horrible frustrations and inescapable traps, and, when I woke in the late morning, I felt as if I had been through a month of hard labor without sleep. While dressing, I was filled with an urge to go to Nugget's bed and tell her how awful it all was, how ghastly I felt. I wanted to hold her and take her round and cheer her up again. And have her cheer me up like that evening together. Her innocence could do that, I was sure, then. Soon I was opening the door to her room, saying, "Nug? Nugget?" But the bed was empty, unmade, sloppy. It was too bad. I headed out of the house.

But on the stairs another impulse stirred. I found myself walking down that hallway again, to that *other* room. I was hoping in a way that the fiend would hear me and scream and curse, and give me a chance to bash her tiny head in. I tried the door, it opened, and there were the two of them, Nugget and Elizabeth, lying together in bed, asleep. Lizzie had one arm tossed casually about her friend. I closed the door and left.

Two weeks to the day I met Nugget, a Friday evening, I was out by the Square walking when a familiar voice said to me, by Holyoke Center, "Hiya, lover boy, how's tricks?" It was Lizzie Forbes, in her khaki jacket, a cigarette dangling from her lips, an Indian band and red feather attached to her head. I stared at her. She shrugged. "Forget me, but Nugget's been missing you something bad, you ain't been around, you know. She's a good kid. She's right over there, with Flash." Across the street, by the corner bank, a small group of kids had congregated. Mostly hippies. The Park Avenue–runaway Indian said something else to me, but I didn't listen and walked across the street. Five or six boys and girls, of high-school and college age, were gathered about a short fellow, perhaps thirty, beneath a bullet-smashed window of the Cambridge Savings Bank. (A typical storefront window in the Square, broken two or three times and then left that way, bandaged occasionally.) Nugget was at the edge of the group and didn't see me. A jovial husky black girl asked me if I had change of ten, and, while I gave it to her, I asked what he was selling. Acid. She turned back to Flash, gave him eight dollars, and he opened a long narrow box, the size of a cigar. From it he gave the girl and her acne-faced blond boy friend four tiny white pills. Then the group hopped away, to Holyoke Square, across the street, laughing, with Nugget escorted by a tall black who held her waist in a vast hand. Flash's friend, a boy with a patch over one eye, wished them "good tripping." I began a conversation with Flash, asking about the stuff. He was very short, with shoulder-length hair, wore an earring, was unshaved and ugly; beneath a light jacket he held an anemic white rabbit to his torn undershirt. He spoke very gently and earnestly, telling me how he himself had "transcended psychedelics" and "had his head into meditation." He also did "OD'ing," which meant handling overdose acid cases at concerts and festivals. He peddled dope now mostly to keep living and to take care of his rabbit. There was something particularly perverse about all that explosive danger emanating from so pathetic a source; it somehow reminded me, later on, of Arendt's thesis about the banality of evil in our time. Anyway, he gave me the rates (two bucks a hit, sixty-five for half a hundred hits, or, if I really had bread, twelve hundred a gram). More: he had some great scag coming in from Berkeley at the end of the week, if I wanted that. With another group of high-school kids waiting to do business, I told him I'd see him later. The street scene was busy.

"Lenny, Lenny!" screamed Nugget, jumping into my arms like a daughter. Two black pals accompanied her, one in a beret, the other in a leather vest. She bubbled an introduction, told them she would "catch" them later on ("Now don't forget the gig," said the taller one), and walked off with me, holding my arm. Before we had gotten out of sight, Lizzie yelled, "Don't punk out on us, baby." Nugget waved.

We left the "greening" culture at Holyoke Center—which

some comrades liked to think of as the center of the revolution—and headed down Brattle Street, past the small shops and the evening people. Nugget was wearing dungarees with a sash, a blouse cut from an American flag, and shiny red shoes with heels. Her hair hung loose, wild and long. Her face was still fine, but made up with excessive eye shadow and rouge. A lovely summer evening, with a slight breeze, and Orion visible, and Nugget delirious over seeing me. Walking through the ordered beauty of that bourgeois promenade—where else could you walk these days where the Flashes hadn't set up corner shop?—past the Longfellow and Lowell houses and other landmarks of American history, and I asked Nugget to elaborate about her home and school and parents. I had that curious feeling of last words and consolations, a priest out with his prisoner for a death-row walk.

She explained, her thin voice precise, how her father had remarried after her mother died and that he seemed "extra strict" with her and her sister. He really disliked her going to "all the concerts"—rock, of course—which she attended, saying that she was "wasting herself." Oh, he was all right, she supposed; but he didn't know when to stop talking after making his point. He kept on and on. And then he was sort of "supercritical" about the boys she brought home, although he was very friendly with them and they thought him a "nifty guy." And life in D.C. was such a drag, when she lived there. Rowena (her new mother) was nice enough, but she was always entertaining. "And I guess kind of silly. Daddy married her 'cause she was really good-looking and he just couldn't be alone after Mom's death . . . I don't think he's too crazy about her." (I hope he is, for your sake, I thought.) At Milton, the boarding school where she was a sophomore, things were much better. At least she was able to come in to Cambridge now and then and sort of "have my own life." I liked those words, as we reached the intersection at Fresh Pond Parkway and turned around. Have her own life, I thought. She held my hand tightly and told me how she had read ninety-nine books the summer previous, to beat all her friends in a contest!

Couldn't I come with her to the party that was on now? she pleaded. Her pale pink cheeks coloring with expectation. I said sure, I'd go, and she kissed me, saying, "Goodie!"

I had been to Louisburg Square before, but never inside one of the grand Bulfinch houses. The red-brick home of old Boston, Brahmin America. A fitting locale for a live rock band and party for freaks, heads, new radicals, adult swingers. I mean, given the confusing times, the bored people, the endless contradictions, new alliances. Several political comrades were frugging with the large group in the main ballroom. Once Nugget was noticed, however, she was gobbled up by male and female admirers who took her to the dance floor. Telling me not to go away, she got out there and became a little whirlwind of ass rhythms and pelvic jerks, with those perfect facial gestures of cool indifference and cold evil. A teen-age powerhouse, out there.

"She's not doin' bad, is she?" said Elizabeth Forbes, a reefer between thumb and index finger. "The kids have really taken to her. And she's got guts. You should catch her ripping things off at the Coop the other day. It shook the shit outa me, I'll tell you. Where'd ya find her? She's liable to be a supergroupie before she's through, if ya don't watch out." She leered between intakes.

There was a kind of idiot malice in her eyes.

"Wanna shoot some scag, lover?"

I caught her by the throat and dragged her to the wall, several feet away. I pinned her there and enjoyed her struggle, like a snake held by the neck. "You ought to be wiped out," I said, "just cleaned up and shoveled away somewhere."

"Do it, baby, do it," came her excited hiss.

I applied more pressure, when my arms were grabbed and I was forced to release her. I stood there breathing deeply from my fury, the music pounding, that wounded creature opposite me, working up a grin.

"You're like me, buddy, not fond of yourself," she spoke finally, massaging her throat. "That's why we're attracted to each other." She smiled, asked a neighbor for grass, and wandered off.

Clever reptile, wasn't she? A few minutes later, someone took my arm. "Hey aren't you Lenny Pincus? I'm Ronnie Stillman, in the sociology department at Cardozo. We've never met personally, I think." He had his hand out. In his thirties, in shades and a beard, white dungarees and striped polo shirt. "I've never seen you at any of these bashes, glad you're making the scene."

At another time I would have been polite and passed on. But Lizzie had done her job. I looked at him and said, "You're shit."

He shrugged his shoulders. "Have it your way, man. See you later."

It would have been good if he had swung at me, I knew. Good for his pride and my stupid arrogance. It might have awakened me somehow.

A tall horse-faced lady, in black silk harem-type pants, announced that we hadn't met and introduced herself. Clarissa Eliot, the hostess. Thin lips, traces of a Canadian accent, the manner of a powerful and independent woman (although only in her thirties). At my name, she said yes, she had heard of me, why hadn't we met before? And this rock group—the Shepherds, were they?—were marvelous, much better than the first party's group. Didn't I think so? My first party here, I said. She gazed, surprised. "Don't make it your last" was her retort, smoking from a golden cigarette holder and surveying the scene like a sea captain inspecting work on the lower deck. "Have you met Leveritt yet? There's the dear," she said, nodding toward a heavyish mustached man, in mod striped suit, dancing pathetically. An heir of Brahmin Boston with a wreath of youth flowers upon his crown. "Making do, I suppose" (eyebrows raised). "He does try his darnedest, poor boy. Well," turning back to me, "we must see more of each other, do come around." She smiled and turned away. Later I learned that this Clarissa, now at the top of the Boston social heap, had come from a middle-class Montreal family, gone to Wellesley, and married Guy Leveritt Eliot, of the old New England family, just after he graduated Harvard. Gradually she had risen in social dominance, opening her—or Leveritt's—Louisburg Square house to "interesting people," like Panthers, freaks, heiresses, Lowells, professors, street people. (Not exactly nineteenth-century puritans gathering, you might say.) "She's really into everything" was the way this tough Canadian ambassador of pop culture was described.

And then I was dancing with Nugget, at first apart, while she gyrated blissfully; then close up, while she stared at me above and rotated her pelvis below.

Soon her tall black friend returned, with two frizzy-haired girls, one brown, one white. They pried us apart. "C'mon, baby, c'mon back with us, the party's just beginning . . . Sheet, this cat can come too if he's a good friend—c'mon, man, come on!"

I followed along, Nugget, with the black boy and girl, stopping to dance while moving out, I with "Jeannie." "She's a gas, just a gas," the girl said, her hair frazzled, false eyelashes huge, wearing a flapper dress from the thirties, with a string of beads, and carrying a fur piece. "The freshest thing I've seen in years in this part of the country." Her accent was deep South, and the expression of her mouth was cynical. "Cheesus, it'll be nice to have someone like her around. The boys go pretty sour on us after a while. And I don't blame them. A groupie's good for three or four times around. That's a year or two, I figure. At least that's how long I've been making the circuit. And I've pretty much had it as a fucker. Oh, I can get a blowjob if I want it, but shit on that as a regular sex gig. So I do other things to stay around. Answer the phone, promote, scout for new flesh." She smoked wearily. "A girl's gotta live." Twenty-four years old, she looked thirty-eight. Originally from Texas, she now belonged on Jupiter or Mars.

"He's okay," Jeannie vouched to a pair of guards in mod outfits at a third-floor door. And we were allowed in, Nugget no longer in sight.

A long rectangular salon, a misty blue-black, with sweet reefer aroma and burning incense. A crowd of twenty-five or thirty people, a few dressed in suits and evening dresses, most in outrageous costumes. Several wearing black masks. The live beat of tom-toms came from one area where two black drummers, waists bared, played. And, in the center, walking in a procession around a lifted platform, eight women wearing black robes. Carrying flaming torches. From the ceiling hung a black flag of a skull and bones, which shone phosphorescent in the flickering darkness.

"Quite a show, huh?" said my newly acquired guide. "Initiation time. And they're all different. Depends on the group, the scene, the place. It's a gas, you'll see." Jeannie pulled at her brown stick.

The nightmarish ritual intensified when a struggling girl in a white robe, her mouth gagged, was borne in by three black-robed men (one holding her arms, the other two her legs). Accompanied by two barking German shepherds on strong leashes, the band's mascots. When I caught a glimmer of what looked like Nugget attempting to hurl herself loose from the men's grip, I restrained myself from running to her and turned to go. I felt near being sick.

"Hey, what about the ceremony, man?" Jeannie grabbed my arm. "You're going to miss the whole scene!"

With pleasure, I squeezed her wrist until she howled, and I got out of the room. Just as the Stones' "Sympathy for the Devil" was turned up high. There, in the splendid corridor, two guards asked if I needed a lift anywhere, but I said no.

Outside the red-brick houses were still standing, the gaslights hadn't gone out, the black rail fences and No Trespassing signs looked as imposing as ever. Louisburg Square was planted neat and orderly, oblivious of its internal gyrations and modern blasphemies. My, how Cotton Mather or any of that bunch would have enjoyed the doings! Was the new witchcraft much different from the old? I wondered, walking down those narrow cobblestone streets toward the river.

And at some point I wondered vaguely what Claude Cummings, Nugget's OEO daddy, would have made of the scene. Or Mrs. Forbes.

But when I heard the full tale a few days later—from the mouth of the head witch herself, the younger Miss Forbes—I saw that another person would have been a more useful guest than the persons mentioned.

Well, I had missed the real fun, explained Lizzie, holding a cigarette between forefinger and thumb, speaking out of the corner of her mouth, in fragments and sadistic hisses. The fun: Nugget brought to the stage and chained to a loudspeaker. (The other one used for the dogs.) The fire kindled and set going. The Stones screaming about the devil, while the robed priestesses chanted and she, Lizzie, applied the final touch: a hypodermic needle filled with H. Part two, with the girl drugged and dreamy, the Shepherds played and their lead man, Big Dog, performed on the makeshift stage. Singing, guitaring, dancing, stripping, with the crowd going wild at the unrobing of his huge penis. Then he got onto Nugget and fucked her. After which, a merry gangbang for all the Shepherds, one after the other. Finally, the audience settled into their own orgy, with everyone on the floor, including host and hostess, joining in.

"But she was the queen of the ball, your chickie," emphasized Liz, about our mutual friend. "It was her coming-out party, and she made it big. And you should see her now. Grooves pretty heavy on the horse." She nodded, smiled, and touched my arm. It stung. "You helped turn on a good sister, lovah."

She began to say something about the "speciality plastercasting" that went on, but I walked off.

Thinking that a more useful guest at that Louisburg Square gathering than the ones I had thought of was the professor from Paris, Lévi-Strauss. Why did that eminent anthropologist need the jungles of Brazil to wander through when there existed the streets and homes of my native land? After all, our primitivism was less shrubbed, our rites more available and equally bizarre, our savagery less studied than the sort provided by our South American competitors. I should know, since I was becoming an authentic native myself.

Was that true, though? Was the new mask of contempt and degeneracy anything more than my own grotesque grafting? Forget that native stuff, a playful rationalization. And there were moments during those frenzied days when the truth hit home. The mask then seemed to slip off me and take on a life of its own, staring at me with mockery and accusation. Such moments threw me into a cold sweat, especially as they came unwillingly; and I'd wonder about my sanity. Quickly, I'd take up the nearest bit of action around—a movie at the Square, ice cream at Brigham's, a pickup basketball game near the Charles. Anything trivial and ordinary would do, so long as it distracted me from myself, my memories, and my incoherent and swirling ideas.

We were into August, about ten days after the party (and the last time I saw Nugget that season), when the story of that summer picks up. The second part of it. The murder.

Late at night, I found myself in the Combat Zone, the red-light district of Boston, just beyond the theater section. Dope peddlers, rough-trade boys, black prostitutes, dingy go-go and striptease dives, police with truncheons—city entertainment, 1972. Exhausted from walking, I went in to see a go-go dancer and had a drink, reminded, when there, of the famous Nobel Prize physicist who found his relaxation in California topless bars.

A good place to reflect. Near 12:45, I walked down to the Essex Street subway station to catch the last train to Cambridge. I waited alone on the deserted platform, engulfed by dirty tile, gray girders, vile billboards, stifling heat. Rattling thunder reverberated closer in that long chamber of darkness, and I soon got on the last car. There was one other passenger, a middle-aged man reading a newspaper in one corner. The fluorescent light was good, and I continued my Nietzsche education. It was a section from *Twilight of the Gods,* called "A Criticism of Modernity," where Nietzsche writes that his society's institutions are no good any longer, but the fault lies with the people, for losing the instincts out of which the institutions evolved.

At the next station—it may have been two—some teen-age blacks came on, and an older black man. I looked up briefly, one of the boys looked at me, and then I returned to my reading. With Nietzsche, you had to stop every few sentences anyway, and reflect, to understand his full force. Presently the subway lurched, there was a sudden low yell, and I looked up to see the three boys in the midst of mugging the middle-aged man. Just like that, as if to pass the time of night, they were hitting and frisking him, and he was sagging to the floor. For a few seconds I was immobile, stunned, the train rumbling; then I got up in a rage and called out, "Hey! Hey, stop!" I ran to midway in the long car before I was met by a boy wearing boots and a tan cavalry hat, and holding a yellow-handled switchblade. "Cool it, baby," he said, the knife held lightly between thumb, index, and middle-finger, palm upward. He didn't smile, his black eyes were brilliantly alive, and he bounced his knife with delicate precision in the air. The seconds were an eternity, the train pulled into the next station, and the three boys fled. Gone. You expected a ride home, and instead your token bought you a beating and a trip to the hospital. I hustled to the man, crumpled amid his *Globe* on the floor. Instinctively, though feebly, he raised his hands to shield his face, as if I had come to finish the job in a rotation of muggers. His lip was cut and blood had trickled onto his open-necked sport shirt, the kind my father used to wear in summer. And suddenly, when he saw that we—that other passenger had joined me now—were not going to harm him and he was safe, he let out a little moan close to a wail and cried. Involuntary tears crawled down his pudgy cheeks. We asked him where it hurt, what did they get, was there someone we could contact immediately?—all the time the train rumbling on—but all he could do was keep his round pleasant face propped against the red cushion, bobbing with pain and indignity, and whimper. It was awful, and I got up and left.

The incident haunted me that insomniac night and the next day, a Friday. The violence committed upon that fifty-year-old man by those boys didn't make sense. Like some stupid accident of nature, a hailstorm in summer that suddenly explodes, ruins your vegetable garden, and is gone, leaving the sun shining. A jab of destruction to remind man of his feebleness. Only now the jabber was man not nature. The incident and my impotence in the face of it, in some strange way, seemed connected to my larger disturbance, of self-transformation, but I didn't know how. But why was I so upset by what was after all a very common event these days? Moreover, most muggings turned out far worse than this one, as I realized from the *Globe*. In three and a half inches of black print, the story was given; it ended with Harry Mandelowitz, age fifty-four, a Dorchester grocer, suffering with bruised ribs, face lacerations, and a mild concussion, and doing satisfactorily in Mass. General. His wallet and thirty-two dollars missing. Not exactly a tragedy after all. Yet it lingered in my head somberly, and I couldn't help cutting out the clipping (tucked away on the obit page—so as not to upset people?) and carrying it with me. Words which brought to mind the face of Mandelowitz bobbing from indignity. And the animal sound of his whimper.

At the Out-of-Town kiosk I bought a *Crimson* and walked to the Yard. In the vast reading room of the Widener, amid the scholars and students, I leafed through it perfunctorily—my mind floating, as usual; that deeper self driving me and seeking expression—until my eye was caught by an announcement. That night, the fourth of August, Norman Mailer was speaking at Harvard. It meant nothing to me at all; except that I kept returning to the announcement, as if for a clue. I was outside again, walking, when a few words from that other story suddenly invaded my consciousness . . . Mandelowitz, a grocer, beaten up. The two began to grow connected in my head, the famous author and the obscure grocer. Mailer and Mandelowitz. Mailer and Mandelowitz. For some reason, I was growing excited.

At the Harvard Book Store I purchased a copy of *Advertisements for Myself*, and, by the calm Charles, read closely the essay on Hipsterism, searching for certain passages. I still didn't know what I was up to with this sudden detective work, but as I did it, as I poured through those daring words and bold ideas, my heart pumped, and I felt as if I were shooting dope. Yes, Mailer was exciting. I found myself reading and underlining and trying to understand, as if this were a test, with my life depending on the outcome. *Literally my life.* Phrases leaped up at me, and I sought to control them with a blue underline.

> In short, whether the life is criminal or not, the decision is to encourage the psychopath in oneself, to explore that domain of experience where security is boredom and therefore sickness. . . . [*That last phrase I truly liked.*]

> What characterizes almost every psychopath and part-psychopath is that they are trying to create a new nervous system for themselves. . . . [*A new nervous system. Yes.*] . . . the fundamental decision of his nature is to try to live the infantile fantasy, and in this decision . . . there may be a certain instinctive wisdom. . . .

To return to or to discover one's "instinctive wisdom" appealed to me. But to try to live the infantile fantasy was only part of the equation; the second part was to recover from it in order to make use of it. Like an artist, say. That was the difference between the two, wasn't it?

> . . . he is looking for an opportunity to grow up a second time, but the psychopath knows instinctively that to express a forbidden impulse actively is far more beneficial to him than merely to confess the desire in the safety of a doctor's office. . . . [*"To express a forbidden impulse actively"— that gripped me. Especially "actively."*]

And then that infamous passage floated before me:

The strength of the psychopath is that he knows what is good for him and what is bad for him at exactly those instants when an old crippling habit has become so attacked by experience that the potentiality exists to change it, to replace a negative and empty fear with an outward action, even if—and here I obey the logic of the extreme psychopath— even if the fear is of himself, and the action is to murder. [*I stopped here, in a daze from the words, and looked at the black river passing and continuing. I read on.*] The psychopath murders—if he has the courage [*again I stopped, in a cold sweat, my hands tingling*] out of the necessity to purge his violence, for if he cannot empty his hatred then he cannot love, his being is frozen with implacable self-hatred for his cowardice. [*I stopped again, reread, and then moved forward.*] It can of course be suggested that it takes little courage for two strong eighteen-year-old hoodlums, let us say, to beat in the brains of a candy-store keeper, and indeed the act—even by the logic of the psychopath—is not likely to prove very therapeutic [*ah, I loved that "therapeutic" just there, in that discussion!*] for the victim is not an immediate equal. Still, courage of a sort is necessary, for one murders not only a weak fifty-year-old man but an institution as well, one violates private property, one enters into a new relation with the police and introduces a dangerous element into one's life. The hoodlum is therefore daring the unknown, and so no matter how brutal the act, it is not altogether cowardly.

How marvelous a paragraph for political implications, and what bold defense of the criminal! More: what open license for killing, like suddenly being given a medallion to operate a taxi without paying a cent! And that "dangerous element," I liked that. It immediately called to mind Conrad's phrase for "immersing oneself in the destructive element." The dangerous and the destructive—didn't they amount to the same exploration? Yes, the article was all that I had bargained for; and more.

As I read on, my head spun from the lush immorality and apocalyptic language! Who would have dreamed that the "nihilistic fulfillment of each man's desire" had a positive side? Or that there was affirmation in violence and barbarism? And who would have the courage to pronounce this perverse ideology in print? And in such an eminently rational magazine as *Dissent* (where it first appeared, according to the credit)? Of course, the famous author could have little idea as to how *I* was going to understand those intriguing ideas, let alone translate them for my own project. When I myself didn't know only twenty-four hours ago that I had a project.

The rest of that afternoon, waiting for Mailer to speak, I walked about half-mad, wild, terrified. The concrete-and-glass buildings around the Square at moments wavered like rubber, near falling. At other times, I expected automobiles to rise up, or pedestrians to float through the air, gravityless. When they didn't, I was surprised. It was like walking around on a new planet, so curious and unpredictable everything seemed. Even the warm August air was eerily still, like packaged heat. Meanwhile, images and thoughts were scribbling themselves in my head . . . *Mailer stabbing his wife . . . Ivan K. accepting the logic of murder and sanctioning Smerdyakov . . . Nugget on her knees begging to be let up and later whispering, "Put it in my hole, please, please." . . . crazy blacks smashing the Matisse and Giacometti in the museum . . . Harry Mandelowitz whimpering, his hands shielding his face from me . . .*

"All right, what's your name, son?" asked the man in blue uniform, staring at me.

Shocked, I could barely open my mouth, and finally uttered, "Lenny. Why, what is it?"

"Lenny?" he stared quizzically.

"Uh, Pincus," I added. "Lenny Pincus."

Suddenly he smiled handsomely. "Take it easy, jaywalking is not exactly murder." And he proceeded to give me a lecture on pedestrian carelessness causing accidents. He wrote out a warning ticket and said next time there'd be a fine.

Still stunned, I said, "Thank you."

He looked at me queerly and told me I could go. I obeyed and turned, urging my legs forward, wondering how the black bulge now in my jacket pocket had not been immediately noticeable. Not to mention thoughts.

Sweating profusely, out of breath from fear and relief, I

headed for the Widener, making sure that I walked instead of following my impulse to dash.

The huge-ceilinged cathedral of a reading room, lined with books and dotted with quiet students reading and writing at long library tables, was consoling. I found a chair at the far end, just this side of the periodicals, in a lone corner. For the first few minutes I stared at the grains in the wood, waiting for my perspiration to cease. To my left, I noticed with odd curiosity, were rows of thick green tomes, a religious encyclopedia, some meaningless dusty conscience of an age gone by.

I got out my Nietzsche, but there were too many thoughts flying through my head for me to concentrate on anything but my night task. Its meaning and its plan. In my green steno pad I wrote my thoughts, at first starting slowly, but then writing suddenly at a feverish pace, like a hawk circling and then dashing straight for his prey.

The museum destruction—where does it take us? What part do I play? Degeneracy, destruction, barbarism. In order to transcend them, one must pass through them. Taste and lie with them, know them intimately.

An inward leap, a leap of the will, to catch up with the knowing primitives. To cut away frozen morals and bourgeois emotions. Nugget a beginning. But I seek a more total break with my grain; a personal gesture that will lead me to . . . bigger game. Right now, this famous author. A sometime hero of mine. Away with him.

Mailer, the perfect victim for my special crime. The true modern designer of *both* our roles! Consider that excellent point he makes in the murder of the candy-store owner, whereby his hoodlums murder not only the man but an institution as well. Surely he'd understand that he, too, was the perfect representation of that which we sought to bring down: culture. How silly and wrongheaded was political assassination—you knock off the attorney general and they have a new one in the next day. Those fellows are interchangeable, like parts in a machine. But an author dead is like a Matisse ruined, irreplaceable. *Yes, irreplaceable.* (How fascinating, to make mortal that which is supposedly immortal, like pictures! Remember this.)

A life of extremity, danger, self-exploration—*what he advocates I shall fulfill.* Anything less than that is cowardly, conservative (according to *his* philosophy). And yet, how often in the past years has *he* taken the victim's role, rather than the executioner's? Yes, this will be educational for him as well as me! Like the homosexuality barrier, which he's refused to cross. Yes, he *needs* my action of tonight, I see this clearly now! I shall do this for *his sake* as much as mine. For both our theories, for both our lives.

Will this act be a heinous crime then or . . . [and here I crossed out several phrases before coming to one that seemed acceptable] . . . will it have its *moral side?* By conventional standards—including my own for the time being, this moment at 3:54, August 4, 1972—it is the vilest and lowest act; but by Mailer's standards, and by mine tomorrow —hopefully!—it will have its own virtues. Strength, a brave step into the unknown, a breaking of moral boundaries. Yes, I Lenny Pincus will become a *true radical.*

Imagine, to have a victim whose ethical credo sanctions and even proposes the very hideous act to be visited upon him. If a man can have a philosophy which includes and blesses his own destruction, surely that man is outstanding? Surely his morality is different, more encompassing than ordinary morals? That was the man to be my judge, not some state-appointed Babbitt! *We would understand each other.*

Time to face the high stakes of our game. If we can't bring down the government just yet, we can at least start anew and build a bridge to the *new man.* First we must bring down our heroes and smash our old feelings. The challenge was in our hands, for we, the young persons, were the only ones confused and angry enough to take chances, risks, court trouble.

A finish once and for all to Greek aesthetics, Jewish and Christian morals, nineteenth-century revolution ideas, and twentieth-century revolution betrayals. A new philosophy is needed. It can only come from the new men.

Tonight, I will be the bridge. *I am what is possible for now.* Later on, there will be an advanced Lenny Pincus, whose moral beliefs and actual deeds will make me look conservative. Fine, this is progress. *He* will have none of my silly terror or sweating fear, or moral uncertainty, but will march ahead into moral adventure coolly, with calm anticipation. How I long to be that boy!

A single negative act, now, will free my comrades from the necessity of repeating it. My individual break is enough to show that we are capable of acting with free will. And today in our land only negative action can demonstrate this. You can't act negatively out there in society unless you begin with the self. In this way, I insure myself against giving in later, to America's tranquilizing powers. *So I shall murder tonight to release hundreds of friends across the country from the pressure to prove themselves in a similar negation.* Thus, my deed, savage in aspect, will also have its beneficial side.

When I looked up, the clock read a quarter to five. I barely knew where I was. I looked around, but everything was peaceful. A young boy was going around collecting scattered books, and I realized the library would close very soon. Summer hours. I glanced again at my pages (two and a half), my eye suddenly stopping immediately at "*So I shall murder tonight* . . ." I smiled at myself with loathing. What a joke! What a sordid stupid naïve imagination! As if I could go through with something like that! God, I was a fool! And a liar! Do you realize what nerve and stamina is involved in such an act? I accused myself. You, a good boy who read books all his life, who still likes cereal in the morning and milk at night, suddenly plunging into a villain's role? Out of spite, I pinched myself hard and held on until I couldn't stand the pain, counting to twelve. And then laughed at my folly!

The bells for departure began ringing, and I stood, feeling relieved. A fantasy, the idle thoughts of a confused student. Nothing more, I told myself with disdain.

I was about to take off when I noticed a stray envelope on the table. I picked it up, and, without quite knowing what I was

285

doing, I tore out the two and a half sheets of lined paper from my pad that I had just written on, folded them carefully, and placed them in the envelope and sealed it. Upon the envelope, used for interdepartmental mail, I wrote, "To Whom It May Concern," and the date, August 4. And then, acting as if I had planned it all carefully, I walked the few steps to the nearest bookshelf and glanced among the various bibliographical volumes. Pretending to look up something at the last second (and nodding at a library worker passing with his collection cart), I took down a thick brown-red tattered book, *Dictionary of Hymnology*. Glancing around, I placed the envelope into the center of the rarely used dictionary. As I did, my eye looked over that curious page 850, where I was placing my note (for posterity?). I glanced down the series of hymns, each preceded by a brief history of origin. Halfway down the page, I lingered amused, and found myself memorizing a piece of a hymn composed by Reverend Haweis, for a dying man:

> O Thou for whom all goodness flows
> I lift my heart to thee:
> In all my sorrows, conflicts, woes,
> Dear Lord, "remember me!"
>
> While in my poor distressed heart
> My sins lie heavily,
> My pardon speak,
> New peace impart,
> In love "remember me!"

At that point—the moment too ironic for fiction, the material too obsolete to mean anything in my life—I caught myself, closed the book with my envelope of pathology tucked securely inside, no ends showing, and set it back into its dusty home. Walking off, I suddenly felt much better, even cheerful, as if I had just completed a nice piece of work. Yet, if anyone were to ask me at just that moment what that work was, or gesture meant, I couldn't for the life of me have told them.

At 8 p.m. I sat in my seat, my head swirling, about ten rows back from the stage of antique Sanders Hall. A packed house, standing room only, of academics, students, outsiders, and one crazy boy. How different it all felt with an appointed task ahead of you, and a black instrument, courtesy of Smith & Wesson, tucked in my pocket. I trembled and smiled, feeling perhaps like a witch doctor holding a magic talisman at an AMA meeting. *Power* from holding a gun and feeling on the outside—certainly he on the stage, eyeing his prey from the lectern, being cheered raucously like a boxer entering the ring—certainly he'd understand, I believed! Although I doubted whether he could foresee how seriously his bold ideas were being taken. If only he could peer through my seersucker to that .38-caliber affirmation of the barbarian!

(And yet he did, didn't he, in his own way?)

An irrepressible smile flickered at his mouth, as the applause subsided. And stayed there during a deliberate minute of theatrical silence. He so wanted to be a national monument like Dickens, and up there I suppose he was in his way, the literary man making like a vaudeville entertainer, as the smile spread into a menacing leer. "Now hear ye, hear ye, 'cause these are hard times, so gather round closely and don't miss what the preacher says. Anarchy is what's on tonight. Anarchy in American literature. With side looks at anarchy on the loose today. And anarchy in me and you. Me at least, and maybe a few of you. So listen good now, hear?" Was he looking at me, I wondered, with that sentence? He proceeded—carnival barker, Southern preacher, Jewish ironist, rolled into one. Holding that academic crowd as well as any Oral Roberts doing his evangelicizing. Looking robust and vigorous, this makeshift city-Hemingway, his fire-red shirt open at the neck (exposing hair), dark jacket, fine Cape Cod tan. A beard, too, and a paunch. Which seemed to amuse and irritate him simultaneously. He ought to play Robinson Crusoe coming to New York, in a movie, I thought.

He lectured, using mint-julep accents, homespun humor, black jive, and staccato Mailer firing. The coeds tittered at the scatology (and took notes in loose-leaf books), the academics shook heads or nodded at leaping insights ("Lawrence," whispered one man in front of me to his friend, indicating the plagiarism), the personality-gazers marveled at the earthy irony and continuous sexual hint. Meanwhile, the New York Champion paid homage to the anarchist trends in Melville, Whitman, Twain, smashing James and Wharton for lacking them; briefly, in a long aside, applauding Burroughs for trying to continue the tradition, putting down Bellow for imitating it "falsely, effetely." (But wasn't *Henderson the Rain King* more truly anarchistic than anything else modern? I wanted to ask, more truly connected to Melville, say? Could I ask him later when we were alone?) Fine wit, sharp remarks about our literature, new twists to old critical insights. But the delivery was what counted, on one side provocative, contemptuous, insulting, on the other vulnerable, compassionate: a brilliant and attractive act. By the time he was through, the audience was angry at their lives, their interpretations, perhaps their professors; and yet exhilarated. I too was seduced: he was all I had expected, all he had written—yes, I secretly knew he'd understand.

Suddenly, in answer to an audience question, he was saying, "Sure, there's someone out there right now, right there among you, with anarchy and blood in his heart. Maybe he even has a knife, a gun somewhere, and secretly wants to use it, but is afraid, dominated, overwhelmed." He laughed like a con-man. "Show me a red-blooded American boy who reads books and I'll show you a potential murderer. Of course, friends, that murderer frequently turns into a writer or a painter. But he's there . . ."

I shook and sweated too much to move, to turn my face or eyes. Tears dropped from fright, and I very carefully wiped them away. The words droned on, more questions, and soon ordinariness was restored. For me.

Joining the awed, wooed crowd in exit, I searched for the right person to tell me where the party would be for the guest speaker.

It turned out to be at his suite of rooms in the Hotel Commander, that old Cambridge landmark near the Square, immediately following the talk. I arrived near midnight on the heels of acquaintances. A filled salon of literary academics, radicals, would-be hipsters, and socialites. At one point, I was introduced to Mailer, who was polite and friendly, saying he'd once read something by me and wanted to talk sometime. I said fine, before he was urged away by a pretty graduate student. I dropped nervously into a corner of a couch, eyeing doors, windows, TV, and radio, while the banter proceeded. Soon I got up, drink in hand,

and wandered pointedly through the two rooms and bathroom, observing carefully, my neck burning. I poured the drink down the drain, afraid of it. In the living room, Mailer, egged on by sycophants, was giving an imitation of the two Republican leaders about to appear in the coming convention, which he was covering for *Life*. It was very funny, even though his self-love kept him from being a first-rate mimic.

My plan became fixed when I heard that the party was near its end, since Mailer wanted to drive back early in the morning to the Cape. I stayed inconspicuous until I saw the last trio of guests preparing to depart, and then I escaped to the bathroom (between the two rooms). When I heard the door click and Mailer locking it, I turned up the faucet, first putting on the pair of black gloves I had brought for the occasion. Mailer called out, is there someone still inside? and I said yes, I'd be right out. The seconds seemed interminable distances, and details riveted my attention. The red-silk bathrobe hanging on the door hook. The fluorescent buzz over the washbasin. An elaborate silver shaving kit, with a strop for honing, on the porcelain basin. Made by Rolls Co., initialed N. M. Saying to myself, "Here goes," like parachuting for the first time perhaps, I emerged from my hideout, leaving the faucet running.

He was drunk, you could see from the way he moved. His boxer's gait enhanced by alcohol, he almost toppled as he approached, his mouth grimacing. As I walked past him—my heart pounding, my gloved hands in my trouser pockets—he asked my name again. I repeated it, switched on the table radio, and found loud rock on BCN. Taking a throw pillow in one hand, I turned and faced him, my automatic out, its snub nose facing his chest. A terrifying and yet calming moment.

His eyes narrowed in disbelief, and then his alcoholic face relaxed into a wide smile. He nodded. "Pretty good, kid. You're the only one with guts." He poked a forefinger toward me. "Faggots, lackeys, parasites. You're right, kid, I gotta do betta." Nodded in agreement, then said, "And now I gotta put up with this," indicating the present annoyance and smiling.

I couldn't help joining him.

"A sense of humor, huh? Good. You need it in this business."

With my okay, he took a pack of cigarettes from his shirt pocket and offered me one. Observing him carefully from ten feet away, I shook my head. He lit one for himself. The rock poured on, deliciously, giving me a whole new appreciation of it.

"Now put the rod away," he began, delivering the Cagney-noun out of the corner of his mouth, inhaling deeply, a brilliant melodramatist to the end. "You've made your point, kid, and you're right. I get you . . . Now give over." He extended his hand, palm out, a priest pleading with a prisoner for last-minute sanity.

I shot him, the pillow muffling the noise considerably, the music doing the rest. Easy. The bullet tore into his shoulder, ripping him back, and then down, into a sitting position. He felt his left shoulder with his right hand and was surprised to see real blood, his own. His look turned to confusion and a peculiar glee.

"This is Mailer, kid, you can't kill me—" his thumb tapping his chest. "Now give me a hand, will you?" He reached out, but I didn't move. "Don't be a punk now, Lenny. Help me up and let's get this wound dressed. Then we can talk. I *dig*, see. But don't fuck it up—"

With his boxer's savvy perhaps, he ducked at the right instant, and the next bullet missed him, ramming into a bureau. The glee on his face vanished, and in its place were sweat, terror, and determination. He breathed heavily through a wide skeptical leer, and he looked suddenly older, his hair grayer and his face more lined. Like somebody's old man being held up in a shop perhaps, not a famous author now. Sympathy flowed through me.

"Whaddya want, kid? What is it you're after, do you know?" Slowly, with pain, he dragged himself to his knees, his eyes alert with fear, and, now, something more. "So you're going to be *a hero*, huh? Is that what you'd like? How? By knocking me off? Cheap. Fit for Oswalds and Sirhans. You know something? You and me deserve something more *inventive*. Yeah, you're probably better than cheap assassination. Don't sell yourself short. You show . . . imagination."

His presence and his words were provocative, captivating, even winning. Sitting up on his knees and haunches, his head bobbing, he was like a brilliant cobra, the words shooting out, testing, like a dazzling fang. Full of dangerous charm.

Was that what I was, in fact, after—heroism? Cheap glamour and publicity? The thoughts confused me.

"Come on, kid, what do you really want?" he said, bolstered now by an idea, the beginning of a handle. "Is it killing? or something else? Sex—is that it? Is that the meaning of that thing in your hand? Be honest." His eye glinted with new challenge.

It grew more confusing as he gained confidence, while I lost it. *Sex?* He was showing me somehow how tepid and repetitive I was being. Banal even, a radical Oswald . . . He should have been a director. I told him so, and he said he was, adding *I* should have been an actor! He knew talent when he saw it, bullshit aside. God, his charm. Containing my excitement, and keeping my words to a minimum, I told him to turn around slowly. And take his trousers down. Moving myself into strange territory. Involved who knew where, or on what level?

"So that's it, kid," he said, nodding with wisdom. He followed the order, still in pain. "Take my cherry, go ahead. Sure, I ain't chicken."

The old word touched me, as he had. Or was he playing it sly and should I just finish him off quickly without the exhibition? But didn't I at least owe it to him to push the event to a Maileresque extreme?

With an effort and still panting from his wound, he positioned himself on all fours, white shorts down, buttocks up.

"This oughta be on film, that's the only thing missing," he said with renewed irony. "Something for the Griffin show maybe. Whaddya think, Pincus, got the guts to do this on TV?"

But it was he who should have had his own TV show, called "Tough Guy."

Smiling, almost laughing in the midst of my fear, I took two steps forward, leaned behind him, and placed the .38 at his anus. He glanced back, but I told him to turn around. "What's that?" "That's 'it,'" I replied, purposely ambiguous. A dead silence; then he said, "You're Jewish, aren't you? Answer me!" "Sure." "Well, you're shitting on my personal torah, kid." "What? You've not exactly led a Talmudic life these years—" Suddenly he had seized my leg, throwing me off balance to the side, and he began biting for the bone. Like being caught in the jaws of a bear. Instinctively I pummeled his back and side with the pistol—then tore him off me (the two of us howling) and in one swift motion put my pillow to his anus and fired. As I myself fell backward, he let out a horrible groan and jolted forward, the blood pouring out torrentially. Dazed, I raised myself and saw his flushed face lying peacefully on the sky-blue carpet.

A last act violent and extraordinary enough, I thought, breathing deeply, to satisfy his wild teachings, my calculating madness. He had been sly all right, and at the end ferocious. Yet, as he lay there, his silver-gray hair and agitated face now seemed to me patriarchal in repose, and I had a curious and powerful urge to touch him.

But the dark red blood forming a puddle was too much for me, and I threw up before I made the bathroom. Shades of *An American Dream*! Inside, I rinsed my face and mouth with cold water, trembling. And when I was ready to leave, I found myself casually slipping the English shaving case in my pocket like a petty thief. How wild you are when doing something totally new, totally insane! Then I fled the suite.

In the hall I looked about and then headed for the emergency stairway. Closing the door behind me quietly, I felt safer, alone there, flying down the stairs.

"Oh, come on, for godsakes, cut it out, will you, he'll never know, and you've wanted it as much as I have—"

I caught my breath, held up suddenly, and saw beneath me, on the next landing, a man with glasses in a business suit, pinning a well-dressed lady against the wall. He continued to implore her, kissing her intermittently, while I stood above, paralyzed. Unbelieving, I held on to the bannister, afraid to move for the noise.

"Come upstairs to *my* room then, for godsakes, Phyllis."

"Upstairs" sent shivers up my spine, and I had to fight to keep from screaming. I stayed put, afraid to move any further upward in the building.

Suddenly the woman cried out, "No, it's wrong, Scotty, please," and she burst through the door. The man ran after her.

Panting wildly, I waited a second, another, a third, then I ran down the stairs, keeping my face away from floor No. 5 as I passed it, expecting it to be flung open and panic to ensue.

As I fled down the remaining flights, I was sure I had left something behind, an incriminating fingerprint or object. *Sure of it*. But it didn't matter at that point, let them catch me the next day for all I cared! The night clerk was busy with a newspaper over his face as I sneaked out of the lobby, from the opposite direction.

Outside, there was a soft breeze, and I realized perspiration was pouring through me, my shirt drenched and sticking. The words of that stairway suitor came back to me, and I laughed aloud. Too bizarre, too incongruous! I loathed myself, but it was *over, over,* I kept saying to myself as I made my way through the Cambridge Common, which smelled fragrantly. And all through that tree-lined lamplit little village, I thought with lucid appreciation of that directorial genius. No, he was no ordinary victim. His presence had made it all exciting, if confusing. Even that last bit of grotesque melodrama, which had ensured that it didn't end banally, was his working. Just as, I reasoned calmly, the idea for the whole project had come from him basically. I moved on as if in a dream or movie, a boy with a gun in his pocket and a killing on his fuselage—no longer a mere student radical, but a new American fantasy-hero in the making, perhaps. Pincus the Kid in Cambridge. Raskolnikov from Cardozo, say.

A policeman swinging his stick idly and walking toward me dispelled my easy thoughts. Afraid to cross over, I headed straight for him, for the hundredth time that day terrified by the ordinary. He nodded and walked on.

When I got into the apartment, I fell onto the bed without removing my wet clothes and stayed there through the night, engulfed by wild images and bled by fitful sleep. A grisly night, which didn't seem to end, and which, as it wrestled on and on, made the earlier events seem more fictional than real.

In the morning, however, I saw the razor kit with the initials N. M. on one corner of the bed, and I knew that the long long night had not been suffered for anything so pleasant as the mysterious or the fictional.

The next days were an abyss of nightmares and insomnia. Getting used to my new condition—outlaw, new man, murderer—was unreal, confusing. Staying inside my friend's Hancock Place apartment—he was away for the summer and perhaps longer—filled with dreams and thoughts, attended to occasionally by Lauri Pearlman (who thought I was depressed). Dreams were adhesions. I remember walking across a sheet of ice and suddenly falling through, not landing or stopping but just falling; and calling out throatily (that too frightening me), while dropping, to no avail. In another, I was being chased by two men with guns, and I hid behind an automobile. Suddenly I was shooting arrows from a bow and hitting one man repeatedly, so that he became a human porcupine. But the horrible pricking of those quills began to pain me deeply; yet I couldn't stop shooting them and piercing him. Also, for the first time in years, I dreamed of my dead father. In one dream, I was four or five, in my crib still, and my father was walking in his undershorts between the bathroom and bedroom. At one point his penis became exposed, emerging enormously from his boxer-shorts fly; enormous even though it was in its detumescent stage. It terrified me. In a second dream, power was reversed. He was in a hospital suffering from a bad cold, and I was visiting him. But when I came into the room, after disappearing for a moment, he reproached me for leaving him alone that way. I had hurt him, he said, his face moving with pathetic injury and feeble scorn. In his hospital gown, he looked defenseless, pitiable—he who had been so strong and overpowering when I was a young boy!

Besides dreams, there were words. First the newspapers with their shouts of HUNT ON FOR ASSASSIN OF AUTHOR! I would have preferred something simpler, more to the point, PINCUS MURDERS MAILER. The one intriguing thing about the articles in the *Times* and *Globe* was the repeated mention of Mailer's "provocative career," and the implied suggestion about the many enemies he had made during its course. Filled as it was, wrote the A.P., with "ex-wives, hangers-on, movie extras, prostitutes and nightclub singers, criminals, boxers, other writers, not a few of whom he certainly antagonized with his aggressive manner." A nice euphemism for a shiv in the back! Anyway, they left students off their list, helpfully. The death was treated as if Tolstoy had been gunned down, so that Mailer had the last laugh after all. As for the "hunt for the assassin," what helped me—if not saved me—was Cambridge. It had become so much of a Kid City, with children dropping in from all over the States, shacking up one night here, another there; forming communes this month and splitting the next; shifting in and out of Project Places and Cambridgeport Clinics, that it was impossible to notice or remember who was transient, who not; or even who was who. (Like the party that fatal night, reported the papers, where persons were reported to be, who were out of the country at the time, or at the Cape.) With everyone looking like everyone else around town, from freaks and hippies to bank tellers and university duds, it was like trying to identify a man in a costume at Mardi Gras.

Other words were written down on index cards and pinned up on a piece of cardboard, in the hope of consolation.

He shall be the greatest who can be the loneliest, the most hidden, the most deviating, the human being beyond good and evil, the master of his virtues, he that is overrich in will. Precisely this should be called *greatness:* to be capable of being as manifold as whole, as wide as full.

—Nietzsche

Real freedom will come when it doesn't make any difference whether you live or not. That's the final goal. . . . Today man is not a real man. One day there will be free proud men to whom it will make no difference whether they live or not. That'll be the new man. He who conquers fear and pain will be a God himself. . . .

—Kirilov

I believe that there is no virtue without immortality. . . . Everything is permitted.

—Ivan Karamazov

The free man is immoral, because it is his *will* to depend upon himself and not upon tradition. . . .

—Nietzsche

But all those past thrilling phrases—"overrich in will," "Everything is permitted," "it is necessary to become really angry"—now failed to grip me. What I had taken for special insight, fragments of wisdom, now were just words. Literary stuff, for students. They provided no consolation, no insight. Worse, they mocked with their phony abstractions! Who had Nietzsche ever killed? I wondered. And that Kirilov, he wound up committing suicide—some new man, dead! Deceivers. Literary tricksters! I suddenly hated them!

295

No surges of guilt or repentance either. Moments of both, but they passed. Instead, there was this strange lack of feeling, as if my life were biological, no more. The heart pumping, air coming in and going out, the brain ticking. What didn't flow was passion, sympathy, or anger. Or anything. It was as if I had expected this splurge of emotions, in one direction or another, and when it didn't come, I sort of took for granted that I could summon it up. But it wasn't true. I couldn't. Nothing came. There was just this dirty white ceiling, stubbled with burst plaster and paint; the bed creaking in the apartment above, along with television melodramas and political candidates; some music, loud, soft, syrupy; and outside the bedroom window, a little protrusion of blue asphalt roof, which in the past had soothed me and made me feel cozy, but which now seemed to squeeze upon me, wanting in.

Sex was odd too, the few times Lauri tried it with me. I mean that all three occasions were failures on my part. Lauri worked and improvised, to no avail. And although it was the first time in my life that I couldn't stay hard, I really didn't mind it. I had no appetite. She might as well have been a lamp or bureau for all my interest. It was a very curious feeling. Every time she came to the bed and started touching me, it was as if I took a walk to the other side of the room and looked on from there. Separated from Pincus that way, I could muster no personal enthusiasm for his success or defeat. Lauri was sympathetic, kissing my forehead and saying, "You'll be better, Len, you'll see." And left the bed to change the mood with Simon & Garfunkel, or else a contemporary composer, Stefan Wolpe. Music of severe dissonance and harsh rhythms, which I found more pleasing than the kindly drifts of those popular boys.

A dry flatness all around, except for the earache. It came on the second or third night (I lost track of those days and nights), waking me out of sleep. I thought it was simply another bad dream, but it was the ear. Not the near-deaf one, but the good ear. Suddenly shooting with pain. The doctor at Mass. Eye & Ear had told me that there was always the chance of that one good ear going bad someday, under the pressure of working alone. The prophecy seemed to be coming true. The pain came at all times of day and night, sometimes getting so bad I thought it was actually on fire. I took aspirin, tranquilizers, painkillers, but they didn't help; the pain rammed them like a bowling ball smashing pins. I'd be reading *Life* or dozing off, and there'd come this *whoosh* sound, rising slowly like a small wave, and I'd be near tears from anticipating the breaking. In a minute or so, it would hit, and I'd be smashed and stunned. There were seconds when I enjoyed the pain and reveled in the punishment, but then it hurt too much and I'd pray for it to leave.

Finally, I remembered a remedy that my mother used on me in childhood, if I had a bad earache. I got Lauri to buy me a bottle of camphor and a box of thick kosher salt. I heated the salt in a frying pan and put it, boiling, into a sock which Lauri then sewed up at the open end. I lay down and had her drop some camphor oil (the bottle warmed in warm water) into my ear and then place the burning sock upon it, as a compress. The thick salt stayed very hot for a long time. Slowly, after one heat burned the other, the shooting subsided, and the pain became a dull bearable ache. Finally, it let up entirely, for a day or so.

But the camphor and salt remedy produced its own form of affliction. For during those moments of being pulled up from that burning hole, and afterward, I was inevitably transported back to those early earaches of childhood. Back to the small living room where I lay on my Hollywood bed, my mother sitting beside me, her hazel eyes and light face looking down upon my eight years with tender confidence and protective love. While her hand stroked my warm forehead and cheek, she told me softly not to worry, the pain would leave, I'd be better soon. Stroking my face and calling me Zshaba, her humorous nickname meaning in Yiddish, "troublesome frog." But now, as the face and the gesture returned with invincible vividness, they cut me sharply with their reminder of happier days. So I fought desperately to shake off that hovering photograph of early love—which I so wanted to have again—even once sitting up in bed and flinging the hot magical sock across the room at the bureau. It made an incredible wet mess over everything that I had wanted to hide from Lauri—handkerchief, wallet, gun, razor—and as I was trying to clean it up, the pounding returned from the vengeful ear.

297

3. Fatherland

Unable to snap out of my doldrums, I decided to move for a few days. So Lauri and I found ourselves in the Gloucester penthouse, one of the tall steel-and-glass skyscrapers in the Prudential complex in downtown Boston. It was a luxurious pad of six spacious rooms, a terrace and sweeping views (twenty-six floors high), automatic air conditioning, which you couldn't shut off (as you couldn't open the windows). Revolution, American-style, courtesy of J. R., a Harvard junior who got his father to pay for the place. The father was a St. Louis liberal, a transplanted New Englander whose family had been friendly with T. S. Eliot's. A factory owner (haberdashery) by inheritance, an art collector by choice; he loved his son and was pessimistic about the country's future. Meaning he was frightened that son Jason would wind up in Nam. Hence the apartment, used as a work area and as a temporary crash pad for a few weeks at a time, before you moved on.

The room we lived in looked out on two parts of Boston, the pretty and the shabby. One tall, glassy, glinting, new American Gothic shooting vertical into the sky. The other spanned the slums of Roxbury and Dorchester, grimy brick and squat wood houses crouched together, with garbage cans spilling over, summer heat sucking up the air along with the stench, square blocks leveled and in rubble, awaiting redevelopment. Here in the Gloucester, you heard Vivaldi and Beethoven through the walls; over a few streets on St. Bertolph, you got the sounds of black whores turning tricks. A country of contrasts; did I want to homogenize it all, take away all the contrasts? And put everyone into plain cotton shirts and baggy trousers? No, I liked the red pumps just as much as the sports cars. It was more decency and humanity that I desired. And institutions that fulfilled them. Anyway, if you peered into the distance, you could just make out West Roxbury, where Brook Farm existed a hundred years ago. Hawthorne's utopia of yesterday become in part a black slum of today. An emblematic evolution perhaps.

Back inside, the sunken living room has been fitted into a

modest newspaper printer's office. Monthly, *Geronimo*, this year's big underground paper, is printed here. Upon the oak parquet floor is a printing press, several desks and typewriters, filing cabinets, folding cots. In the corners, alongside back packs, stand the mandatory KLH speakers, with Aretha and Otis, Joplin and Dylan, the Stones and the Band coming through constantly. Figures who provide more quotations for my colleagues than Chairman Mao. Hung on the walls are the latest fun-posters, a modest achievement of my friends. One shows Comrade Ho in Uncle Sam's stars-and-stripes hat, pointing. The inscription says, THE GUERRILLAS WANT YOU. Another shows a series of airplanes lined up in the sky, automobiles below on the road, with passengers sitting and reading on the airplanes' wings; the inscription, SEE THE U.S.A. ON YOUR TWA. A third, my contribution, had Nixon sitting on a shrink's couch, wearing a football helmet and tossing up a football, perspiring; across from him sat a little girl of seven, a picture image of Tricia, sucking a lollipop. The shrink says, "Now try to relax, Mr. President, and pretend that the two of you are alone."

More impressive than the posters are the floor-to-ceiling corkboard charts on the center wall. The epigraph above reads

THE ONLY NEWS THAT'S FIT TO PRINT

On one chart, beneath the listing THE DEAD is a meticulous handwritten list of Vietnam war dead, according to the year and month of death. There are Vietnamese (NLF mostly) and American boys listed, with small snapshots interspersed. Neil Gumpert, of Grand Rapids, Michigan, in baseball uniform, is looking for the signal from his catcher. A Polaroid snap. A red asterisk by his name indicates a letter has come in about Neil. I go to the files and find this note from his mother:

> Neil liked to tinker with engines and throw baseballs and hunt. He was shy with girls, I'd say, but he did have a girl friend before he left. A nice girl named Jane Wolpert. . . . He had no thoughts one way or the other about the war, except that he thought it was his duty to serve his country.
> In answer to your last question, I only think that it's wrong that he's dead. So wrong!

Beneath Neil a few lines is Long Dan Phong, a Cong boy who looks about twelve, on his bicycle. His dates are the same as Neil's, 1950–68. No letter.

There are thousands of names, a few hundred pictures possibly—boys in canoes, in high-school graduation cap and gown, sitting with the family on the front porch—and a fair number of red asterisks. The bottom is a number in ink, changed weekly, of the entire toll: 32,456 U.S., 152,420 V. (all listed together). Like a parimutuel board with the betting totes.

The adjacent chart is titled THE LIVING. It is a listing of American draft resisters, submitted by themselves and friends, with more pictures and correspondence. Unlike the first chart, many of the notes here are from the boys themselves. Here's a typical section from one, written by James Collins III, Louisville, Kentucky.

> And I don't really know when I decided that the war was bad and I wouldn't fight in it. One thing for sure is that I never thought of myself as radical. I still don't. I still think of myself as a good American.

Beautiful touch, that last. Collins is now in federal prison, Ashland, Kentucky, serving a five-year sentence. He makes one request, for mystery and spy novels. ("I'm sure I can take what they dish out if I have a good supply.") A 3-by-5 filing card shows that we've sent him two packages thus far (Christie, Gardner, Chandler, Le Carré, Sayers).

I took little part in the proceedings. Most of the time was spent in my room, alone with Lauri. Taking her cue from the autobiographical atmosphere and my own gloom, she shrewdly got me to talk about myself, the younger Pincus. Over a period of three days, I narrated family history, growing up, and my early, complicated rebellion. That jumbled talking set my memories whirling and provoked me to put them down in a more organized fashion, words on paper, so as to make sense of them to myself.

Childhood was on the edge of Brownsville (in Brooklyn), a cozy neighborhood of first- and second-generation Jewish immigrants from Poland and Russia. (Merchants, small entrepreneurs, garment-industry people, they made a modest living, and for that most became superpatriots.) I knew my six- or eight-square-block area as well as any Kansas boy knew his barns or fields—every alley and doorway, vacant lot and butcher's shop, rooftop and beneath-the-stairs hideout. I could tell you what brick wall was good to lean against if you were the pillow in Johnny-on-the-Pony; what street was clear enough of traffic for Spaldene punchball; what gasoline pit good for hiding in, in a game of ring-a-lievio, or hiding out if the Syndicate Midgets gang (thirteen and under) were looking for you; what orange crates were useful for making wooden rifles or linoleum-firing pistols. In that Sutter Avenue–Howard Avenue–East New York Avenue Ralph Avenue square of asphalt territory, I was a little lord. Called by my first name by shopkeepers (Simon the jeweler, a balding bachelor who, with his sister, drank tea in the afternoons; Charley the dry cleaner, a gaunt and sweet Gentile—besieged by a huge Jewish wife—who always slipped me pennies; Sally and Walter of haberdashery, my surrogate grandparents, orthodox Jews and fierce merchants, and more), I was also adored by them, because of my five-year-old towhead looks, my semi-English accent (no H's pronounced), my precociousness (I read at three and a half), my vulnerability (bloodied head and battered body from bullies). I was mad about sports, playing stickball and basketball in the P.S. 189 schoolyard, baseball (softball early, hardball later on) and handball in Lincoln Terrace Park; and was taken to Ebbets Field by Burt, the ex-air force navigator from upstairs, where I watched Jackie Robinson, Carl Furillo and Pee Wee Reese, my favorites. Saturday afternoons was movies at the Sutter Theater, a nice break from Hebrew school five times a week after regular school. Platinum hair, tiny nose, and blue eyes notwithstanding, I was, at a prepuberty age, a rather typical young Jewish boy, smart, good, annoying, irreligious, and a solid American citizen, trained, obedient, blissfully patriotic.

Born two years after Hiroshima, three after Anne Frank in Belsen, several before our nation involved itself directly in Indochina, it took me fifteen-odd years to learn of those items of interest on my planet. But it did not take me that long to discover, in a curious way, my own direct intimacy with the enemy.

I forget now when or from whom I first heard the word Communist—was it from my father, when he held my six years on his lap in 1953 and pointed to the black arrows of the Chinese troops on the *Times*'s battleground maps of Korea? (Or those earlier World War II maps he had kept of the German Army fighting in Russia and being pushed back, back?) Was it from the sprightly voice of that white-haired elf on television when he questioned the burly American senator, who fiddled with his hands and sometimes got very angry, right there in my living room while I did my homework on the floor? Or from my mother, who, in a burst of twenty-year anger, would mutter sardonically about my father's friends? Or even, tracking back through the camouflage of time, the insidiousness of memory, did I first hear the ominous word from the kids on the block—that teeming herd of second- and third-generation patriots—when they heard that I was enrolling, at my father's enjoinder, at the Sholem Aleichem cheder instead of the Orthodox Tomah Torah school? After all, the Bund cheder was taught by smooth-shaven, bare-headed Chaver Gittelman, who was, according to Joel Nieman's father, a "Red," a mysterious term meaning to us, I think, the absence of yarmulkes (for teacher and students), calling the teacher Chaver (which he explained on the first day meant friend), the school's location in a seedy Brownsville basement in a two-family house. For the Tomah Torah, in contrast, was eminently respectable, evidenced by an imposing three-story brick building in East Flatbush, black-hatted and forest-bearded rebbes (they weren't at all), rigid instruction, in Hebrew only—Yiddish was a sure sign of degeneration—and strict observance of laws, codes, pieties (no school on Friday, instead on Sunday). Moreover, it had to be *good* and *fine* and doing its job, since everyone who attended it—most kids that I knew—hated it fiercely. (*Plus it cost more.*) Whereas, at the Sholem Aleichem school, your feelings were liable to be much more mixed. Orthodoxy and patriotism and Hebrew versus no yarmulkes and Yiddish and Reds, was that the equation in my eight-year-old head? Who knows.

But in whatever guise it first appeared, through taunt or complaint, approval or vile dismissal, it never really registered, I think, until the third grade at my Public School, 189. (Across the street from Lincoln Terrace Park, a mecca in those days for young DiMaggios and Sniders, plus little white-bearded ghosts from Russia or Poland who preferred chessboards to *Das Kapital*, walking sticks to guns, while at night the park was taken over by budding American gangsters). In all likelihood, I heard it mentioned somewhere along the way before my fourth year, where you are fed who knows what intravenously, during an auditorium period of important speeches served up by the benign principal, or in your current events show-and-tell lecture (weighted with *Book of Knowledge* wisdom and *National Geographic* photography), or perhaps in some little patriotic homily delivered sternly after I had made Steven Werter giggle irreverently by crossing his heart instead of mine during Pledge Allegiance time. In any case, it was my 3A and 3B teacher who impressed the word upon me, although with consequences that were not known to her and probably not intended by her. Or so I imagine.

A four-foot-ten-inch spinster, either forty or sixty in age, Miss Bidden wore no makeup, rimless spectacles, high black shoes, and tied her hair in a bun. Dresses were long, shapeless, flimsy. She had a small round face, with a child's smooth skin, and she could smile wonderfully. But every so often her mouth would constrain tightly and she scolded viciously, the crazy gypsy turning into a Presbyterian minister. Her name—when your report card announced it the previous June—meant striking eccentricity, evidenced immediately in her perennial habit of cooking a midday meal over a hot plate set up near her wardrobe in the classroom. Arriving with trepidation in September, I found myself settled with contentment by November, due to my cleverness, which she appreciated. And, since she taught me long division and multiplication tables in a few weeks (the latter by means of droopy circles on the blackboard containing seven, eight, or nine eights, say), while the rest of the class took months to learn them, I found I had ample time for mischief and fantasy, my favorite classroom pastimes.

Contentment; well almost. Clouded contentment, let's say. For she had another habit which disconcerted me. Often she asked you questions that had nothing to do with the lessons, questions that were difficult to answer, without your knowing exactly why. When I look back, I see why: they concerned your personal life—outside of school, at home—and I, for one, was shy about revealing such matters. Like most, I guess. It was as if, when she talked to you, she was always on the lookout for some hidden information, some secret perhaps, which would drop out of your mouth involuntarily, and which was much more interesting or important than any arithmetic lesson or spelling quiz. My intuition, I think, read that she was bored with trying to teach twenty-eight boobs and three or four clever children, and so she sought relaxation and pleasure beyond the class curriculum. In your life, if she could get there. Questions which were posed from her special perch on a high wooden chair, where she sat propped higher by a pillow because of her diminutive height (her elbows just barely extending to the wide wooden arms); a small mysterious lady peering at you from a tribunal like some inquisitor or magistrate.

One winter afternoon, perched high and breaking chicken legs with her hands, she announced that we would go all around the room and one by one say out loud what our fathers did and what we wanted to be. A harmless enough gambit, delivered through greedy gobbling and rancid fried odors. One which, at first, seemed pleasant. A break from workbook dullness. A chance to hear from the deadly dodoes who were condemned to silence by books, numbers, words, teachers. So that I am unsure as to when the lump began living in my stomach, with the initial announcement or with the first stumbling and excited monologues by my pals. But it was rising by the time Richard Foodman spoke gravely about his father's women's-wear store on Utica Avenue, and prophesied that he would be "a fighter pilot." And edging northward as curly-haired Irwin Goldfarb sopranoed the news that his father was a doctor, and he would be one too. I waited with enthusiasm for him to elaborate dully—his characteristic—but this time his self-importance was served by silence. (Just when I could have used his verbal pomposity!) Disappointed, I swallowed harder. And blushed deeply when my eight-year-old Betty Grable, named Ellen Levine, put forward with daughter-pride the imposing shingle of her father, "Certified public account-ant." Syllabic officialdom which impressed me more than her own hopes for turning into Florence Nightingale.

As the voices bellowed with pride and giggled with prophecy, I sat huddled behind my fourth-row desk, scratching the long woolen socks which, by my father's edict, accompanied the tweed knickers I was to wear to school once a week. Another Friday of old-world humiliation. The lump choking me as the voices snaked closer, I realized that what was on the tip of my tongue had to be shoved back to where it came from, the stomach or the head. That what had to be said instead was that my father designed ladies' hats and pocketbooks, and occasionally operated millinery machines. For what I felt Miss Bidden was after was that *something else,* that lump of information, which, just in those moments, I had discovered the meaning of, and which I knew must be kept secret. For suddenly, from nowhere, had erupted in my head the four or five times when Miss Bidden had hissed *that word,* as if she were naming yet another poison for us to watch out for (poison warnings, another of her hobbies). For the first time, I knew what my father was, what he was called: Communist.

I waited my turn with fear and trembling, praying to God—whom I called on in crises, like when I couldn't move my bowels in the bathroom—that I wouldn't blurt out what was suddenly—had to be—a secret.

"Embroidery," I mumbled finally. "My father is an embroiderer. Of pocketbooks and hats." Heart pounding, I waited for Maxwell Lubin to begin talking.

Silence.

Then, from Miss Bidden, still munching, "Come on, Leonard, speak up."

She had me!

"What would you like to be?" she repeated, irritated.

Be? When? Who? I sat speechless, trying to breathe, scratching.

Miss Bidden, wiping her fingers, descended from her chair and, walking to her desk, searched my face. I was sure *she knew.* But all she said was that I could certainly talk when I wanted to, but not when I was supposed to. And passed on to Maxwell.

Instead of attending to long-division problems the rest of the day, I found my mind rerunning certain scenes with my father. His fine pencil drawings on paper napkins of his home and land in Russia, done for me specially on the kitchen table. Late-evening talks with old friends from Minsk, Leo, Jake, and Marc, with my father warning the others about keeping their allegiances more quiet. While I lay in my living-room bed, straining to hear in the darkness, thrilled by the smell of coffee and argumentative male voices raised in Yiddish, English, and Russian. I thought of the three shelves of hard-bound books in the windowed Empire secretary which he would sometimes read. Black and brown books in Russian mostly, Dostoevsky and Tolstoy, Marx and Lenin. When no one was around, I would stand on a chair, turn the key, open the protective glass doors, and leaf through several, longing to read Russian. And then, of course, there were Sundays, spent wholly with my father. Mornings I went down for the *Times* (for my father) and the *Mirror* (for my mother) and then watched him prepare for me hot Ralston and boiled eggs. I would dip fresh challah in his hot coffee, and we joked over my mother's sleeping late. Then, dressed in my tweed knicker suit and long socks, I accompanied him to the Brownsville Air Raid Wardens Club, on Union Street, where cigar smoke and thick gossip and World War II memories floated through pinochle and chess. At age seven I played a fair chess game, and at eight (to his credit and restrained approval) beat everyone in the club. By afternoon we were ready for the trip uptown, via the IRT, to the Stanley Theater on Fourteenth Street, where I crouched in the leather seats, watching Russian-made melodramas and Charlie Chaplin shorts. The furry soldiers, the drifting snow, the guttural Russian, the heavy romantic music, the worn faces in the audience—all cast a mysterious Slavic spell upon me that was made up of joy and fear: a bond of ambiguity. And finally dinner with my father at a Hungarian restaurant on the Lower East Side. Those were Sundays which I kept hidden from the rest of the week. And now, now! In the classroom, I understood why: I saw what tricks and deceptions those pleasures were! For behind it all—the drawings and talks and books and dipped challah (which he had taught me!) and strong *chrane* (horseradish) he made—lurked the Enemy, who, if Miss Bidden found out, would expose me to the whole class, not to mention before some higher, more official jury. *Communist.* The classroom became a cage, and I was weak all day until the three o'clock bell signaled freedom. I grabbed my hooded mackinaw from the wardrobe and ran home, abandoning the after-school punchball game.

Toward evening, after cheder, the school chill returned to grip me. I was sitting in the tall upholstered chair in our living room, trying to do my homework, but not really concentrating, when I heard my father's footsteps approach on the concrete landing. Suddenly nervous, I got off the chair and began to walk, instead of run, to fulfill our ritual of evening affection. As I walked the dozen steps down the long narrow foyer, encased in darkness, I arrived at a bitter decision: I hated him. A decision made with vengeful derisiveness, for his having tricked me all that time! And so, moments later, when my father swooped me in his arms (the *Post* cold in his overcoat pocket) and asked how his *boitchek* was, I wanted to cry back, "You're a Communist, and you love Russia better than America! I know, and one day Miss Bidden will know too and it'll be your fault!" Keeping back my tears by pressing my teeth together hard, I mumbled, "Fine." For the first time, his ten-hour stubble, which I had so adored against my cheek, felt harsh.

I had no idea then as to why the political affiliation of my father infuriated me and turned me against him. I had no idea of the complicated web of ideology that could envelop an eight-year-old's feelings, a web that began out there in international diplomacy and State Department policy, filtered down through the *Post* and popular pundits to my third-grade teacher, and traveled in a similar way to my mother, whom I loved a great deal. For even she, a saint to me then, who bore unnecessary abuse from my father, often made corrosive references to my father's loyalty to his land of his birth rather than to his land of tenancy. Just then, with that stubble of my father's rubbing my cheek with accustomed affection, her remarks and his abuse exploded upon my consciousness. In a fury that startled him, I struggled free from his bear hug, grabbed my face in histrionic pain, and told him, "Don't do that!" He stood there, I recall, stunned, unbelieving. "You hurt me," I continued, crying. "You purposely hurt me." With a little maniac's joy, I watched his bewilderment turn into pain, and then ran away.

From then on, I felt like a spy; more precisely, a double agent. Aware that my father was a criminal, but unable to turn him in, I was an accomplice; full of deep feeling for him that I tried to repress, I was seized with guilt for not shielding him, and felt like an impostor. A secret agent of Miss Bidden, posing as an eight-year-old son! Doubleness of perspective disturbed me everywhere: in the classroom Miss Bidden was a moral investigator, beneath the guise of teaching multiplication, peering at me through fingers full of chicken bones; in Hebrew school Chaver Gittelman pretended to read Sholem Aleichem but was really a "Red"; at my father's club, the men played pinochle and chess and blew smoke rings, but were waiting like a jury to assess the evidence. The thrill of certain radio and television shows now turned to terror: the grotesque tales of "Escape," the squeaking-door fear of "Inner Sanctum"; the eerie laughter of "The Shadow"; the machine-gun rattling of the "F.B.I. in Peace and War." For turning my world inside out this way, I blamed my (unwitting) father more. And one day I made an ingenious discovery, while waiting in left field for a fly ball to come my way: I realized then and there that all his character defects were derived from his political heresy. His disdain for my friends and for all things American, his periodic use of force (his fist, his open hand, his belt), his cruelty toward my mother and sister. Another way it entered my mind was this: communism meant my father's personal rigidity, arrogance, elitism, physical force. My deliberations sunk me deeper in shame and bewilderment, so that I wasn't prepared for a line drive which came my way. When I played the routine out into a triple, I was shifted to the job of catcher by our thirteen-year-old captain ("You schmuck, what are you doing out there, dreaming about girls?"). No, thinking about fathers. My new odious role was my father's fault too!

What complicated matters was that I loved him. I cherished our Sunday rituals, was proud of his letter from F.D.R. (for air-raid-warden work) and awed by his real World War II gas mask, admired secretly his intelligence and arrogance. And of course I couldn't drive from my mind, no matter what my new-found ideology dictated, memories of being in his arms when I was two, three, and four (holding me by the radiators, and teaching me to say "hot"), or surprise gifts he had given me (a red fire engine with an adjustable ladder, an Erector set, my first wooden chess set, with weighted pieces). Nor did I forget those exotic tales of his vanished history, where he was the prince of his small village outside Turov (thirty miles from Minsk), and had his own pony, tutor, and valet. I gasped at the family history of tragedy, his father, a wealthy timber dealer, murdered by a marauding Czarist general during the post-Revolution chaos; and his own adventure story of European wandering and work (mining in Belgium for six months, odd jobs in Germany—my father doing hard manual labor thrilled me!) before coming to America at age seventeen. His American years, recounted to me mostly by my mother, filled me with emotion. In six months of New York night school, he learned English, and, with the hope of returning to the country and revolution that he believed in, he abandoned pharmaceutical training a few months short of a degree in order to make quick money as a milliner. (A gamble resulting in forty years of embroidery work, almost a half century in sweatshop lofts and worse, as part-owner or operator-designer, with shtetl Jews whom he considered peasants.) His one opportunity to return to Russia halted by bizarre luck, when my sister's throat grew badly infected while aboard ship and they had to take her to the hospital. By the time she had recovered, a few months later, the Second World War had officially started, changing the travel situation. The Russian "village prince" (his nephew's term for him) was thus condemned to permanent American exile.

An "exile" never more painful or vivid than when I visited him at his work on occasional Saturdays, to run errands for him. Visits which intensified intimacy, welded son-father bonds, for better or worse. My memory of them is distinct, undiminishable. During the period I am speaking of, when I first discovered that he was not merely my father but a Communist criminal, he had his own shop several bus stops from our Brownsville tenement. And although I would have preferred playing ball on that occasional morning, still I was always filled with strong boyish pride during the routine: the bus ride, the lunch, the adult errand. On my own, at eight a little man.

On the Saturday following my revelation, however, I rode the bus alert to each bump and jolt, my nose tucked against the cold window as we passed from the fine clothing stores and Saturday shoppers of Pitkin Avenue toward my destination, a decaying grotto of tenements and private houses inhabited by Negroes and Jews. February sun flashing harshly off store windows, car chrome. Reluctantly, I walked down Dean Street, past the fading brick houses, avoiding sidewalk cracks to propitiate the Powers for my approaching trial. The cellar at the bottom of a two-family house was Glamour Products, my father's business. Obeying habit, I paused halfway down the eight concrete steps to peek through the iron-barred window (a protection from gangs). A hanging electric bulb shed a dim circle of light on a man sitting hunched over a black machine, running the pedal with his foot and cutting material with his hand. An image of my father etched in my brain, projected in later years onto the work of Daumier or Dickens. That day, seeing him in his black hole, at his hapless labor, provoked in me fury instead of sympathy. Emotional vengeance for all the sympathy he had tricked me out of.

When I entered the shop, he rose from his machine, removing his glasses, and said, arms out, "Sonny boy!" Stepping toward me, his look was vague embarrassment, as if to say, "Some surroundings, eh? Not very nice, *boyala*, is it?" He bent and kissed my cheeks—a favorite pastime, along with pinching them affectionately—a gesture of Russian-Yiddish intimacy which I had adored but now resented. A sturdy man of five-foot-five, wearing a double-breasted serge suit, and, to stay warm in the chilly cellar, a thick woolen vest, heavy scarf about his neck, and gray fedora on his balding head. "Your cheeks are ice, *boitchek*," he said, his brown eyes delighted. "Sit, I'll wash up and we'll *nem essen* and a *gloz tay*." The oval face creased by a crescent smile— a smile of self-effacement that again stabbed me.

He went to wash, and I wandered about the crepuscular cellar, a grim rectangle of cement and stone, peering at the familiar piles of sequined hats (for the jobber), the swatches of cloth and assorted designs, the four rusting black machines set into wooden tables, for embroidery and sewing. The fetid odor of the toilet mingling with that of cloth and camphor. A world of exotic mystery and dungeon iconography, the cellar exerted upon me a contradictory force of appeal and fear; sympathy and love for the man who spent six and a half days a week down there, a Brooklyn version of a coal miner. I punched the palm of my hand as if it were a mitt and tried to steel myself against my vulnerable feelings by remembering his inner corruptness. He emerged from the broken toilet with a towel flung over his shoulder, appointed us seats, and proceeded to open the brown paper bag which he had prepared at seven that morning. Lunch was unvaried and, I realized at last, un-American: several slices of stale pumpernickel (the staler the better), a thick hunk of Farmer's cheese, two hard-boiled eggs. On a gas burner he boiled water for tea. Pushing aside swatches, he cut for me a slice of cheese (which I hated so thick) and placed it with pride on the dry hard pumpernickel. He peeled an egg for me, oversalted it, and began to narrate a new business hardship. He talked and ate; for spite, I stayed as silent as possible, still bundled in my woolen mackinaw. I wanted desperately to take the tied parcel on the table (some hats for neighbors, I understood) and be off; the tensions of sympathy and anger were unnerving. Sucking his sugar cube in his mouth and drinking tea, he asked me about school during the week. My replies were curt. Not knowing that ideology (or *which* ideology) was stifling intimacy, his dark eyes flashed in temper. "What's the matter," he said, venom joining his sucking, "I'm not good enough for you?" Ears and cheeks burning, I longed to blurt out, once and for all, the burden of the week. The seconds seemed like eternities. I might have, in any case, had not his anger overflowed. He struck me twice with his open hand, stinging each cheek, the tears flowing. "Come on, get out!" He took me by my collar roughly, "Not good enough for you, eh? *Du goy!*" He wasn't, but not in a way that he meant or understood. And, of course, alternately, I was not good enough for him, which hurt me too. Crying, confused, tormented, I was shoved out of the door. In the streets, at the bus stop, and all the way home, I cried uncontrollably.

From that day on, I was relieved by my father of running Saturday errands. Instead, I was free for stickball in the 189 schoolyard or hardball in Lincoln Terrace; but in both open playgrounds that Dean Street cellar would close in upon me like an eclipse. In left field, I too had become an exile. Like him. A crime and a punishment that struck both ways, erecting the first of many walls between us.

Willful and misguided, accounting each blow he delivered to the family as stemming from malignant politics, I continued in my own way to do underground work for Miss Bidden. And one day, when I was thirteen, I helped my mother pay him back for

311

two decades of misery by buying a new lock for the front door and by delivering his clothes to a mutual friend. Naturally, I had taken her side through their increasing battles (witnessing in terror, for example, an orgy of cruel slapping and cursing when my sister's Gentile boy friend was uncovered and my mother tried to intervene in my father's beating her). Not to mention my unbearable fear and anger when my father would slap her. Acts of violence much harder to take than the few beatings he administered to me—kicking me around in the dark landing when I disobeyed an order, or slapping me dizzy for insisting upon seeing my friend Joey, whom he didn't like. After the lockout, I saw him regularly for a year or so, meeting him weekly at Dave's Blue Room on East Ninety-eighth Street, beneath Abie's pool hall, where I hung out, to accept his three-dollar allowance and to hear his pleas to return to the house. Terrible pleas ("Do you think she's right what she did after all those years? I was such a bad father to you? You never had what to eat?") like some awful stuck record; they repulsed me. Finally, when the allowance became irregular, I broke off meetings and relations altogether, missing in part the reversed role of power which had suddenly become mine and which I had enjoyed. A son's brutality for a father's brutality was the way I looked at it; the small inevitable arithmetic of family tragedy, as I look back upon it.

We skip a few years, to when I was a junior in high school and still living with my mother. (My sister had married that "goy," a lovely Italian fellow who made an excellent husband. My mother, meanwhile, flouting bourgeois convention with the strength of personal experience, had taken up with an old family friend, also unhappily married, a kindly Long Island Press photoengraver. For taking my place, I used to fight with Sam Lerner fiercely.) One November Saturday, the doorbell rings and a man named Pritchard asks to see my mother. Opening his wallet, he explains to her that he is from the F.B.I. and asks to speak with her alone. I leave them in the kitchen and, in the living room, turn on the camouflage-tube to an old movie. Through one melodrama, the other comes in clearly; Pritchard's voice (Midwestern?) makes it easy to eavesdrop.

Had my father corresponded frequently with his brothers in the Soviet Union? Did the correspondence continue after the war? Who were his close friends here? How often had Leo Markson visited the house? (The name rescued a lovely smile from childhood oblivion, and evoked warmly those resonant late-evening talks.) What organizations did my father belong to? Had he ever joined the Communist Party? My mother's answers, as far as I could hear them, were a mixture of honest ignorance and shrewd evasions. Leo was a very old friend who had visited them since they were first married and had stopped coming around years ago. She didn't know which organizations he belonged to, outside of the air-raid wardens. He received an International Ladies' Garment Workers Union newspaper. And so on. When the man began asking about personal habits of my father, I was suddenly resentful and bitter. I sat with bewildered fury, watching the flickering screen and hearing my mother answer the official questions with more vagueness.

After an hour, she came into the living room, in sweater and skirt, her fine brown hair now bleached auburn, her once-firm breasts sagging. Her hazel eyes remained expressive, luminous. "Leonard, he wants to speak with you," she announced, somber, dutiful, burdened. Answering the agent without vindictiveness, with shrewd vagueness, was impressive for a woman who had been beset since age sixteen by a domineering tyrant twelve years her senior. My father had crushed her youthfulness, but she had preserved generosity and nurtured a quiet dignity. A peasant woman with the best of instincts. She touched my shoulder as I moved past her.

Hugh Pritchard, a tall slim man wearing a striped tie, nicely colored vest, and gray suit, shook my hand cordially. He might have been an alumnus of a college fraternity, hygienic, forthright, businesslike, inviting me to join the alumni club. We sat, and instead he explained that I had a right to consult a lawyer if I wished before answering any questions. "That's all right," I said, answering obliquely his oblique query. The inquisition began. Had my father ever attempted in any way to indoctrinate me into "Communist thought"? Given me Marx or Lenin to read? Taken me to any secret meetings ("Leonard, have you ever heard the term 'cell meetings'?"). My mind replayed scenes of going to the Stanley Theater (a cell meeting?), of reading the Nimzovitch chess book he had gotten for me from the public

313

library (was chess subversive because the Russians played it so well?), of the Russian textbooks in our Emperor secretary that I used to love to handle but could never read. (Indirect indoctrination?) "No," I answered, shaking my head, "he never did." More questions, and I focused on the kitchen table, that ancient wooden relic covered with cheap plastic, where not so long ago my father taught me Hebrew (for my bar mitzvah) and where, much earlier, he would draw, for my delight, sketches of his Turov childhood, the land, the stables, his father's house. Covering that same area of the table was Mr. Pritchard's black-leather portfolio, with monogrammed initials (H. V. P.) and a shiny gold clasp. When I raised my eyes, I hated him. The parrying continued, the agent speaking politely through thin lips, my heart pounding furiously. Finally, in an attempt to round off cordially the talk—to euphemize its deadly significance to a teen-age boy— he asked, smiling narrowly, what I was studying and what I wanted to be. *What would you like to be?* The question transported me to 3A and the perched Miss Bidden, waiting nervously upon that same question that began my education in patriotism. For a moment, Pritchard had smooth skin and a small round face and was gobbling chicken. I said I didn't know. In the next instant, asking quickly if he wanted a glass of water, I sprang from my chair and deliberately brushed the edge of the portfolio, knocking it into Pritchard's coffee cup. "Gee, I'm sorry," I offered, as he hastily wiped the dripping leather, disconcerted. I ran the faucet with satisfaction, and faced Mr. Pritchard, feeling better, though I was tremblingly uncertain about the meaning of his gaze.

His presence and departure forced to the surface old ambiguities and guilt. Immediately I left the house and immersed myself in a schoolyard stickball game, following the curve of the tennis ball and trying to forget events in the kitchen, except that torpedoed portfolio, which I remembered with pride.

A week later, my father phoned and told my mother that he was being investigated, with the threat of deportation. On account of his political sympathies, the government was checking into the validity of his original passport, issued in the twenties. He was worried, scared. What he wanted from my mother was that she should say that she, like him, had joined the International

Labor Organization, which was non-Communist. "Are you crazy? I'm supposed to lie for you now to the F.B.I.?" a thirty-year bitterness in her voice. "What do you take me for, a complete fool?" When she explained that the F.B.I. had already visited, and she told him with reluctance that she had said nothing that would get him into trouble, he replied—I could tell—with skepticism of her abilities and doubt of her motives. He had, one way or another, to demonstrate her inferiority, whether it was real or not. When the argument turned to (his) obsession—his forced departure from the house two years ago—my mother hung up. The rage in her eyes was betrayed by the croak of her voice and the exhaustion of her body, that housecoated prisoner of time and male imperiousness. Their incessant struggle and frustration, long after their lives were separated, were like the two halves of a worm jerking spasmodically after it has been split asunder. The undying bodies more painful, in a way, than the dead corpse.

Pritchard and the F.B.I. never returned. And my father was not deported. But for two years, I learned later, government agents hounded my father's life, trying to hang some treason-noose around his wasting neck. So that at age fifty-two he was driven into a corner of fear and persecution, his every move observed and recorded, facing the United States government without the comfort of a lawyer, a family, a decent place to live. Plus old age and sickness without money. The Free World had its disadvantages, you might say.

Leap several years. I'm in college, and exchange letters with my father about once a year. From my sister—who, along with that goy husband for whom she was once beaten and chased from the house, treated him very kindly when he paid visits to their suburban house—from her, I heard that he lived a dog's life in a downtown Brooklyn tenement and that he had had serious stomach surgery the year previous, to remove a malignant growth. On the whole, I had done an excellent job of putting the entire business of my father and me out of my mind, like a bad investment. Meanwhile Cuba had occurred—the missile crisis, the Bay of Pigs—and I had been provoked into serious political education, moving leftward the more I read. So that when I received a letter from him, written in his florid calligraphy, with

315

an allusion to Trotsky casually stuck in, I was impressed and surprised.

With the curious letter in my jacket pocket, I remember walking around my adopted home, that sun-filled Cardozo campus—a springtime Lotus-land of nubile coeds, red sports cars, lazy willows, an America brimming with promise and hope, so different from the one he knew—feeling odd, alien. And bewildered. With thoughts. A letter from a vanishing world was one. A letter from an interesting life buried beneath a father's mask was another. A letter from a man I never really knew. *A plea from a father. Mine.* Near the hillside statue of Justice Cardozo, I cried.

For the first time in several years, I decided to see him. In New York, I phoned and he was astonished to hear my voice.

Soon I was on Bleecker Street, heading north from the Village, looking for number 19. Winding, narrow, dark (the tall buildings blocking the light), Bleecker led me back into a childhood of candy stores and cheap luncheonettes, populated (now) with Puerto Rican and black sweatshop operators, the Jewish boys now jobbers and bosses. Fresh from campus kid stuff and political awakening, I was aghast at the grimy brick, the greasy odors, the gaseous airs. The city of fun, the capital of culture and finance, America's finest, sinking in soot, nerve-jangling with noise, cracking from racial heat and social discrepancy. One minute I was in a fourteenth-floor Park Avenue apartment, a maid serving me a cocktail, while I chatted with a school friend's father; the next hour I was climbing the filthy stairs of a dilapidated building, on my way to another sort of father. At the door of yet another Glamour Products, Inc.—the success illusion didn't die easily anywhere—a pretty black operator pointed out to me her boss, Harry Pincus; otherwise I probably wouldn't have recognized him. He was where and how I left him over a decade ago: a hunched figure in a black shop bent over a black machine. But he was different. Looking up, he stood in surprise, a piece of material clinging to his hand, his spectacles drooping on his nose. Hitching his trousers over his protruding belly, he waddled toward me like an emperor penguin. Time had distorted him into a ludicrous lute shape; sickness had eaten the flesh from his face, leaving shriveled bags for cheeks and shaping his nose into a grotesquely bulbous lump. My father—or a vaudeville clown performing a cruel imitation? He was crying. He reached out and embraced me, saying, "Sonny boy." The childhood fondness crushed my defenses. The caricature in my arms blasted the forged complacency of college years, my adolescence of vengeance. Time's caricature and "sonny boy." Slowly I eased him off, confused and shaking at the unexpected immensity of the moment.

We spent a little more time in the soot-gray loft, while he answered phone calls and made arrangements to leave. Seated at a decrepit wooden desk (its roll-top gone), he was still inept at business; a man on the run attempting to ward off his host of creditors. The old authority returning only when a Puerto Rican operator was about to leave and Harry questioned him about a certain hat order. The skin on his neck had turned yellowish, like nicotine stain. Using words like "debt" and "bankruptcy," he laughed embarrassedly, his shoulders hunching in bewilderment. As if all this *weren't real*, as if he still didn't believe in the last forty-five years! And, for a moment, through the decaying American body, I perceived the handsome young Russian, the self-styled aristocrat in a snapshot I had once seen, lounging with confidence. The moment vanished. What remained was a dying father in business debt talking to his son, also in debt.

At dinner in a Second Avenue restaurant, he recovered his usual arrogant self with the jacketed waiter (another old-world Jew), but was meek and deferential toward me, the American. I tried not to notice the sudden reductions, reversals. He began talking about my mother, but I couldn't take that and closed him off with peremptory pleasure.

The name of Kennedy came up, and we began talking politics. My vigor in denouncing our government's Vietnam involvement surprised him. About Cuba, he hesitated a timid critique, still using his European habit of two utensils to eat with. Cutting him short, I stated authoritatively that Kennedy had endangered the world with his dangerous rhetoric and hypocritical policy. His eyes widened. In a twenty-year-old gesture, reminiscent of his cautionary warnings to Leo Markson, he glanced fearfully around the room, filled with transplanted shtetl Jews munching corned beef and drinking tea. Smiling abjectly, he put his finger to his lips, murmuring "Ssh, ssh," to quiet my voice, still my charges. His look said, "Who knows who is sitting here, listening?" For a reason I didn't understand then, his fear infuriated me. "Oh, come on!" I hissed bitterly, "where do you think we are?" And gazed fiercely at his frightened eyes. A complicated exchange, as I now perceive. By loudly proclaiming my dissent and by mocking his timidity, I was not merely enjoying my new power over him, I was also trying to pay back America for its part in my deception. And I was angry at him—and them—for not being stronger. Let the whole fucking restaurant know that I was not Harry Pincus, but his son.

And then, in the next moment, the entire rhythm changed. He was seriously afraid, I realized, through that clown's mask. The years of his political persecution, when agents did follow him to restaurants like this one (as he narrated later), came home to me. I pictured him sitting down to supper here, alone, trying to relax with a schnapps, wondering if it was safe to open his family mail (those white envelopes with the strange Russian stamps and the exotic handwriting of his Smolensk brother that turned up in the mailbox throughout my childhood). In a softer tone, I asked after Leo Markson. What had happened to him? The reflex of persecution—the sideways glance and the abject smile—then he explained how he had lost touch with him years ago. The last he had heard of him was when Leo phoned to borrow money, after he had been fired from two jobs when they found out he had been a Party member and was on the verge of jail. Furthermore, Yetta, his wife—did I remember her? That short dark woman?—shamed by him, picked up and left, taking the two boys with her. My father had sent him fifty dollars and told him not to bother him any more. ("What could I do? They would have thrown me out of the country if he came around." His palms out, pleading painfully for being forced to abandon old friends.) He narrated the persecution tale in a hushed voice, his brown eyes dead. And I thought, Was this dying bag of fear advertised over those Voice of America programs? Was this what was meant by a citizen of the land of the free? Earlier I had wanted to shout at him that this wasn't Russia, but I realized, that for him, it might as well have been.

Outside the spring evening had turned cool, as we walked toward the Bleecker Street subway station. Looking up at me from beneath his fedora, he remarked, with a smile, how surprised he was at my sharp interest in politics. What he didn't realize, of course, was the lesson in American politics I had just learned. A sleek black auto suddenly shot around the corner, just missing us, its horn jangling my nerves. "Ah, *meshuggaas*," my father said, indicating the natives. I was still shaking when we paused by the subway entrance, chalked with obscene graffiti. "It was nice to see you, Dad," I said, looking at him and using that title for the first time in years. "Take care of yourself and I'll write to you."

"You can't stay around another day, Leonard?"

"I'm due back tonight." Then, on an urge, I added, "Mother asks about you from time to time, how you are and so on."

My lie brought some light to his dead eyes.

"She does?" he repeated, not with understanding but with hope.

I nodded, and took his hand. He embraced me, his cheeks wet, shaking. This time I pressed him to me, kissing the indented skin. I was crying too.

Breaking from him gently, I said, "We'll be in touch. Answer me when I write, okay?"

He waved and I descended the stairs, taking his potato-sack figure and frightened smile down with me. My cheeks burning, I ran to catch my train.

Soon afterward I flew off to England, where I spent a summer at the University of London.

Robert Kennedy was killed in June of that year, and my father died two months later. The grief and commotion in England over the assassination were great, naturally, but I, though shocked, could never get up too much enthusiasm for mourning. His fame, I thought then, was more derived from position, title, and family than accomplishment. About my father's death, from stomach cancer, there was less fuss, naturally too. He had been in the hospital for four weeks prior to death, it turned out, but my sister hadn't let me know about it for fear of interrupting my work. Also because she felt that I wasn't that interested. A small logical miscalculation. When a letter finally arrived and I phoned from London, he had died early that morning. I was too late.

Piling books and packing suitcases in my Hampstead room, I

319

roamed from my father to the Senator and suddenly realized that beneath the rank there was a father there too. I found myself feeling abashed, guilty; I had a new private slant on the assassination. Poor Robert was just as dead as poor Harry. Tying up loose ends on the telephone, I was able to leave for New York that night.

On the streamlined jet roaring through the sky, coated by Sidney Poitier on celluloid and leggy Southern stewardesses in the aisles, I sunk into the bulky *New York Times* and observed the clouds. Floating gobs of white cotton, they presented at once a grand illusion of heaven and splendid evidence of worldly beauty. Somehow they led me to the obituary columns. An editor of the Boston *Globe* had died at seventy-four, of a circulatory ailment. The wife of a Philadelphia civic leader passed away at age forty-one of septicemia. A Hollywood director was hit by a fatal stroke at fifty. Stories of the successful, the well known, the accomplished. To the right, in small-print columns, were the more anonymous finishes. Parry, Peyser, Pollard, Prince, Protofsky. No Pincus.

On an impulse I released the tray-desk from the back of the airplane seat in front of me, got out a yellow legal pad, and composed.

HARRY PINCUS, AN UNHAPPY FATHER, DIES

Aged sixty-seven, Harry Pincus died today, August 24, in Brooklyn, New York. An American citizen, he remained a permanent exile from Russia (attested to by our government); a milliner by trade and Communist by ideology, he was always an aristocrat by temperament (ask his workers and friends); a most respectable father on the outside, he died unfulfilled, unloved, and mostly unforgiven (see his family).

The causes of decease were complicated, let us admit. Just as it would be inaccurate to attribute the death solely to early infidelity by his son or lack of family love later on, so it would be mistaken to isolate the cause as cancer of the stomach. Both, physical disease and human neglect, played their part.

It's unfortunate that there is no place here to explain in detail the subtle role played by a nation's malice in individual lives, for the nation has played a part in this particular life. And since civilization has not as yet advanced to the point where Laws and Courtrooms exist to try nations for the effect of their propaganda, it cannot now be charged that America is guilty. Only that she stands accused.

The father is mourned mainly by his son, whom he early wronged and who in turn wronged him. Both, however, it should be added, were victims of larger and more insidious forces, patriotism and family relations.

For most of the ride through the night and clouds, I was intent on sending off my little account to the *Times*, challenging them to print it. So what if it bordered at times on unmanly self-pity or resounded with lofty almost unprovable national charges? Or if it missed the terrible guilt and forfeited love that hurt so much? Didn't a small, rather ordinary and unhappy life deserve its place alongside the more heralded and prosperous? When was the *Times* going to print the essential qualities about a life—its unhappiness, frustrations, fears, failures? The state of its spirit rather than its body? Anger, which had been rising slowly alongside sorrow, now peaked.

But when we had landed at Kennedy and began descending the windy ramp, I stopped, crumpled the page, and tossed it away. A yellow speck of a life important really only to me, not to the public. Did I smile? In any case, I'm sure I lingered to watch the scrap obituary disappear down the green-lit runway, for the next thing I knew, I was being prodded by a finger to get a move on. As I did, I suddenly felt more firmly than ever an enemy of the state, only not exactly in the way that my father or the fatherland or even I had anticipated. In fact, I felt propelled by a feeling that surprised me with its focused intensity, though perplexing me with its layers of ambiguity.

> *I myself am a pacifist, but I think our system can*
> *bear, and ought to get, a good deal more roughing up*
> *than it has. And I do not much distrust that the young,*
> *white and black, know where to draw the line.*
> —PAUL GOODMAN
>
> *Do we, Paul?*

4. Bigger Game

It was a few weeks after the Mailer incident when I saw Luis Rodriguez sitting on the white steps of the Widener, eating. I waved and climbed the sixty steps to join him. He was just finishing a sandwich. In his wraparound sunglasses, striped polo shirt, and dark curly hair, he looked like some glamorous hood. His famous gray fedora hat, which he sometimes wore, was missing.

I asked what he was doing around there, and he replied that he had taken a part-time job at the Widener for the summer. He took out a pack of cigarettes and lit one, his innocent matchbook recalling to me that other infamous one. He stared out at the tree-shaded Yard, where students sat lunching and reading.

"The word is that someone from the Movement did the killing," said Luis quietly, working a wooden match on his teeth. "Imagine the gink who did that."

He was always finding nice words for derision. "Why?" I asked. "What do you mean?"

He lifted his glasses and looked at me with smart black eyes. "Killing that nobody was a waste of energy. He was a writer, man, just a writer. It's this stuff that counts." His thumb pointed over his shoulder at the massive library. "Buildings, universities, that's the gimmick. Or pictures and museums, like the brothers started to come down on, in June. That's what scares the Man—touching his pro-per-ty. He don't give a fuck if some silly-assed poet gets done in. But touch his buildings and he's going to jump." He inhaled and twirled his match in a groove. "I bell-hopped for a while at the Americana in New York, and there was this protest one week by kitchen help and chambermaids for higher wages and all that shit. Well, everything was cool until this one cat, who used to shovel grease for the cook, got excited and started writing some shit on the corridor walls. That was it—boom, boom, boom! Two bouncers were on that cat in a flash, and he was carried out of there. And this little ofay manager comes on and says, 'We will not tolerate any damage to the property here.'" He smiled at his fag imitation and put back his dark glasses.

"But certainly Mailer meant something important to some people," I argued. "And his death meant more. It was a signal, to the intellectuals at least. A warning that things can't be carried on the same way any more. At least we're upsetting them"—as soon as I said this, I felt frightened at that "we" and went on quickly—"I mean, have you seen the special *New York Review* on it? Three separate essays trying to figure it out and declare the implications."

"*New York Review*," Luis repeated slowly, as if I were talking about J. Edgar Hoover. "Man, when *The Wall Street Journal* writes three essays on it, then you got yourself a piece of the action. But that *New Review?* I've seen that around. Small-time stuff. Where you been all your life, in schools?"

I shut up, my head faint from anger and confusion. A murder for nothing and for nobody was not exactly what I had had in mind. Or was Luis missing the point?

"No," he continued, reflecting, "the brothers knew where it was at when they went after the pictures." His hand sliced the air easily. "Too bad they didn't take down the museum with it. What are you into these days? Ain't seen you around."

I stared at his olive skin and long, sideburned face. Twenty, and he knew more about degeneracy than I'd know at eighty, for all my trying. An education on 106th Street was hard to match.

"Not much," I replied. "Just doing some reading and thinking."

"That's your trouble, Pincus. You think too much. Get on the stick more. Get busy, man!"

Was it a perverse joke? Had he seen through me right along? I searched his face, hidden again by the dark glasses.

He laughed suddenly and tapped my arm. "Don't look so serious, brother. I'm just kidding." He stretched himself and stood up. "I'll catch you later sometime. Let me know if anything's happening." And that slim and cunning counselor bounced slowly down the steps, surveying the quiet square of traditional soil as if it were Gaul dirt and he were Caesar. A Puerto Rican Roman in bell-bottom dungarees and sharp sideburns, come to the university to get his spoils.

Cunning Luis had set my ideas in motion again. His critique of the murder left me gasping, almost laughing. Frantic laughing. How little it could mean to someone like him! Of course. But the question was, whose troublemaking was this, his or mine?

Both, I thought, as I wandered inside the Widener, looking about idly. *Both.* Gazing at the model scale of Harvard College when it was first founded in 1636. At the special exhibition in glass cases of Russian Revolutionary materials, housed by the library. How curiously old-fashioned Trotsky and Lenin looked, dressed properly and staring sternly. A pair of college presidents today, perhaps. Trotsky at Buffalo, say, pushing social change. Dr. Lenin at Bennington, a strong suffragist. And finally, on the first landing, a pair of huge portraits by Sargent. I stared at the formal clothes and poses, the pink faces and ornate backgrounds, thinking how camp it looked.

"Impressive, isn't he?" A lady smiled at my side. "To my mind he was the best American portrait painter."

I nodded vaguely, and she apologized for interrupting me.

I moved off, my brain suddenly whirring. I hurried down the stairs, out the door—holding my hands high to indicate I had taken out no book!—and down the steps of the Widener. Quickly I made my way along the dirt path leading out of the Yard and across the street to the Fogg. Much too excited to remember my original task of retrieving that envelope I had left behind a little while back. Too excited with my new plans and the hideous future to worry just then about the dead past. I spent the rest of the afternoon in the Fogg, enjoying myself thoroughly for the first time in a museum.

I outlined the plan in a large house off Brattle Street, courtesy of Felicia C., a woman in her forties who, in the past, had contributed money to help us with hideouts, printing, bail, and lawyers. I had never met her, however (it turned out she was the elder sister of Kove's Melissa and had met the Dean once or twice) or been to her house. How odd to walk up that long flower-lined entranceway to the gabled house with columns in front and be ushered in by a Scottish maid in uniform. All that aristocratic splendor on behalf of proletarian havoc! What might husband Tommy C. think, a retired tennis champ who lived in the Caribbean and followed the big fish? Curious times.

My audience of nine was waiting in the library, a sunken room with oriental rugs, deep love seats, velvet chairs, imposing pictures, leather-bound books, and autographed photographs from important figures. (Eleanor Roosevelt wrote, "To my dear protégée Felicia, whose future in noble causes is assured." And RFK had written, "Charm, wit, beauty, and reads *The New Republic*, a dangerous lady!") Felicia, tall, salmon-colored, lovely, introduced herself long enough to explain where to find coffee, liquor, bathrooms, and then left the room. A graceful swan arranging a Duma of hawks and buzzards.

And so, a few doors down from where some of our founding fathers and great generals had first fought for a nation, I laid out my plans for shaking it. One patriotic act for another, given the different conditions.

Using my spiral notebook set upon a wooden lectern (already set up), I narrated what I knew about the Fogg and Busch-Reisinger Museums, my projected targets. Nervous at first, noting several strange faces immediately—a young black girl, barely listening; a thin man wearing a tie and goatee, a blond boy with adolescent pimples—but I got better as I went along, citing guard schedules, coffee breaks, door and window exits, accessible rooms, and alternate targets, provisional timetables.

"Hit the pictures *or* the museums," inserted a balding middle-aged man who I knew to be a Harvard professor of physics. Brilliant, authoritarian.

"The pictures, primarily."

"But why? I don't get it." Speaking from his lotus position on the floor.

I was unsure how to put it, since my ideas were still fragmentary, unsettled. "I think we have to hurt those with the best minds. Make them see that we're not kidding. Those who care about culture, books, art. If we want a better life here, it's they who can design it. At least they should think about it. On their

325

own, they won't. We need to prod them. I want to impress them that the stakes are higher nowadays. Intellectuals live and think in special sanctuaries of privilege, and this seems to me to be one way of piercing them."

"And once they're pierced?" asked Lauri Pearlman, in Levi jacket and loose hair, casually riding the arm of a chair.

"I don't know, we'll have to play it by ear, I suppose."

"Without a precise theory, you're done for," countered Thompson, the physicist. He began to argue for demolishing government buildings.

"If you're talking about open warfare," spoke up the thin man with the tie, "they have more guns, tanks, ammunition. If you're proposing guerrilla tactics, the shopkeepers and farmers and mechanics around the country will knock our heads in. And instead of swimming in the water of the people, we'll be drowned in it, by them."

How nice to see one of Mao's analogies twisted into native sense.

"Isn't that elitist what you're proposing as to who's going to plan the good life for us?" The young blond boy's voice squeaked horribly, in contrast to his articulateness. "It sounds like Plato's *Republic,* with the philosopher-kings directing the state."

"Yes and no," I answered. "I should have prefaced all this by saying that the basic idea came from our friends at the Berg Art Museum last June. Not from philosopher-kings but from blacks, Puerto Ricans, students. As for it becoming elitist later on, we'll have to watch out for that. Guard against it. Make sure that there's a healthy mix of . . . democrats and theorists, kids and teachers, old and young." I turned around. "Like there seems to be here."

The boy, Joshua—he gave his first name when he spoke—nodded reasonably, and questions immediately were put about museum details. I answered as best as I could. Guard routine meant three regulars in the Fogg during weekdays, two at the Busch-Reisinger (which I scouted after the Fogg). No one carried a gun that I could see. Coffee breaks were at 11:15 and 2:15, with variations. Busch-Reisinger had fewer office personnel around, generally a secretary and the curator (when he was there). The Fogg had several more, and I explained where the offices were. The matter of hostages came up, and I really didn't know what to say. But Monroe Rules, a neatly dressed black boy, said the fewer the better, they only added extra weight. If there was a shootout situation, he said, then they could come in handy. (That movie-word sent a ripple of fear through the room.) We then discussed the subject of weapons and the method of destruction to be used. Napalm and knives for pictures, I said; Mace or its equivalent for guards; guns for self-defense. Immediately questions came about where we'd get all this, what kinds of guns, what about those who had never used tear-gas canisters, et cetera.

God, who had figured all that! "It all has to be worked out, I guess," I stammered.

"Don't sweat, Luis and I can handle that end," said Monroe in his barely discernible Southern accent. He said something about a Boston armory where National Guardsmen who were brothers could pick up stuff easily enough.

"Anything else major to tell us about?" asked a boy in glasses, beard, and excited face. Ronald Kepfner, an M.I.T. teaching assistant in biochemistry.

"Well, I thought of having a couple of reserve units, say of about fifteen kids each, waiting in adjacent buildings, the William James and the Visual Arts Center. These kids will be in complete ignorance of who we are or what we're up to. All they'll know will be written down on slips of paper, and on an appointed signal they can leave their buildings and cross over to the target areas— to create diversion, havoc, whatever's necessary for the moment. I'm thinking of peace-marcher types or McCarthy kids of a few years ago, to be used just in case we need them."

Addie, the black girl, smiled lazily and raised her hand. "Kind of pointless, isn't it, to have thirty bodies just sitting around, when they can be used? Why not give them something nice to do, while we're doing the bad stuff? A protest, like." She shrugged her shoulders. "That'll do. A nice protest somewhere at Harvard or the Cliff to draw attention. They needn't know anything of what we're up to on the other side of campus."

God, how stupid you could look when you were trying to present a plan! What I thought was simple and clear was being punctured everywhere. The general idea and rationale had so excited me that I had forgotten the hard part, the details.

The Radcliffe black girl and Joshua Greenberg, a senior at the

327

Cambridge school in Weston, were assigned the protest arrangements.

"I'd like to make another suggestion, if I may," said the same thin man. "I'd like to suggest a third hit, the Clark Art Institute in Williamstown. This will give friends out our way work to do. It also adds some breadth to the strategy, which I think can be helpful. Instead of a purely local affair run by Cambridge fighters, this will indicate a much wider syndicate is at work. Furthermore, the Clark, as you probably know, Mr. Pincus, has as good if not a better permanent collection than the other two museums." I asked Kepfner who he was, this funny guy. Peter Briggs, a young composer and professor of music, from Smith.

But I was against the proposal, since it involved an area and museum that I was ignorant of and persons that I couldn't account for. A discussion followed, a vote was taken, and the Clark Institute joined the select crowd of art victims. Shakedown trips to the three museums were immediately planned.

It was nearly eleven, three hours after we started, and I was about to call a halt when Luis, caressing a cat on the marble mantelpiece, began talking.

"It all sounds cool to me, except that we're not taking any property down with us." He smiled narrowly and lit a cigarette. "I've been working at the library the last few weeks, and I think we could have some fun there without too much trouble. That same night when we hit the pictures, I'd like to see us take on the library."

"What library is he talking about?" whispered Thompson the physicist loudly.

Luis looked at him patiently. "The Widener."

"What?"

"Are you crazy?"

"The Widener?" I found myself saying, perplexed. "How do you mean?"

"Burn it. Burn it down."

I smiled, the idea was so unbelievable. Those books burning? It struck me as thoroughly incredible, so totally different from slashing pictures.

Thompson said he wasn't going in for any crazy pyromaniac stuff! Ronald Kepfner was shaking his head in dismay. Lauri looked like she was going to cry.

The idea hung like a nightmare in the air for a few still moments, then Luis spoke again. Quietly. "I say take the Widener that night. If you're really interested in shaking up people." And he stayed against the fireplace, dark glasses on, smoking, frail and indomitable, stroking his new furry friend, with tenderness.

Tense, afraid, angry, they threw questions at the solitary boy who had waited three hours before challenging them, us. I vaguely heard some of the answers—a series of small fires set on different levels—in the stacks, the basement and first floor, carrels and cubicles—by means of old tires stuffed with newspapers and kerosene. Like they did for sugar-cane fires in the Caribbean, he added. No, it had to be the same night as the museum hits, otherwise there'd be too many precautions taken. He'd need about eight or ten kids, which he could get easily enough. And so on. Confronted, with the chips down, he was stone and ice, immovable.

I was too staggered to listen with exactness. The Widener! I could barely speak. So Luis was putting it to me once again. I took one leap—proposing the museums—and there he was, there *they* were—bounding ahead with two, easily and casually, looking back skeptically to see if I'd make it.

By an eight-to-two vote, the Widener was added to the list. The dissenting votes came from Thompson and Kepfner.

Five hours after we had begun, we called a halt, arranging to meet in ten days with details of personnel and run-throughs. We'd plan then on an exact timetable.

As we left the room, Felicia asked if any of us would stay on for coffee or a nightcap. No one seemed in the mood.

"I just wanted you to know," she said to me on the side, her eyes lake-blue, her cheekbones high, her face spirited, "that I heard you talk about a year ago, at Cardozo, and I thought you were marvelous. Professor Kovell recommended you as a radical who was interesting, and I took up his suggestion. I mean, you were the only one then to say something positive, when everyone else was so negative. Do you remember that talk?"

I nodded vaguely, sardonically remembering the boy who spoke then. A boy sane, hopeful, civilized. I eyed the tall grandfather's clock, pendulum swinging.

"Forgive me for putting it so awkwardly, but I truly would

329

like to know more of your personal feelings these days. I don't mean anything about what you've been discussing here. Just your ideas about what . . . what a revolution like yours can come to?" She smiled with perfect white teeth, and her look was a mixture of aristocratic grace and impressive modesty. "Would you talk to me one day about the future? I mean, if you think I could understand what your ideas are." No, she belonged more to Henry James than to Lenny Pincus.

But I was confused. "Yes, we'll talk sometime. When I'm . . . more free." And I said good night, not understanding anything, what she was saying or my feelings.

Outside in the warm September air, Luis Rodriguez sidled along suddenly. "You were tough tonight, Pincus. Good. You've changed, brother."

"How so?" I asked, nervous.

"More ready for action. Less talk." He shook his head. "A few months ago you never would have come around on the library. It would have offended you. Anything happen to change you?"

We walked down Brattle, the trees swaying and the large houses looming imperiously behind gates and hedges. How peaceful, I thought. Was there anything evil about that? About Felicia?

"Just events," I answered. "I suppose they've made me come around."

He took gentle hold of my shoulder and stared at me, nodding. "Any personal events, like?"

"Oh, shit, get off my back, will you? What I do personally is my business, no one else's!"

"The man's hot. You're wrong, Pincus. Your business is my business, from now on. Remember that. But there you go again . . . uptight for no reason. Why?" He nodded. "You watch yourself. I'm getting *concerned* about you. We're brothers, remember." He smiled, squeezed my arm, and turned away, heading for the river.

I stood on the street for a minute or two, watching the red light scatter on the asphalt, feeling the pressure on my arm. Crummy sly spic!

I walked up Mt. Auburn and through the Square, where

freaks and heads and kids with guitars and dope peddlers and local blacks and high-school students lounged, waiting. But all that a few weeks back had seemed so degenerate and bad now looked like toyland, with tricycles, taffy, children. How reality can change after you've gotten yourself in trouble. *What did Luis know or sense? And what did his being my "brother" mean for the future? Was I his brother? Did I believe in his brotherhood?*

The Widener suddenly loomed in front of me like some massive medieval fortress, surrounded by gates and stones. A fortress which washed away doubt and confusion, bringing instead grim determination, a sense of encirclement—as if the gate and the stones were circling me. How I longed to be on the road to Canada or New Mexico, and out from under—Luis Rodriguez, Cambridge, libraries and museums, my life. As I walked along Mass. Ave. that long face of Luis's, with his narrow smile, pencil mustache, and baleful eyes, came back to me, blocking escapes.

It took two more meetings before everything was ironed out, final plans made. In the interim, we—the nearly two dozen kids scheduled to hit the two Cambridge museums, went through the Fogg and B-R twice more, taking mental and written notes, talking afterward. Each trip increased in nervous excitement—through the austere stucco-and-tile Busch-Reisinger, with its imposing Teutonic floors, stone walls, and awesome Flentrop organ (which I had never seen or heard of before); and through the monastic arches and winding stone stairways and imitation Renaissance interior court of the Fogg. Next to Luis or Adelaide or a Nam veteran named Jimmy Haggerty, I was a novice at the scouting business, not really knowing where to look first, what to check out. Addie located two telephones in the Fogg that I had never noticed; Luis cited a guard downstairs who carried a gun; Jimmy H., a tall pink-faced Boston Irish boy, with a couple of medals for heroism, found two extra basement exits in both museums. Meanwhile, I would tell myself that it was going to be child's play, only to have a guard in green uniform walk toward me and convince me on the spot that it was all over, we were suspected and known. I froze, and the guard walked by me to check on an overeager patron who had started to touch a small sculpture. My perspiration and shaking hand suggested something other than child's play.

The meetings were filled with details, details, more details. You couldn't do anything without a problem appearing, an unanswerable question arising. To be checked out and rechecked. But the single most memorable item from those last two meetings was Luis Rodriguez's presentation of his Widener plans and research. He produced a set of drawings of the great library which seemed to my amateur eye a beautiful piece of work. Drawn in pencil and ink on large oaktag, soft brown pattern paper, and sketching sheets, they showed the library from a vertical in-depth view downward, and a cross-section horizontal perspective. (Did I take to them especially because they reminded me of my father's drawings of his house and land in Turov, which he would compose for his six-year-old son on the wooden kitchen table? Perhaps. From White Russia to Puerto Rico, a longer distance than Columbus traveled.) Small red asterisks and arrows indicated fire and bomb sites: for example, in the Binding Room in the basement, where there were stacks of periodicals; the Catalogue Room on the first floor; three different stack levels; two professors' studies. (How did you get into a professor's study? I asked. Good skeleton key, bobby pin, or thin manila folder inserted between lock and jamb.) Small time bombs would be set off first; afterward, during commotion-time, students would ignite "manually" the stack fires. At one point, he indicated matter-of-factly a section of jagged lines, Harry Widener's personal library in the mezzanine. Pretty tough. How would he get in there? I wondered aloud. A file box behind glass doors would be replaced by one of Luis's specially made ones—containing black powder in a small pipe, or dynamite—when a book was removed from the case. A precedent he had already set down. Again came the questions—about timing, "cadres," extent of damage, high-percentage risks—and again Luis was audacious in his new role of architect-designer. The blueprints and sheets carefully laid out on Felicia's long fine library table, the small melodic voice that occasionally spoke the wrong idiom, the calm and conciseness of the answers, all this impressed me in a wholly new way. I had been wrong too about Luis; besides being a cunning street crook, he was a fellow with real talent.

Outside, after the last meeting, I asked him about architecture or design school after Cardozo.

He played with the wooden match in his teeth. "Sure, amigo, if this job works out, perhaps I can apply to Harvard with a Widener reference."

A new sympathy and those Widener plans suddenly stirred an impulse, almost forgotten. I asked Luis if he could retrieve for me that special envelope I had left in the Widener, and explained where it was. "A letter home?" He smiled. "Something like that." He nodded, we talked about a girl he had run into—he making funny imitation of her burdensome breasts—and then we split from each other, feeling good. With two days to go, it was nice to suddenly have a new friend.

At home during those last days, I rechecked details and glanced over some notes of the past few weeks. Especially at night when sleep was impossible.

> Doing away with art, culture. Cutting down great pictures, destroying fine books. We're not the first boys to think of such sabotage. There are useful precedents. Pissarro, an Impressionist painter, had a detailed blueprint for getting rid of museums and libraries and starting over. A nice document for art appreciation classes. The Italian Futurists wrote: "We want to destroy the museums, the libraries, the academies." The Russian Constructivists proclaimed: "Art must die; only useful objects are worthy of being produced." And the Dadaist exhibit currently in the B-R is full of anti-art art. *Down with Art* is a real slogan on one of their posters. We student barbarians have a very eminent tradition behind us. Will our critics see this?

> Art, literature, music, the opiate of the intellectual, the refined citizen. An opiate especially valuable when the moral and political life of the nation deteriorates. Seeing a Picasso the equal of an opium pipe? Partial truth, perhaps. A book, the smart man's pleasure. A symphony, the luxury of the sensitive. Remove the comforts. Make the intellectual bleed. Make him face life without his escapes and pleasures. Put him into the frame of mind of a peasant beneath napalm

skies, a migrant worker, a garbage collector. Get the refined citizen angry. Upset and insult him. Injure his pride. Then try to change him. Create a new value, a new man. How? That's where he—that same smart citizen—would help out. He who would survive. He could teach us, the jailors and troublemakers.

What a nice little nuisance you're making of yourself, LP.

Meanwhile, I learned by heart the floor plans of the Fogg for the two main floors we were to strike. A friend in the director's office secured the plan (it was not in the same category, in terms of aesthetics, as Luis's master drawings of the Widener). With red asterisks, I indicated the targets for our three teams and other small directionals.

The Friday morning of S(iege)-Day, the twenty-second of September, was sunny, pleasant, conveniently cool. Jackets were appropriate. I walked by my museum at 8:30, found everything in order, and made my phone calls. To Cambridge and to Northampton, saying, "Classes are on today, let me know how the lectures go." Back at the apartment, I got my masks (Halloween and gas), Mace squirt can, hunter's knife, pick hammer, napalm canister. (Designed by Kepfner in his M.I.T. laboratory, helped along by the formula given in a *Scientific American* article on Fort Detrick, the experimental lab in Maryland.) Using a clever system of money belts and ropes—the inspiration of Jimmy Haggerty, recent vet—I tied the weapons and toys around my body, on top of my special undershirt. Padded and bulky, I felt like Neil Armstrong headed for the moon in a space suit. Except that I wore a sports jacket and slacks, and was headed for the Fogg. The walk there from Hancock Place was like walking a last mile, though it took five minutes.

We filtered in ones and twos into the museum, nine of us inside by 10:50. The antiwar protest, meanwhile, had begun at 10:30, outside the president's office. If the run-throughs had been nerve-racking, they were nothing next to the real thing. Looking at a Byzantine madonna, I was shaking. What would happen when I'd have to begin? Colleagues carried pocketbooks and light portfolios—checked out beforehand to see what the guards would allow through—and wandered about, Lauri P. taking nice notes, Addie pointing out Chinese scrolls, Kepfner walking round and round an abstract sculpture in the modern exhibit. Trouble-makers playing patrons, students. We had a total of eight rooms targeted, with an alternate four available, depending on guards and visitors. At 11:10 I would go to the Oriental room, begin my work there at 11:15, when done move on to the ancient Buddhas; if there was still time, take up the modern show. At approximately 11:15, three comrades wearing their horror masks were scheduled to enter the curator's office and, at gunpoint, tie up everyone, cut phones, post the CLOSED TODAY sign outside. (We were aided here by a recent Radcliffe graduate who worked in the curator's office. A tall quiet girl who loved baroque music, and whose father was a civil-rights lawyer.) Simultaneously, the same sort of plans were scheduled for the Busch-Reisinger, a few blocks away, and the Clark Institute, eighty miles away. Later I would check in with Thompson and Briggs, the brigade leaders there.

The first problem occurred at 11:08 when a new guard told Lauri that she had to check her straw shoulder bag, it was too large to be carried around. She reddened, and I thought for sure she was going to faint. I caught her attention, nodded, and she followed his order without breaking down. My stomach sank until I saw her return, which was time for me to take my station. Trembling, I moved into the Oriental room down the left corridor, where Chinese and Japanese scroll paintings, dating from the twelfth century at least, and other ancient vases, jewelry, and *objets d'art* were displayed in glass cases. I darted about, the guard came in for a routine check, my heart fluttered wildly, and he walked out again. I had a minute to go, and I picked out my first target. It seemed to me more tense there than being in the hotel room with Mailer. I remembered that, and Kovell's class-room words about how art lived on while we died. Its immortality was its glory.

At 11:15 I had my pick hammer out and poised, but all I seemed able to do was stare down at a long picture of a mountain, a sea, a man contemplating, peasants with a mule, a fisherman, a tea ceremony. I stood there, paralyzed, trying to make sense of the picture. An elbow in my side and Addie's fierce "Move!"

335

broke my inertia. I smashed the long glass with my light hammer, finding the glass more durable than I imagined, and having to hit it harder before it cracked and came apart. I poured napalm on the scroll, and it leaped into flames. Shoooosh! Frantically, I made for the next case and was in the middle of smashing it when the first guard appeared, running and calling out, "Hey, are you crazy?" He was tripped by Monroe and squirted (Mace) by Addie. When I first saw them in their gas masks that way, with the narrow tubing leading forward like elephant tusks, I thought I was in a movie or Brazilian jungle. I went back to work, Monroe joining in, wielding a small ax. Shouts and screams sounded from far off; otherwise there was just the cracking of the cases and the crackling of burning scrolls. Breaking apart the vases and fine bowls was more fun, as they shattered easily and you could throw them against walls and floors. When I looked up, the room was smoky and gassy, glass lay in bits everywhere, along with broken pottery and jewelry. A junkyard of pretty pieces and colored bits. My watch read 11:28. God, the time ran!

In one motion we ran to the nearby room containing the ancient Buddhas of all sizes and proceeded to work there. This was much more difficult, since the largest of the creatures, which we attacked first, was enormously heavy. Set up on a four-foot pedestal, it looked like a monstrous ape or grizzly, and it took all of Monroe's and my combined effort to topple it. It fell to the floor almost in slow motion, hit with a thunderous crack, and smashed like a bomb. By that time I had lost any idea of a plan or order and was grateful when Addie called out, "C'mon, c'mon, baby, let's get going, time's moving too fast!" Swiftly we began collaborating on another large fat ape—only it didn't crack! Jesus. Not enough height for a real fall. The smaller Buddhas went easier, thrown against a wall and broken. Monroe and I took care of the Buddhas, and Addie cracked the smaller glass.

Eleven forty-two when we hit our final stop, the large end room displaying the modern exhibit. I was exhausted at this point, but also curiously vengeful, feeling as if it were the fucking paintings and sculptures that had lured me into this in the first place. All those odd shapes and stupid abstract canvases suddenly struck me as so much fodder, to be mashed and reduced. Animal glee replaced civilized tremblings, fears. I pulled down the tall vertical painting with the crazy texture and incredible mishmash of lines, and slashed away at it with my knife. I tried to light a match after pouring fluid on it—my canister empty or not working—but my hands were unsteady and I couldn't get it going. Monroe caught sight of my fumbling and helped me out, on his way to another piece. Next, I got hold of a black-smear-on-white canvas and ripped it down and apart, saying, "I'll rip your fucking heart out!" when it gave me trouble. I turned, and my eye sighted a small sculpture resembling a musical instrument, and I grabbed it and flung it against a wall. It bounced off zanily but barely cracked. Fuming, obsessed, I raced to it, and, winding up like a baseball pitcher, fired it across the rectangular room. It cracked apart with a small tinkle and I felt relieved, glorious. "Two minutes!" warned Addie. "Two minutes!" It was like being in a playpen where you were allowed to encourage your destructive desires, with orders given every so often reminding you of society. I was in the midst of burning a picture of a woman split into three heads when out of the corner of my eye I noticed a man standing there. It was only a second, then Addie saw him and tried to squirt him. But the slender man in a suit got to her first, knocked the can away, and headed for Monroe. I waited two long seconds before calling Monroe, somehow mystified by this stranger. Was he part of the game? Monroe ducked and dived at the intruder in the same motion. But the citizen began to put up a good fight, getting Monroe's leg in some kind of bending lock, while having his windpipe choked. My instinct was to break them apart, tell them to stop it, and settle it by talking. But Addie was up and screaming by then, and I was urged once again by her voice. Yet when I got to the battle, I wasn't quite sure how to get him to let go. I tried his arm, but it wouldn't budge from Monroe's leg. The citizen, whose face was twisted in pain, gasped, "Delinquents, lousy vandals!" I had an urge to tell him no, we weren't that at all, we—"Hit him with the fucking hammer," ordered Monroe. I stared at the object in my hand and hit the outsider beneath his arms, first lightly, then harder. At the second blow he grunted deeply and left off Monroe, grabbing his own side in anguish. I dropped the hammer and leaned toward him, trying to loosen his tie. Addie grabbed

337

my arm and jerked hard. Monroe pulled at me. Finally he slapped my face hard and I came around.

We were in the corridor running, Monroe limping (humorously). Down the metal stairway, leaping two at a time, and then racing through the basement to the back exit. I couldn't think, it was happening so fast. At the door, Jimmy Haggerty urged, "Mask, mask!" and then, eased us up, when we had removed them, one at a time like parachutists, into the street.

Outside was sunny, peaceful. Two female students hurried by, a woman pushed a carriage with a child and packages. Five of us piled into the Ford parked across the street back of the museum. An overtime parking ticket was set into the wiper, indicating that the Law had been right there, two hundred feet away. As I worked on the ignition, Joshua was crying, Lauri Pearlman was near hysterics, Addie was saying, "Ho-ly shit, just ho-ly shit." A wind stirred the maple branches through the windshield as the engine wouldn't catch. "I hope you didn't kill that guard," Kepfner was saying to Haggerty, who guarded the curator's office. "You didn't have to hit him that hard." Jimmy looked at him disdainfully. Exhaustion and helpless fear traveled through us all, I thought.

"Start this mother, will you? Or let's dump it!"

Finally the '59 Ford caught, and we pulled out. As we turned right at Broadway, my watch read eight after noon. No sirens yet. My hands were sweatbands around the wheel, and kids were changing clothes, mumbling and shocked as if they were wounded, just returned from the front. It had all really happened, this past forty-five minutes or so; and it began to sink in, incredibly. I turned at Ellery for Mass. Ave., then went right by the Yellow Cab street, right again at Green to Putnam, down Putnam to Western, finally over the bridge and the river to Cambridge Street. At Harvard Stadium, I turned in and parked by the fence near the football field. As the others left the car for the huge grassy playing fields, I changed my own clothes and took a football from the trunk. We walked maybe four hundred yards to a far-off field where friends were already throwing the ball around, waiting. Our alibi, just in case. Soon our crew was playing, while we waited for Thompson's group. If they weren't there by 12:30, we'd split. But they arrived soon afterward, at

12:20, and started toward us, an odd-looking pickup team wearing football jerseys and carrying canvas bags. Soon they were removing sneakers from their bags, having left the weapons in the trunks to be buried later.

At 12:40 two teams of nine were playing touch-tackle football. On the sideline Richard Thompson informed me about B-R doings. Things had gone okay, except that the kid named Gold— my old enemy from Cardozo—had suddenly slumped to the floor while working on the organ and hadn't moved. His face had gone white, and he had lost his pulse. They had to leave him there. I vaguely remembered something about his having a heart murmur. Thompson explained some smaller difficulties, but my head went back to Marty Gold. He was twenty-one and had wanted to be a surgeon, before hearing about neo-imperialism and getting consumed by it.

After an hour of play, four of us drove along Memorial Drive to the Magazine Street pool, where we parked. We walked a quarter of a mile down the shoddy grassland, just past the new overflow tank or cesspool for the polluted Charles. Then, with Kepfner trailing behind as chickie, Monroe, Thompson, and I began depositing used canisters, lighter-fluid cans, masks, and ropes along the rubbish and mud of the embankment leading to the black water. Guns, which we had placed in Baggies and paper bags, were set beneath old tires or piles of rocks or dirt. It didn't take long, and we soon returned with our lighter canvas bags to the car. I felt grateful once again for the city's sponsorship of sordid and rundown sites.

I phoned Peter Briggs at three o'clock from a gas station along the drive. In his deliberate and articulate voice, he explained how there had been some problems at the Clark. They had gotten the pictures all right—Turner, Sargent, Renoir, Rembrandt—but getting away was difficult. A guard got loose and shot a girl, a Mt. Holyoke junior. And in leaving the parking lot, one of the getaway cars had skidded and hit a tree, with two of the kids ultimately getting caught. Briggs relayed all this as if he were giving me football scores, and I imagined him working on the pictures with his tie and shirt collar in perfect order. He asked how we were and I said frightened. Resentful, I left him.

To sweep away the morning and to try to forget the approaching night (and Luis's activities), I went to Boston for a movie. A murder-and-arson story with romance thrown in was the surprise second picture. How pretty and adventurous crime seemed up there on the Technicolor screen, so different from the gray ordeal of the real thing. But instead of Tony Perkins, I kept seeing Lenny Pincus, hammer in hand, going after pictures and then that citizen. God! Murdering Mailer for the sake of some theory was one thing, but going after an innocent man with a hammer? Was I turning into a violent psychopath without my own cooperation? I longed to run to that flickering screen and slash away its lying glamour and deceitful imagery!

Later, on the MTA back to Cambridge, I was furious that we had planned for more trouble on the same evening. I was too tired, even if I had nothing to do; too weary to start worrying again. You needed time, time! But Luis had said no, tonight or no go. So, tonight. During those waiting hours, I saw how men got bad hearts, migraines, shot nerves—the dull anxiety never left for a moment, no matter what the escape.

The Harvard FM station announced an 8 P.M. university meeting to discuss the "tragic events of the day." Oh, boy, the poor suckers will have their noses rubbed in it, I thought, while scrambling two eggs. Their endless discussions! Why didn't they go out and catch us, run us down like dogs—but do something other than *talk*. On the same news program, I learned that Gold was dead from a heart attack; the Holyoke coed was in critical condition; a B-R guard, thought to be seriously hurt when knocked downstairs (why hadn't Thompson informed me?), was all right, with a bad ankle and slight concussion; a Midwestern art professor, "pummeled by two of the attackers" (two?), had bruised ribs; the two "guerrillas" caught were being held without bail, with no names given, except that they were from Amherst and Smith. (I knew no one there.) There was nothing said about sweat, fear, or madness—my memories of the events.

At 8 P.M., I was sitting in Sanders Hall, along with very serious students and bewildered adults. By that time, I was numb from terror, and feeling something like a mole, up for air temporarily. If they had come for me then and said, "You're under arrest," I would have gone along gladly, with relief.

The first speaker was the president of the undergraduate

student council, a blond boy who initiated the theme that in one way or another dominated the discussion. The country was as much to blame as the particular mad and misled students who perpetrated the morning disaster. Applause. Next, the curly-headed *Crimson* editor, a Farber from New York, laid the blame more directly on Vietnam, prophesying that this sort of thing would continue for as long as we burned people and destroyed land over there. And which was worse—he asked us to contemplate—the destruction of pretty pictures or the taking of human lives? A good part of the audience stood to clap. A lean, handsomely graying Harvard psychiatrist, known for his radical sympathies, spoke next. He began by acknowledging the accuracy of the analysis that had preceded him, and somberly explained that the real tragedy was that "most of us here know this, but they in power don't and won't." He proceeded to announce that "we are all guilty" of what happened today, just as all Americans to one degree or another were responsible for what was happening in Vietnam. "Yes, it's hard to accept responsibility for the heinous acts of today, but those who performed them, let us remember, are our sons and daughters, our brothers and sisters, perhaps our colleagues. In important and symbolical ways, *they are us and we are they*." In the midst of the steady applause, an elderly lady behind me whispered to her friend, "My God, can't that man think?" A youngish wife turned to glare at the shrewd lady.

I contemplated the argument, looking around at the concerned and innocent faces of most of the audience, trying to compare their morning—attending classes, taking notes, lecturing, talking—with the morning of the maniac boy with his hammer and ax.

The next three speakers disagreed sharply with the doctor. The first, a historian, said that what had occurred was either the beginning or the end of an era, and hoped for all our sakes it was the end. The second, a philosopher, demanded the apprehension of "this morning's lunatics" and proposed student and faculty vigilante groups to find the culprits. The students booed his angry proposal, though I thought it made sense. The third speaker was Paul Goodman, who had been spending a few days at one of the Harvard houses. Short, bespectacled, he cautioned in a quiet voice that the attack was dangerous because it was a "case of

341

displaced anger," like a boy hitting his sister after his father has given him a beating. "That's what's disturbing to me, that the act has been perpetrated against the innocent and the incorruptible—the one institution that clearly has nothing to do with our vile politics and that remains always a brake against political tyranny." He was cheered loudly. "I think that's what we have to turn our attention to—the reasons for this confusion and displacement, so that those who committed the offenses may perhaps come to their senses before it *is* too late." "Too late?" I wondered. What did he mean by that? Perhaps I could ask him afterward, if there was time.

As he went on, a disquieting rumbling began at the fringes of the audience. Heads turned, students got up, and finally a man at the side cupped his hands and called out, ". . . Widener!" More disorder. Spectators stood, some to get out, others to find out what was said. When the moderator repeated the word, a kind of tidal groan swept the wooden auditorium, and there was a mad dash for the exits. "The Widener?" asked a man, trying to get out of his aisle. "Oh, God, not more of this stuff!"

As soon as you got out of Sanders Theater and Memorial Hall (five minutes?) and you saw the sky above the trees and buildings, you had your answer. Chimneys of black smoke funneled upward, discernible in the moonlit night. I ran in the cool darkness across the Yard; flames flickered into view, sirens screeched in the air. Closer, and a massive building was burning in the night, with people still trickling out like ants from their heated hill. Breathing hard, I slowed up near the spectacle, and it was fantastic, yellow and red flames licking at windows and wood like hungry tongues, gorging black holes. From professorial fire-and-brimstone to the student reality. From Quaker meditation to bonfire radicalism. A crowd of a few hundred had formed, with small circles gathered around those coughing and crying, actual victims of the attack. The firemen had set up ladders and hoses and had begun spraying silver water upon the billowing black. I moved between the front and the western side, listening to the wood crackling like a country fire, watching the blue-tipped yellow and red flames; a sight of such awesome power, destruction, and color that it made you want to become a professional arsonist. I felt the momentary urge to gather up everything around me—grass, trees, fire trucks, books, clothes, students, anything I could get my hands on and toss it into that library dragon.

A girl to my right stood with hands on hips, chewing gum obsessively, enraptured. I walked about, listening to talk of punishment and shock, but also picking up other reactions. Two professors observed the matter with concerned irony, the tall pipe smoker saying something about the *Arizona* and *Oklahoma* going up in Pearl Harbor. I recognized a white-haired librarian from Periodicals, who was shaking her head. When she saw me, she lamented in her Midwestern voice, "Those poor boys. Those poor boys who did this." How interesting to see how extreme events seemed to bring out one's essential characteristics; anger, vengeance, or, in this case, the desire to forgive.

The Widener raged. Not like a battleship or aircraft carrier, which were, after all, replaceable, but like itself, a great library in severe trouble. That was the whole point of it: one of a kind, built up over a period of time, in fact *relying on time* for its achievement. No Detroit assembly line could turn out Wideners like Fords, nor Xerox machine duplicate it, making the original ordinary and almost irrelevant. The Widener was unique. Like Mailer, like the paintings. While I watched those scorching, fantastic flames, it occurred to me that it raged like some ancient ritual resurrected suddenly in the middle of Cambridge, a primitive sacrifice to something like City Gods. Or a Judgment Day for the scholars and intellectuals.

My arm was taken, I froze, and the narrow smile of Luis appeared out of the unlit darkness. "Keeping warm?" he asked, and took out of his jacket pocket an envelope. "Here's your mail, by the way." I didn't understand at first, then took the envelope and saw my handwriting on it, and nodded. But Luis was off by then, away, and I put the still-sealed envelope in my inside pocket.

His appearance suddenly made me think of the books inside: *books burning*, I imagined the fire creeping closer and turning them to ashes. *That* I couldn't take, as much as I had steeled myself for it. I walked away, thinking of Conrad, Yeats, James going up in flames. Out of the Yard and back to the apartment, sick all over again. One moment a tough new boy of the future

343

and the next the same old *feeling* Pincus. From power to . . . confusion. Clearly I had a way to go yet in my personal retraining and overhaul.

In the morning and during the next few days, I read the newspaper accounts and editorials. They were interesting.

There were three headlines in three-quarter-inch caps, which, along with the stories, I couldn't help clipping and carrying around with me, like an artist carrying reviews of his opening show perhaps.

TERRORIST RAIDS ON FOGG, BUSCH-REISINGER, AND CLARK ART MUSEUMS: DESTROY PRICELESS PAINTINGS AND SCULPTURES, DAMAGE ESTIMATED IN MILLIONS—*Times*

HARVARD'S WIDENER LIBRARY SET ABLAZE LATE AT NIGHT, STILL BURNING!—*Globe*

PRESIDENT TO ADDRESS NATION ON ART DISASTER
—afternoon *Herald Traveler–Record American*

Cambridge, Mass., September 22

At approximately 11:15 A.M. this morning, well-trained and well-armed cadres of young radicals attacked three Massachusetts museums, the Fogg Art Museum and the Busch-Reisinger Museum in Cambridge, and the Clark Art Institute in Williamstown, destroying beyond repair some thirty to forty major works of art, and damaging countless others. The raids, considered by historians and museum officials the most spectacular and most devastating in recent history, were executed with remarkable precision and efficiency, lasting from thirty to forty-five minutes. Obviously following a meticulous and brilliant plan, the marauders, wearing Halloween masks and using expertly a variety of chemicals, completely overwhelmed the modest security forces on hand, while holding at gunpoint administrative officials and the few visitors.

When asked to estimate the financial damage incurred, the Fogg Museum director, Mr. Daniel Robbins, who had been away for the day, broke down and could barely speak.

In one hand he held the charred remains of a Sung Dynasty scroll painting, and on the table before him were the mutilated shreds of what used to be a Jackson Pollock painting.

How curious to see those words and to try to connect them with my actions of yesterday! Sung Dynasty, Jackson Pollock, Franz Kline—was Lenny Pincus connected to them?

I was able to make more sense out of the interview with the Widener head.

The damage is inestimable, now and in the future. When the fire stops, we can go through the building and take some sort of inventory, I suppose. But that will be a very crude and misleading measure of what's been lost. How do you replace a man's work of seven years? Or the only medieval manuscript of its kind? Or an archive that no one has ever looked at and wouldn't have for another 75 years? These are the things that make a library outstanding. What's happened here is the greatest tragedy since the pillage of the great Alexandrian libraries in the fourth century A.D.

I was flattered by the comparison, but I didn't think it held up. At Alexandria, truly irreplaceable manuscripts were lost—much of Aristotle, Greek drama, philosophical works. Checking a reference book, I discovered that, in the drama alone, the losses were fantastic: of Sophocles's 116 plays, *seven* survived; Aeschylus wrote ninety plays and *seven* again remained; and for Euripides the figure was *nineteen* extant out of ninety. Now those numbers indicated a major or near-fatal injury. As far as I knew, not one important original manuscript was housed in the Widener for which there was not a duplicate. (The archives of men like Trotsky were a considerable loss, but still it was not as if *The History of the Russian Revolution* had been *lost*.) If, for example, the one and only copies of the novels of Faulkner, Melville, and James had been destroyed, leaving perhaps three books of their entire total corpus, a comparison with the Alexandrian tragedy would have been in order. What was in the Alexandria library was the heart of a great literary and humanist culture; what was inside the Widener were the reproductions of a small part of the culture. Now destroy a great *science* library and you're talking about true Western accomplishment.

Taking down the Widener was a humiliating insult to refined minds, just as mutilating a flag injured simple-minded patriots.

High-falutin' talk. One picture hurt me more than the grand remarks of pundits and curators. It showed a young man of thirty-three, turned sideways in casual distraction, his tie loosened, who had just lost his manuscript of three years' work. Assistant Professor Hal Brookings's book on Dickens would have to be done over again, his carrel charred, his pages ashes. I thought of some essays I had written—on Chekhov, Dostoevsky, even Dickens—and tried to imagine myself coming home after spending those long days and painstaking nights getting one done, only to see it gone, burned. And a three-year effort?

Compared to that photograph of real grief, the newspaper editorials struck me as bombast, hypocrisy, pious anger. Consider the *Times*.

September 22, 1972, will go down as a day of infamy in American life.

The madness of events that has been spiraling downward in American life reached its violent and degrading bottom in yesterday's wanton raids on the Massachusetts museums and the world-renowned Widener Library. These are more than acts of crazy vandalism; they represent a criminal felony of the most outrageous and most heinous sort.

In the last few years, we have heard a great deal of explaining and apologizing on behalf of students, concerning their plight in a society where racism remains a problem, where foreign wars continue to occur, where nuclear armaments proliferate, where the human being is no more than a computer number. Moreover, we here have not been without sympathy. But no matter what the half- or near-truth of these charges, nothing will now do to excuse in any way the monstrous acts of September 22. For these acts of arson and wanton violence are a blow against the one institution—art—that has nothing whatsoever to do with political wrongs and social ills. They are grossly senseless, and can only be the products of demented—"confused" will not do any more—and dangerous young persons, who must be caught immediately and punished appropriately.

The monstrosity of these acts is such, however, that no punishment—yes, even the death chamber—can be equal to their crime. For that crime is not merely against the Fogg Museum or the present American government, it is a crime against the whole history of civilized man. Is there a punishment to fit such a deed? If Hitler or Stalin had been tried in a court of law, for example, would there have been a commensurate punishment for the injury they brought upon all of mankind and its past and future as well? Hardly. The names of these horrible totalitarian creatures are not used in vain here, for once the present villains are apprehended and named, they will take their place alongside these archcriminals as enemies, not of this or that nation, but enemies of all mankind.

For such enemies there is to be no such thing, in this world at any rate, as charity, compassion, or understanding; they are like mad dogs infected with rabies who have already bitten children. They must now be hunted down and dealt with before they spread their disease.

Mostly a thicket of platitudes. Tired analogies. Grand distortions. Me with Stalin and Hitler. Not quite. Someone less significant. Not an archcriminal, but a very troublesome, even dangerous, boy.

But I felt healthier, angering them. I recalled a few years back during the ABM debate when one of the leading presidential advisors, a respected businessman from a large California company, gave the names of two eminent scientists whom he said had spoken in support of the system. In the course of the next few days, each of these scientists reported separately to the newsmen that the advisor's testimony was not true, but on the contrary, each was against the employment of the missiles. I waited that day, the next, and the following for the *Times* to editorialize about this deceit, it being so clear and so dangerous, but nothing came. Silence. Instead there was a sudden barrage of editorials attacking vehemently the influx of pornography and sex in our literature and culture, and the corruption of the nation's morals. I didn't understand this. They seemed to be confusing ideas, *words*. What did they mean by "morality" if the advisor's dismissal was not immediately and obviously called for? For he was tampering with the survival of millions of lives with his lie, while the book or play they were so hot about was a fiction, a make-believe. I wrote them a letter, advising them of these matters, but it was never printed. And when the government advisor, who stayed in office, was spoken of again, it was with the tone of respectability, of pious reverence. This seemed to me to be truly immoral. Were our Presidents and national leaders Popes, and the *Times* a clerical journal in Rome?

So the present editorial almost made me feel good about our actions. Though, in reminding myself of my political anger of a few years back, I realized how far I had come from that world. The world of politics. Of the "right" political strategies. Of socialism and capitalism and Communism. I had been traveling on a different road this past year or more. One which I found it hard to give a name to, but which was more personal, more privately intense, more problematic.

Other newspapers and commentators were also excited, but in different ways. Especially those outside the West.

Take the Chinese People's daily, *Renmin Ribao*, and its headlines:

AMERICAN PEOPLE STRIKE BACK!
DESTROY MUSEUMS AND LIBRARIES ACROSS U.S.A.!
WORKERS AND STUDENTS UNITE IN PEOPLE'S
    WAR AGAINST CAPITALISM!

Even though they had invited our President there, they couldn't resist this plum of propaganda. But why couldn't they tell it straight? Did they need the embroidery of foolish slogans? Wasn't the truth strong enough—some students got angry and did some crazy things to pictures and books? (Admittedly only part of the story; but nearer to the truth than those slogans.) The only workers I saw around were a few hard-hats and police at the fire who nearly foamed at the mouth in anger at us. Proletarian heroes in Peking fairy tales, most of those fellows were in real life rednecks who'd have loved to drop The Bomb on China, if given the chance. A sad commonplace fact.

Less exuberant was *Pravda*, who covered it with their usual blend of cave mentality and bureaucratic lingo:

> The fact that no member of the working class was present in these raids proves once again the utter futility of the student movement, and the great danger of terrorist brigands calling themselves social revolutionaries. While the C.P.S.U. stands ready to back any serious revolutionary movement that struggles against American capitalism, it regards with total condemnation these senseless acts of violence committed against institutions of culture. If the idiotic terrorists or their leaders believe that they are in any way furthering the international socialist cause, they would do well to read—before their next itch for action—the classical analysis of their confusions, Comrade Lenin's text, *Left-Wing Communism: An Infantile Disorder*. Meanwhile, we can only express our shock and offer our sympathy to the innocent victims of this madness, the American people, especially the artists, scholars, and academicians.
>
> Yet, it should be said that the events do signify the increasing desperation and division in American civil life. It is clear that the hour is approaching when internal chaos will break out into the open. It is, therefore, all the more urgent that the C.P.U.S.A. reinvigorate itself as soon as possible, so that it may be in a position of assuming the reins of power when the opportunity arises. . . .

Poor *Pravda*, with butchers for authors and seminarians for thinkers, was missing the boat. No self-respecting writer would be caught dead in our company; and no enlightened radical could do anything but smile at the American Communist Party appeal. A few of the dilemmas of history disregarded by our Soviet detractors. Why didn't they offer Dostoevsky instead of Lenin? And, while they were calling for the C.P.U.S.A. to reinvigorate itself, why didn't they also beckon the D.A.R. and American Legion to wake up and stretch after their quarter-century naps?

349

Reading these news clippings was a welcome break from reality.

Naturally the law got excited by these small assaults and went to work. First, it went around arresting everyone in sight who had ever been involved in the Movement, or been seen marching in protests. (The few times it traveled to the suburbs, it kindly came with warrants, unlike the illegal Cambridge arrests of students.) Of the 340-odd persons rounded up in that first week, I knew of five students and one adult who might be of some help to the police. Happily, however, none was chosen to remain among the dozen held over in custody, after the masses were let go, three days later, with A.C.L.U. pressure. (The police were sure that local heroes like Chomsky were directly involved, and so kept that sympathetic, innocent professor on hand for a whole week.) The police received their one substantial aid from the Amherst marauder caught at the Clark Art Institute; he broke down, cried, and listed eight names that he knew or heard about. So there was Pincus plastered across the Boston newspaper the next morning, along with the others. But the picture was of me at sixteen, beardless, hearing-aidless, beaming widely.

Still, they knew that I had changed. And to prove it, a week later the headline read, N.J. STATE POLICE NAB CARDOZO TERRORIST. PINCUS IN PRISON. How curious to read that while having breakfast in Lexington! Anyway, it turned out that they had arrested a boy with a long sharp nose and a hearing aid, a Princeton dropout. For forty-eight hours Harvey Rich protested his new identity, before he was allowed to call home and get his father to come East from Bloomfield Hills, Michigan. The portly high-school principal at his side, Harvey appeared on television that night for an interview, wearing a headband—couldn't they tell Harvey from Lenny from that?—and brandishing his fist. At one point he shouted, "Viva Pincus! Viva Pincus!" Now that truly embarrassed me, to hear that Brando-Zapata slogan transferred to NBC, while I watched from a comfortable den.

Playstuff compared to the real thing—that notorious arm of the law actually reaching out and gripping me. Back from an overnight shuttle trip to New York to raise funds, I was eating a hot dog at a cheap counter at Logan Airport when a man was suddenly at my arm saying, "If you try to make a run for it, I'll be forced to use this." He indicated a bulge in his coat pocket. "I'm taking you in, Pincus. You're wanted for questioning in relation to the recent museum fires."

The pronounced Boston accent belonged to a man in his thirties, dressed in regular attire, his face blue-eyed and handsome, with a shock of black curly hair. He flicked out his wallet, using one hand, and his badge flashed. The identification read, "Patrick Higgins, Patrolman, Twenty-third Precinct, Boston."

Stunned, I mumbled something about his lack of uniform, and he, smiling with sympathy (I thought), told me it just wasn't my day. He had only come to drop his brother and family off at the airport when he spotted me. Tuesday was his day off this month!

I asked to finish my food, and he nodded, warning me calmly not to try anything foolish, saying he would shoot if necessary. I believed him. He wanted to make this as easy as possible for both of us. Was I carrying a weapon? No. He told me to lift my hands as if to brush my hair back, and when I did, he ran his hand inside my windbreaker jacket and along my belt. Causing the black counterlady to peer oddly. I returned to my tasteless meat, my heart quivering.

I thought of protesting my identity, but that was useless, he'd just take me in any way. A break was possible, but not just then, there. Out in the lobby, perhaps, amid the moving crowd. I remembered the loose money I had just secured in New York.

Not looking at him, I said, nervous at what I was doing—as if the bribe was more criminal than my previous acts—"I have a few hundred in my pocket, could you use it?"

He smiled, I saw, and said firmly, "Not yours."

Another exit closed, I thought.

As we started walking—per instructions, I to the right and a few steps ahead of Higgins—I began to chat, confused. I asked him where he had gone to school. At first quiet, he answered Boston College, for three years. Why hadn't he graduated? Marriage, kids. How many? Four, he said, and added, "With one in the hopper now." The phrase struck me, fondly, and I liked Higgins, walking amid those hygienic corridors and polished travelers. And I recalled why he was there in the first place, this family man and apparently decent guy. I asked him about his brother, and as he started telling me about Tommy, a high-school

351

Latin teacher, I became convinced that I was mistaken about that closed escape route.

We approached the airport exit doors, and I paused to face Higgins.

"What do you earn a year?" I asked, with new focus.

His face went blank, then his eyes and mouth moved—so it seemed to me—with pained uncertainty.

"How much do they pay you a year?"

He angled his head, like a fighter who's belted you with everything and is now watching dazzled as you still stand and face him, and I felt sorry for him.

He didn't or couldn't answer. Finally he muttered, "You'd better start—"

A lady in a cape, bearing two small children, burst between us, startling Higgins and giving me my opportunity. But I stayed put, restraining my impulse to run. Higgins gazed at me in surprise. That fifty-fifty chance against his shooting was not as good as my twenty-percent dark-horse hunch.

"What do you make a year from patrol work, Pat?"

He wavered from the first name, and the words slipped involuntarily from his full lips, like a man hypnotized. "I'm up to eleven eight."

His choice of verb fitted appropriately.

I took a step closer, frightening Higgins.

"Let me walk out of here," I spoke slowly, "and I'll get you half of that salary in a few hours. Don't answer, Pat, just consider it for a minute. In a few hours, I'll give you *six thousand dollars*." I added, "In tens and twenties, say." My heart shook like mad; I had no idea of what I was saying or how to get that dough, but my voice was steady. It sounded official, aboveboard.

A couple this time barged between us, muttering something about standing in the path of people.

Higgins and I barely noticed them or the rest of the airport. I observed those blue eyes blinking, and his cheeks bunching and reddening.

I spoke very softly. "Half your salary by . . . two o'clock, say, no questions asked, wherever you want it. Let's walk toward a phone booth, and you can think it over."

For thirty seconds neither of us moved, and he looked as if he were going to cry. I began walking, staying near him so as not

352

to shake that fragile perplexity, as if my physical body could comfort his moral doubt. God, how new arrangements in life could confuse!

When we arrived at the phone booth, I turned and faced him.

He told me to make my call.

Inside the glass box, I breathed deeply, furtively, afraid I was going to fall over. What kept me going was the next obstacle, getting that dough. I had just finished dialing when he told me to put the phone down. So close, so close!

He proceeded to give me detailed instructions on delivering the money. So he had been thinking too; good. Afterward I went back to dialing. Two calls got nobody. A third found a friend who said it was out of the question, not in two hours. I sweated, to myself. It was almost noon. Finally I got Lauri P., and told her the situation—she knew our contacts—and she said she'd call me back in a half hour if anything was up, or in an hour. If I wanted to wait a day, of course . . . I looked over at Pat Higgins, struggling on his side, and I said it wouldn't wait. She said she'd try.

Before we went to find seats to wait, Pat went into the booth and made his own phone call. To tell the wife not to worry, he'd be home a little later than he thought, he explained to me.

To the right of Eastern Airlines there was a long open lounge, where we sat and watched the planes. I tried to read *Time* but couldn't. At a half hour we were by the booth, but nothing came. The full hour dragged like two weeks, and finally we were back at the booth. Only there was an executive in there, and we had to wait. Five long minutes. Finally he exited, and I got inside and waited, more. "Come on, baby, come through," I cheered to myself, like praying that a foul shot would go in while standing at the line.

The phone rang, I picked it up, identified myself, and shared the receiver with Higgins. The money would be gotten, but only from Providence, not Boston. This meant getting somebody down there and back, at best a two-hour trip. Pat looked at his watch and told me to tell her that we had till four o'clock. That was it. I relayed the message, wished her luck, and hung up, breathing easier before worrying anew.

We returned to the curved cushion seats, magazine flipping,

the drone of announcements, an occasional policeman strolling by in the distance.

After twenty minutes, Higgins offered me a cigarette, which I took, and he started talking. "I'll bet you think I'm corrupt for doing this, huh? Maybe I am. But I'll tell you, if you were a killer, I'd have taken you in, and not for a million bucks would I . . . As it is, I'm willing to ease up on . . . principles." He was pleased with that word, and shifted territory, happily. "You know something else funny? I'm offered bribes all the time, down in that lousy combat zone, and I've never taken one. And won't either. Not from those pimps and prostitutes, and I've been offered some beauties too. Those *boys* are not poor, you know. Cheesus, it gets to me when I see 'em in their Cadillacs, not caring a dime about twenty-buck parking tickets, but laughing. Cheesus!" He paused, puffed, and waved his hand in disdain at that low life. "Some job, having to work down there." He was quiet for a few moments, and started again, half looking at me, half staring in front of him, at the wide window and somewhere beyond. "For three years my wife has wanted new furniture, and for three years I kept saying we can't afford it. How's that? A lousy dining-room set at Jordan Marsh, and I keep putting it off for another year. Or the bedroom stuff, hand-me-downs from my sister-in-law. There's a limit to what I can take of that. And yet, if I go into debt any more—I mean I'm up to here." His palm paralleled his chin. "So what am I to do? And you know, we've been lucky with the kids. But a year ago, Mary, she's three, couldn't hold anything down, and she kept getting skinnier and skinnier, and they started taking these tests and naming some disease, well, it turned out to be nothing. An allergy. Go beat that. But if it were real, I'd be sunk. Up to my ears for the rest of my life, no coming up." He turned more to me now, less to his conscience. "Is it so awful if I let you go, and get some furniture for Donna? We'll catch you some other time, don't worry. So I spend six hundred for a dining-room set without having my balls squeezed, is that so awful? It'll be nice for a change. I mean, if some black pimp can make that dining-room set in *a night or two* and get away with it, while I go around tagging him with tickets and he laughs and I can't make it in three years, well, Cheesus! I mean, I'm not exactly gonna go to the Caribbean with the money,

I'm just looking for some room to breathe! That's all, some room to breathe. Does that sound so corrupt? Tell me honestly."

It did, but I decided against pointing it out at the moment. Besides, I did sympathize, and told him so.

He picked up another cigarette and glanced through a *Reader's Digest,* which he evidently had been carrying on him.

I concentrated on the big gleaming silver-and-yellow steel birds, the small creatures scurrying about them. The airport seemed the right place for conducting our business and for making modest confessions.

The boy who carried the *Life* magazine and stood by the far left corner of the spacious window arrived at 3:43. Seventeen minutes to spare. He wore a buckskin jacket, buccaneer boots, his hair was shoulder-length; he read the magazine and started eating from a Hershey bar. Pat Higgins stood, lit a cigarette, and looked around; then nodded to me. I rose and headed for the modern messenger, with Pat angling to my side. The boy, who recognized me, gave me the *Life,* with the fat manila envelope inside, and walked off, not looking around. I read through the pages and, when he was gone, I headed in the opposite direction for the far exit.

When I reached the automatic doors, Pat Higgins was again at my side, and he led me to his car, a '69 Ford. I sat in the front and handed him the envelope. I'm sure he didn't get all the way through the counting; in fact, he got so nervous that he began dropping some tens and twenties. Angry and embarrassed, he told me to beat it—I thought he was going to hit me just then, he looked so out of control—and I scrambled out of the car and weaved through the parking lot, not looking back. The image of Pat dropping those bills and growing red in the face stayed with me, sympathetically. At the exiting highway, I got a hitch while walking toward the bus, and I was on my way home. Grateful for Catholicism, for debts, for bigotry. And, of course, for money, that great pusher, so much more universal than its competitors in drugs or ideology.

How did I stay free the rest of the time? Mainly through the aid of the New Underground in America, a surprising territory nowadays. (Look around you at the Most Wanted list, by the way, and you'll be amazed at how few students and comrades are caught these days.) For when you made use of the underground network setup, the first thing you realized was how much *above-ground* it was in crucial ways. Instead of cellars and dim garrets, there was an abundance of pleasant rooms in respectable houses. I stayed two days with an architect in Lexington, three with a psychiatrist in Chestnut Hill, a long weekend at a philosopher's in Lincoln, split two weeks between Felicia's off Brattle Street and a lawyer on Beacon Hill, and even got in several days with an English professor in Concord. The talk was first-rate, you never got questioned, you could eat in the dining room or in your room, and so on. Privacy and personal volition were assured. Interestingly enough, Luis and Monroe were the orphans most welcomed by these new-styled moral foster homes. Fine, it had been the other way round for a long time. Anyway, you'd get an address in Lexington, say, and either get out there yourself (hitching, buses) or accept a lift. Up Route 2, right on 4-225 past Wilson's Tree Farm, then left to Lexington Center, a short turn to a white colonial house, with shutters, gables, and a woman in tweeds who greets me at the door. I'm shown to my dormered room, where there are clean sheets, towels, and a view of the Battle Green and the Minute Man statue. Patriotism, contemporary style, meant what it used to mean, I supposed, looking out the window—good citizens had become fine rebels. All that talk about the horrors of the middle class seemed to me so much misinformed rhetoric as I sat over dinner and listened to that tall fifty-year-old architect espouse his ideas on social reconstruction, while his schoolteacher wife kept trying to add irrelevant militancy to his clarity and common sense.

Amazingly, mail turned up at least once in every place, if you stayed more than two days. Through box numbers in various cities and towns, and through these same impressive citizens who took it upon themselves to participate in troublemaking in their own dutiful way. Did the government, the magazines, or my colleagues know what excellent and sophisticated rebels lived in our suburbs? Had anyone gauged the depth of their disturbance with our government or, better, their quiet courage? No, they were being short-changed by everyone, these patriot rebels.

Oh, they were not interested in doing violent things, and some gave up on us when the museums and Widener were attacked;

but others stood by their moral commitment to help change the country, even if they disagreed profoundly with our methods. (A standing rule was to ask no questions.) Weren't they, in fact, a more sophisticated *kind* of rebel in acknowledging a split in feeling and acting anyway? Most comrades disagreed with me when I tried to make this point aloud, smiling at me and saying I was just a sucker for comfort. These "patriots" of mine, they said, were no more than bourgeois types, becoming unsettled, and perhaps guilty. And maybe I was "selling out." No, I wasn't. I was trying, rather, to take note of what I saw before my eyes, rather than relying on past history or present mythology. To my relief, Luis got the point, in his own fashion, and had a marvelous time at these stopovers.

"Do you think they'll let a spic buy a house out here?" he said to me, amused, as we walked around White Pond in Concord. "Why," I asked, "do you want to?" He reflected. "Well, Pincus, I might like someday to show some subversive cat where the stables are, in case he wants to ride while he's hiding out. Man, did that ever throw me the other day, when I was offered a horse and saddle for the afternoon!"

The most memorable stopover was an unlikely one, at the Kirshner house in Chestnut Hill. The surprise was not in the hero's welcome I received from Sarah, a frizzy-haired Jewish beauty of fifteen, or Joey, a scholarly sixteen, who had cut out my picture from a magazine and placed it alongside their other idol, Dylan. Rather it was to be found in the amiableness of their father, Sam Kirshner, a smallish taut man in his fifties with the brutally craggy face of a villain wrestler I had once seen on television. Starting as a Dorchester eighth-grade dropout, he had worked as a light-fixture salesman and eventually made a small fortune in manufacturing (from fixtures to small electronics), the journey appearing in his face. He was not a deep or subtle fellow, his reading was the *Boston Herald Traveler–Record American* and *The Reader's Digest,* and his affections were not books or politics but his family, puttering in the yard, good restaurants. That this self-made capitalist was against the war was mildly surprising; what started that was a godson who had been crippled in Nam. But that he allowed his house to be used in the underground was startling.

357

More. After a first evening of bad loud jokes, good cowboy pool, and much teen-age adoration of me, the second evening produced its share of pain and poignancy. We were at dinner when Sam, mildly distracted all evening, suddenly started shaking. His hands, holding a lobster tail, trembled noticeably. Ruth set her food down and asked if he were well. Sam paid no attention, Ruth repeated the question and then said, "Sam, Sam!" Peering through his hands at his plate, Sam said in his crusty voice, "They're doing me in, *Ruchel*, they're doing me in." Tears rolled down his cheeks, heading for his white bib. He shook his head from side to side slowly. "They're going to get me, it's clear now. There's no way out. It's all over with Kirshner Enterprises. They're squeezing me, the banks, the creditors, and Bradford with his two new plants. Squeezing me until I break!" He looked up at his wife fiercely. "And do you know what, Ruchel?—there's at least six months or a year to go of it. Think of that. And *then* court litigation. Yet, I can't get out of it, *now or then*. I'm trapped, Ruchel, trapped! That fool of a C.P.A. and Mandel, of course, that shyster, I should have gotten rid of years ago, of course, they keep telling me not to worry, anything can happen, and all that *narishkeit!* But it's all over, all gone, thirty-eight years down the drain, and I can't even pull out of it but have to wait for the end . . ." He broke off and held his hands over his face. Joey started crying, Sarah ran to her father and hugged him, Ruth sat astonished. I felt very out of place and conspicuous but dared not move. Finally, Sam looked up self-consciously, pulled away his bib, stopped his tears, and left the room like a wobbly boxer. Ruth called the children back and followed her husband's path.

The incident stayed with me powerfully as I slept in the spare Kirshner bedroom that night. The next day, Sam had returned to his tough cheerfulness and startled me again by taking me aside to apologize for the previous evening. It was beyond me to express my sense of humility and sympathy. Even his melodramatic hand on my shoulder was moving under the circumstances, this man battling for survival, opening his house and hospitality to some strange kid. Who spoke and acted against his country, against his (Sam's) life's work.

Out of curiosity and fear about that long-term despair, I

called a few days later. Sarah answered, said things were fine, Daddy was all well again. I was about to hang up when she added, "Len, do you think I can come along with you on your next job, say? I mean, I'd like to spend some time with you. School's so much less important than what you're doing."

I paused, amused, flattered, tempted. I told Sarah to look after her father, he was a worthwhile project.

Mail contained more surprises. A few were addressed to me directly (on the inside), others were passed along with the general heading of the Cambridge chapter. The international set of troublemakers was as small and intimate in its way as any small circle, academic, theatrical, governmental. Four of the letters were especially interesting.

Mon cher Pincus,

Je vous félicite, vous et vos frères, pour vos nobles et courageux efforts. Vous nous avez donné, à nous autres européens, la force de formuler des nouveaux projets.

Une rumeur significative, bien qu'amusante, circule déjà dans les circles officiels qu'il faut renforcer la surveillance à la Bibliothèque Nationale. Et l'on dit que le grand traître, Malraux lui-même, demande d'urgence un rendez-vous avec Sartre pour discuter des affaires culturelles des jeunes. Cela promet! Sartre, avec qui je viens de parler, ne sait que dire de vos actions. Comme toujours, d'ailleurs! Mais je crois qu'il se laissera convaincre à la fin.

Vous nous avez indiqué, à nous tous, des nouvelles pistes à suivre aussi bien que de Nouveaux Espoirs.

A bas les chefs-d'oeuvre!

A vous, en toute fraternité,
Daniel Cohn-Bendit

With the aid of a Larousse dictionary, I was able to appreciate the redhead's good cheer, once I deciphered the tiny chicken scrawl.

The second letter was printed in large block letters. I gave the postage stamp of the sickle and hammer and a rising Sputnik to the S. child, who collected stamps.

359

Esteamed Comrade;

In your country I was two yeers, and speek your language therefor. It is much difficult to understande what you do to libraries and museums. Notwithstanding I am much pleasing! What you do hurts the government, no? That much is good. Here we heard in enthusyism that news. Mine famous library is Lenin Library, maybe you hear it? Maybe we try famous plans to it now, no?"

Szogniorveff

A nice note from that Russian Smith, opened over boiled eggs, muffins, and bird feeding (through the window) on Francis Avenue, Cambridge.

Then this note from a London friend:

Lenny, that's not very funny. I don't know if you had any direct hand in that incorrigible mess, but a mess it was. To me it made no sense at all, and you know that I speak from no old-fashioned radical bias. Just speaking as a civilized member of the species who also happens to want a better and more just society in both our countries, I think your acts were cruel, counterproductive, and indefensible.

I take it that you have heard by now of one of the nastier consequences over here of the Cambridge business. I mean the sudden growth of a group called the New Oxford Movement, a parody of Newman's nineteenth-century movement to bring reform to the college. NOM's aim is to "bring down the old buildings and values and start from scratch." The only thing to be grateful for is that NOM makes no pretense at being leftist.

Are you all right?

Juliet

I answered my new correspondent Danny fondly; and, to Juliet wrote, "No, I'm not well. Haven't been for a while."

The most moving letter was also the most problematic, the most seriously critical. (Delivered via a New York publisher.)

My dear comrade P.,

Please forgive this intrusion into your affairs, your very complicated affairs. My friends and I have read with much interest about your group's unusual activities. These have certainly been newsworthy, and probably very well-intentioned. Certainly it is difficult for you and your friends to stand by with arms folded in these times of crisis in your nation and around the world.

But may I inject my very personal opinion into your public affairs?

You see, my friend, I am—or was—a writer, of stories and novels, and four years ago, in 1968, spent fifteen months in your country at Texas University in Austin. The experience was most interesting, most educational, especially in Texas, as you will imagine. What surprised me most, or perhaps what I was most interested in observing, was the relationship between the artist and the government. I was quite astonished, to speak boldly, at the total freedom of the artist to say or paint what he wished, about politics, morality, or sex. The lack of an official censor, appointed by the government to oversee cultural matters was a new sight to me. (My own works have been banned here in C. ever since our neighbors from the East have decided to look after our affairs for us.) No matter what your foreign policies of deceit and cruelty, no matter what the internal injustices concerning poor and black peoples, I still couldn't help but be astonished at the protected freedom of the individual to have his say against the government in public. In my country and others around me, the individual is rewarded in other ways than television and news coverage for speaking out, whether as a private citizen or as a writer.

I appreciate such freedom very much, since for the last three years I have been asked to work at two new jobs, trolley conductor and building janitor. I take tickets, make small change, advise passengers what stops to get off at. Or I sweep hallways, empty trashbins, and tidy offices for important bureaucrats to feel comfortable and clean the next morning. Comrade, both are not difficult jobs; they are slow and monotonous, and one has much time to reflect and to imagine.

And late at night, after I have attended to family duties, I sit at my desk and write. Of course I shade the bulb so as not to arouse undue notice of my subversive habit.

I appreciate the freedom to write what one wishes and not to be censored, at the same time that I regret and repudiate government policies that destroy people in foreign countries. I realize that we live in different cultures, and that there are always aspects that a foreigner doesn't quite understand. Perhaps you don't know what it is like to live in a country ruled by national betrayers and foreign overseers; and ruled not by TV manipulation, perhaps, but by guns, tanks, and secret police. Perhaps you will visit Prague sometime and give us your impressions?

And in the meanwhile, won't you please explain to me why you have chosen to punish the artists for the sins of the government?

Yours sincerely,
Joseph B.

A heartbreaking letter, from the world's Heartbreak Capital. What could I say? We had different problems and different governments to overcome, both of us. Yes, I would like to try Prague sometime, my friend, and have you try Cambridge. Have you try my intellectual frustration and political impotence and moral rage, while I try your all-around terror. Who's to say which condition is worse? Perhaps if I were a confident literary man, I might have tried art against barbarism—although history has proven the inadequacy of that form of protest. For myself, an apprentice guerrilla, I was trying barbarism against art. For the time being anyway.

Through these interim weeks, our groups met with broken regularity, generally in twos and threes, in ice-cream parlors, nice homes, town greens. Excitement, fear, and curiosity about the future, however, emerged more than careful plans or theories. The students remained children with strong feelings, not Marxes or Lenins. And I was a tense boy, wondering what next.

What next came by chance, when one of our patrons couldn't make a concert in Boston and offered me his two tickets. I said no, but he insisted, declaring it'd be a nice change for me.

Out of apathy I went along, taking Lauri P. A young conductor from Harvard was handling the Boston Symphony Orchestra, and we sat midway up in the first balcony of Symphony Hall, listening to Brahms, Tchaikovsky, Prokofiev. It was in the middle of the Tchaikovsky violin concerto that it happened. At some low point in the music there rose from behind us a strange harsh sound for a second or two. Tchaikovsky thundered back, but five minutes later, at the next low interval, bang! the definite and embarrassing beat of rock! I turned around and, along with hundreds of others, saw a red-faced father fighting to take a transistor radio out of the hands of his pudgy daughter. The girl, a heavy wallflower type with dull hair and freckles, had obviously adjusted her transistor to block out the Tchaikovsky, but missed badly the last two times around, leaving the rock blaring in the air, a humorous and emphatic annoyance to the audience. Well, Tchaikovsky returned for good, wallflower was admonished, Dad blushed, the audience turned with relief to the serious music. But I was excited. And couldn't help turning once again to that chubby teenager, who was now blowing bubbles with her chewing gum. My freckled friend had little idea that her small revolt was setting off larger ideas for cultural annoyance.

From that night to our first siege took approximately two weeks. I planned it with five others and picked the Loeb Theater to begin with. But it turned out that, after the Widener troubles, Harvard had hired a team of guards to patrol the Loeb, which made it too risky for our first effort. So we switched targets. A friend of Luis's worked as a part-time usher in Symphony Hall, and through him a time device was set into the theater on the afternoon of a scheduled performance. Meanwhile, on that same Friday, October 13, at 5:30 P.M., six friends and I entered the Cheri I Theater, across the street from the Sheraton Plaza Hotel. The theater was nearly empty at that twilight hour, before the Friday night crowds. Still, we chose an area close to the screen and on the side. In pairs we settled into a kind of chessman's Indian Defense, two in front and two in back (not in symmetrical order), and three of us in the middle row. Jane Fonda was playing an angry squaw on the screen, and I tried to get into it, but the attaché case at my feet was like a live wire. A seat apart sat Luis, who, after five minutes, had begun to cut with a razor the red velvet of the empty seat bottom in between us. He worked from a design on tracing paper, made beforehand, which he now laid on the seat, and followed the outline with that special cutting edge. Then he removed the paper and cut directly into the material. Jane was resisting the lust of Lee Marvin, white trapper, when Luis nodded to me. I leaned forward to snap open the case when Kepfner, from behind, tapped my shoulder. Immediately I sat straight, eased my jacket over the seat, and in a moment a uniformed usher was shining his flashlight at my hands and asked if I was smoking. I uttered no, sweating, and he told me scornfully where the smoking section was. I looked back at the screen and put my arms around Lauri, to my right. He departed after two more minutes of overseeing. We waited five or six minutes, and this time I leaned forward and brought the case onto my lap, where, at the sound of hoofbeats, I snapped the locks open. Meticulously I removed the green lead filebox, the ticking barely audible through the lead and foam, and set it down into its velvet rectangle of space. Whereupon Luis proceeded to complete the operation, first placing a strip of foam on top of the filebox, then closing the incision with red masking tape, while I lowered the attaché case to the floor. I was as worried about that *thing* going off in our hands as about getting caught. Meanwhile, Jane was begrudgingly aiding a young white boy, hurt in the woods.

You couldn't hear the ticking from its new home, and I breathed easier. We sat on another hour or so, and then filed out, in pairs. I was the last to go, and as I sat there, along with the bomb, I had a terrific urge to rip it free and take it out with me and be done with it and the whole business. Conceiving the plans was always so much fun and play next to the business of carrying them out. That was always tedious, terrifying. The details to be accounted for seemed in the thousands, with even the most trivial weighing upon you enormously. Pleasureless and burdensome, all of it! Where was the fun sitting in that lonely seat, next to that stupid thing, unable to enjoy the pretty fantasy on the screen? Tedious and desperate, I repeat. And *lonely*. Where was fraternity, closer friendships? I hadn't found them in our acts; all I had discovered was ear-splitting tension and the nervous strain of doing desperate, unlawful deeds. I looked over at that narrow rectangle of red tape and imagined myself lifting it up, making myself very small and climbing down in there, tucked away, the velvet top zipped close over me. But then a couple strolled by and found a seat ahead of me, returning me to the real, the necessary. With an effort of will, I rose. Carrying my case like a good graduate student going back to his study, I walked wearily up that narrow aisle, which seemed long, endlessly long, remembering bitterly how much I used to love going to the movies.

The phone calls to the police and theaters were made at 8 P.M., the crowds were evacuated in a mad rush, the explosives went off at approximately 8:20 (five minutes later than planned, curiously), and the new curriculum was started. The Culture Business was under siege. The actual damage done to the theaters was small, modest next to the psychological pressure exerted on audiences, owners, and performers.

After the Widener, there had been talk of setting up cells in different cities to carry on the work. Once that freckled girl's transistor signaled the new plans, word was given out to implement the idea. Cells were to be limited to six friends who had known each other over a period of time, as an insurance against government agents and police informers. (The two kids who had been caught knew only two more kids involved, it turned out; both were local to the Amherst area. And the police had gotten no more names out of them.) Furthermore, by operating autonomously, if one cell was discovered it would not mean the breakdown of the entire chain, but the end of that single unit only. The risk of duplication was measured against the danger of exposure, and preferred. It turned out to be a small risk because, on large tasks, like the wiring of Lincoln Center, more than one unit was obviously needed.

At first I tried to keep abreast of events and cells, but it was hard concentrating on my own effort without also trying to be an official national scorekeeper. Besides, newspapers and magazines like *Time* gave out enough general information. In the first few weeks the statistics seemed to me either exaggerated or awesome. Had we in Cambridge created a Frankenstein of sorts? Perhaps. At least Pincus and his pals had put our Cambridge on the historical map, so that no longer would it be asked *which* Cambridge—England or the U.S.A.—but THE Cambridge.

Homemade guerrillas ambushing our culture centers, making them unsafe, useless, empty, temporarily obsolescent. Lenny Pincus, who at one time threw his body into second base, now throwing it into the culture machine; from a would-be Dodger to a would-be Luddite. Kids on the loose, more everyday, turned on to pranks, annoyances. As I said, those figures seemed unreal. Of twenty-seven major concerts scheduled in ten major cities in the third week of October 1972, half were canceled ("In the interest of the public safety," read the official notice on standing bulletin boards). The attendance figures for the remaining thirteen did not together add up to a single full house for the New York Philharmonic. Of the major museums in America, according to *Time* again, three were closed down until further notice (the Phillips in Kansas City, the De Young in San Francisco, the Frick in New York); six were opened on weekends only; the museums that chanced to stay open cut back their public hours drastically. (The Museum of Fine Arts in Boston, for example, reduced its hours from 11 to 2 P.M. daily, and Friday night from 7:30 to 10. This was the only way the museum could receive sensible insurance coverage and also pay its new teams of guards.) In Boston, movie-house attendance was down 87 percent from the previous October (*Globe*).

Only a handful of theaters operated with any regularity (mostly Sack theaters), and those with stress. A long slow line waiting to be searched, bright lights on while the movie played, armed guards patrolling the aisles, all this had changed movie-going. Leaning down to light a cigarette surreptitiously could mean, as it did for a young secretary, a week in Mass. General Hospital. A patrol guard, seeing her, cracked her head with a truncheon and dragged her out into the aisle, much to the sadistic delight of the small frightened crowd. A thorough search, however, revealed nothing except blood, innocence, and a Ronson lighter on the floor (*Herald-Traveler–Record-American* item, October 18). University theater dwindled to a standstill after the Yale fire in their drama church. Two phone call threats closed down permanently the Loeb Drama Center and Kresge Auditorium, turning those theaters into tombs, patrolled day and night by uniformed men. As for the libraries and concert halls . . .

I attended a concert to experience the chaos for myself. Or

to flirt with getting caught. Or to flirt with Felicia, who invited me—to a previously scheduled charity concert, to be conducted by Leonard Bernstein. Perhaps it was Bernstein who tempted me, for the only other concert I had ever attended took place in my high-school days, when we were given special free tickets to watch a Thursday-afternoon rehearsal of the New York Philharmonic. Perched high up in Carnegie Hall and peering down that funnel of darkness was like sitting atop a volcano, and when the music pumped upward and ricocheted around the walls, it amazed me with equal force. And watching the feverish director in black turtleneck stop the orchestra to instruct them, and then turn to explain to us, made Bernstein some sort of exotic hero in my boyhood head. So I stood in line, Felicia next to me, splendid in evening dress and dark cape, waiting for the search to reach us. I was bearded, and wore a suit and tie, and had removed my hearing aid. The line of about seventy-five or a hundred inched along, and just as we became the next couple to be searched, the man in front of us suddenly bolted like a horse, saying, "This is ridiculous. I'm not stepping into that contraption for anyone!" And he pulled his wife out of the line and away. But as he did, he was immediately seized by two burly civilians and brought briskly to the side. They were taking no chances.

With us, Felicia went first, shaking her head with cool disdain and stepping past a turnstile to be inspected electronically. Then she disappeared inside the lobby. I was next, and had to urge my knees to move. A pleasant pallid agent asked if I carried anything of metal to declare, besides keys, and I said no. He guided me through the gate and onto a small platform, where a photoelectric mechanism eyed me quietly, its dial staying still. The guard smiled politely and helped me along. Suddenly I was jerked into a screened-off voting booth, and two men were frisking me, reaching under my trouser legs, beneath my shirt, and around my back, and, with apology, down my buttocks. It all happened in a minute or two, and then I was out of the makeshift booth and into the carpeted lobby where Felicia waited. "Rather sexy, aren't they?" she inquired. "Yes," I replied. And observing her layers of beautiful fabric, I asked, "Did they get around to all of you?" "Not quite," she rejoined, "but they got their money's worth."

We sat in the sixth row center, with eight persons in a row of about thirty-five seats. How curious to see that huge auditorium, with gilt-edged and velvet reminders of a grander fuller age, now a nearly empty mausoleum. Soon the orchestra appeared, took their seats on stage, and began to tune up. Each new couple or spectator who entered drew a mild stir, there being so few. We glanced at the program (Mahler's Ninth Symphony the feature), and Felicia twice waved to persons she knew. When they started to move in our direction, she stood and went to them, shrewdly. Approximately at 8:30, there was applause, and Bernstein, accompanied by the Boston conductor (Steinberg, Felicia informed me), appeared onstage. As he moved toward the center, the audience stood and further showed its appreciation of his courage in fulfilling the engagement. Handsomely gray and tanned in a tuxedo, he reminded me of Mailer. When Felicia joined the others on her feet, I followed suit, and it was very moving as Bernstein, obviously touched, bowed graciously. Looking up, he said in a firm voice, "Come, please move forward, everyone. You too up there, won't you come down and sit with us here?" More applause for his special intimate style. In a few minutes the first ten rows or so were filled with spectators.

The first piece, by Prokofiev, was light and spirited and lasted twenty minutes. Bernstein conducted with great vigor, his long mane of hair bouncing youthfully, his hands flying. He was cheered before turning around, and immediately asked members of the orchestra to take bows. Then he started to walk offstage, but hesitated, turned, and went back to the podium, where he changed scores.

"This will be interesting," whispered Felicia, radiant. "He loves Mahler and the Ninth Symphony may be his greatest."

The baton rose magisterially and dropped slowly, and those first low-keyed chords of French horn, double bass, and violin set a stark muted mood. And gradually, at Bernstein's low contained direction, the romantic harmonies of Mahler filled the hall, with their curious combination—to me—of Hollywood-epic optimism and dark foreboding. The contrasts were intriguing, and I welcomed the melodic release from grim tasks and subversive scenarios. The music began to carry me—how did you ever describe that stuff, I wondered then—so much so that I barely noticed when some ten or fifteen minutes into the symphony, an odd thing occurred. As if in slow motion, Bernstein's baton came down but didn't rise back up, and the conductor suddenly lay half-slumped over his podium. It was quite incredible.

"Oh, my God, no!" came Felicia's cry, and she grabbed my hand, breaking my revery and making me see what was happening.

Had they—we—shot him? Was he dead? The fools, the stupid fools! Why? Wasn't one death enough? Hadn't they *understood* me? or my deed?

Mahler sloughed off. Thirty seconds of incredulous shock and paralyzing, painful silence. Finally Steinberg ran onto the stage, breaking the stillness, and as he did, several spectators reached up from the orchestra.

Bernstein moved, his back still to us. His left hand waved Steinberg back and away, and with his other hand he warded off the spectators. Another five seconds and then, utterly alone again, he turned around for the first time since the terror began. Staring straight ahead at a point above our heads, he took several steps forward, moving unsteadily like an old man. His face was ashen, as if he had seen a ghost, and when he was near the lip of the stage (held there by hands on his ankles), the baton dropped feebly from his hand and bounced on the boards, that little wooden sound heard clearly in the silent house. The conductor's large white hands swayed in the circle of light, fumbling; his lips moved but no words came; was he wounded or had he suffered a stroke? The tension and the drama were high.

"What are we to do?" he began, low, so that you had to strain forward to hear him from thirty feet away. "How long is this . . . this madness to continue? . . . Why? . . . Why are they doing this to us? TO US?" The sudden shriek made you jump. "One hundred and sixteen people at a concert," he forced the words out, "one hundred and sixteen." He made the number sound sacrilegious, villainous. His head shook very slowly, his body virtually trembled, and he looked up, beyond us, for Higher Aid. "What have we to do with . . . governments? With policies? With Vietnams?" His palms stretched forward, Job pleading with Jehovah to cease his fierce scourges. "This is . . . art. A holiness. *Why to us?*" Standing there, he cried, not moving to cover his tears with his hands, but offering his face boldly in anguish.

Slowly then and amazingly, he sank to his knees and, face turned upward and hands clasped, he bobbed his head in prayer. In Hebrew he pleaded richly, and I followed the first few words: *Ribono shel olam! Yirhavu hanaar* . . ." It was incredibly moving, and I was eager to find out what it meant.

Felicia was sobbing, handkerchiefs were out everywhere, you could hear low wailing, and Bernstein stayed right there, for three or four more extraordinary minutes. Finally, three musicians, along with several spectators, bore the conductor off the stage. A kind of religious silence and awe pervaded the auditorium. All told, there had been about ten minutes of unbearable melodrama and real pain, in which the artist and showman-celebrity had joined to form a single posture of grief and mourning.

The climate of terror successful. Bernstein down on his knees, helpless and wounded, without any bombs or guns. An absurd figure, out of opera, melodrama. But strangely, I didn't feel any triumph or joy. Project accomplished, but the feeling in me doubtful, negative. I didn't understand it! Instead I had an urge to run across that long stage and *explain* to that Lenny—*that poignant Lenny*—how it all occurred, what I meant by our disruptions, how once things got started it was difficult to stop them or control consequences. "We're hurting you now," I wanted to explain, "in order to make things *better later*." But as I sat there searching for the precise words and philosophy, my mind kept rerunning the scene I had just witnessed.

Felicia asked if we could go, and I took her arm. On the way out, I noticed Rabbi Silver from Cambridge, supporting his tearful wife in their seats. I felt too badly to stop.

Outside, waiting for a taxi in the October fragrance, Felicia said, "It's awful, just *so* awful. The poor man must be suffering so—I mean regardless of his way of showing it. That's his whole life." And for the first time her clear blue eyes were clouded over with doubt, fear. And searching mine for answers.

In the taxi I tried to reassure her and myself. I don't think I was too convincing. At her door, I declined her plea to come inside and calm her doubts further, and walked back to my apartment.

We are out to hurt you in order to make society better. Progress and health can only be preceded by pain and upheaval. If we don't cause discomfort now for a select few, it will be catastrophe and disaster later, for everyone. Logic is on our side. I repeated these lines like catechism or litany, whenever the anguished face of Bernstein or the questioning face of Felicia permitted me respite.

Walking amid the embracing trees, the cozy circles of light from lampposts and bedroom lamps, passing an occasional couple strolling arm in arm in the soft autumn evening, I suddenly felt a growing and irrepressible loathing! How I resented all those signs of peace, order, man's ease, life's loveliness! In a rage, I stopped at Ellery Street corner and got down on my hands and knees and dug out dirt from a patch of lawn. Looking about frantically, I took four steps to a dumpy red, white, and blue iron mailbox and shoved the dirt down its gaping patriotic mouth. I did this twice more, carrying the dirt with meticulous care, as if the task depended on it. And I would have gone on, maybe even stuffing the mailbox to the brim with that acrid earth, but a car drove up the narrow street and I walked on, casually, in a fearful sweat.

The next morning I phoned Rabbi Silver, an old acquaintance from the local Hillel Club who had always been personally sympathetic. For a half hour on the telephone, Rabbi Silver labored to discover and translate the three Bernstein lines, meticulous in his distinctions, gentle in his manner, Yiddish-European in his accent. They turned out to be, first, a rabbinical phrase (*"ribono shel olam"*); second, from Isaiah in the Bible (*"Yirhavu hanaar bazeken vehanikleh banichbad"*); third, from the Psalms (*"bauh mayim ad mafesh"*). Silver translated:

> Master of the Universe!
> Shall the young be insolent to the old
>   and the base to the honorable?
> Waters have reached us all!

This last, he explained, was a deeply moving expression of despair, meaning, "We're drowning!" I smiled, without pleasure, thinking, First fire, now water. The rabbi asked if I had been at Symphony Hall the night before. I said yes, and added how

371

disappointed I was that the concert had been cut short. The rabbi, speaking with Talmudic ambiguity perhaps, said he hadn't realized that I was so passionate about fine music. He'd think of me next time he heard Mahler, and hung up, politely. Fortunately for me, I knew that Silver would relay his doubts to the Higher Law only and not bother with the law a few streets away. But his personal displeasure with me was clear enough, and, since I liked and respected him, that hurt.

No more teachers,
No more books . . .
from a jingle

5. On the Re-Education of Intellectuals

A Note on the Letters of the Alphabet

In what follows I have not used the real names of the professors and intellectuals whom we took with us to New Hampshire. In place of their real names I have identified them by the letters of the alphabet, beginning with A. and moving to B., C., D., E., etc., in order to emphasize this self-imposed censorship.

Why censor myself? To begin with, it is difficult to see what useful purpose can be served by naming these gentlemen here. Obviously, it is not as if I were trying to conceal their identity entirely, since most citizens who followed their ordeal in the newspapers and on television know well enough who the prisoners were. But there is a more compelling issue here. For in these next pages, the crucial point for the reader is to observe what *the prisoners are put through, and not to wait breathlessly to discover* who *suffered* what. *My aim is not to create TV melodrama or to compile a* Who's Who of Political Captives, *but to describe faithfully a serious political project. To use real names here would, in my opinion, divert attention to personalities and away from method and purpose.*

After all, it is not with these particular professors that our over-all success or failure will be measured; it is rather with all intelligent citizens of the nation. Our beginning is with this handful of distinguished men, but our end is with the majority of men. When I speak of Professor A. or Professor B., I mean to be speaking about every intellectual in the country, be he connected with a university, the making of artistic works, the critical disciplines, the dissemination of ideas, or the development of sensibility. In other words, I mean to be addressing You, You, and You, Enlightened Citizens. I hope by means of these ABC's to make it easier for you to slip into the prisoner's skin and experience his ordeal. In this way, the full impact of our re-education program and our urgent message, visited currently upon those ten eminent men, will not be lost upon you, reading as you doubtless are in a quiet room, in a comfortable chair. It seems to me that at the very least you owe it to the real professors to put yourselves in their roles and insert your own names for A., B., or C. Anger and resentment against me and my colleagues are fine, but easy; empathy with the prisoners is a harder and, I think, a more "progressive" emotion in the long run.

But perhaps, finally, there is a more personal and more simple reason behind my decision. It is my belief that the professors have suffered enough real trials and real pain without my rubbing salt in the wounds. Comrades and budding comrades: I may be a monstrous boy, but I am also a civilized young man. Difficult as it may seem, a murderer, kidnapper, and culture-bandit can also retain a measure of civility, courtesy, and public decency. Remember, these are outstanding thinkers and teachers whom I respect very highly, no matter what I am forced to do to them. Though I could not spare them the larger humiliations, perhaps by this small act of discretion, I may spare them further unnecessary shame or scandal.

It goes without saying, I hope, that throughout my Mischief Making, there have existed two strands of motivation, the political and the personal. While I have constantly tried, and still am trying, to unite the two, differences, even contradictions, perhaps of an irreconcilable nature, remain. Need it be said, for example, that all along it has been my "personal" side—the self sensitive to feelings and sympathetic to the humanistic tradition—that has constantly put up the best battle against the political Pincus? Then how nice for a change to find an issue on which the two sides can be joined. For it would not only distort what is truly important about our task to cite those men, but it will only *humiliate* me *further to subject the prisoners to a further humiliation here in print.*

Once you got going on making trouble, you looked for it in every direction. You became more and more alert to the various ways of disturbing the national peace; especially the peace of established systems, official persons. Contributing to chaos became as natural as building for order, playing the outlaw as routine as acting the good citizen. Every newspaper story, movie, or individual developed into an unknowing source for doing bad. So a boy with narrowed interests can be quite dangerous if he's out there on the loose, in the midst of American variety, prepared to fulfill his obsession in reality and not let it drain off in private fantasy. Much of this, I found, was a question of confidence, in which, to use Yeats's phrase, you had the courage of your conviction, even if that conviction involved the most extreme aims and produced the most preposterous notions.

When I read one day in some journal about the government's proposals for detention camps for political subversives, an idea we had all heard about and experienced before (e.g., Washington, D.C., Spring 1971), I called a lawyer friend and got hold of the *Congressional Quarterly,* the original source of the material. The first proposal, in 1950, Title II of the Internal Security Act, was a full-scale plan for constructing such camps for boys like myself. It listed six geographical sites for camp construction, including one in New Hampshire. The second document, a follow-up to the 1950 idea—itself a development of the World War II Camp for Aliens—was put forward in 1963 by the House Committee on Un-American Activities, and suggested that these camps be implemented as soon as possible. (I found out from asking around that initial work had actually begun, new painting, reconverted bunkhouses, new barbed wire, before things were temporarily laid at rest, waiting.) This interesting blueprint for taking care of subversives was entitled "Guerrilla Warfare Advocates in the U.S." Now I mention this background so that, if our history books get around to documenting the present small wars, they record correctly the origin of my ideas. Not from Red Star or hammer-and-sickle directives did I receive my inspiration, but from Washington, D.C., documents; from the democrats not the totalitarians. And from my unpoliced imagination.

Getting the campsite was a page out of Americana. Money for the project was provided by several sources (again, capitalists aiding rebel patriots). One was the same father, Mr. R. of St. Louis, who had subsidized our luxury apartment in the Prudential Center. Another source was a Sephardic Jew from Providence, Rhode Island, who sent us a note saying it was "in the family tradition to support radical projects and dreams in the adopted land." Did he know the kind of dream I had in mind? Had some of our immigrants really kept such a healthy head about patriotism? It seemed so from that Portuguese helper. And finally, we received aid from Felicia, who said the idea of a camp reminded her of Brook Farm. Well, there was an idealistic side to it, that was true.

With particular satisfaction I remember the journal that gave us the actual site. Not the *New York Review of Books*, as was rumored, but the *National Review*. Leafing through that Wheaties, Breakfast of Champions, view-of-America magazine, I came across an interesting advertisement in the back for a "country estate in the north country." Large house and barn, complete privacy on two-hundred-plus acres, bordering both sides of a private dirt road—all that was pleasant enough. What caught my attention, however, was the phrase, "Includes a fully equipped bomb shelter, large enough to house a small community." Hyperbole to sell the place? Did such things still exist? All I could do was to try, and so I dialed that 603 number. It was answered by a rough, impatient voice, "No, I'm not joking, you fool! And there's no use your wasting my time talking about it on the damn phone. If you're interested, come up and see it!" Before he clicked off, I managed to get directions out of him and was on my way that afternoon. Up route 93, toward the foothills of the White Mountains. Exhilarated by the road, the mountains (once you passed Concord and turned off on routes 3 and 4), the striking October colors, I found it difficult to believe my underlying purpose.

Simon Stillwagon was short, wiry, a sixty-five-year-old schnauzer with a Walter Houston voice, who, fearful of the "goddamn socialistic takeover" of this country, was leaving for Australia. Simon showed me around the place by crashing through the woods in his Land Rover, or by walking, talking, and pointing. Perpetual man-in-motion. All the time he carried around with him an assortment of small tools tucked everywhere into white Carter overalls, held up by bright red suspenders. A millionaire inventor and one-man dynamo with his screwdrivers, handsaws (large-toothed), Swedish knife, cutting down brush or stopping to fix wires. The place was grand, lots of forest and woodland ribboned with brooks and trails, twenty or more acres of open meadows, an enormous rambling house that ran on and on like a train or boat. Of the twenty-odd rooms—the place had once been used as an inn—the most impressive was Simon's workshop, a private wing of four rooms. The thousands of tiny gadgets and mechanical items that he had collected there—for sliding, screwing, fastening, hooking, magnetizing, sharpening—and his impatient manner of picking up each item and showing me how it worked, suggested a Dickens character, crazy, eccentric, incredibly human. Stillwagon not only knew every bolt and washer in the rooms, he had invented half of them. (Three of his inventions stayed in my head, though they were of very different sorts. One was a buzz-and-light mechanism for announcing the arrival of the mail, some two hundred yards down the road. Another was a small steam engine, pulling three other cars, which would deliver messages from Mrs. Stillwagon at one end of the house to Simon at the other end. This wooden toy train ran on tracks high along the walls for the entire length of the house, dipping down at the end to wind into Simon's workrooms; inscribed CANADIAN PACIFIC on the locomotive (and CP on the cars), it was inspired by that famous train, when Simon took vacations on it to Banff and Vancouver. Finally, there was a large electronic board, with an aerial view of his land, set on one whole wall, with blue, yellow, red, and orange lights flashing on and off periodically. These lights signaled who was on the property and approximately where—deer, hunter, or bear, each light registering according to the weight placed on the wire. When I muttered something incredulous, Simon grabbed my arm and, without saying a word, ran me down to the woods behind the house, dug up a buried line there which connected to a soft mesh of intersecting wires; alongside it was the clear print of an animal's paw. He held that "trap" to my face, saying, "You can do anything, son, if you put your mind and body to it!" His zeal for work made you want to get at it yourself.

The Bomb Shelter. What can you say when you see a huge underground area cut out of thick cement blocks with a cement floor, totally equipped for everyday living, with single beds, electric lights, faucets and refrigerators, and two huge freezer units, lavatories, neat wooden shelves built incredibly onto cement slabs, a kitchen with a huge iron stove fit for a restaurant? A shelter that made you want to stay down there and not come up, so much was it a showplace of one man's fastidious genius. "Yeah, I thought the bombs would be here by now. But don't you worry, this'll hold you secure when they do come. All reinforced concrete two foot thick; they thought I was crazy when I put the shit in, but one day they'll see who's crazy. Hmm!" Yes, I thought, my heart trembling, you could fit a dozen persons in there all right. "Snug as a bear for the winter once you settle down here. Me and the missus know," Simon said, coming close to pride for the first time. "We tried it for a winter. Hibernated along with the bears, you might say. Got a lot of work done, too."

Buying the place took ten minutes, ten incredible minutes. "Two hundred seventy-five acres more or less—and that could mean two twenty or three twenty with these surveyor jokers!— is what you'll get on the deed, along with the buildings. If I had her all over again, I'd rip it down and start from scratch." (That phrase!) "I like to live in things that I built. What do you think the whole shootin' match is worth, fella? I'll tell you. A hundred fifteen thousand, and that's modest. Now, what will you give me for her?" He gave this little speech while using a chain saw on a cut maple tree a hundred yards in back of the house. The suddenness of the question, and the price, which was about twice what we could afford, confused me. He must have seen this, for he looked up and said, "Speak your mind, son, I won't bite you. I can only say no." And went back to making that cutting shriek. "We have fifty-five thousand, Mr. Stillwagon," I managed to get out or gulp. This little dynamo was the first man, besides Luis, to put me on the defensive in months.

He lifted a booted leg onto a stump. He squinted in the sun, eyebrows bushy, matted. "You Jewish?" he asked.

Completely taken back by the question, I nodded, weak. "Yeah."

He nodded back. "Well, I grew up in these parts believing that Jews ran those socialistic countries, and I'm not sure I still don't believe that. But the only live Jew I ever met saved my sister's life over in Grafton. A doctor up for the weekend. Operated on her and removed a burst appendix the size of an Idaho potato, when the other fella in town wouldn't touch her, said take her to the hospital in Hanover. Only there was no time to get her there, any fool could see that. I did, and so did Levine. Morris Levine. How's that for a moniker? Saved her life, and you know what? She wasn't worth saving!" He threw his hands up. "But that don't mean that she should have died, you see. Me and Levine still correspond, every year or so. He comes back every so often to fish, but he can't do that worth a damn."

He finished sawing his log, looked up, came closer, and put his hand out, muttering, "You're gettin' a nice piece of land, son. Be nice to it." A paranoid little right-winger, half a pain in the ass, half an inspiration.

Irony Day in the American mountains had ended. The *National Review* contributing to a Fund Against the Republic. Sweet Simon Stillwagon's bomb-fantasy of the fifties to be converted into a surprise children's camp of the seventies. A Trojan horse of conceited boys and girls set down in the midst of Minuteman patriots and flag-waving Yankees. I waved goodbye to Simon, going off in his Land Rover ("I'm taking this rig to Australia, you can bet your life!"). A few weeks later, Larry S., our lawyer—who insisted that we tell him nothing of what the place was to be used for, or in any other way inform him of our activities—completed the transaction at the bank, buying the place under its new name, Hibernation House. What else could I name it?

There remained at least two tasks, getting some furniture and getting some campers. Luckily, we didn't need too much furniture, since Simon left most of his (including a handwritten letter of directions for operating the place, which took up seven packed pages). And in a few weeks an antique dealer called to tell us that he had twenty-four desks for sale at three bucks a piece, but that they were the old-fashioned kind, would we want them? They turned out just fine, with their inkwells and slanted tops and slat for books beneath—they set the mood of what I hazily had in mind for the place. What was more of an immediate problem, one which I hadn't anticipated—that phrase could be repeated in every sentence—was the sudden introduction of new colors and new odd skins into that uniformly lily-white mountain town. A solution was discovered when I took a walk along the town's best street, a broad avenue lined with white federal houses which, three years back, had been converted into a liberal-arts college. School would again bail us out! White Mountain College, in case anyone inquired, was the breeding ground of the new foreign population. But inquiry was hardly necessary, as was demonstrated in the local grocery one morning, when a native lady saw Addie and myself shopping and said to the cashier, "Do you see what that college is already bringing us, can you imagine the future?" (Addie smiled and greeted the ladies.) In fact, what White Mountain did bring was longhaired Long Island chicks and bearded Westchester dudes, who were in the hills partly because of romantic illusion, partly because of failure elsewhere. Middle-class pioneers who would provide a nice camouflage for Roxbury and Harlem colleagues.

Good enough, but still, what about the campers? In other words, how were we going to get the intellectuals and professors up to the hills? Which ones, and how to recruit and select them? Go around the nation and nab a likely liberal from Ann Arbor, by helicopter? Steal a philosopher from Cambridge via the MTA? Flag down a Maoist on the Bayshore highway on his way to S.F. State? The decision to kidnap was one thing, which would present its own problems; figuring out the victims and their whereabouts seemed insurmountable.

Seemed. Once again chance and circumstance suggested resolutions. Going through my mail in Cambridge one day, I discovered a folder of a few weeks back, a reminder of the annual Socialist Scholars Conference, to be held that weekend, the third week of October, at Hofstra College. I didn't think twice about it, putting it in a pile of left-wing and liberal announcements and invitations which threatened to swamp the room. But as I was at the stove preparing dinner, a name from the folder suddenly shot into my mind. I took it out again from the drawer, and sure enough, listed as the moderator for the special panel on the culture crisis: "Bernard Kovell, Cardozo College, Dean of Humanities." Back at my overdone hamburgers, I thought about the weekend.

On Friday noon, I got a hitch at the Mass. Pike from a Wellesley girl and Harvard boy going down to New York City (in her new Volvo). From there, I took the LIRR to Hempstead and soon was walking on that pleasant tree-lined campus, prepared for boring rhetoric, but also curious about Kovell and that panel. Imagine my surprise when, walking from a seminar called "Plantation Masks on Corporate Faces?", a mass of huge figures blasted out of a nearby dormitory and headed straight for me. Sociologists and political scientists charging like buffalo? If only they would. But as they clacked by, I saw the name JETS emblazoned on their gray sweatshirts. My God, Jets and eggheads—were these socialist scholars also directorial talents? Later it was announced that this would be the last year that Socialism would compete with Football. But why? Tell me, what American wouldn't vote for revolution and chaos if Namath were on our side? How else would our citizens wise up to fraud and hypocrisy if it were not through its idols and heroes? One Namath was worth ten thousand Maos when it came to influencing the American masses.

I attended two other sessions that day and night, "New Forms of Monopoly Capitalism" and "Colonialism in California." The first suffered from the gray matter of heavy abstraction, the second from mistaken terminology. But what was really wrong with it was that it was a conference—vast audiences, papers read aloud instead of passed around beforehand, an excessive variety of styles and assumptions. As I walked along the corridors bubbling with booksellers, pamphlet hawkers, academic gossipers, I thought how the Democrats might lend the Socialists some bands and girls, while the scholars would in turn give the Dems some real substance to talk about. In short, mix the two convention styles and help each other out.

I was stopped by an old acquaintance, a thin pleasant lawyer who had come to radicalism through ecology. A wealthy boy interested in conservation, he had become convinced, in discussions with me partly, that there was a direct tie-up between land destruction, water pollution, and the profit motive.

"Is that really you, Lenny? *Jesus*, I barely recognized you.

The beard, and you've lost weight, haven't you? You look . . . different, just completely different!

I shook his hand, smiled, and told him to go easy on the identity, I didn't want it spread around.

He nodded. "Man, am I ever impressed with you," he said in his high singsong voice. "I didn't think one guy could shake up the country the way you have. They're going crazy. Even Nader must be jealous."

"There's really more than just myself, Jamie. And I don't know how much we've really shaken it." I paused. "But there's still time."

We gossiped about old mutual friends, and then Jamie asked if I wanted to make a guest appearance on tomorrow's culture panel. "It would be terrific. Bring back all the young radicals who are boycotting the thing in the first place, because there are too many respectable liberals and social democrats doing the talking. If word got around to the right kids that you might show, say . . ."

I declined the offer, told him I was there just to listen, and asked for his program for the next day, with the full list of speakers. He gave it to me, I reminded him again of my anonymity, and we split amiably.

At the cafeteria I had a sandwich and coffee, and read the impressive list of intellectuals beneath the title "Culture-Siege: Progress or Primitivism?" All the eminences of the day—A., B., C., D., E., F., G.—it went on and on. How did they ever get that bunch to sit down together? I wondered. A.'s anarchism alongside E.'s conservative liberalism? C.'s traditional Leninism next to D.'s freewheeling shifting politics? These were battlefield enemies, not bed partners and symposium friends. It could only be anger that united them, anger and resentment. *At us.* Good. My friend's words about "boycotting" came back to me. I liked that too. When *they*, my side, boycotted, it never failed to stir in me certain . . . impulses. Spite. Perverse humor. A chance to turn tables. Impulses which I'd smile at but which would linger. An example perhaps of my private malignancies spreading to my political plans.

In my dorm room that night, I came across the Jets' lineup for Sunday in the *Post*, and I shifted back to that other lineup.

My heart leaped. I got up and walked downstairs and out into the quiet night air, amid the still dark lawns and pacific walks and strolling couples. My stomach quavering . . . The components were there, if only there was *time*. Luis liked surprises, but on such short notice? I gathered dimes, nickels, and quarters, found an outside coin booth, and started calling. Cambridge, New Hampshire, Manhattan, Amherst. There was skepticism, but also excitement and encouragement. "If it was anyone else," Luis said, "I'd say no. But with schoolteachers, let's try it." That telephone, what an invention. Can you imagine what Napoleon or Caesar would have accomplished with that eight-inch arm and long black box? what nations trembled when they dialed? Look what Pincus had done in an hour of phone talk, preparing for tomorrow. Upstairs, an old habit hit me, and I threw up in the bathroom. Wheeling and dealing in being bad had made me a nervous wreck at an early age.

On the bedside table in my small room, I set my trusty Zeno (nickname for my Zenith Z-70 hearing aid) next to gun, glasses, watch, notepad. Smoking, I thought back to that lovely afternoon several summers past, when, in a friend's basement, I worked on an essay while two comrades made bombs. The sudden explosion, the total shock, my friend's arm dangling and shredded, my hearing gone. After the first weeks of intense solitude and sense of deformity, my hearing returned in one ear, and I came to adopt a new attitude toward my wound: pride. I was a soldier in the new army, clearly *marked;* there was no backing out. As Luis said to me, "You know what, Pincus? I like you better with that thing sticking in your ear. Yeah, I think you hear sharper what I'm saying, brother." He was right in his way; physical wound was an added impetus to vengeance.

Of course, my infirmity had its particular circumstances which added humor and ambiguity to that vengeance. For it was inflicted by allies not enemies, and therefore was not exactly a powerful reminder of heroic battle. And then the object itself lacked distinction, nobility; it was not a black patch over one's eye or a wooden leg left by a whale. No, Zeno as a trophy was about as dignified as a mobile home, but also, perhaps, just as American. Being wired electronically, in fact, listening in to beeps, signals, words, made me feel very modern, like a C.I.A.

spy, an astronaut, a football coach. Didn't criminals need to be up-to-date? And wasn't it appropriate in a sense that my greatest admirers were young children, who excitedly pulled at their mothers in supermarkets or else directly at my ear contraption as if it were Santa's beard? (I returned the favor by suddenly creating loud static with Zeno. Some cried, some squealed in delight, suggesting to me that my injury was more childlike than Hemingwayish.) Childish and technological, another native association.

Zeno on my night table, a heartfelt symbol. Like the Benrus watch, a memory of good-boy high-school days; my eyeglasses (now wire-rimmed but also a pair fitted out with volume control, receiver, battery, microphone, printed circuit chassis, and my own On-Off switch), a memento of the dangerous habit of reading; my Smith & Wesson, a potent L-shaped reminder of my recent dark side; and now little Zeno, the tiniest of the lot, my link to talk, my device for cunning silence, a declaration of the dangers and humors of my new trade. No other of my posses-sions was as marvelously efficient as that miniature gadget, hold-ing within its flesh-colored plastic shell a brilliant network of operations, with transistors, magnets, coils, capacitators, amplifier assemblies—all those magical words that made little sense to me but which brought sense to my beleaguered ear. Could I construct a similar efficient network the next day? I wondered.

And what good was a hearing aid if you didn't develop a philosophy of sorts to go along with it? I often had thoughts of what it was like to be totally deaf—not merely deaf to the small criticisms, complaints, and skepticisms of everyday life, but deaf, too, to history and society and great men's teachings. Then you'd be free to knock things over all around you with no qualms whatsoever, just like kindergarten days when you—or I—saw a long trail of carefully laid blocks for railroad tracks and station, and you got ready your ambush plans. And did it, bang! Sadly, I wasn't totally deaf and therefore not totally free (even after that murder). With one bad ear, you were sort of in be-tween, one ear still over there with respect for and training in things adult (history, reason, restraint, consequences), the other deaf to all that, allowing your imagination to roam and be on the lookout for kindergarten railroads. Do you see what I mean?

How I felt limited and also licensed? How I had one ear in both camps, to mix metaphors. Like having Zeno, it was a dilemma I had come to live with steadily, listening and dreaming, abiding by elders and idly wondering how to plan ambushes, remembering concentration camps and totalitarian societies and authoritarian leaders, and then listening to my high-frequency signal, trying to follow it up and down a sound spiral, like a tiny brain trapped and running inside a giant bell ringing, quivering as yet with unborn societies and new men and women, remembering vaguely what adults looked like and how they talked, and then making them smaller, their words more garbled, their habits more scrambled, until they were unrecognizable in their old form and I had created new creatures. Sometimes I even thought, during those strange minutes and at other idle hours, AWAY WITH ALL ADULTS! But of course that was just a one-ear fantasy, a one-ear slogan, not to be construed as the whole hearing by any means.

Much of the rest of the night was spent jotting down details to remember, and when I awoke at eight, I felt more exhausted than when I had gone to bed. The night life of a daytime rogue meant diarrhea, insomnia, endless notetaking. At 8:30 I was in front of the administration building, with two pals already there. By 9:15 four more had arrived, and we went to the student-union building, where the panel was scheduled to be held, and walked carefully through it, veterans of casing. Over coffee we planned and diagrammed, while older academics, sitting all around over breakfast, also theorized and plotted. Theirs about theory, ours about action. I tried to pretend to myself that what we were doing was prankish not criminal. But my heart pounding signaled otherwise. Still, I thought aloud, socialists would understand, wouldn't they? They wanted serious change, right? These fellows weren't law-and-order automatons ready to use truncheons and Mace at the first sign of democratic chaos, but intelligent men and women ready to try something new for the sake of a Grand Idea!

"Easy, man, easy," cautioned Luis, holding my wrist. "You're liable to believe that jive."

My head swirled, I stopped the schoolboy talk. Besides, what Grand Idea did I have in mind? Wasn't our revolt against such nonsense?

With more sobriety I proceeded to the panel discussion.

There were, fortunately, at least a couple of hundred people in the banquet hall, and it was easy to lose myself among them. The speakers sat on a low platform up front, Dean Kovell in the center to introduce them. It began at 10:15, and by one o'clock, the lunch break, my head was spinning. You thought one speaker was intelligent and correct, until the next got going and developed *his* idea. God, could they talk! Trained since adolescence on polemics the way I shot basketballs or Luis flashed razor blades. A different species from us, I thought, while listening to their verbal brilliance. A., the anarchist, spoke about "the crisis of faith and the need for a new belief"; Professor E. explained that "the end of liberalism means much more than the end of a mere political ideology, it means the disruption of a moral continuum, a line of feeling extending back as far as the Greeks and adapted ever since with increasing complexity"; the critic C., in his hoarse voice, warned against "terrorist tactics posing as a socialist movement, and neo-anarchist tendencies replacing party discipline and order." Of course, what they all called for—with the exception of D., the wild pacifist, who was much more ambiguous in his critique—was reason and coherence, and an end to "the lunacy of recent events" (B.). All of it, as I said, argued impressively as just those men could argue. What would happen to the culture when they departed the scene I wondered. Now, when we had them, and later, after they died? Who would replace them?

My head whirled from ideas and from nervous anticipation of the afternoon.

By 3:15 when we made our move, the crowd had dwindled to perhaps a hundred. We walked out, too, to get on our Halloween and actors' masks and returned to set up guard, two at the far door, two each at the side doors, and four of us directing operations. We used pistols and sawed-off shotguns, taken from briefcases. We told the eight men around the oval table to stand, and the audience to sit right where they were, as we went through them, searching for other interesting men who might be there. Well, the reactions were various and fascinating. There were the expected indignant cries and incredulous shock, but also clapping and open cheering. Wow! Some of these fellows really were confused. A bearded radical novelist on the panel raised his hand and cried, "Right on, right on!" With his childish slogan and copycat fist, he clearly wasn't for us, and I put him down for the decoy truck. Another fellow, a New York editor who I was told was severely militant, came forward with his wrists out for manacling, offering to help us bind his friends. He seemed curiously satisfied with the situation if not exactly happy, and I declined his aid. But I kept him in mind. Even in some of those who were most against us, I thought I detected a certain primitive joy in being in on the act. Like C., whose swarthy face lit up with delight as he chastized (correctly), "Roughnecks, adolescent roughnecks!" At last these men—who had been for decades discussing and arguing about the right strategy and the right theory—now were personally involved, directly implicated. This was real! From perennial Talmudic scholars we were already making them over into Jobs and Abrahams, demanding their bodies on the line instead of their *print*. And instead of false Jehovahs and religious Bolsheviks transforming them, it was young boys and girls with scary masks and desperate ideas.

When we actually had them lined up, it was dazzling. These were stars, and I had an inclination to get their autographs, as I walked among the rows of seats, looking for a few more spectators to take along with us up north.

A dark-haired woman wearing dark glasses touched my hand, and I leaned down. "I'm H. Would you mind if I came with you? My camera's in Manhattan and I could easily stop off for it."

An enchanting thought, from the renowned critic and moviemaker, and I said I'd think about it.

White-haired D. suddenly caught hold of me. "You kids are loony, just absolutely loony, but I love you! You've been the first lively thing on the Left since I've known it." And he grabbed my cheek and kissed it!

Of course, there were other sentiments, other sentences.

"Has the Movement taken a vote on this action? Have they democratically elected you as their representative?" (B.)

I shook my head, conceding both points.

"I told you all along how dangerous they were," cried a lanky fellow whom I didn't know. "Now you're finding out for yourselves. These kids are not leftists, they're maniacs! You didn't need this conference or panel to discuss them. They should just be put away, period."

I asked someone in the audience what that fellow did for a living, and he said he was a sometime playwright, sometime professor. He mentioned his name, it meant nothing to me, but I liked his angry spirit and so directed him to the group marked North. In the other group, headed for Jersey, I put Miss H., the editor, and a half-dozen others. It was all hectic, confusing.

Just then Kove was close by. "Again, Pincus?"

It was half-humorous. "Yeah, again. But the last time, I promise."

He didn't smile. "Maybe the last time you play the host and I the guest. Next time we'll switch roles."

I walked off.

I tried to take ten men whom I thought could stand the strain, at least physically, and so asked if there were any diabetics or heart cases? It turned out that C., whom I wanted to take along, had recently had an operation. I think he felt a little left out too, not coming. Mr. D. I sort of worried about, but I couldn't resist him. The prospective campers tied and blindfolded, we herded them out at 3:45 into the corridors, at a sign from Monroe that the coast was clear. We left four guards, including a black and Puerto Rican—"Believe me, they're insurance colors with those cats," advised Addie—to keep the audience in tow for a while. (Another pair of guards stood outside the door, just in case.) Finally, we were into the three trucks waiting at the doors, with me in front driving the U-Haul, someone behind me in a Ryder, and Luis in the third, a National. (We had checked beforehand and discovered that these trucks were the easiest way of moving to and from campus without suspicion.)

And so I pulled out, nervous, my head congested, but knowing that I'd get more air before the six-hour trip was over. Lauri was at my side, Kepfner next to her, Jimmy Haggerty riding shotgun and playing nursemaid in the back with the bound prisoners. It was going to be a long six hours though, my eyes and stomach and neck muscles told me.

We were out maybe twenty minutes when, through my side mirror, I no longer sighted the Ryder truck behind me. Anxious, I pulled over to the side and got out. About two hundred yards behind me, down the road, the yellow-and-red Ryder truck was parked by the shoulder of the road, and a boy was standing outside it, looking around. *My God* who was he? I wondered as I raced toward him.

He was curly-haired, round-faced, and I vaguely remembered having met him that morning, hanging around a New York friend. A dark-haired girl sat in the cab.

"Look, I know you guys were counting on me, and I said I'd do this, but I just can't make it, I'm sorry, really I am. But I . . . I have to get back to L.A."

My head was a switchboard of details, suddenly flashing everywhere. I tried desperately to make sense of it, and remembered something on the telephone about "possible sickness . . . a short-term driver . . . a girl Bobbi, and Stuart, her brother." Who had told me that? When?

"L.A.?" Do you mean Los Angeles?"

"Yeah, I really have to get back, I'm sorry." He was struggling, in pain himself. He just couldn't go through with it, I saw immediately! He wouldn't have any part of it. Of course! But who had brought him along? *How could they be so careless.*

Cars whizzed by on the Hempstead Turnpike, and I wanted to cry. It was all over because of this . . . this freakish accident.

The girl crying in the cab caught my attention, and, without knowing what I was doing, I went around to her. She was heavy, dark, wearing a long gypsy dress.

"What is it, what's wrong with him?" I asked.

She pouted, looked away melodramatically, then looked at me boldly. Finally, she uttered words, saying something about it being unfair to ask him to spend the day driving, he really hadn't come to New York for that, and he was upset. It grew worse, crazier.

I went back to Stuart and apologized for having presumed to take his time up this way. He said it wasn't my fault, it wasn't that at all.

My eye caught that amateur actress in the cab tossing her hair, and suddenly I had it.

"It's her, isn't it? You don't want to be with her."

"Look, I don't mean to hassle you, honest. I'm sorry, really. I just can't go through with it. I know I'm hanging you up." He glanced imperceptibly toward the cab and then quickly away, across the busy highway.

"It's her, isn't it?"

His mouth struggled, and he looked like he might cry or hit me. "She's just so bad, honest," he pleaded, seeking understanding and forgiveness for letting go of the secret. "I mean, she hasn't changed at all in nine months. I thought something would happen when she left L.A. and the family and college, but she's only gotten worse! She's so incredibly self-centered and false, and everybody knows it, too. They make fools out of her. And she makes such a fool out of herself. You should have seen the people we visited last night, who she called her 'friends.' They were just some people she met! Like you guys, she said you were 'friends' too."

A Jewish bitch, her confused brother, and the perfect madness of everyday circumstance threatened to accomplish what the federal government, local police, and the most refined citizens in the nation couldn't, with all their plans: knock us over.

Now Luis and Addie had gotten there from the third truck and listened to the gist of it with consoling calm. It turned out that they were surprised, too, thinking that this pair were to be used for provisional helpers and not as main truck drivers.

Luis, fiddling with his match, suggested that Bobbi travel in another truck. The boy shrugged, and I thought it would work, but Bobbi would have none of it, insisting that Stuart be allowed to go back to L.A. while she drove the truck alone. Luis smiled narrowly, and I was hoping at that point that he would use the razor blade. What about calling one of the familiar guards still at Hofstra to come here and take over the truck? Too long a wait, too chancy. We had already spent over ten minutes there.

I fixed my gaze on the Long Island commuters driving by, on the orange Gulf station up the road, and then at the yellow-and-red Ryder van holding E., A., B., and the others. I found the situation hard to believe.

Should we invite them to go all the way north, instead of having them drive to the change point? No. That young viper was too dangerous to have up there. Poor Stuart's twenty-one-year struggle was not over nothing.

The alternatives were running out.

Twenty minutes passed like twenty years, and I was about to give it up, let the truck stay there and just walk off, call it quits, when Stuart came over and said he'd do it. Reluctantly, but he'd do it. Addie had done it. Powerful with me, Bobbi and Stuart were helpless before a black girl. What pair of young liberals had a chance against her these days? When I returned to my U-Haul, Jimmy Haggerty looked at his watch and cursed, the first time I saw him lose his cool. I didn't care. I climbed up, started my engine, and pulled out. After five minutes, I looked in my mirror, and the Ryder was right there in its place behind me. For the umteenth time in those weeks, I couldn't care less if we were caught or not, it had all gotten so ridiculous, so tangled and difficult. You tried for something grand or important, and a bad ear or banal stairway couple or crazy brother-sister team suddenly entered your plans, threatening to upset them.

I drove, seeking consolation by thinking of those zealous radicals who had practically volunteered themselves, turned loose in the wilds of the New Jersey woods and walking three or four miles to discover Short Hills. Not exactly the kind of kidnapping you'd want to tell your grandchildren about. But across the Hudson was a good enough Long March for the likes of H., that hip editor, and some of their pals. I didn't think they were dressed to travel too far.

Meanwhile, I drove. And drove. And drove. Through those endless highways with the green-and-black guide signs announcing destinations, the brightly festooned gasoline stations competing for attention, the zippy and huge automobiles in a thousand colors pushing forward, the white lines looking like they'd lead you anywhere, to the darkly gathering sky or beyond it, to some silver or golden or chrome point of your imagination. Steel, glass, engine purr, asphalt, billboard ingenuity, and industry spires worked to calm me.

Somewhere near Hartford, I pulled in at a Howard Johnson, and the girls went to get sandwiches for the captors and the prisoners.

"I've been trailing you for the past ten miles, buddy," announced a slack-jawed thin man wearing a windbreaker, standing beside me suddenly, "did you know your back lights are gone? I tried to pull up to you to tell you, but I could never catch you in my own buggy. You better do something about it, or you'll get stopped or killed. The fine's fifty bucks, I think, for traveling without them."

I breathed easier, thanked him, got in the truck, and tried the lights—brake, signals, tails. No go, said Jimmy, checking me out. Dead, all of them. Good old U-Haul. Do we risk going?

Stopped or killed, I thought, both a nice release from highway 91 north and from that crazy day.

We got to the house near midnight, both trucks. A *true* Adventure in Moving, as U-Haul advertised on its side panel. I learned later that the New Jersey haul had made it okay, sibling fights restrained by Addie. No wonder she got a Radcliffe scholarship. She should have been given Miss Bunting's job for keeping that Bobbi under control without sabotaging the trip or driving her brother off the road. As for us, we got the campers down below, and most of them were so shocked and exhausted that they fell into the cots and beds without too much struggle. A few gave me "the silent treatment," while others began immediately denouncing and cursing. "Don't you think we've had enough for one day?" I pleaded. "It's 1:30 in the morning, can't you save it for another day? I'll be here. I won't run away, give it to me then." And I left them for the second-floor porch.

Up there it was cool and lovely, and I sat on the white railing, looking out at the blue-black sky, the jagged mountains. It was really happening, I thought; those men below were our prisoners. The crazy dangerous scheme had been translated, through luck and work, into an ordered dangerous reality. How pleasant, how relieving. Pincus's professors were gathered below like Conrad's "Chinamen" huddled in the boiler room of the *Nan-Shan*, before the typhoon. We would have ours, too, I imagined, before we were through. Sitting there smoking, seeing the red blinking light of an airplane-warning station, a certain calm slowly swept over me. A settling confidence that washed away the day's uncertainty and chaos.

The mood transported me back to my murder, and those subsequent days of inescapable regret, despair, emptiness. *Old-world feelings*, I realized suddenly, smiling narrowly. That's what they had been. The night and the day's success were encouraging revelations. Yes, I had fumbled along, but on the right road. Spilling a little blood was good for the spirit, the mind, the body. The Romans had done it (among others), then the Christians, now the Americans. Why not Pincus? For the first time I took pride in the act and felt strength from it. From the power of breaking through one's own inhibitions as much as anything. I had an inkling of what those pilots felt who dropped those bombs in Nam, or the muggers of thirteen and fourteen who seemed to get a special kick out of shoving their switch-blades into their victims after having already robbed them. Oh, it was thrilling that power over other lives, especially for the young (see Miss Lizzie). With Nugget, I had sensed it; with Mailer, the shock to my system was too great for me to be able to experience it. Now, just then, it was spreading through me. God. Yes, there was something special about abandoning morals or transcending them. Something wild and free, once the message hit the visceral cords. It fired up the adrenalin, whirred the brain, made you electric. By contrast, the world, once so fast, now seemed like a small town of slow tumbleweeds and tired cowboys. Pointedly, Mailer knew better than anyone about this. No wonder he hadn't been able to write fiction any more: life was too hot and too exciting. Oh, that prick knew it all right. And I sitting there on that white porch in the superb October night knew it too.

It was not the whole truth, friends, not the sum of my knowledge, be assured. I understood perfectly well the direction of my thinking, by civilized criteria: immoral, brutal, vicious, maniacal. And knew how I deserved jail, chains, punches, a hard sentence, or the chair. I knew, I knew. I hadn't turned into a total criminal baboon or self-deceiving moron. But what was *progressive* was that I was able to separate the actual feelings of the moment from my old morals system. A system of inhibitory criticisms and prescriptions. A societal superego. A system which I'd try to get rid of here at the camp, I surmised; a skin to shed in order to see what the next skin would be like. I didn't exactly know what the next morals—if that was the word, or if there was any—would be; but I did know then that operating from within the old system had kept me from realizing my new potential. In short, I was feeling in my own way as much student as the professors below, at Hibernation House.

For two days I stayed away, leaving the prisoners in the hands of the guards and wardens (and Kovell, who had been used to this sort of thing, his last "removal" lasting just a few hours). There was also a fantastic amount of plain business and administrating to do, both in the city and in the country. I tried to be on hand for oil and gas men, the roofer and plumber, wood cord deliverers, New England Electric, the prospective snowplower (for the garage and driveway), an insurance agent. Fortunately, most of their services had been rendered beforehand, when the kids were running the place without guests, without me. This was tidying up things, getting introduced, paying bills. (Out of our recently formed corporation. Yes, that's right, it was easier to run a radical house through a legal corporation than any other way. Subversion, native-style, remained a very curious matter.)

I was scheduled to address the prisoners on the third day, and the night before and that morning, I found myself nervous and unsure. Furiously, I wrote down various little lectures, about the deficiencies of past leftism, the evils of present capitalism, the spiritual exhaustion of modern man. It all seemed, however, banal, irrelevant. More talk, rhetoric. Didn't they know all that? These weren't sophomores, I kept reminding myself, but sophisticated men. Much more sophisticated when it came to analysis and philosophy and words than I. It was only in my will toward negation, really, that I had the upper hand.

When I first entered that curious shelter, and saw the men wearing their white gowns and striped pajamas, I was even more awkward. It is one thing to give orders for hospital attire, another to actually see it. Professor E. looked like a slender aging girl, with bony knees showing beneath his gown; Professor B. was an impressive Roman consul, tall and wise with wire glasses; F. in a football jersey, was in the Lombardi mold, I thought, tough and sentimental at the same time; Kove, arms crossed, glared so strongly that I barely noticed what he wore. My reaction was awe. The men before me, to repeat, were not stars, they were gods, my old gods. Whose words and thoughts had molded my thinking about literature, morality, society. It was something like bringing a little Greek boy up to Mt. Olympus to see Zeus and Poseidon, an American boy to home plate to meet Mantle and Mays.

I started to blubber something about one's will under extreme conditions, but immediately felt it was all wrong, pompous. Scratch that, I said, standing at my table, upon which was set a small lectern. I took out my composition notebook, nervous. The preachers had had experience with this sort of thing. Begin with the texts. But which ones; weren't they all obsolete? Wasn't that one of our major tasks up here, to create new ones? I found some quotations which I thought might impress them with their appropriateness.

> The false role played in our society by science and the arts is due to so-called civilized people being led by scientists and artists with a privileged existence like that of priests.

My voice was shaky at first. The lanky playwright, smoking, interrupted in his whiny voice. I asked him if he would please be quiet until I was finished. To my surprise he obeyed. I read the second passage, calmer now.

> The conviction has been growing up in me, that things of fundamental importance to the people are not secured by reason alone, but have to be purchased with their suffering.

"What's that supposed to mean?" jumped in a man with glasses, round in his white cotton, from the third row. "Who are those people?" he stammered, angry. Was that Professor G., the noted end-of-ideology sociologist?

"Tolstoy and Gandhi," I replied.

"It's a disgrace, a sacrilege, to be using those names here!"

"But don't you think they're interesting?" I fumbled, confused by his anger. "Aren't those men to learn from? Isn't that your heritage? I'm not exactly quoting from the Beatles, Mr. G. Tell me, should artists and intellectuals like yourself have a privileged existence? Behave like mandarins and be cut off from the ordinary citizen the way you are? Isn't that dangerous, as Tolstoy suggests? Or, to take the familiar point that Gandhi reiterates, real change can only come about if it's deeply felt. If it hurts even. Even Freud—"

"How dare you speak this way under these . . . these illegal and immoral conditions! And pervert great men of humanity this way with this . . . this filth. These dirty shenanigans! You should be ashamed of yourself." His eyes grew wide with barely controlled scorn, and his face grew redder.

It was scary and fascinating, especially the words. I saw that

making them lose control, however it might be done, was a
fundamental principle of operation. Did those specific terms of
abuse originate in a deep Jewish background, where bad and
dirty were equal?

As Mr. G. quivered with anger and perhaps panic, E. and
Kovell went to him, consolingly. I was moved by it, and I'm sure
I reddened. The learning for all of us was beginning. Perhaps not
so much for the guards standing at the edges of the room with
guns, but for me and for some others. I didn't like those weapons
there, and I made a mental note to remove them.

I got ready to read the texts and asked if they would kindly
copy them into their notebooks. They stared at me and didn't
move. It was A. who said, "Go ahead," and prepared his pen at
his desk. I read, A. copied, then several others did, looking
around self-consciously. I wished strongly that I had movies of it
all, those eminent men sitting there and writing on small desks the
new lessons. Above all else, it was incredibly touching.

I couldn't resist moving down then, among them, trying for
. . . casualness? To be one of the boys? It amazed me to see the
child's block letters of D. A.'s was a tiny mad scrawl.

"Come on, explain yourself," cried I., that playwright, rising
and talking from the corner of his mouth. "What's your basic
position? Do you know it yourself? Without a theory or idea,
you're not going to carry this off. Without ideas it's all silly.
Well, where are the *ideas*? Where are they?" Cocky, brown-
faced, in his fifties, I imagined.

I was about to answer I. when Luis stood up. A cigarette
dangling, fedora slanted. He started speaking:

"That's one of our problems, baby, and that's why we have
you here. Those old 'great ideas,' as Pincus might call them,
Christianity, socia-lism, liberal values"—he spoke those words like
a professor saying shit, fuck, piss—"all those are shot now, and we
want something new. And it ain't going to be any great idea at
all, the way we see it. Maybe just a series of small ideas—friendships instead of Parties and Correct Lines; larger families in place
of state rules and state dictators or Presi-dents; and something like
'con-tin-gent' philosophies, one- or two- or five-year programs
rather than 'mill-ennium' plans and thousand-year dreams. No
more of those Idea Machines, brothers, which have given 'cam-

395

ou-flage' to widespread murder and legal-ized *ex-ploi-tation*. If things are going to be immoral and vicious, then let's name them that, and not cop-out by tagging them Socia-list *progress* or Capita-list *law*. Uh-uh. That's why we got you here, man, to help us *look into* how to dis-mantle the apparatus here, while others go to work to take down the state machines elsewhere. Now there's your ideas, baby."

Well, coming from Luis, it was pretty startling. Obviously he had memorized bits of my speeches to young true believers and now was showing off his mental stuff to the new guests. Fair enough. Later I'd try to explain to my pal the difference between crude Stalinists and (these) serious intellectuals.

"Mr. I.," I now interceded, walking closer to him, "we've been going it alone now for quite a while. We'd like *help, advice*. That's what I'm after. That's what this is about. Now you know it wouldn't have come about unless . . . unless we took these measures. Measures which are not pleasant, I agree, but which have been—"

"You're nihilists, that's what you are, Pincus. A stinking little nihilist, bankrupt of real social and political ideas!"

"Look, I., we've taken you ten men because you're the cream of the crop intellectually, and if you can't help us to plan a new society, who can? A presidential commission? The Soviet Polit-buro? The Rand or Brookings Institutes? This is just the point, *you're the ones* we're hoping will come up with new ideas, new visions, once we make you see and feel our point of view. This last," I said, thinking of my new use of that literary phrase, "is our task."

I. whined the same accusation, and I let go and turned away.

"Do you realize the consequences of your actions for your own side?" put forth Professor B., whose political and literary works I had always learned something from. "This'll mean the police and the F.B.I. will be after every single person who has been connected with the Movement, all because of you. I find this a totally self-defeating and counterproductive gesture, for which, I'm afraid, you must be willing to accept full responsi-bility."

His hair had whitened as he had moved into solid middle-age, and it seemed to bring forth a certain luminosity to his character, a certain new mature substance of sorts. Or was I reading into things out of shame?

"What do your friends think of your actions," he continued, after the pause, "or have you bothered to ask them?"

But it was they who had shown me, B. They, the street kids. I was their vehicle as much as they were mine. It was so, wasn't it? How did you separate us? I suddenly wondered. Was I that sly brown boy in the corner, fidgeting with his shotgun and looking like a comic-strip character with his bandolier? Yes, I must get those weapons out of there.

I nodded finally. "Responsibility? . . . Yes. Yes. I accept it. Sure. That's true. It's my responsibility." Hadn't I assumed that role long, long ago, in that Commander Hotel room? Of course!

How curious though that I was still . . . unsure in my answers here. Where was the superfirmness that was supposed to come with the pressing of that trigger? Where was it? When would that . . . that release come?

"Now what I should like to ask you," began Mr. E., one of my first heroes, his face now craggy from time, worry, "is exactly what kind of *power* are you interested in obtaining by this kidnapping? I mean this question very seriously, Mr. Pincus." He lit a cigarette and inhaled in a kind of precious way.

The question would have been all right, that is, I would have tried to consider it, but Mr. E. then went on, making qualifications, adding subtleties, calling forth references, which amounted to a lecture in the political history of malevolence. The words came, fluently, brilliantly, and I saw how they got high on talk, these fellows. Like some of my pals who shot speed or H, they shot words.

Finally, I held up my hand and replied that I'd consider that question later. "But please don't go on just now. Please."

I smiled at Kove, or offered him a smile. But he fixed upon me in return an emphatic unrelieved glare, all hardness and rejection. I believe I shook my head, not wanting him to be that way. Do you see how weak I was there, in my position?

The literary critic, F., was speaking. "And what about the humanitarian tradition that I've been hearing you're interested in? Tell me, young man, how do you account for your present action in terms of *feeling* for other human beings? If not us, what about our wives, our children?" He blanched momentarily at the slip, for his colleague's son Larry was a trusted comrade. It got him angry, evidently. "I want you to account for this here and now." A short man with Asian eyesockets and a Bessarabian-Brownsville background. He had lived about eight blocks from where I had grown up, which linked me with him in a curious way, especially since the neighborhood was no more, and we were shared survivors of it, from different times.

I was so struck with gazing at him—I had never met him before, but had read with great feeling his book about old Brownsville—that I didn't speak. I said nothing about the obsolescence of the humanitarian tradition, but considered his dark brow, the energy left in his hair, which curled upward.

Unfortunately, my silence was taken as contemplation by playwright I., who dug in and rattled off about Enlightenment Man, Pascalian wagers, and Kierkegaardian "leaps of faith" before I knew what was happening. And I realized then, from the way he spouted all that, that it really meant little to him too.

"Just knock it off, I. Just stop."

When he raged at this, two guards came to him and sat him down. I didn't like to have to use those fellows, but what else could I do? Swing at him?

By now I had a better sense of what needed to be said, for the time being.

I told them to take it easy, get established, get the feel of the place. As I had to, too. There were large problems before all of us, and I was hoping that we could work together to solve some of them. To change society and to make better citizens, stronger men and women. I was hoping we could begin with them. ("No, you won't, I've read all about such maneuvers," shouted G. "You won't thought-reform me." I waited till he settled down.) New gestures, new vocabularies, new men—that's what we were after. Of course, it would be hard, I didn't have the answers. But it would be hard for me too, I pleaded. I didn't like this role of authority particularly. That's what we wanted to do away with— such hideous and awkward and misleading and, yes, dangerous roles. And if we couldn't change them in *their time*, perhaps in the next generation, their sons and daughters. Like myself. Or even younger.

To myself, I was Hamlet trying to tell ten Horatios about a larger world than their philosophy and emotions allowed for. I could see they weren't understanding.

I called a halt and said, "Just take it easy, get a routine, and things'll go better. After a while, and a certain period of isolation, you can establish contact with your families again. But first . . . let things go: I mean your old lives, your old ways. Drop them. See what it's like. Is that so awful to ask? Is it so terrible to be men without women for a while? Look, have some fun," I waxed enthusiastic. "Play some volleyball and ping-pong. Who knows, perhaps by next summer we can get a swimming pond in and—"

"Next summer, you madman! Next summer!" F. had gone hysterical. "Your determinations will be the end of us!"

I started to walk out, not wanting to pursue it. As I passed Kovell's desk, I couldn't help suddenly turning his notebook to read. Between the two copied passages he had written, "P. seems to be inoculated with some sort of serum. He really believes in this lunacy. Can he be saved before it's too late for all of us?"

I tried to touch his shoulder, but he shuddered and turned away. His profile suggested, of all things, asceticism. Kovell ascetic? Things were changing.

How must I look?

Before departing, I gave one last glance around, my eye fixing on interested comrades and armed guards. I felt the impulse from the other night swelling up.

"Do you know what, Mr. I.? I believe you were partly right a minute ago in your implications," I said calmly, the other Lenny pushing forward. "We are nihilistic, but from feelings, not ideas." I paused, trying to say it as simply as possible. "It's true, we're out to destroy. The frustration of the last few years— and in my friends' cases the last few hundred years—has built up steadily, so that our concern is to rip apart your institutions, your culture, your way of life, your morals. And your bodies, if that's the only way of getting through to you. (I noted the twinge in several faces at that.) "Sshhh, just listen, F. The truth, indiscriminate as it may seem, is that I and my brothers have grown sick from you and your government and your society; it's only fitting then that we wish to destroy them all. And break apart your private libraries. And possess your wives. And steal your sons and daughters, already accomplished. An end, friends, an end. I wish I could put all this with more subtlety or with some refinement, but I can't just now. So bear with me. Oh, we want also to make a new society, a better life, a more democratic place, but right now we want to destroy. I know it's not easy to contemplate, but I hope you understand. In the last few years, we've become angry, cumulatively angry, you might say, and *destroying what is* has become a way of life, an obsession. And I'm afraid you're just going to have to put up with it, the way we have."

I paused, pleased with my crudeness, and followed a new direction.

"Let me try it this way. Perhaps what I've been saying is really a metaphor, or better yet, perhaps a camouflage for a hidden assumption. Which is this. Our Movement may in fact be very simple, or very complicated, a Movement of young persons against older ones. A basic desire *to impose youth* upon the country, upon your sensibility. I don't think I need belabor here how frozen your feelings are, how set your attitudes, how fixed your responses; if you doubt these commonplaces, ask Mr. A. or Mr. D. Obviously concepts such as Liberal Imagination or Moral Judgment"—I looked at Dr. E., who stared at me, smoking furiously, and at Professor B., who shook his head in disappointment—"are outdated, discredited, no longer usable. To insist on applying them to politics, morals, culture, or art at this late date is ludicrous. What's new, I think, is youth. But youth conscious of itself, liberated from parents, the state, and assorted pieties; youth then can be a very bold movement. And I think that we've been motivated as much by this new-found freedom and self-conscious power as by any strict political notions. The First Adolescent International? The First Narcissistic Movement?" I joked. "Perhaps." I looked about in vain for smiles. "You see, youth becomes interesting once it frees itself from the burden of trying to be adult and concentrates instead on fulfilling its own potentials and bringing them into the society at large. It becomes interesting once it takes itself seriously: its eroticism, its impetuosity, its adolescence, its essential playfulness and troublemaking." I paused and looked around, some faces bewildered, others openly angry. "Anyway, Professor Kovell here has had his . . . periods of immaturity, and I think he can tell you something about its attractions. Maybe there's an analogy there. I suppose we're something like Gregor Samsa's young sister, who, at the end of that little story, is finally released from the burden of her insect-brother and displays her new sense of herself, her youth, by stretching out her young body. Society is *our* insect-brother, and perhaps Kafka, not Lenin, has had a hand in fathering us.

"All right, perhaps this is outrageous, but it is also exciting, daring, truly interesting. Now can anyone here apply honestly such adjectives to his recent thoughts or life? Or to any political movement or idea of the last twenty or thirty years? This may at first sound nonsensical or pathological to you, a kind of Norman O. Brown political theory—by the way, he's not a favorite author of mine—a cop-out from reason and explanation, an evasion of politics, a loathsome and immoral way of proceeding, and so on. But there are pathologies and there are pathologies. Some are worth investigating, thinking about. Consider what I'm saying. Refine my thoughts. At the very least, what I've been describing is the growth of a feeling in myself, as I've been trying to understand my own personal struggle. Need I say to gentlemen like yourselves that for a bookish boy like me, it has been a great struggle to work this way? I sincerely hope not. Certainly I've been as brainwashed as the next smart boy about growing up and becoming adult. Fortunately, my colleagues here have taught me otherwise, although not with words. What is natural to them, I've had to learn. *What they feel in their bones, I have to first get through my brain.*

"Yes, this may be impudent talk and wild, outrageous ideas, but it's impudent talk that's to be taken seriously. I'm sure of that. And governments everywhere, not only in America, can vouch for it. Now wouldn't it be interesting if ten top-notch intellectuals came to serious terms with it? We have a vital strength here, a vital erotic strength that I'd like you to move with. If you do, this camp will be a valuable experience. After all, voyeurs have as much to contribute in their way as the fornicators. Instead of one staying behind the bush, however, while the other copulates, how much more interesting if contact is made! Come out, be with us, try it."

Nervous, I tried to end on a note of humor—something resembling an Alka-Seltzer ad—but again no one smiled, or sympathized.

401

A stunned silence lasted for almost two minutes, or until I had reached the door. Then, like one of our own rallies, the prisoners began yelling, cursing, and fist-clenching. I was surprised. The loud abuse lasted all the way up the stairs, until I closed the cellar door.

Outside was a fine autumn day, and I headed for the rising meadow where Simon's flagpole and American flag still stood. It felt good, coming clean that way. Speaking from the hearts of the brothers, and perhaps a little beyond. Firmness, crude truths, and extreme speculations were much more satisfying—after a point—than fine distinctions and ambivalent hairsplitting.

"That was sweet, brother, real *sweet*." Addie gleamed, at my side, a slender ebony cowgirl in blue denims. "Especially that part where you talk about 'possessing' their women. A c-o-o-l rap. You surprised me. I didn't know you saw things so whoosh!" Her hand sliced the air. "Baby, I think you made brother Luis sit up and listen some, shooting from the hip that way. Upstaged him even." She laughed, her dark eyes shining. "Even if some of that Youth jive is a bit heavy that you lay on, it's still plenty groovy for a Cardozo ofay."

I smiled to her straight face. She patted my arm and turned back.

Indian summer in the foothills of the White Mountains glowed around me. How false for me all those brilliant vermilions and golds, the fluffy summery air, the brown mountains curving on the azure horizon. What was real was that pressure-cooker basement behind me. Was I as sweet in conviction as in rhetoric? As sure as that pretty cowgirl?

I left nature for my room, and for some private subversiveness, called William Faulkner.

On my way to my room, however, I noticed Luis sitting alone in the paneled commons room and walked in. He was leafing through a *Life* magazine (a pile of *Liberations* lay unevenly on the coffee table) and stroking a fluffy tiger-striped cat, which I realized had become a camp fixture.

I sat down and tried to explain what I had meant down there by my intrusion. About the differences between young Maoists and those men below.

He listened impassively, turning the pages, smoothing the fur of the cat in his lap.

No response, and I finally shut up. The sound of a popular song floated through the walls, and intermittently there was the calling of birds outside.

The tender stroking reminded me how emphatically impersonal he was to people, especially to girls. Not that he didn't have them, but that he treated them all alike, with a kind of neutral coldness that was not unkind particularly, just impersonal. The girls were attracted, nevertheless, and at times I wondered what went on behind his bedroom door.

"I didn't know you were so fond of cats," I said. "How come?"

His face turned for the first time, and those black, baleful eyes held me momentarily. The long piano-fingered hand, however, shifted from its casual stroking to a deliberate massage of the cat's throat. The cat began to purr richly.

"How come?" he repeated, the question gathering weight as the silence continued, like a rolling snowball. During those seconds, which perhaps totaled sixty, he seemed to be making a decision. He might just as well have decided to take his razor to me, I thought, as answer my query with words. Yet I couldn't withdraw the question without calling attention to it and to my own fears.

"She's soft," he spoke quietly, relieving me. "And I like soft things. And she's on her own, depending on no one. Her own boss, and her own lover. Yeah, she does it by herself."

The commonplaces disappointed me, struck me as anticlimactic.

"And, oh yeah," he added, as if he had heard my thoughts, "because the one thing I remember well about my mother was that she hated cats, and wouldn't let my sister keep hers." He grinned now, showing nicotine teeth, and also revealing a certain adolescent and Latin ludicrousness which was very appealing. Speaking to his revery as much as to me, he went on: "One day she caught her playing with a stray cat in the apartment, and without a word she took the pair of them, Theresa and the cat, to the kitchen window. She opened the window, which looked out on a parking lot, and, in front of all five of us kids, tossed out the cat. We lived six floors up."

I waited. But there was only the purring, the massaging, the radio.

403

"What happened to her?" I ventured, hearing for the first time a detail about his personal life. "Your mother?"

The grin narrowed, and the vulnerable attractiveness was gone. "Are you writing a book about my life, Pincus?"

"Just curious," I said, sounding casual.

He shook his head and fixed my gaze. "Don't be."

He set the magazine back on the table, the cat carefully onto the floor, and he stood. As he proceeded out of the room, the cat hastened after him. They left me sitting there, nervous, wondering, warned. Among our other differences, I found myself understanding, we had different sorts of mothers, didn't we?

After several days of settling in—certain classes beginning, rules laid down, a routine established—a young guard appeared at my converted office and announced that a "Docta E." wanted to see me. Surprised, flattered, edgy, I invited him in.

Clacking in, in his football cleats—the Jets at Hofstra were useful after all—the silver-haired gaunt man in the hospital gown nodded, and I offered him a chair. I held up a pack of cigarettes, he took one and glanced around. His gaze stopped at the triad of photographs I had put up, Ty Cobb, Dostoevsky, Melville. "Three angry loners," I explained. He lit a cigarette with a lighter from my desk, and I was dazzled by the contrast— the professor with his number 86 jersey over his gown, and I with corduroy trousers and white shirt, waiting to see what was on his mind. I had an impulse to ask him about "moral perspective in George Eliot" or "images of grotesquery in Dickens," the way I had always done in professors' offices. When, in fact, he had come to see me about such matters in life, not art. A prime shift, from aesthetics to survival. And in roles.

He had come to discuss the situation on behalf of the others, he began, his shrewd face creviced with deep riverbeds, intelligence flickering in his sharp gray eyes. In his high gravel voice and occasional English affectation, he produced a complicated prelude which I barely understood. Dear Dr. E., are you a prosecuting attorney or an appellate judge? I wanted to ask, but restrained myself.

"The point that I wish to stress is this, Mr. Pincus. I'm afraid for several of the prisoners. Are you prepared to accept the consequences if certain men . . . crack up? You see, some of them are long-time friends. They mean a lot to me." He went on to describe his own New York City background, army and O.S.S. days, Wisconsin, Columbia, citing along the way his friendships with several of the prisoners. All the time holding that cigarette in his faintly faggish manner—a gesture eliciting sympathy, as I realized all his many years as the lone Jew wolf in Waspy English departments. What could he do but adopt others' mannerisms? Anyway, it was all a touching plea, by way of personal experience not abstraction.

Noting a book on my shelf, he paused and leaned forward, the cat-gray eyes daring alertly in the aging skull, hatcheted by time. He shifted his tone abruptly. "So *that's where* that phrase came from. I want you to know, Leonard, that if you have Bettelheim as a model here," and he nodded toward *The Informed Heart*, a bookmark sticking from it, "you're going to be badly disappointed. I mean his thoughts on how to survive in the concentration camps. These men will never hold up the way Bruno did, not even Professor Kovell. I know Bruno, and it's not psychological defenses that kept him going. Forget that, Mr. Pincus. It was youth and constitution. The man's a brute, and that saved him. Not worlds of 'internal integration.' Brute strength. Just look at that scene in which he relates how the S.S. carved the flesh off his frostbitten hands and he didn't budge or utter a sound, let alone pass out. That man has the pain threshold of a rhinoceros. Don't try to compare men like D., B., or myself with Bettelheim. It won't do. We've been here not quite a week, and F. has already begun to cry at night. Mr. Pincus, I want to warn you that I won't be a silent party to his breaking down. I—and the others—*won't*. Should you recover your *conscience* at any point, you'll have F. on it, if this continues. And us. Even prisoners of war have rights, protections. I'm here to demand ours. Not to ask, by the way, but *to demand*. Non-negotiable, I think the phrase is these days."

And to my amazement he proceeded to read from a lengthy list.

During the last part of his speech, a growing hardness of spirit and certain bullying manner had developed, which I wouldn't have imagined from reading his wonderful prose and emphasis on gentle, sane civility. How print deceived at times!

I leaned back in my wooden chair and gazed out the window at the pleasant field and distant mountains.

Partly from his own increasing superiority, partly from my own ambiguous mission, my perverse will was spurred into action.

"Doctor E.," I began, nervous beneath the surface calm, "forgive me for putting it this way, but could you say something about your personal life? Sex, for example?" I could see immediately that Family Talk was a useful text for opening the teachers up, though *we* desired different directions.

E., who had been leaning forward with his demands, stood up as if pierced. He took a series of small puffs, holding the cigarette between forefinger and thumb, movie-style. His long face reminded me of one of those fine Byzantine portraits in the Fogg. His momentary fierce gaze confirmed my track.

"You're ill," he began, checking himself, trying reasonableness. "You're confused. Why don't you try psychiatric help, before it's too late? I mean this for yourself, Leonard, as much as for us."

"Sex in the family, to start with," I said, pushing myself, him. "Tell me about it."

His face tightened. "Do you think you'll get me to go along with such insulting play? You had better save such sadism for your fantasy life."

Intelligent, always. That's why they would make interesting prisoners. I refocused my memory on the progress cards my colleagues insisted on keeping. On Tuesday, for not asking permission to go to the bathroom, he had been slapped twice and reacted badly. God, the Orwellian primitives!

"You won't get me to grovel in dirt," he added. "I assure you."

I could have proceeded with calling in Harold and Tyrone, waiting outside. But it went against my grain.

I spoke casually. "Oh, I don't know, if *I* were a well-known professor, who for years had been a good fellow say, reading and teaching about bad fellows—Dostoevsky's characters, for example— I'd be tempted to try out some of their actions." I shrugged. "You know what I mean. Crazy things, sordid impulses, 'man's base desires.'" I smiled. "Screwing one's students, perhaps. The younger the better as you went on. Or even, I should imagine, trying out new things with my wife. Personal things. Take buggering, for example. You take a nice Jewish woman, intelligent and moral, and you try to get her to turn on her—"

It was fine then, as he lunged for me and I caught his blow on the side of my arm, just before it grazed my cheek. His awkward punch—the first for this verbal heavyweight in how many decades?—threw him off balance, and when I pushed him, he fell over easily.

He lay on the floor, curled like a dazed fighter, breathing heavily, holding his back. Frightened and remorseful, I kneeled beside him. I moved to massage his back, but he jerked away in terror. Shades of that subway victim! I tried to hold him, as softly as possible. His white hair up close that way was very fine, like a child's. It was poignant. He smelled—from age, fear?—and panted, still in shock from the fall. Finally I lifted him up and slowly settled him into the upholstered chair.

I gave him a glass of water and he sipped at it. I offered Scotch, and he nodded.

I spoke gently. "You've been in a fist fight, E. That's all."

He shook his head. I handed him the drink.

"And over what?" I continued, trying to understand it myself. "Over some kid talk. That's all, kid talk. Like when you were eleven"—yes, he was looking up at me now, with more openness?—"and someone called your mother a whore and it got you blind with anger. Nothing more. Stop protecting people, E. Stop protecting yourself. Be a man. Stand up and be honest. I know it's tough. That's what we're asking here . . . The incidents, the questions, the classes—they're all geared to that one simple project—to make you stronger, not weaker. To make you a man again."

"Like you, you mean?"

His energy and combativeness were returning. Good.

I paused, considering his charged question. I half smiled, stood, and went to the hallway, where the two black guards were sitting playing cards. I asked them for a favor and returned inside.

407

"Okay, let's change subjects for the moment. Let's talk about one of yours, not mine. Matthew Arnold, E. M. Forster. Those fellows. Do you think, for example, that their views of life are taking hold in America? I mean, is their world view or way of proceeding, their values, to be seen in the American government or people?"

"Arnold, Forster? How can you drag them in here?" he asked with replenished anger, smoking energetically, drinking. "Those men stand for everything that's antithetical to you and your bunch. For decency, for humanity, for going forward not backward."

"I don't think you've answered my question, however. Do you think Sweetness and Light or Hebraism and Hellenism have become part of the American system or way of life?"

Of course he could tear into this, in a way, but that was all right.

A small knock came at the door. I called for my favor to come in.

"Hi, sweetie. Say hello to Doctor E. This is a friend of mine, Nugget."

She smiled shyly, my weekend guest, wearing white bell-bottoms and a blue Cardozo sweatshirt. Her hair was tied in a ponytail. E. nodded to her uncertainly and gazed at me for the meaning.

"Tell me, go ahead," I said to the professor. "Hebraism and Hellenism in New York? Sweetness and Light at the White House? If they're not working, those humanistic concepts and values, why not try our way?"

I reached out my arms for Nugget, and she came into them. I sat on the wing chair opposite E. and took the trim teenager on my lap, stroking her hair. I concentrated on Mr. E., however, and urged him to answer.

"I can't believe you're serious," he began, concentrating too.

"But I am. Very."

He hesitated, looking at the girl. Finally he said, "The principles those men advocated are goals toward which a culture strives. The leading figures of the civilization. What's important in all of it is the striving toward it, not the slinking backward, toward some grotesque and miserable . . . sordidness. It's a matter of degree, of sharp degree, my ingenious friend—"

He stopped talking when he saw that I had placed Nugget's hand on my penis, opening the zipper. She blushed but obeyed.

E. stood fiercely.

But when he opened the door to leave, Harold and Tyrone grinned at him. When he tried to push through, they pushed back. And shut him back into the room.

"Oh, come on, forget what she's doing. You were saying, a matter of sharp degree. Can you honestly say, however, that the men who have power in this country could even have a conversation with the man who wrote 'Only connect'? Now be honest."

Without losing E., I eased Nugget off my lap and arranged her down on her knees. Her face reddened deeply, and I squeezed her hand. "Go ahead, sweetie, don't mind us. We're just having a grown-up conversation." She frowned.

"Young lady, you don't have to do that," said E.

"She knows all about free will, Professor. Don't you?"

She shrugged, in her sweatshirt.

He appealed again, "Why don't you use common sense?"

"Oh, shut up," she responded.

"There's a tiny bit of free will," I noted, proud of her articulate assertion.

And returned to seriousness. "Come on, be honest, E. Do you think Forster would say that our country, our civilization, was moving toward *his* goals or values?"

But when Nugget had taken my stiffening penis into her mouth, the professor had turned away toward the bookshelf. I called the boys in, and they turned him back again. Also, at my request, they placed him in the chair, opposite.

"Now come on, E., open your eyes and talk," I pressed gently. "I'm not interested in having my friends here convince you of that, okay? Just answer."

He stared at me bitterly, emphatically avoiding Nugget's pumping labor.

"You're a thousand times worse, Pincus, than any Nixon, any Agnew. Your mind is a thousand times more sordid, more sadistic, more twisted."

"You're speaking from anger now," I said, swallowing hard, trying to keep control. "And exaggerating. I'm not *hurting* you, you know that. Offending you perhaps. But that's not the same as real hardships, E.–poverty, injustice, racism, bombs. You know that. Only connect, E., only connect!"

I found myself gasping.

His face was a creviced mask of vengeance and hatred; the boys kept it focused on the scene.

"You're just angry, you're not answering the issues. Only connect with our Vice President, huh? That's what you opt for?"

"You're a psychopath," he pronounced slowly.

"You're a hypocrite," I said, coming close. "A hypocrite and a moralist. And you worry more about this"–I indicated the labor–"than you do about important things." I shook my head slowly, near ecstasy, trying for subtlety. " 'Only connect,' E., 'only connect.' It pertains to you more than you think . . ."

I stopped to breathe in deeply, very deeply, my eyes on the professor. It felt very very queer, the pleasure that way.

Afterward Nugget looked up at me, slightly dazed. I leaned forward and wiped her lips with my handkerchief. Bravely, she tried to smile. Turning her about so she sat at my side, I held an arm around her tenderly.

"Do you want to say anything to the professor?"

"No. I don't like him."

"But why not?" I asked the pouting face. "He's a very distinguished gentleman."

"I don't like him. He makes you, well . . . sort of act weird."

"But what's weird, sweetie?"

She shrugged. "Oh, nothing."

I leaned down and kissed her forehead.

"She knows about tenderness, too," I commented to the professor.

Then, to Nugget: "You want to leave, don't you?"

She stood, frowning away from the guest. "Okay."

"Go read a book." I smiled.

Adjusting her ponytail, in a gesture of maturity, she proceeded to practically skip out, in her sneakers.

"Talented for fourteen, don't you think? Would you like some of this sort of attention, sometime?" I inquired, well-meaning. "As recreation? Let me know."

He stared beyond me, imperially beyond me.

410

"So you think I'm as bad as the Auschwitz guards, huh? I'm not, E. I'm not. That's what I'm trying to explain to you, some differences between life and literature. Some distortions in your morals."

"You're a criminal."

"Just a student, still learning." I nodded to the boys and they prodded him. He stood wearily, and they guided him out, his gait unsteady.

Outside it was hazy, and I ambled along the dirt road, happy for the air. I should invite the professor out here one day, I thought, to talk about Wordsworth, Keats. And do other things. I myself felt cleansed, detached. I wasn't sure of the path to those men, the path to breakthrough in their morals and feelings. So I had improvised. What I knew was that the professor had come in to reprimand and take charge, and had gone away somewhat defeated. And upset. Yet I felt little sense of victory. We were exploring new territory, I knew, where the rules of the game were yet to be established, let alone the winners or losers.

Back in the office I noted on a card:

Sex-talk and sex-action provoke new aggression, new fears; tantamount to physical punishment

I doodled a bit—smiling at my decadent sex loops and prurient arrows, and thinking of Kove—and then wrote, by Treatment:

Begin first stages of homosexual advances;
Suggest New Morals text and Nuclear-Accident plans

Feeling headachy, I got out of the pressure-cubicle and went for another walk, this time taking Dylan, the camp Weimaraner, and Nugget, my cheerleader.

Later I took down my Mentor Plato and read my notations in the back. In Book III of *The Republic*, I reread Socrates's explanation of who the rulers of the city should be and the kind of strict training they were to receive. I admired the way Socrates spoke of the city, like a father talking of his young son; hence his sharp demands upon the guardians made sense. He went on to describe, in the passage I wanted, how the guardians could lose

411

their way through fears or pleasures. Therefore, he proposed tests, severe tests. "You know," he said, "how they bring colts among noises and tumults and see if they are timid; in the same way while the young men are young we must bring them into situations of terror, and again change the scene to pleasures, and test them even more than gold in fire." How interesting that Socrates, not Goebbels, could talk of "situations of terror." Then why not Pincus? "Then whoever is thus tested among boys, youths and men, and comes out immaculate, he must be established as ruler and guardian of the city; honor must be given him while he lives, and at death public interment and other magnificent memorials." Nice stuff. How fitting if I could get one or two of these men, say Kovell and A., to come out *immaculate*, and serve as our nation's guardians. With national honor and public memorials thrown in for them. (Kove's girls could cater a special affair perhaps?) Obviously I was hindered by not having these men from childhood, but only now, in their middle-age and older. My tests, therefore, would have to be an *untraining*. Also, I was *acting out* what the philosopher was *imagining*, always more difficult. But basically we, Plato and I, wanted the same thing: men who were capable of being the best and who would care deeply for their land. Care more for their country's good than for their families or careers. Care to the point of jails, banditry, exile. Outlaws first, then caretakers and leaders of excellence. Could honest and strong leaders be made from any other mold in our time?

How much more pleasant were books and visions than real life! I put aside my Plato and thought of the next day and seeing those men again. Luis and other colleagues at the little talk would provide an extra incentive. Or pressure? I lay in my bed, staring at the funny green wallpaper of Mr. Stillwagon's, wondering about Plato's *Republic* and that of my colleagues. Were they the same? And were my tests the same as theirs? Situations of terror. Did I want to use such terms tomorrow?

Luis, Addie, Monroe Rules, and Kepfner, along with other wardens, were in the back watching, arms folded. They, along with the guards with their weapons—no, they wouldn't let them go, despite my protest—ringed the intellectuals, who sat by their desks, looking small and foolish. I didn't go for that, but I was there to talk.

I started with Plato, using my thoughts of the night before. Neither party seemed to get excited, comrades or prisoners. I changed directions, speaking from the lectern, wondering if the heat had been turned up.

Our purpose was in transforming men, I said, stripping the philosopher-intellectuals down (the "untraining"), so that they got the feel of life of the peasant; the bracero; the migrant; the janitor; the miner; the radical organizer; the civil-rights worker (jeers from the back); the delinquent in East Harlem, kids like us here, tailed, hounded, cracked with billy clubs, shoved by unsheathed bayonets in broad daylight, by government buildings, tapped and wired, made into outlaws. A new breed we wanted to create from E.'s and Kovells, the B.'s and A.'s, and so on. (I looked down just then and saw a slip of paper had been handed to me. It disturbed me. I looked up and saw that ring of faces back there staring at me, Luis with his match in his teeth. I read the quotation declaring we wanted men "with no alternative but death or victory, at moments when death was a thousand times more real, and victory a myth that only a revolutionary can dream of." Che Guevara. Melodramatic? I asked aloud. Sure, but why not? Did I believe my new confidence?) How else to spur people to significant actions? "To your dreary landscapes of civilized maturity," I hastened on, with a bitter zeal, "we hope to add hills of melodrama, abysses of urgency, points of terror. Into your Morningside Heights and Cambridge lives, why not some Hollywood luridness, Texas erotica? I can't help mentioning here, in fact, a tale told by one of your own, Professor Kovell, of his visit to a Galveston whorehouse where University of Houston coeds worked their way through college. It's that kind of down-to-earth work for a high cause that I'd like to get you interested in."

No smiles, anywhere.

A cosmetic of masks and roles to insure fun and pain, I continued, in the pursuit of transformation. We'd play games. *I* smiled. Serious games. They would have to be turned into the victims of our native contradictions—and for some reason I found it hard to concentrate here, I thought of other contradictions.

413

More personal ones . . . "Victims of contradiction" . . . I was paralyzed.

To my relief, Addie suddenly stood in the back and rattled off equations. "Victims of American contradictions, Lenny Pincus just said. A black child of Mississippi suffering from rickets while his fascist senator was paid by the government to throw out surplus wheat; a Puerto Rican janitor living in two squalid rooms with a family of seven, while his employer, a corporation tax lawyer, lives five minutes away in ten rooms of luxury with his wife and daughter; a Brazilian peasant slowly starving while the U.S.A. program for food supplied his dictatorship government with munitions and guns; a Kansas boy brought up on the *Star-Spangled Banner* and Pledge of Allegiance scorching Asian families and defoliating their land . . ." Addie went on and on, enumerating the discrepancies with poised clarity. It was not that she was wrong or that there was not truth in those parallels, it was just that these men knew these things, didn't they? I mean they weren't dumb or vicious or reactionary, they were men on the fence, knowing what was right but temperamentally unsuited to take the leap into action.

I took up the thread in my own way, after another few minutes. "The days of leisure and books for the sake of academic, abstract, or Talmudic truth are over, I'm afraid. For you as well as for me. From now on, no more compromise, no more pragmatism, no more civility, no more order. And instead of steaks and chops and gourmet dinners, perhaps we'll try some peas and beans, a piece of fatback and cold string beans, some sodden corn bread—in other words, the diet of a poor Southerner headed for trouble. The classes are intended to accomplish the same ends, to make you feel personally the disgust of the victim in our land, and then to move you onto the road of permanent resistance. Gentlemen, these are not qualities which can be developed by reason or words alone. Surely you understand this? Hibernation House will combine Stanislavsky . . . and Strindberg . . . with marine boot camp at Fort Benning, Georgia. From professors to beggars and victims, to honest and strong men; from tinkering with a society to taking it apart, to making plans to reconstruct it. Some such stages we have in mind here."

I paused, searching for a new way into the problem. "What

we want," I began, using a certain simple-minded and perverse analogy, "is what the founding fathers wanted, a democratic place to live in. When things were simpler, this was more easily gotten, obviously; partly because a man was less specialized in his functions; partly because the private and the public sides of his life coincided more, out of necessity. Whether he was a Minuteman, a Berkshire Hills farmer, a New York City lawyer—making the new country meant struggle, revolt, public participation. Wait, wait, just let me finish. What I'm onto here is something we used to do, something the Chinese have been doing only recently—*forcing* democratization. And that means the removal of private privilege and status. There is considerable merit behind the notion of removing the profs from the university classroom to the factories and fields. Why not a modified form of that for us here in America? Instead of a sabbatical year in London or California, writing yet another book on Hardy or *theories* of work"—I gazed at B. and G.—"why not a sabbatical year in Mississippi at a black college? Or a semester in New Mexico teaching high-school Indians and Chicanos? Or, instead of collaborating on yet another literary anthology"—I gazed at E., who was putting out an anthology with a half-dozen colleagues when we grabbed him off—"why not collaborate on resuscitating a city high-school system that's all shot to hell? Yes, I think Mr. McCoy would welcome the assistance of persons like Mr. F. in his old stalking grounds. I know, you'd rather not; you'd rather stick to your own ways, doing what you want; and from one point of view I appreciate that freedom. But from another, from these boys' and girls' views"—now I peered at my own colleagues—"I don't and can't appreciate that freedom. Just now in our history, I call that by another name, *unwarranted privilege*. Which is why we have you here, to *de-mandarinize* you."

At that point I backtracked and quickly pointed out a lot of other things the Chinese were doing, which we, in our future society, wanted no part of. The forced collective life, the absence of civil liberties, privacy and dissent, the homogenization of the society. And then went forward again. "But the point is, you're not going to change men by ideas alone. A certain amount of dramatic action is necessary to re-educate intellectuals and re-invigorate adults. Dramatic action. Dunce caps on professors' heads? Ink spilled on useless manuscripts and assignments? Public confessions of guilt? Okay, over here there have been other more private methods of re-education—principally, of course, therapy, analysis. Is it possible that we can find a way of joining the private and the public at some point? Of getting you away from literature and onto life, away from refined books and onto more common problems, out from intellectual remoteness and into common people's needs? I hope so. And I like to think that such direct touch with people again can only help you when you return to the world of ideas and social visions."

I stopped, this time for good, as I realized I had nowhere else to go for the time being. Before stepping down, I asked if there were any questions.

"There's no need to beam or put on false modesty or even speak politely when you're delivering your torture sentences," declared E.

Is that what pressure and confusion looked like, angelic beaming?

He continued, "What I want to know, Mr. Pincus—and from your friends here too—is whether you too intend to be 'stripped down' or is that a pleasure reserved only for us? Are *you* going to be reconstituted also?"

Excellent! To the heart of the matter.

"Yes," I said, pausing, considering. "Yes, I should think so. I have already, in some respects . . ."

Professor J., the linguist, whom I had hardly remembered was with us, so incredible were those first days, then asked complicated questions about the classes and their ideology, stating that he could see their initial premise—the change of roles from a professor to a Southern slave—but what were they going to lead to? How was the new knowledge going to be implemented in action out there in the society if they were to be locked away for months? And so on.

I said I couldn't answer those queries now, they would have to wait awhile. God, had we gotten that moral and spiritual leader also? All that was missing was Dr. Marcuse from California. Would he join us if I wrote him?

"What a lot of old-fashioned bullshit, if you want to know the truth," asserted I., standing. "You're getting China and these ignoramuses mixed up with your literary imagination, Lenny. What precisely do you mean by all that vague talk of transformations? What precisely do you mean by making me over into a migrant or garbage collector. Or a delinquent from East Harlem? Now tell me, what does that mean? Anything? I submit to you that it's metaphorical talk, not meaningful language. Metaphor-rhetoric which has diluted and deluded your thinking as much as it has our national government's. Now why don't you come off it, unless you can show *here and now* how to make me over into some Harlem dropout or junkie."

What did I mean? Was it only metaphors? But I believed in those words and ideas, I did. I believed they were real. And yet, right here and now show him, how? . . .

I stood dumfounded, more and more convinced that he had me, had us. If you couldn't show them tangibly—

Out of the corner of my eye, I caught sight of . . . Rodriguez slipping slowly and narrowly, with a cat's grace, diagonally across the room. He stopped a few feet from I., who towered above him. The professor stared at Luis as if he were a raccoon who had paused to chat. From where I stood, on the small platform in front, I watched Luis's mouth move at the corner in the direction of a smile, his inimitable smile, which could signify anything from appreciation to disappointment.

I., derisive, challenged, "Come on, what do you want?"

I saw Luis's head beneath the fedora shake ever so slightly, then he removed from his shirt pocket a pack of cigarettes. He offered it to I., who, hesitating at first, selected one and put it in his mouth. My dangerous friend, moving slowly, reached for his matches.

Paralyzed with awe and perplexity, I finally yelled, "Luis, wait, wait!" Scrambling down from the platform, nearly going over headfirst, running between the desks, I raced the fifty feet to the pair, afraid to look up when I got there. But the professor's face was still clear, as authoritative as ever, no blood running. Breathing deeply, I put my arm around Luis, who edged it away.

"I'll explain it to him," I said to Rodriguez. "He'll understand . . ."

Luis calmly lit the cigarette for I. and one for himself, and I staggered off, needing air.

Outside, I kept imagining the professor's angry face suddenly streaming bright red, and I felt weak in my stomach. No, I hadn't made it yet, despite the murder, despite the tough talk, the vile thoughts. My instincts were still strongly bourgeois, weak. I hadn't as yet learned to let go, be an animal, and watch the professor bleed for his answer.

Two nights later, I was reading in bed—Baudelaire on Goya, which reminded me how little literature was read here, only political tracts and pamphlets, but didn't they know that this was the more dangerous?—when the doorknob turned and the door creaked open. I sat up straight and reached for the gun on my night table when I saw first Addie, then Monroe, Luis, and Joshua enter, somewhat stealthily. My colleagues gathered by the bed, in the dimly lit darkness. My watch read 1:35. A late visit.

I started to rise when Monroe said there was no need.

"We wish to tell you simply," began Joshua Greenberg, who had taken to wearing a worker's cap with a red star on it around the camp, "that we've spent the evening talking about you, and we're worried. We're not sure you've the spirit to carry this out. This is a People's War and a People's Camp, Lenny, and we're not totally convinced that you're one with the people. That book, for example"—and he reached down for my Baudelaire paperback, took it, adjusted his glasses, and said—"shows a clear predilection for bourgeois habits. Precisely the kinds of habits that we are trying to exculpate from the professors downstairs."

Addie jerked at Joshua's sleeve and spoke to me. "Baby, you seem up and down—one day terrific, the next day shaky. Are you all right?"

I guess I nodded, thinking how much prettier Addie used to look in her brief skirts and stockings than in the gray pants and shirt she wore now.

"You've been a valuable member of our corps since we started, Lenny." She spoke in her lovely, gravelly voice, and I remembered that she used to be called Sarah for Sarah Vaughan, when she was little. So she collected all her records. "Is there any reason why you've grown more . . . skeptical? You can speak freely with us, you know."

Could I? I wondered, seeing that circle of intent faces.

"I just couldn't see Luis going through with that sort of lesson with I. I guess that's what upset me."

"He was asking a direct question, wasn't he?" put in Monroe, standing against a sloping ceiling, wearing overalls. "The man was challenging you, and us. Luis was responding to that challenge, not initiating one."

"Besides," said Luis, "we're not here for fun and games, are we? That's not why we soused the Widener or performed the other little acts, is it?"

It was no time or position to argue—in bed. The mood was one of . . . trial, and it called for my "apology" or understanding of error. Something like that. At another time, I could explain my doubts, make my criticisms.

"I guess I have been shaky," I offered.

There was a pause; then Addie said, "That's cool, honey. You been into the thick of things. We just wanted to see what was happening." She shrugged and smoked, and I felt relieved. "Take a few days off, why don't you? Go back to the city if you want, huh?"

"Yeah, maybe I will soon enough. If I don't relax, maybe I will."

Addie came over and kissed my forehead. "Sleep well, brother."

"Cool, brother, cool."

Joshua was leaving in silence, taking my bourgeois paperback.

"Hey, Josh, why don't you leave it? Baudelaire was *bad*, believe me. You ought to read him sometime. He was as anti-bourgeois as Mao. Or maybe more." I smiled.

The thin young boy with the thick glasses laid the book down and left. The others followed, leaving friendly good nights.

Luis turned at the door. "Joshua is right. Those books are going to fuck up your head. Lay off 'em, Pincus. They're not worth it." Unsmiling, and without a good night, he left.

The surprise visit served its purpose, and I stayed awake through the night, gauging its implications. The one time I picked up my paperback, it felt like a hot coal, and I found myself setting it aside, my hands and cheeks burning.

419

6. Young Goodman Brown, Young Lenny Pincus

How curious to be up there in the hills trying to concentrate on "being good" again. This time on the side of the devil and his new adolescent helpers. But good was good, wasn't it? It meant no personal deviation, no subversive thoughts, no idle meanderings off the main prescribed path. Was the Establishment really everywhere, in radical foothills as well as government offices, so long as there was an organization you were hitched to? If this was so, it was a dirty trick. I tried to believe that it wasn't so.

Thus, into the soil of those well-protected and well-ordered lives, I tried to plant disorder, vulnerability, anger. I'd remind them of our heritage of "natural manure" (Jefferson). Upon their sacred privacy I'd intrude profane thoughts, dazzling obscene deeds. And on occasion, as we went along, reproduce via films and tapes the scenes in which they themselves were the actors. I rephrased the old radical saying this way: "To each according to his fears, from each according to his fantasies." E., the Jewish puritan, an authority on E. M. Forster, would learn by doing about his idol's secret desires. G., the theorist of work ideology, might be put onto a diet of hash and speed and clever tranquilizers, to experience idle dreams, the helplessness of an addiction. B., the strong upholder of high morals and complex experience, would have young brown and tan girls—volunteer teenagers from Roxbury, Brownsville—teach him new habits. And so on. Already we had some visual recordings of this semester's course in shame and humiliation. With suggestions for sending these new-style flicks home to families and citizens for education, uplift.

In trying to match the camper with a particular project, I too, of course, was obtaining an education—in perversity, willpower, negation. I took a certain pleasure in going against myself in various ways, alternating between self-contempt and outward civility, kindness. Be nice to others, so long as you were despicable to them and to yourself, was an unspoken rule of thumb.

Gradually we would prepare for the day when all of us joined together to create national disorder and disturbance. (It

420

was amusing to read in the newspapers that my "motive" for the kidnapping was a direct ransom: if America would release its political prisoners, we would release ours. I'm afraid my mind didn't move in such one-to-one categories.) Boys and men like boys planning at their desks blueprints for turbulence. Taking a certain pleasure in figuring out how to set off a nuclear disaster, for example. One that could instruct and teach rather than just kill. Whether in New Orleans by shrimp boat or, more remote, in Smolensk by MIRV. *Force disarmament, not plead for it. Blow up for it, not march for it. Use the language of those in power, not literary gestures.* (A. J. P. Taylor, the English historian, was useful reading material here.) Other projects too. To take one or two of the chemical and biological germ centers in the country, such as Fort Detrick in Maryland, and upset them profoundly, so that our natives could get a taste of what was planned for others. Another project, nicely named "Le Sacre du Printemps" after the 1913 riot at Stravinsky's opening—named by a young art-comrade—was to plan similar disturbances at new painting and music openings, to close the doors there. And I thought of using that decoy truck of editors and related friends, once we had made our plans to disrupt printers' plants and publishing houses. Such doings, I explained to myself, would be a return to kindergarten sabotage (knocking over that train of wooden blocks, say) or writing down in print one's strongest fantasy of destruction (arson, or bridge detonation). Enjoyment embedded in the midst of revulsion and unwillingness. Special pleasure found amid terror and pain. You can see I had high hopes and ideals, naïve as they may sound.

There was no limit to the disquiet and turbulence that a small group of intelligent men, working in concert toward that goal, could create in so vast a country as ours. Just as, conversely, there was no limit to the varieties of excellence and pleasure that these same men could add to our daily lives. Once the nasty work was done, or better, congruent with it, plans for a spiritual reconstruction—implemented through political, social, and economic blueprints for a new republic—would proceed. As much as we clearly needed an end to one, we needed and desired the making of a new one.

Already, in those first weeks, we had brought these pro-

421

fessors from the doldrums of aloof university life to the excitements of street fun. From Brattle Street to Massachusetts Avenue, from Morningside Heights to Central Park at night. Journeys they could never undertake by themselves, burdened with the heavy baggage of civilized adulthood (families, wives, jobs, age, habits, stamina). The marijuana flowed, the hash pipes were lit, white and green and sky-blue pills were popped. At all hours Cream pounded, Traffic thundered, the Stones mocked. No Mozart or Bach to soothe the nerves, or Beatles to entertain. (I never knew how powerful rock music could be upon sensitive minds until the professors begged and protested against "the continuous raucus insanity.") Sharp and violent contrasts were presented, to reduce overcomplex minds to important simplicities. Eight-millimeter news films of napalm burning children, policemen clubbing students, private guards beating migrants, were run alongside speeches by our national leaders about freedom, democracy, and justice. Clips of sheep dying in Nevada from escaped nerve gas next to official stories about animal safety and citizen protection. Nuclear explosion tests followed by Bergman's *Shame* and British documentaries. And then more personal at-home movies, like F. entertained by two Puerto Rican girls, teenagers in pants suits carrying transistors, who giggled and danced, teased and fucked with the esteemed literary critic. (How interesting to watch those cunning girls go to work on one of the nice Jewish professors to try to get him over his personal and celluloid embarrassment.)

In all of this I was kindergarten teacher, perverse guide, pressured boy, spiritual criminal. And beginning swimmer, who had gotten in over his head and was making do as much as the next fellow, arms flapping, feet wiggling, hoping against hope I'd wind up breathing comfortably and not going down, gasping, drowning.

The routine went something like this. The campers were awakened at 5:30, made their beds, washed up, and had breakfast (by electric light, downstairs). From 7:15 until 8 A.M., there were exercises (calisthenics and yoga) and a brief meditation period, to contemplate "past bad habits and new changes to look forward to." (Curiously enough, it was this little twenty-minute session that provoked intense disgust in some of the men. B. and

I. found it repellent to have to contemplate anything at that time of morning. I'm afraid I didn't blame them there. It was not I who had set up such an early-hour practice.) School began at eight sharp, and ran until 1 A.M., when lunch was eaten. (Lunches were given in black workers' pails, with red thermoses, both of which were tagged with the camper's name.) In the afternoons, there was either private work on projects, play and games, or occasionally, outdoor exercise, carefully supervised. In those first weeks, raking of leaves was a desirable task, since it wasn't all that difficult—though even here men of fifty found it harder than they had imagined—and gave them some air. For such work, the prisoners were given overalls and Levi jackets and looked like farmhands of sorts. Only an occasional car traveled that private dirt road, and we were signaled of its coming by a guard posted at the edge of the property. Since we had more than a half mile of frontage on the road before you came to the house, there was little problem moving the prisoners to the side or back, once the walkie-talkie announced an approaching vehicle. After dinner at 5:30, evenings were spent in reading, journal-keeping, consultation with wardens. Contact with the outside world just then was forbidden. That is, there was to be a complete withdrawal period for a few months, in which the prisoners were to break ties with their old world and get used to Hibernation House and their new future. At least this was our plan.

For diversion once a week, we expected also to bring in a common citizen, a janitor or seamstress or migrant or bus driver, who had a story to tell. A story expressing grievance, anger, or grief.

Again in the classes the essential purpose was to plane down overrefined minds, to bring them back in touch with reality as it was known, in the past or present, by the common people of the world. So there were classes in colonial consciousness, for example, in which the professors took the parts of black slaves in real case histories, with the guards playing their masters and judges, sometimes using white masks. (Punishments, consequently, were meted out, which could mean anything from embarrassing slaps to slave-whippings to isolation-box containments. For my part, I voted against these actual sentences and proposed instead symbolical payments. My proposal lost.) Another course, which to my personal embarrassment was taken from my ideas, only to be crudely fulfilled, was entitled Auto-Critique, in which the prisoner traveled back in his memory to explore a moment of racist feeling or hatred, which he would then have to act out. Films were made of these scenes of humiliation and run at night for the benefit of the other prisoners.

My own course was different, since I centered it in readings, especially from what was becoming a favorite project—inspired perhaps by my new habitat—The Thoughts of Herman Kahn. (And others like him.) How much more real than the thoughts of that other moon-faced Chairman seer (whom many comrades wanted me to quote from), or more powerful than other so-called tragic literature (which the professors were used to). No, my Herman was better than both. What excited me was that this contemporary Herman was as obsessed with the bomb and its aftermath as that older Herman was fixed on the Whale and His consequences. We had a modern Melville here, I explained to my bewildered students. For adults today, I said patiently, the real thing was *On Thermonuclear War*. Next to that, works like the Bible, *Macbeth*, and *Oedipus Rex* were more properly put into a category called "Grown Children's Literature," a subject fit for undergraduates, actors, humanities' professors.

Kahn's opus was exciting and breathtaking, and constantly put one in a state of wonder, fear, and helpless awe. (At man and his capacities, naturally.) Why? Because, like all great works, it was determinedly anti-romantic, supremely impious, and it dealt with a grand—or the grandest—theme. Death. And death on a grand scale. Furthermore, it dealt not with myth but with *the real* at a moment in history when the real was much more overwhelming than the mythical. Along the way, it dispelled the kind of apocalyptic romanticism held by the prisoners and most other enlightened citizens—including myself, during my days of innocence—namely, that nuclear war meant the end of civilization. For 650 pages this jolly pragmatist, embracing facts like a brown bear approaching food in the fall, declared and demonstrated that this end wasn't true, and went on to delineate the alternatives facing us. Not fantasies about a golden love-future created by songs and bell-bottoms, or nostalgic dreams about a pre-machine utopia (which never existed), but the practical consequences of thermonuclear warheads exploding in the atmosphere or at sea or upon cement, bursting buildings, razing the earth, burning people, radioactivating America. In short, the real and probable future—showy summits and SALT agreements notwithstanding.

And instead of the old Grown Children's Lit. terms like catharsis, tragic flaw, conflict between society and the individual, internal struggle, nemesis, unities, Kahn tried to teach with more concrete words, like roentgens, radioactive isotopes (strontium 90, carbon 14, cesium 137), lethal radius, hostile environment, PD (permittable dose), local fallout, external gamma emitter, radiation meters. (All of which I had my students copy in their notebooks and learn, the way the old high school teachers made their little campers memorize lines of poetry.) Kahn himself was kindly in evicting the old romanticism:

> It does no good to use expressions such as *intolerable, catastrophic, total destruction, annihilating retaliation,* and the like. These expressions might be reasonable if it were really true that in a modern war the goal target system is "overkilled" five or ten times. It would then be unimportant to calculate the exact degree of overkill. But such expectations do not seem to be realistic, and it is important to get some understanding of what the levels of damage might be.

How sweet and reasonable that last chastisement; how calm and understated his words next to the declaiming poets and critics. Tough Thomas Huxley wrapping the knuckles of the sentimental Matthew Arnold. And the main point was not whether Kahn was right or wrong in his estimates and recommendations; after all, only priests, fanatics, and American Presidents pursued absolutes in this world. Rather, the important thing was that he was investigating realistically a very important subject, probably the most important in the world today. Now where were you going to find such discussions, except among a very select few—and those, scientists?

True enough, any scientist might have written *On Thermonuclear War,* but this was precisely the difference between the old tragedy and the new: the old was artistic and conceived by

425

one man in a personal voice; the new was scientific and produced in collaboration and written impersonally. It was manifestly more boring, more styleless, more devastating, because it was real, not metaphor or fiction. It was conceived in the true modern signature, the Anonymous.

Appropriately enough, the tragic scientist had developed his own form of tragic chorus. That is, instead of the groups of people used by Sophocles and Aeschylus to warn of and lament the oncoming tragedy, Kahn used tables, charts, statistics, numbers. In *On Thermonuclear War* there were no less than seventy tables and charts concerning nuclear-war devastation, postwar environments, prewar plans. *Seventy*, in 651 pages. This compares favorably to the forty-eight choruses in Sophocles's seven plays, or roughly three hundred pages of text. Again and again, Kahn's narrative is interrupted and supplemented with those numbers and statistics that announce tragic doings. It was interesting to observe a few of these tables and compare them with the more traditional and far better known choral odes of Sophocles:

From *Oedipus Rex:*

II. 1

Woe, for unnumbered are the ills we bear!
Sickness pervades our hosts;
Nor is there any spear of guardian care,
Wherewith a man might save us, found in all our coasts.
For all the fair soil's produce now no longer springs;
Nor women from the labour and loud cries
Of their child-births arise;
And you may see, flying like a bird with wings,
One after one, outspeeding the resistless brand,
Pass—to the Evening Land.

II. 2

In countless hosts our city perisheth.
Her children on the plain
Lie all unpitied—pitiless—breeding death.
Our wives meanwhile, and white-haired mothers in their train,
This way and that, suppliant, along the altar-side
Sit, and bemoan their doleful maladies;
Like flame their paeans rise,
With wailing and lament accompanied;
For whose dear sake O Goddess, O Jove's golden child,
Send help with favour mild!

TABLE 4   A COMPLETE DESCRIPTION OF A THERMONUCLEAR
WAR

Includes the Analysis of:

1. Various time-phased programs for deterrence and defense
   and their possible impact on us, our allies, and others.
2. Wartime performance with different preattack and attack
   conditions.
3. Acute fallout problems.
4. Survival and patch-up.
5. Maintenance of economic momentum.
6. Long-term recuperation.
7. Postwar medical problems.
8. Genetic problems.

TABLE 3   TRAGIC BUT DISTINGUISHABLE
POSTWAR STATES

Dead	Economic Recuperation
2,000,000	1 year
5,000,000	2 years
10,000,000	5 years
20,000,000	10 years
40,000,000	20 years
80,000,000	50 years
160,000,000	100 years

Will the survivors envy the dead?

TABLE 22   MORBIDITY OF ACUTE TOTAL
BODY RADIATION

	Instantaneous	Semiacute (1 month)
Some die	200–300r	~300r
50% die	350–600r	~600r
All die	600–900r	~900r

And later:

I. 2

       Pride is the germ of kings;
Pride, when puffed up, vainly, with many things
   Unseasonable, unfitting, mounts the wall,
   Only to hurry to that fatal fall,
Where feet are vain to serve her. But the task
Propitious to the city GOD I ask
       Never to take away!
GOD I will never cease to hold my stay.

II. 1

     But if any man proceed
     Insolently in word or deed,
     Without fear of right, or care
     For the seats where Virtues are,
     Him, for his ill-omened pride,
     Let an evil death betide!
If honestly his gear he will not gain,
   Nor keep himself from deeds unholy
Nor from inviolable things abstain,
     Blinded by folly.
In such a course, what mortal from his heart
     Dart upon dart
   Can hope to avert of indignation?
Yea, and if acts like these are held in estimation,
     Why dance we here our part?

TABLE I   ALTERNATIVE NATIONAL POSTURES

1. Internal Police Force plus "World Government"
2. *Minimum Deterrence* plus *Limited War* plus *Arms Control*
3. Add insurance to the *Minimum Deterrent:*
    (a) for reliability (*Finite Deterrence*)
    (b) against unreliability (*Counterforce as Insurance*)
    (c) against a change in policy (*Preattack Mobilization Base*)
4. Add *Credible First Strike Capability*
5. "Splendid" First Strike and no Limited War Capability
6. Dreams

TABLE 43   TO PROTECT ALL DETERRENT FORCES

1. More shelter, concealment, dispersal and control
2. Late-strike facilities and use of improvised forces
3. Warning and defense against second and later strikes
4. Protection against postattack blackmail

TABLE 51   THE EIGHT WORLD WARS

I. (1914–1918)	An Accident-Prone World
	Unexpected Operational Gaps
II. (1939–1945)	The Failure of Type II and III Deterrence
	The Technological Seesaw
	Unexpected Operational Gaps
III. (1951– ?)	A Peacetime Revolution in the Art of War
	Unexpected Operational Gaps
	Re-emergence of Russia as an Eurasian Power
IV. (1956–?)	The Problem of the Postattack Environment
	The Waning of U.S. Type II Deterrence
V. (1961)	S.U.–U.S. Parity
	Emergence of the S.U. as a World Power
	No Type II Deterrence Programmed
	Potential Failure of Type I Deterrence
VI. (1965)	Prematureness of Minimum Deterrence
	Possibility of S.U. Strategic Superiority
VII. (1969)	Possibility of Reliable Finite Deterrence
	Emergence of "Third" Powers?
	Arms Control or "?"
	World is ⅓ Rich, ⅓ Aspiring, and ⅓ Desperate
VIII. (1973)	Thirteen Years of Progress (or 50,000 Buttons)

And still later:

I. 1

O generations of mankind!
　How do I find
　Your lives nought worth at all!
For who is he—what state
Is there, more fortunate
Than only to seem great
　And then, to fall?
I having thee for pattern, and thy lot—
Thine, O poor Oedipus—I envy not
　Aught in mortality;

II. 2

Time found thee out—Time who sees everything—
　Unwittingly guilty; and arraigns thee now
　　Consort ill-sorted, unto whom are bred
　　Sons of thy getting, in thine own birth-bed.
　　　O scion of Laius' race,
　　Would I had never never seen thy face!
For I lament, even as from lips that sing
　Pouring a dirge; yet verily it was thou
　　　Gav'st me to rise
And breathe again, and close my watching eyes.

TABLE 11   RADIOACTIVE ENVIRONMENT THREE MONTHS LATER

Standard	Early Attack		Late Attack	
	NAS	100 × IND.	NAS	100 × IND.
U.S. Maximum	26,000	17	110,000	75
	(660)	(0.4)	(2,900)	(2)
U.S. Average	1,200	0.8	17,000	11
	(31)		(430)	(0.3)
Northern Hemisphere Minimum	10	0.007	130	0.1
	(0.25)		(3.3)	
World Minimum	3	0.002	52	0.03
	(0.08)		(1)	

TABLE 9   RADIOACTIVE ENVIRONMENT 100 YEARS LATER
(As measured by ratio to NAS or Industrial Standards)

Standard	Early Attack		Late Attack	
	NAS	IND.	NAS	IND.
U. S. Maximum	11.0	0.75	48.0	3.0
U.S. Average	0.6	0.04	7.0	0.45
Northern Hemisphere Minimum	0.004	0.003	0.06	0.004
World Minimum	0.001	0.0001	0.01	0.001

TABLE 7   GENETIC ASSUMPTIONS

Normal congenital abnormality rate	4%
of genetic origin	2%
Normal early deaths (including late miscarriages)	13%
of genetic origin	8%
Dose to double normal mutation rate	50r
Rate for expression of genetic defects	
First generation	10%
later generations	4%
First generation expression rate for 100r dose (factor)	0.2
First generation expression rate for 1,000r dose (factor)	2

Obviously, Sophocles was in over his head with Kahn. Ancient Zeus was no match for contemporary Poseidons and Atlases. This much was clear. In fact, the only way that you could read those old-style choruses without smiling was to replace Oedipus with America (or Civilization):

> For who is he—what state
> Is there, more fortunate
> Than only to seem great
>   And then, to fall?
> I having thee for pattern, and thy lot—
> Thine, O poor America—I envy not
>   Aught in mortality.

Carefully, I went around the room watching the prisoners paste Xerox copies of the new tragedy alongside the old in their scrapbooks. When Kovell was about to cut the vague gray borders of the Xerox away, I told him not to, since the resemblance to mushroom clouds was appropriate decoration. He looked at me with anger, and did as he was told. I. tried to engage me in an intellectual debate on the comparison, B. told me I was being overwhelmingly crude and perverse in my distinctions, D. took my arm and said, "Brilliant, just brilliant!" Which buoyed me.

And could any reasonable adult have compared the forms of literary tragedy today, in movies, poems, or books, to those stunning *numbers?* No. Tables of Truthful Alternatives made literary scenes and poetic lines look like so many cartoon strips. What counted nowadays for the intelligent man were bombs that could kill you, and the chances for survival; the rest was soap opera, euphemism, trivia. A lecture I repeated resolutely, to the discomfort of the professors.

If Oedipus blinding himself was hard medicine for the Greek citizen to swallow, so was the prospect of America killing sixty to eighty million Russians, or vice versa, hard for us to face. So we didn't. But at Hibernation House we would. The enemy was liberal piety and ignorant, dangerous romanticism. ("Have you thought of trying for funds from the federal government?" put in A., "for this Hudson Institute or Rand on the Left?" I considered the thought and replied that one day, why not?)

433

Subsequently, whenever one of the prisoners protested that my plans could very well drive the planet to ruin, I would pick up my Herman and quote from page and chart. (Not to mention becalming exaggerated claims concerning my capacities. I wasn't Zeus of Olympus or Kissinger of Washington, but Pincus of Cambridge.) I never tired of preaching those realistic texts:

> If we assume that people could survive the long-term effects of radiation, what would the standard of living in their postwar world be like? Would the survivors live as Americans are accustomed to living—with automobiles, television, ranch houses, freezers, and so on? No one can say, but I believe there is every likelihood that even if we make almost no preparations for recuperation except to buy radiation meters, write and distribute manuals, train some cadres for decontamination and the like, and make some other minimal plans, the country would recover rather rapidly and effectively from the small attack. This strong statement is contrary to the beliefs of many laymen, professional economists, and war planners.
>
> If we assume that the destruction has been as specified [the total destruction of the 53 standard metropolitan areas], we then might ask, "What's left?" The first reaction of many people is that there is practically nothing left. The United States is an urban country. These areas—New York, Philadelphia, Chicago, Detroit, Los Angeles—*are* the United States of America, they believe. Destroy them and you have nothing left. Not quite so. Simple subtraction demonstrates that the statement is too strong.
>
> If these cities contain about one-third of the population, then almost two-thirds is outside. If they contain half the wealth, another half must be outside. If they contain slightly more than half of our manufacturing capacity, then slightly less than half remains outside. They do contain an inordinate amount of our war goods manufacturing capacity, true, but we would not be trying to produce jet engines in the postwar world—we would be trying to survive and reconstruct. What is outside the large metropolises—construction, mining, agriculture, consumer goods, and the like—is what we would need to do this.

How lovely that "Not quite so." And the following phrase, "Simple subtraction." Like teaching schoolchildren their multiplication tables. But it was like that when you were dealing with two-thousand-year-old men who hadn't progressed beyond Mt. Sinai Commandments and Sermon on the Mount ethics. Little schoolchildren.

And this piece of instruction:

> The only point to be made now is that those waging a modern war are going to be as much concerned with bone cancer, leukemia, and genetic malformations as they are with the range of a B-52 or the accuracy of an Atlas missile. Senior military advisors in particular will increasingly be forced to deal with what once would have been called "nonmilitary" problems.

Useful for my prisoners too. Not only would they have to deal with moral and social problems, but they too would have to expand their range to include the military and the medical sides. That's what serious works did to the intelligent man—made him painfully aware how ignorant and naïve he is about himself and the world, and how immense was the task that lay ahead. Kahn knew this as well as Sophocles, as well as Freud. And Pincus knew it too.

Why did I belabor the boys with Kahn? For two reasons. One was that they needed to be prodded to stick with the real and the significant, otherwise they'd return to their trivial and academic concerns. (It was K., a Cardozo philosopher of ethics and education, who came to me one night and said, "Kahn's obsessed, but I'm convinced now that it's a healthy obsession. I'm ready to investigate it seriously, and I thought I'd tell you." He had clear blue eyes and had spent his last twenty years studying the fine nuances of ethical problems. I appreciated his words.) The other reason was that I was obsessed too. For in the midst of the chaos engulfing me, and the high-pressure zones approaching every day, Kahn was a calm place to be.

Boys, I called the professors. At least that was part of the goal, to make them young again, so that the old rules and old assumptions wouldn't count any more. When the world was new and wondrous and they could come to it like Columbus and

Cortez coming upon the Americas, not fatigued husbands and schoolteachers tracing the same paths every day, every year. An education in being bad, in acting roguishly, was in part an attempt to reintroduce long-abandoned habits and outlawed feelings. To rip loose those nets of ideas, prohibitive rules, inhibitions. When looking at those scrawny chests and spindly legs and balloon paunches, the appurtenances of a Still Life, I couldn't help wondering what had happened to the apple cheeks and round bottoms, the signs of running, and awe of subways, grownups, baseball fields, new schools. They had struggled so hard to become secular Popes, pronouncing moral judgments and quasi-legal evaluations on all of experience (condemning a bad book as if it were a felony), that they had forgotten about play and the mischievous side of childhood. Hence their conspicuous lack of wild humor, invention, unpredictability, the capacity to play-act and mimic, to indulge in fantasy worlds. (Of course, Kove was in a special category here. Family Talk had taught me a lot about the whole subject. And A., too, I presumed, was outside their Adult Pale Zone.) In shedding their boyhoods totally, the professors had lost their youthful vertebrates and had become city gastropods and cephalopods; their brains had tired from running the same grooves; a half century of decent citizenship had made them fossil-like. What could be done?

Try to unwind them and open new grooves. One was the new play of sexuality, just begun. (What was wrong, for example, I mused one day, with resurrecting those city puberty rites, where the boys threw their bets in the center of the floor and then, in a circle, jerked off communally, the first one to come taking the pot? Or perhaps a gang-bang with a young girl? Certainly it was worth trying. You tried anything with a terminal cancer patient, didn't you? Why not a terminal spiritual patient?) Another was the constant humorous racket of rock sounds. And the color and excitement of uniforms. What child didn't love them as much as a new toy? (Besides their football cleats and numbered jerseys, we also purchased baseball uniforms and caps for them, to go along with the gowns for regular attire.) And on the cement walls, next to their beds and lockers, we placed photographs and drawings of baseball giants alongside culture heroes: Honus Wagner, the slugging shortstop, at the plate, next to Stephen Crane, the lanky poetic realist, at his desk; the ferocious Cobb sliding spikes-up into second base, alongside Saul Bellow in his beautiful youth; Bobby Thomson smashing his Cinderella homer next to young Einstein, dapper and fastidious like a young pre-Raphaelite, standing over a lectern. No, you couldn't beat pictures. Too bad we couldn't get Willie Mays to come up and run a Spring Instructional League, with the professors as rookies. Silly and dangerous nonsense? Certainly.

And more: after a hard morning of classroom work during recess, an old-fashioned Good Humor wagon would roll around with the bell clanging, and vanilla cones, pops and fudgicles, ice-cream sandwiches would be sold to the students, who paid for it out of their allowance. And two afternoons a week they would play in their specially made indoor sandboxes, digging tunnels and making castles and getting muddy. Absurd? Possibly. Degrading? Not at all, once they got into it. The point to remember is, it wasn't all Kahn and prison and destruction that I was after, but a character change deeper and richer, more ambiguous and more outlandish.

Games naturally were big. For instance, in that eighteen-room, two-section house, hide-and-seek could be a marvel. Especially when surprises turned up, as they did frequently. (And naturally I too preferred the games to some of the more . . . necessary doings.)

I remember being It once and searching for players hiding, when, next to a tall linen closet, I heard a strange noise. Opening the door, I saw, peeking out from the bottom a man's leg. I kneeled down and there was K., rolled up like a foetus in the cramped space. He was hysterical, shaking, and, when I asked him to come out, his refusal was a cringe, like a terrified dog hiding under a bed from his brutal master. K., what happened? I asked. Tell me. What's wrong? Slowly, not looking at me, but blubbering through his hands, he explained how he had been knocked down and his glasses smashed in the morning class, while playing the role of a black sharecropper accused unjustly of raping a white woman. Knocked down and kicked by the guards and then sentenced to two weeks of isolation, beginning tomorrow. (Isolation consisted of standing in a tall dark closet for eight to ten hours a day, with little food, no space, no light; a punishment mistakenly modeled, not by myself, on the ingenious tiger cells in Indochina.) Finally, after he got his story and fears off his chest, I was able to persuade him to leave his burrow hole. I helped him out and up (like a giant unwinding from a VW in the circus), and, seeing that he was still shaking uncontrollably, I led him to a nearby room. There I sat in a cushioned rocking chair and took him onto my lap, where I rocked softly and said things were okay. While he sat boyish-helpless and startled, I began to be struck with the overbearing sensation of holding my father, as I held this balding man, with oval face and stubbled cheeks and sharp blue eyes. It transported me to my own father's lap and reading the *Times*'s Korean War maps and World War II Russia maps (which he kept), or feeling his cheeks when I ran to kiss him coming home from work. It was I who shook now, and I fought to restrain my emotion. I told K. that I would get him new glasses and try to arrange for a modified punishment. I got up and left him in the chair, sobbing. And for the rest of that day I yearned for the days when I was younger and happier.

In sum, the combination of hard tasks and childish play (or vice versa) produced confusion, anxiety, fears. It had been a very long time since these men had had their emotions ambushed, their behavior challenged. That was the important thing. For the first time, they were being asked and coerced into betraying an adulthood of reason, civility, and propriety, by means of boyish chaos and prisoner hardship. Certainly the contrast between these last two, the boyish and the prisoner, didn't help the adjustment any.

The most consistently approachable of the prisoners—apart from D., constantly enthusiastic—turned out to be A., who came to see me a few days later. Fifty-seven, wavy-haired, communitarian, anarchist, experimentalist, A. was the Natty Bumppo of the tribe, a veteran scout familiar with forests, adventure, and personal risks.

He sat in a stuffed chair—how different from E., who selected the straight hardbacked one—opened his lunch, and began right in. Saying at first how, of course, something had to be done, with the shape the country was in, both in official places and on our side. His and mine. It was all the same old routines and had to be "broken through." This was a start. He knew it for sure when I was junking Sophocles for Kahn, though that particular switch may not have been the best substitution.

"I think what you're doing is interesting and suggestive," he continued in his faint New York accent, crossing his legs, "much to the chagrin of my colleagues. Whether all this will turn out profitable in the future who knows. But who ever knows? The least trustworthy agent to bet on, along with governments, is history. And these men, whom I grew up with in the thirties and forties, know this better than anyone." He drank coffee from his thermos cup. "Everybody's overexcited right now. You've offended their morals, which they think are their feelings. Well, good. I've been offending them for years now. It doesn't change them, but at least they learn to live with it. What you're doing, however, is unique. The first national event in thirty-five years that has actually *touched the lives* of American intellectuals. And the Spanish Civil War was far away, just as Stalinism was in fact a fantasy-fight, a pseudo-event. But this is affecting them personally and immediately. It's something I've tried to do for years, without success. So congratulations."

I nodded, grateful and flattered.

He ate from a sandwich and spoke again, his voice full-bodied, unwavering, measured.

"As you know, I've been dreaming and writing all my life about social experiments, and this is the first one that adds up to anything. I always thought it would start with the schools somehow, but I was mistaken. The experimental colleges in San Francisco and New England turned into great busts. Not enough brains. And suffocated by dogmatic kids and macrobiotic fools. But at least my basic intuition was right, it would be the students who would start a new direction. You kids, not me and my pals. I just had to be patient, which was harder than I thought." He shrugged and lit a cigarette. "Pals. I always thought so much of friendship. And yet how many friends can I count from among these men? Not many. They're . . . afraid of me. Distrustful. They think I'm vulgar. I'm sort of an untouchable among them. Why? Because I go down on stevedores." He shook his head. "Not very nice for a Jewish *luftmensch* from the Bronx. Either you love according to their rules or you're a witch. Salem and Zion, Puritans and Jews, the same . . . It's their fear that dictates their principles, of course. Their repressed fear. And do you know what? It's been exactly that fear that's kept them from being truly outstanding men. Einsteins or Freuds. Their fear has kept them back; and not being pushed. Never being bombed or put in exile. Literary men, especially Jews, I think, are personal cowards generally. Terrible. All connected with being tied to Mama's apron strings. That's why I stopped hanging around with them long ago. Physical and sexual cowards. I never knew it so clearly until now, in these several weeks. We were here just one night and G. was crying how strange it was and how he'd never make it. *One night.* As if he'd never spent a night in a Holiday Inn in a strange town." He paused and went on. "What you're doing brings all this home emphatically. And it hurts to watch it; to watch cripples. But keep it up. The ones who pull through might even turn into great critics."

My God! My head was swimming.

His look alternated between radiant cheder boy, in love with ideas and the world, and dark neurotic, haunted by an inner devil. Floppy boyish hair and fierce mouth and eyes. The split of his life in that face.

"I have one serious criticism," he continued in his unmelo-dramatic, determined way, "and that is to watch out that you don't overdo things. Total freedom is hard for anybody to handle, citizens or jailors. Ironically, it usually makes prisoners out of us. Make limits for yourself, your ideas. Whatever you wish. But real limits. Otherwise you'll have excesses on your hands that you won't know what to do with. How to judge or measure, to see what's worthwhile, what's not. I say all this from personal experience, Lenny. For too long I had some cockeyed idea of being a totally free person, and I was self-destructive and destructive to others. It was naïve and dangerous. I think at times you fall into that trap."

He bit into his fruit and recrossed his football-trouser legs. This critique was very different from the others. It seemed to me free of hysteria and reflexive accusation.

In a while, he said, "I thought I'd come around and say these things in light of that petition for non-negotiable demands. They've even stolen their means of protest from you. Besides," he paused, "you should probably receive some encouragement and some criticism from someone on this side of the fence. If you're honest, which I think you are."

I told him I appreciated it indeed, and added spontaneously

that I had always admired the spirit and energy of his books. And his courage in writing the one about his down-and-out years. "You still seem to have all of it," I said.

He closed his pail, adjusted his thermos, and stood to go.

"If you have any suggestions for us," I offered enthusiastically, "let me know them, if you care to. . . . I can use them."

His face narrowed. "I think the kind you mean would make for a complicated moral problem in view of the situation."

"Do those kinds of problems still exist for you?" I retorted.

His face changed abruptly. "That's the first adolescent remark I've heard you utter," he countered sharply. "Of course, they exist. Otherwise my life would be utterly happy and utterly senseless. What do you think all this . . . *struggling* is about? Do you think it's all libido and games?"

I reddened.

A moment passed. A. took a step closer and put his hand on my face, freezing me. He ran the length of my cheek with his cool palm. "You have lovely smooth skin, Lenny." He smiled, showing crooked, space-filled teeth. The sallow aging color and ungainly features were washed away in a bliss of light.

His free hand sought mine, and my heart trembled.

"Don't be afraid," he said gently. "Isn't that what you're trying to teach us?"

He moved his face toward mine, and somehow I was able to turn away and move off. He stood a moment, said something conciliatory, and departed.

By the narrow window, I stared at the stillness of the hills and sky, and at the blue fog wrapping them. My cheeks burned and my head was spinning. His caressing hand and the desire in his eyes transported me back to jail days.

Still shaking, I thought of my recent prescriptions, so casually written down, for "opening up" Professor E. How painful to have one's nose rubbed in one's ideas!

I sat by my desk, near tears, and jotted in my notebook, "Watch out for Excess" and "Try on a prisoner's skin once a week."

It was all so hard and unpredictable, every step, every step. When would it cease? Was I unable to face my own prescriptions and challenges? Was I pushing these men indiscriminately

441

with force and small violence? Were my games useful as humanist experiment or closer to primitive sadism? Where was spontaneity, which I once so prized? Or that clarity which Addie had so admired? These were the doubts that flooded my mind after A.'s departure.

But that's what was finally so impressive about these particular prisoners, the way they could constantly teach you something if you cared to listen. Where else could you get prisoners like that? Or teachers, for that matter?

But then, in their way, my own colleagues were good at instructing too, weren't they? Consider my recent education, stemming from their (instinctive) tutoring. But precisely this vexed me: that at times I felt as if I were the only real student in the entire place, receiving lessons from both ends, lessons which frequently contradicted each other. Was it that I was more divided than I would acknowledge, or that both sides had their element of validity, as well as shortcoming? overwhelming shortcoming? I left off my questions and went for a solitary walk in the cold white sunshine.

Weeks went by, peaceably enough. Fights, verbal ones, broke out among prisoners (J. and I., for example, and D. and B.), and among ourselves (mostly my objections to certain practices suggested by several strange black guards). But they were not major and were always mediated by someone like Addie or Monroe on our side and Kovell on theirs. A thousand small items came up: would I please get some special migraine pills for K.; perhaps I would permit just one letter home from all of the men? to take care of mechanical things like bankbooks, checking accounts, mortgages, etc. (permission granted); a dripping water pipe downstairs, which necessitated evacuating the men to the woods, and the desks to another room, while a local plumber came to repair it; a serious fist fight occurred when a black boy had his best sweater stolen by a newcomer friend of Luis; and so on. The sheer administrating of the place took at least thirty hours a week, worked at collectively. A process which made me admire an area of competence that I had previously scorned as if it were evil personified.

Where were the police and federal agents all this time? Looking for us, though not with the zeal reserved for missing diplomats, politicians, or business leaders. You see, the kidnapping of ten eggheads, most of them Semitic busybodies and troublemakers in their own right, was not slowing the nation down or disturbing its conscience. Simple enough. Occasionally you'd read on page 56 of the *Times* a letter written to the President, signed by the wives and relatives of the missing men—I nearly laughed aloud when I read "Grace Lawrence and Angela Michaels, on behalf of Dr. Bernard Kovell"—asking him to please take a "personal interest in the case, in which the lives of ten distinguished citizens were involved." But with Chou En-lai and abortion and the Miami Dolphins still on his mind, the President remained detached. All of which is not to say that they weren't hunting for us. They were, but mostly in the wrong areas—in Southern rural regions, and in New York and Boston. For among our precautions was the use of a fleet of a half-dozen rented trucks which headed south and southwest, on the same day that we had kidnapped the professors. Meanwhile, we returned our three trucks early the next morning to Boston and New York; these had been taken out in the name of respectable citizens, who accounted for them perfectly well when they were checked. (Most of the other trucks were leased on stolen credit cards, of which there was a constant supply for a moderate price. Other trucks were leased from Movement cash or Movement cards, provided by donors, with no questions asked, on a rotating basis.) The result of this decoy-envoy and subsequent hunt was the breaking up of many communes, from South Carolina to New Mexico, in those first days especially. Another precaution, already suggested, was the use of legal procedures to secure the house and the setting up of a corporation and trust to run the place. Seeing titles like Big Springs Trust and Hibernation, Inc., on checks made local merchants and individual workers feel easier. It was clear that Simon Stillwagon's successors were very American; besides, would he sell to anyone less than that? Then, too, some of the kids attended classes at the local college and applied for winter admission on a resident basis. All of this was to familiarize the town and the college with strange faces.

Anyway, it would probably be spring, if then, when the north country was checked out intensively. Winter up there discourages mobility and inquiry, just as the bears know. Which

443

is not to say that you didn't have to be constantly alert for slip-ups and still have a lot of luck on your side. Like when two federal agents, investigating a statutory rape case that involved crossing state lines, came to the tiny depressed town and stayed a long weekend. With nothing to do, they uncovered a nice marijuana field and business in a commune set on a hill not five miles from where we were. I remember seeing those two agents, accompanied by the local policeman, Chief Edmund Jones, taking into the courthouse three hippie-looking kids, while I filled Kove's Mercedes—borrowed with his keys, a N.H. license put on it—with gasoline across the street in the Texaco station. At such moments you were reminded emphatically all over again how thin the line is between disaster and good fortune, far finer than the black hose I held in my hand. The big crooks were right: if you were going to commit a crime, go all the way. The penny-ante stuff will always get you caught faster. I loved to amuse myself with such Underworld Wisdom.

One day in early January, I received this note from Kovell, who had remained rather cool and composed, I thought.

Dear Lenny,

I don't know how to talk to you any more, so I'm trying it this way. I've waited patiently for things to change or signs of civilized life to reappear, but it's been in vain. I'm now thoroughly frightened of you and frightened for the others. I also somehow have retained enough feeling for you to be frightened for you too. I think you're out of control. Out of your *own* control.

What are you doing?

Whose flag are you saluting? Do you know?

When will it end?

These are the questions that I think you must answer. To yourself and to me. Otherwise, this is all lunacy, pure and dangerous lunacy.

I want to be as straight with you as possible. It's my opinion that what's happening to you is something like what happened to Young Goodman Brown in Hawthorne's tale. Do you remember him? The young Salem boy who enters the forest in the middle of the night, sees how terrifying and evil it is, wants to turn back, but finds that he can't. Len, don't be trapped the same way. If there's a mad part of you, a demon who suddenly takes hold, remember that he visits us all at one time or another. But he's *not uncontrollable.* You *can* pull back, force him away. Believe me, we have all given him freedom at some point in our lives, to some extent or another. But don't give up the reins. There's always time to leave the forest, no matter how far you've entered it, no matter what you've done. Leonard, let me plead with you, beg you at this point. Don't go down in history as a crazy and dangerous fiend. I know that once you used your energy in other directions; it's still possible. *Call it off.* Leave the forest. Go away somewhere, if you don't want jail. But stop this before your will is helpless before your desire.

There are men's lives involved here, besides your own.
Your old friend,
Kove

I found myself smiling wickedly at the reasonable note. I think it was that I resented his ability to be calm and reasonable at this juncture. I was jealous of that civilized pleading. So I interpreted the letter within the context of my sudden peculiar emotion. He was always the literary man, down to the last drop. Books instead of reality, when it came to moral guidance and advice. Perhaps Kove knew or would know now what his girls felt when they, in Family Talk, tried to get through to him via the U.S. mails. I'd remind him of that. Yes, *getting through* was difficult. As for Goodman Brown, too bad that Hawthorne didn't live today—his antique tale of evil might have been written with the kind of pornographic detail and sense of explicit depravity that it called for. It would then be convincing today. Or if Céline were given it to rewrite. As it was, Goodman Brown was a tepid creature and the tale dated; both author and hero lacked the strength to fulfill their unholy fantasy. Whereas I was trying to find and fulfill mine. I enjoyed the forest more and more as I discovered it, didn't I? That's what made Hibernation House so interesting—it was beyond my expectations in negative possibility.

Yet the letter stirred in me two other impulses, one educational, the other more personal. The first had to do with literature, with the classics. They would have to be rewritten, I saw clearly, in order for them to mean anything again. Rewritten with the knowledge and freedom of today, without violating the story's basic idea or thrust; in other words, fulfill the story's true promise which, in past times, had been stifled because of literary convention, bourgeois social pressure, psychological inhibition. Otherwise, what was the point of the new freedom if we couldn't make use of it to resurrect the past? Any sensible adult reading the Masters knew they needed refurbishing. For a start, Kove could rewrite Goodman Brown, describing a true black mass, with limbs climbing and orifices opening and spirits lusting. (Hawthorne, of course, begged to be rewritten, with his sack of unconscious terrors and desires. And who better than Kove for the job?) Professor E., that devotee of English classics, could go to work on James, his old master, and develop for real the varieties of homosexuality implicit there; that was a lifetime job, certainly. (And why not Lawrence too?) Professor B., meanwhile, an interpreter of Hardy, could explore in detail the sadomasochism of his heroes and heroines, beginning with Sue Bridehead and Jude and taking up that lustily confused Mayor of Casterbridge. Do you see how real those now silly incomplete scenes of Henchard and Donald Farfrae together, or Hyacinth Robinson and Paul Muniment sitting by the banks of the Thames, arms around each other's waist, could become, with the correct doctoring? And that's what I was thinking of, doctoring, not distorting; the new scribes, the professors, would be acting like restorers of great paintings, who worked on the old masterpieces for months to bring out the lost nuance, the decayed color and texture. Literature over the years had accumulated the dust and soot of time gone by, of customs and morals grown obsolete; the great works were weighted down and clogged with the conventions and inhibitions of their time. Do you see what was possible with the new conception? How literature, great literature, wouldn't be a grandfatherly hoax any more, but a living thing? No longer a sport or joke, it could *mean* again. Enthrall for real, not out of duty. A writer like Borges had the right inclination, but he was too old, too weary. The professors could begin the job, redo Hawthorne, Melville, Poe, Hardy, James, Lawrence, Kafka (a more delicate job)—the obvious ones first. Novels, far from being dead, were waiting to be born anew. Or born for the first time. Is it any wonder that of the ten or so major writers who ever lived, there is hardly any one of them who did not suffer the ignominy of a novel banned, a work treated like a crime? Dostoevsky and his Stavrogin, Tolstoy and his Anna, Hardy and Tess or Jude, Lawrence and Chatterley, Joyce and Bloom, Flaubert and Emma, Proust and Swann, Dreiser and Carrie—the list of punishment by society is endless. An interesting and important footnote to the relationship between great literature and *society's feelings*.

No, there was nothing so fine as the general principle of digging for the seamier side of sanctity and exhibiting it. All fine flowers had their roots in dirt, and these men would dig them up. The sanctity of literature, the sanctity of morals, the sanctity of men, would have to be overturned. Instead of heaven and its opposite, hell (it too by now literary-fied into piety), we would investigate, and talk about, manure.

Such thoughts had been uttered before, I knew. Any thinking citizen knew that every hundred or two hundred years there needed to be a thorough housecleaning, a complete inventory of culture-stock. To get rid of useless junk, period pieces, culture obsolescence; all that clutters the mind and prevents clear sense. So, for example, Emerson thought—I explained to the class— more than a hundred years ago when he wrote, "The books which once we valued more than the apple of the eye, we have quite exhausted." Even the scholarly Emerson was brave enough to admit that the new culture and the new strength would not come from the sophisticated and the professorial and the old.

> Not out of those, on whom systems of education have exhausted their culture, comes the helpful giant to destroy the old or to build the new, but out of unhandselled savage nature, out of terrible Druids and Berserkirs, come at last Alfred and Shakspeare.

Now that wasn't bad, was it? I never quite thought of myself as a terrible Druid, or of some of my friends becoming Shakspeares. But why not? Who else? What was so nice about actually reading the lines of the ancients like Emerson was that they knew very well that they too were headed for the dustbin one day. And that we, unhandselled savage nature, would be the helpful giants to put them and their work there. So what if these helpful giants were just out of their teens, some of them not even quite there?

The second impulse led to my surprising Kovell a few days later, against the wishes of several wardens. That letter had kindled certain memories after all. When Kove came to the long sitting room, somber in baseball cap and football trousers, he was suddenly stopped in his tracks, just beyond the door, by the sight of Grace, standing to greet him. As she ran to him he kept his eye on me, wondering what the trick was; but he was smothered by Grace's adoring kisses and caresses. (How many light years away that night in Cambridge seemed, when I had had an occasional dinner with them.) In her bundled sweaters and tweed slacks, Grace looked perfect New England countryside; Brahmin jaw and forehead didn't hurt. She was just what the doctor ordered for a man in isolation almost three months now, especially with Kove's leanings. (He had had some sex with the camp girls, that was all.) But still he stared at me across her shoulder with skepticism. An appropriate enough response from a humanities teacher who has been force-fed on depravity by his old student. What was up now? his look read. But all that was up, on my part, was surprise and sentiment; and so I left the room.

But remember, as I've said, I too was a beginner in my profession. Perhaps I should have guessed that a camp prank was in the air from that early opposition to my surprise suggestion at our weekly powwow, but I didn't. Anyway, Kove and Grace had the rest of that day and evening to themselves, and the next day, a warm January afternoon, a thaw day, I allowed Grace to make a picnic lunch for them. Walking outside at 12:30, probably out of a desire to be with them like old times, I found myself following the footsteps on the snow-covered path. Sure enough, there were Kove and Grace, in a clearing, settling down. Near a fallen tree, Kove prepared the blanket, Grace the food from the straw basket. It brought back an emotion that I had just had the other day, nostalgia. I wanted, I realized, to join that old-world scene, to have a brief interlude from Hibernation House games. I smoked a cigarette, debating, and was on the verge of going over, when Kove reached out for his old girl and began kissing her. At it again, right there in the open, up to old sex tricks. If he were walking down the corridor on his last walk, and his guard offered him a woman or escape, you can guess which he'd choose.

As I started to walk off, I noticed out of the corner of my eye a slight movement behind a tree. Surprised, I looked over quietly and observed Tyrone White, a black guard in a turtle-neck and holding a bat, watching the scene clandestinely. I didn't get it. What was he up to? I moved a few steps closer and there, behind another oak, was a brief view of Harry Cinqua, an Indian boy from Cape Cod. They were on their own, not acting from my directions; it made me furious. I stood my ground, feeling like a dumb fool. And as Kove and Grace began to fuck, his trousers down and her pants and underwear off, the scene grew enigmatic. A modest circle of guards and wardens, perhaps eight or ten, left their posts behind the trees and quietly moved closer to the jerking pair. Like Birnam wood moving to Dunsinane. Or a group of silent Indians in a John Ford classic.

But what followed was stranger and meaner than Metro-Goldwyn-Mayer melodrama; real life. That circle of guards, a mix of melting-pot bloods, from brown girl to red-face boy to dark-haired spectacled Jew to slim olive Puerto Rican, slipped silently up close to the lustful Dean and his blond lay, like brilliant foxes stealing upon a chicken coop. They stood silently, observing. Their exquisite control was startling. Kovell, spent, lying across Grace, jumped about, shocked. Grace screamed. Frantically she sought her slacks, which were grabbed by a female guard. Naked from her sweater down, the sun splashing her lovely pale skin, she scrambled desperately behind Kove for protection, wedging herself between a pine trunk and him. For a whole minute or two, it grew perfectly silent; my impulse to run to help my old friends was strangely becalmed by the beauty of the afternoon, the sun-dappled snow, the motionless green pines and white birches, the thin air like heady quicksilver. I stood still, seventy-five feet away. It was their show now, another marauder show against my good boy's grain. Would they beat them? Rape her? Stand and make them perform again? Or all of those, in an orgy of vengeance? Once more, as during those nights of June, I was at the mercy of the occasion and the spontaneity of primitives' desires.

Still quiet, some now smiling, several jailers crouched to

449

their haunches, eyeing their prey in a formed semicircle, twenty feet away. I must admit that I never fully realized how emphatically and collectively *pretty* my comrades were until I saw their flashing colors—glistening black and full-bodied chocolate, red-tinted and subtly olive, the burnt red-brown of Indian—against white snow and clear blue sky. And in their carefully chosen garb of striped bell-bottoms, bright turtlenecks, billowing shirts and leather jackets, they were certainly the best-dressed gang of guerrillas that you could imagine. I suppose the scene was very movielike, deceptive with glamour and exoticism. Kove, meanwhile, had begun talking to them quietly, with control, after having covered Grace's legs and pubic area with the blanket. The cast of Gilbert-and-Sullivan outlaws stood and smiled, or sat and looked impressive, suggesting a band of New Hampshire cannibals who have discovered a Victorian couple poaching in their hills. Save that here the dress and behavior was in reverse or upside down, and the well-dressed cannibals looked on with native curiosity and patient delight at their primitive guests. Yes, if you had a photograph of just that moment, you'd have to concede that the colonials deserved to be boiled and enslaved, while the cannibals clearly deserved to rule and to eat.

I walked closer, into view, and Kove, seeing me, tightened and directed his words to me. It was so peculiar and intense a moment, and I was so unsure of my own desires, that I barely heard him. Or understood his sense, as he uttered strange accusations about "trap" and "betrayal" and "some surprise!" I just shook my head, I recall, the effort to communicate sensibly beyond me. Who was he talking to, Goodman Brown or Lenny Pincus?

Finally a black girl, hands on hips, called him to a halt.

He glanced angrily at her, then was grabbed by three boys who pulled him away from Grace, while he fought furiously. Immediately she too was held from two sides by a pair of female guards, one black, one white, while a third pulled the blanket from her front, exposing her long pale legs and downy pelvic region. Her legs thrashing like a fish flapping in a net, she was pinned securely, with only a sweater on. To my surprise, she began to curse tremendously. ("You fucking morons!" from a Brahmin mouth was hot stuff.)

What followed was breathtaking and wicked.

Tyrone White walked to the center, between Kove, Grace, and the guards, unzipped his fly, and took out his penis. Long, chocolate, still hooded with prepuce. Cupping it underneath and dangling it loosely like a knife, he smiled earnestly, planted his feet apart, and began to pee. A rising arc of thick yellow urine that fell, at first, two feet short of Kovell; then, slowly, the spray inched closer, until it showered him as he tried to duck away. Finally he stopped trying, the liquid running down his face. Tyrone finished and walked to Kovell. Kneeling down by the anxious professor, he kissed him on his forehead. Gently he took Kove's hand and placed it on his soft brown member, as if he were selling him merchandise which he wanted him to test out for himself. Then he stood and strutted slowly back to the seated group and joined them. It must have been strange indeed for Tyrone, a Dorchester black recruited to Cardozo under a special program, to do that to the program's original sponsor.

In a few seconds, a rock song crashed from a little transistor, and sister Adeline, attired in trousers and boots, danced to the center. It thrilled and amazed me to see sophisticated Addie suddenly performing at the barbarian ritual. Radcliffe had joined Roxbury for real now. After doing steps to the slow rock rhythm, Addie moved toward Grace's direction. Dancing all the while, she opened her belt and wriggled out of her tight suède bells. She wore white panties and did some fine steps to the music, her behind trim. Then smiling sweetly, she peeled down her panties and stepped out of them. Again she picked up her rhythm and now moved to within three feet of Grace, where she danced this way and that before lowering herself in a squat, her backside facing the mesmerized blond girl. Grace shrieked and struggled, but was held securely; she squeezed her eyes shut, but they were opened and also held. As Addie began to defecate, kids shouted encouragement, as if she were doing a jazz solo ("Go on, bring it all home, baby!" and "Get it all together now, sister!"). It was a very long minute or two, as transcending perhaps as watching a great blaze or pulling a trigger, and yet curiously ambiguous with the winter sun and snow so particularly striking in beauty. She stood up then, grinning proudly, moving away to show off brown turds in the snow. But she wasn't done, you saw then, as she bent to scoop the feces carefully into cupped hands. She danced the few steps to the blond girl, a few of the kids good-naturedly applauding her sporting gesture. Addie kneeled by Grace, whose head sought desperate but vain release. Very kindly, like a nurse caring for a patient or a nun for a novitiate, Addie displayed the treasure in her hand and said, "See, honey, it's just like any other shit, yours or your man's. No different, sweetie, here smell it." She brought the feces up to Grace's nose, having shifted it to one hand, holding Grace's face with the other. Grace squealed like a hit animal and coughed violently. With ceremony, Addie waited a moment and another, and then proceeded to touch the excrement to Grace's glistening forehead, anointing her as if it were Ash Wednesday and rubbing her cheeks, too. "Just a black Eucharist, dear," Addie said, smiling with what seemed to me sincere sympathy. And she stayed there, offering the victimized girl the consolation of her presence.

Then she got up, danced across the circle to Kovell, and repeated the anointing ritual, saying, "Some black affection for you, too, Professor."

When Monroe Rules turned his face in gentle smile at me, I sensed who was next. I wanted to run, and as if they had read my mind, I was suddenly gripped tightly, and it was the museum all over again. I sensed Luis at one arm, in fact, as Addie rocked toward me, a sparkling black snake coiling and shaking amid the dazzling white brilliance. My heart trembled, and I was near tears. This will be hard to understand, I didn't understand it myself, but as Addie's brown face drew nearer, as I was forced to my knees in the soft wet snow, as I awaited my fate, I grew happy. It was all now resolute and clear. Addie brought the dark smear of brown to my nose—I tried to observe it precisely, and saw about two inches of brown fecal matter, striped just the slightest in pale gray—and held it there for me to inhale. I whiffed it willingly, the aroma making me swoon as if it were the richest perfume from the East Indies. I was pierced with the pungent attraction of repellent smell, and I had no hatred or anger. I was reduced to a dog who reveled in shit and sought eagerly to roll in it. But all Addie did was to rub my forehead and cheeks, and then lean forward and whisper, "Don't be nervous, brother. Just believe in us."

I found myself nodding and understanding.

She eyed me clearly with her two small alert pupils, and I nodded, for a long time, I think, for when I looked up, she was gone.

I remember seeing Grace and Kove pulled away, I remember getting sick right there in the snow and heaving, I remember it being all still and lovely in the forest again. I got up then, too groggy from the experience to think or reflect, and took about ten or fifteen steps before I realized I was going nowhere and the path was the other way. I felt all right, peaceful even, as I headed back. It was only when I reached the house and a guard chuckled that I realized the stuff was still smeared on my face. I returned his smile and cleaned my skin with the fine snow.

In the next few days, though I was ill with an earache that extended to my head, I tried to discern the source of my peculiar joy during the revolting scene. And what I discovered was that it was clear once and for all that I was as much prisoner, in my own way, as the professors downstairs. The anointment with the excrement signaled emphatically that I was neither leader nor counselor, but rather a sometimes useful serf to the new lords; a grain of sand serving the new shore. Now while this should have perhaps upset me in theory, it, in fact, pleased me. I felt released from a weighty burden and, like any man released, appreciated my new freedom. My comrades didn't want a leader and resented me for being one. Second, they resented me for myself—for my skin color, my upbringing, my way of thinking and reasoning. They wanted to rely wholly on themselves and their instincts for conquering. If I was useful, it was as a function of the animal, a head for the body; however, this head was to be severely limited in its powers and controlled authoritatively by that body. When *it* wriggled, I—the head—was its helpless victim.

The animal was right, I thought. Just as the professors were right too, for their time, in their way. For what had impressed me about the professors was how right or valuable each of their views was, B.'s democratic socialism, A.'s anarchical man, E.'s sensitive literary creature, in terms of the old society where the single individual counted a lot. Not only did each view contribute something positive to the making of the whole, but you could also take each apart and argue with each ideology separately.

453

How different from what was happening here, with my comrades. First, "arguing" itself was an obsolete gesture, so far as I could make out. For whom would you argue with, if there was only the Whole? Could you argue, for example, with an atom that constantly moved, split apart perhaps, and changed its shape? My colleagues, while not exactly forming an atom, did represent a force, a collective and anonymous force; thrust forward by instinct, spontaneity, and accumulated anger, it headed in the direction of *against*. (I had shared this particular direction, but from the wrong perspective, as I shall explain.) Now, Addie, even though she had worked to make herself individual and distinct, had understood this and was able to accept it. Which meant that she was able to accept her own obsolescence and glisten with new pride as part of the new animal's body. I myself, until that ritual in the snow, was cloudy and confused about all this. When I did perceive once and for all that, for my colleagues, instinct was going to dominate planning, the barbaric rout the civilized, the collective annihilate the person, the body master the head, I was happy for the clarity.

I made these divisions without reference to moral judgment, but rather as an artist putting landscape lines down on paper. Just as the professors had been right for their time (the recent past) with their emphasis on reason and proper order, so my colleagues were right for the future because they represented what was new (right now their procedures in flux, their final values uncertain).

This new clarity forced me to face anew my deed of murder. For what had struck me then as an extraordinary and bold act, risking moral and physical danger, was, by my comrades' terms, a silly and useless gesture. (Luis's words returned to me, with the derisive movement of his lips.) On the contrary, far from it being a daring act, it was actually cowardly and retrogressive, an attempt on my part to play a *strongly individual role* and set myself above the crowd and the people. This was wrong, an old-fashioned error. (Errors and mistakes were more appropriate words of the future than right and wrong.) The act was bourgeois, by the new morals, no matter how criminal it might have been by liberal courts. I found this assessment good news, after the initial alarm. You see, it relieved me of yet another burden and yet another illusion. *I was not a murderer in the new world, but a boy who had committed a bourgeois error.* Constantly, my colleagues were convincing me, by their upsetting and repulsive acts, that most of my burdens were small illusions whose purpose was to enlarge my private ego. This self-concern was obsolete and dangerous.

Animal, force, or atom were simply various ways of describing what hit me intuitively the afternoon of that special black sacrament.

Meanwhile, at the house, news of the ritual sent fresh waves of fear and anxiety through the professors, who doubled their petitions about "Geneva rights of prisoners," "negotiating committees," and "the desire to participate in camp decisions." That last was a nice demand, since it reminded everyone of the student desires to run the universities, a point denied vehemently by many of these same men—F., E.—a few months before. But all of the petitions were gratifying, since they showed a new assumption about the camp's permanence and possibly even its right to exist. Hibernation House was Little Israel up there in the New Hampshire hills. As for relations between the comrades and myself, they seemed to grow warmer in those next days, as if I were a patient or penitent slowly recovering, needing tender care. (Roxanne, a tough ugly black woman of thirty, who hadn't spoken a friendly sentence to me in three months, now voluntarily brought me tea and a sandwich in bed when my ear hurt too much for me to get up.) I had played doctor for so long, as I have indicated, that the role of patient was consoling. At least that's what I told myself while I concentrated on my long-range interpretations.

I continued also my accustomed planning for the camp, again taking my cue from the ritual. It was clear that play with feces was no humorous matter, but deeply offensive and alarming to the professors. A matter of cultural heritage and toilet-training. Antics could be planned here, a mixture of subtle pressures and dangerous pleasures. Playing with turds in their sandboxes; the end of privacy in single toilets; some playful diapering by the female guards after bowel movements; a return perhaps to the language of childhood for feces. Hadn't Kove himself at one point told me the kind of curious pleasure he had found, once he got beyond self-consciousness, in playing with sand, water, and mud for a few hours a week? When I announced such thoughts at the weekly meeting of wardens, they were given hearty approval. Though it seemed to me the thrust of the satisfaction in that meeting room, with Mao and Che and Malcolm X looking down from the walls, was different from the way I presented it, more angrily sadistic than playful and experimental. I declared so, but it was countered that I was not envisioning the complete logic of my proposal, which they had.

It was at the end of that first week after the snow incident, and I was lying propped in my bed late at night, reading and idly thinking, when I heard a faint approach on the stairs. It produced in me a sudden pleasing and controlled fury, and I got out my revolver from the night table. The first black or Puerto Rican head I saw I was going to blow up; it was as simple as that. A low knock came instead. I was perplexed and didn't move. The knock sounded again, and I barely heard my name called. My mechanical joy of a moment ago vaporized into perspiring bewilderment. I crept out of bed in my pajamas, and ran silently to the door, standing behind it. Another knock, and then a whisper, "Lenny, can you hear me? Are you asleep?" I still didn't answer, uncertainly familiar with the voice.

Finally, I reached across and slid the bolt from the latch and leaned back again behind the door, terrified.

The doorknob turned, the door squeaked open slowly, and the curly-haired head of A. poked through. "Lenny? Are you here?" he whispered, and stole in his nightshirt into the room. Following him stealthily were B. and Kovell, all in their stockinged feet.

"What is it?" I asked, as Kove closed the door.

They turned in a circle, startled.

A tense moment of stillness ensued.

"Put the gun away, for godsakes!" commanded B.

I obeyed, weakly lowering it.

In the crepuscular light of the double-gabled bedroom, at 2:10 A.M., the three professors looked like a humorous routine in their garb, A. in his Victorian nightshirt, Kove in a maroon-and-gold football outfit, B. in a striped terrycloth robe, a boxer's relic. The Three Stooges performing in a nihilist play.

A. removed from his shirt somewhere an off-print pamphlet

and held it up, brandishing it slowly, like an attorney presenting key evidence.

It grew more bizarre and ludicrous.

"Kovell found this on your shelf the other day," A. began. He adjusted his wire glasses and read, " 'An Analysis of Technique in Chekhov's "Anyuta," ' by Leonard Pincus, *Studies in Short Fiction*, Winter 1969. And under Contributors' Notes, it says about the author, 'Mr. Pincus is completing his junior year at Cardozo College and has an article forthcoming in *Sewanee Review* on *Great Expectations*.' Not bad for an undergraduate, Lenny. Furthermore, I read the piece last night and found that, except for the opening paragraph of bull, it was first-rate right down the line. It had real University of Chicago excellence to it."

If they had sneaked in at 2 A.M. to recite a Zen sutra or announce the bar mitzvah of a nephew, it would have made as much sense.

"Here, look at it," and A. handed me the yellow offprint, with my handwritten gratitude to Kove on the cover ("It's awful of you to make me publish these things").

I sunk, bewildered, into the green upholstered chair, Kovell gently taking my gun and putting it on the bureau.

Just then the door opened, the robust body of D. barged in, bickering began about his sudden appearance, and I stared dumfounded at a nostalgic prize of Lenny Pincus's youth.

B. broke from the squabble and turned to me, his face alive with eagerness for the first time in weeks. "Look, man, anyone who can produce that at your age doesn't want all this. You should be back there, with literature. Writing literary reviews for *The New Republic*, say, for a beginning. You had to write those essays out of love. Kovell said they weren't produced for any class, but just because you got excited about Chekhov and Dickens."

What were they getting at? What did they want? The silly offprint stayed in my lap, an irritant.

"Call it off, Lenny. Stop the whole thing. Get yourself out, and us. This is what you want to do, battle with books and write about them." B., crouching, tapped the offprint.

Stop it? How?

"You're a literary boy, Lenny, a literary boy," pleaded A.,

by my shoulder. "They don't make them any more. I've seen your generation, I know. The breed is vanishing, it's a rapidly extinct species. Today's kids do movies or rock music, you know that. Don't throw your special talent away."

The group gathered around me as if we were huddling to plan a tricky play. Kneeling and sitting, with Kove standing a few steps back.

I was confused by the strangeness and offered, feebly, "How . . . how'd you get up here?"

"Forget that for now," spoke up Kovell, moving closer. "This is what we're talking about." He took up the article and began reading aloud, a paper that he had spent half a day correcting before allowing me to send it in.

A simple story, it is interesting in showing that before Chekhov proceeded to chisel his "artless" fictions, he was busy learning how to master the basic ingredients of "artful" storymaking. This meant learning about his materials and tools—wholesale strategies as well as nouns and verbs—how he might use them in the service of his vision. It is a stage in an artist's development when technique is as paramount as substance, if not more important; for technical competence in art is an acquired skill (through endless hours and pages of revision), whereas subject matter is much more of a "natural" heritage. That "Anyuta" is, let us say, assured now of its place in relative anonymity (because of the many great stories in the Chekhov canon) may be beneficial to the critic interested in analyzing technique; for technique here is more exposed, more observable than in later work. It is perhaps axiomatic that one can learn more about an author's battle with technique from his years of apprenticeship, when work is skeletal and flawed, than from his work as a master, when form and content are welded firmly together, almost inextricably. Imperfection and even failure have their uses for the critic as well as for the artist.

I squirmed, as if Kove were reading a dirty confession of mine. The language and interest struck me as so odd, so curious. He was still reading in a quiet voice, crouching down, looking at me every so often. I tried to smile, embarrassed.

The temporal sense then, to begin with, determines the structure of "Anyuta," breaking it up into five discernible blocks of action. The "present" is not one continuous line of action, flowing smoothly and uninterruptedly; it starts, stops, then starts again. In other words, each time we return to it, it has been modified in one way or another (by the character's or the reader's new knowledge or feelings); modified at first by the past, then by the future. It is constantly being revised, changed. Such dislocations of time are clearly unusual and even precarious in so brief a story (four pages). As we shall see, they reflect aspects of technique that serve as forces of literary liberation in terms of character and thematic development.

I asked Kove to stop. He said it was almost done. I asked him again. He looked at me, then returned to the text, a prosecutor proceeding with incriminating evidence. He read on and on. Finally, like a doctor seeing his patient in pain, he announced that it was the last paragraph.

Put another way, what one feels at the end is no less than that special sort of savagery that only civilized human beings are capable of. Crueler than the primitive sort that is dependent on physical torture, civilized savagery violates another's soul, manipulates another's psyche. That Klockkov is a potent physician and that his friend is an artist are a secondary irony (useful for thematic purposes, unnecessary for the soundness of effect of the story itself). They serve to remind us that a man is neither protected nor defined by the titles or rewards conferred upon him by society, that those to whom we refer frequently as society's saviors—in this case the doctors and artists—may be in person humanity's enemies, cruel and venal individuals. Superior as professionals, inferior as men—it is a contradiction that Chekhov sensed so acutely in "Anyuta," one that our own age knows only too well. On this level, "Anyuta" strikes me as a small but relevant parable.

Kovell looked up, finished and pleased.

" 'Forces of literary liberation in terms of character and thematic development,' " repeated B. "*That's* your bag, Len."

"Civilized savagery, not the primitive sort," added A.

I breathed hard, trapped, hot.

D. broke the torture by grabbing my knees suddenly. "And the thing is, Pinky, that you've won, you've won! Most of us have become convinced *here* of the *urgency* of changing things and stopping the present order. Not everyone of course," and he glanced around, "but most of us realize how authentic, how angry, you all are, and how immediately pressing are the national dangers. We've changed to some extent, believe me. I, at least," he fumbled for the right phrase, his face red with enthusiasm, white hair wild, "am prepared to do extreme things. Take up arms, perhaps!"

More modestly A. approved. "Yes, to a certain extent we've changed."

After a moment's pause, B. spoke up authoritatively. "Others have felt differently, *quite* differently. I, for one, have excused no blow or humiliation for some *higher good*. And I'll add something else. There's even a right wing developed here among us that thinks even harsher of you than I myself do—which is harsh enough. I mean you personally. Let's face it, you've driven us with very little letup or mercy. And they're angry. Only, instead of being angry at the society"—and here B. glanced at the last speakers firmly—"they're angry at you, Pincus, and out to get you."

Out to get me? How? With words, did he mean?

"There are schlemiels in every group," retorted D. "They were there in the thirties and forties, and they'll be around in the seventies."

"I don't think this is the moment to start arguing again," interceded Kove.

"We better go," said A. "You understand me, I hope. Get us out somehow, and yourself too. Think about it, and we can talk more. We can plan together." He took my hand, sending shivers up my back. "You can't stay split for too much longer, Len, without breaking down. The boy who wrote this about Chekhov is a boy on *our* side as much as *theirs*. Remember."

He stared at me for half a minute, and stood up, the others joining him.

"A victory, I tell you, nothing short of a victory," D. leaned to repeat, "I want to write about it and let the other adults know. Wait till M. hears, it'll bring him back to America! We mean business; at least I do. No more inertia! You've rejuvenated me and I thank you." He was kissing me again!

They were leaving quietly.

"Kove, wait just a minute, huh?"

He turned and motioned to the others to go on. He came back into the darkened room, and I stood up and walked back and forth. I didn't talk, and after a few minutes I noticed him sit down and hold up a pack of cigarettes. It was a few seconds before I realized he was waiting for permission to smoke. I stared angrily and nodded.

The evening wouldn't leave my head, so that I could say what I wanted to say. Especially D.'s words about victory.

I walked back and forth, counting the ten steps eight times between the small mahogany writing table at the far window and the space between the bed and the sloped wall.

"What's up? I don't have all night," said Kovell. "I have to be up at 5:30."

I smiled to myself and turned to face him. "Of course," I said. "I'm sorry for all the melodrama. This has been silly. Anyway, this is what I wanted to tell you." I shook my head, in self-reprimand. "It's not that important to me any more."

I pulled up a straight wooden chair, sat down facing him, and proceeded to make a full confession of the murder.

Interestingly, I found it easier to tell it in the third person, referring to Lenny rather than I. It was easy that way to insert small criticisms of the murder and the murderer, which I did frequently. I spoke without rancor or guilt or pain, but narrated the tale with a calm, even casualness, that surprised me. It was as if I was describing a course I had taken, which hadn't worked out.

Kovell, who had listened in silence during the confession, sat back in the chair when it was finished and smoked.

I didn't understand his apparent nonchalance.

461

He proceeded slowly to ask me questions in a firm but detached manner. Very specific questions.

This pleased me, and I answered as best I could. What was fascinating—and I told him so—was the way an interrogator expected you to remember every single detail about a brief episode that had happened months ago.

"I only came to kill the guy, not to memorize the scene." I smiled.

He didn't, but put the same questions in different ways. No, of course I didn't find out the names of the couple in the hallway. Was this the same revolver that I had shot Mailer with? I almost laughed, he was really a child. No, no, that .38 automatic was disposed of long ago. Where? Dropped from the B.U. bridge into the Charles, attached to a lead pipe. How many minutes did it take from the moment of the first shot to the moment when I left the suite, the victim dead? How did I know, I replied. Ten, I speculated, maybe less, maybe a little more. But why did I stay so long? We were talking, I said impatiently. His brows lifted perceptibly. What did I do afterward, whom was I with, who saw me, where did I stay? I explained, I walked back to my apartment—my friend's, he was out of town—no one saw me, and I stayed alone for the whole night and perhaps the next day, I forget.

I thought I detected a flicker of condescension on his mouth, but it passed quickly and he returned to his questions, beginning with the afternoon.

After a few of these, I grew exasperated by his obstinacy and finally said I had had enough. It was nearly 3:30! Yet curiously, I had enjoyed the session immensely. I liked talking with Kovell again, and, for some reason, it was exhilarating to describe the murder to someone. It was the first time I had talked about it, and I realized I had stored up a mountain of memories, criticisms, and reflections.

Kovell stood, put out his cigarette casually, and said, "I don't believe you."

His smile was almost scornful, for wasting his time. I wanted to shoot him.

"Why?" I pleaded, almost frantic. "Why not?"

"You don't know enough about it, and at other points you know too much. For a starter."

The arrogant fool. The stupid arrogant fool.

He started to walk out when I suddenly remembered something and called to him to hold on.

In my closet, buried beneath window screens and shoes, I found the shoebox I wanted and untied it. From beneath the small Giacometti sculpture, held from the Berg Art Museum, I removed Mailer's silver razor. With controlled glee, I handed it to the Dean, explaining what it was.

"You could have gotten this anywhere, from an antique shop, from a junkyard, or even from the real murderer," he explained, twirling the object once and setting it down on my chair. "Get me the F.B.I. on the phone and I'll check it out with them. Until then, I'll remain unconvinced."

He paused. "You haven't murdered yet, but you might one day. The way you're going. And then it will be too late. You won't be so calm and collected about remembering such an event, the way you are now. No, right now you're a young man who's finally grown tired of mocking others and has now begun to mock himself. It's the last abyss of self-contempt. What's next may be real disaster, a real killing. Then it's all over. The Chekhov in you will be dead as a doornail and you'll be an animal."

He walked to the door, opened it cautiously. He turned back momentarily. "I'm sorry for you despite my anger. If I can be of help, you know where you can find me." And he left, sneaking out silently.

I decided that I would find out how they had gotten up there and punish them accordingly.

But by the time dawn came, that thought had long since passed. The house had squeaked from wind and age, and the storm windows and wooden shutters had banged all night, accompanying my confusions and rent loyalties. The mountaintops were snow-covered and wrapped in gray-blue rings of fog, a morning ambiguous and deceptive, out of some Chinese landscape scroll. Like the ancient one in the Fogg, perhaps.

At breakfast I asked Luis to call an impromptu meeting of wardens, and at 10:30 I was in the pine-paneled powwow room, addressing Monroe, Joshua, Luis, Addie, Kepfner, and others. I had never before been so conscious of the room's environment as

I was then—giant rubber plants, two fish tanks, South American masks, and African drums. And, on the walls, alongside highway STOP signs and subway-train "AA" and "New Lots Avenue" mementos, were blowup posters of Jimi Hendrix, Fanon, Roberto Clemente, William Du Bois. An arrangement of homage to primitive energy which made me fumble an introduction and remain as nervous as when I first spoke to the prisoners downstairs. That new energy—undifferentiated, unfocused, unleashing itself—worked upon me as I spoke, a visceral adversary to my words and logic.

"These prisoners are the best men around, that's what I think we ought to remember," I said softly. "They're complicated organisms, like very fine clocks, and therefore they can't be treated as if they were Vice Presidents, attorney generals, or other crude items. Look, one way of looking at these men is that it's taken some two thousand years of hard work to make them what they are now; that's a long, long labor process. So we just have to be careful, even delicate in . . . tampering with them. Understand me, I'm saying this as much to myself as to you, for I've been just as responsible, if not more. I've acted . . . crudely, insufficiently. It's like having a million dollars' worth of hi-fi equipment—you just don't want to go banging it around casually. Our accomplishment here has been precisely in choosing sophisticated men rather than ordinary citizens and national leaders. Wouldn't it, therefore, be a great shame to have these fellows here and not to come up with some sort of . . . philosophical therapy which matches their complexity? And matches our own rich desires? That's really what I'm asking us to consider, to reflect upon. Do you see what I mean?"

And just as it hit me how much those prisoners meant to me, Joshua, Monroe, and Tyrone walked out.

I gazed at Addie smoking, Luis fidgeting, a fellow named Walker doodling. There was an awkward minute of silence.

"You're missing it, man," drawled this Walker, a big fellow with a handsome mustache. "You're too snowed by those cats. Cool it."

"They're just schoolteachers, you know," said Addie kindly. "No use making them into gods, Lenny."

I appreciated the use of my name. Catching sight of Kepfner, I said to him, "Don't you think one Einstein is worth ten peasants? Come on, be honest, be realistic."

"No," replied Kepfner, peering at me steadily, *"we* don't. That's the whole point. One peasant is as valuable to us as one Einstein. It's the only way we'll ever get peasants one day to become Einsteins."

"Would it make a difference if I used clerk or rabbi?" I responded impatiently. "And there's no such thing as *Einsteins*, that's the whole point of what I was trying to say."

"You're off the track," Kepfner asserted, closed his folder, and left.

No more rational arguments, I recalled. A force versus reason, say.

"You're upset by the other day, baby," spoke Addie, standing. "Calm down, take off for a while. Maybe you need a change." Her smile was sympathetic, her face dark brown, warm.

The wardens passed by me, talking to themselves casually, and departed the room.

I stood numb. Luis, holding his cat, was motioning me to the far wall, and I followed his urging. There, touching my shoulder, he said, "Remember this?"

I stared at the small framed poster I had made, in imitation of a college diploma, and placed there the first week. It read, in my large script,

> To speak plainly, it is necessary to become really angry in order that things may be better.
>
> —Nietzsche.

My cheeks burned.

Luis's face was smooth beneath his glum fedora when I looked up at him. He stroked his friend. In his melodious accent, he said, "Maybe you're losing your anger, Pincus. Maybe you need to get it back."

I nodded in a daze, thinking about a quote, some quote, from Chekhov to put up on that wall. And wouldn't D. testify to my anger?

"Forget that 'complexity.' Forget those thousands-of-years shit. They're gone, man, gone. And we're here. The brothers and sisters. That past is shit. It no longer counts. Just like those pictures you helped to cut up and destroy. Just get angry, brother, and you'll be well again."

I walked off, thinking of "well again." And "shit." Anger and feces equaled health somehow.

I was weak but satisfied. Solid defeat. I saw for sure that I had to get away, to think things through. A furlough away from the pressures of the combat zone, where now there were two armies to contend with instead of one. And how confusing to be disliked and distrusted by one's colleagues, while being relied upon by one's enemies. I'd get away.

D.'s praise from the night before sung in my ears in a steady mock refrain. It was countered by Luis's cutting words and touch. I'd have to outrace both.

In my room. Will replacing energy, I began to pack some things. It was gratifying to be on the run again, I thought. I enjoyed with delight the image of my friends' and enemies' faces when they found me missing.

Of course, I did no such foolish thing, but told Luis during the afternoon that I thought I'd take up their recent suggestion and leave for a little while. He took the news easily, not at all surprised, cleaning his teeth, and said it was a good thing. He even reminded me to have some fun. His look was openly sincere, and I thanked him, feeling once again that ambiguous bond between us settling on the trusting side.

The day before, it turned out, the news had broken about the camp in the Boston newspapers, as we had anticipated. The reason we returned Grace was, first, you didn't want an innocent mother kidnapped, then they'd really be after your ass; and, second, I had the thought of showing our financial backers some proof of our . . . success. Operating Hibernation House was not unlike trying to get a play to Broadway—the publicity could be useful for obtaining more financial aid.

Of course, we had taken necessary precautions, driving Grace blindfolded on an eighteen-hour trip up through Quebec (where we ate in a French-speaking restaurant), and then back down again, so the papers were hot about the camp being in Canada somewhere.

The *Globe* headline ran:

In any case, the *Globe* didn't give out any real truth—out of fear
for Kovell? or because Grace couldn't herself admit the details?—but told in vague generalities about "dreadful ceremonies
of humiliation and perverse classroom lessons." It sounded like a
routine night in the theater.

But old Pinky was back in the news, this time as the "youthful Rasputin and Guevara rolled into one, and masterminding this
incredible incident in American history." I read this with some
amusement, pressured as I was to leave the hills the next morning.
Che and Rasp had become more like Huckleberry.

We needed more accurate news, I saw. A national television
crew to come up and document "A Day in the Life of the Professors." It was one thing for us to film in our amateurish 8-mm
way, for special private purposes; quite another for a regular
ABC or CBS team to go to work in the interests of the general
populace. Live action, if it were possible, was the best arrangement. Live-action TV, especially if it could be advertised in
advance, not only would be a dramatic and educational first, it
would attract, I imagined, a wide wide audience. "Pincus and His
Bandits," for an hour of prime time, might be as good as "Broadway Joe and His Jets." The fantastic made into the actual; little
criminals-at-work; prisoners of Civil War II shown into suburban
living rooms. Narrated by Cosell, Meredith. Not bad. What
better way to raise consciousness *and* funds? Not to mention the
station's Nielsen ratings. An hour like that could easily compete
with "The F.B.I." or some other fictional crime show. Naturally,
careful advanced preparations were necessary—blindfolds and
checkpoints, security guarantees and secrecy promises, etc.—but
it could be done. And should be done. Cronkite coming to the
hills of New Hampshire at the request of Pincus—whom he had
once interviewed in New York City at his, Walter's, request—
would be more of a coup than our President going to meet Chou.
And after all, wasn't it only fair that I, a native radical, share
equal media time with that foreign mandarin-revolutionary? And
Hibernation House with the Great Wall?

The day was sunny, but the evening grew harsh as the wind

gathered and the snow began falling. Yet, perhaps because I knew I was departing soon, perhaps for other reasons, I was more restful and at peace than I had been in weeks, with the small exception of the earache which had lingered on, unnecessarily, I thought.

7. Zshaba; Over and Out

February 4

Fantasies of self-transformation in the air. Persons hoping to escape their own masks and try on someone else's. Authentic Babbitts playing at bohemians, fashion designers at rebels. Thoughts inspired by the Mt. Washington weathercaster on TV. Devilish sideburns, long hair, mustache, dapper double-breasted blazer. Was he Edwardian actor? *Esquire* model? No, just plain Tommy Gorman, citing barometer pressure, shifting cold fronts, snow outlook. A New Hampshire weatherman "dressing up," now that it was permitted and called for. Like the excitable children of a few years back who called themselves by that name.

I, who've caused some disturbances in the New England region, feel old-fashioned. Wanting no one else's mask, but grimly accepting my own. Using a mask as disguise only, a conscious actor for a day, a month. Like my tie and suit. Or the pseudonym *Zshaba*, my occasional alias lately.

February 5

Tommy was accurate, a fierce snow-and-sleet storm this morning, as I drove down to Cambridge. Instead of the three-hour trip, a scary five hours. Through slush, freezing sleet, icy tire grooves. Forty mph tops. No heat in Kove's 1962 Mercedes. Forced to stop periodically to wipe windshield and move my feet. James (Henry) was right, New England weather juvenile.

Life on Interstate 93 lethal. First accident occurs twenty minutes out, a green Porsche turned upside down and smoking, a huge white station wagon perpendicular to it, nose into the island, smashed; a man bleeding on the ground, a woman in shock helped by two policemen. Forced to watch it up close, at 15 mph, like slow motion. Another accident twenty miles later, as neat rectangles of hay dot the slushy road, stopping autos in their tracks, some nicely, others not. Two truckers running back from their open-backed tarpaulin-covered truck to retrieve bundles, see who's injured. A scene out of a war-torn country (perhaps), with bundles looking like relief drops.

Radio for escape from highway blood-and-death brings in intermittent beeping and cracking voices. More astronauts on the moon, doing EVA, says the announcer repeatedly. (The way he puts it, extravehicular activity sounds like lunar-sodomy.) The banalities of the talk contrast with those sharp tongues of the professors, and I turn it off. If the Cronkites are for America, those prisoners should be for the moon. Then we could contrast the progress of the two spheres in a few decades.

Soon visions of Kahn (not Johanna) transform the landscape. The sky bursting blinding white, showers of radioactive dust falling invisibly; Chevrolets and Pontiacs, containing families, stopped on the smoking asphalt, mangled, burning, charred.

The small car becomes a miniature nuclear accelerator, and I'm in the center, smashed by atoms of uncertainty and fear. Does Cambridge mean freedom, New Hampshire, victory? I smile and perspire.

Arrive late afternoon at Hancock Place, this winter's digs. Ear acting up after being good on the road. On the B.U. FM station, around seven, I hear a snatch of a curious record, about a concentration camp during World War II. I call them up, find out the name, and promise myself to buy it. Dinner is peanut butter and jelly, a banana, and milk. I try to settle down with Faulkner.

February 7

At twilight out walking the slushy ghetto trails behind Mass. Ave., Green, Franklin, and Kinnaird Streets. I pass by the battered house of Melissa, an old Kove girl. As I walk on, I suddenly have an inspiration and change directions. At the Square, two radicals hawking newspapers sneer at my suit and tie when I refuse their wares.

Sophie, dark-faced, hair up, in pink wool sweater, greets me warmly, after breaking through the beard to recognize me. In her neat living room/study, painted bright orange and white, a

469

change from Kove's days, we chat over coffee. The comfort of bookshelves, typed pages, paperbacks, a respectable household working. She tells me about dissertation (on the painter Vermeer), teaching. For no reason I start crying. After an awkward minute or two, she gathers me, cradling me to her full breasts. The affection and acceptance are better than sex. Tender feeling, so long missing in me, surges up. A conversation with Sophie from the past, in which she reminded me above all to be true to myself, flashes by. Which self? I want to ask now. She's forty or so but might as well be twenty: she's that alert, open, curious. Expressive eyes, wonderful dark hair, a brown birthmark beneath her left eye.

At about midnight she makes me a chicken liver omelet, and I feel like a mandarin. It's a hundred times better than feeling like the commissar.

Afterward I talk of the camp, though she hasn't prodded me about it. I explain how my interest has been serious games and complicated play, not bureaucratic pain or sadism, 1984-style. An effort to open the men up, to make them intellectual Robin Hoods, outlaws and rebels first in the service of the future society. Heady talk. She mentions the recent *Globe* article and wonders if there are other aims too? I shrug and look at a paperback (Ortega, *The Dehumanization of Art*).

Then I look back and answer that there are other aims and methods, and, yes, I've been responsible for those too. She nods and I say nothing of what's eating me.

Shrewdly she shifts the subject to an article on Mangaia, a South Sea island where the pleasure principle is still going strong. An interesting place to visit, I speculate. Didn't Melville love his Marquesas? And Kove dream of playing Roheim and going to meet the aborigines? Primitivism and intellectuals, a Pincus tour of the Cook Islands. For my playful imagination, she kisses me and says to count her in. But haven't we been having a similar tour up there in the hills? I think privately. Haven't we put the American version of aborigines next to the intellectual aristocrats?

Near 2 A.M., she hugs me goodbye warmly and says it was nice. May she see Kovell sometime? And me too again?

All across town I'm high with Sophie and think of the different 2 A.M. meetings I've been having lately.

Why not invite her back with me to New Hampshire, I wonder. It would be nice to have Sophie there, for a mistress even, in front of Kove. You could do wonders with the emotion of jealousy. And who knew what a steady dose of tenderness would do to Pincus? Already it was making him nervous and perverse.

February 12

A visit to the red-brick University Museum (at Harvard). Impressed by the room of prehistoric animals, ancient rhinos, two-horned dinosaur head, 42-foot-long kronosaurus, mastodon reconstructed. The white bones of extinction. In an adjoining room, stuffed African animals—zebras, horses, tigers, apes. One mountain gorilla, in particular, caught in 1926 in the jungles of the Congo, catches my attention. Five foot three, 450 pounds, pitch-black fur that drips like black crystal, insanely prognathous jaw, terrifying eyes. A mad brute, arms akimbo, about to thump his chest. Ancestor. And, I thought, namesake. Will I be in that glass cage one day, a specimen of guerrilla, five foot eight, 150 pounds, captured on the streets of Cambridge, 197– . . . One of the new armed policemen walks my way, and I move on.

In the attached Agassiz Museum (Comparative Zoology), I'm reminded of yet another Kove girl named Polly. Like footprints left across town, a kind of Lewis-and-Clark sex trail. Poor crazy Kove, better off where he is than out on the loose.

The Peabody (archaeology, anthropology) offers a fine collection of skulls on the fifth floor. In corridors, rooms, labs. Evolution of man, beginning with australopithecine, Java, Steinheim to Homo sapiens. How about Pincus Man, a rare deviant breed, destroyer of himself?

In a lab, a grad student records the data of Yemenite skulls from 1933, for no explicit purpose save *preservation*. A folly unique to the species.

And more skulls in the glass case. What a lovely little instrument, the brain. A few inches in diameter, no more than a few pounds in weight, yet responsible for the edifice called civilization. Not bad, the ratio between that size and its various productions.

Outside again, across the street, the vine-covered Center for International Affairs. Modern fluorescent lights and conference rooms, where they lend the government a hand in planning destruction. How convenient is American symbolism, one side of the street for preserving the species, the other for liquidating it.

While up the street sat squat Busch-Reisinger Museum, closed and bandaged, a casualty of the culture wars.

A quiet little street called Divinity Street. Truly Dead End.

A trip to take my mind off pressing questions works nicely the other way. Emphasizes them.

February 13

Mid-afternoon at Trowbridge and Broadway, across the street from Cambridge High and Latin School, Lizzie Forbes appears. By the greasy sub sandwich shop, a high-school hangout. With white boots, miniskirt, black leather jacket, yellow leer. A little gun moll pushing H. Greets me with casual, "Hiya, lover boy, long time no see." Tells me Nugget is back in town, left school, eager to see me. And informs me, with her nose for carnal news, that "that Dean cat" who's my pal likes "young pussy" so I might want to take Nugget back for him. She winks. Our Iago. Invites me to come around sometime to see her (Liz) myself; to make up for lost chances last time. And goes off to peddle her horse. Trembling, I walk off, wondering what Salem trial she's escaped from? Or is she Hawthorne's Pearl, updated one hundred years?

Television back home to shake off the spell. Scenes of new Laotian refugee families, out on a desolate plain, waiting for delivery somewhere. The camera pans to an eight-year-old boy, bandage across his eyes, being led by his teen-age sister, then a desperate mother searching for her child. And a close-up of an American colonel talking of "resettlement camps." The language reminds me of Liz's, dirty in a special native way.

Why not Lizzie for Kovell, while I board with Sophie? Not bad, Len, I think, scrambling eggs (with more beans).

My fantasies fill me with perverse amusement and self-loathing.

February 14

A double bill at the Orson Welles Cinema. Packed house. One cowboy, the other a gangster, called "sleepers." This means the killings were missed by aficionados. I stopped counting at fourteen in the Wayne movie (*Rio Bravo*). In the lobby later, a bearded professor teaching film at Tufts (I hear) talks to students about director's "love of pastoral" and "use of lighting" to hypnotize audience. Hilarious. The killings do the hypnotizing. Gangsters, shoot-'em-ups, lurid thrillers—an American way of life. How convenient (for my hopes) that the popular imagery is now infiltrating the academic world. M-G-M come to M.I.T., Bogart to Harvard. For the American mind, the real desperadoes, criminals, and the fictional players merged and mixed, Wayne, Earp, Steiger, Capone, Dillinger, Cagney, Billy the Kid, Newman. These were the real heroes of the land, stamped so by celluloid. The true Underground heroes. Lenny Pincus, with his naïve philosophical killing and intellectuals' kidnapping, was small-time stuff next to those serious killers.

No wonder I felt emphatically native back there, outside the Commander.

Would they make a movie of my life too? Enshrine me in celluloid into the permanent folklore of the land? Who would play me, Dustin Hoffman? Perhaps even, if I were still alive, I could help the actor with the part. Tell him what it's like, for real. So what if the large screen turned the sickening and the crazy into the pretty and the glamorous? It would be a useful illusion, useful propaganda for types like me.

February 17

Teach-ins at several universities—usually a combination of high-school debate, P.T.A. meeting, fundamentalist service. At Sanders Theater again I sit and listen to the words; it's a good place to think and plan, or forget, among the peasant-students and mandarin-professors.

Usual rhetoric bath, save for the Southern journalist who talks about *redemption* of the land and the people with particular fervor. Quentin Compson returned to Harvard. Then, in an answer to a question about me and my actions, he says that he believes I am basically "a religious boy," searching for "a way to believe." And that my "soul," like America's, needs to be saved if the country is to survive.

How nice of him. I'm moved and flattered. And appreciate

473

the preacher's innocence. Lenny Pincus, Cambridge Nietzchean and part-time psychopath, deemed worthy of redemption and compassion by that romantic journalist. Move over, Raskolnikov, here I come!

But later, on channel 4, the twentieth century and America returned. There were five stories. One, a piece of pipeline that had been held up as evidence of military success a week ago, turned out to be fraudulent. Two, the head of a labor union was being indicted for embezzling union funds. Three, an eminent army general was accused of having run a blackmarket and illegal PX operation, involving bribery, kickbacks, prostitution, blackmail. Four, six L.A. policemen had violated the constitutional rights of five persons in critical situations, while several others were involved in "mistaken" killings of an unarmed black Vietnam veteran and a Chicano newspaperman. Five, the governor of California, in order to balance his budget, cut back on money and welfare to poor people, closing down immediately hospitals and nursing homes.

Why did the news intrude in one's private thoughts constantly? Couldn't there be a letup?

Could any man of our country, any humane and honest citizen, believe in authority any longer? Was there any institution or group, moral, religious, or political, whose authority had not become absurd and discredited? Was there a more obscene noun in the English language today than "authority," especially government authority?

Did the country really have a soul any longer to save?

February 18

The morning *Globe* had a story about one hundred coeds from Northwestern University who answered an ad in the student paper concerning a "scientific experiment" to test the sexual consequences of spanking. It turned out that the man who placed the ad was an ex-convict, that he had no credentials to prove his scientific interest, and that the laboratory was his motel room. Despite this, said the AP, not one of the girls backed out of the proposition. Nice. It made my own doings with Nugget and Liz seem like cookie-jar raiding. With morning coffee in our land came sports, jokes, and Dostoevsky. So long as your reading material was not the *Times*. Then you got no jokes and all the Piety and Earnestness that was fit to print.

At three o'clock I found myself with Lizzie and some of her pals, wandering through Memorial Hall. Amid the aisles of that huge examination hall, observing the marble busts of past Harvard dignitaries staring down from inlaid pedestals. Emerson and Lowell face each other across the hall. Next through Sanders, across the corridor, with the little band of street kids. (I've shown a Harvard ID to the custodian, who tells me about meeting Adlai Stevenson and Diana Ross and "other famous celebrities.") Soon there's dancing on the stage with the aid of a transistor. Then sister Liz, climbing on the marble arm of Josiah Quincy, a past president of the place, gives a little speech (at my request). A speech in sharp contrast to last night's teach-in religion and government sham. About growing up in America. Blunt, vicious, honest, mad. Against Mom and schools for "laying a lot of shit on you." Not very different from the "shit" (favorite word) the government "gives in Ve-etnam." The only thing to do is to "spit at them" and "go off with an upper." Or become "a Bokononist." Otherwise, they'll "fuck up your minds and waste your bods."

A wonderful package of venom and dirt, I think, as I leave the assembly hall. She ought to have gone on Mailer's "Tough Guy" show, he would have appreciated her.

Meanwhile, I'm hot again with a plan for fun.

February 19–23

January thaw arrives a month late down here.

Days of scholarly research into local history archives at the Cambridge Public Library, Unitarian and Christ churches, local historians. The only way to discover the real past.

February 24

Exciting prank night.

While rock band plays in Sanders to packed house, we go to work in the Old Burial Grounds just off the Square. An exchange of marble busts for slate tombstones; Lowell and Emerson for Neptune Frost and Cato Stedman, black slaves from colonial days buried with their masters. Exalted Yankees for anonymous and

475

forgotten boys. An act of democracy which I imagine Emerson would have okayed. Though his marble face looks stark, severe, authoritative as I lower him.

Three cadres do the digging, with Nugget at my side in pea jacket, black sweater, snug dark corduroys. My graveyard digger, who's developed a twitch in her face. The rest of the diggers are an assorted lot from high school and college; plus an A.W.O.L. GI and a draft resister. A nice mixed crew.

(John Adams once described the insurrectionists who attacked the British with snowballs and were shot in return this way: "a motley rabble of saucy boys, negroes and mulattoes, Irish teagues and outlandish Jack Tars." Well, the rabble had changed, into saucy coeds and teenybopper Teagues, A.W.O.L. Jack Tars and outlandish Jew boys, (free) angry blacks and High Church blondes. And dumping tea had now changed into snatching tombstones. So I amused myself, as the rabble went off to Mem Hall to celebrate.)

While I took my teen-age doe to Christ Church for some private celebrating. On the red-velvet pew benches, by light of a flashlight. And slim Nugget down on the kneeler, on her knees, face flushed. Very disturbing moments even for perverse Pincus.

George Washington, an old Christ Church–goer, and a pretty good lover himself, would have appreciated the night's work, I think. You can't beat clever plans and patient execution. Any general knew that, Pincus or Washington.

February 25

Buchenwald comes to Hancock Place.

My record arrives at Coop. The one that I had first heard a few weeks back, on the B.U. station. Edward R. Murrow's World War II reports. Murrow lean and aristocratic, in leather gloves and fine raincoat and hat, getting into London taxi on boxed-set jacket. A handsome prelude to disaster times.

The titles of the pieces on inside cover impress me: "Children evacuated from London." "On rooftop during airraid." "D-day." And the section I'm interested in, which I heard a piece of on the radio, "Buchenwald, April 15, 1945." I turn to this first and listen to it. Startled. Yet puzzled. Without quite knowing why.

A walk in the bright winter sun. Turning cold again. Newspapers filled with headlines of the night previous: BOSTON TEA PARTY TWO HUNDRED YEARS LATER? (*Globe*). PINKY ON THE LOOSE AGAIN IN CAMBRIDGE! Absconds with Ralph Waldo Emerson and James Russell Lowell! (*Herald Traveler–Record American*).

Late afternoon, some student marauders arrive to tell me of the fun at Mem Hall. Roosevelt Johnson from Texas, now a freshman at Cardozo, does the talking. The ceremony of the tombstones was followed by dancing and playing (in Gilbert-and-Sullivan costumes, discovered in balcony). With music piped in from Sanders, according to plan. Smooth, he smiled widely. "Colonel Johnson," I call him, and he refers to me as "General Pincus." A nice change-over from colonial days when the officers were respectable gentlemen, white and Waspy.

The other four kids had been listening to rock, and I decided to try them on Murrow. The sonorous voice, the pontifical generalizations, the soapy rhetoric. And then Buchenwald again. It lasted about eight minutes and was framed in majestic tones of warning at beginning ("If you're having lunch now, you may want to turn off the radio . . . for I propose to tell you about Buchenwald"), and noble realism at end ("I pray you to believe what I have said about Buchenwald. I have reported what I saw and heard. . . . If I have offended you by this rather mild account, I am not in the least sorry"). And during those seven other minutes, there was more "realism": about the ghastly smells, the human bodies piled like cordwood, the walking skeletons, the tattooed numbers, the starving children, two men crawling toward a latrine ("I saw it . . . but I won't describe it"). The statistics too were impressive all over again, five thousand killed in March (the last month), nine hundred a day when the camp was operating at full efficiency, at least sixty thousand during the history of the camp. "Men from all over," said Murrow, "Frenchmen and Czechs, Poles and Germans. Men who helped build America," he declared with controlled anger.

A bell-bottomed boy said, "Man, those cats had a *down* experience, didn't they?" And a pug-nosed girl, chewing gum, offered, "Those Euro-peans almost went "out of business."

"Cats" and "Europeans" struck me suddenly. And I went through the record again, paying astonishing attention to phrases like "A Frenchman came up to me, a professor from the Sorbonne" and "This man, the mayor of Prague." And finally, "Dr. Paul Heller, a Czech doctor at the camp, offered to show me the courtyard." A *Czech* doctor? A *French* professor? A *Polish* writer? What about that other word: "Jew?" Where was it? The word, the name that united all these men, women, and children? Had this "tough" courageous reporter thought it too impolite, too vulgar for Americans at home that day? Or was it unnecessary? Then why mention that the jailors were Nazis? That too then was unnecessary. But that fact was given. Jews, Mr. Murrow, that was the heart of the matter. Without that, it was all meaningless. But he didn't mention it. Was that preserving history or distorting it? And what about all those Gentile Americans out there, eating lunch, what would they think Buchenwald was all about—only European horror, like the young teenagers sitting around now? (Perhaps some giant billboards of Sophie holding up her Auschwitz jacket and barbed wire could be placed at certain points, for reminders? Like at drive-ins?)

Again I put needle to groove and replayed the ending. It turned out to be a paean to F.D.R., which I had missed before. How the "men at Buchenwald" had cheered for F.D.R. just a few days before his death. And how Churchill had told the reporter that the Americans were led by a great leader. A patriotic homage fit for the Broadway stage. A curious finale to this scene of genocidal evil, one of the great instances of systematic malignancy in man's history.

It was interesting, all right. Once again I had to learn about my government and history. Once more about euphemism and hypocrisy. Yet another time about the official discomfort with truth. The kids sat entranced as I explained my feelings.

The organized slaughter of Jews by Nazis was better swept under the rug. It was the American way. Like the piecemeal but steady slaughter of blacks and Indians by white Americans. That too had been obliterated, until recently. For hygiene and for comfort. The power of America to forget and to wipe the slate clean was impressive. In its own way more insidious than the hammer-and-sickle method, where the revised distortions of history were embarrassingly obvious.

As for Mr. Roosevelt and his image of hero-savior to the

Buchenwalders and many Americans, well, we all now knew that he was something less than that in relation to the Jews in the camps. In fact, we knew now that he, like Mr. Churchill, had behaved badly. Very badly. They just weren't interested when they had the chance, and when they were informed of what was going on, in saving those "men from all over Europe." They could care less about those . . .

Would some patrician Murrow come around to our camp in April 1975? The story might be different then, the black guards brutal, the Indian boys duped, the Jew leader an evil maniac. With an analysis by Sevareid about what can happen when an enraged minority group, especially children, take things into their own hands. No, our camp, like Buchenwald, called for a peasant not a patrician. A Mailer, say, not a Murrow. Someone who could tell the truth about dirt, shit, men in trouble. Someone to record the new approaching history—its violent excesses, its general disagreeableness, its sordid energy, its pent-up vengeance, its gallows humor, its *outsider chutzpah*. For the first time I recalled that Commander Hotel room with remorse, pity. For the victim and for the boy with the gun.

Kovell would have to replace Mailer and record our children's games and adolescent adventures. I'd ask him.

No, Buchenwald didn't exist for these kids, or for my other friends. History didn't exist either. (Or parents.) There was a point here. Boys and girls were freer now to do what they wished. They were not hampered by old events, old morals, or existing traditions. Luis knew this, and Addie too. Knew it instinctively. It was I who resisted this. Wrong training, bad upbringing. Pincus with his Chekhov, with his concern for old teachers and surrogate fathers. Pincus with his reading and *learning*. He hadn't as yet been able to let go fully and follow the flow of the new.

He would, he decided then, for sure. He would.

While Murrow intoned, the phone rang. And rang. Either Sophie, who was supposed to call back (about that trip north), or Nugget, whom I also had travel plans for. Maybe south.

But it was Addie from the camp instead. In her high sultry voice, she explained that something "heavy" had happened. A break yesterday. A. and G. had been caught; F. was hurt; Kovell had

479

escaped. She gave me some details about a chase through the woods and the proposed punishment for the prisoners, but I didn't listen too closely. *Kove out* was what I thought about. Intriguing. Well, good for him. Let's see how he'd handle his freedom.

Luis got on then and asked me if I knew anything about a revolver lost? The prisoners had a gun, it seemed. Of course I had mine? I shook my head, not knowing . . . Yes, I had mine, I lied. He said good and asked if I was enjoying myself. Sort of, I answered. Sort of. He'd see me soon then, and clicked off.

I was bewildered. The revolver. I hadn't seen it since . . . the late-evening visit of my literary guides. Kove put it on the bureau—Kove! So he too was a cunning thief. Everyone was. Okay.

The kids had finished off Buchenwald and were back to music. From hard history to hard rock; if only one day *I* could make that instant shift. Roosevelt and his blond girl were dancing slowly, and he smiled at me, wide and gleaming, a nice fellow. A group drummed and screamed, blasting monosyllables about rev-o-lution. Sweet almost.

I found myself packing in a distant room, trying to measure things. In a while, I heard the kids tire and split. I saw that I no longer knew how to measure. And where was I headed? I sat on my bed with a pair of socks and undershirt. I felt like a weary thousand pounds, couldn't keep myself from crying.

I had recovered and resolved, by the time Nugget came, about six. In long Afghan sheepskin, second-hand and raggedy, she looked sad, except for the ribbon in her hair that offset it and her worn looks. She had come a long way in a few months, all downhill. As we got into the streets to go for a bite to eat, she gave me a warm smile, and I couldn't help twisting her wrist. Her child's face turned to hurt and shock as I moved her to the car. Fine. She should rid herself of any new illusions as soon as possible, if *that* was possible. A fourteen-year-old junky whore up with the professors as their plaything would be a scene all right, I'm sure Luis and the others would agree. And I could explain the nonsense about the gun when I got there.

She was still tearful in the car and I told her to knock it off. Obediently she did, sniffling (her cute Mick apertures still huge). Perhaps we could plan some surprises for her on the way up, I thought. And later on, in the hills too. My last consolations, it seemed, surprises and pranks. My embarrassing tag-end of theory. Just give me five years or even three, and we'd really make some trouble. Me and the philosopher-outlaws I was cultivating up north. Plant them in the winter like bulbs and watch them spring up in May, little Kropotkins and Genets. Stupid Kove! He'd have more real fun up there than back in Cambridge, hunting cunt. Well, next time we'd get him, we'd keep him.

As I headed for the Somerville drive-in, my soiled doe lost her baby grief and regained her irrepressible cheekbloom and spirit. As if she too were planning conversions. How sweet. It made me smile and take new delight in the moment. So I suddenly pulled over and, on a dark narrow street, printed a message in yellow chalk:

BANDITS, STUDENTS, AND HONEST CITIZENS OF AMERICA, UNITE!

Squeezing my arm and giggling, Nugget said how it was always fun to be with me! You never knew what was coming next!

We walked back to the idling Mercedes, crazy Zshaba in his World War II pilot's jacket and his high-school A.W.O.L. in pink ribbon and sheepskin. The literary boy turned barbarian and the fourteen-year-old virgin turned hustler and junkie. A nice pair to hand the future over to. With *Mutual Aid* (Kropotkin) and *Sanctuary* for company in the back seat.

A few blocks down, I pulled in at Dunkin' Donuts, and we bought four hamburgers, French fries, a pile of glazed doughnuts, and two chocolate malts. We ate them there in the car, beneath the lurid glare of the white spotlights, Nugget spreading napkins for us with her proper training. I liked that. And I thought what a perfect place for one of those Auschwitz-billboards, a history lesson for Americans right there on one of its native landmarks.

I dropped Nugget off at Prospect, near Trout Fishing, and told her to be ready in a half hour. Yes, I thought, driving back to my hideaway, it'd be nice to have her reading to me about Popeye and Temple while soaring north. And maybe have her do some naughty things on the way, just to stay in practice.

But as I was driving back, my mood changed abruptly. Fear

and an aching loneliness seized hold of me. I didn't quite know what to make of it. Fear of going back? A desire for respite from my new resolve? Was Nugget too painful a reminder of my inner life these days? Had that phone call threatened in ways that I hadn't fully understood? Thoughts which flashed through my mind, as I parked the car on Harvard Street, where I could leave it for a few days. In the apartment I got together some underwear and paperbacks and headed with my brown bag for Trailways, via the MTA. The sudden impulse to see my mother, and to rest there, was compelling me.

Some five hours later, I was on the A train, IND subway, marked Mott Avenue, headed for the Rockaways. The refurbished IND rocked and heaved, the conductor shrieked the coming stations into the car, and I sat by a window, baffled by my motive and inclination, but sure of my determination. In the car, a boy with a yarmulke was reading, briefcase at his side, two teen-age blacks preened through, a middle-aged woman sat stone-faced. The train rumbled out from the tunnel finally, past dirty pastel-colored roofs and TV antennas, back yards with blue plastic swimming pools, past junkyards, churches, Aqueduct Raceway. As we got into Jamaica Bay, on the track joining Brooklyn with that long sliver of land called the Rockaways, a huge blue-trimmed Pan Am plane gently lifted itself into the sky from Kennedy International. For a moment my heart fluttered at the big bird's slow contained rise into the clouds, its red and yellow lights blinking escape into the blackness. It grew smaller and smaller, and I lowered my gaze to the choppy waters of Broad Channel and to the ink-black distance. Soon we were lunging by tracts of desolate land—with my memory filling in partly for my eye—and piles of assorted rubble, smashed autos, soaked timber, all cordoned off protectively by barbed wire. A madness, I reflected, but a better one than Buchenwald.

I got off at Beach 60th, and walked the few blocks to my mother's apartment house. The elevator took me up to the sixth (top) floor. Her grating voice, slightly better since polyps were removed from her throat, asked who it was, as she got to the peephole. The chain was released, the door opened, and as we embraced (she planting a wet kiss on my cheeks), she said, "With that beard I barely recognized you. Why didn't you call before and tell me you were coming?" I hadn't seen her in over a year—though we had spoken on the phone and corresponded—or since I had come in to stay with her when my stepfather was dying, in Rockaway and Memorial Hospital (Manhattan). In the small pink kitchen, fluorescent light glaring, she asked how I was feeling and boiled water for tea. From a bread basket emerged yellow sponge cake, a childhood favorite. Could I eat a snack? Yes. She went about preparing a plate of pickled herring in cream sauce, with lettuce and tomato. For a moment I was back in that Bleecker Street loft with my father; then I was back in the pink kitchen, with the shock of a wasting mother. Nursing Moishe, a printer's assistant, through three years of cancer of the lymph, mostly in one room of a huge but empty house by the beach, had made its mark on every point of her anatomy. The cheerful buoyancy of pink flesh had evaporated from her arms, her legs, her face; her dyed auburn hair lay lifeless on her scalp; her face was carved deeply into a lined mask of nervous ravage. She asked why the sudden visit, and I said it was a long time since I had seen her. She responded with a long face of kindly irony, bottom lip forward, and said, "My son is suddenly changing his ways." While I ate, she told me about my sister's family on Long Island, digressing when an old name came up, or to ask me if I wanted more herring, or to narrate an incident that took place in the building the other day. Patiently I listened to the scrambled talk, surprised by the wealth of feeling stirred by this lady with whom I presently had so little in common. I appreciated the periodic glimpses of humor that came through. Near 1:30, we called it a night. I slept at her insistence in the one bedroom, she on the Hollywood bed in the living room.

Huge jets rumbled overhead, shaking the room as I tried to sleep. I summoned up a swarm of images from childhood in an effort to wash away my present. No use. I was a new Zshaba now, not my mother's. Lying there, I felt strange and frightened, wondering if I was ever again going to feel the special bond with the woman in the next room, the deep consolation. Or was that all in the past? I shifted to her. A good woman who had deserved a better fate than a premature marriage to an older tyrant (my father), an abortive affair with a man who couldn't escape his own bad marriage (and who had died in middle age of a cold which became pleurisy), and a second husband who turned terminally ill soon after marriage. With me, another man, she had had a mixed fate, always being able to talk frankly and easily, yet never seeing me much after I was eighteen. About my life as a celebrity, she was very funny. Being a guerrilla was not much different to her from being a TV personality or eminent doctor; the picture on *Time*—cut out and saved by my brother-in-law— and the various gossip and news notes that she herself picked up in the *New York Post* and *Daily News* signaled to her success, for which she was happy (for me). And when she saw an item or rumor of particular ugliness, she'd immediately write and ask if it were true, and when I'd answer and say no, she was relieved. Of course, she quite realized that, unlike Carson or Salk, there were dangers and even evils in my "work" (Mom's word). A fact brought home to her the first time she saw my new Zenith aid; she gasped with puzzlement, fear, and indignation at my vague explanation. Still, her concern was with the injury, not the ideology. Always she came back, like a homing pigeon, to *emotions and feeling;* that's what got to me. And confused me. Like her last words of the evening, her familiar refrain which referred to my accident as if it had occurred several days and not several years ago, "Your ear, Zshaba, it's feeling a little better?" An expression of sympathy which stabbed me, coming from her.

Early the next day, her fussing in the bedroom woke and irritated me. The next three things I did—bathe, eat breakfast, and try to read—were undercut by her nervous words or trivial instructions ("Lenny, please, the eggs'll get cold," "You're going to read right now, it's so lovely out?"), so that, finally, I blew up at her, told her she had become impossible and was "a great pain in the ass." I got on my jacket and flew out of the apartment and onto the elevator. When I arrived downstairs, my fury had dissolved, and in its place were regret and sorrow. Back upstairs, I apologized to her, which she handled nicely, and said I was going to go for a walk, I'd be back after a while. When she cautioned me about walking alone on the deserted boardwalk—an elderly lady had been knocked down with her groceries two months back and killed for her purse by a fourteen-year-old boy—I knew she felt okay again. Outside, it was brisk and sunny, old people lined two benches in front of the housing project and, across the street, kids screamed from basketball and handball games. Coincidentally, the junior high was named Cardozo.

I walked along the boardwalk, the Atlantic slapping the sandy shore impressively, with hope, it seemed to me, some fifty yards away; to my right, however, acres and acres of empty ground, where houses and summer cottages had been leveled for urban renewal three years ago, leaving a dumping ground of holes, rubble, piled dirt. A patient lying on the operating table, anesthetized and cut open, waiting for the surgeon to finish the job. Still, the walk was exhilarating, releasing me from anxieties with its flood of open space and sea. At one point, a few blocks off the boardwalk, I stood at a corner and gazed hypnotized at huge airplanes appearing out of the sky every forty-five seconds to glide in for landings, looking so close that you wanted to wave to the pilots. I weaved my way back through the schoolyard, seeing my own give-and-go youth replaced by a more spectacular jump shooting, wondering which of those potential pros would leave off rebounding for mugging. Leave off to walk (as I did) across the street, where elderly Jews, thirty-year tenants of the neighborhood, sat like bundled clay pigeons, waiting to be picked off by the new young sportsmen.

Upstairs, Sol Fingerman, seventy, spry, fastidious in newly laundered white shirt and pressed trousers, was obtaining my mother's signature on a tenant petition for an intercom between the apartments and the front door. The petition would go to the city housing authorities, where it would rise slowly through the bureaucracy and be acted upon who-knew-how-many-months-and-muggings-later. In an era of non-negotiable demands, in an area of administrative negligence and juvenile chaos (when they caught the fourteen-year-old murderer of the old woman and confronted his parents, they pleaded, "Do whatever you want with him, please, we can't handle him"), shtetl Jews continued doing things in the old way. (Along with the few older black couples in the buildings.) I sat, enchanted, after being greeted affectionately by Fingerman, my radicalism meaning less than my manners. The rest of the day was quietly settling. The afternoon was spent in the crowded living room, where my mother chronicled what it was like to take care of Moishe for those three years, wondering whether she'd find a dead man in the bathroom

485

in the middle of the night (when he went there and moaned from an infected spleen), transporting him, without a car or money, from Medicaid blood specialist to welfare-nursing home to cancer hospital, back to the one-room (and then three-room apartment), suffering his last days of vengeful anger at her for not being able to tolerate more than two hours a day at Memorial Hospital during that steamy September week of his dying. (After two hours there, and bus rides of two and a half hours each way from Rockaway, she felt faint, utterly alone, hopelessly depressed, and lived on tranquilizers, at sixty-one.) A narrative without tears or maudlin sentimentalizing, just unpleasant facts and repugnant insights, especially the one that the longer his sick life continued, the shorter her healthy one would be. In fact, it was only a month previous that she had regained her appetite.

In the evening, I watched the Knicks beat (Kovell's) Celtics on television, while my mother had tea, cake, and gossip with Jake Rosen, a widower from the floor below. A firm man in his sixties and also a helpful suitor, Jake was the only one in the building who had some real sense of my doings and reputation. It turned out that we argued heatedly for an hour about blacks, crime, social injustice. Working from a perspective of history and an abstract ideal of justice, I patiently tried to explain that we were in the midst of a period of transition which was difficult for everyone. Rosen, spare, strong, well-kept, grew furious, chronicling his East Side poverty in the thirties and working his way up to the recent change in the Rockaway neighborhood. He got through to me, but I doubted if the reverse was true. Sponge cake barely reconciled matters.

The next morning, I rose rested and fresh, and treated with a newly found humor my mother's blue-jay pesterings. Her hazel eyes also seemed to glint with her old charm; two days put in there had made things easier. Breakfast of lox and bagels was accompanied by the incessant AM radio noise, which I quieted, and then I was out around 11:30 for my solitary oceanside walk. It was nice, this second time around, with the familiar sea, sand, and slatted boardwalk. Suddenly I felt very glad and confident about our kidnapping, recognizing its historic significance and bold ambitions. Even if it didn't work out with great success, and no real projects or great ideas were produced, we would have tried, I surmised. And perhaps D. was right, perhaps some of those men saw the urgency of thinking about the nation's plight —not in an abstract sense but in an immediate one.

As I walked along, the air cool, the day gray-blue, a new calm settled over me about returning north. Luis, Addie, and the other guerrillas could use me, and I, them. They and I were, I knew, right after all in our basic anger and revolt, despite my old feelings and nagging cultural schizophrenia. A condition that I would have to live with, until—if ever—I overcame it. Otherwise, what had been the point of putting those bullets into Mailer? What I had discovered, however, was that firing bullets didn't bring instant or complete release; only time and determination could do that. Ideas about projects popped into my head, and I sat on a decayed wooden bench, facing the blue-green ocean, and jotted them down. For the immediate present, I'd invite Professor E. to abandon his literary anthology and collaborate instead, with Professor B. perhaps, on a high-school history text chronicling the Cold War and continuing to today's erosion of civil liberties. The second project was more long-range and envisioned a Blueprint for a Future Society, to be worked on in stages, and encompassing morals, philosophy, politics, economics. (We did have an economist up there, didn't we? Well, we could pick one up.) Jotting the notes in my small pad made me feel attached and purposeful again. I grew excited about elaborating upon them in my large notebook and also about calling Hibernation House to tell them to expect me back shortly. The ocean air caressed me as I retraced my steps, and for the first time in thirty-six hours I looked upon that small apartment as a true rehabilitation center. A visit with my mother was resulting in propelling me forward into my new adventures, at the same time that it had transported me back into my past. A therapeutic irony.

It was 1:45 when I turned the key to the apartment door, remembering my mother's words about going out shopping. For a split second, I saw her face as she sat in the living-room chair; her eyes were fixed upon me, with inexpressible sadness, before she lamented, "Oy, Zshaba." For a second, I say, because immediately I was seized by two pairs of arms and twisted backward. My nose pressed against the foyer wall, my neck encircled by a thick arm, I had to struggle for air. Hands roamed my pockets, legs, and torso, swiftly and roughly; they entered my under-shorts. The words "F.B.I." and "Take it easy" very strange when you're being felt up and choked. Once again, nearly a decade later, that organization was visiting the Pincus household.

When they spun me back around, my hands were squeezed together and pinched into manacles. Mr. Stepanowski, forty-five, with a sharp nose and slicked hair, introduced himself. His associate was younger, with guerrilla hair and student clothes, and was faintly recognizable. A planted provocateur, I surmised. The background of fake flowers, forties' furniture, and Victoriana pictures made them look like characters out of Dickens, agents of Mr. Jaggers, say, while my mother, sad, awkward, and loving, was Joe Gargery. It was only as I was led to the deep upholstered chair on the far side of the room that I noticed the third man, standing by the entranceway to the bedroom. It was Professor Kovell.

Seeing my attention, he said equably, "Hi, Lenny." Meanwhile, Jake Rosen, accompanied by a third F.B.I. man, entered the scene, to escort my mother out of the room. She said, before leaving, "I can see him before he goes, Mr. Kovell?" The Dean nodded sympathetically. "Of course, Mrs. Pincus." He turned to the pair of guards: "Okay, can I get my end of the bargain now?"

I sat huddled in the chair, fascinated by Kovell as if he were an apocryphal figure coming to life as he moved closer. My stomach was slowing down, and my breathing was somewhat easier. I longed to dive headfirst through the window, and would have, possibly, if it was the Hancock Street apartment on the street level. But it was not. It was Rockaway, with schoolyard shouts screaming through the window and the feel of the shtetl surrounding me, where the new history was being made—the student recaptured by his old teacher.

"Good for you," I said with controlled emotions to Kovell, comical in his tight and shiny suit, an obvious police replacement for his camp football gear. "Good for you for proving how right I was all along. You're the System, Mr. Kovell, the System straight and pure. All that playstuff with sex and women is a shallow cover after all, isn't it? What you're after is what those poor goons and their stupid sirens outside are after—*preserving things.* Preserving order. Preserving the state. Preserving the American empire. Okay, you've helped them do it now. *Temporarily.*" Words of anger and injury as much as sense.

"Come on, Lenny, you can do better," said Kovell, smoking, sitting opposite me. "Your terms are inflated. Grandiose. It's much simpler than all that. And more honest. You killed a man, right? That he was a famous author, that you had certain strange ideas for motives—beside the point. If you had shot one of these agents, to me the problem would be the same, friend. You murdered someone, and now you're going to pay. And secondly, you and your crazy friends destroyed some works of art. Not Nixon's pictures, or the government's, but pictures that belonged to everyone. Those pictures were immortal, as Malraux might say, and now they're gone too. Now you can't get off free for that kind of stuff, Lenny. You know that yourself."

In silence, I gazed at him, his sandy hair thinning, his face developing new lines. Furious and strangely pleased. At what? At his calm, his new assurance, at the latest twist, where he was again bossing. It felt comfortable. Yet I couldn't get over how this ordinary-looking man with that tormented and diseased interior life had fingered me! Was this purposeless decadent going to be out on the loose, while I, a boy with a cause and serious work to do, went to the hoosegow? Again I longed to jump from my chair, this time to squeeze that steady look from his face and turn him upside down to see his life! The pressure of my hands pulling at the iron handcuffs cut my fantasy.

I asked how he had found me.

"By crazy luck, and odd doings," he said. "First the luck. There was a crumpled, almost unreadable note in my mailbox, written a few days ago, saying that if I returned to town and wanted to find you, you were at the Hancock address. Some friends had visited you there. It was signed 'Lizzie.'" He put his palms up and shook his head. "Know her?"

The name registered, I began nodding, and even laughing. My naïveté was amusing.

"Now the odd doings," he continued, making a face. "It turned out to be the same address that your friend Luis—uh—"

"Rodriguez?"

"Rodriguez. The same address that he had given me. Of

489

course, I hadn't taken that seriously; in fact I almost threw it out. But when I got this other note and found signs of you in the apartment, I remembered another address on Luis's note, searched for it, and—here, I've kept it around."

He handed me a lined page from a small spiral pad, which recorded, in Luis's incredible crooked print, the two addresses. (Address spelled with one "s," and an "e" at the end.) After the Rockaway information, Luis had written, "Mothers, where they all run in the end."

Brilliant Luis! He was doing the upstaging now.

I looked up, curious and baffled anew. "But why did he see you in the first place? Why?"

Kove stared a moment, then reached in his jacket pocket, pulled out an envelope, and brought it to me.

Feebly, I opened it, looking up at him as if he were a magician. I removed two sheets of Xerox paper. At the top, in my handwriting, was written, "To Whom It May Concern," and the date, "August 4." A Xerox copy of an envelope front. What followed beneath that was the incoherent philosophy of a young lunatic, the reasoning feverishly consecutive and madly logical. Some of my words were hard to make out, even for me. But my old pal had gotten it all re-pro-duced (as he might put it).

I was dumfounded but admiring, thinking how brilliant the world was when it wanted to get you.

"You see, I didn't believe your confession at all, not a word of it. Just as I told you. *I* wasn't lying either. And then, strangely, Rodriguez came downstairs the next night and asked to see me. You were still there that night, if I recall correctly. The black girl was with him, the clever and crazy one. Anyway, the talk got onto you after a while, and he explained rather casually that you hadn't been the same since the killing of Mailer. I said I had heard that rumor but didn't believe it. To my amazement, he then produced this little document, which you have in your hand. I recognized the handwriting immediately. I began to believe it then . . . I realized I had to try the break immediately then. It was 'too late,' so far as you were concerned."

I tried to control my breathing.

"You can't expect this to hold up in any courtroom," I offered.

He shook his head. "It's just part of the evidence. I went back and got that shaving razor you showed me, which I had resisted so obstinately." He glanced at his watch. "They're probably dragging the river by the B.U. bridge now for the gun. You probably weren't lying about that either."

I smiled, dazzled.

"You stole my revolver that night, didn't you?" I asked eagerly. "And still have it, don't you?"

To his credit, he didn't laugh. "Oh, I took it, but I don't have it. A. had it last I knew, and since he didn't make it I assume your pals have it now. The whole thing was curious, including the break. I still can't understand how I was the only one to make it out."

The last dazzling pieces to the puzzle. So they knew that all along up there, about the gun, and just wanted to have me confirm it, which I did by lying. And they planted him on me, thinking I was helping them! How brilliant it all was, the conspiracy of circumstance, accident, and design! You had to get in trouble, real trouble, to appreciate it.

"No, don't give me that stuff about systems, empires, or selling out, your next accusations," he went on, warming up. "You're more sophisticated than that. Think instead of how you got into this mess. Too much Dostoevsky, I'd say. *Crudely* digested and transferred to life. And not Stavrogin as your museum poster flaunted, but his curious buddy, remember him? Peter Verkhovensky." He shook his head slowly. "I think you've been turning into a version of that maniac, Lenny. Too bad, especially since *without* Stavrogin, Peter is not nearly as interesting. In fact, he's just some creature masquerading as human, but who really has little to do with human beings. Moral idiots never do."

Back with fiction, even then. God!

"Can't do without literature," I said, "can you, Kovell? Without those analogies you're sunk as to how to interpret things. Verkhovensky? Maybe. Sure, why not? He has his virtues. He's less self-deceiving than the others, isn't he? And more forceful too. Yes, so what if he is *part* of me—where does that lead you? It's your Stavrogin who commits suicide as I recall; Stavrogin who admits defeat. Meanwhile, Peter V. takes a train out of town and disappears. Now, Doctor Kovell, if you really thought

491

I was Peter not Lenny, you would have ended this episode with some literary propriety—instead of this banal finish—by buying me a ticket on the next Pan Am flight out of the country."

Kovell smiled appreciatively. "This is less fanciful, true."

I asked for water, and, when the slick-haired Pole brought it to me, his cheap metal tie clasp suddenly transported me back to a portfolio of ten years ago and another agent. How circling it all was! I drank, amused.

"Don't you find it interesting," I pursued, "that Dostoevsky could have been so antiradical in *The Possessed* and in his own life, and yet at the same time *set Peter free* at the end?"

He gathered my implication. "I guess I'm less lenient than Dostoevsky. Also, I've had to live with you, in *real life*. That makes a difference."

"Perhaps there was more of the 'moral idiot' in him too. And," I added softly, "perhaps more boldness and more forthrightness . . . Don't you think you *deserve* prison, Kovell? Some sort of prison? Come on, be honest. Don't you think you've abused the ladies as much as I've abused the museums? And which is more important in your philosophy, people or property?"

He looked at me unsmiling. "What do you think?" he replied. "Have you turned into a little judge over some spilled semen? Use your head, boy."

It was my turn to smile. "Well, maybe jail's not for you after all. Real jail, that is. Just go back to the old prison—the saddle. The hairy saddle." I shrugged. "For a break, you can come to Walpole and visit me, and tell me all about your views on 'human dignity and survival.' Just after cheating on Melissa, say. You know what's funny, Kovell? You didn't have to turn me in. Honest. I mean it's not in your line. All you wanted was to get out, to get free, to get back to those cunts. How ironic! And I wind up paying for your pussylust."

His face began to tighten in that special camp way, his eyes growing venomous.

"I made an error," I admitted, "a serious one. I should have brought them up there for you, on a permanent basis. Then it would have been all fine. You would have been happy. I should have rounded up three or four of the girls. Of course, you would have loved it, it would have been an 'experiment' for you. That's all you would have needed. A pair of new bloomers every other day and you would have cooperated politically. What a schmuck I was, treating you like all those Good Husbands."

He shook his head. "You're too far gone. You're talking gibberish."

"You're Stavrogin, all right. A lightweight version. Without all the literary fervor and open dilemmas, et cetera. What you need is a Lisa on your lap for you to fuck. Or these days, who turns around and knifes you while you're sleeping. Yeah, a Lisa or a Lizzie. You might look that girl up, Kove. She has a cute pal, too. Oh, God, it's all too much! Hey, you guys, get rid of me, will you? Come on, let's split!"

I stood up, and Mr. Stepanowski and his friend took my arms.

Kovell stood too. "You're a maniac, a crazy little animal. But again, I'm . . . sorry, Lenny. Again, if I can be of help with a lawyer or something, let me know."

To my guards I said, "Can we go now?"

At the door to the apartment, my mother stopped me (Jake waiting ten feet off).

"You'll take care of yourself, yeah, Lenela?"

"Sure, Mom."

She looked at me, without tears, as if my face would provide some answer. She took my face in her hands and kissed me on the cheek. "You'll write me, yeah? And let me know . . ." she moved her head puzzled, ". . . what's going on? They'll give you a trial, I suppose?"

I smiled. "I'll write. They'll give me a trial. It'll be all right."

She shook her head, in lament.

I said goodbye, hurting and detached, and they took me to the elevator, my hands handcuffed to Stepanowski and another agent who had come up. Downstairs, a small crowd of young blacks and old Jews had gathered outside the door, attracted by the squad cars.

"What'd whiskers do, huh, man?"

"Who is the cat?"

"Is that Rose's Lenny? She said he had a beard. *Sei gesunt!*"

The three agents led me into a plain Plymouth sedan, four-

493

door, green. Stepanowski and Pete, the new agent, rode with me in the back, while the provocateur was up front with the driver. Police cars escorted us in front and back as we drove off, the basketball games receding, the ocean on my right hidden by the elevated tracks. I was offered a cigarette and puffed on it with "Step's" aid. (His nickname.) They flattered me for being so hard to catch and recalled two times when they had come close, in Cambridge. Quietly stunned, melancholic, I didn't pay much attention. Instead, my mind roamed with nostalgic imagery, shooting basketballs in high school, watching the Red Sox in Fenway, Kove's classes, driving north as I had planned, with Nugget at my side. But the images of freedom dejected me further, and I tried to put them aside.

In twenty minutes we were at Kennedy, and soon I was walking up the aisle—with my Siamese attachments—of a nearly empty Northeast Yellowbird jet, just in from Miami. Three or four passengers had boarded with us, and there were two suntanned middle-aged couples already there, flying on to Boston, having a good time with their Polaroid and memories. Otherwise the big plane was deserted, like the carcass of a dinosaur, and we sat near the tail, Stepanowski taking a *Life* and Pete reading a travel magazine. Meanwhile, the Florida vacationers had grown wide-eyed and slightly awed by the sight of the handcuffs. Presently, one of them, a handsome gray-haired man in a Hawaiian shirt with a camera slung over it, sauntered down the aisle, ostensibly to the bathroom, but eyeing us and nodding a greeting. On his way back, he paused, unfurled the cellophane from a cigar, and offered it to Step, who shook his head. In a thick voice, the man said, "The ladies were wondering, could he be one of the leftover Manson kids?" Step looked up, said no, and returned to *Life*. The vacationer tipped his straw hat back from its front perch and inquired again, "Is it dangerous? I mean to be on this flight . . . with him?" He reminded me of Sam Kirshner from Chestnut Hill, so I said, "I'm pretty pacified. No bombs, no Havana." He blinked, then smiled and laughed, and sauntered back to his eager group. Immediately, they began citing loudly all the recent criminal cases in an attempt to recognize me; throughout the forty-five-minute ride, I was the subject of backward glances and excited loud speculations. The women, especially, gazed at me with earnest curiosity, their broiled faces a mixture of fear and . . . attraction?

So I was getting my ride in the air after all, as I had first anticipated on that IND to Rockaway and later, watching the jets nose in for a landing. But it was a different sort of ride than I had wanted. Yet, curiously, there was a peace in all this, which broke in upon the melancholy as we streamed through the floating clouds. For there was something consoling in being driven and flown to an appointed destination without the need to plan, to rehearse, to check and recheck alternatives, to up the old ante—all my old tasks. Something surprisingly consoling in having those two simple bears beside me, their thick hairy fingers practically touching mine, their job to protect me as much as to hold me. It was a great change of pace. I even saw a bright side to it all. Kove's words about a proper ending came back to me. Perhaps *caught* was good in the end, or at least useful. For a while, anyway. It would be horrible for sure, I knew that (though I also knew that I'd get much better treatment this time, for my royal crime). But, I thought, wasn't behind bars the destination of all truly honest boys these days? All true patriots of America? Hadn't I (and others) uttered such beliefs in speeches and written them down? In jail, these days, meant you had committed a virtuous deed, if the crime was political. Which, to me, my murder and my museum destructions were—political and philosophical. Surely my victim, at least, would have agreed and taken up my part, were he living now.

Caught. Headed for prison. Maybe worse. While the real large-scale criminals went free, were saluted by chambers of commerce and veterans' clubs, and given daily publicity by our newspapers and television stations, ruled the nation, frightened the world. No, there was another side to getting put away, a side that had a deep logic and that was comforting. And the companionship, it would be topnotch. (Especially once I got off death row, which wouldn't be too long, I hoped.) The companionship of teachers and priests, pacifists and internationalists, honest lawyers and brave army officers, GI's and students who wouldn't kill, men who wouldn't lie. A whole band of American idealists and patriots, growing steadily, mixing with the thieves, the forgers, the killers. I smiled, thinking how I, being of both parties, would mix well. Behind bars told the truth about how we felt just now toward the homeland and about how it felt toward us. On the inside, looking out. Like some of the Russian and Czech prisoner-patriots, say. Honesty International.

And more. Perhaps Sophie'd bake me cookies, while Kove could keep me supplied with paperbacks. And with pen and paper, and a period of uninterrupted time, who knows, maybe I'd be an author after all. Once I got the documentary work out of the way. From literature student to dangerous barbarian to jail-bird author, why not? So I tried to surmount my sympathy for myself, and concentrate on doing my work from my new base, for as long as it lasted. Once again, it seemed that Luis knew more about my nature and my mission than I had given him credit for.

Caught. It'd test me. Good.

Walking down the windy airplane stairway, I was at last recognized by the celebrity fans.

"The kid from Cardozo, I'm telling you! Pincus, Pinky the Red!" The taller lady was gleaming with pride and grabbing her friends. "The kid who burned down that library, sitting right there on the plane with us. And you said he was okay, Lou? My G-o-d. He looks so much . . . weirder than his pictures with that beard and all. So, Lou, what are you standing there for, get a picture, will you? Terry'll just die when she hears about it."

Harassed, the man snapped two pictures as we walked along. When we stopped momentarily by the gate, however, the short dark-haired lady suddenly caught my eye and flashed the peace sign to me very quickly. I wanted to hug her. "Peace to you too, friend," I said. Furtively, she began to tell me about her grand-daughter who went to Cardozo and idolized me, when her husband pulled her away.

Inside Logan Airport, more photographers and news media people, who followed us, snapping flashbulbs, firing questions. ("Is it true, Lenny, that your mother didn't mind when she heard you were a murderer?" "What would you think?" I replied. "Were you really in Red China last February?" I nodded. "On a mission from Kissinger." "How do you feel about *Time*'s doing another cover story?" "I think I could reveal more in a *Playboy* interview.") My F.B.I. seconds soon escorted me to another anonymous sedan, and Pete was kidding Step about his "photogenic mug." The young provocateur agent now returned, obviously having been on the plane with us all along, and sat up front with the new driver. The old team talked about their kids and families.

We drove through the toll booths and dark Sumner Tunnel and soon were on Storrow Drive, the deceiving promise of Boston glittering on the left. Then we were turning up Charles, moving slowly past the new government center, where my eye caught a glimpse of "Thermopylae," a bronze sculpture we had thought of knocking off at one point. As it approached and fled in the twilight, it lingered in my mind, but not as an abstract symbol of heroic defeat. Instead, it twisted and fidgeted into some sort of mechanical contraption for implementing the law. Sagging against Pete, whose breath I had tried to avoid, I shuddered as if electric circuits were shooting through me.

Another sort of crowd awaited us in front of the tall federal courthouse building, where I was to be held until I was indicted. Obviously, the word had gotten out about me, and about fifty to a hundred supporters had shown up, shouting my name, raising their fists, cheering me with those slogans that I so loathed. Walking through them ("Viva, Pincus, Viva!"), I caught sight of the first agent, now back at work in the crowd, roaring against the pigs and yelling for Lenny. I waved to him and asked if I would see him later during the questioning. A moment of confusion as I was whisked away. In the gray-walled rectangle lifting me upstairs to my new home, the crowds and children's wisdom receded, and my body and brain traveled back to my electric version of Thermopylae. God!

When they had settled me into the five-by-nine cell—with the iron plank for a bed, the gray cement-block walls, the dirty latrine that never lost its stinking stench—and the days went by, it got worse, not better. I had dreams of that horror machine sculpture grunting toward me, aided by items of my new life— huge metal keys dangling, shiny silver badges, black bars crisscrossing, high leather boots. Sadistically, Thermopylae tortured my nights. My only release has been finishing these notes, and even then it's like piling stones for one's own graveyard. Mail appears, but it's very different when it comes to you opened, censored. It's been a mixture of radical criticism (why did I kill someone "frivolous" and "on our side"?), anti-Semitic hate (these letters are worth a book by themselves), and angry letters from academics and professors. They have a point. The most intriguing note, I suppose, arrived from an old Mailer wife, saying how much she wished to meet me, in jail or out.

A note from Lauri (signed "L"), saying don't worry, we'd see each other again soon. Are they planning a break for me? My mother's letters, written in her large handwriting on very small sheets, are the hardest to take, with their avowals of love, trivial gossip about familiar persons, and direct questions about why I killed that writer. Had he done something to me?

Visitors try to see me, but if they're not wearing gray wool with stripes and aren't awaiting sentences or indictments, how can they interest me? Felicia swooped in like some noble queen, but left crying when I told her yes, it was true, I had killed. Sophie was much better, she had had a taste of this. She even made me laugh by telling of seeing Kovell in the Square with a young girl who looked like a high-school senior but whom he nervously introduced as an old student. I asked if the girl had a twitch in her face and long brown hair. Sophie said no, she was tall, blond, and well dressed. Too bad. When the cocksman himself appeared (back in his old corduroy jacket) and I told him we were both losers, he on the outside with his sex-dependence and me on the inside with my own lack of freedom, he still didn't get it. Neither of us was good enough, I suggested. He got upset and asked how I liked prison. Calmly I replied that Hibernation House was much more interesting, the comrades and wardens sharper, the reconstruction program more varied and more intelligent. Didn't he think so? Then I asked him about his new young girl friend, and he departed. The talk of decadence still offends him. For me, it's the open life that makes me a prisoner; for him, the hidden life.

Finally, my lawyer, a slender fifty-five-year-old with soft gray-white hair, a pacemaker in his heart, a cataract in his good eye, and a consoling deep voice. Why he stays on, I don't know. A Jewish Lincoln who loves justice and human beings about equally—therefore, what can he love in or about me? He brings his chessboard along in the hope that I'll say something useful to my cause. But I have nothing useful on my behalf, do I?

Which reminds me: no word from Cronkite, just a note from Cavett. He'd like "very much and very sincerely" to do a Special, an hour and a half interview with me, here in my cell. To give "my side of things." No, Mr. Cavett, no, I'm not up to that television first just now, not up to giving my side just now. But I do see clearly what that gentleman from Prague meant in his earlier letter to me, about rewards for crimes. Of course, they've asked me to turn state's witness and help myself, but I figure they'll find Hibernation House on their own. Naturally, I'd love to see Luis here and get to know him without his safety razors. (And to see how he'd react to these walls and bars.) But I'm also intrigued to see how long H.H. can be kept going. After all, you wouldn't ask Pavlov to dismantle his laboratory or Plato to turn in his Republic because of a few errors, so why ask Pincus to bring down his edifice? Besides, I gave up helping people awhile back.

About the citizens one encounters here, while waiting indictment, they're poor company. There's one fellow who's tolerable, a University of Michigan graduate (history major) in for grand larceny, but I only see him once a week. Otherwise, the talk up here on the fifth floor, Block 10, Charles Street jail, concerns what you're in for, how long you think you'll get, attorneys and bails, and varieties of "ass" (boy and girl). As a steady diet, sex-and-crime talk, especially as practiced by these high-school dropouts, wears thin quickly and mires you down. So much fantasy and lying. (At least Family Talk gave you some convincing details.) Without a college education, I see now, men remain brutes and cave dwellers. *And whoever claims that criminals are interesting men should be condemned to live among them.*

I hear March has been a terrible month, full of the worst winds and rain. Not inside here, I can tell you. Couldn't they allow prisoners to walk the streets on those days when ordinary citizens wouldn't dream of going out? What I'd give to spend one day outside in the worst real storm!

Nights are the hardest. I've become an insomniac. If it's not your thoughts and memories, it's a man suddenly cursing or coughing (so many of these guys seem physically ill), another taking a loud piss and flushing his latrine, or even, somewhere, an attempt at rape, which you come to wait for, expect. And then there are the idiots who jerk off loudly and exhibitionistically at 3 A.M. Words fail. And whatever you think about, your thoughts always turn back to the three walls, the cement ceiling and cement floor, the sixteen iron bars, the futureless years ahead. I've devised a nice game, attributing to each bar a different number of years in prison: one, two, three, four; at four I get forty-eight, at five, eighty. Eighty years. Which I'll never make. Contemplating a mere year apiece and adding them up makes me cry, I can't help myself. A mere *sixteen years*, and it brings tears. I try my best to keep this down to once a night, it's more depressing than masturbating. I try to think of comrades working, of some sort of International Cause that I've played a part in, of the varied inmates to be found in the federal penitentiary (but when will that come, months? years?), of the book I'd like to write about life here (shouldn't every citizen be forced to spend three or four months a year in jail?)—but then the black bars return and the giant numbers. I see my flesh decaying, my teeth rotting, my hair going, here, where it's been useless. Myself turning into . . . a madman at forty? . . . a weak or brutal homosexual at thirty? . . . Insomnia, fed by those images, ravages me. I twist and turn on my plank, feel the iron, and fall into cold sweats and pray for sleep, like a man whose bones have been crushed in a fall but has no painkiller or medical aid and awaits self-healing, knowing it's hopeless.

And when I get a cold, a simple cold, it's the most torturous. And you get them easily in jail, or at least I've had two in the six weeks I've been here. A common cold drives me into a panic. For it not only stays on and on, it travels to my ears. My bad ear hurts then. It rings with a steady ache, and once or twice a day pumps me with a half hour of sharp pain. And the other ear seems permanently drafty, cold. They've brought me general medications, but it doesn't help. And when I worked up enough nerve to ask the doctor for my childhood relief of salt-in-the-sock and heated camphor, he laughed raucously. The next day, the guard, with a wink, asked me what else my mother brought me with the sock. When my lawyer took the situation to the warden, that gentleman answered that he had upward of fifteen hundred inmates, was he going to worry about warming camphor? Not unless the ear needed taking off. Then take it off, I screamed sometimes, take it off! The guard's there with his stick, and, after getting belted once in the ribs, I'm good now and quiet down. Do you see how silly it is? I want to think about the new values, the new man, about Hibernation House diversions and plans, about troubling society from within here—but a stinking trivial cold ruins all that. I wait for change, for some new medication, but it doesn't come. It doesn't come.

And meanwhile it hurts.

It hurts.

It hurts!